EROTIC
FAIRY TALES

A ROMP THROUGH THE CLASSICS

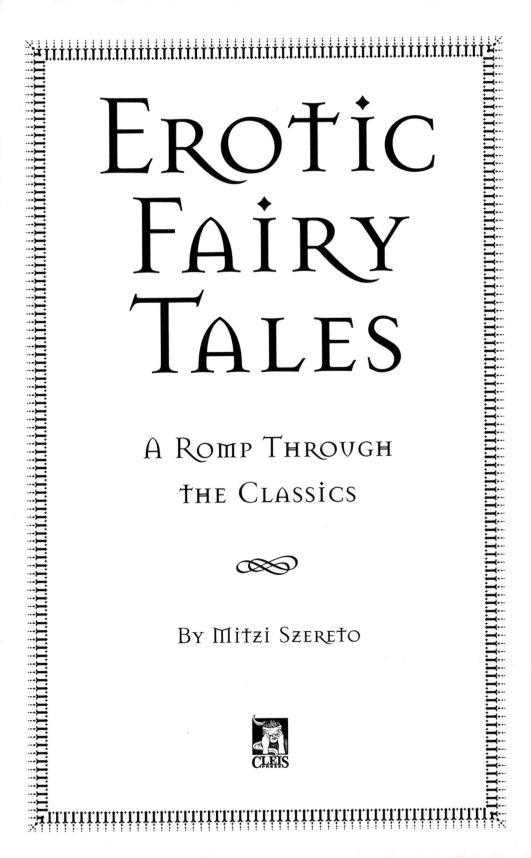

EROTIC
FAIRY
TALES

A ROMP THROUGH
THE CLASSICS

BY MITZI SZERETO

CLEIS
PRESS

Published in the United States by Cleis Press Inc.,
P.O. Box 14684, San Francisco, California 94114.
Printed in the United States.
Cover design: Scott Idleman
Text design: Karen Quigg
Cleis Press logo art: Juana Alicia
First Edition.
10 9 8 7 6 5 4

LIBRARY OF CONGRESS CATALOGING-IN-PUBLICATION DATA

Szereto, Mitzi.
Erotic fairy tales : a romp through the classics / Mitzi Szereto. — 1st ed.
p. cm.   ISBN 1-57344-124-4   (pbk. : alk. paper)
1. Erotic stories, American. 2. Fairy tales — Adaptations. I. Title.
PS3569.Z396 E76 2001
813'.6 — dc21   00-065634

CONTENTS

Introduction

The fairy tale has no landlord...or so say the Greeks. One has only to initiate a cursory investigation into the origins of any common fairy tale to discover the truth of this. Fairy tales that at first glance appear easily identifiable to the reader may in actuality have roots reaching back to the Middle Ages and even into antiquity. Such tales are believed to have originated in oral form (the word *tale* deriving from the Anglo-Saxon *talu,* meaning *speech*) as folktales of the common people, taking on the character and imagination of the storyteller in accordance with the culture in which they were told — only to undergo further development and refinement as they came to be written down. Indeed, traces of what we consider the "classic" fairy tale have been discovered in written form in Egyptian records dating from 1600 B.C. as well as in Indian, Persian, Greek, and Hebrew writings and inscriptions more than two thousand years old.

Of these known and lesser-known tales, variants exist throughout the world. In fact, it would seem that there is rarely a story for which a parallel cannot be found in the folklore of another people. Scholars remain convinced that these folktales originated in Asia and were brought west by the Crusaders, the Gypsies, the Judaic peoples, and Mongol missionaries. In the nineteenth century, Sanskrit scholar Theodor Benfey provided evidence that a significant portion of what has been widely considered traditional European folklore came from India via Arabic, Hebrew, and Latin translations. However, many anthropologists are likewise adamant that this folklore has its true grounding in the "savage superstition" of the primitive cultures. Regardless of where they began, all folktales deal with the basic motifs of human existence: good and evil, life and death, weakness and innocence, temptation and intrigue. Such themes know no boundaries of culture or time.

By the tenth century, much of the material attributed to the Late Classical period would be imported from the Mediterranean by traveling entertainers and missionaries following pilgrim routes. During the time of the Crusades, folktales from places as widely dispersed as Ireland and India managed to make their way onto the fields of Europe and, hence, into the ears of those who tilled them. (Around this same period the Hindu *Panchatantra* would for the first time be translated into a major European language, offering readers a glimpse into the exotic East—a glimpse that would later turn into a grand passion.) As the Crusades reached an end, the lusty prose of the late medieval towns came into popularity. This signified the first major flourishing of a literature of the common people in Europe, and perhaps the first appearance of material of a sexual nature. Since these stories were relayed at adult gatherings after the children had been tucked safely into bed, their peasant narrators could take considerable liberties, thus indulging their natural penchant for sexual innuendo. It would not be long before such erotically charged folktales insinuated themselves into the literary works of the late Middle Ages, the Reformation, and the Renaissance.

Only in the late seventeenth century did a conscious literary interest in the folktale begin in earnest. Around this time it had become the fashion for the upper classes of France to seek out their entertainment from the ways and amusements of the common people, whose folktales were often markedly unpretentious in manner. Up until the late 1600s, the oral folktale was not even deemed worthy of being transcribed, let alone transformed into literature. The aristocracy and intelligentsia of Europe had banished it to the realm of the peasant, associating such material with pagan beliefs and superstitions no longer relevant in a Christian Europe. If acknowledged at all, the stories were at best considered a crude form of entertainment, anecdote, or homily passed on by peasants, merchants, clergy, and servants—and, as such, something to be chuckled at or clucked over by the upper classes.

From the late Middle Ages up through the Renaissance, the oral tradition of telling tales proved popular with many groups. Nonliterate peasants told them among themselves at hearthside or in the fields. Nevertheless, these folk narratives were not relegated exclusively to the illiterate. Priests quickly discovered their value, utilizing them in sermons in an attempt to reach out to the peasantry. The tales eventually received an even wider hearing by the members of all classes, as literate merchants and travelers relayed them at taverns and inns, while in the nursery wet nurses and governesses told them to the children in their charge. As the stories of the common folk spread from place to place and from person to person in their many variants, they grew to be more cultivated, eventually entering the French salon by the middle of the seventeenth century—and, in the process, losing much of the unpretentious quality that made them so appealing and entertaining in the first place.

In what can be seen as the rise of the literary fairy tale such as those attributed to Charles Perrault in his *Histoires ou Contes du Temps Passé* (Tales of past times), one must look to the Paris salons formed in the 1600s by women of the French aristocracy. Because they lacked access to institutions of higher learning, these ladies of the boudoir organized gatherings in their homes, inviting other women and eventually even a few men to discuss art and literature. Narratives based on oral folktales would be introduced and continually improved on, thereby setting the standard for the *conte de fée*, or literary fairy tale. As a consequence, the peasant settings and content of the tales would be restructured to appeal to a more aristocratic and bourgeois audience, including that of King Louis XIV himself.

By the close of the seventeenth century, the salon fairy tale had become so acceptable that women as well as some men (including Monsieur Perrault) wrote down their tales. Eventually these tales made their way into the public arena in the form of publication. Yet such elegant reworkings of what had once been the folktale of the peasant were not always intended as an innocent form of entertainment. A crisis was brewing in France; living conditions had deteriorated at every level of society, leaving neither aristocrat nor peasant immune. With Louis XIV waging costly wars and annexing more and more land, it had become a time of high taxes and poor crops, not to mention a time of rigidity caused by the king's ever-increasing piousness. Ergo, these salon tales eventually began to be utilized as a means of criticism, prompting many writers to fall into the king's disfavor.

By the 1700s, the lure of the exotic rather than the common had captured the fancy of the French, with *The Arabian Nights* and the Hindu *Panchatantra*. The diminishing grandeur of the court of Versailles and the continuing decline of France further fueled this intense interest in the Orient, and by 1720 the once-irresistible appeal of the literary fairy tale had all but diminished, resulting in a conventionalized form suited more for pedagogical purposes than the sophisticated entertainment of the aristocracy. *Colporteurs* (peddlers) took these tales into the villages in the form of the *Bibliothèque Bleue*, which contained abbreviated versions of literary tales adapted for use in oral presentations. With this continuing institutionalization of the literary fairy tale, people of all ages and classes could have access to them, thereby creating still more diffusion of the tales throughout the Western world.

In the Germany of the early 1800s, former law students Jacob and Wilhelm Grimm collected more than two hundred tales in their *Kinder- und Hausmärchen* (Nursery and household tales), of which seven editions were published during their lifetimes. The project initially began as a scholarly enterprise, their goal being to capture the German folk tradition in print before it died out. Since the brothers believed that the idiom in which a story was told had as much value as the content, they were extremely devoted to the oral folk tradition. Indeed, early-nineteenth-century Europe was possessed with a romantic admiration for the simple folk—an admiration that encompassed a decidedly nationalistic concern with local traditions. Although it has generally been assumed that the Grimms collected their folktales directly from the peasants who heard and retold them in the oral tradition, in fact they took them from nonpeasants (often the brothers' own relatives) on whose memories the Grimms had come to rely.

Up until the Franco-Prussian War, the art of composing the narrative folktale remained popular with adults in many parts of Germany. As the Industrial Age took hold, the necessity for the types of collective household and harvesting activities that had once provided a perfect forum for the oral narrative began to be eliminated, thereby bringing an end to the folktale as a form of public entertainment for adults. Fairy tales soon fell out of favor worldwide as more and more young people became educated. The household arts would all but vanish, as would local dialects, which were usurped by the use of a widespread language. With the arrival of the newspaper, the reading of serious material had supplanted the more frivolous entertainments of the past. Wars and issues related to government captured the attention of the reader, not the romantic awakening of a beautiful princess.

By the twentieth century, adults had turned away from fairy tales altogether, leaving them to the domain of the nursery. Because so many of these tales had been written down in literary earnest during the time of the Grimms, it had become the norm to expurgate fiction, especially with regard to sexual matters, thus further relegating the fairy tale to the only audience apparently remaining to enjoy them: *children*. Nevertheless, it is interesting to note that despite the brothers' efforts to sanitize elements of the tales they found objectionable—or believed their audience would find objectionable—the Grimms appeared to have no qualms about perpetuating the unwholesome themes of cannibalism, murder, mutilation, and incest.

Although expunged in more modern times by various authors and collectors, eroticism was alive and well and, indeed, flourishing in the oral tales of the peasant and in the literary works of such authors as Boccaccio, Chaucer, and Straparola. Yet no matter how cleanly excised from the stories of our childhood, elements of sexuality still remain even today—if only in subtle form. Perhaps our normal human interest in matters of the flesh inspires the fairy tale to live on and on. For whether curious child or curious adult, we all have the desire to know The Forbidden.

No matter where they came from or who has had a hand in their retelling, fairy tales have captured the imagination of the world and the imaginations of writers such as Charles Dickens, C. S. Lewis, and George Bernard Shaw. It is in this very same creative spirit that I continue the age-old tale-telling tradition by offering my own variations on these fairy tales, choosing to rely not on the unexpurgated versions of the past, but rather on those considered suitable for *all* eyes—including the eyes of children. By working in this way, I can remove myself from all previous erotic influences and make these tales my own.

Mitzi Szereto
January 2001

Cinderella

❦

Scholars and lovers of fairy tales will no doubt agree that "Cinderella" is one of the most popular and widely known stories of all time. Nearly a thousand versions from Europe and Asia have been collected—a number that indicates that "Cinderella" has probably undergone more versions than any tale known to us today. For whether appearing during times of famine or in the elegant salons of Paris, the lowly hearth dweller who has lost her shoe can always be recognized.

"Cinderella" has witnessed a long and varied history, hence its present form as known to the Western world is simply a variation on an already existing folktale dating back to antiquity. Although its earliest written form has been traced to a Chinese book from the ninth century, even before the arrival of the Ch'in dynasty "Cinderella" lived in the story of Yeh-hsien— a poor wretch of a girl ill-treated by her stepmother, but aided by a mysterious man from the sky. In fleeing her family at a festival, Yeh-hsien loses a shoe, which eventually falls into the hands of a king, who orders every woman in his kingdom to try it on. Finding the shoe's rightful owner, the king marries Yeh-hsien.

Despite the great age of this Chinese "Cinderella," many scholars believe that the tale actually originated in the Middle East. In the story of Rhodope, collected around the time of Christ, an eagle absconds with the sandal of a beautiful courtesan, only to drop it onto a pharaoh—who finds himself so taken by it that all of Egypt is searched for the sandal's owner so that he can marry her. However, some elements in the tale may be far more ancient than even those found in the stories about Yeh-hsien or Rhodope. In the primitive hunting and grazing societies appearing at the end of the Ice Age, the female was placed at the center of society and, as such, would often be sacrificed so that she could return as an animal or tree—as did Cinderella's mother, who after death returns in some versions of the tale in the form of a calf.

Although Charles Perrault and the Brothers Grimm (with whom we equate "Cinderella") are household names, less familiar to nonscholars is Giambattista Basile, a Neapolitan of seventeenth-century Italy. In his collection of tales derived from the Neapolitan oral tradition entitled *Il Pentamerone* (The five days), a less ancient precursor to "Cinderella" can be found in the tale "La Gatta Cenerentola" (The hearth cat). Interested in manipulating circumstances to suit herself, Basile's protagonist, Zezolla, conspires with her governess to murder her stepmother. But matters do not turn out as expected, for Zezolla's new stepmother (the governess) has several daughters, all of whom are placed above her in importance. Hence a life of drudgery of even worse proportions is bestowed on Zezolla. Indeed, this prevalence of stepmothers in folktales and fairy tales resulted not merely from creative license, but from the reality of the times. Many women died young from frequent childbearing and unsanitary conditions, only to be replaced by the husband's new spouse, which usually left the remaining offspring at the mercy of the not-always-kindly stepmother.

A literary critic, poet, and court attendant during the reign of Louis XIV, Charles Perrault created the version of "Cinderella" that seems to be the most preferred. Since he intended his tale to suit the refined tastes of the court of Versailles, anything considered vulgar was removed. Published in 1697 in his *Histoires ou Contes du Temps Passé*, Perrault's "Cendrillon" is a cleaned-up version of its Neapolitan predecessor. Unlike Basile's murderous Zezolla, Cendrillon sits passively by while those around her act with the utmost cruelty. Changes

2

in social attitudes would contribute much to the folktale's evolution into literary tale, for it was in Perrault's day that the motif of the passive female appeared—a motif that served to reinforce the patriarchal values of the times.

In the versions collected during the nineteenth century by Jacob and Wilhelm Grimm in their *Kinder- und Hausmärchen*, the protagonist is as passive as her ash-bespattered counterpart in Perrault. Aside from being a reflection of contemporary standards, this indicates a possible diffusion of the Frenchman's literary tale into German oral tradition. The brothers' "Aschenputtel" restores much of the violence and gore of earlier non-Perrault versions by including the stepsisters' mutilation of their feet. Of course, this particular element demonstrates that still more diffusion may have tainted the supposedly German versions of the Grimms via the Scottish tale "Rashin Coatie"—in which the stepsisters compete for the slipper (and the prince), resulting in the mutilation of Rashin Coatie's stepsister's foot. A story in *The Complaynt of Scotland* dating to 1540 is considered the basis for the tale, which makes it predate not only the versions of the Grimms, but Basile as well.

Perhaps not as erotically infused as other fairy tales with so lengthy a history, "Cinderella" is not altogether lacking in matters pertaining to the sexual. Clearly, the presence of the slipper is the most important element in the story and, as such, can be construed as an object of eroticism. Indeed, in a variety of Chinese folklore, the slipper serves as a symbol of the vagina, with further evidence of Cinderella's link to Asian cultures being assumed from the ancient practice of binding a woman's feet. A small foot was considered sexually appealing—and much mention is made of the petite nature of Cinderella's feet. With this in mind, how could any self-respecting prince possibly resist worshipping the slipper into which so dainty a foot could fit? ❧

CINDERELLA

THERE ONCE LIVED A WIDOWED GENTLE-
man of minor distinction and much loneliness.
Although he had a daughter of his own, it was
the companionship of a mate he desired most. The
daisies had not even begun to spring up from the
freshly turned earth beneath which his poor late wife
had been buried before he took for himself another
wife—the proudest, vainest, and haughtiest woman to
be found in the entire kingdom. It so happened that
she had a pair of daughters herself, both of whom possessed even greater pride, vanity, and hauteur than
the mother who had given birth to them. The three
came to live with the unsuspecting widower, whose
own daughter had the sweetest, most temperate
nature imaginable and was the complete opposite of
her father's new wife and stepdaughters. Hence the
trouble begins.

For no sooner had the ink dried on the parchment of the couple's wedding decree than the new
bride made the true wickedness of her character
known. Unable to bear the goodly virtues of her pretty
young stepdaughter—for they served to make her
own flesh and blood all the more abominable—the

woman took it upon herself to foist on the girl the dirt-
iest and most disagreeable of household chores:
chores that only a common char would have performed. Each day from sunup to sundown the
stepdaughter washed dishes and scrubbed floors; she
polished silver and emptied chamber pots. When she
had finished, she swept out the cellar and gathered up
cobwebs from every corner of the house—and all
while being at her stepmother's constant beck and
call. For the grand lady had a good many garments to
be laundered and much dust to be cleared from her
bedchamber.

As did her two spoiled daughters, both of
whom had been given rooms of their very own with
fine parquet floors for their oversized feet to walk
upon and tall gilt mirrors to reflect their lumpen forms
from top to toe. At night they slept on the softest and
most luxurious of beds, their heads resting comfortably against fluffy pillows stuffed with goose feathers,
the costliest of lace-trimmed duvets tucked cozily up
beneath their disdainful chins. Meanwhile, the girl in
whose father's house they dwelled had for her solitary quarters a cramped space in the corner of the
dark and musty attic, with only a small oil lamp to see
by and the squealing of mice for conversation. Since
she owned no bed of her own, she slept on the stone
hearth among cinders remaining from the coal fires
that provided heat for the rest of the house, cinders
that she purloined when no one was looking and took

to her room. Although terribly uncomfortable, at least they were warm.

As a consequence of this sleeping arrangement, the girl became known in the household as *Cinderwench*. However, the youngest of the stepsisters, who was not quite so cruel in temperament as her mother and elder sibling, would instead bestow upon her new sister the more melodic appellation of *Cinderella*. Even in her ragged old garments and clumsy wooden clogs, the girl possessed a far prettier face and figure than either of her two stepsisters with their grand dresses and glittering jewels. Despite her dismal situation, Cinderella dared not complain to her father, since he would have scolded her most severely and taken his wife's side. For ever since the wedding day, the woman had made it her mission to control her husband's every breath, especially those drawn in the household.

With the impending arrival of spring, the King ordained a festival of food and dance at which his young son and sole heir to the throne would choose a bride from among the many guests. He invited all persons of social standing, and, being well known in society, Cinderella's two stepsisters received an invitation, thereby creating still more work for the poor girl. There was linen to be ironed and ruffles to flute, along with a myriad of other personal tasks in need of attending to. In the preceding weeks the sisters talked of nothing but the nightly dances and what they planned to wear to them; not even the most minute of details would be overlooked. They ordered special headdresses stitched from the finest silk with rows of pearl trimming, and they selected beauty patches from the best maker in the town, their pride not allowing them to accept otherwise. The sisters next summoned Cinderella to solicit her opinion, for, irrespective of her lowly appearance, she had been endowed with an innate sense of taste of which the two desired to avail themselves. Being dutiful and kind at heart, this unwanted female relation provided as much assistance as she could, even offering to personally dress her stepsisters' hair—an offer that both enthusiastically seized. The King's son was very handsome and stood to inherit great riches, not to mention the wealth of the entire kingdom. Why should it not be one of *them* whom he takes for his princess?

While pressing yet another perfect ringlet into place above her older stepsister's temple, Cinderella was asked with an unmistakable mocking of tone whether she might like to accompany them to the royal ball. Naturally, she realized that she was being teased, since who would desire *her* unworthy presence at such a grand event? "Oh, sisters, whatever would I be doing at the Prince's ball?" she said with a laugh, trying to cover the bitter sting of tears.

"Indeed," snorted the eldest, "whatever *would* a miserable Cinderwench be doing at the Prince's dance? How people would laugh!"

7

One might imagine that the humbled girl would have used this opportunity to sabotage her stepsister's hair after having been made the victim of so heartless a joke, but Cinderella had such a sweet and loving nature it would not have been in her mind to do so. Instead she continued pressing the ornate ringlets of hair into place, refusing to cease from her labors until both sisters were ready to have their expensive headdresses placed atop their stylishly coifed heads. For luck, Cinderella tucked a tiny gray mouse beneath each headdress, her sisters having told her that mice brought very good fortune and that she should be grateful to have so many of them living with her in her attic quarters.

So excited were the two siblings as the hour of the Prince's dance approached that they refused to eat a morsel all day, desiring only to spend their time preening and primping before their mirrors and ordering their exhausted step-relation to lace their waists tighter and tighter till they could scarcely draw a breath. Cinderella found herself being dispensed time and again to the cellar to fetch rags so that the wilted growths on her stepsisters' chests might be granted an opportunity to project more conspicuously outward from the tops of their corsets. (Unbeknownst to Cinderella, the proud swellings atop her own chest had provided her stepsisters with yet another reason for their hatred of her.) Fortunately, there would be rags aplenty for the task,

Cinderella having just that morning used them for cleaning the chamber pots.

That evening, Cinderella watched her stepsisters' elaborate departure with melancholy eyes. No sooner did their elegant coach disappear from view than she hurled herself among the cinders in the hearth and wept. Although she occupied an inferior position in the household, she was still a young woman with a young woman's dreams and desires—dreams and desires that did not preclude meeting the handsome son of the King. As the torrent from her eyes formed salty puddles on the cold flagstones beneath her, she sensed another presence in the shadowy attic. Suddenly through the sheen of her tears she saw a wispy, winged figure hovering in the air. It lit up the room, radiating a quality like sunshine on a summer's afternoon. "Do not weep, dear one," came a voice as pleasant and musical as tiny bells. "I am your fairy godmother, and anything you wish for, it shall be my duty to fulfill." As her visitor drew nearer, Cinderella noticed something curious that seemed to jar with the creature's tinkling tones and diminutive dimensions—a something that took the form of a prickly black stubble on the face and a proliferation of curly black hair on the forearms. Having never before met a true-to-life fairy, she thought no more about it.

In a mad rush of words, Cinderella began to tell of her heart's desire, her plaintive pleas mingling with her hopeless sobs. Needless to say, the gist of her plight would be easily understood. "Of *course* you shall go to the Prince's ball!" trilled the fairy. "But first you must fetch me a pumpkin from yonder garden."

Although puzzled by this demand, Cinderella did as she was told. While on her quest, she came to find herself momentarily distracted by a patch of parsnips. She had oftentimes observed her two stepsisters stealing out in the dark of night to collect the stout white root, which they took back to their rooms for use in a special ritual. Cinderella knew this, because she would steal up to their doors, only to hear a tremendous commotion coming from the other side consisting of a whining and whinnying that reminded her of her father's favorite horse. The following morning when she went in to clean, she discovered a heap of wilted parsnips on the floor by their bedsides. Taking a cue from her older and wiser stepsisters, Cinderella thought she should collect some parsnips as well, so she uprooted several from the soil and placed them inside the frayed pocket of her apron, deciding not to mention this extra acquisition to her stubble-faced fairy godmother.

With the biggest and orangest pumpkin Cinderella could locate cradled in one hairy arm, the little fairy scooped out its pulpy flesh until all that remained was the shell. Satisfied with her handiwork, she touched to it her tiny wand and lo! The pumpkin was no longer a pumpkin, but a fine golden coach.

"Now fetch me that mousetrap," she instructed, pointing to a corner where six gray mice squeaked and complained inside a wire cage. Another stroke of the magical wand, and three pairs of horses rose up in their place, each a lovely dappled gray. Cinderella pinched herself to bleeding, unable to believe her eyes. Nevertheless, she did not hesitate an instant when charged with the disagreeable task of checking the rat-trap for new arrivals. Three large and very black rats glowered indignantly up at her. The fairy considered them carefully, selecting the one with the most imposing set of whiskers. As her tiny wand glanced its spiny head, up sprang a coachman dressed in shiny black livery, his mustache as grand a specimen as could ever be seen and covering nearly half his face. The snug hide of his uniform rippled with the sheer bulk of him, and when he turned away to take his place alongside the golden coach, Cinderella flushed with embarrassment, for the seat of his pantaloons had been cut completely away, revealing twin globes of pale flesh. Never having seen such costuming on a servant, she looked to her fairy godmother for confirmation that this was, indeed, proper attire for a coachman, only to find the fluttery-winged sprite fixing the exposed flesh with a wicked eye. Alas, Cinderella's discreet clearing of the throat resulted in the wearisome requisitioning of six squiggly green lizards, which instantly sprang to attention as an equal number of green-liveried footmen. "You may now go to the royal ball," announced the fairy with a hint of irritation, the girl having returned with the lizards far more swiftly than expected. Even the coachman appeared put out as he plucked at the seat of his uniform, as if it required adjustment.

Cinderella danced happily about, her mind filling with glamorous images of herself and the handsome Prince. Then, just as suddenly as she had started, she stopped, glancing down at herself in dismay. "How ever can I go to the royal ball in these old rags?" she lamented, indicating her soiled and tattered garments. Why, she could not even recall the last time she had been allowed to wash them. Her mean-spirited stepmother scolded her endlessly about wasting soap — unless, of course, it was intended for washing the lady's garments or those of her two spoiled daughters. In response, the magical wand came down on Cinderella's head and the dirty rags covering her body dissolved into a magnificent gown woven from threads of silver and gold and encrusted with precious gemstones.

All at once Cinderella felt herself in danger of toppling over, and she flailed her arms about in an effort to regain her balance. Upon discovering the reason for this sudden unsteadiness, she cried out in astonishment, for the chipped wooden clogs that swam about on her tiny feet had been replaced by a pair of delicate glass slippers. Indeed, the heel was as tall as the slipper was long, tapering down to a piercing spike. "Oh, Fairy Godmother, how ever shall I walk in these?"

"Some people are never satisfied," grumbled the fairy, her hairy forearms crisscrossing one another in annoyance.

Feeling like a real-life princess, Cinderella wobbled regally up into the waiting coach, its golden door held open for her by the mustachioed and scantily seated coachman. "Remember, you must return by the stroke of midnight and not a moment later," cautioned the fairy godmother with undue sternness, "or everything will be as before." By now the little fairy had become all too accustomed to these flighty young things paying her no mind, and she sometimes wondered why she bothered any more, particularly when so many others in the profession had long since retired. Promising to be home at the appointed hour, Cinderella rode off to the royal ball, too delirious with joy to have taken any notice of the meaningful looks being exchanged between her fairy godmother and the muscular coachman.

As it happened, Cinderella's glass-encased feet had not even teetered across the threshold of the King's palace before the Prince received word about the arrival of a beautiful Princess. Although no one claimed to know the identity of this Princess, her appearance garnered considerable attention from those in attendance, including the two sisters, whose envious eyes almost sprang from their sockets when they saw the eligible young Prince putting forth a velvet-clad arm to escort the unidentified Princess into the ballroom. They scratched their heads with apparent curiosity, although perhaps this scratching had been brought on by the tiny mouse placed beneath their headdresses by their lowly relation.

At the couple's grand entrance, a hush fell over the crowd and the instruments stopped playing and the dancers stopped dancing. Never had any of the King's guests set eyes upon such an exquisite creature, let alone such extraordinary footwear. The ladies made a careful note of the elegant style of Cinderella's hair and gown and the dagger-like sharpness of her heels, while the gentlemen willed the turmoil taking place within their tightening breeches to cease lest they make public spectacles of themselves. The ornate bodice of Cinderella's garment had been cut immodestly low in the front, placing on view two graceful and luxurious mounds of milky-white flesh that formed a neat and most eye-catching crease down the center. As for the glass slippers, the height of the heels directed the wearer's carriage into that of an *S* shape, forcing Cinderella to walk with an exaggerated out-thrusting of the posterior and thereby inspiring desires of a not altogether chivalrous nature to ferment in the minds of the gentlemen in attendance.

During the entire evening the King's son refused to stand up with anyone but the mysterious Princess, and hence when the hour came for the magnificent supper to be served, he insisted that Cinderella be seated in the place of honor at his side. Alas, the Prince would be incapable of swallowing even the tiniest bite of the fine fare that was displayed. Despite the many attempts made to engage him in conversation or draw his gaze toward a succulent cut of meat, his attention could not be swayed from the ever-more succulent presence of his female table partner. Be that as it may, the Prince would not go hungry on this eve, for his bewitched eyes gorged themselves on the heavenly movement of his companion's primrose lips as she chewed and on the gentle rise and fall of her chest as she breathed and on the delightful wriggling of her tiny feet in the spiked slippers as they sought to create for themselves a restful position beneath her chair. Later, the Prince's chosen companion wobbled purposefully past her stepsisters, who even close up failed to recognize their Cinderwench. As she was about to identify herself, Cinderella heard the portentous striking of the clock. With a hurried curtsy to all, she dashed outside to the golden coach, arriving at her father's home mere moments before it and everything else returned to their original humble states.

As Cinderella replayed in her mind every magical detail of the glamorous ball and the King's handsome son—who had extended an invitation to her for the following evening—a presumptuous knock sounded at the attic door. Without waiting for a reply, the two sisters barged into the little attic room and proceeded to regale their step-relation with tales of the royal events and the enchanting Princess who had turned everyone's head with her beauty and her extraordinary glass slippers. "It is unfortunate you did not choose to accompany us," replied the elder sister with intentional cruelty. "For she was the loveliest of princesses and paid us a good many compliments on our dress and hair."

"Indeed," interjected the youngest, whose fingers scratched and poked persistently beneath her headdress. "She has promised that I may have personal use of her slippers whenever I wish."

Swallowing a powerful urge to take them both to task about these bald-faced lies, Cinderella instead inquired as to the identity of this Princess, only to be answered by a matching pair of shrugs. Yet one thing the sisters *did* know—the King's beloved son had withdrawn to his rooms in great despair, telling anyone who cared to listen that he would be willing to forfeit half his father's kingdom to discover the identity of the lady who had stolen his heart. "Dearest sister, might I borrow your old yellow frock so that I, too, may catch a glimpse of this beautiful Princess?" asked Cinderella, eager for some evidence that deep down her stepsisters possessed kind hearts. She was well aware that the garment in question had not been worn in many years and now hung like a discarded rag on a hook in the rear of its owner's wardrobe.

The elder sister snorted. "Lend my dress to a miserable Cinderwench? Why, I should be frothing mad to do such a thing!" Apparently finished with their torment of her, Cinderella's stepsisters fled the musty attic room, their scornful laughter echoing through the house and piercing the heart of the one who had inspired it. A moment later, they could be spied in the moonlit garden, where they set about pulling up the largest and meatiest of parsnips from the earth to take back with them to their rooms. For the remainder of the night, a cornucopia of whinnying and neighing could be heard coming from behind their doors till dawn finally broke over the horizon, at which time Cinderella would be required to undertake the monotonous task of clearing up after her stepsisters, each of whom had left a mound of broken and wilted parsnips alongside their beds.

The following evening at twilight, the two sisters set jubilantly off for the King's palace in their stepfather's horse-drawn coach, leaving behind a disheartened Cinderella, who watched their boisterous departure through the soot-covered panes of the dormer window. The *clickity-clack* of hooves had not even faded before she fell weeping to the hearth, receiving no solace from the cold flagstones. As all hope of ever again seeing the handsome Prince seemed forever lost, Cinderella heard a familiar fluttering of wings, followed by the diminutive sight of her fairy godmother, whose facial stubble had grown noticeably denser since their last meeting.

Moments later, yet another from the household was riding happily off to the Prince's ball, albeit with an entirely new coachman, the previous one having been recruited to remain behind with the little fairy. On this occasion Cinderella would be attired more magnificently than before in a gown stitched with rubies, its snugly fitted bodice propelling the fleshy swellings on her chest outward like offerings of fruit. The very same glass slippers encased her tiny feet, but by now she had become more accustomed to walking and dancing in their steeple-like heels and did not in the least mind the attention that both her footwear and her out-thrust posterior garnered. Having been for so long an object of neglect, Cinderella enjoyed the appraising looks and suggestive comments directed her way by the gentlemen guests, and for some inexplicable reason she found herself thinking of parsnips.

Once again the Prince refused to be parted from Cinderella's side, even to the detriment of neglecting his other guests, many of whom were titled young ladies most eager for his company and whose families were still more eager to experience a commingling of fortunes. Of course, no one thought the least bit ill of him for his unintended rudeness, for the charm and the beauteous attributes of the glass-slippered Princess were far too great for any humble mortal to resist. The King's son lavished so many compliments upon Cinderella that she forgot the warning issued by her fairy godmother. For who could worry about pumpkins and mice, with the fire of the Prince's breath in her ear and the scorch of his fingertips on her arm? Nevertheless, the clock's first strike of midnight reminded Cinderella that she must take heed, and, without a word of farewell, she fled into the night, her impassioned suitor dashing after her in frenzied pursuit. Try though he might, the Prince could not keep pace with the spike-heeled apparition who had captured his heart. He stumbled and fell to the dew-dampened ground in an unroyal sprawl. He had been tripped by a tiny glass slipper. Its distinctive heel glittered provocatively in the moonlight, bringing a cry of longing into his throat.

Cinderella arrived home breathless and shaken and minus the pomp and glory of her coach and footmen, her garments once more the tattered rags that designated her subservient position in her father's household. All that remained of her former splendor was a glass slipper, its delicate spike-tipped mate having apparently gotten lost somewhere along the way. To look at her now, one would never have guessed that Cinderella was the mystery Princess who had twitched her hips so invitingly on the dance floor or who had willfully encouraged her royal suitor to press his foot to hers beneath the supper table for a time far longer than one might have deemed prudent. For when the Prince quizzed the palace guards as to the direction in which this Princess had fled, he was informed that they had seen only a poor peasant girl hurrying toward the road.

A short while later, Cinderella's two stepsisters charged into the dusty mice-ridden attic to entertain their miserable drudge of a relative with still more tales of the glamorous proceedings and the unnamed Princess whose behavior on the dance floor they deemed highly scandalous...though neither sister would be above claiming that *she* had been personally singled out by the glass-slipped Princess as an arbiter of beauty of fashion. This time Cinderella was pre-pared for them and their outrageous falsehoods. "Dearest sisters, I have collected for you some very fine parsnips from the garden, since you must be greatly fatigued from the Prince's ball." She gestured toward a basket of straw filled to overflowing with parsnips, each one fatter than the next. Having returned home well in advance of her sisters, Cinderella had rubbed them with the crushed seeds of chili peppers — her stepmother's favorite condiment and one that undoubtedly accounted for the woman's perpetually pinched expression.

The two sisters flushed to a dark purple, only to reclaim their usual braggadocio when pressed by Cinderella for further details of the royal festivities. The eldest spoke in excited tones of the rather hasty exit of the lady in question and the glass slipper that had fallen from her dainty foot. It appeared that for the remainder of the evening the King's son had gone moping about the palace grounds, clutching the spike-heeled little slipper to his chest and gazing forlornly at it as if it held his heart imprisoned inside. "Imagine that a prince should fancy himself in love with a shoe!" snickered the older sister, whose crude cackles were immediately joined by those of her younger sibling.

Had Cinderella's stepsisters but known the truth of their words, they would have flushed yet again. For the good Prince swore a solemn oath that he would locate the owner of the glass slipper, no matter if it took him till the end of his days. On that night he would be granted no sleep. The last of the guests had not even been escorted out through the palace gates before the King's son bolted himself inside his rooms, his unfulfilled passions making him dizzier than all the mead he had drunk during the evening's merriment. "Oh, my lovely one, where art thou?" he wept, pressing the still-warm hollow of the fragile slipper to his nose and breathing in the faint scent of the tiny foot that had occupied it. With trembling fingertips, he caressed the heel, savoring the smooth perfection of the glass as it tapered down to a sharp point. While doing so, the embarrassing affliction that had disturbed so many of the gentlemen guests when confronted with the charming presence of the slipper's wearer began to make itself known inside the Prince's breeches. Indeed, it afforded a constriction that proved extremely distressing, and he nearly collapsed to the floor in a faint. "I must seek relief from this wretched suffering!" he gasped, reaching down to loosen the straining laces that kept the front of the garment closed and his manly modesty intact.

No sooner had the Prince succeeded in doing so than an object of substantial length and girth sprang forth from the escape his fumbling fingers provided. The weeping purple crown at its apex jumped wildly about in his palm, growing so fat that his fingers could no longer contain it. The aggrieved heir to the throne stuffed as much of it as could be gotten inside the diminutive slipper, the fleshy mass bursting out from the jumble of unfastened laces and swelling even larger within the narrow glass confines. Had he not been in such desperate straits, the Prince might have thought better of his actions. The bloated entity promptly became stuck and commenced to throb most painfully, matching the wild throbbing of his love-stricken heart.

Taking great care not to shatter the translucent contours, the Prince twisted and joggled the little slipper about until he had regained some freedom of movement. Satisfied that matters were at last under control, he cleared all thought from his head in readiness for the task before him. Allowing his instincts to rule, he urged his hips forward and back, thereby encouraging the bulbous protuberance to slide across the slipper's slender instep. By this time the surface had become suitably moist and slippery, and the

Prince discovered that he could slip along it quite easily and with considerable enjoyment to himself. And indeed, the impassioned young royal spent several luxurious moments doing so until, in a sudden flash of memory, the image of the slipper's lovely owner materialized in his mind's eye. Ergo, both hands would be grasping onto the heel with such desperation that its gleaming point cut the flesh of his palms to ribbons. A garbled groan caught in the Prince's constricting throat, and he shuddered as the glass filled to overflowing with an endlessly spurting stream of hot, frothy fluid.

The very next day, the King's son sent forth several teams of trumpeters with a proclamation that he would marry the lady whose foot fit the glass slipper. Not surprisingly, every young woman in the kingdom, and even those no longer young, offered up a hopeful foot for the royal equerry, praying that it could be squeezed into the impossibly tiny shoe. At first all the princesses tried, followed by the duchesses, each grouping of toes being greeted by a marshy warmth. For when the avid aspirant removed her too-large foot from the dainty vessel of glass, her bruised and battered toes would be sticky with cream.

As the search for the slipper's owner expanded, it eventually came to the house of Cinderella's two stepsisters. They tried every trick they could think of to force the slipper to fit, curling and contorting their proffered extremities until they scarcely resembled feet. Determined to see a match take place between one of her daughters and the handsome young heir to the throne, their mother brought forth a carving knife so that they might slice off their toes—a tactic that was summarily thwarted by the horrified equerry. All the while, Cinderella had been quietly observing these activities from a shadowy corner, having immediately recognized the distinctively heeled slipper as the mate of the one she had kept with her since the night the chiming of the clock had forced her to flee the Prince's ball. "Please allow me to try," she pleaded, stepping boldly forward.

The two sisters squealed and guffawed, jabbing their fingers mockingly toward Cinderella's cobweb-covered form. The Prince's equerry, who had been endeavoring in vain to wedge their clumsy feet into the narrow slipper, looked closely at the raggedly dressed servant girl and, taking note of her natural comeliness, agreed to give her a chance. His instructions had been to try the slipper on every woman in the kingdom—and he dared not disobey an order from the palace, if he placed any value on his head. Gesturing for the pretty wench to be seated, he knelt low to slip the delicate spike-tipped slipper of glass onto her dirt-smudged foot, availing himself of this convenient opportunity to steal a glance up her skirts. Concerned that her foot had become swollen from performing chores all day in her wooden clogs, Cinderella parted her knees just enough to afford the walleyed equerry a better view, thus ensuring that this imperial deputy would do his utmost to make certain that the slipper met up with its rightful owner. And to everyone's astonishment, it was a perfect fit.

Turning her glass-slippered foot every which way to admire it, Cinderella removed from the frayed pocket of her apron a slipper identical to the one the equerry had placed on her. All at once a fluttering could be heard, and from out of the air materialized the Lilliputian form of the fairy. Seeing Cinderella wobbling unsteadily on the impossibly tall heels, the stubble-faced sprite broke into a mischievous grin. A hairy arm clutching a tiny wand shot forward from beneath one iridescent wing to tap the girl's tattered garments, changing them to a gown woven from threads of gold and trimmed with diamonds.

Recognizing the beautiful Princess they had seen at the Prince's ball, the two stepsisters threw themselves at Cinderella's glass-encased feet, begging for forgiveness and lavishing her with honeyed flattery. They even went so far as to bequeath to their previously unwanted relation the next harvest of parsnips in the garden—which, under the circumstances, was no great sacrifice, for their nether parts had been suffering a terrible burning of late. Indeed, the sisters' woeful braying would keep the entire household tossing in their beds till the wee hours, inspiring many a black look and cross word at the breakfast table.

A magnanimous Cinderella placed a regal kiss upon the tops of their falsely bowed heads, bidding her stepsisters only the kindest of wishes, the words tasting bitter on her tongue. Although vengeance might have sweetened them (as might the act of driving the deadly heels of her slippers through their imploring hands!), surely the best revenge of all would be her becoming the bride and therefore the Princess of the King's handsome son. Besides, she could always issue a decree for a sisterly beheading at a later date.

Attired in all the magical finery her fairy godmother had bestowed upon her, Cinderella was escorted to the palace for her wedding to the Prince, who found her even lovelier than she had been in memory. Upon seeing *both* of the exquisitely heeled glass slippers on her dainty feet, he gathered her teetering form into his arms and carried her up the stairs to their matrimonial bedchamber, which had been thoughtfully prepared for this special moment with candles and perfumed sheets and a lute player strumming and singing in an antechamber. Making haste to draw the bolt on the door securely behind them, the Prince placed his beautiful bride with marked gentleness upon the satin-covered bed, where she lay flushed and trembling. Thanks to the parsnips procured from her father's garden, Cinderella had some small knowledge of the matters that transpired between a man and a woman. Furthermore, she frequently overheard her parsnip-collecting stepsisters discussing the subject with a markedly unwholesome relish, and she closed her eyes in happy anticipation of the loving lips that would soon be covering her own.

Rather than presenting his Princess with a tender kiss, however, the bridegroom, who had by now grown quite feverish with desire, plucked the glass slippers from Cinderella's tiny feet, chafing the flesh of her heels in his impatience to remove them. Ripping the laces from the perilously straining front of his specially embroidered wedding breeches, the Prince plunged the bulky protuberance he had released into the right slipper, babbling incoherent words of love as he drove it back and forth across the foot-heated instep. Paying no mind to the damage inflicted upon his hands from the dagger-sharp heel, he performed the same ceremony with the left, his hips charging faster and faster, as did the purple-crowned object jutting out from his unfastened breeches. By the time he finished, frothing lakes of equal depth and stickiness filled the glass of each slipper.

And the Prince and Princess lived happily ever after. Especially the Prince, who had at long last located the missing mate for the dainty little spike-heeled slipper that had fallen from a dainty little foot. For now that he was in possession of both, he vowed to fill them with his love each and every day.

As for the Princess, she would seek her own marital bliss by paying frequent visits to the palace gardens in search of parsnips, as well as by visiting the home of her father and step-relatives, in whose kitchen she collected the crushed seeds of chili peppers to store inside her glass slippers expressly for her beloved husband, the handsome Prince. ❧

THE MAGIC MUNTR

"The Magic Muntr" comes to us from *The Three Princes of Serendip,* or *The Serendipity Tales* — a collection of stories from the fifth century and earlier, considered to have their roots in Persia. Although originally the ancient name for Ceylon, the word *Serendip* evolved into *serendipity,* which in its more modern context would be used to mean the gift of making fortunate and unexpected discoveries by accident. It is a theme that can be found throughout "The Magic Muntr" and its accompanying tales.

Contained in *The Serendipity Tales* are the seven stories heard in the seven palaces of the Emperor Beramo—stories told to him on the advice of three brothers, who suggest them as a means to cure the illness brought on by the emperor's love of a slave girl he believes he has sent to her death. According to the frame story, in the Far Eastern country of Serendippo there lived a king and his three sons. So that the young princes could experience knowledge, their father sent them out into the world. During the course of their travels, they come upon the kingdom of Emperor Beramo. When the emperor falls ill, the brothers advise him to build seven palaces and place within each one seven virgins and seven of the kingdom's best storytellers. Hence the tale telling begins.

Translated from Persian into Italian, *The Serendipity Tales* originally underwent publication in Venice in 1557 as *Peregrinaggio di Tre Giovani, Figliuoli del Re di Serendippo* (Peregrination of the three sons of the king of Serendip). However, the stories were already known in Venice at least a century before their publication, being told in oral form and performed before an audience. And they might well have also been known elsewhere, for despite the ascription in the title to its translation, uncertainty exists as to whether the stories are, in fact, Persian. The *Peregrinaggio* contains tales that may have their origins in the Indian *Panchatantra* and the *Jakata*. A further connection to India can be seen by the character of the parrot, which appears quite prominently in Indian folk literature. So, too, does the theme of humans being transformed into animals (as is demonstrated by the characters in "The Magic Muntr"), the concept of one's soul entering the corpse of an animal being a commonly held Indian belief.

Although the arguments for India may be convincing, the evidence supporting Persia as the *Peregrinaggio*'s true place of origin still cannot be denied. The adventures of the three princes who supply the narrative framework for the seven stories appear in strikingly similar form in the Persian epic poem *The Seven Beauties*, attributed to Nizami. Like the Emperor Beramo, the ailing and lovesick Behram (who regrets his decision to expel from his empire his favorite slave/mistress) is told seven stories by seven princesses in seven different palaces in the hope that he will become well again.

As the Italian *Peregrinaggio* came to be translated into other languages, much of its content would likewise undergo change—including content of a sexual nature, since many of the tales were considered quite ribald in character. Indeed, "The Magic Muntr" does not lack its share of sexually oriented material. The original story concerns an emperor with four wives and an insatiable interest in the wonders of nature—an interest that leads him into being deceived by his chief counselor, who fools the emperor into exchanging spirits. In his new form, the counselor decides to indulge in intimate relations with each of the emperor's wives, finding the youngest so desirable that he returns to her a second time. Noticing that the caresses of her "husband" are not like those of the emperor, the young empress claims to have experienced a terrible vision and must henceforth remain chaste, therefore he cannot approach her bed again. Meanwhile, the real emperor — who has exchanged spirits with a parrot — experiences adventures of his own as he adjudicates an argument over the financial negotiations between a prostitute and the man to whom she wishes to ply her wares. Eventually the emperor-parrot returns home and plots with the young empress to trick the impostor by having her agree to sleep with him if he can change himself into an animal, thus offering proof of being the true emperor. Finally able to resume his original human form, the real emperor dismisses his other wives, keeping only the youngest.

Such frank and, indeed, highly adult content as that seen in "The Magic Muntr" appears regularly in folktales from the Middle East and India, demonstrating that, despite their strong ties to religion, these cultures possessed far less sanctimonious-ness in sexual matters than their more modern Christian counterparts in post-seventeenth-century Europe. Therefore, it is with this very same sense of frankness that I have turned my lit-erary attention toward "The Magic Muntr" and its serendipitous protagonist, whose gift of finding the valuable may well prove to be his undoing. ❧

The Magic Muntr

I N A FARAWAY LAND RICH WITH THE SCENTS of tamarind and jasmine and shaded by the branches of the banyan tree, there lived an inquisitive young ruler named Vicram. Known to his people as the Maharajah, he felt undeserving of so grand a title. He also felt unworthy of so beautiful a Ranee. For Anarkali possessed the exquisite beauty of a flower—a beauty that frequently left her husband wondering whether she might have been dazzled into becoming his wife because of his place on the throne rather than by his average countenance.

Indeed, Vicram's curiosity about matters both great and small extended far beyond the domain of his household, as did his reputation. So powerful was his desire for knowledge that he undertook to erect a temple dedicated to Saraswathi, the goddess of learning. The eager ruler spent many an hour in the jungle, organizing every detail of its construction, convinced that the temple's completion would augur well in his ceaseless pursuit of intellectual fulfillment.

One day as the jasmine exploded into fragrant bloom, a pair of travelers claiming to be philosophers arrived at the gates of the Maharajah's palace.

Although one was in truth a very old and learned seer, the other was but a demon rakshas in disguise. Hearing that such men of erudition had condescended to grace his doorstep, Vicram ordered them to be made welcome. Each was given comfortable robes to wear, woven from golden thread, and a tasty meal to eat of curried rice with slivered almonds and sweet figs plucked from the trees growing in abundance on the palace grounds. After a good night's rest in the finest guest quarters the household had to offer, the two were brought before the Maharajah, who had much of interest to discuss with his guests.

Sensing opportunity in the air, the wicked rakshas wasted no time. Instead of involving himself in a lengthy and arduous discussion of philosophy and politics, he bowed his head low to the floor and tendered his services for the post of prime minister, which by some coincidence just so happened to be vacant. Of course Vicram felt extremely flattered; his government would be most fortunate to secure such a learned individual within its humble ranks. After putting forth a series of difficult questions and receiving the answers he desired, the Maharajah appointed the rakshas to the office with the title of Prudhan. As for the new prime minister's aged companion, he lowered his head in sincere homage, asking only to be granted the supreme privilege of sharing wisdom with the young Maharajah. Vicram could not have been more delighted, for he now had at his constant beck and call two men of great learning. Surely no other ruler could lay claim to such intellectual prosperity.

As the rakshas used his newly acquired authority as Prudhan to plot mischief, the Maharajah and the old philosopher met together daily so that the younger could learn from the elder's tremendous store of wisdom. This ancient savant had come to witness many remarkable events in his travels. Yet perhaps the most wondrous had taken place while he was out walking along a dusty road where he encountered a boy and his dog, the latter of which lay fast asleep in the cooling shade of a banyan tree. The youth had placed his hand over the animal's heart and mumbled a strange and eerie muntr the likes of which had never before been heard by its venerable listener. And there before his rheumy eyes the young master's spirit had slipped into the slumbering form of the hound, whereupon the animal had hopped up onto its four paws and proceeded to sing and dance as its human companion fell lifeless to the ground, his once-robust body an empty husk.

Such a tale sounded amazing, if not impossible, to the Maharajah, yet many more amazing things were to come. After some hours had passed, the dog returned to its master and, placing its front paw over his heart, let loose with a series of barks and whines strikingly similar to the muntr recited earlier. The boy's spirit instantly returned to his body and all became exactly as before, with the hound sleeping peacefully beneath the banyan tree and the master resuming his activities of collecting twigs for the night's bedding.

At this point the philosopher grew uncharacteristically reticent, for he thought it unwise to elaborate further on what had transpired that day. When prodded by the Maharajah—whose curiosity to learn more of these astounding goings-on had lodged itself like a dagger in his chest—the aged seer finally admitted that he had pursued the youth and begged from him the secret of the muntr. "I journeyed with him for many moons so that I might prove myself worthy of owning so dangerous a piece of magic," he explained. "I can now make my spirit pass into that of another living creature at will."

"Oh, Great Sahib, I beseech you to teach me the secret words!" cried the Maharajah, certain he could not live another moment without possession of this valuable knowledge. "For, with all due respect, I must see for myself that this is true."

Although he held grave doubts as to the wisdom of sharing such witchery with the earnest young ruler, the philosopher felt it was not his place to refuse. During their exchange, a sparrow had alighted upon the windowsill and he caught it gently in his hand. With a finger placed over the creature's tiny heart and the utterance of a few mystical words, the savant's ancient body crumpled into itself, dropping to the silken carpet in a withered heap. Shaking off the cage of fingers imprisoning it, the little bird flew up onto Vicram's shoulder and began to sing in the croaking voice of the old man. Yet before its final note had even been released from its warbling throat, it flew back down to settle upon the seer's unmoving chest, with each spirit once more residing within its proper home.

In this way the Maharajah came to learn the secret of the magic muntr. Being of an inquiring nature, he could not wait to try it for himself. That evening as dusk blurred the viridescent landscape, he sallied forth into the jungle, vowing to experiment by changing places with the first creature he encountered—an owl that had made the mistake of perching upon too low a branch. Vicram flew far and wide over bucolic farmland and village rooftop, stopping frequently to rest and to listen to the conversations of his people. As he grew more daring, he ventured into the cities, his feathered ears aprickle for the words that might help him to better understand those over whom he ruled. And indeed, the more he learned, the more he desired to learn. Hence the Maharajah would often be gone from the court for long periods of time, leaving government matters in the wicked hands of his new prime minister, who could not have been more pleased about this recent and unexpected turn of events. For perhaps, he thought, the vacancy in the lovely Ranee's bed might be in need of filling as well.

Wishing to ascertain the cause of these mysterious and frequent absences, the Prudhan decided to follow Vicram into the jungle, where he witnessed an amazing sight—that of the Maharajah exchanging spirits with a bright-green parrot. Now here was a piece of magic of which the demon rakshas could make use! He immediately committed the strange words of the muntr to memory, since one never knew when the opportunity to apply them might present itself. For no sooner did the parrot spread its multicolored wings and fly out of sight than the scheming Prudhan would be kneeling over Vicram's inanimate body, repeating what he had heard and placing his hand over the heart as he had seen demonstrated.

Wearing his new armor of youth and power and with a sprightly spring in his step, the evil rakshas left behind the tired husk he had formerly occupied, returning to the palace to serve in the Maharajah's stead. However, he would not do so without first issuing a fateful curse: that Vicram's inquisitiveness should never be satisfied and that his most primal urges would henceforth be his guiding spirit.

Unaware of the mischief that had just transpired in the jungle, the curious young ruler soared far and wide in his flamboyant form, savoring the sensation of the cool wind against his opened wings. Indeed, the body of a parrot proved far superior to that of a stodgy old owl, and Vicram found himself riding the currents with mellifluous ease, allowing them to take him to places exotic and unknown. He even joined up with a flock of geese heading south, delighted to discover that he could understand their unique language. From them the Maharajah learned many new things and would, in fact, have learned still more had not the sight of an uncurtained window and the shadowy form beyond beckoned him toward it.

Drawn by a force beyond his control, the Vicram-parrot landed atop the sun-warmed sill, his talons softly raking the stone surface. He cocked his tufted head sidewise so that he could peer inside the room, which revealed itself to be a private place for bathing. Almost every piece of furniture, including even the walls themselves, had been covered in silk damask. Had the Maharajah been his normal human self, he might have wished to study the weave of the cloth to better understand the intricacies of its warp and weft. But a curse of great evil had been laid upon him, so instead he found his curiosity ensnared by the stone bathing vessel occupying the center of the room and, in particular, by the provocatively posed figure balancing in a half-crouch within its flinty contours.

A young woman of exceptional beauty appeared to be in the process of washing herself. Hair as black as the blackest of raven's wings draped itself in long, spirally ringlets over a pearly back and shoulders as she stood aggressively lathering a thatch of equally black ringlets growing like a jungle from between her parted thighs. Vicram observed with his left eye (for he could not see in the same direction with both) while this enchanting maiden heightened her cleansing ministrations, her head lolling about to the soapy music being played by her nimble fingers as they blissfully lost themselves within these sudsy nether-curls, their movements accelerating to an impassioned crescendo. By the time they finished their work, she was bucking and grinding against her palm and crying out in the voice of a sick lamb, her dark-fringed eyes raised toward the heavens.

Curious to learn whether others utilized the same bathing technique, the bewinged Maharajah flew from window ledge to window ledge, hoping that he might further his education through a course of stealthy observation. As luck would have it, he located many a shapely female engaged in this fascinating ritual, albeit with slight variations. Some preferred to concentrate their efforts upon the deep crevice located below the graceful arches of their backs, their industrious fingers digging deeply and with unabashed joy into the apparent treasures to be found there until it looked as if their entire arm had vanished in their enthusiasm. Vicram could only marvel at the infinite variety of washing methods employed and the frequency with which they were applied, since many bathers deemed it necessary to repeat their ablutions twice, if not thrice, before finally sinking into the watery depths of their bathing vessels with a ragged sigh, their foam-flecked hands dangling limply over the sides.

Although each individual approach proved highly entertaining as well as educational, the Maharajah's favorite were those seekers of abstersion who, in their feminine cleverness, succeeded in simultaneously cleansing themselves both fore and aft. Indeed, it would be they who bucked and grinded the most, bleating like hysterical ewes as their knees went every which way, their bellies billowing with all the sinuosity of a kohl-eyed desert temptress. Whenever this occurred, Vicram—momentarily forgetting that he had donned the guise of a parrot—hitched up his feathered shoulders and strutted about with masculine pride back and forth along the windowsill, his talons clicking and clacking as he endeavored to gain these lovely young maidens' attentions. Yet rather than having the effect he had hoped for, all it did was result in his being repeatedly shooed away from the window by these bathing beauties, who considered the bird's brightly feathered presence a minor annoyance in the performance of their daily lavations. For their eyes saw not the great Maharajah who ruled over their vast land, but instead a silly green parrot waddling to and fro on its spindly little feet and flapping its red- and yellow-tipped wings. During his travels, poor Vicram felt the threatening breath of many a broom, narrowly escaping with the loss of a feather or two.

In his quest for knowledge, the Maharajah journeyed across the length and breadth of the territory over which his human self reigned. He soared from steppe to sea in his insatiable need to learn more of the mysteries that had so recently consumed him, all the while continuing to be swatted at with brooms or the swishing silk of undergarments still warm and fragrant from their wearers. One evening Vicram became so exhausted from the coarse words and gestures directed his way that he was forced to seek rest upon the branch of a sicakai tree. He felt most unwell. Out of hunger he had eaten the seeds of the tamarind, some of which had gotten lodged inside his tiny throat. Soon a fowler happened by and, seeing the colorful bird fast asleep on the branch, snared it inside a cage. Because of his misfortune with the seed, the Vicram-parrot was powerless to call out his true identity; the only sound to emerge from his throat was a choking croak. The following morning he discovered himself being offered for sale at the bazaar, his brilliant green plumage being remarked upon and haggled over by all. It appeared that in his never-ending search for intellectual enlightenment, the young Maharajah had unintentionally traded his palace for a cage.

While Vicram endured the chaotic clamor of the marketplace, his wife, Anarkali, was made to endure something of an entirely different nature. The beautiful Ranee was becoming increasingly puzzled about the changes that had recently come over her usually predictable husband. Suddenly the man known to his wife and his people as the Maharajah no longer concerned himself with the acquisition of wisdom, but rather with the acquisition of gold and the pleasure derived from merriment. Not even the construction of the temple for the goddess Saraswathi held any interest for him. Instead he ordered the workers to dig a pool so that he might cool himself on a hot afternoon, in the interim converting the half-completed temple into a distillery. He refused to partake of his favorite foods, insisting upon being served dishes of a highly unsavory nature most unlike the flavorful curries and honeyed fruits the palace cooks had always prepared for him. Yet strangest of all was the Maharajah's abrupt dismissal of the old philosopher, whose scholarly presence he had culti-vated with a near-religious devotion. Indeed, the only knowledge for which this once-inquisitive ruler now demonstrated any desire was that of the lovely Ranee's physical self.

For whether morning, noon, or night, his hands were roaming busily about her person, poking and prodding in the rudest and crudest of fashions. "Open your sweet lips to me, my lovely queen," the Maharajah-rakshas would order in a rasping voice most unlike the gentle timbre to which Anarkali had grown accustomed from her mild-mannered husband. "Unlock your thighs so that I may gaze with rapture upon your juicy pomegranate!" commanded this wicked impostor, only to trespass with far more than merely his eyes.

Confused and frightened — and, above all, made increasingly sore by her unremitting ravishment at the hands of the man she believed was her husband — Anarkali sequestered herself inside her private apartments, where she hoped to gain some peace. However, there could be no deterring the determined Maharajah, who took tremendous delight in breaking through the series of iron bolts his wife drew across the door. It seemed the Ranee had no choice except to relinquish herself to these perverse claims upon her person. And she did so with gritted teeth, wondering how her unassuming spouse had gotten such peculiar ideas into his head. For no more was the good Maharajah heard to speak of music and poetry and the plight of the poor, but only of matters pertaining to the pleasures of the flesh.

When not busy accommodating the Maharajah's fleshly demands, Anarkali would take to her bed in exhaustion. Sorry for her mistress, a faithful attendant who had gone shopping in the marketplace happened upon a cage containing a brilliant green parrot. Although it required the entirety of her month's wages, she purchased the bird from the fowler and brought it back with her to the palace, hoping it might bring cheer to the Ranee, who had come on rather wan and poorly of late.

Anarkali accepted the gift with sincere thanks, placing the cage and its feathered occupant alongside her bed. She spent many solitary hours talking to the parrot, which had apparently taken a liking to her, for it would raise its tufted head and splay its wings to show their spectacular reds and yellows, winking an eye in suggestion of something the Ranee could only have guessed at. Despite its outwardly healthful appearance, something seemed to be wrong with the bird. Every time it opened its beak, out came a terrible choking squawk. And it grew even worse whenever the Maharajah called upon his wife in her bed, which would often be several times within a single day. No sooner did the masquerading Prudhan order the trembling Ranee to offer up for his meticulous inspection her juicy pomegranate than the parrot staged a fit. It thrashed about in its cage and beat its red- and yellow-tipped wings, emitting a screeching and squawking the likes of which could not be heard in the wildest jungle. It came to be such a nuisance that the Maharajah-rakshas threatened to have the bird served up for that evening's supper with a sauce of cherries and figs and a topping of shredded coconut. Obviously it never occurred to him that this vexing entity of feathers and mites was the very man he had taken it upon himself to impersonate. Had the demon rakshas known, matters would have turned out very differently, indeed.

To placate the agitated parrot and thereby gain for it a temporary reprieve from the supper table, the Ranee began feeding it by hand pieces of dried fruit and nuts and even some bits of peeled cucumber.

Perhaps it might have been the latter that finally inspired the lodged seed of the tamarind tree to go sliding down the bird's slender gullet. For one morning when they were alone, the parrot suddenly announced to the Ranee that he was her husband, the Maharajah. At first Anarkali refused to believe such a fanciful claim. But after hearing Vicram's astonishing adventures as a winged creature of flight and all that he had seen and learned in his travels, she accepted his claim as fact. It would have been exactly like her inquisitive husband to venture forth on such an incredible mission in the guise of a parrot. Nevertheless, one mystery still remained unsolved: that of the true identity of the villainous impostor who now occupied the Maharajah's throne and his wife's bed. When queried by the bird as to whether anyone had gone missing of late, the Ranee replied without hesitation that the new Prudhan had done so—and, indeed, done so on the very day her husband, Vicram, had come to her so greatly changed. The pair then proceeded to hatch a plot that would soon set all to rights.

That evening the rakshas appeared as was his usual custom in Anarkali's bed in the guise of her husband, his gait unsteady, his breath stinking of distilled spirits. He fell heavily onto the mattress alongside the frightened figure of the Ranee, unperturbed by her violent trembles or the expression of revulsion in her kohl-rimmed eyes. "I demand that you once again give up to me your pomegranate, for this afternoon I did not find it nearly so sweet and juicy as usual. In fact, I'd say it was extremely bitter," he replied with a scowl, his hand scrabbling up Anarkali's thigh.

At this the parrot flew out from its cage, the door of which had been left intentionally ajar by the Ranee, and landed atop the traitorous Prudhan's chest. "You jackal! Give back to me my body!" screeched the bird, whose voice sounded oddly familiar to the drunken rakshas. Yet before he could identify it, the Vicram-parrot uttered the words of the magic muntr.

The demon rakshas, who had abandoned his body in the jungle without a thought toward ever making use of it again, found himself imprisoned within the bright green body of the parrot and, for that evening's supper, was served up on a golden platter with a sauce of figs and sweet cherries and covered from beak to talon with tender shreds of coconut. And not a single feather would go to waste, for even his carefully plucked plumage later served as excellent writing quills.

·However, the wicked curse that had been placed upon the Maharajah by the rakshas had not been lifted and, with that evil one's death, never would be. Although Vicram once again wore the comfortable body of his old human self, he was greatly altered in mind. While he would be as inquisitive as ever before, his was an inquisitiveness that manifested itself in ways most dissimilar to the learning gained through lengthy philosophical discussions or solitary rumination. Surprisingly, the Maharajah no longer cared for such matters, but only for matters concerning that of his short-lived parrot self. Henceforth he spent his days peering into windows at the bathing figures of lovely young maidens, who, upon recognizing the flushed and ecstatic face of their ruler, dared not shoo him away with a broom as they might once have done.

As for Vicram's nights…well, there was always the Ranee's juicy pomegranate to consider. ❧

THE GOBLIN OF ADACHIGAHARA

Japan is believed to have more folktales than any of the countries of the Western world. Yet its folk literature, although quite varied, gives the impression of being conspicuously sparse when placed alongside its tale-telling counterparts in the West. This is due to the fact that the scholarly collecting of Japanese folktales would not even get under way until a century later than that of Europe. Indeed, only in 1910 did someone finally take on the task of recording the tales of the people, thereby providing proof of Japan's long storytelling tradition.

An inspector for the Japanese Ministry of Agriculture, Kunio Yanagita started the movement to collect his country's folktales by setting down some oral stories he heard from a farmer. However, this is not to say that no written form of the traditional folktale existed prior to this time, for folktales appeared in print as far back as the eighth century. In contrast with the West, the oral tradition remained popular in Japan long after it had diminished in Europe, with the *hanashika* (public storyteller) practicing into the early twentieth century.

Japanese tales consist of *mukashi-banashi* (fairy tales) and *densetsu* (legendary tales). While the former have always been considered fiction, many of these *mukashi-banashi* evolved over the years into *densetsu,* which belong to the living folk culture that even now continues to be supported by the cultural institutions of the people. In an environment consisting of little social change over long periods of time, these local legends were allowed to flourish, experiencing repeated tellings over many generations and taking on ever more fantastical elements as they went along—only to undergo further evolution via the various travelers, peddlers, performers, and itinerant monks who visited the villages, bringing with them their own tales and traditions. The three centuries of isolation imposed on Japan by imperial decree, together with an absence of colonialism, kept its stories uninfluenced by the outside world and therefore purely Japanese.

Because of its shortness of length and sketchiness of detail, "The Goblin of Adachigahara" may actually be a legend instead of a fairy tale. It contains the three important elements that comprise *densetsu:* an extraordinary event involving the presence of a supernatural being (the goblin), a reference to a particular locality (Adachigahara), and an attachment to a particular place (the ever-popular derelict dwelling). Yet unlike Western fairy tales and legends that tend to be relegated to the category of fictional and—thanks to the Brothers Grimm—pedagogical entertainment, the line between fact and fantasy is less pronounced in Japan. Even today *densetsu* are alive and thriving in the villages and cities, for the people believe them to be true.

Of the many Japanese folktales passed on down through the centuries, a substantial number of them have always been considered unsuitable for children. These stories tend to be filled with much lampooning of bodily functions, featuring copious references to scatology, flatulency, and sexual humor—particularly with regard to human genitalia. Happily coexisting alongside such bawdy subject matter are tales involving suicide, cannibalism, and the supernatural. Indeed, themes of demonology and spiritualism occur quite regularly in Japanese village tales. Like the religious pilgrim in "The Goblin of Adachigahara," villagers fear a variety of demons, which are thought to be the degenerate corruptions of ancient divinities.

49

The most popular demon is the *kappa*—a water monster that appears in boyish form. As one of the busier categories of demons, the *kappa* spends his time raping women and dragging his victims into the river so that he can pluck out their livers through their anuses. Another renowned demon known as the *tengu* haunts mountains and inhabits trees and can be identified by its wings and beaked nose. Demons such as these are still seen and talked about in Japanese villages today.

Although the type of demon featured in "The Goblin of Adachigahara" has not been clearly identified, it would appear that this goblin (especially in my version) possesses the characteristics one might expect to see in the *kappa*. For surely a more randy demon cannot be found. ❧

The Goblin of Adachigahara

THE SPRAWLING, WIND-SWEPT PLAIN OF
Adachigahara was a place spoken of with
great fear. All who knew of it believed it to be
haunted by an evil goblin that donned the disguise of
a feeble old granny. The locals told terrible tales of
how unsuspecting folk had been lured into the hob-
goblin's derelict abode, where they found themselves
being devoured from top to toe, with only a bloodied
sandal left to indicate they had ever existed. Not surprisingly, no one dared venture anywhere near this
ramshackle residence after dark, with those of a wiser
nature avoiding it altogether, no matter how brightly
the wholesome rays of the sun shone upon its decay-
ing exterior. Yet every so often a traveler might pass
through having no knowledge of the dwelling or its
fiendish inhabitant—a traveler whose sudden disap-
pearance further fueled the grisly stories circulating
around the countryside.

One young man on a pilgrimage to spread his
message of faith to the people had been walking for
many days with his religious pamphlets and his cup
of coins when his footsteps led him to Adachigahara.

He had been told by the last person whose door he had knocked upon before it got slammed in his face that many generous benefactors lived in the area, therefore this was where he should go if he expected to collect donations. Not one to be easily discouraged, the pilgrim's persistence had resulted in little to fill his cup other than foul words and tobacco spittle. With a renewed sense of purpose, he counted the number of pamphlets he had remaining in his rucksack, hoping he would have enough to meet the demand. Indeed, he was most appreciative for the advice given him and intended to rattle his cup beneath the noses of all those he met until they sent him on his way with a coin or two.

Unfamiliar with the local lore, the religious traveler roamed the endless terrain without concern of mishap. As night moved in to cloak the land in its thick black curtain, he realized that he had lost his way. Having been on his sandaled feet since the rising of the sun, the pilgrim was weary and hungry, not to mention quite chilled. The air had grown cold, and a hint of snow threatened to spill from the darkening sky. If he could only locate some shelter, all would be well. However, this prospect looked less and less likely as the worn reed soles of his sandals tramped the dusty ground, for not so much as a friendly curl of wood smoke could be glimpsed along the monoto-nous plain. Just when the exhausted fellow began to lose heart, he spied a cluster of barren trees in the gloom-tinged distance—and through their sickly branches a welcoming glimmer of light.

Alas, the pilgrim's relief would prove very short-lived. Despite a battered sign proclaiming "Inn for Travelers," this light came from a dwelling so wretched and ill-kept that it gave him cause to wonder whether anyone lived beneath the rat-chewed straw of its roof. A worm-eaten front door stood wide open. Rather than having been positioned so in invitation, it accomplished the less-lofty function of allowing the fresh air from outside to flush out the insalubrious smells coming from within. Beyond this gaping threshold an old woman could be seen sitting on a mat as she sorted strips of hide into bowls filled with a yellowish-brown liquid, her bent figure illuminated by the jaundiced light of a lantern.

Swinging open the splintered bamboo of the gate, the pilgrim called out to her a tired greeting, barely managing to paste on the beatific smile he always kept ready when approaching strangers for donations. "Forgive the intrusion, Madam, only I have lost my way and am in need of shelter for the night." Contrary to his usual practice, he stuffed the religious pamphlet he was holding back inside his rucksack, since it did not appear particularly promising that any donations would be forthcoming from the inn's owner.

The ancient figure raised her grizzled head and focused on her visitor with crinkled eyes that, beneath their milkiness, were as sharp and watchful as a hawk's. "I am sorry for your plight, but as you can see, my establishment is small and I am fully booked for the night."

Although this could have provided him with a graceful out, the pilgrim found himself in circumstances of some desperation and would have been happy for any accommodations—even those as disagreeable as what he now saw before him. With the temperature outside steadily dropping, he could ill afford to put his nose in the air. "I ask merely for a square of floor on which to make my bed," he implored, "or I shall be forced to sleep out in the cold."

The wizened granny nodded thoughtfully, at last indicating that she had relented by building a fire in the hearth. Once the flames had caught, she invited the weary pilgrim to warm himself before it, furthering his sense of sanctuary by bringing him a tray of supper, which consisted of a bowl of possum stew and some wilted greens. Her guest ate of it gratefully, all the while chattering blissfully away about his theological convictions with the aged woman, who—first impressions aside—had shown herself to possess much kindness and hospitality. How extremely fortunate he was to have happened upon her! Perhaps in the morning he might ask if she cared to make a modest donation in return for one of his inspirational pamphlets.

As the fire burned down to a smoldering ash, the old woman announced that she planned to gather up some additional sticks of wood before her guest got cold. Although deliciously lazy from the warmth and the contents of his belly, the pilgrim reluctantly volunteered to perform the task himself, reckoning that this would ingratiate him for later when he put forth his pitifully empty cup for her consideration. For despite the wretchedness of her establishment, its proprietress apparently augmented her income from the tanning of hide. Refusing his offer, the kindly woman proposed instead that her guest remain behind, since he would be of far greater use if he kept watch on the premises during her absence. However, she did not leave without first imparting a warning. "No matter what happens, do not go into that room," she cautioned, indicating with a twisted finger a red door the garrulous religious traveler had earlier failed to notice.

The pilgrim nodded his head in enthusiastic assent, hoping to further loosen the old woman's purse strings with his trustworthiness. Unfortunately, the seed of curiosity had already been planted and after her departure, he could think of nothing but the door and the mysteries contained behind it. Without any fire, the icy daggers of wind sluicing through the unpatched roof had become even more formidable, and the shivering religious trekker took to stamping about in an effort to keep warm. With each clippity-clomp of his sandaled feet, the forbidden door took on the guise of a harlot, beckoning him nearer and nearer its red-painted presence. Summoning up the courage to place his hand against it, he heard the aged granny's premonitory refrain echoing in his ears. Suitably chastened, the pilgrim returned to his post before the cold hearth, his heart hammering with the realization that his hostess was due to return at any moment and would likely be very angry at finding her generous hospitality rewarded in so thankless a fashion—in which case he could kiss goodbye any chance of a few coins being thrown his way.

Only the old woman did not return. As the darkness outside the ruinous little inn grew thicker and blacker and, indeed, more menacing, the religious traveler began to feel uneasy at having been left on his own for so long. Although concerned for the absent proprietress's welfare, it was his own that concerned him the most. He kept hearing a mournful howling—a howling that became louder and more lamenting with each passing minute. Yet rather than being the sound of the wind gusting through the vast empty plain, it seemed to be coming from behind the red door. If he did not learn what lay on the other side, he would go completely mad. Besides, what possible harm could it cause? As long as he did not leave any evidence of his presence, the moth-eaten granny need never even know he had peeked.

The curious fellow moved with trepidation toward the mystery door, steadying himself with a series of deep breaths before placing the perspiring palm of his hand against the paper surface. *The old woman probably stores her fortune in here,* mused the pilgrim, fully expecting to be greeted with dust-covered sacks of coins. Instead he discovered what appeared to be the inn's one and only guest room.

And indeed, the wizened old proprietress had not lied when she claimed to be fully booked for the night. For shackled to a wall was an assemblage of guests, all young men of extraordinary pulchritude and vigor. Their muscled flesh had been partially covered with a supple black hide that stretched across their brawny backs and chests like a second layer of skin, offering little in the way of protection to those parts traditionally in need of protection. The contrast of dark against light further accentuated the areas that had been left exposed, as if the intent was to call attention to them. While this was an incongruous enough costume by itself, even more so were the ornamental accessories accompanying it. Bracelets of an unpolished iron encircled the mighty wrists and ankles of each of the inn's guests. A chain constructed from the same iron had been attached to these cinching cuffs, thus preventing the wearers from straying beyond the confines of the mean little room.

Upon seeing the curious pilgrim peering in at them, the young men began to gesticulate wildly about, the chains keeping them imprisoned rattling and clanging with enough noise to summon the old woman back from wherever she had vanished to in pursuit of firewood. Several attempted to call out to their would-be rescuer, their hopeful faces swelling purple with the effort. For a braided cord of hide had been fitted between their lips, muffling all sound save for the slightest of incoherent murmurs and the occasional frustrated wail.

One of the room's tethered occupants remained slumped by himself in a corner, making no effort to join the inarticulate pantomimes of the others. He was far handsomer than his fellow companions in both face and form, with an athletic chest and backside that had been generously marked with red stripes of varying degrees of intensity and deliberation. Like the establishment's more effusive guests, he, too, had come to be attired in only the most inadequate of vests fastened in the front with cords of the same hide as that which subdued his mouth. The garment failed dismally to safeguard his lower portions, which, despite the cruelty of the temperature, had been left totally bare and vulnerable to the elements. As a direct consequence of such abbreviated costuming, the sturdy muscle of his manhood was plainly visible to all, and it remained in a state of perpetual agitation, the ring of plaited hide embracing it at the root having inspired a severe engorgement of blood to occur. The condition looked quite painful, judging by the moans of those afflicted.

For once the pilgrim had finally unfixed his disbelieving eyes from the lethargic figure in the corner, he discovered that the others suffered from this discourteous malady as well. Indeed, the braided rings of hide encircled the upstanding members of everyone in the room, lending a livid and not altogether unappealing purple cast to these thickened pillars of flesh. Several of the shackled young men clutched themselves in poignant anguish, their eyes rolling upward in their sockets as the lustrous black hide of their vests and those of their immediate neighbors became splattered with a thick white froth, which dripped slowly down the robust cylinders of their thighs. Stepping forward, the religious traveler reached out a hand toward the man nearest him, hoping to provide some comfort. As his tremulous fingertips caressed the bulging arc of flesh held imprisoned by its plaited ring, he found himself being sprayed with the same spumy substance that stained the captive's costume and those of his unfortunate comrades. As if in sympathy, the pilgrim put forth his own contribution, discharging it discreetly within his loose-fitting garments. Nevertheless, his corresponding cry of pleasure was anything but discreet, and he stuffed his fingers inside his mouth to quell it, inadvertently tasting the pleasure of another.

Horrified by his actions and what they had brought about, the pilgrim looked down at his sandaled feet in shame, only to be even more horrified by what he saw on the floor, for its sticky surface had been littered with inspirational pamphlets just like those he carried about the country with him. With his future suddenly laid out before him, he fell backward in a panic, his frantically pumping elbows jabbing holes into the flimsy red door and leaving irrefutable evidence that he had seen inside the forbidden room.

Collecting his rucksack containing his precious pamphlets and his chronically empty cup, the pilgrim dashed out into the chilly night, leaving behind the lurid montage of his enslaved brothers. However, he would not even reach the broken bamboo gate before a loud cry pierced the silence. From the far side of a dead tree appeared the old granny, her ancient form squeezed into a corset of buttery black hide. A cat-o'-nine-tails swung from one withered arm, cracking dangerously through the air. "Stop!" she screeched, her once-feeble voice like rusted nails being hammered into the pilgrim's ears. The kindly, crinkled face she had worn for her unsuspecting guest had melted away, revealing the sadistic visage of the Goblin of Adachigahara.

The religious traveler's journey-worn legs sprouted invisible wings and he ran like the wind, the tails snapping closely and threateningly at his heels and sending up an explosion of sparks from the frosty ground. He knew now that the old woman's warning had been intended to lure him into that vile lair, where she planned to catch him in his spying and make him a prisoner. Indeed, two empty sets of irons awaiting the wrists and ankles of some unfortunate soul had been set to one side, eager to be used. How many other unsuspecting pilgrims had come knocking on the door of this dwelling of the damned in expectation of a donation?

The terror-stricken fellow ran and ran until a pink dawn began to break over the great plain of Adachigahara. He ran until not a scrap of flesh remained on the bloodied soles of his feet. Only when the white of his bones showed through did he stop. Although the goblin had vanished into the blackness of the night, her eerie wails continued to haunt him — as did those of the men he had seen imprisoned behind the red door. To think that he had been so close to becoming the fettered amusement for the inn's godless proprietress. Why, she had not even bothered to read one of his inspirational pamphlets!

The next place the pilgrim came to would be the place where he chose to spend the remainder of his days, but not without first setting fire to his remaining pamphlets in symbolic thanks for being spared such a fate. Here he met many others like himself, all of whom had managed to escape from the Goblin of Adachigahara. Indeed, some still wore their plaited rings of hide and appeared not to mind in the least when the newest among them stroked their straining flesh to a frothy fulfillment.

For the pilgrim could not so easily forget those he had left behind. ఴ

Rapunzel

∞

Most familiar to us by way of Germany and the Brothers Grimm, "Rapunzel" originated many centuries earlier in Mediterranean Europe. Perhaps the farthest back it can be traced is to the ancient Greek folktale "Anthousa the Fair with Golden Hair." Despite its already lengthy past, the possibility remains that the rudiments of this so-called puberty tale may stretch all the way back to the primitive societies living in the days before recorded history.

For long before the *Kinder- und Hausmärchen* or the tales of the ancient Greeks, it had been common practice among tribal societies to confine a young girl of Rapunzel's age inside a "puberty hut" during the time of her menstruation. In their construction, these structures often took the form of a tower. Most ancient cultures practiced some manner of isolation of a young girl, separating her from the community at the first onset of her menses. She might be placed in the hands of the elder women of the tribe, who then prepared her for womanhood. Indeed, Rapunzel's confinement within a tower took place at the age of puberty—with her guardian being an old woman. In Mediterranean versions of the tale, the old woman who takes the girl from her parents is no nurturing mentor, but a flesh-eating cannibal. So gruesome a character could provide further evidence of Rapunzel's connection to primitive societies, for cannibalism was a part of the belief system and social reality of these cultures, which may have practiced the consumption of human flesh in puberty or religious initiations or even as a result of famine.

By the time of the Grimms, the cannibal character had evolved into a witch/enchantress. In their earlier renderings of "Rapunzel," the brothers, rather than concluding with the shearing off of the girl's hair, allow the story to continue with Old Gothel using the shorn tresses to lure the character of the prince into the tower. Seeing this hideous impostor in place of his beloved, the prince leaps from the window, losing his eyesight in the fall. For many years he blindly wanders the desert into which Rapunzel has been banished, along with her twins. Upon their reuniting, Rapunzel's tears fall into the prince's eyes, restoring his vision.

As the Grimms continued to revise their story, this second part would eventually be lost, along with any references to procreative matters. Yet this was not the case in the "Rapunzel" appearing in the first edition of the *Kinder- und Hausmärchen*. In referring to the prince's visits to the tower, the Grimms wrote: "The two lived joyfully for a time, and the fairy [witch] did not catch on at all until Rapunzel told her one day: 'Tell me, Godmother, why my clothes are so tight and why they do not fit me any longer.'" Here is a blatant indicator of Rapunzel's gravid condition—an indicator that in subsequent versions loses its initial punch as the issue of overly tight clothes evolves into the anger of the witch caused by having been told by her ward that she is a good deal heavier to pull up into the tower than the handsome prince. Deeming the tale unsuitable for children, the brothers moved to clean up any objectionable content, which included the apparently unwed and pregnant state of the protagonist.

Although the Grimms thought "Rapunzel" came from an eighteenth-century novelist who heard it from a member of the common class, the German text they adapted was actually a translation of a French literary tale composed by a lady-in-waiting at the court of Louis XIV—which she in turn based on a French folktale. In Charlotte de la Force's story "The Maiden in the Tower," the beautiful Persinette finds herself confined inside a tower to prevent her from being carried off and, no doubt, ravished. Yet ravished she will be, as Mlle. de la Force makes no secret of the fact that the unwed Persinette becomes pregnant as a result of the daily visits of a prince.

Indeed, sex and eroticism would make an appearance even before the arrival of the French literary tale. In Giambattista Basile's story of "Petrosinella" from his volume *Il Pentamerone,* the prince maintains no qualms about the partaking of fleshly pleasures from Petrosinella as "...he sated his desire, and ate of that sweet parsley of love." (Note that in some versions, *Parsley* is also the name for the protagonist, perhaps providing a duel meaning.) Be that as it may, by the time the tale of "Rapunzel" fell into the bowdlerizing hands of the Grimms, any such feasting had been turned into sexual famine.

Since no man would likely scale the wall of a tower just to hear a song, I have revived the erotic spirit from Rapunzel's early days, for I could not allow such masculine efforts to pass unrewarded. ❧

Rapunzel

I N A PASTORAL LAND OF GREEN WHERE nature's bounty thrived in abundance, there lived a husband and wife. Although it was their greatest wish to have a child, the fertility of their surroundings did not seem fated to extend to their household. To ease the pain of her emptiness, the wife took to blanketing her sorrows in food, growing outward in girth until her husband thought she could grow no more. Indeed, his wife had discovered that there was more than one way to fill a hollow belly.

By some coincidence, the farmhouse located directly adjacent to the couple's cottage boasted a splendid orchard that had won many awards. It contained the ripest and tastiest of fruits whose delights were enjoyed solely by its lone caretaker, an unsightly crone who went by the name of Gothel. With such choice edibles only a few steps away, it was inevitable that a certain neighbor should find herself obsessed with the desire to visit this rich piece of earth and partake of its verdant contents. Of course it also stood to reason that easy access could not be gained to a parcel of such wondrous fecundity. A high fence topped with barbed wire surrounded it that not even the heartiest and bravest dared venture to climb. For it had been rumored that this orchard belonged to a witch of great power…and an even greater temper.

One morning as the wife stood before an upstairs window gazing longingly down into the perfect rectangle of green on the far side of the fence, her eyes suddenly alighted upon an alligator pear tree. She cried out in what sounded like a fit of agony, for she preferred the alligator pear to even the sweetest of cream cakes brought daily to her by her thoughtful husband. The leathery-skinned fruits dangling weightily from the branches called to her, boasting of the delicious buttery meat that lay hidden beneath—a buttery meat that appeared to be going to waste, the owner of the orchard having made no attempt to harvest any. Every day this bereft neighbor could be seen hovering at the window, the imagined taste of alligator pear on her tongue turning her into a mere ghost of herself.

Returning home one evening with a box of fresh cream cakes—only to discover the previous day's cream cakes sitting out on the kitchen table uneaten—the woman's husband could bear no more. "What ails you, Wife?" he prodded gently, believing it to be the absence of the child they could not have. He would be quite taken aback by the explanation for his spouse's misery—that being her tearful proclamation that she would die if she did not receive at least a tiny serving of the savory alligator pear growing within the fenced orchard. It should be noted that the man loved his wife very much and that it tore at his heart to observe her wasting so pitifully away. Preferring her former buxom self to what now lay beside him in bed each night, the husband decided that he would happily risk the wrath of Old Gothel the witch, since *anything* had to be better than the skin and bones into which his good and faithful helpmate had turned. He could not endure another night of reaching out and sinking his fingers into the flattened disks of her breasts and the concave pit of her belly where there had once been layers and layers of plush, jiggling flesh.

Under gloaming's protective cloak, the husband climbed over the barbed-wire fence, cutting himself to shreds in the process. Although all remained quiet at the farmhouse, he made haste as he plucked from the bountiful tree an alligator pear for his wife's supper. With bleeding hands, he delivered it to her like a bouquet from an enamored suitor, basking in the brightness of her smile as she prepared from it a salad and ate of it joyously. Alas, so modest a sampling only piqued the woman's appetite for more, and by the very next twilight the husband could again be seen scrambling over the high fence separating the two properties, knowing that he would not be granted a moment's peace until his wife had finally had her palate for the fruit satisfied.

Perhaps good fortune had been at his side the previous day. As for the occasion of his second visit to the forbidden orchard, fortune apparently chose to be elsewhere. The lacerated fellow had barely finished gathering his leathery spoils when all providence took leave of him. "Halt, thief!" came a voice so horrible that it felt as if hundreds of hot needles were being thrust into the hearer's ears.

The terror-stricken husband straddled the tall fence with great precariousness, with one trembling leg dangling toward the orchard and the other toward freedom, the barbs jabbing purposefully into the crotch of his trousers. Yet he would not have been able to flee if he tried, for the hideous figure of the orchard's owner held his foot tightly within soil-encrusted fingers. "Please, Madam, have mercy on this poor soul!" he pleaded. "I am here on behalf of my dear wife, who is near to death with longing for a taste of this fine alligator pear."

"Near to death, say ye?" echoed the keeper of the alligator pear tree.

The man nodded sadly, praying that the old witch's heart could not possibly be as ugly and malevolent as her face.

"If such a claim is true, I may be of a mind to offer my charity."

Weeping with relief, the grateful husband thanked his gap-toothed capturer and proceeded to shift himself back in the direction of home.

"*On one condition,*" added Old Gothel in an ominous tone.

The alligator pear thief froze, dreading what would be coming next. Indeed, it was not considered prudent to strike a bargain with a witch, especially *this* witch.

"Ye must bestow unto me the child that shall be born of your wife."

Out of fear and desperation and the fact that he had just been caught in the act of stealing, the husband readily agreed. Despite an icy quiver of foreboding in the vicinity of his testicles, he felt confident that his promise would come to nothing. In their many years of marriage, his wife had never once been able to conceive, no matter how frequent or carefully timed their nocturnal encounters. Therefore he returned safely home with the precious alligator pear, pleased at the oh, so clever bargain he had struck with the foolish hag next door.

Within three-quarters of a year an infant was born to the couple—a delightful baby girl who emerged from the womb complete with a full head of golden locks. No two people could have been more astonished by her arrival. By this time, the husband had forgotten all about the silly pact he had made with their green-thumbed neighbor. However, Old Gothel had *not* forgotten and within a matter of days appeared at their door to lay claim to her half of the bargain. The wife had been consuming alligator pears from her orchard at an alarming rate—a fact that could not be denied by the new parents. Conferring the name of *Rapunzel* upon the gurgling infant, the witch took her back with her over the high fence, the little one never again to be seen by the couple who had given life to her.

Rapunzel was a beautiful child — her beauty so striking that it actually seemed to emphasize the ugliness of the individual who had taken over her care. When the girl reached the age of twelve, Gothel shut her up inside an abandoned tower set deep in the wilderness, no longer able to tolerate being daily cuckolded by such physical perfection. On those occasions when she visited her banished ward, she called up to her from below: "Rapunzel, Rapunzel, let down your hair!" This would be the agreed-upon signal for the girl to assist the witch, for Rapunzel possessed a head of hair that had grown so long throughout her many years of solitude that it could easily suffice as a rope. Since the tower had neither steps nor door, she cast these golden plaits out the window some twenty ells below to enable Old Gothel to climb up. The witch had been the only mother the girl had ever known, therefore she was most eager to have her company.

Rapunzel's beauty continued to flourish as she blossomed into young womanhood, resulting in a conspicuous lessening of visits from the evil one who had wrenched her from the adoring arms of her parents. Out of boredom and loneliness, the girl sought to pass the endless hours of the day by entertaining herself with the rhythmic lyrics that played inside her mind. She often spent entire afternoons in this way, hopping from foot to foot and stabbing the air with her fingers. On one of these afternoons a local survivalist had been out riding in search of his dinner when he heard a voice of such sweetness and purity that he could go no farther. Tethering his horse to a tree, he settled himself on a patch of scrubby grass, his heart soaring with love for the voice's unseen female owner as he listened to her stirring song.

> *Yo!*
> *Whassup?*
> *Don't gimme no shit,*
> *Motherfucker!*

And indeed, the voice belonged to none other than the beautiful Rapunzel. So moved was the horseman that he arose from his listening place and encircled the tower several times in search of a way inside its crumbling walls, baffled to find none. He returned home to his cabin in anguished frustration, only to ride back to the forsaken tower the very next day, and the next as well, his heart tormented by the curious cadences coming from within — and stirred by the young woman he imagined to be their composer.

One afternoon as the horse-riding survivalist sat listening to his favorite rapstress, he witnessed the arrival of a horrible creature. Never before had he laid eyes on such a misshapen form or a countenance of such utter hideousness. Frightened that she might see him and place upon him an evil hex, he secreted himself behind a large sycamore, his camouflage fatigues blending him into his surroundings as he kept a watchful eye on the witch who hobbled toward the ruinous tower, and hence toward its musical mysteries. The voice caressing his appreciative ears continued to haunt him, and he took comfort from pressing himself against the rough bark of the tree, moving in rhythmic concert with each exquisite word. However, the restless young man quickly discovered that what had originally brought comfort would instead bring agitation, and he all but drove to tatters the front of his fatigue pants in his quest for relief.

"Rapunzel, Rapunzel, let down your hair!" bade a voice that flayed the tender insides of this concealed music lover's ears and proved as offensive in nature as the voice coming from the tower had been pleasing. The rap abruptly ceased as two golden ropes dropped down from out of an indistinct little opening set high up in the tower wall. The horseman nearly kicked himself for his folly, for in his single-minded search for a door, he had neglected to notice the presence of the window. He watched as the hands of the crone grabbed hold of the braided cords and employed them as a means to climb up the tower's ruinous exterior, at which point she leapt through the window.

After several days of stealthy observation, the young survivalist arranged to return on his horse before twilight, certain he would go mad if he did not meet the rapstress whose rousing words had forced him to rub himself to a frenzy against the coarse bark of a tree. Satisfied that the grotesque creature who had visited in the daylight would not be returning in the eve, he placed himself directly below the little window and called: "Rapunzel, Rapunzel, let down your hair!" And like clockwork the golden ropes were flung out, this time to be seized by a masculine pair of hands.

The figure climbing boldly in through the small opening heretofore reserved exclusively for Old Gothel's entry led Rapunzel to cower against the wall in fear and confusion. Thanks to her many years of confinement by the witch, she had never set eyes upon a man. Nevertheless, her handsome visitor spoke so softly and lovingly to her that her unease vanished, especially when he implored her to sing for him. Indeed, Rapunzel took tremendous joy in her little raps and launched into one at every opportunity. Unfortunately, Mother Gothel did not like for her to sing and would always issue a stinging slap across the mouth whenever she caught the girl doing so. Yet this stranger was kind of heart and pleasing to the eye—of *course* she would sing for him!

A rhythmic cadence began to issue from Rapunzel's graceful throat, rising and falling in pitch while gaining in strength. Its devotee instantly recognized it as the rap he had heard on that first day he had hidden himself behind the trunk of the sycamore. All at once a familiar sensation seized hold of him. Seeing nothing resembling a tree in the tiny room of the tower, he installed himself directly behind Rapunzel, pressing the front of his camouflage fatigues against the pleasing roundness he encountered there. It felt far nicer than the coarse, unyielding bark of the sycamore to which he had grown accustomed. Why, there was even a convenient and warm groove into which he could fit himself most comfortably and agreeably.

Happily situated, this visitor to the tower loosened Rapunzel's hair from their restrictive plaits, freeing up the long tresses of gold. With her voice filling his ears and her silken locks filling his hands, he forged ahead, thrusting forth his pelvis and raising himself up onto the very tips of his combat-booted toes, each note inspiring its appreciative listener to rub harder and harder and faster and faster. Indeed, the more force he exerted, the more passion the lyric seemed to possess, and before long Rapunzel would be rapping with all the force of a gale wind.

> *Yo!*
> *Whassup?*
> *Don't gimme no shit,*
> *Motherfucker!*

Like his earlier encounter with the sycamore, the young survivalist's comfort swiftly turned to agitation. Yet still he did not cease from his strange gyrations, for he sensed that relief would very soon be his—a relief that promised to be a good deal more satisfying than any that could be gotten from a mere sycamore. Within moments a powerful explosion took place, sending Rapunzel's musical admirer soaring high into the cloudless sky. He whirled about like a falcon in flight, swooping upward on a current of air, then dropping back down again. The aqueous roiling of seed taking place in his congested testes erupted in a tempestuous storm, flooding his fatigue pants and leaving behind a masculine signature that even their camouflage pattern would fail to conceal. Never had the survivalist experienced such a wild journey! It was then that he made the fateful decision to visit this enchanting rapstress each and every twilight, regardless of the perils involved.

Rapunzel, too, desired her intrepid suitor's return, wishing only to sing for him and him alone. From this day forward her throat refused to release a single note until the handsome horseman came to claim his place behind her. So happy had she been made by his secret visits that one day when Old Gothel was paying a call, the euphoric girl suffered a devastating slip of the tongue. The witch had taken a particularly long time in reaching the window, placing a nearly unendurable burden on Rapunzel's golden plaits. "How is it, Mother Gothel, that you climb so slowly while the good horseman moves with the swiftness of a deer?"

"Wicked child!" shrieked the witch. "What is this I hear? Ye have betrayed me most grievously, and for this I offer punishment." Seizing Rapunzel by her golden tresses, Old Gothel removed a pair of gardening shears she always kept handy in the pocket of her smock and severed the plaits clear down to the pale white of their transgressor's scalp.

Rapunzel collapsed to the floor, her fingers clutching hopelessly at the fine filaments of hair that lay all around her like sunlit sheaves of wheat. With a satisfied cackle, the witch leapt from the high window, landing unharmed on the scrubby grass below. "Ye shall die an old maid!" she cried victoriously, taking pleasure from her cruelty. In fact, it was highly probable that these vicious words would come to pass, since many years would be required for Rapunzel's lustrous tresses to grow back to the glorious length they had once been—and by then it would be too late for *any* man to come courting.

Be that as it may, there was one thing that Old Gothel the notorious bargainer had not bargained on. That same day the young survivalist returned before twilight to the crumbling tower in the wilderness. "Rapunzel, Rapunzel, let down your hair!" he called from below, his heart pounding in anticipation of the rhythms that would soon be filling his ears and the rhythms that would likewise be filling his loins. Hearing his voice summoning her, Rapunzel touched the stubbly wasteland of her freshly shorn head, devastated by the loss of her beautiful locks. Yet her love for the handsome horseman could not so easily be thwarted. For in her rage, Gothel had overlooked some locks as fine and golden as those that had once adorned Rapunzel's head.

Placing herself before the little window, the girl raised up her skirts, thus allowing the cascade of golden curls previously hidden from view to tumble down to her waiting lover. Grabbing hold of this fragrant, silken ladder with his hands, the young man climbed up the exterior of the tower...where he and Rapunzel remained till the end of their days. Indeed, the most pounding of raps could be heard both day and night, their singer never tiring of singing them, or their listener of listening. Their aficionado would even add his own contrapuntal cadences, accompanying each word by scratching with his penknife against the broken-off bark of his favorite sycamore.

> *Yo!*
> scratch —
> *Whassup?*
> scratch —
> *Don't gimme no shit,*
> scratch —
> *Motherfucker!*

As for the loss of Rapunzel's head of golden tresses, this did not make her in any way wanting to the handsome survivalist. In fact, he barely noticed their absence. For with Rapunzel's every rap, his fingers joyously entwined themselves within the spirally tresses of gold growing beneath her skirts as he rubbed himself silly against the delightfully grooved roundness he found at her back.

And not even Old Gothel the witch could climb up to stop them. ❧

THE
SWINEHERD

Scandinavian literature has long been fraught with extremes—
extremes that likely take their cue from climate and geography.
As one who found his inspiration from such extremes, Hans
Christian Andersen would become the individual most commonly associated with the folktales of Scandinavia. A favorite
story of the king of Denmark, "The Swineherd" was often given
a royal recitation by the author himself, for Andersen's tales
charmed one and all.

Unlike his nineteenth century German contemporaries
and friends Jacob and Wilhelm Grimm or his European predecessors, Andersen would be the first writer of fairy tales to come
from the humble class for whom the oral telling of tales was a tradition. Although a number of his works had been claimed by him
as a product of his own imagination, he was known to have
crafted stories heavily influenced by the folktales and legends
told to him in childhood. Of those most thought to be original
creations (and some that were not), many end on an unhappy
note, apparently influenced by the Dane's personal life. Indeed,
themes of suffering and misery appear in abundance all throughout his tales, including "The Swineherd." Unlucky in love,

perhaps Andersen incorporated his own unsuccessful romantic experiences into his work.

Basing his "Svinedrengen" on the folktale "The Proud Maid," Andersen discovered that his source material contained parts he considered unsuitable for his readers—such as the female protagonist's allowing her suitor to spend a night in her bedchamber and, later, in her bed. Many versions of the story show the princess trading her chastity for objects of gold, which Andersen (likely influenced by the religious climate of his country and the moral tastes of his editors) changed to the more innocuous kisses. A woman's desire for material possessions—a desire that eventually leads her into trouble—has become a well-established theme in the folktales of Scandinavia. The message in "Svinedrengen" appears to be that a woman will dispense her favors for the mere possession of a trinket. Of course, proud princesses with a love of the superficial are not exclusive to Hans Christian Andersen. In "King Thrushbeard" by the Grimms, a disguised suitor attracts a spoiled princess with the aid of a golden wheel that makes music, much like the waltz-playing rattle of Andersen's swineherd. Indeed, it happened that the Dane's tales held such appeal to their nineteenth century audience that some would be passed on in oral form, only to turn up in the subsequently published work of the Grimms.

Two centuries before Andersen wrote "The Swineherd," there existed a counterpart not only to his work, but also to the folktale that inspired it. In Basile's "Pride Punished," a king rejected by the proud princess Cinziella alters his appearance and takes employment in the palace gardens, whereupon he entices Cinziella with a robe adorned with gold and diamonds in return for sleeping one night in her apartments. The disguised king next tempts the princess with a beautiful dress, if only he may sleep for one night in her antechamber. Lastly the disguised king offers Cinziella a special undervest in exchange for one more night in her room. Having thrice agreed to his terms, the princess draws a line on the floor to separate them. However, no line can deter her determined suitor. "The king-gardener awaited till she was asleep, and thinking it was high time to work in the territory of love, he arose from his seat, and laid himself down by her side, and before the mistress of the place was well awake, he gathered the fruits of his love...." And such lusty activity apparently continues as Cinziella witnesses her belly growing rounder by the day. Humiliated by her pregnancy, she runs off with the man she believes to be a gardener—a man who forces her to suffer numerous indignities for her initial rejection of him.

Rather than meting out various forms of punishment in the manner of Basile or the Grimms, Andersen's swineherd prefers to do so by revealing his true royal identity, even as the princess laments her loss of the prince who once courted her, thereby prompting his declaration of contempt. For the princess has rejected an honorable prince, yet kissed a common swineherd just to gain possession of a toy. Perhaps the socially dejected Andersen has slipped a message into his tale. In the swineherd's attempts to be accepted into high society, the shallowness of this very same society has been exposed.

Nevertheless, a good deal more will be exposed when the swineherd in my version demands his hundred kisses from the young woman with whom he has fallen in love. ❧

†he Swineherd

IN A TIME OF SPORADIC WARFARE AND
political upheaval, there lived a young gentleman of title who possessed a great wealth of
appearance. Alas, such wealth fell short of extending
to his noble pockets. The coffers belonging to his
family echoed emptily in comparison to the bountiful
coffers of his aristocratic neighbors, who, unlike him,
did not find themselves obliged to throw open the
doors of their stately homes to visitors for an entry fee.
To compensate for his financial shortcomings, he
always needed to be cleverer than others in his
endeavors, especially when those endeavors involved
wooing a potential bride.

Being of an optimistic character, the bachelor
nobleman saw no reason why his lack of riches should
thwart him in his quest. He knew of others who had
married successfully with less wealth, therefore he felt
certain that many a fine lady would be pleased to
accept his proposal. Unhappily for this marriage-
minded gentleman, the bewitching daughter of a
notorious warlord for whom he had set his cap could
not be counted among them. Indeed, there were those
who might have said that by offering his heart to one

so far out of reach the gentleman invited the lady in question to trample upon it.

In a small patch of garden he tended himself, the nobleman had cultivated a very rare plant that came from the distant fields of the tropics. Unlike the more commonly held varieties, its leaves and clusters of greenish flowers when dried and touched by flame emitted a fragrance so sweet that anyone who inhaled it would instantly forget both sorrow and trouble, regardless of their gravity. The nobleman also had a special pipe whose wood he had carved and painted so beautifully that it put the finest works of art to shame. Since these were the most valuable of his worldly possessions, he decided to fashion by his own hand two silver boxes into which he would place these treasures and have them presented as gifts to the unmarried daughter of the warlord. Having a flair for the theatrical, he made the boxes oversized so that their contents would be even more of a surprise to their recipient. For the nobleman had quite set his foolhardy heart on wedding the young lady, with whom he had fallen desperately in love the moment he had seen her snapping her scourge at the vanquished townspeople as she passed through the pillaged ruins of the city on the uniformed arm of her father.

The warlord's daughter was busy improving her technique on the already scourge-toughened back-sides of her handmaidens when a pair of servants brought the nobleman's offerings up to her. Seeing the large silver boxes, she clapped her hands together in delight. "Oh, I do hope one of them contains a new pillory!" she cried, for she very much wished to install one in her room. Yet no sooner did she hoist up the gleaming lid of the first box and discover its contents than her mouth shifted into a petulant pout—a pout that bore the beginnings of a dangerous grumble of discontent.

"The box itself is quite prettily constructed," offered one of the handmaidens, hoping to stave off another of the young woman's infamous temper tantrums. "In fact, that filigree work is the finest I have ever seen." Although little more than a servant, she knew a great deal more of such matters than her mistress, the handmaiden's late father having been the deposed monarch in whose household the warlord's family now lived.

"Aye, it is uncommonly lovely," remarked the warlord with effusive jocularity as he entered the room, sharing a similar hope to that of the handmaiden who had just spoken.

The warlord's disappointed daughter dipped a hand inside the intricately tooled box to touch the leafy plant. As her fingertips brushed against the clusters of greenish flowers, she yelped as if stung by a bee. "What is this ugly thing? Surely I cannot be expected to allow this to take the place of my trusty nettle scourge?"

"We should say not!" chimed the handmaidens, knowing it was best to agree with their capricious mistress. Nevertheless, they gazed at the gift with bittersweet forlornness, for its leaves would have been preferable to the stinging nettles they were made to endure.

"Now, Daughter, perhaps we should investigate what awaits us in the other box before we allow our tempers to get the better of us," admonished the warlord with a long-suffering smile. He wanted only for these proceedings to be over and done with so that he could return to the important business of seizing territory.

With the raising of the lid of the second box, the pipe that had been placed inside with such tender care by its owner came into view. Its exquisitely carved presence stilled the tongues of all those in the room. For a moment it appeared that no one could find fault with this gift, until the warlord's daughter ascertained that the pipe was not made of painted porcelain, but rather of ordinary briarwood. She immediately ordered its return, dispatching along with it a message to the gift-bearer indicating that she would not *under any circumstances* permit a miserable worm like himself anywhere near her. Why should she bother with the likes of so inconsequential a suitor when she had turned away far better from her door? As for the plant, she gave it to the cook, who chopped up its leaves and mixed them into the bread that would be baked for that evening's supper.

Having nothing to lose but his manly pride, the enamored nobleman refused to let this curt rebuff discourage him. If anything, it made him even more determined to ingratiate himself with the warlord's daughter. The young woman's mean disposition had long been a popular topic of conversation at many supper tables, and this most recent indication of it simply confirmed that he had made the right decision in settling upon her to be his bride. Hence this undaunted suitor decided to modify his courtship tactics, since it had become apparent that his status as a nobleman was of little consequence.

After selectively blackening the contours of his face with boot polish and placing on his head a tattered old cap he bought off the head of a passing vagabond, the nobleman journeyed to the former palace of the ousted monarch to inquire of work. Because so many had already been rendered into poverty since the arrival of the warlord, every post was filled save for that of the warlord's swineherd. Although the prospect of spending his days and nights in the company of pigs did not exactly inspire joy in the young gentleman's heart, he accepted the position, only to find himself being led to a mucky little stall directly adjacent to the pigpen — the room that was to become his new home.

When not tending pigs or shoveling dung, the new swineherd spent his time fashioning a cane from the local hickory, which he imbedded with beads made out of clay baked to a hard finish inside the cast-iron stove that provided his sole source of heating and cooking. All around its gracefully turned handle he attached a string of tiny silver bells that, when turned at a certain angle, played the most jolly of melodies. But perhaps the most distinctive quality of the musical cane was its amazing ability, just by grasping its handle, to allow one to hear the whistling whack of wood on flesh produced by every cane in every household in the city. Surely such a clever creation would be hard to resist.

One rain-freshened afternoon while the daughter of the warlord had been taking a turn in the palace grounds with her handmaidens, she heard the playing of music. Although not unusual in and of itself, the fact that it seemed to be coming from the pigsty *was*. Indeed, what transpired next would rouse her interest to impassioned proportions as the music became abruptly supplanted by the unmistakable sound of hickory hitting flesh. Panting with excitement, the warlord's daughter ordered the most attractive of her handmaidens to seek out the new swineherd, for she very much desired to own the instrument that created such sublime sounds and was prepared to pay a goodly sum for it. However, the musical cane could not be purchased for any amount of gold. After several minutes of failed negotiations, the thwarted handmaiden returned to her mistress, a furious flush staining her plump cheeks.

"Well?" snapped the warlord's daughter, who was impatient to get on with the proceedings. "What is the swineherd's price?"

"I dare not say," stammered the handmaiden, her neck turning as red as her face. "For it is very naughty."

"Oh, for pity's sake, I do not have time for such foolishness! You may whisper into my ear if it is so difficult to speak of it aloud." And so the embarrassed messenger revealed the swineherd's price: ten kisses from her mistress's lips.

Clearly such a price could not be paid, for no daughter of a successful warlord would ever condescend to kissing a common swineherd. Upon being informed of this impudent proposition, the affronted young woman went storming off in the direction of the palace. At that moment the bells on the cane chose to play their special music, followed by yet another rhapsodic session of wood against flesh. Envisioning all those upraised backsides quivering with each biting kiss of the hickory, the warlord's daughter spun about on her heel and grasped the startled wrist of the handmaiden who had spoken with the instrument's maker. "Ask that cheeky swineherd if he would be satisfied with ten kisses from my handmaidens," she demanded. If he had any sense, the mud-caked brute would consider a kiss from the lips of *ten* women a superior bargain to the kiss of one.

The daughter of the warlord did not seem to realize that it was her lips alone that the lovesick swineherd desired most, therefore her latest proposal would also be met with rejection. Indeed, she was growing extremely annoyed with the pig-man, whose stubbornness only strengthened her resolve to own the instrument capable of such dulcet tones and—if the fantastical story told her red-faced handmaiden could be believed—capable of making her privy to the activities of every cane in every household in the land. With no other choice remaining, the warlord's daughter accepted his terms. For them to be administered with the least amount of indignity to herself, she required that her handmaidens form a circle around the two of them and open out the folds of their skirts so that no one could view this scandalous kissing of the swineherd.

Finally face-to-face with the presumptuous underling whose talented hands had fashioned the musical cane, the daughter of the warlord was astonished to find that the fellow was by no means as grubby or repulsive as she had anticipated. "Very well," she snapped, the corners of her mouth twisting downward with a disgust not entirely genuine. "Let us get this disagreeable business over and done with."

Just as the warlord's daughter took a step forward, the swineherd's mud-stained breeches dropped to his ankles. An object resembling the imperial scepter her father had ripped from the monarch's dead hand pointed up at the cloudless sky, swaying unsteadily from its weight. For some mysterious reason, the swineherd had stuck a very large purple plum on the end of it, which probably accounted for so much unwieldiness. Curious though she was to learn why a common keeper of pigs should go about with a piece of fruit attached to the lower half of his person, the warlord's daughter refused to flatter him with such inquiries. Yet she did put forth the issue to one of her handmaidens, only to be informed with an embarrassed giggle that what the mistress had before her was *no plum.*

"And now for those kisses you promised?" prompted the swineherd, unable to drag his eyes away from his intended bride's stern mouth. He thrust his pelvis forward, prompting the weighty protrusion at the end to bob up and down. Its throbbing contours had grown so fat and purple that it looked in danger of bursting, in which case the young woman's fine frock would be ruined — an occurrence that would have been difficult to explain to her father, who had acquired the pale-yellow silk for his daughter during his recent annexation of Manchuria.

Such concerns for her garment began to appear ever more likely to come to fruition once the warlord's daughter realized that the ten kisses the presumptuous swineherd demanded as payment for the musical cane were not to be bestowed upon his lips as she had assumed, but rather upon the bloated specimen thrusting out from his pale loins. Perhaps this need not be so terribly unfortunate, however, since she found it preferable to lavish her kisses upon this robust offering than upon the mouth of a strange man—especially one who earned his keep tending pigs all day. Thus cloaked in the shelter of her hand-maidens' skirts, the warlord's daughter went to her knees before the expectant swineherd. Had her father discovered her in such a pose, he would have sent her off to tend soldiers savaged in battle, not to mention stringing up the poor swineherd from the nearest tree and letting him dangle by the neck until dead. Yet, whatever the risk to herself or another, she simply had to own the musical cane.

The rigid set of her lips relaxed and softened as the young woman pressed them warily against the wildly bouncing object with which she had been pre-sented. The exhilarating warmth from her breath inspired it to dance about with such recklessness that she would be forced to grab hold of the stout stave with both hands just to keep it still. As it turned out, the swineherd tasted so pleasant that the daughter of the warlord had no difficulty in fulfilling the remain-der of their bargain. With kiss number ten still shimmering upon the purple flesh of the pig-tender, she snatched up the musical cane and ran off, her con-cerns about stains to her frock forgotten.

For the remainder of the day, the warlord's daughter and her handmaidens entertained them-selves by dancing to the tunes of the musical cane and taking turns grasping the handle until scarcely a cane remained in the city whose lusty activities were unknown to them. As one might have expected, it did not take long for the capricious young woman to grow bored with the game, not to mention irritated with her handmaidens' silly titterings over the private lives of the townspeople. Not even the repeated application of the cane to their reddening backsides could return her to the spirit of things. No matter how hard she tried, the warlord's daughter could not banish the image of the swineherd from her mind...or the taste of him from her lips.

In the meantime, still more miraculous creations would be forthcoming from the pigsty. The nobleman-turned-swineherd refused to sit idle for a single moment. Over the next several weeks, a great deal of sawing and hammering could be heard, keeping the warlord's daughter tossing in her bed at night. Needless to say, her curiosity had been piqued to such a level that she dispatched her most trusted handmaiden to spy on the nocturnal activities of the swineherd. Fatigued from spending all day meeting the demands of her mistress's new cane, this chosen emissary promptly fell asleep outside the pigsty window and would have no information to impart in the morning.

Since being in the employ of the warlord, the swineherd had heard of the daughter's desire to own a pillory into which those whom she deemed in need of punishment could be locked. Having already enjoyed a fair amount of success with the musical cane, he decided to set about constructing one, confident that the finished product would win her over completely. For this would be no ordinary pillory, but one that replicated the cries of those locked into pillories all throughout the land. To make it as attractive as possible, the swineherd melted down every last piece of silver in his pockets, applying this glittering liquescence as trimming for the framework. He also took special care to buff away any roughness inside the holes carved out for the hands and head, hoping in his heart that his own might one day be fitted into them.

While out for her usual constitutional with her handmaidens, the warlord's daughter thought she could hear the tortured groans of men and women originating from the muddied recesses of the pigsty. She came to an abrupt halt, causing one of the more distracted of the handmaidens to collide with her. "What is that exquisite sound I hear? I simply *must* own the instrument that is the source of such delight!" She gave a push forward to the handmaiden who had trod on her heels. "Clumsy oaf, go and ask the swineherd what he wants for it. Only this time I shan't kiss him."

The handmaiden disappeared inside the pigsty, only to reemerge with a furious flush on her cheeks. "Oh, Mistress, now the beastly swineherd desires from you a *hundred* kisses!" she wailed, her umbrage so great one might have thought the demand had been made of herself.

"The fellow must be mad," declared the warlord's daughter. "Who does he think he *is* to request such a thing?" And indeed, she genuinely believed that this time the talented swineherd had gone too far. With a disdainful toss of her head, she went striding back toward the palace, the handmaidens hastening after her in a flurry of ruffled white. However, she did not even reach the ivy-covered colonnade before the mournful strains of an agonized wail teased her ears. "Hmm…perhaps a kiss is not such a costly price to pay for so magical a contrivance," she murmured. "Very well. You may inform the swineherd that I shall grant him *ten* kisses. As for the other ninety, they must come from my handmaidens."

"But we do not desire to kiss the swineherd!" protested the handmaidens in horrified unison.

"I assure you, it is not so disagreeable as you may imagine," replied their mistress with a secret smile.

As before, the pillory's marriage-minded creator could be neither tempted nor negotiated with. "If your mistress wishes to own the pillory, then she must grant me one hundred kisses," he stated resolutely. "I shall not accept a deputy in her stead." The swineherd knew he was pressing his luck, yet he would have done anything for such a bounty of kisses from the warlord's daughter.

And so the bargain was struck. A pillow would immediately be secured, the dispensation of a hundred kisses certain to place a considerable strain upon the knees. Without needing to be told, the handmaidens gathered in a circle around their mistress and the swineherd, fanning out their skirts to ensure that the activities occurring therein could not be monitored by passersby. Secure in her privacy, the daughter of the warlord found herself oddly flustered at once again being confronted with the swineherd's prodigious offering, for it had been revealed to her before she had even gone to her knees.

The handmaidens counted off each kiss aloud so that this impertinent tender of pigs would not be given any more than his agreed-upon due. Nevertheless, it soon became too difficult to keep a running tally, as each kiss lingered longer and longer than the last, their bestower's lips shining with the sweet juices they had inspired. The warlord's daughter executed her side of the bargain with unladylike relish, repeatedly squeezing her thighs together and riding the heel of her slipper as she alternately sipped and slurped the swollen purple object presented to her, unconcerned with the rude sounds her mouth made or the disconcerting effect it had upon those who listened. Indeed, the daughter of the warlord drew on the swineherd with such ferocity that he let out a tremendous roar, his legs folding in upon themselves—and still she refused to cease from her kisses. Even after the aggrieved pig-man had crumpled to the ground in anguish, she could be seen clutching his depleted flesh, her tongue fluttering to and fro within its drooling little cleft long after her handmaidens had called *"one hundred."*

Unbeknownst to the participants or their con-
spirators, the warlord had been seated at an upstairs
window planning the tactics for his next invasion
when he became distracted by the commotion occurring in the vicinity of the pigsty. Annoyed at having
his concentration interrupted—for it so happened that
the land he planned to invade was, by coincidence,
that of the nobleman-turned-swineherd—he set aside
his work to investigate the reason for this disturbance.
Certain that some devilment was in the works, he
crept up on the ring of women until he had gotten
close enough to peer over their heads. Observing his
daughter crouching over the groaning swineherd
whose breeches lay suspiciously rumpled about his
ankles, the warlord slipped off a shoe and set about
striking the handmaidens on the tops of their bon-
neted heads. "What is this mischief?" he bellowed as
he made his angry way toward the center of the circle.
However, no sooner did he reach the source of his
daughter's disgrace than he slumped forward, his
heart giving out, and he fell lifeless to the ground.

It would have seemed fitting that, with the
unexpected death of the warlord, the swineherd
should have chosen to disclose the truth of his situation to the warlord's daughter and return with her to
his home. Instead he remained silent, preferring to
reside with her at the palatial residence of the
deceased warlord. The nobleman continued to wear
the garments of a common swineherd, the muddied

breeches of which would frequently be loosed so that the new warlord (the daughter having taken over from the father) could apply the musical cane to his backside all through the day and long into the night as he stood with his hands and head locked into the glittering pillory he had built.

For what better form of annexation could there be? ❧

THE SHOES THAT WERE DANCED TO PIECES

Tellers of folktales have always been known to bring their personal experiences as well as their social environments into their stories. Although the peasant narrator generally reigns as supreme, there exists yet another voice — a voice belonging to one who has experienced the battlefield. Such a voice can be heard in the soldier's tale called "The Shoes That Were Danced to Pieces."

Equally well known as "The Twelve Dancing Princesses," the story tells of a poor discharged soldier who manages to rise in status by using his ingenuity, gaining for himself not only the crown, but also a beautiful princess. This type of tale likely arose from the inspired imaginations of the many soldiers all throughout history who, on finding that their services were no longer required, had nothing remaining to them except a life of poverty. Ergo, the creation of stories like "The Shoes That Were Danced to Pieces" provided these soldiers with adventure and a means of once again being useful, even if only within the boundaries of folktale reality.

Exclusive primarily to Central Europe, the tale is believed to originate in Russia. More than a hundred variants of "The Shoes That Were Danced to Pieces" have been recorded, the majority reaching from Serbia to Finland, which makes its diffusion quite limited when compared to other European folktales. Although scholars consider it doubtful that the story of the princesses and their worn-out shoes came into existence any earlier than the seventeenth century, elements occurring in the tale already have their antecedents in works of antiquity. The presence of the underground tree bearing jewels from which the soldier takes a sampling can be seen in the four-thousand-year-old Sumerian epic of the Mesopotamian ruler Gilgamesh. Like his more modern-day counterpart the soldier, Gilgamesh must make his way through an underground world, crossing over waters and encountering along the journey vines and bushes that bear jewels instead of fruit. And indeed, the tale may reach back farther yet by way of the coat the soldier wears to make himself invisible—an element indicating a possible connection to the folklore of primitive cultures and their belief in metamorphosis and magic.

Most familiar to fairy tale fanciers will be the version put forth by the Brothers Grimm. Coming upon elements of their story "The Twelve Dancing Princesses" in their travels throughout various regions of Germany, the Grimms found that not every story contained twelve princesses. One version involves a princess who supposedly wears out twelve pairs of shoes. They are in turn repaired by twelve apprentices, the most curious of which hides beneath her bed to learn how so many pairs of shoes could possibly be worn out by one wearer. In so doing, the apprentice discovers the existence of eleven other princesses, leading to the inevitable reward of being allowed to marry the first. In another version collected by the Grimms, three princesses wear holes into their shoes, thereby inspiring the announcement that anyone who can solve the mystery of the worn shoes will receive the hand of the youngest in marriage.

Present here for the first time is the character of the soldier who pretends to drink the drugged wine given him by the princesses—an element that became permanently incorporated into the tale by the Grimms, along with the gruesome disposal of those who tried and failed to solve the mystery of the worn-out shoes.

Indeed, Victorian editors would have a difficult time with the fatal and unjust disposition of the candidates who failed to learn where the princesses went at night. For the concept of those who strove yet failed despite their valiant efforts was not a theme held in particularly high regard by the Victorians. Nonetheless, these very same editors who objected to the dismal fate allocated the many candidates did not appear to pose any objection to a soldier's surreptitious spying on the intimate doings of beautiful young princesses or the princesses sneaking off in the night to meet with young men. Perhaps the bolting of their bedroom door by their father had been intended as a means of protecting their virtue, since surely a good deal more than a dance was on the princesses' agenda...as it would be for the young women in my version. ❧

The Shoes That Were Danced to Pieces

H IGH IN THE CARPATHIAN MOUNTAINS where counts came a dime a dozen, there lived a wealthy widowed Count who had for his pride and joy twelve daughters whose smiles warmed their father's heart. Concerned about untoward influences affecting the wholesome innocence of their lives, the Count insisted that his toothy offspring share the same bedchamber. Fortunately, it was a very large room with space enough to accommodate twelve satin-upholstered beds, which had been custom made from the finest mahogany and trimmed with bronze. Each evening at twilight, their father locked the young Countesses in, placing the one and only key within the pocket of his cape, thus ensuring that no one could go in or out but he himself.

Despite these paternal precautions, something always seemed to go seriously awry. For just before sunrise when he unlocked their bedchamber door to check on his daughters before retiring for the day to his own bed, the Count discovered that the soles of their shoes had become worn through from their nocturnal activities—activities that had evidently

been of so strenuous a nature that twelve corresponding pairs of underdrawers lay discarded beside their
owners' beds, one damper than the next. The continually thwarted Count was eventually forced to post a
notice in the village, announcing that any man who
learned where his twelve daughters went at night
would be granted the countess of his choice to take for
his wife *and* — upon the father's death — would inherit
vast wealth. As with most bargains of the day, there
was a slight caveat to this generous proposal: Not only
had the Count already lived for many centuries and
would likely live for many more, but if the man who
offered his services had not made the discovery inside
of three nights, he would have every drop of blood
drained from his body.

Within hours of the notice's posting, the son of
the burghermaster presented himself at the castle. A
notorious gambler, he owed money to nearly everyone in the village and had twice suffered a broken
nose as a result. He was immediately assigned a small
room across from that of the twelve Countesses in
which a pine box had been conveniently placed for
him to rest. So that the Count's ungovernable daughters might be more effectively observed, the door of
their bedchamber would be left fully open, placing
their every activity within plain sight of this sentinel.
Indeed, the burghermaster's son took considerable
delight in watching such fine young ladies dashing to
and fro in petticoat and chemise as each performed

her toilette, for the twelve Countesses possessed figures of great allure that not even the modest cloak of
their undergarments could hide.

Although such visual pleasures had never
before been made so readily available to him, this new
arrival had undergone a tiresome journey from the
village, and his eyelids began to droop with heavi-
ness, bringing with them an unwanted slumber.
Having found no coachman willing to transport him
to the Count's castle, he had had to walk the distance,
most of which was uphill. Only the rising of the sun
could finally prize the burghermaster's son out from
his sleeping box. The following morning he awakened
rested and refreshed...until suddenly he remembered
the reason he had come to the castle. Stealing into the
bedchamber of those over whom he had been
assigned to keep watch, he was greeted with the reassuring image of the twelve Countesses sleeping
peacefully in their mahogany beds, a toothy smile of
contentment on their pale faces. Alas, their guardian's
relief at his findings would be very short-lived.

For abandoned alongside each sister was a pair
of shoes, all of which had fresh holes worn into their
soles. Stuffed carelessly inside the left foot of each was
what at first glance appeared to be a kerchief.
However, a more thorough investigation revealed not
kerchiefs as originally thought, but ladies' underdrawers. The burghermaster's son pulled them out one by
one the better to examine them, his fumbling fingers

encountering a mysterious dampness upon their silken gussets. So intrigued was he by his findings that he took the pair assigned to the shoe of the youngest of the twelve Countesses back with him to his quarters to contemplate it at his leisure. And so it would be on the second and third nights as well, which explained how this luckless betting man came to be bled dry.

Be that as it may, there was always some desperate soul willing to risk his life-giving fluids for a chance at possessing great wealth in his pockets and a beautiful young bride in his bed. Indeed, both tradesman and peasant would be left with an emptiness in their veins, thereby necessitating a continuous supply of pine boxes to the castle. For not only did they function as beds, they could be utilized to bury their users in as well, proving the ultimate in multipurpose efficiency for the economically minded Count, who, it should be noted, had not accumulated his fortune by being a spendthrift.

One day a soldier passing through the village heard of the Count's unusual proposition from an old woman selling garlic in the marketplace. No longer in the sweet bloom of youth, he found the prospect of seizing tremendous riches greatly appealing. A wound incurred during the heat of battle had prevented the soldier from remaining on in service, leaving him in a position of poverty and lowly status. He beseeched the garlic seller to direct him to the castle until she grudgingly obliged, albeit not without first issuing a garlic-breathed warning: "You must refuse to eat or drink anything the Count's daughters offer. For if you fall asleep, your blood will be let by the close of the third night!" Apparently taking pity on him, the old woman placed a cloak of the blackest and most supple rubber across his arms. "Wear this and you will be protected from evil."

In appreciation, the soldier bestowed upon the marketwoman the one thing of value he owned: the silver crucifix he wore around his neck. Then he set confidently off on the road to the castle. Like his inauspicious predecessors, he would promptly be conducted into the little room across from the bedchamber of the Count's daughters. Accustomed to sleeping rough, the soldier found no fault with his accommodation. As darkness descended over the Carpathians, he lay in repose inside his pine box, observing the twelve Countesses through a crack in the wood. The moment the eldest came toward him with a cup of what looked to be wine, he began to snore loudly and with great enthusiasm, for he thought it best to heed the old garlic-seller's advice. With cup in hand, the Countess returned to her eleven sisters, whereupon they tittered merrily, no doubt heartily sorry for the doomed fellow who, at the conclusion of the designated three nights, would be obliged to spill his blood.

With the soldier snoring safely at his post, wardrobes and cupboards were flung open and garments were draped over every available surface. The Countesses dressed both themselves and each other, dancing gaily about on shoes whose soles had yet to experience wear. Despite such girlish gaiety, the youngest of the Count's daughters did not act nearly so carefree as her siblings. "Sisters," she addressed them portentously, "I fear an obstacle shall be placed in our paths on this eve."

"What nonsense!" retorted the eldest. "Can you not see how the fool sleeps?" She indicated the slumbering soldier, who had not altered his position since dusk. One might even have imagined him dead were it not for the guttural snorts and rattles emanating from the pine box. To make certain all was well, the sisters performed a closer inspection of their inharmonious sentry. Confident that he posed them no threat, they returned to their bedchamber, forming a line before a painted landscape of an ancient necropolis whose ghoulish iconography had sent shudders through the soldier on his arrival. The first-born rapped her knuckles thrice against the gilt frame and the immense canvas swung inward, revealing the entrance to a passageway. Although many castles had been designed with such secret labyrinths, it was the Count's servants whose persistent indolence prevented this particular one from being sealed up. With toothy grins, the twelve Countesses vanished into the black tunnel, the oldest going first, the youngest last.

All the while, the ostensibly slumbering soldier had witnessed everything, including the very pleasurable sight of the sisters' disrobing. Why, his famished eyes had roamed over vistas the likes of which had never been theirs to roam! With such fleshy scenarios still vivid in his mind, he undressed down to his boots before fastening at his neck the cloak of black rubber the old marketwoman had given him—only to discover that it rendered him completely invisible. Armed in his protective garb, the fearless soldier followed the Count's giggling daughters into the cobwebby darkness and down a succession of narrow steps. The smell of the rubber and the feel of it against his bare skin proved unexpectedly stimulating and in his distraction, he accidentally trod on the hem of the youngest's gown. "Eeek! Who goes there?" she shrieked, swatting her hands about as if to ward off an overly persistent bat.

"Hush, you silly!" hissed her sisters in annoyance. For they needed to remain absolutely silent until they had left the castle grounds and, most especially, the range of their father's highly acute hearing.

The twelve Countesses and their unseen pursuer emerged from the musty passageway into a small family graveyard whose ancient and crumbling tombstones lay in the moonlit shadows of trees. Unlike ordinary trees one might encounter in any graveyard, these arboreal specimens were dappled with shiny leaves of silver. The soldier decided to collect one as a token, figuring that he could secure a good price for it in the village in the event that matters did not conclude as favorably as he hoped and a hasty escape proved necessary. As he reached up to break off a leaf, the sound of its stem snapping fractured the stillness, alarming the already-alarmed younger Countess. "Sisters, did you hear?" she cried.

"Shush! It is only the sound of a gun being fired at a werewolf," scolded the eldest.

"Must you always be such a ninny?" reproached another sister, her sharp eyeteeth gleaming in the darkness.

The graveyard eventually opened out into a slightly larger graveyard whose leaning tombstones were overhung with trees containing leaves that appeared to have been hammered from gold. Regretting that he had not gathered for himself more of the silver, the soldier happily settled for a token of the gold, since it would fetch an even greater price than its more modest predecessor. Hearing the loud crack the stem made when broken, the youngest Countess jumped in fear, only to do so again when she and her sisters entered a graveyard of immense proportions whose more recent tombstones were eclipsed by trees that dangled glittering diamonds like ordinary raindrops. Having lived a life without anything of value in his pockets, the soldier wished to acquire a sampling of this as well. Indeed, with graveyards such as these in his environs, no wonder the Countesses' father possessed enormous wealth.

Having by now resigned himself to spending the entire night stalking the Countesses through graveyards, the soldier was startled to see the sparkling water of a lake at the terminus of this dominion of the dead. A dozen rowboats had been moored along the pebbly shore, and at each of their helms sat a handsome young squire, all of whom held a cudgel in their laps to ward off any blackguards who might happen by. As the twelve sisters fanned out to join their waiting sweethearts, the rubber-cloaked soldier attached himself to the youngest and, in his opinion, the prettiest. Since arriving at the castle, he had grown quite enamored of the little Countess, who seemed so much more ingenuous than her older and toothier siblings.

The boats and their occupants cast off toward the opposite shore of the lake, where the sound of music and laughter could be heard. Lagging far behind was the young Countess, whose robust companion rowed with unexpected difficulty, a labored sweat breaking across his smooth brow. On this particular evening the vessel felt unusually heavy—a phenomenon that he blamed on a fatigue brought about by too many nights of carousing with the Countesses, rather than on the presence of their invisible stowaway. As the rowboats touched land, the sisters took off in a run along the beach, taking care not to move too swiftly for fear they might outrun their handsome escorts. Furthermore, the pebbles hurt their feet, the soles of their shoes not having been intended for such rough terrain. Seizing the Countesses in their arms, the squires raised up the hems of their gowns, bringing into exposure their underdrawers, the already-dampened gussets of which were immediately drawn to one side. In this manner each couple danced on the shore, although instead of the partners being face-to-face and palm-to-palm, the gentlemen stood behind the ladies in close tandem.

In his position of newfound invisibility, the soldier could move freely among the twelve dancing couples with no concern for being made a victim of the squires' weapons, for, indeed, some of the larger ones looked quite menacing. Admittedly lacking in the social graces, this unseen spectator considered their jerky dance steps most peculiar and not at all in keeping with the elegant style he expected from those of their station. Yet perhaps even more peculiar was the fact that the squires insisted upon hiding their cudgels inside the disturbed gussets of the Countesses' underdrawers. Each charged forth with warlike impunity, his handsome features distorted with the effort of lodging his armament as deeply as possible before moving on to impale the next eager sister. Those gentlemen of a less robust physical nature paused to rest in between and give their spent weapons an opportunity to return to their former defensive mode, leaving their female partners swaying and shuddering in a solo dance before yet another squire moved in to claim them. The soldier placed himself before his favorite of the Count's twelve daughters so that he might get to the crux of the matter, the crude objects in the squires' care offering a bitter reminder of how skillfully he had once wielded a bayonet in battle. In his opinion, such masculine horseplay would be certain to result in serious injury to the Countesses, if it had not done so already.

Indeed, the youngest moaned wretchedly as she shimmied beneath the imprisoning arms of her dance partner, who had lifted her completely off the ground, leaving her legs to dangle beneath her upraised skirt. She clutched her ruffled bosom in distress, pleading with the grunting and grimacing squire to release her from her misery lest she die before the next sunrise. However, the fine fellow appeared not even to hear her. Instead he stepped up his vicious attack until the Countess began to howl like the creatures of the night of which her father was so terribly fond, her pointy eyeteeth bared to the moon. Before the concerned soldier could intervene on her behalf, he spied a tiny hole that had been forced into view by the retracted silk of her underdrawers. Although at first glance it was black as pitch, a closer inspection showed it to be as red and flamboyant as the poppies he had encountered in his desert travels. It was here that the squire's great cudgel vanished time and time again — as did those of his male companions, all of whom seemed to have the same effect upon the frantic young Countess. As the rubber-cloaked soldier proceeded to monitor the other dancing couples, he noted that all twelve of the Count's daughters sported a similarly outfitted hole.

The revelry went on well into the small hours of the morning until even the moon itself had gone to bed. Each squire performed this awkward dance with each Countess until all parties had been happily paired together, the wolfen howls of the sisters and those of the squires creating an eerie symphony of night music. Despite such equitable arrangements, there were those who desired a second dance with a partner already known to them. The eldest Countess, in particular, was shockingly bold in making her wishes manifest. Before the night was through, she had enjoyed two or three dances each with all twelve squires, hanging forward over the bridge of their arms as they swung her wriggling and baying figure about, her sharp teeth snapping at the air. Unlike her greedier older sister, the youngest seemed modestly content to partake of one promenade per squire, after which she dropped to the pebbly ground in quivery exhaustion, the soles of her shoes worn clear through to her feet. As she occupied herself readjusting the disarranged gusset of her underdrawers, the soldier would once again be granted a glimpse of the little mystery hole the dozen squires had used. To his astonishment, it had grown as large as the one belonging to her eldest sister.

The pink light of dawn was almost upon them by the time the squires rowed the dance-weary Countesses back over the lake. As the rowboat in which he had been traveling approached its pebbly moorings, its invisible mariner jumped out, charging ahead of the Count's daughters and reaching his quarters before the first-born had touched the tattered bottom of her shoe to the top-most step in the secret passageway. Flinging himself into his pine sleeping box, the soldier let loose with his most boisterous snores, his heart pounding furiously from his exertions and the curious events he had witnessed. Fortunately, the sisters had no reason to check on their unwanted sentry, who had forgotten to remove his rubber cloak and thus would have been invisible to them anyway. They instead fell into their mahogany beds in lifeless slumber, their battered shoes and moist underdrawers forgotten on the floor beside them.

Following in the wake of his unsuccessful fore-runners, the soldier also made the tantalizing discovery of the dampened wisps of white that lay crumpled up within the left shoe of each Countess. Something compelled him to try on the pair belonging to the youngest, which hugged his masculine curves and lumps with the snugness of a fine glove and left him gasping for breath when he ran his hands over himself in an appreciative caress. He so enjoyed the delicacy of the silk beneath the putty-like feel of the rubber that he sampled them all, since they proved so much more pleasing against the skin, what with their pretty owners a mere arm's length away. Indeed, this fallen warrior all but scraped his battle-scarred knees to bleeding, so much furtive crawling about the floor did he do in his self-appointed quest for fulfillment.

On the second night of his stay beneath the Count's roof, the soldier again feigned sleep so that he could slip back into the black rubber cloak and pursue the unsuspecting Countesses to their illicit assignations. Only now, rather than collecting silver or gold or diamonds, he had a far more valuable token in mind.

When the moment arrived for him to be summoned before the Countesses' father, this former combatant went armed with his precious leaves, which he presented to the Count, along with a circuitous explanation of the lake and the twelve boats and the twelve squires whose handsome presences had rowed them. He spent an inordinate amount of time belaboring details of lesser consequence such as the quality of pebble on the shore and the motion of wave on the lake, even going to the trouble of describing the color of the moonlight. Despite his anger, the Count was relieved to have finally received an explanation for the disgraceful condition of his daughters' shoes and underdrawers…although he was not given the exact specifics of the dancing that had taken place or the cudgels that had been wielded with such impunity by his daughters' dancing partners. For it appeared that the soldier had come to an arrangement with the Countesses.

The Count next called upon his recalcitrant offspring, who, in the face of the evidence against them, were obliged to confess. Apparently satisfied, he instructed their garrulous sentry to select for himself a wife from among the twelve. It would not be an easy choice to make. Each of the sisters possessed considerable appeal in face and figure, although in the soldier's eyes their smiles left a great deal to be desired. It might be thought that he would have taken for himself the youngest, since he had so admired her vernal artlessness, not to mention the poppy-like redness of her little mystery hole. Yet instead he claimed the eldest as a bride, her boldness and commanding nature offering him a battle he very much desired to fight with his bayonet—even if it was *not* so stalwart as a squire's cudgel.

The couple took for themselves a private apartment in the castle, one located near the bedchamber now occupied by the eleven remaining Countesses. With the Count's troubled mind at peace, his daughters resumed their nocturnal activities with the complicity and silence of their new brother-in-law, who was most eager to make good upon his bargain.

Night after night, the sisters stole away to meet the handsome young squires at the lake, only to return before dawn, at which time the soldier would be waiting to collect from each of them his token. Unlike a glittering memento of silver or gold or diamond, the token he wished to extract from his sisters-in-law commanded a value well beyond that of the monetary. Indeed, he did not need to await his father-in-law's death to become a wealthy man, for he attained his riches in other ways—and that is how it came to pass that the soldier acquired such an extensive collection of ladies' underdrawers. ∝

THE EBONY HORSE

A tale of the exotic East, "The Ebony Horse" can be found in *The Thousand and One Nights,* or, as it has come to be more commonly known, *The Arabian Nights*—an anthology of tales assembled from remote parts of the Islamic world over several centuries. Although admired by the West as a work of literature, *The Arabian Nights* has always been held in low esteem by the Arab world. In fact, were it not for the Europeans, it might never have made its way into our literature.

"The Ebony Horse" is one in a series of stories told over a thousand nights by Princess Shahrazad to her husband, King Shahryar. The princess used such stories as a form of entertainment and distraction and—most importantly—as a means to keep her life. For these stories served to prevent her husband from continuing with his pastime of marrying a different woman each night and, after taking her virginity, beheading her in the morning. Having discovered his first wife in sexual dalliance with a blackamoor slave, the king vowed to take no more chances. After experiencing a night of erotic pleasure with a steady succession of wives, he ordered them all put to death. However, he would soon run out of marital candidates as

"...parents fled with their daughters till there remained not in the city a young person fit for carnal copulation." Fortunately for all parties concerned, by the time Shahrazad finishes spinning her tales, she will have borne the king a son—and will thus be spared the fate that befell so many of her sex.

Much speculation exists as to the true origins of *The Arabian Nights*. Although the flavor of the work is distinctly Middle Eastern, with the core of the collection believed to represent medieval Cairo, its earlier tales, such as "The Ebony Horse," likely originated in either Persia or India, only to be passed down from generation to generation in the oral tradition by the storytellers of the Arabs, Egyptians, Iraqis, and other Mohammedan peoples. Over time, more and more stories came to be added, and by the fifteenth century the collection had been set down in manuscript form.

Yet, many centuries before the tales in *The Arabian Nights* even appeared in the Arabic language, they may already have lived in print. In the *Hezar Efsan* (A thousand stories) from Persia, the frame story also consists of a king who puts each of his wives to death, only to be distracted from this practice by his latest wife Shahrazad—a concubine of royal blood who keeps her husband entertained for a thousand nights with a series of stories. Despite its parental connection to *The Arabian Nights*, the *Hezar Efsan* likely has its own parent in India. The idea of framing stories within stories to provide a pretext for their telling is widely regarded as an Indian invention.

The Arabian Nights eventually made its way to Europe, undergoing various translations and revisions to suit the tastes and mores of the day. Just as Charles Perrault and the Brothers Grimm stamped their personal imprints on the folktales of Europe, so, too, would the translators who chose to tackle *The Arabian Nights*. Since many of the stories had been composed during the golden age of Baghdad—at the time a city of both pleasure and a marked licentiousness among the upper classes—the Middle Eastern reader would not need to look very hard to locate seduction, adultery, incest, and orgies on its pages. But all this would change, along with much of the integrity of the tales, as Western scholars of the eighteenth and nineteenth century got their hands on the Arabic manuscripts. Although the original work treated matters of sex in an uninhibited manner, such frankness was deemed unacceptable by the "modern" reader. A gulf existed between standards of morality and taste in Eastern and Western cultures — a difference made all the more intense by the developing prudery of middle-class readers, which prompted a continual expurgation of sexual content in *The Arabian Nights*. Nevertheless, one translator refused to shrink from such frank sexuality. In reaction to the Victorian prudery of his day, author and explorer Sir Richard Burton decided not only to include, but even to *emphasize*, the erotic content in the tales, thereby making his work the closest to the original.

Considered one of the oldest stories in *The Arabian Nights*, "The Ebony Horse" appears to be of Persian extraction and may be a survivor of the *Hezar Efsan*. Although not as sexually infused as some of the neighboring tales, it is not without the occasional erotic passage. Unlike his blushing predecessors, Sir Richard seemed to relish such passages, especially those describing the prince's desire for the beautiful princess. "...[T]he fires of longing flamed up in his heart and pine and passion redoubled upon him. Grief and regret were sore upon him and his bowels yearned in him for love of the King's daughter...." Such extravagance of language cannot easily be found in similar works. This literary style would prove quite popular as more and more readers (and even a few writers) came to discover the lure of the exotic and, indeed, the erotic in *The Arabian Nights*. ॐ

THE EBONY HORSE

I N A LAND OF GOLDEN DESERT SANDS THERE lived a great and powerful sultan named Sabur. He was much loved by his people, such that each year the day of his birth came to be celebrated with more lavishness than those that had gone before. As he sat upon his jeweled throne surrounded by his loyal courtiers, dervishes would dance, slave girls would serve, and cooks would proffer exotic victuals capable of pleasing the most fastidious of imperial palates. So revered was the Sultan that on his birthday every road in the empire stood littered with gifts, each finer than the next. But on the day marking his fifty-fifth year, one gift surpassed all the others.

An old sage who dwelt in the cave of a mountain presented himself to the Sultan, bowing with extravagant ceremony to kiss the ground between Sabur's large feet. On this special occasion he had brought a life-sized horse carved from the finest ebony, with eyes of glittering diamonds and a mane and tail created from the cocoon of the silkworm, the quality of which surpassed even that of the Sultan's best robes. The tooled red hide of the saddle, bridle, and stirrups had been inlaid with gold and every precious jewel that could be cut from the earth. "Your Majesty, this horse has the power of flight. It can leap higher than a rainbow and cross the seven seas," boasted the sage, his claim generating no less than a few scowls of disapproval.

"If what you say is true, then I shall reward you with your dearest wish," replied Sabur with an amused smile, convinced that this unctuous braggart was endeavoring to get the better of him.

Upon hearing these words, the sage leapt up with startling agility onto the ebony horse. Rotating a peg hidden beneath the saddle, he flew off through the arches of the palace gallery and high into the pinkening sky. By the time he returned, the Sultan was beside himself with excitement at the notion of possessing the splendid horse. In his eyes, no wish would have been too grand to fulfill. Therefore when the sage requested the one thing of value belonging to the Sultan, it could not be denied. As a result, Sabur's only daughter came to be promised to the sage in marriage.

Outraged by this impetuous peddling of his young sister, the Sultan's son found himself obliged to intervene in this unwholesome bargain, fearful that the outcome would not bode well for his unworldly sibling. "Father, this wicked man is a common sorcerer. Surely you cannot trade your precious daughter for a toy horse?" Kamar al-Akmar protested in horror.

Sabur raised a hand to still his son's heartfelt remonstrations. "A sultan's word is his bond—and my word has been given. Perhaps you might elect to ride upon it yourself to determine if your opinion is in need of altering," retorted the Sultan, who did not take kindly to having his decisions questioned.

All the while, the old sage had been standing silently by, cloaking his instant hatred of Kamar behind a habitually sour visage. "Simply turn this little peg and you shall partake of journeys it would require ten lifetimes to experience," he croaked, grinning yellowly and bowing toward the young Shahzada with false respect.

Being of a fair mind, Kamar al-Akmar felt himself relenting. And indeed, no sooner did he climb up onto the saddle and touch his fingers to the peg the sage had indicated than the ebony horse went bounding off over the gallery and high into the desert sky. At first he enjoyed this amazing sensation of flight, but the heights he reached and the speed with which he traveled soon became too much for a young man created from flesh and blood, regardless of its royal content. The panicked Shahzada barked out a series of frantic commands, his words failing to penetrate the horse's delicately carved ears as all he had ever known faded to an ochre haze beneath him.

As the shadows flickering upon the marble walls of the palace became absorbed into the night, the Sultan grew increasingly concerned. He ordered his slaves to fetch the old sage, who claimed that nothing could be done. "The good Shahzada departed

with such swiftness that I did not have an opportunity
to explain to him about the second peg," he shrugged
in exaggerated dismay, his black heart swelling with
joy at Kamar al-Akmar's apparent misfortune. Only,
rather than being allowed to console the Sultan with
hollow declarations of sympathy, the sage found himself banished to a cell, where he would spend his
tenure being whipped by the palace slaves. Since they
were so often whipped themselves, they took great
satisfaction from inflicting pain upon the body of
another and performed their task far beyond their
ruler's most stringent expectations. Needless to say,
the Sultan's earlier matrimonial promise of his
daughter was promptly rescinded, thereby further
blackening the sage's heart and setting him toward
what would become an unwavering path of revenge.

By this time, Kamar had traveled a considerable distance and, while battling to control the
ebony steed, he called upon Allah to bring him back
down to safety. It was then that his furiously searching fingers alighted upon a corresponding peg
located to the far side of the saddle—a peg so seemingly insignificant that one might have thought its
presence was not meant to be detected. His fingertips
barely grazed it before he discovered himself plunging perilously toward the converging rivers of the
Tigris and the Euphrates. Further adjustments managed to slow the wooden beast's progress, and the
young Shahzada was soon journeying at a more

leisurely pace, marveling at the vast desert landscape laid out below him. As the veil of night cast itself over him, he was drawn toward the shimmering lights of Sana, where he had seen a magnificent palace whose marble exterior still glowed with the heat of the now-sleeping sun. Certain that he would be welcomed here, he maneuvered the ebony mount steadily down-ward, landing atop a flat portion of roof.

Since the hour had grown quite late and was thus not an appropriate time to presume upon the hospitality of strangers, Kamar al-Akmar stole into the palace via a carelessly unbolted door, moving with winged feet along the polished marble floors of the topmost corridor in search of sanctuary. Just when he despaired that he would never locate a place to rest his weary body, he arrived at a small vestibule. A slave stood guard outside, fast asleep on his bare feet. Tiptoeing past so slowly that he did not even disturb the air, Kamar drew aside the heavy velvet drapery concealing the entranceway, discovering a private bedchamber.

Commanding the center of the room stood a round bed constructed from the rarest pink-hued agate and studded throughout with the same precious gem-stones that adorned his father's crown. Flames from a bevy of candles repeated themselves in miniature within the brilliant reds and greens and blues, giving the illusion that the source of light originated from the bed itself. Little else in the manner of furnishings appeared to be present, which only made this solitary specimen for sleep all the more spectacular to its observer. Voile curtains hung in a graceful drape from a canopy of intricately carved rosewood, and they fluttered slightly at Kamar al-Akmar's approach. They had been tied back in one place with a gleaming silken cord, as if offering to him an invitation.

And he would accept it most gratefully, for just behind these curtains was the most enchanting creature the young Shahzada had ever seen. The one he gazed upon could be none other than the famous Shahzadi of Sana—Shams al-Nahar. Kamar had heard a good deal spoken of her legendary golden hair and tiny white hands; they had been the subject of many a male dream in empires far and wide and in dreamers both young and old. The Shahzada all but dropped to the floor in a faint as he spied the beautiful Shams lying in graceful repose upon her back, her perfect alabaster form untainted by cloth save for a gauzy veil concealing the lower portion of her face. A pair of half-lidded eyes the color of smoke had been caught in a trance-like state as two pretty slave girls knelt over her, dutifully administering to their beloved Shahzadi. They wore scarcely more than their highborn mistress, their own veils having been pulled immodestly down to reveal mouths with lips as lush and red as fine wine and nearly as wet. From what this stealthy encroacher could discern, the duo appeared to be bathing the Shahzadi with their tongues, as Shams al-Nahar possessed skin of a remarkable delicacy that would have been marred by the common crudeness of a sea sponge.

Kamar watched in spellbound silence as the slaves licked slowly up along the silken lengths of each lovely thigh, urging them gently apart to gain access to the innermost potions. The Shahzadi sighed softly as they worked, the sighs turning into low throaty moans as the diligent pink tongues of her two attendants moved toward a dainty little pleat located at the junction of her outspread thighs, at which point the pale swell of her belly began to undulate like waves on a storm-tossed sea. The cleft flesh reminded its captivated beholder of a cowry shell that a visiting ship's captain had given his childhood self, although this version proved far superior in every respect. Why, one could almost liken the slender seam running through it to a tiny mouth—a mouth that, unless the Shahzada was greatly mistaken, actually smiled at him.

Indeed, the closer the two slave girls got to this special place, the more force with which Kamar al-Akmar's heart beat. Encouraged by his friendly reception, he placed himself to the farthest end of the bejeweled bed and, with furtive deliberation, raised up the voile curtain to better observe the enchanting Shahzadi's evening bath. For the first time in his privileged life the Shahzada actually found himself envying those of menial status, for it did not seem so terribly unpleasant to pass one's days attending a mistress in possession of such beauteous attributes. He started to tremble as the slaves' feline tongues reached the charming little pleat between the Shahzadi's thighs, the trembles graduating into violent shudders when each placed a well-acquainted thumb along the polished sides, drawing them tenderly and lovingly asunder.

Out from this artificially widened rift grew the petal of a rose, its pink more vibrant and lustrous than any Kamar al-Akmar had ever come across in his journeys. It bloomed with all the vernal freshness of a new spring, offering up a perfume as subtle as it was sweet. A breeze blew across the silken surface, causing it to flutter and billow and surge forth with vigor, as if straining to declare itself to its captivated onlooker. Although Kamar would have liked to press his yearning nose against it, he did not wish to frighten the Shahzadi. Instead he kept his desires mute, watching with breathless rapture as the two slave girls bowed their heads to lick the richly shaded pinkness surrounding this newly revealed treasure.

Alas, Kamar al-Akmar's restraint did not last for long. A strange and most disconcerting occurrence had begun to take place inside his garments. He thought that perhaps an adder (for the desert was abundantly populated with them) had slithered its sinuous way in among the linen folds, and he shimmied about to set it free. When this failed to work, he took to slapping and rubbing himself, which only served to exacerbate the problem. In frustration the Shahzada reached up underneath his garment to grab hold of the offending entity, feeling it spasm and jerk in his hand. Suddenly it spat a hot stream of venomous fluid onto his belly, extracting from him a tormented groan. Indeed, Kamar created such a disturbance that Shams al-Nahar and her female attendants leapt up in fright from the bed. "Who are you?" cried the wide-eyed Shahzadi, straightening the veil over her flushed face. "What is your business here?"

Unconcerned for their own modesty, the two slaves fetched the flustered Shahzadi's nightdress and assisted her back into it. However, it did little to cloak her nakedness. Kamar could scarcely drag his eyes away from the place that had caused him such agitation, so mesmerized was he by the silken whorls that the diaphanous linen failed to conceal. With a regal bow and as much dignity as he could muster, the Shahzada introduced himself as the son of a great and mighty sultan and proceeded to explain the unusual nature of how he had come to be in the palace of the Shahzadi. Of course Shams al-Nahar refused to believe such an impossible tale and demanded to be shown the ebony horse. Apparently, this handsome trespasser took her for a fool if he thought he could coax his way into her bed with such a fantasy. Even her two attendants could only shake their heads and titter behind their veils at hearing the lofty claim that Kamar al-Akmar had put forth.

Although this self-professed son of a sultan who had so rudely interrupted her slaves' very pleasant laving of her person readily agreed to escort the Shahzadi to the wooden horse, Shams took note of his fatigue and condescended to grant him a few moments in which to rest and refresh himself and perhaps partake of a light meal. Despite this generous offer of hospitality, Kamar dared not tally for too long in her bedchamber. The guard posted in the corridor was bound to awaken in due course, and once it had been discovered that this presumptuous foreigner had spied upon the beautiful Shahzadi during her bath, the dogs would be set on him.

Shortly before daybreak and with the discordant music of the barefooted sentinel's snores in their ears, Shams al-Nahar and her male intruder stole up to the palace rooftop. At the sight of the ebony horse with its flashing diamond eyes and jewel-encrusted accouterments, the Shahzadi leapt about in girlish delight. "Oh, do let me ride upon it!" she squealed, so excited that she dislodged the veil from her face. Only it would not be what lay behind the veil that tormented Kamar's thoughts and sent a scimitar arcing through his belly.

Swallowing hard, he pondered the eager Shahzadi's request with some deliberation. For, like his father and the wicked sage, Kamar al-Akmar, too, could strike bargains. "Your Highness, I shall be both honored and pleased to accommodate your wish. But I have a wish of my own."

"Oh, yes! Anything!" cried the Shahzadi. "Is it gold you desire? Or land? I can speak to my father —"

"It is neither gold nor land I desire."

"Well, what then?"

Kamar cleared his throat, for suddenly it felt as though the pit from a date had gotten lodged inside it. When he could finally speak, his words came out sounding rough and raw and not at all like the mellifluous tones to be expected from one of his position. "I should very much desire to sample the perfume of your rose petal."

"My *rose petal?*" echoed Shams al-Nahar in confusion. Indeed, she truly did not understand to what the owner of the ebony horse could possibly be referring. When the red-faced Shahzada indicated with his eyes the area beneath her garment to which he was alluding, the Shahzadi began to giggle. "I am certain that can be arranged," she replied with a diffident smile, raising up the gauzy hem of her nightdress.

Falling weakly to his knees, Kamar al-Akmar pressed his nose against the velvety-silk softness of Shams' proffered gift. "*Ahh*...my desert rose," sighed the enamored Shahzada. "You have been sent to me from the heavens."

Such worshipful words could not fail to ignite the Shahzadi's passions. "Take me with you!" she pleaded, driving Kamar's flushed face hard against the bisected shell-like promontory beneath her belly.

As the sun squeezed slowly out to fill the eastern horizon, Kamar al-Akmar and Shams al-Nahar together mounted the magic horse. A quick flick of a peg sent the couple soaring high into the early morning sky, the palace of Sana receding to an orange-toned speck of marble beneath the beast's ebony flanks. It would not be until the following sunrise that they arrived in the sultanate of the Shahzada's father, for they had stopped many times along the way to rest and for Kamar to once again stimulate his senses with the Shahzadi's exotic endowment.

Leaving Shams and the ebony horse behind at his summer palace, the Shahzada traveled by foot the remainder of the distance to the palace of his father. Although he had not been gone from his homeland for very long, he discovered the city and its inhabitants greatly altered. People had taken to dressing in the black of mourning and walked with their eyes cast downward in sadness. Even the imperial banner atop the palace roof had been respectfully lowered in a manner indicating that a member of the Sultan's family had died. As Kamar al-Akmar approached the gates, excited shouts could be heard coming from every corner of the palace. "The Shahzada is alive!"

Seeing the face of his son before him smiling and beaming with health, the Sultan's tears of sorrow turned to tears of joy. Many hugs came to be exchanged, after which Kamar told his father of the beautiful Shahzadi he had brought back with him.

Orders were immediately given to release the old sage from his prison cell, his evil intentions having resulted in good after all. Fully expecting to be put to death at any moment, the sorcerer was quite taken aback by his pardon, although this in no way lessened his searing hatred of the Sultan's son. On the contrary, many cruel days and nights of bloody whippings had honed and refined it; hence the happy news of the young Shahzada's return with the enchanting Shahzadi who awaited his hand in marriage did not sit well with the embittered sage, whose taste for revenge had grown ever stronger.

As celebrations were planned for the wedding of Kamar al-Akmar and Shams al-Nahar, the newly freed wizard hastened to the Shahzada's summer palace, planning to arrive in advance of the official messengers who had been dispatched by the Sultan to collect the bride. He came upon the Shahzadi sitting alongside a gaily tinkling fountain with the ebony horse, whose silken mane she combed lovingly with her slender fingers. Having departed from her own home in such haste, she had not been given an opportunity to change from her nightdress into proper street attire.

"Oh, gracious Shahzadi, allow me to kiss the ground betwixt your imperial toes," croaked the sorcerer, who could barely conceal his excitement at the sight of his enchanted horse or the alluring young woman who stroked its glossy black mane with her tiny hands. The image of those caressing fingers stirred something raw and primeval within him, and all at once the sage felt a lifetime of need welling up inside him. He knelt to press his withered brown lips against the sun-warmed earth at the Shahzadi's feet, his tongue slithering boldly and wetly between her dainty toes and eliciting from her an astonished yelp. As he sucked the flavor from her smallest toe, the sage glanced stealthily up to behold her startled face, only to have his attention waylaid by something a good deal more savory than a toe limned beneath the thin cloth of her garment. "The Sultan has sent me to bring you to the place of your wedding," explained the old wizard in a voice careening high with strain.

Shams al-Nahar arose from the stone bench encircling the fountain, pulling her toe with considerable effort out from the sage's mouth. "Then I must locate something into which I may change, for I cannot be presented to the Sultan thusly," she chuckled self-effacingly, indicating the obvious unsuitability of her attire.

"But your Highness, that is entirely unnecessary. A gown of watered silk embroidered with every precious jewel in the sultanate awaits you at the palace. Come," invited the sage with a courtly bow, mounting with unexpected difficulty the horse's elegantly outfitted back. An incommodious swelling had begun to make itself known inside the lower portion of his shabby vestments, hampering his every movement and necessitating a need for further furtiveness lest the unsuspecting Shahzadi take heed of it. "We must make haste, as it would not do to be late for the Shahzada and Shahzadi's wedding!"

Since Shams al-Nahar, indeed, did not desire to miss the day of her own wedding, she allowed the Sultan's peculiar message-bearer to assist her up onto the saddle in front of him, where he assured her she would be safe from harm. The sage knotted his long belt securely around her waist, thereby linking it to his own. With an expert twist of the peg, the ebony horse bolted high into the endless blue of the desert sky.

Although unfamiliar with the foreign landscape of her future husband, Shams knew with reasonable certainty that the palace of the great Sabur was located to the west, Kamar al-Akmar having earlier set off by foot in that direction. Therefore she grew extremely alarmed when the jackal-faced messenger piloted the magical horse toward the morning sun. "Look here, this is not the way to the Sultan's palace!" she protested. "Why do you not obey your master's orders?"

The sorcerer chuckled wickedly, displaying to the anxious Shahzadi a generous assortment of jagged yellow teeth. "I have no master!" he snorted contemptuously, cinching the belt binding them together even more tightly to emphasize his words.

"But the Sultan—"

"I, who command the secret of flight, do not require a master. As for that worthless horse thief

Kamar, I heartily advise you to forget him. I shall give you all the kisses you require and *more,* once I take you as my bride!" For in having been originally promised a bride by the Shahzada's father—who promptly reneged on the arrangement—the wizard felt entirely justified in acquiring another, especially when this other happened to be betrothed to the son of the one who had cheated him.

With so foul a proposal resounding in her ears, the Shahzadi struggled to free herself, only to discover that the sage's belt held her like a chain of iron. She tried everything in her ability to thwart the villainous wizard, her threats and entreaties having little impact. It was not so much that she possessed an actual aversion to being restrained; for in the evenings Shams would often presume upon her personal slaves to bind her wrists and ankles as she awaited their devoted ministrations. However, the unsightly visage of the old sage bore no resemblance to those of her pretty slave girls, and despite the increasingly excited shivers that shook her slight frame, the Shahzadi found herself protesting with unexpected vigor, her words seeming to encourage her abductor to commit even greater improprieties upon her person.

Laughing like a madman, the sorcerer grabbed hold of the hem of her garment and tucked it into his belt. With Shams al-Nahar's pale thighs stretched wide and clinging in trembling desperation to the horse's wooden flanks, Kamar al-Akmar's cherished rose petal became fully exposed to the elements. The cold wind lashed cruelly against it, causing it to ripple wildly about as the image of her wedding to the evil sage stung the Shahzadi's eyes and caused a corresponding burning in her loins.

By mid-afternoon, warder and prisoner approached a misty landscape of white-capped mountains and rushing blue rivers. The ebony horse finally set down in a rich green meadow. After securing a struggling Shams to its saddle with his belt, the wizard went off in search of food and drink—albeit not without first giving his captive's windblown petal a vicious tweak, which was followed by a burst of vicious laughter and a suffusion of redness to both the Shahzadi's cheeks and the object of the sage's torment. Shams al-Nahar vowed to herself that when she returned to the land of her Kamar, she would see to it that the old wizard's testicles were skewered and cooked over flame for their wedding supper.

It so happened that the ruler within whose empire the ebony horse had alighted had been out riding with his companions and had stopped to watch the amazing spectacle of the flying horse and its two equestrians, one of whom had gone scurrying off on some mission known only to him. The party of men discovered the beautiful Shahzadi bound to the finely tooled saddle of the beast with her diaphanous garment rolled up to her waist, her sole concession to modesty the gauzy veil covering the lower half of her face. She lay in helpless repose upon her back, her wrists and ankles cinched by a belt, which had been secured beneath the horse's wooden belly. Left to stare up at the darkening sky, Shams did not see the group of horsemen until they were almost upon her. However, the telltale sound of hooves tramping the earth made her tremble and writhe with a fire that grew ever hotter as the riders drew nearer.

As the riding party galloped determinedly toward her, Shams al-Nahar cried out with what sounded to the men like relief, although the breathless Shahzadi knew different. The ruler of the land had barely managed to rein his steed to a halt before her recumbent figure when Shams was already halfway through the story of her life, unable to temper her outrage as she spoke of the evildoer who had brought her to this place. "You must arrest this *shaitan* and lock him inside your securest jail!" she implored of the astonished ruler and his equally astonished companions. "For he has stolen me from what should have been the day of my wedding."

Despite the calamities this improperly posed equestrienne claimed to have suffered at the hands of the now-absent wizard, the master of this misty landscape was unable to concentrate on the torrent of words tumbling like a waterfall from her lips. For his attention had been claimed by what lay beneath the uplifted hem of the foreign Shahzadi's nightdress — as had been the attention of every man in his riding party, save for the slender, falsetto-voiced one who was summoned nightly to entertain the royal sons in their private apartments. *It must surely be more fragrant than any flower in this meadow!* mused the ruler, a powerful shiver shaking his stalwart form. In a strangled tone, he commanded his followers to locate the fiendish sorcerer and escort him to the palace dungeon. Clearly disgruntled, the men galloped off to carry out their detested orders, leaving their leader and the provocatively tethered horsewoman alone.

Without the watchful presences of others upon him, the ruler had taken to drifting with subtle stealth nearer and nearer the ebony horse and its solitary female rider, whereupon Shams al-Nahar began to writhe against the hard surface of the saddle with renewed excitement. Indeed, it appeared that her royal liberator did not act with any particular haste toward releasing her from her bonds. Although propriety demanded that she bid him to let down the hem of her garment, the Shahzadi held her tongue.

"And what might you have there to show me, my lady?" inquired the ruler, the intensity of his gaze making his point of reference unmistakable.

The Shahzadi flushed hotly, as did the object of his interest, which actually seemed to flourish with the ruler's attentions, putting forth a series of come-hither twitches—a phenomenon Shams al-Nahar had yet to experience even under the dutiful ministrations of her two slaves. Of course, she did not consider it at

all appropriate to respond to such an inquiry, therefore she continued to remain silent, hoping that this
seeming rescuer would accept her reticence as a sign
of acquiescence.

Thusly encouraged, the ruler inclined his tur-
baned head toward the exaggerated junction of the
Shahzadi's thighs, the discerning tip of his nose grazing the velvety tip that thrust boldly upward to meet
him. His stiff black mustache tickled the shell-like surroundings, whose lustrous pink had been forced into
the open by a pair of outstretched knees. As he
embarked upon a leisurely nuzzle of this distinctly
foreign terrain, several droplets of moisture adhered
to the waxed hairs on his upper lip, and he licked
them furtively away, reveling in their nectarous
sweetness.

Shams could feel the twin breaths from the
ruler's nostrils blowing warmly upon her, followed by
their sudden reversal as they drew in the surrounding
air, taking with it the fragrance of her arousal. "Please,
your Majesty, I am already promised to the Sultan's
son," she appealed shakily, the sensation of those stiff
black hairs on his upper lip stealing away what little
remained of her composure. For the ruler's nose was
significantly larger than that of her dear Kamar.

Without warning, the mustachioed ruler drew
forth his golden saber and sliced cleanly through the
belt keeping the Shahzadi bound to the ebony horse.
Rather than allowing her to go free, he seized her

139

bodily and heaved her atop the saddle of his steed, taking care that the hem of her garment remained as before—rolled up to her waist. "And now you are promised to *me!*" he bellowed, roaring with laughter as wicked as that of the sorcerer who had stolen Shams al-Nahar from the young Shahzada. Holding her imprisoned within one powerful arm, the ruler brought his great thighs down over hers so that they were kept as deliciously parted as when he had first encountered her. Their pale inner flesh had already forgotten the luxurious memory of her slave girls' diligently laving tongues. Now they only experienced the coarse licking of the wind.

In this manner they galloped off, followed by two trusted members of the riding party who had returned to the meadow to fetch the magic horse. Approaching the fortified walls encircling the palace, the ruler shouted out orders for the household to commence wedding preparations. Indeed, the land would rapidly be abuzz with comment, a good many people having witnessed the shocking spectacle of the beautiful Shahzadi being paraded through the streets with her thighs held open and the lusty emblem of pink at their crossroads pointing the way like a defiant finger. With the eyes of hundreds of men and women burning between them, Shams al-Nahar experienced a deep thrumming in the place that had attracted so much public interest—a thrumming that reached all the way to the tips of her fingers and toes, curling them tightly into themselves. Within moments the Shahzadi would be bucking wildly about on the saddle. A tiny vermilion pearl formed on her lower lip as she bit through the flesh, the tooled red hide beneath her becoming hot and slippery with her private pleasure as her ears devoured the ruler's crude words. If only her beloved Kamar could have spoken to her like that!

Despite her present abductor's apparent gift for verbiage, it did not take long for Shams to realize just how tedious life would be to find herself wedded to this hulking tyrant upon whose horse she had ridden and in whose household his slave girls possessed the faces of boars. Therefore she devised a scheme in which to delay the taking of vows and, in the process, spare herself from being subjected to the daily, if not *hourly*, interrogation of the ruler's great hair-fringed nose. Thus it happened that the Shahzadi refused all food and drink, preferring to spend her days hurling about in a maddened fit until the ruler would at last be forced to release her. So successful was this performance that not only did he postpone the marriage ceremony, he refused to permit his dejected nostrils to graze anywhere near his stolen betrothed's fragrant attributes. Not even the household's finest slave girls could calm the feral Shahzadi. No sooner did they enter her room than she bit them, taking pleasure in the shrieks of terror she inspired. Determined not to become a topic of ridicule for his people, the ruler next summoned a succession of doctors, although he feared her condition to be beyond cure.

All the while, a grief-stricken Kamar al-Akmar had been wandering far and wide in search of his beloved Shams. Everywhere he went, he made inquiries, hoping that someone might have seen her riding the ebony horse with the old sage. Why, he dared not ponder what evils might have befallen her at the sorcerer's filthy hands. Stopping briefly to partake of food and drink at a small inn, he heard talk of the sudden and inexplicable illness of the ruler's recent betrothed—a beautiful young Shahzadi who had the petal of a rose growing out from the meeting place of her thighs. All who had been out and about on the afternoon the ruler had ridden through the streets with her had viewed it, the gentleman having gone to great pains to keep the hem of her garment raised. One might imagine that he should have desired to keep such matters a secret lest a competitor throw down his glove in challenge. But, being of a rather advanced age, the ruler wished to flaunt his good fortune by offering conspicuous evidence of his youthfulness and virility.

Hearing this strange and remarkable tale, Kamar knew at once that the demented Shahzadi was none other than Shams al-Nahar. Filled with renewed hope, he hastened to the ruler's palace and presented himself as a doctor who could cure the Shahzadi's mysterious illness. "I have repaired the broken minds of many," boasted the Shahzada, his newly sharpened saber twitching in its sheath with the desire to pierce the heart of this recent thief who had stolen his near-bride.

Overjoyed at the appearance of this specialist in madness, the ruler explained in some detail the unusual circumstances in which he had encountered the Shahzadi and the old sage, the latter of whom was at this very moment hanging from his toes in the palace dungeon. Naturally, he intentionally omitted the Shahzadi's more intimate specifics, the ruler not wanting to draw the handsome young physician's attention to those things of which he himself had been so sadly deprived. Kamar al-Akmar was next escorted to the room of the afflicted one, who, hearing the approach of footsteps, threw herself to the floor and snarled like a demon, her hands clawing at her much-tampered-with nightdress. As the disguised son of the Sultan stepped forward, the ruler took several steps back, unable to mask his fear. It appeared that his sons had been correct when they had advised him so strongly against taking a foreigner for a bride.

Kamar squatted beside this wild she-beast whom he believed to be his beloved Shams. As she continued to thrash about, her garment became even further torn and upset, when suddenly the disconsolate Shahzada spied something familiar in the place where the young woman's thighs came together. With the hovering figure of the ruler only a saber's distance away, Kamar al-Akmar placed his flushed face as close as he dared, his sick heart soaring with happiness. For not only was this tattered madwoman Shams al-Nahar, but she had been feigning her illness all along. *How extraordinarily clever of her to have devised such a plan to save herself for me,* Kamar thought with pride, confident in the knowledge that his virtuous Shams would not have allowed the ruler to so much as wash her feet. Now he, too, needed to be clever. "Your Majesty, has the Shahzadi been in contact with a wooden figure of any kind?"

"To be sure, she has!" cried the ruler, thrilled to be of assistance to the gifted young physician. If all went well, perhaps he would soon be spending his days and nights in some delightfully fragrant company. "She was found with an ebony horse."

"Then this horse must be brought here at once so that I can break the spell of evil it has cast, for its spirit has entered the Shahzadi's head."

The ruler summoned his most trusted servants, who fetched the magic horse. Kamar al-Akmar next requested to be left alone with the Shahzadi so that he might begin the difficult and dangerous process of curing her. The ruler's thundering footsteps had not even receded down the corridor before a laughing Shams al-Nahar leapt up onto the tooled red hide of the saddle, with Kamar buttressing her from behind. With a twist of a peg, the ebony horse raised its front hooves into the air and leapt out through the window, taking its two runaway riders.

Hearing the commotion, the ruler raced out into the courtyard, shaking his large fists threateningly at the sky. "Come back here, you foreign horse thief!" he bellowed. "I demand you return to me my rose-petaled bride!" A storm of arrows from the palace guards lanced the air, but not a single one managed to touch the horse's wooden flanks. By now it had soared so high that even the most courageous of hawks could not have reached it.

Kamar al-Akmar and Shams al-Nahar returned in victory to the sultanate of the great Sabur. Celebrations were held throughout the land as their wedding took place, yet no celebration would be as full of joy as the one that took place when the Shahzada came to be reunited in private with his bride. Although never to be parted from her again, Kamar quickly discovered that his newfound felicity would have to be shared with his people. For Shams required her husband to secure her daily to the saddle of the ebony horse, where she rode writhing through the streets, her cries of shameful rapture resounding over the rooftops.

Word eventually got around, and the city of the Sultan became a much-sought-after destination for visitors, who journeyed from far and wide to see the famous Shahzadi riding on her magic horse. As for the old sage, he knew an opportunity when he saw one. Having managed to escape from the foreign dungeon in which he had been imprisoned and tortured, he made his way home, where he set up shop outside his cave by selling tickets to tourists foolish enough to pay for what they could have enjoyed for free. ⁊

Michel Michelkleiner's Good Luck

Undoubtedly one of the most obscure folktales in all of Europe, "Michel Michelkleiner's Good Luck" comes from the tiny country of Luxembourg. However, the tale was formally collected only in 1960. Had it not been for a decision by the Committee of Ministers of the Council of Europe to sponsor the publication of a collection of works on European folklore, Michel Michelkleiner's auspicious adventure might never have become known beyond its oral form.

When compared with the other countries of Europe, Luxembourg has not enjoyed a great deal of study of its folktales, let alone their historical foundation. Nevertheless, folktales help determine a people's unique character and outlook, and in Luxembourg one particular theme seems to crop up quite frequently—that of the poor man who turns out to be much cleverer than the rich man. Such a cleverness might come upon him in an uncontrived way; like Michel Michelkleiner, these folktale heroes are usually far too simpleminded to be calculating. Indeed, this motif of the naïve character or simpleton can be found world-wide, for he (rarely if ever does one encounter a female incarnation) symbolizes the basic genuineness and integrity of the personality. Perhaps such traits are what have made this character so popular in folktales. By pitting protagonists like Michel Michelkleiner against what is bad and having it all come to rights, these tales offer hope by demonstrating that even a simpleton can win in the end.

Despite its lack of written history, evidence can be found to indicate that "Michel Michelkleiner's Good Luck" has experienced a fair amount of diffusion. In fact, an almost identical folktale exists in Costa Rica. In "The Witches Ride," a bobo (simpleton) who beds down in a hut for the night ends up taking a wild and uncontrollable ride on a broom left behind by some witches, only to find himself plunging toward a group of robbers. Believing him to be a devil, they run off, leaving behind their booty—which is then confiscated by the broom-riding bobo, whose earlier misfortunes have now left him a very rich man.

The theme of the naïve young lad going out into the world and, after being repeatedly taken advantage of because of his guileless nature, finally encountering good fortune, can be seen in somewhat different form in Grimms' "Hans in Luck" from their *Kinder- und Hausmärchen*. Like the highwaymen in "Michel Michelkleiner's Good Luck," an endless string of opportunists strike bargains with the trusting Hans, each being analogous to thievery. For, having initially given up his lump of gold, Hans discovers himself saddled with a series of animals—none of which proves in any way useful to him. However, unlike his counterpart in Luxembourg, Hans has willingly (albeit stupidly) parted with his possessions.

My version of "Michel Michelkleiner's Good Luck" parallels the folktale from Luxembourg, except that I have continued young Michel's journey as a man of means. Alas, he seems to be no wiser for having found his fortune. Indeed, he, too, is willingly made to part with portions of it—only to be even more willingly made to part with a good deal more. ❧

Michel Michelkleiner's Good Luck

ON THE DAY MICHEL MICHELKLEINER turned the age of eighteen, he was taken aside by his father, who told his son that he had now become a man and must go out to try his luck in the world. With a bundle containing all he needed to start him on his journey slung across one shoulder, Michel bid tearful leave of his father, grateful for the confidence that had been shown in him and excited about the adventures that lay ahead.

Alas, Michel's bundle would grow to be as heavy as his heart as he walked the whole day long, the distance separating him from all he had ever known increasing with every footfall. As darkness drew close, the woeful lad realized from the rumblings inside his belly that he was hungry. He had not eaten so much as a crust of bread since sunrise. Eager to put still more miles beneath his feet, he ignored the desirous pangs in his gut and continued on his way long past the last saffron glow of the sun, until he reached a dense woodland. Most would have elected not to enter so perilous a place in total blackness, but Michel was certain that he had seen a fire burning not too far distant. And where there was fire, there must surely be friends—and perchance some nourishment for his hollow belly. "Why, they might be travelers like myself," he mused as he made his hopeful way through the fragrant pillars of pine and camphor toward the nucleus of light.

Only Michel Michelkleiner met neither trekker nor tramp nor even a caravan of motley tinkers. Indeed, those he had desired as friends turned out to be a raucous band of highwaymen, all of whom were being sought by the authorities. Each brutish fellow held a stick out toward the snapping and popping flames upon which a chunk of bloodied meat had been haphazardly skewered. The smell of grilling flesh prompted Michel to groan with hunger. Why, he would have kept company with the Devil himself if it meant that he might be given something to eat. Tipping his trusty cap, he bade the party a polite *good evening* and humbly inquired if they had anything to spare a poor traveler who had only that morning left behind the safe embrace of his family to seek his fortune in the world.

Upon seeing the young stranger, the robbers pounced on him en masse, wrenching from his slender arms his precious bundle and stripping from his travel-weary body every item of clothing he wore, including his woolen socks, which were in need of a good mending—and, after so many hours of walking, a good wash as well. Not even Michel's old felt cap was sacrosanct as it made its way onto the laughing heads of his hecklers, eventually being settled atop the cabbage-shaped specimen of the fellow who appeared to be the group's leader. Suffice it to say, a purloining of possessions would not be the worst of the lad's troubles on this eve.

Having been so rudely divested of his garments, a naked Michel Michelkleiner next found himself being passed around the cooking fire so that each of these larcenous brigands could have his illicit way with him, for the young fortune-seeker was of a highly agreeable countenance with eyes that sparkled like the blue of the sea and hair that shone like the finest gold. Indeed, the highwaymen chose to weave their calloused fingers into these glossy, sweet-smelling strands, making use of them to anchor young Michel more solidly against their stout, hairy thighs as they fitted themselves against his slight backside, seemingly determined to both take from him and give to him at the same time.

With their hot breath branding the back of Michel's tender neck with whiskey-stained scorches, the men set out to amuse themselves, spurred toward greater heights of barbarity by the woeful whimpers of their victim, who remained bowed forward at the waist with his bare knees digging holes into the cold damp earth, along with his elbows. Michel's golden hair fluttered wildly in the breeze as the robber positioned behind him performed a most extraordinary jig—or at least it seemed extraordinary to his unversed prey. It appeared to consist primarily of a repetitive thrusting of the haunches that eventually reached its ungainly conclusion with a convulsive tensing of the limbs and a guttural animal growl, intersecting with an ear-piercing squeal from Michel, who felt as if a pillar of fire had been shot through him. Several times during the course of these events a substance similar to that of clotted cream spurted forth from the lad's loins, landing on the flaming logs with a telltale hiss and leaving him weak and confused, his ensuing shudders attracting much in the way of laughter and jeers from his thieving tormentors. Dawn was barely beginning to show her shy face by the time the gang of men had finished with him, and by then Michel Michelkleiner had forgotten all about his empty belly. For he had been filled in ways he had never before imagined.

When they no longer had any use for him or were too fatigued to continue with their fleshly plunderings, the highwaymen heaved their victim into an old cask, covering it over with a lid and securing it up top with a heavy log. It would be in here that Michel remained, bruised and smarting in places he never knew could smart, as he listened to the contented snores of the marauders who had misappropriated his person until he, too, fell into a slumber. Unlike the peaceful oblivion of the ruffians surrounding the fire, Michel's sleep would be a troubled one. The unsavory business of the night had left the lad with a nagging sense of guilt. Although surely it had not been *he* who had done anything wrong?

By the time he awakened, Michel realized from the intense quality of light squeezing in through the gaps between the staves of the barrel that morning had turned to afternoon. The silence proclaimed that the highwaymen had evidently chosen to take their leave. Only the cheerful chirping of birds disturbed the stillness. Anxious to once again be on his way, Michel flung himself from side to side within his slatted prison. His slight shoulders butted painfully up against the walls confining him, the purple marks left on his flesh by the grasping fingers of his tormentors growing purpler in his struggle. The log keeping him penned inside the barrel was extremely heavy. Yet it was also round and, after a good deal of movement on his part, it rolled onto the ground with a defeated thud. Michel Michelkleiner had been freed.

The boisterous band of highwaymen was nowhere to be seen, the once-tenanted clearing now vacant of their sweating and groaning presences. Rather than relief, their young victim found himself overwhelmed by despair, especially when presented with the charred remains of the previous night's fire — a night that had been a veritable festival of male savagery. Michel stood in the middle of the dead embers, hoping to elicit from them some heat. The robbers had left him without a thread to call his own, and the chill breeze of an early autumn evening had already begun to blow. It seemed that he had no other recourse but to continue on his way where, in the course of his travels, he might happen upon a good Christian with a mind toward lending him something with which to cover his bruised and battered flesh.

Hence a shivering Michel Michelkleiner tramped on bare feet through the woodland, convinced he would reach its terminus before nightfall. Having never made the journey, he did not know that this was an unusually deep woodland, requiring those of far heartier stature than himself a full two days to traverse. The birds of darkness had taken up their posts on the cone-laden branches, and they hooted at the naked lad as he passed, reminding him of his poignant lack of success in securing for himself a chunk of fire-grilled meat. By now, so many echoes could be heard inside his belly that Michel would not have refused even the tough flesh of an owl for his supper. Yet perhaps good fortune would very soon be his, for up ahead in the dusky gloom he discerned the outlines of a tiny hut.

Having recently learned that one must not rush willy-nilly into situations unknown to him, Michel approached with caution. The hut had been constructed out of packed mud that had turned ashy-gray with age, and its thatched roof boasted the slanting remains of a smoking chimney. Although not a particularly impressive structure, it gave the appearance of being habitable in a pinch. A square opening cut into the facade glowed invitingly from the flickering flame of an oil lantern within, indicating that someone in more dire straits than this young fortune-seeker had decided to seek shelter. It was through this rough-hewn window that the identities of the hut's occupants came to be revealed.

For whom should Michel Michelkleiner see seated around a tottery old table but the very same gang of highwaymen that had robbed and then taken such brutal advantage of him? At the memory—a memory as raw and vivid as his wounds—a powerful quiver went through the lad's unclothed body, and he moaned with remembered helplessness. Despite the chill night air, his flesh grew extremely hot, as if he were burning up with a terrible fever. He even needed to reach out a hand to steady himself lest he fall to his knees. For it had been on his knees that his tormentors had placed him.

The men in the hut appeared to be in the process of dividing up their spoils. Several stacks of gold coins had been arranged on the gouged-out surface of the table, the tallest of which teetered precariously before the group's ringleader. Michel immediately recognized the silver coins his father had given him and of whose value he had been in great awe; they had been set to one side as though unworthy of being counted. The head robber wore looped around his thick neck the scarf Michel had carried in his bundle—the scarf he had been saving for the day he arrived in the city and, as a matter of convention, needed to spiff himself up. It was the same robber who not only had been the one to have broken him in, but had used him a second time as well. Michel would never forget that throaty laugh or the labored sounds of his breath, which had stunk powerfully of spirits. The sight of the man's coarse fingers allocating out the coins to their appropriate stacks inspired a tortured sigh to escape from Michel's parched lips, and he came close to giving himself away but for a sudden chorus of larcenous chortles that intervened to save him.

As these transitory inhabitants of the tiny hut continued with their unlawful pursuits, Michel Michelkleiner conceived of a plan. "I will steal in through the chimney and take these dastardly villains by surprise!" he said to himself. For in so doing, the thieving brigands might then be that much more the angrier at having had their important business interrupted, which should undoubtedly provoke them to do their worst. The mere thought of once again being so roughly manhandled by this uncouth lot of criminals was sufficient to make their erstwhile victim risk tackling the dangerously slanted rooftop to climb inside the smoking chimney. Unfortunately, Michel's bare feet could locate nothing on which to secure themselves, and he found himself sliding down through the narrowly bricked gap, the soot from many winters coloring his fair flesh black. He landed in a heap of burning logs, letting out a roar as if the gates of Hell had been opened and all its residents let loose.

The highwaymen scrambled about in terror, failing to recognize the golden-haired lad who had just the night before been the source of so much raucous revelry around the cooking fire. To them he could only be a devil, with his wild eyes and his flesh charred black from the punishing fires of Hades. The head robber was convinced that this hellish being possessed a tail and intended to sting him with it, for something long and sharp stuck out from the demon's skeletal body, the glistening red tip of which dripped with a deadly poison. Certain that they were all about to be dragged down into the underworld for their misdeeds, the men scurried off into the woodland, vowing never to rob or pillage again.

Michel Michelkleiner called out after them, but the highwaymen had run too far to hear. Crestfallen, he sat in the ringleader's chair before the table upon whose scarred surface the gold coins had been stacked with painstaking care. Perhaps if he waited long enough, the robbers might see fit to return, since surely they would wish to collect their ill-gotten pickings. To help pass the long hours of the night, the soot-covered lad counted out the shiny disks, discovering that he had a fortune at his fingertips. Although it could not make up for the absence of the villains who had manhandled him, it might be of considerable use when he reached the city.

Reclaiming his well-rummaged bundle that had been tossed carelessly into a corner, the newly prosperous Michel Michelkleiner donned what little remained of his garments—albeit not without first cleaning from his besmirched flesh the gritty black residue from the chimney. After a satisfying meal of bread and cheese left behind by the highwaymen, followed by a good night's sleep, he set off in the direction of the city, his bundle jangling with gold. In the villages and towns through which he passed along the way, he purchased new items of clothing, and by the time he arrived at his destination, he looked quite the young gentleman.

The first thing Michel did was to avail himself of a small lager in the scruffiest tavern he could locate, his engaging presence immediately attracting the unruly attention of a gang of ruffians who had been making a contest out of who among them could consume the greatest volume of spirits in the least amount of time. Bets had been placed by the establishment's equally unruly patrons, and with an impassioned quaver of voice, Michel placed a glittering gold coin in with the tarnished silver ones, stating his preference for the burly fellow who appeared to be the leader.

When the game had at last reached its conclusion and the well-attired newcomer scooped up his winnings from the table (for Michel had guessed correctly), the rowdy party led him into a dimly lit back room to celebrate with still more laughter and drink, which the blue-eyed and yellow-haired young stranger paid for and was eagerly encouraged to partake of...whereupon each man proceeded to pass around the squealing lad just as the lawless band of highwaymen had done at the cooking fire, with the burly fellow going first, and, indeed, closing up the circle by going last.

And that would be how Michel Michelkleiner came to find his good luck. ❧

Punished Pride

Classified by folklore scholars as a seduction/humiliation tale, the punishing of prideful princesses always takes center stage in the many versions of "Punished Pride." Known from the shores of Ireland to the steppes of Russia, the tale even has echoes in Shakespeare's *Taming of the Shrew,* which clearly indicates that the theme of prideful females who must be subdued has been the fodder for storytellers both peasant and nonpeasant alike.

Collected by the Brothers Grimm in the familiar form of "König Drosselbart" (King Thrushbeard), "Punished Pride" is believed to have arisen in Central Europe during the Middle Ages, with Italy being the likeliest candidate. However, its actual roots may go beyond those of the medieval, for elements in the story can be traced to pre-Christian days in the legend of the Teutonic god Wotan, who (like the folktale king) goes about in the guise of a beggar. In fact, the German name for *Thrushbeard* closely matches in meaning that of Wotan — that is, *Horsebeard,* thereby providing evidence of a Germanic influence upon the tale's development.

As the Baroque flourished in Italy, Giambattista Basile would create his own version of the story. In "Pride Punished," the haughty princess Cinziella—for whom no suitor is ever good enough—rejects a king, who later disguises himself so that he can take employment at the palace of the princess's father. Although the first part of Basile's tale parallels "The Swineherd," the humiliation of the princess soon becomes a major theme as she finds herself greatly humbled by a pregnancy caused by a man thought to be the palace gardener. As Basile wrote, "The miserable Cinziella, agonized at what had befallen her, held it to be the punishment of Heaven for her former arrogance and pride, that she who had treated so many kings and princes as doormats should now be treated like the vilest slut." Hence the princess is forced to flee her father's kingdom with the man responsible for her condition, whereupon the disguised king inflicts upon the banished princess indignity after indignity. Only when he believes that she has finally learned her lesson does he reveal his true identity.

Although Basile would carry forth the sixteenth century's tolerance for sexual frankness in folktales into the seventeenth century, in the years following his *Pentamerone* a change in attitudes began to take place—a change exemplified by an increasing shame and embarrassment about bodily functions, specifically those related to sexual matters. By the nineteenth century, references to sex were all but gone. In "King Thrushbeard" by the Grimms, not a word can be found of the princess becoming pregnant. Instead, her lessons of humiliation derive solely from the tasks she has been made to perform, rather than from any unsanctioned sexual behavior. It would appear that the men have acted in conspiracy against her as the princess's father arranges for his daughter to take for a husband the first beggar who comes to the palace door—in this case, a common fiddler. In reality the fiddler is a rejected suitor, a king who, according to the mocking princess, has a chin that resembles a thrush's beak. She makes no secret of her contempt as she tells her suitor that he is unworthy of even cleaning her shoes—a contempt that has on occasion been expressed with slightly more erotic overtones via her suitor's apparent unworthiness to *unstrap* them. Having succeeded in winning her with his music, the royal fiddler subjects the princess to a life of poverty by sending her out to perform menial work in the palace of a king, which leads her into thievery.

The version of "Punished Pride" from which I received my inspiration flowed from the pen of the nineteenth-century writer Bozena Nemcová, who is considered one of the greatest names in Czech literature. Although her tale does not contain the sexual candor present in Basile, Nemcová was not shy in making the occasional subtle reference to passion. Indeed, her gardener/prince would find himself *burning up* with love for the princess—a burning that would be reciprocated in kind. However, no mention is made of the princess being forced into thievery or of her untimely and shameful pregnancy. Perhaps Nemcová had more sympathy for her fellow female, for it must be remembered that the other versions of "Punished Pride" were all composed by men.

Such sympathies aside, I have devised far more ingenious punishments for the prideful protagonist—punishments that, depending upon one's point of view, may not really be punishments at all. ❧

Pvnished Pride

YOUNG MIROSLAV POSSESSED ALL THAT a czar could ever desire...except a czarina. Within days of announcing his decision to marry, the portraits of every imperial daughter from every neighboring empire began to arrive at the palace, each sender hoping against hope that *hers* would be the portrait that the bachelor Czar chose. Although the subjects of these painted works proved most agreeable to the eye, it was the portrait of the spoiled and prideful daughter of the Kaiser that finally captured Miroslav's heart.

With the selection of a bride settled in his mind, the Czar summoned the most famous and sought-after painters in the land. He wished to commission each to paint his portrait—and the more portraits he had to pick from, the better. Attired in all his finery and with a wreath of easels surrounding him, Miroslav sat in thoughtful repose upon the throne that had once belonged to his father and to his father before him, his outward calm concealing the powerful stirrings he felt at the thought of the beautiful Krasomila, whom he hoped to entice with the gift of his portrait.

The master portraitists were most eager for their subject to decide which of their efforts he liked best, and each outdid the other in an effort to please, going to exaggerated measures to flatter the Czar in paint. Yet to the astonishment of all, Miroslav expressed a preference for the painting bearing him the least compliment, his intent being for Krasomila to find herself pleasantly surprised when she discovered her suitor to be substantially more appealing in the flesh than in paint. To further diminish the impact of his canvas image, the Czar ordered the work set into a massive gold frame studded with gems of every conceivable size and tincture. He then bade two of his finest-looking courtiers to deliver it to Krasomila, along with a request for her hand in marriage.

Miroslav waited anxiously as day after day went by without a word. When at last the messengers returned, they did not bring the answer the lovesick Czar expected to hear. Indeed, Krasomila had earned a reputation for spurning all suitors, no matter how eligible or handsome. "We were received most graciously by the Kaiser," they began with clumsy tongues, hoping this might soften the sting of what next needed to be relayed. The Czar had been known to possess a mean temper when roused, and neither desired to be made the recipient of his brutal lash. "Yet when we presented the painting to his daughter, she scarcely gave it a glance. Truth be told," they stuttered out haltingly, "she replied that the gentleman in the portrait was not fit to tie the laces of her shoes." By now the two messengers were trembling in terror. Miroslav could have ordered their heads chopped from their necks for being the unfortunate bearers of such unpleasant tidings.

"The Kaiser pleaded for us to wait," piped the older and more diplomatically experienced of the courtiers. "For it appeared that he wished to use his influence and impress upon his daughter how greatly she had erred in her judgment. Only we thought it prudent to take our leave, as we did not believe she would make a suitable czarina for His Imperial Majesty." With the words that might end their lives irretrievably spoken, the men bowed low to the floor, expecting at any moment to feel the cold blade of an ax against the prickling flesh of their necks.

"You did very well," replied Miroslav, his words resulting in a sigh of relief from the two anxious courtiers. "Perhaps I have underestimated the lady."

For nearly a fortnight Miroslav pondered the issue of the spoiled Krasomila before formulating a strategy. Delegating all matters of consequence to his trusted ministers, he embarked upon a journey that would be of some length, taking with him a few modest garments of little fashion along with a handful of coins that clinked sadly in his pockets. He refused to speak to anyone of where he was going or what he would do once there. Indeed, his business with the Kaiser's daughter was *not* finished.

One might well have wondered why a man in Miroslav's position should have bothered to pursue so callous a woman when those of finer character had made their interests known. But in his mind none could measure up to Krasomila, whose icy beauty had come to be admired in empires both distant and near. Although she could on occasion be kind and even grow tearful upon hearing of the plight of those less fortunate than herself, she actively shunned beggars for fear they might tarnish her with their dirty hands. Yet the prideful daughter of the Kaiser spent her days shunning far more than the common beggar. For numerous gentlemen of importance had put forth proposals of marriage to the haughty Krasomila, without a one being met with acceptance, let alone civility. She had requirements to which few could rise, and she made no secret of her contempt for those who failed. The man she would finally deign to wed needed to be not only highly cultured, but superior in appearance and manner as well as hailing from noble birth. Should it have been surprising that so many suitors found themselves spurned?

One afternoon as Krasomila sat in the shade of a willow tree reading her favorite prose, her father decided to seek out her company to consult her on a matter of minor consequence. "Daughter, I should very much like to solicit your good opinion on the gardener I have engaged—a most extraordinary fellow who appears to be as knowledgeable about music as he is about horticulture."

Although impressed by her father's claim, Krasomila never took anything at face value. "Just the same," she responded, "I prefer to withhold my judgment until I have met with him personally. If he is as you say, then perchance we might presume upon him to teach me to play the harp."

And so it was decided. Later that day, the new gardener presented himself to the Kaiser's daughter, his cloth cap clutched in one soil-smudged hand. He looked uncomfortably out of place in the refined surroundings of the music room, with his shabby garments and mud-stained boots, which he had made certain to brush off before entering. "Your Highness, this humble servant awaits your command," he addressed her in a husky whisper, bowing to kiss the brocaded hem of her robe. When at last he raised his head, the eyes that gazed into Krasomila's held an expression most unprecedented for one in so lowly a position. For, unbeknownst to the Kaiser's daughter, this scruffy fellow was no ordinary gardener, but Czar Miroslav himself.

Of course Krasomila failed to recognize him, having only been presented with his poor likeness in a painting—and that likeness had been attired in the grand robes suited to his high birthright. In any event, the contact had shaken her wintry composure. "Tell me, Gardener, what is your name?" she asked in a quavering voice conspicuously lacking its customary authority.

"Miroslav," replied the Czar, noting with displeasure that the name failed to inspire even a flicker of recognition upon Krasomila's face.

"Well, Miroslav, for a long time I have desired to play the harp. Are you of a mind to teach me?"

The Czar bowed again. "I shall be pleased and honored to do so."

Seeing no further necessity for his inferior presence, Krasomila dismissed the new gardener, surprised at finding herself so unsettled after their meeting. A fire raged within her body, setting her heart to burning like a flame in her chest and chasing out the breath from her lungs. It became so distressing that she was forced to seek out the sanctity of her bed, where her hands moved of their own volition beneath the woolen covers, the fingers rubbing and prodding with a desperation previously unknown to her. Krasomila passed the remainder of the afternoon in this fashion, imagining that it was Miroslav's earth-stained hands upon her, her resulting cries losing themselves beneath the heavy bedclothes. She did not show herself again until suppertime, when she was joined by her father, who promptly inquired of his unnaturally flushed daughter as to whether a suitable arrangement had been made between the gardener and herself. "His name brings to mind your thwarted suitor, Czar Miroslav. Perhaps you should have considered his proposal of marriage more carefully before acting with such haste to dismiss him," said the Kaiser in rebuke.

Nevertheless, the father's sentiments were not shared by his offspring. At the mention of her snubbed suitor, Krasomila wrinkled her nose in distaste. "Please, Father, do not speak of it again. I am certain I would have been extremely unhappy as his Czarina." And indeed, she remained wholly convinced of her words.

With the arrival of the new gardener, much would change in the Kaiser's household. Rather than spending her afternoons reading, Krasomila could be found sitting before her harp, as enthusiastic to learn as the gardener was to teach. Beneath his gentle coaxing and generous praise, the iciness of his pupil's demeanor began to thaw, becoming a much-favored topic of conversation among the maidservants. "The Kaiser's daughter is very greatly changed since taking up the harp," they would whisper conspiratorially to each other. "Before, no one could come within a footstep of her. Now she cares not a fig if that grubby Miroslav licks her hand!"

Such domestic observations held more than a smattering of truth in them, for of late the Kaiser's daughter had developed a restlessness of manner and a strangeness of temperament that did not go unnoticed by those who knew her best. Being of proud bearing, Krasomila refused to acknowledge the true reason for these symptoms. However, every morning she could be spied in the gardens, acknowledging Miroslav with a haughty nod as she loitered in the vicinity of his barrow, appearing to investigate the quality of the bulbs contained therein. Curiously enough, when it came time for her music lesson, she suddenly lost all desire for the gardener's company and dispatched one of the maidservants with an excuse for her absence, only to dispatch a second to cancel out the words of the first. It was said that Krasomila suffered considerable confusion.

One evening, as she entertained herself playing her harp and singing, Krasomila's teacher unexpectedly appeared at her side. His presence did not even allow her to reach the second refrain before her fingers ceased their graceful plucking. "Play for me," she commanded of Miroslav, her voice ragged with despair.

Taking over the instrument, the gardener selected a melody favored by his pupil. As he sang the lyric, Krasomila began to weep, overcome by her imprudent love for the handsome young man who tended the palace gardens. She hung her head in helpless surrender, a hot tear spilling onto Miroslav's expertly moving hand. Her sobs continued long after he had finished, especially when she heard the words that followed his sweet song: "This is my farewell, for I must depart on the morrow."

"But you cannot!" protested Krasomila, seizing the gardener's soil-spattered hands between hers and pressing them to her heart. "You must never leave me."

Drawn downstairs by the music, the Kaiser discovered the couple in a rather compromising and inappropriate placement, the gardener's hands having been relocated inside the swelling bodice of Krasomila's gown. Taking note of the frantic state of his daughter, he understood what had just transpired. "Is this the man you love?"

"Yes, Father. I love him with my entire heart and soul!" cried Krasomila, lavishing kiss after kiss along Miroslav's warm palm, her tongue furtively collecting the salty dampness it found there and eliciting a powerful shudder from Miroslav.

The Kaiser's face sagged with disappointment. "Are you aware that he is greatly wanting in two of the qualities set forth by you for a prospective husband?" For Miroslav the gardener neither hailed from noble birth nor possessed a noble fortune.

"It matters not to me. I should love him even if he swept out chimneys."

"Then you must marry within the hour, at which time you are to leave this land, never to return."

Despite Miroslav's protestations that he did not wish to be the cause of Krasomila's misery and loss in stature, the die had been cast and the Kaiser's will could not be swayed. A hasty taking of vows took place in the music room; it would be attended by only one witness—the harp that had brought the couple together. Stripped of her title and all her jewels and dressed in garments as ragged as those on the beggars she once shunned, Krasomila walked out of the palace gates with her new husband, banished from her father's realm...*forever.*

The newlyweds made their way on foot to the frontier of the land the Kaiser's daughter had one day been meant to rule. "We might be wise to go to the town," suggested Miroslav, indicating a miserable cluster of soot-stained structures in the equally sooty distance. "My brother lives there, and he can find a post for me."

"I, too, shall seek work until matters right themselves," Krasomila assured her husband, although she had no notion of what type of work she might be qualified for, if any.

Miroslav let for himself and his wife a shabby room from a sickly old widow whose house smelled of boiling cabbages. "I must seek out my brother," he told his apprehensive bride as they arranged their few paltry possessions inside their cheerless quarters. "If good fortune shines upon me today, he may know of a post for the both of us."

The bridegroom was absent for the entirety of the day, leaving Krasomila in the company of their landlady, whose rattling coughs came straight from the grave. Finally Miroslav returned at sundown, bringing with him a parcel containing fine linen, which he placed expectantly before his wife. "If you can sew with a perfect stitch, you shall be well recompensed."

The young bride set to work with a vengeance, determined to sew the most precise stitches anyone had ever seen. She toiled night and day, leaving the linen unattended only to prepare her husband's meals. When the pieces were completed, she delivered them to a grand house located in the center of town, placing them in the hands of a lady's maid. The maid immediately found fault with the stitches and refused to grant payment. Unused to being the recipient of such cavalier treatment, Krasomila appealed to the woman's sense of fairness, adding provocation where none was needed. For the maid possessed a most vinegary temperament, especially when dealing with the more well-favored members of her sex. Greatly humbled by the experience, the disowned daughter of the Kaiser kept the incident to herself, too embarrassed to speak of it to her husband.

Miroslav next made it known that the post of maid to a very fine lady had come available. Certain that she would make a lady's maid far superior to the disagreeable specimen to whom she had earlier handed over her sewing, Krasomila accepted, giddy with delight to leave behind the wretched room that served as the couple's home so that she could move into the lady's stately residence for a trial period. As it happened, the new maid would not be allowed to take the weight off her feet long enough to draw a breath. Krasomila performed her employer's bidding from sunup to sundown, running errands, bathing the lady and dressing her heavy black hair, lacing the lady's voluptuous curves into her fine garments—and all with a cheerful smile and an offer to do still more.

Indeed, the lady of the manor summoned this recent addition to the household at all hours, each request being more toilsome and tiresome than its predecessor. The deeds were often quite peculiar in nature, the undertaking of which left the new maid with an uncomfortable sense of wrongdoing. During the lady's bath, Krasomila would be required to spend a considerable amount of time in the laving of her demanding mistress, who disliked the coarseness of a cloth against her skin and preferred that the comely young domestic use her hands. They felt extremely soft for one employed in the lowly capacity of servant, an admission that, when offered aloud, inspired a shameful flush to stain the Kaiser's daughter's cheeks. For, like the lady to whose pampered flesh she now found herself attending, this high-blooded underling had once been accustomed to having a maid assist her with her bath.

Settling into her new routine, Krasomila spent the early hours of each evening drawing soapy circles on her mistress's back and shoulders, rinsing them away with fresh water that had been heating over the fire, only to begin the process all over again by directing her attentions to the fore. Although this might not have sounded particularly difficult in itself, the lady had been endowed with two very large conical objects that she wore proudly upon her chest, and the maid was required to employ both hands in their simultaneous laving, kneading the soft doughy sections with her palms and tweaking the stiff mahogany tips between thumb and forefinger — tips the overworked domestic was instructed to pinch with such severity that the mournful sounds soughing upward from her employer's throat could only have been those of agony.

However, it would be those unseen parts that lay far beneath the warm sudsy water that always seemed to demand the most care. Krasomila could not for the life of her fathom how such a fine lady could possibly get so dirty. She often spent upwards of an hour rubbing at the soiled areas with her fingers, reaching her hand deep into the bathwater until even the crinkles of her elbow had disappeared. No matter how thoroughly she scrubbed at the wriggly little knurl she found and the two furry puffs encasing it, her mistress refused to be satisfied. "Do not stop just yet," the lady commanded in a strangled whisper, "for I am certain that there are many more particles of dirt in need of unearthing." Hence the new maid continued to scour the region with fatigue-numbed fingertips, applying them with a palpable lack of gentleness in hopes that the infernal woman might see fit to release her from her toils. Why, not even her husband when in her father's service as gardener had been in need of so aggressive a wash!

To Krasomila's dismay, this intentional roughness only made matters worse. Within minutes her other hand had been drafted into reluctant service, the soapy middle digit of which would find itself sluicing in and out of a snug trough located at the terminus of a graceful slope of back—a trough so fiery hot it scorched the flesh of her finger. Just when the poor, forsaken daughter of the Kaiser feared her cramped hands were in danger of being permanently crippled, her mistress suffered a fit, gasping and moaning and hurling herself about in the tub, heedless to the sudsy water splashing over the rim and onto the serviceable surface of her attendant's shoes. "Yes, yes!" howled the aggrieved bather. "Oh, *yes-s-s!*"

The startled maid nearly called out for assistance, concerned that her hysterical employer might drown—and that *she* would be blamed for the mishap. Then, as suddenly as the fit had arrived, the woman returned to normal, stepping out from the tub as if these extraordinary events had never occurred. A relieved Krasomila wrapped the heat-suffused body standing before her within a fluffy white towel and proceeded to dry it off, too discreet in her duties to reflect upon the bright-red snippet jutting out from a nest of fur as she knelt to wipe the moisture trickling down the insides of her mistress's legs, most of which did not look at all like water.

It might be expected that the lady should have retired to her bed to spend the remaining hours of darkness in contented slumber, thereby allowing her hard-working domestic to get on with the normal business of laying out her garments for the morning. Instead Krasomila discovered her implacable mistress sitting up in bed, waiting impatiently for the summoned reappearance of the comely young woman in her service. "Krasomila, I fear you were very negligent in your washing," scolded the lady, throwing down her embroidered coverlet and revealing the furry creature that had only moments ago been lurking beneath the steaming bathwater.

The maid found herself shivering, for what next took place struck terror into her heart. With a hand situated upon each pampered knee, her employer extended them fully and salaciously outward, coaxing this bristling denizen of the bath even further into view. The creature appeared quite fierce as it was forced out of hiding from the safe haven between the woman's thighs, no doubt irritated at having been disturbed. A vermilion tongue of a dichotomous structure stuck rudely out from a dense coat of black fur as if in silent rebuke of this seemingly incompetent servant. Krasomila took several steps back, frightened that it might attack, as it had begun to salivate most profusely from its blood-red gash of a mouth.

The lady cleared her throat in a not-so-subtle prompting, her eyes glowing with an eerie luminosity. All at once it became clear to the weary domestic that her unappeasable mistress expected additional efforts to be expended with regard to her ablutions — as did the hirsute creature glowering at her from between the exaggerated *V* of the woman's thighs. For it, too, stood by in a state of expectancy, its flickering tongue distending farther and farther away from the furred halves of its body and bringing into exposure the dripping red maw below. As Krasomila moved to fetch a bowl to fill with warm water, her employer gripped her wrist, this minor physical contact most uncharacteristic and, indeed, most unprecedented for one in her mistress's position. "I shan't be requiring water or soap. They contain properties that have proven to be an irritant to my delicate skin."

Although she yearned very much to do so, her lowly status in the household prevented the maid from remarking that perhaps her delicately skinned mistress should not have lingered for such a long time in the bath, for, indeed, the woman's flesh always looked as puckered as a prune's after stepping from the water. But before Krasomila could inquire as to precisely what method her tiresome employer expected her to use for this washing, the answer had already reached her ears. "I believe your tongue shall suffice quite nicely," her mistress replied matter-of-factly.

With no allusion to ceremony, the lady launched her loins high into the air, drawing her knees up to her shoulders and extending them wide, propelling her furry companion completely and helplessly into the open. Left without their safe camouflage of thighs, still more of its ferret-like features had become visible. The creature appeared to observe the anxious maid from upside-down. A solitary, crinkle-edged eye as black and unfathomable as midnight peered at her from beneath its drooling mouth, blinking with such frequency and intensity that the bifurcated tongue above had taken to flickering right along with it.

Concerned for her safety — for the great hairy thing had been hissing at her ever since her first glimpse of it — the disowned daughter of the Kaiser had little choice but to comply with her mistress's wishes. Placing herself where she could best reach the spitting creature, Krasomila promptly set to work, employing her tongue as one might a cloth, albeit with far more delicacy and pliancy of touch. Perhaps if she did an especially fine job and distinguished herself from her predecessors, the creature would see fit not to harm her, and she might then be allowed to remain on in service. Although Krasomila did not comprehend this obsession with cleanliness by her employer, what did it matter as long as it put food on the table and a roof over her and her husband's heads?

At the thought of her dear Miroslav, who was probably right at this very moment also engaged in servile pursuits not entirely to his liking, the new maid applied herself to her duties with greater enthusiasm, closing her eyes to the hirsute visage before her. She swabbed and swabbed and swabbed again, traversing the same slippery terrain several times and from several different angles to ensure that her mistress could find no fault with her work. To be as thorough as possible, Krasomila smoothed back the shiny black fur with her thumbs to reach any hidden folds or fissures that might have been obscured, the creature's tongue fluttering with a companionable friendliness against her diligently licking one. In fact, she was pleasantly surprised at how tame it proved, although this in no way lessened the labors that had been foisted upon her. But no matter how exhaustively her tongue searched, not a particle of dirt was to be had. Nevertheless, the grand lady continued with her sharp harangue, ordering her frantically licking servant to clean a bit lower, then higher, and then lower again.

This eventually accounted for how Krasomila was gotten to extend her fastidious lavings to the gaping red maw that was clearly the source of so much discommode. Its sticky dribbles had been growing steadily more profuse by the moment, thus necessitating frequent and skittish forays of the domestic's tongue into the hissing mouth. By concentrating her ministrations below the location specified by her mistress as being the most heavily soiled, she hoped to put a halt to the problem before the woman took note of it and offered up yet another vitriolic scolding.

Krasomila spent a long time in the application of her duties, her neck and jaw aching with the strain of washing the hairy denizen that lived between her employer's thighs. Every time she lifted her head to smooth out the knot into which her neck had tied itself, her mistress boxed her on the ears, only to push the maid's face right back into the furry black nest with its serpentine tongue and frothing mouth and vigilant eye. More than half the night was passed in this fashion, with the lady barking out instructions and her flustered servant following them to the letter. "Clean me there!" shrieked the undulating figure on the bed, her breath coming faster and faster, her fingernails digging painfully into Krasomila's furiously moving head. "Do not cease for an instant, for I am so very, very dirty!" However, no sooner had the maid's weary tongue located the spot her mistress had specified than an entirely new one would be proposed.

The Kaiser's daughter knew full well that she was being hoodwinked by her employer, for, unlike those who had come before, she had not been born into the ignorance of domestic servitude. As tears of injustice filled her eyes, the lady of the house began to emit a series of mournful wails, followed by a violent thrashing. Her actions were very much like those she had performed in the bath, only instead of sudsy water, fluffy goose feathers went flying to the floor, having been summoned out from the pillows and coverlet by her pounding fists. Indeed, Krasomila's mistress was truly very, very dirty!

At the conclusion of her trial period as lady's maid, Krasomila returned home to her husband, weakened and defeated and having no intention of remaining in domestic service a moment longer. Upon being queried by Miroslav as to her reasons, she flushed hotly, replying that the work demanded of her had been far too difficult—as was the lady herself. Why, just because her employer had riches and possessed a grand title, she was not therefore superior to others.

Not even a week passed before Miroslav informed his wife that the Czar had chosen a bride. "The palace shall be in need of cooks to prepare food for the celebrations. Perhaps you might offer your services." Krasomila found herself in agreement. The couple could do with the money and, besides, kitchen work would surely be easier than being lady's maid to some titled virago. As for the irony of being in the employment of the Czar, so much had happened to her that his proposal of marriage had become less than a distant memory—as had the proposals of the others she had spurned.

Not surprisingly, the daughter of the Kaiser had never been inside a kitchen before, and she nearly wept when her husband deposited her in the toil-worn hands of the head cook. Without so much as a sip of water to sustain her, she was placed into service. As in her previous post, Krasomila labored so hard she scarcely knew whether the sun or the moon lighted the sky. The splendor of the arriving guests gave her much reason to bewail the lowly position to which her pride and hauteur had led, and she hung her head in shame, which was how the new kitchen maid came to collide with a grandly attired gentleman in the process of descending the stairs. "You!" he bellowed. "The laces of my shoes need tending."

The regal finery of his clothing told Krasomila that this majestic figure was none other than the Czar himself who addressed her. She dropped to her knees to perform the task, not even daring to sneak a glance at his face. Afterward as she squatted in a dim corner of the kitchen peeling her fourth bushel of potatoes, a manservant arrived to inquire as to the identity of the comely young kitchen maid who had tied the Czar's shoelaces. Raising her hand in humble identification, Krasomila discovered herself being escorted upstairs to some exquisitely furnished rooms that, with a heartfelt pang, reminded her of those she had occupied in the palace of her father. It was apparent they had been prepared for the bride. Could it be that the new kitchen maid had been drafted into personal service for the future Czarina?

Before Krasomila would be given a reason for her presence in such luxurious surroundings, a lady's maid appeared. "Select a gown and some jewels to accompany it," she invited the kitchen maid, indicating with a sweep of one leg-o'-mutton arm the magnificent garments and glittering gems that had been laid out upon a luxuriously outfitted bed. "In reward for your earlier courtesy to him, the Czar requests the pleasure of a private dance."

Krasomila could hardly believe the woman's words. She stood docilely by as she allowed the maid's expert hands to dress her, her heart pounding with excitement. It had been so long since she had worn such finery, not to mention being attended by a servant. By the time the gown had been laced and the jewels clasped into place at her ears and throat, the kitchen wench resembled the beautiful young woman she had once been. Alas, such fleeting joys did not come without the proverbial caveat attached to them. "You must not look His Imperial Majesty in the face," cautioned the lady's maid, her tone chillingly ominous. "It is considered a sign of disrespect and therefore worthy of the penalty of death. Now stand facing the wall and remember: Under no circumstances must you look upon the Czar till he bids it."

How strange it felt to be the recipient of these instructions. It had always been Krasomila or her father who granted such a permission to others and, indeed, meted out the penalty to transgressors with generous discretion. With a nervous swallow, the Kaiser's daughter took her designated place at the foot of the bed with her elegantly draped back facing outward. As she waited for the great man who desired from her the simple merriment of a dance, she studied the tapestry hanging above the bed's ornately carved headboard, her drastically diminished status making her appreciate the labor that had gone into creating so many colorful stitches. It depicted a soldier in uniform riding on horseback, his crop raised high to strike the fleeing half-clad figures of his slaves. The scene had been executed with such fleshy realism that it inspired an icy shiver to slither down Krasomila's spine. Before she could ponder her reaction to the tapestry's disquieting subject matter, she heard the door through which the lady's maid had exited creak slowly open, followed by a sumptuous swish of satin as a stately presence came to stand behind her. All at once she began to tremble, for she could feel the closeness of the Czar and smell his grassy scent—a scent that stirred something familiar within her.

Without so much as a cursory greeting, the Czar urged the tremulous kitchen maid forward until she was bending over the bed. Had Krasomila not been quick to put out both hands, she might have fallen on her face. Nevertheless, it would not be her face in which His Imperial Majesty displayed an interest. A sudden coolness gusted over Krasomila's thighs and backside when the beaded hem of her gown was flung up to her jeweled neck, exposing her to the waist. A deep, masculine sigh shook the room, sending another shiver through the young maid's stooped form. Unlike its icier predecessor, this one was made of fire.

Within moments a sharp crack fractured the static silence, leaving in its wake a stinging burn. Its recipient yelped in surprise as a swarm of leathery tails raked over the twin hills of trembling flesh the Czar had unceremoniously uncovered. Krasomila had not even recovered from their first application than a second ensued, crisscrossing the crimsoning tracks that had already been laid and creating the pattern of a draughts board. Although she wished to flee from this terrible torture, an exit would have meant turning to face her assailant—and she could not forget the portentous warning given her by the lady's maid. Hence Krasomila remained bent fully forward over the bed, staring through a salty curtain at the tapestried scene of the slaves trying to escape their fates as she relinquished herself to hers, enduring lash after lash and wondering when it would ever cease.

For apparently the dance the Czar had in mind was a dance that could only be performed solo. The Kaiser's daughter wriggled about in a frenzied waltz of pain as the punishing tails licked over her wildly shimmying backside, which had turned the shade of a setting autumn sun. A sticky substance similar to that which had earlier bedeviled her when she had been in the demanding employ of the fine lady coated the insides of her thighs, increasing with each searing crack, as did the igneous heat in the place of their convergence. When Krasomila glanced down at herself to investigate, she saw a fiery red flame extending out from her body. To her astonishment, it looked exactly like the vermilion tongue belonging to the furry creature that lurked between her former mistress's thighs. Had it somehow managed to follow her to her new post?

Before she could shoo it away, something hot and wet sprayed the kitchen maid's smarting flesh, inflicting additional distress as it insinuated itself within the raw striations that had been carved by the sizzling tails. The liquid trickled steadily downward, making its way through the quivering archway of Krasomila's thighs and toward the flickering, tongue-like flame to the fore. "You may now turn to face me," came a familiar, albeit strangled voice.

Krasomila gingerly hoisted herself up from her stooped position, only to learn that the one who had wielded the weapon that caused her such torment and, indeed, such intensity of sensation was her husband, Miroslav. "Why?" she gasped weakly, the fire between her thighs demanding further fuel from his lash.

"Because I am Czar Miroslav," he said simply, the leather tails in his hand twitching in their desire to prescribe still more of their rousing remedy for prideful young daughters of Kaisers.

At last Krasomila recognized the suitor she had so cruelly spurned. From that day forward, she remained in the palace, since it was the palace of her husband the Czar, as were these elegant rooms those of the Czarina. All concerned lived happily ever after—especially the local whip makers, whose services would be required on a weekly basis. For Miroslav wore out many a lash on his beautiful and once-prideful Czarina. ❧

A Tale of
the Parrot

Acknowledged as the home of some of the oldest stories in the
world, India is considered by many scholars to be the original
birthplace of all folktales. Indeed, one of the oldest collections of
folktales can be found in the *Jakata*, which contains fables and stories in the ancient Pali language that date back to the time of
Buddha. However, there also exists a collection of lesser promi-
nence in another ancient language—that of the Sanskrit
Sukasaptati, or *The Seventy Tales of the Parrot.*

The folktales of India have traditionally been told by
singers and tellers who traveled from place to place as well as by
bardic troupes, family members, and servants. Like the French
literary tales presented in the Court of Versailles, these stories
eventually came to be set down in writing for the sole amusement of royalty. Despite their primary function as a form of
entertainment, one could often find more lofty purposes at work,
for it was standard practice in Hindu medicine for the mentally
disturbed to be told tales, the contemplation of which would
help overcome emotional disturbance.

"A Tale of the Parrot" is believed to be part of the much
larger Sanskrit work called the *Sukasaptati,* which possibly dates

back in written form to the sixth century. A sacred language, Sanskrit was used by the educated class, therefore the *Sukasaptati* would likely have been enjoyed by the highborn rather than by those of common blood. Like the stories contained in *The Arabian Nights* and *The Serendipity Tales*, those in the *Sukasaptati* were used as a form of distraction and, as such, often proved extremely erotic in nature. The Indian folktale can be characterized by its distinct sense of candor—a candor that manifested itself in matters pertaining to the sexual.

In the frame story of the *Sukasaptati*, a garrulous parrot relays a string of stories to a woman as a means of preventing her from committing adultery. (Conversely, many of the parrot's stories involve faithless women.) The theme of woman as fickle creature forever waiting to cuckold her husband is widespread in Indian literature, therefore much emphasis has been placed on the importance of a woman's chastity. Serving in the *Sukasaptati* as an instrument of this chastity, the parrot has become a popular central character in Indian folktales. In fact, speaking animals have appeared in some of the most ancient Indian texts, many dating back centuries before the birth of Christ.

The *Sukasaptati* traveled out of India, reaching the Middle East by about the fourteenth century in the form of the *Tutinameh*—a translation of the Sanskrit into Persian. Unfortunately, the *Tutinameh* does not contain all seventy tales from the *Sukasaptati,* and the plots and characters of those it does contain have been so altered that they have become unrecognizable. However, the *Tutinameh* has at least managed to retain, if not exceed, the original erotic spirit of the *Sukasaptati*—an excess I, too, have endeavored to create in my refashioning of one of the parrot's many tales. ❧

A Tale of the Parrot

A MAGNIFICENT GREEN AND GOLD PARROT had been sitting on the branch of an acacia tree for many days, observing the activities of those who passed. Annoyed that no one paid it any heed, the parrot finally decided to speak. For it had a tale to tell about the only child of an emir who received a message indicating that the great Khan who ruled the Turks desired to marry her. A dutiful daughter, she had vowed not to leave behind her widowed father, therefore she made it abundantly clear to anyone who would listen that she had no interest in the Turk, let alone his presumptuous proposal.

Within days of declining the Khan's offer of marriage, the Emir's daughter lapsed into a strange illness—an illness made all the more extraordinary by the fact that the young woman had never suffered a sick day in her life. Those of a superstitious nature entertained the belief that the rejected Khan had had a hand in it, although no evidence could be found to corroborate such meddlesome prattle. In his desperation, the Emir called out doctors from far and wide, yet none could agree on a diagnosis for the malady plaguing his daughter. Finally the wise men were summoned, their clever counsel providing the anguished father with his first real glimmer of hope. Apparently what would be required was the presence of the imperial daughter of Spain—the Infanta who had aided in the rescue of so many royal children from the clutches of an evil cult. No corner of the world existed where her name was not uttered without wonderment. If she could liberate someone from the crazed members of a cult, then surely she could help the Emir's stricken daughter.

The Emir ordered his entire fleet to set sail at once, vowing to wage war against Spain if her leader refused to relinquish to him this miracle-producing offspring. For no amount of spilled blood would have been too great in the quest to cure his daughter, who now languished by the day in her sickbed, shivering and moaning in heart-wrenching misery. There was not an eye in the emirate that did not overflow with tears for this much-adored young woman.

When the King of Spain read the message that had been dispatched to him by this faraway Emir's envoy, instead of compassion for an anguished father, he experienced a powerful rage. He, too, was willing to pick up arms rather than allow his daughter to undertake so dangerous a mission. Having already been informed by a personal spy of the distressing news that had arrived by way of a foreign emissary, the Infanta insisted upon offering her aid to this distant sister, assuring her apprehensive father that she would return swiftly and without harm. Hence she departed with the Emir's envoy, sailing across the sparkling sapphire sea to a place whose name evoked exotic images of desert caravans and black-eyed houris.

No sooner had the Spanish Infanta set foot onto the arid soil of this strange, sun-baked land than its aggrieved leader came forth to greet her with offers of tremendous riches and even his crown—if *only* she could cure his beloved daughter. Naturally, she politely declined such effusive generosity. The King of Spain's daughter had her own crown, not to mention the vast wealth of her entire country at her disposal. Indeed, her motive for coming was one of pure philanthropy.

Upon being led to the young woman who lay wasting away in her bedchamber with her once-vibrant eyes sunken to two shallow pits and her once-lush mouth a rictus of faded black, the Infanta promptly set to work, for there was no time to lose in this battle against approaching death. Smoothing back the sodden straw framing the chalk-white face against the pillow, she ordered a virtual feast to be prepared and brought up to the sickroom—a feast of food and drink sufficient to last for three days and three nights, which would be the amount of time this visitor required to effect her cure. Yet for it to be successful, she needed to be left in complete privacy, without so much as even a brief visit from the patient's devoted father. "No one must be allowed to enter this room," the members of the household were instructed by the Infanta, her tone of voice making it clear that there would be no exceptions. As per her directive, a series of iron bolts were fastened onto both the inside and outside of the bedchamber door, which the Infanta slid into place on her end, as did the anxious Emir on his.

Later that day, as the Spanish Infanta sat silently by the sickbed in the failing light of the window, it came to her notice that the servants had neglected to provide any tinder for the lighting of candles or the stoking of wood in the hearth. With winter close upon them, it was rapidly growing dark, not to mention quite cold. Loathe to spending the evening in pitch-blackness, she began to rummage about in cupboards, hoping that a few pieces of tinder might have been left over from the previous night. The King of Spain's daughter found bottles of ink for writing and sticks of charcoal for drawing, yet could not locate a single twig that could be used to induce light or warmth. Only one door still remained to be opened—and it led not to a wardrobe as expected, but to a small room. A window scarcely of a size to allow a child to pass through it beckoned the Infanta toward it. When she leaned out to look across the sand-covered landscape, she noticed an eerie light flickering in the hazy distance. Fortunately, the little window was not situated so very high up off the ground. With the ladder of rope that had been left forgotten in a corner, she should surely be able to climb down without too much risk to her person. For the increasing chill in the air made this daughter of Spain most eager to secure a source of tinder so that she and her patient would not be forced to pass the next three nights in shivery darkness.

The source of this light revealed itself to be nothing more mysterious than an ordinary cooking fire. An iron cauldron had been placed directly above it, the crackling flames licking its blackened surface like dozens of red tongues. A muscular Turk stood over this great kettle, diligently stirring the contents with a stick. Whatever kind of stew he was in the midst of preparing must have been very thick, since he required both of his hands to agitate it.

"Noble Turk, what is it you are cooking there?" inquired the Infanta, who suddenly found herself quite peckish. She had not eaten any of the fruit and cheese or broth and game delivered to the sickroom door, preferring to save it for the young woman under her care. Yes, she did, indeed, fancy a hot, tasty meal in her empty belly.

"The Khan desired the hand of the Emir's daughter in marriage," explained the sad-eyed Turk, gesturing with his dark head toward the palace. "Only she did not desire his hand in return. Therefore I must stand here and stir this pot as a bewitchment."

The Infanta patted the emissary's continually moving arm in an effort to comfort him, for it had become apparent that he was most distressed over his assignment. "You poor fellow! How tired you must be, stirring for so long."

The Turk nodded miserably, his brawny arms persisting with their steady and monotonous motions. He gripped the base of the cooking tool held out before him with such force that the brown skin covering his fingers had blanched to the white of a fish's belly. "If only someone would render me assistance!" he bemoaned.

"Then it is most providential that I have come along," relied the daughter of Spain. To provide proof of the unfailing generosity of her heart, she placed her hands with some caution upon the stirring stick (for she did not wish to pick up any splinters), thereby replacing those of the exhausted Turk. The texture of the implement felt surprisingly smooth and sleek and not in the least likely to produce injury, its surface pleasantly warm against the tactile flesh of her fingers—although this might have been a result of the poor Turk's having already held it for so prolonged a period. "Am I doing it correctly?"

"Yes, lovely Infanta," sighed the vengeful Khan's emissary, the glittering topaz of his eyes rolling upward inside their almond-shaped sockets. "But perhaps it might be more efficient if you placed your hands end to end, since they are so very, very tiny." And the Turk spoke the truth, for the hands belonging to the King of Spain's daughter failed to cover even half the surface area that he had easily enfolded with one.

Desiring only to be helpful, the Infanta did as was suggested, no longer concerned about catching splinters in her fingers. "Is this acceptable?" she asked, her hands dwarfed by what she held in them.

A garbled groan escaped from the Turk's saliva-moistened lips. Nevertheless, he managed an affirmative nod. "Squeeze while you stir," he directed, his voice a raspy whisper. "That way you shall maintain a better grip."

The Infanta tightened her slender fingers on the cumbersome instrument, which had begun to lengthen and thicken in her diminutive hands. As it turned out, the instructions given her would be of great benefit. Her grasp immediately improved, and she soon found herself wielding the stirring stick with all the culinary skill of the most favored cook in her father's kitchen.

"Now slide your hands up and down," wheezed the Turk, whose nut-brown face had turned a bright shade of henna, as did the implement clutched in the Infanta's hard-working fingers. It had absorbed so much heat from the fire-fueled kettle that her hands needed to move with ever-increasing speed just to prevent her flesh from becoming scorched. This had a profound effect upon its swarthy recipient, whose constricting throat issued a succession of alarming gurgling noises. "Faster, Infanta, faster!" came the Turk's strangled plea.

As she performed her task in accordance with the Turk's wishes, the Spanish Infanta decided to investigate the steaming contents of the black cauldron, only to learn that it contained a rich, creamy stew. Suddenly it occurred to her that she might be able to use the maliciously intended brew to benefit her ailing patient. If the Emir's daughter actually *consumed* the sorcerous stew, it could well produce the opposite effect intended, thus breaking the spell and curing her of her malady rather than being the cause for it. It certainly seemed worth a try, as the young woman's health was fast failing.

By now the Khan's emissary appeared to be breathing with considerable effort, his broad chest heaving beneath his vest with every laborious exhalation. Sweat had broken out upon his brow, the droplets gleaming against the darkly flushed flesh like beads of glass. Placing his large brown hands over the Infanta's tiny pink ones, he guided them on their journey along the ever-increasing length of the stirring instrument, moving faster and faster and inducing this surrogate cook to exert a pressure far beyond her natural strength. The Infanta's hands went skimming across the heated surface with such swiftness and absence of caution that she feared that this time she truly would receive a splinter—and that it would be driven deeply and irretrievably into the tender flesh of her palm, perchance to lie within and fester until she, too, required the healing touch of one like herself.

The Turk's spittle-flecked lips had taken to flapping open and closed like that of a sea bird desperate for a meal. He seemed to be trying to say something, although the words that came out sounded hopelessly foreign to their listener. Despite having been schooled in the tongues of various lands, the Spanish Infanta found this particular form of parlance as alien and complex as if the aggrieved speaker had simply invented it on the spot. She strained her ears to decipher the gurgling syntax, only to have them abruptly assaulted by a primitive cry. The Turk's body froze, his stilled hands crushing hers against the flint-like hardness she had been battling to contain in her fingers. For it had apparently taken on a will of its own, thrusting deeper and deeper into the fire-blackened cauldron until the simmering broth had reached the level of the iron brim, whereupon it went splashing out onto the flames below, nearly dousing them.

Fully expecting the battered flesh of her palms to be chafed and flayed and, indeed, blistered beyond repair, the King of Spain's daughter gingerly unlocked her cramped hands, finding instead a healthy flush of red upon their sticky cushions. She pressed at various points with a tentative fingertip, meeting not the slightest soreness. The exhausted Turk had fallen shuddering to the sandy earth, his hands continuing to clutch what he had used to agitate the stew. For some inexplicable reason, it had greatly diminished in size. To see it now, the Infanta could not imagine how so insignificant a tool had ever been successful in preparing the hearty brew that was cooking inside the iron pot. A drinking vessel of tarnished pewter lay on the sand alongside the panting form of the Khan's emissary, and she borrowed it to collect what she could of the overflowing broth. Although she would not have minded sampling some herself, there could be no time for delay. The Emir had placed his only child's life in her hands—and she dared not fail in her task.

The Spanish Infanta hastened back to the little window and up the ladder of rope, taking care not to spill a single drop of the precious panacea she had stolen from the Turk. Upon reaching the sickbed, she propped up its frail occupant with one arm, holding the pewter cup to the cracked lips she located with the other. The pungent steam that arose from it seemed to activate the young woman's nostrils, for they twitched and flared with hunger. A skeletal hand crept shakily out from beneath the woolen blanket to grasp the life-giving vessel, pressing it more forcefully against the shriveled hole located in the center of the pillow. And in an instant the entirety of the cup's contents had vanished down the patient's wasted gullet.

Encouraged by her success, the Infanta searched her ward's bedchamber for a more sizable container. A chamber pot had been placed discreetly beneath the bed; fortunately it had recently been emptied and scrubbed clean by a servant. With this in hand, she once again sought out the Khan's emissary, whom she found just as before—lying lifelessly upon the sand, his trusty cooking accomplice having by this time dwindled to the size of a twig. As the Infanta strode purposefully toward him, his topaz eyes flickered in recognition…and perhaps something more, for the shrunken stirrer of sorcerous stews managed to produce a few forlorn twitches. Ignoring the Turk and his feeble attempts to once again solicit the aid of her hands, the daughter of the Spanish King used the pewter cup to fill the chamber pot with still more of the creamy brew, emptying out the entire contents of the cauldron in the process. Although it required extra time and effort for her to mount the ladder of rope, this dedicated healer of the sick managed to reach her patient with hardly any spillage.

In the morning, when the Emir's daughter awakened, she was given a second cup of the curative stew, followed by another at lunchtime and yet another at supper. By the third day the young woman's condition was markedly improved. Her face and figure had filled agreeably out, their cavernous hollows only a horrible memory in the concerned eyes of her father. The rosy bloom had returned to her cheeks and lips in full force, and after one final cup the adored daughter of the Emir was up and about as if she had never taken to her bed. Upon witnessing this remarkable transformation, the Emir offered the miracle-producing Infanta all that his desert emirate could provide, and more. Nothing else mattered to him but to have his only child back, happy and healthy. As before, the Infanta declined his generous offer and bid her leave, wishing them both well.

Rather than keeping her promise to return home to her own father, the daughter of the King of Spain returned to the source of the flickering light—and to the Khan's dutiful and topaz-eyed emissary, who had once again taken up the indomitable task of stirring the now-empty cauldron. And it was fortunate for him that she did, for the great pot most assuredly needed filling. ❧

Little Red Riding Hood

Possibly the most analyzed fairy tale in existence, "Little Red Riding Hood" has long been fraught with controversy over its purported sexual meaning. Many experts suggest that the story of the pretty red-hooded girl is but a thinly disguised parable of rape. Yet if one looks back at the tale's more cannibalistic ancestors, it will easily be discovered that this interpretation results more from the cultural notions of sex roles in post-Renaissance Europe than the historical reality.

Having experienced a long oral tradition in Asia, "Little Red Riding Hood" takes its roots from the folktale "Grandaunt Tiger," in which an old woman who consumes human flesh disguises herself as an elderly relative to lure a pair of sisters into her bed the better to eat them. On being offered her sibling's finger, the surviving sister outwits the old woman by claiming a need to relieve herself, thereby making her escape. Widely found in China, Japan, and Korea, "Grandaunt Tiger" likely gave birth to the European oral tale believed to have evolved into the "Little

Red Riding Hood" we know today. In "The Story of Grandmother," a werewolf disguised as a girl's grandmother fools his young victim into cannibalizing her elderly relative, only to coerce her into a ritualistic disrobing—whereupon the girl joins the werewolf in bed. The story ends much the same way as its Chinese counterpart, with the expressed need for urination/defecation, followed by the escape.

Despite its Asian origins, elements in "Little Red Riding Hood" can be traced to tales of antiquity. In the Greek myth of Kronos, the Titan swallows his children, one of whom has been replaced with a stone (a motif featured in the versions by the Brothers Grimm). The use of trickery to deceive the innocent can be seen in a fable by Aesop, where a wolf disguises its voice like that of a mother goat to fool her young. Other elements adding to the tale's development appeared in medieval days, such as in the Latin story "Fecunda Ratis," in which a girl wearing a red cap is found in the company of wolves. Even the distinctive repartee occurring between the wolf disguised as grandmother and the girl has its historical counterpart in the Nordic fable "Elder Edda," where it is explained why Thrym's would-be bride Freyja (the thunder god Thor in disguise) possesses such unladylike physical characteristics.

In Europe, "Little Red Riding Hood" began in the oral tradition during the late Middle Ages in France, northern Italy, and the Tyrol, giving rise to a series of warning tales for children. Indeed, hunger had driven people to commit terrible acts, and the prevalence of superstitious tales circulating in France during early Christianity and the Middle Ages resulted in an epidemic of trials against men accused of being werewolves (and women accused of being witches)—with the accused werewolves routinely charged with devouring children. Yet these so-called werewolves may have existed in primitive cultures as well, which could make "Little Red Riding Hood" far older than initially believed. Puberty and religious initiations practiced by ancient tribal peoples often consisted of sending an initiate into the forest to learn the secrets of nature by reverting to animal ways, only to return reborn to the community. Those who failed might out of hunger resort to cannibalism—and were thus considered werewolves.

With the decline of the witch-hunts in post-seventeenth-century Europe, werewolves lost their significance, which might explain why Charles Perrault changed the figure of a werewolf to that of a common wolf. In "Le Petit Chaperon Rouge," Perrault omits many elements from the oral tale, regarding them as too shocking and improper for his courtly audience. No mention is made of tasting the flesh and blood of grandmother, let alone a desire to urinate or defecate. Nevertheless, Perrault had no qualms about the girl undressing and joining the wolf in bed. A man of his time, he changed the nature of his protagonist to suit prevailing gender roles. Whereas in the folktale the girl is brave and shrewd, by the time of "Le Petit Chaperon Rouge" she has become gullible, vain, and helpless—and, as such, brings her fate on herself for dallying with the wolf.

Perrault's popular version inspired a massive circulation in print, resulting in the tale's reabsorption back into the oral tradition—which later led to "Rotkäppchen" (Little Red Cap) by the Grimms. The brothers likely got their story from a lady-in-waiting raised in the French tradition and already familiar with "Le Petit Chaperon Rouge," only to be doubly influenced by Perrault by means of Ludwig Tieck, who based his verse play *Leben und Tod des kleinen Rotkäppchens* on the French literary tale. Yet while Perrault mostly intended his tale as a form of amusement for adults, the Grimms aspired to a more didactic tone, hence they revised the tale for children, eliminating any erotic undertones—and, in the process, stressing the evils of unsanctioned conduct. For the girl's freedom from restraint as she frolics through the forest enjoying nature (and perhaps her own budding sexuality) was not a thing to be encouraged in the nineteenth century. The only allusion to any prior sexual content seems to be in a later version of "Rotkäppchen," in which the rescuing huntsman calls the wolf an "old sinner"—an expression used to represent one who seduces, particularly young girls.

Having already followed in the footsteps of the Grimms by taking inspiration from their standard version of "Little Red Riding Hood," I find that I have apparently done so again. Only rather than stopping with the wolf, I have extended the lecherous qualities of the Grimms' "old sinner" to those of a less furry nature. ❧

Little Red Riding Hood

THERE WAS ONCE A YOUNG LASS WHO owned a hood of the reddest and plushest velvet. She wore it upon her pretty head at every opportunity, for it had become her most treasured possession. Mind you, this was no ordinary shop-bought hood, but a special one presented to her as a gift by her grandmother, who had toiled many long hours stitching it with failing eyes and quivering fingers. Indeed, its delighted recipient could rarely be seen going anywhere without it. The hood suited to perfection her fair coloring and bright eyes, the intense shade of red kindling their innocent blue into two twinkling sapphire stars. With such a distinctive fashion trademark, this much-favored granddaughter came to be known as *Little Red Riding Hood*.

Or, to those with whom she was on more intimate terms: *Red*.

Now it so happened that Red adored her elderly relative, therefore she made no protest when called upon by her mother to deliver some teacakes and a pot of strawberry jam to the old woman, who had been feeling poorly and could not leave her sickbed. "Now, set out before the sun grows too hot," came the maternal warning. "And mind not to stray from the path, as thou might suffer a mischief." Of course the dutiful daughter promised to do just as her mother said, although she could not for the life of her imagine what sort of mischief could possibly befall her upon such a fine spring morn. However, the mother knew her offspring far better than her mildly creased brow indicated; residing in a village, it usually proved difficult to keep one's activities a secret.

Grandmother lived in a tiny, shingled cottage set in the middle of a vast woodland, a fair distance from the bustling village of her granddaughter. Armed with her precious gifts, which would be certain to add cheer to the convalescing woman's day, Little Red Riding Hood sallied happily forth on her journey. The distance and the isolation did not for a moment concern her. She liked taking solitary strolls along the periphery of the wood, although she had never ventured out this far all on her own. Yet it seemed like such a grand day to be strolling among the invigorating scents of pine and rain-soaked earth that any dangers awaiting her would surely be minimal. Besides, Red had heard that the wood contained handsome young huntsmen and thought it might be of benefit to ascertain the truth of this claim, since those of the local variety were already familiar to her. Many a time did she go skipping by the village tavern in hopes of meeting one of its rugged patrons, her red-hooded presence in the vicinity inspiring considerable gossip, which undoubtedly accounted for this sudden dispatch to Grandmother's. Indeed, Red had become very well known in huntsmen's circles.

Just as she would likewise become well known in other circles…. Despite the fact that she had no legitimate business in the vicinity, Red frequently made a point of passing a busy construction site located down by the docks on the east end of the village—a place notorious for its unsavory activities and equally unsavory characters, several of whom appeared to have been hired as laborers. These men worked outdoors in the open, balancing precariously upon planks of wood as they slathered mortar onto bricks and joined them together to form sections of wall. Beads of sweat glistened like diamonds on their sun-bronzed flesh. They had stripped down to their dungarees in the heat of their labors, exposing their naked chests and backs to onlookers. The pretty, red-hooded presence of Little Red Riding Hood was most inconsistent with these rough and grubby surroundings, to say nothing of attracting the kind of attention on which her mother would likely have frowned. For each time she approached the brick-strewn rubble of the construction site, the workers called down to her in greeting: "Oy, Red—show us yer hood!" Whereupon they grabbed hold of the bulges at the front of their sweat-stained dungarees, shaking them about as they blew her a noisy kiss. In response, the beneficiary of this friendly salutation twirled merrily about, leaving her sweaty admirers with the memory of a forbidden flash of skirts…and what had lain beneath.

As the hooded lass made her carefree way along the woodland path toward Grandmother's cottage, the wind of a departing wintertime set the hem of her garments aflutter. Giggling good-naturedly, she smoothed her skirts back down to rest flatly and neatly against her hips, only to be forced to repeat the process again and again with each successive gust until she ultimately abandoned her efforts. For who was there to take heed? Red quite enjoyed the stimulating sensation of winter's cold breath swirling about the bare flesh of her thighs and nether regions. To derive the maximum benefit possible, she hitched up her dirndl skirt and ruffled pinafore to better appreciate what the season had to offer, fully aware that by doing so she was providing the casual observer with amusements of an altogether different nature. Indeed, Little Red Riding Hood took tremendous delight in displaying what others may have regarded as shameful.

Beneath her cherished hood, Red's face glowed with all the luminosity of a full moon, her eyes a sparkling set of perfectly matched gemstones against the surrounding mantle of red velvet. Several wisps of springy yellow curls escaped to frame her face. Rather than tucking them back up underneath the hood as modesty would have advised, she allowed them to have their freedom. How wonderful it felt to suddenly be unburdened by the opinions of others! Creatures both great and small emerged to watch this blithe damsel as she passed, hanging precariously from the branches of trees or scuttering up from holes dug into the winter-encrusted earth. Perhaps it was to be expected that this spirited bearer of gifts should come to the attention of the local wolf, who made it his vocation to be conversant with the business of the wood.

Having never before made the creature's acquaintance, Red had no knowledge of the wickedness of his character and his cunning lupine ways. Therefore, when he stepped boldly out from behind the frosted trunk of a fir, she experienced neither fear nor distrust. "Good day, my pretty one," the wolf greeted, his grin framing sharp yellow teeth whose greatest desire was to sample the supple young flesh he had seen parading with such insouciance through the shadowy woodland.

"And good day unto thee, kind sir," answered Little Red Riding Hood with an amiable nod. She had always been told by her mother to demonstrate the utmost in politeness in her dealings with others, even if those others might only be strangers. Of late, though, her mother had been given much cause to regret such counsel — if the village gossips were to be believed. Since Red had no reason to be wary of this pitifully unprepossessing creature whose intentions seemed merely to while away a few dull moments of the morning engaging in carefree banter, she acted in the manner most natural to her.

"And where art thou off to on so fine a day?" inquired the wolf, his sanguineous eyes gleaming with an unwholesomeness far beyond the worst imaginings of the mother of his chitchat partner.

"I am going to visit my gran, who is feeling poorly and hath not the strength to leave her bed."

"Indeed…" mused this hirsute busybody of the woodland, his broad grin never once wavering. A trickle of saliva had begun to make an escape from his darkly furred mouth, and a carmine tongue darted forth to collect it before it could cause offense. "And where might she live, thine old granny?"

"In a cottage ringed by hazel bushes and situated beneath three large oak trees. It is the only dwelling in the whole wood." Red stated this with pride, as if the old woman's isolation were a thing of status.

The wolf nodded thoughtfully, scarcely able to contain his mounting excitement. "Pray, may one be so presumptuous as to inquire what treasures thou hast got hidden there?" For the hooded lass appeared to be in the process of transporting a receptacle of some sort. With any luck, it might contain something tasty to eat. The poor wolf was growing quite weary of a diet of small animals and the occasional bit of gristle procured from a woodland neighbor's leftovers.

Deliberately misinterpreting the object of the inquisitive creature's interest—for she could never resist an opportunity to flaunt herself—Red raised up the hems of her skirts and pinafore, revealing to a vigilant pair of eyes a little cherry. It had been the source of great pleasure as she went skipping along the earthen pathway with her garments aflutter, just as it had been when she twirled about for the bricklayers at the construction site, each of whom had been most effusive in his praise. It boasted a hood of the same shade of red as the one she wore upon her head, and as the gift-bearing granddaughter stood indulgently before the wolf, a gust of wind inspired this velvety sheath to flutter festively in the breeze. All at once the sinewy legs of the beast threatened to give way beneath his weight. This must be the hooded lass of whom he had heard all the huntsmen speak. And she had just revealed to him a treat for which his discontented palate had been desperately longing.

A fruit of unparalleled glossiness sprouted forth from a downy vale, its plump contours bursting with a succulent sweetness that caused its beholder to sway in drunken delirium. This lone harvest had reached the perfect pinnacle of ripeness, all but demanding to be plucked and, indeed, consumed. *This pretty maiden shall provide me with a very choice morsel,* mused the creature with an impassioned shudder. *Yet perchance if I am clever, I might also manage to secure a somewhat less tender bill of fare to help remove the edge from my appetite.* For in having just set his lupine sights upon Grandmother, the greedy beast planned to save the juicy tidbit before him for dessert. "My, what a nice little hood thou hast there," remarked its furry admirer in a strangled tone, the unwavering direction of his stare clearly indicative of which hood he meant. "Wherever did its charming owner manage to acquire it?"

"Forsooth, I cannot say. For it has always been there whenever I look beneath my skirts."

Aye, it shall not be there for long! the wolf snickered inwardly, an image of the blue-eyed damsel staring up her skirts and discovering a vacancy in this once-fertile dell giving him even more to chortle about.

Red coughed as if trying to free something from her throat, her patience with the beast wearing dangerously thin. "Sir, hast thou perchance spied any young huntsmen about?" she interrogated, hoping this unprepossessing creature might actually be of some use to her. After all, she had better things to do than pass the time holding up her skirts for silly wolves. She needed to make the obligatory visit to Grandmother, then get on with the *real* business of the day.

"*Huntsmen?* Nay, there are no huntsmen in this wood," lied the wolf, in whose best interest it was to avoid such bloodthirsty individuals in the first place. Putting forth a courtly bow, he accompanied Little Red Riding Hood through the wood, pointing out all the colorful flowers that had turned their faces toward the slanted rays of the sun. "Perhaps thine old granny might like a nosegay," he suggested, his motive being to delay the granddaughter's arrival at the old woman's cottage, which would grant him the running start he required.

Red gazed all around her, the melodic singing of birds and the busy buzzing of bees seeming to encourage her in this pursuit. Why, a cheerful bunch of blooms sounded the very cure for her ailing relation. Perhaps she might even locate a blossom whose narcoleptic petals could be brewed into a tea, thereby sending the old woman to sleep, at which time her gift-bearing granddaughter could make her escape. For indeed, Red had no wish to listen to laments of aching joints and failing eyes when there might be handsome young huntsmen about.

With this in mind, the dutiful daughter disobeyed her mother's strict instructions, leaving behind the wolf and the earthen pathway so that she could set about collecting the most perfect and beauteous of blossoms. With each stem she pulled from the earth, yet another floral specimen of greater beauty sprang up within her line of vision, drawing her deeper and deeper into the wood and farther and farther away from the path that would have taken her to Grandmother. To keep her skirts and pinafore from getting soiled, Red tucked them up out of the way, which would also prove advantageous in the event a huntsman might be passing, since she did not entirely believe the wolf's protestations to the contrary.

Meanwhile, the crafty creature dispatched himself with lightning swiftness to the tiny, shingled cottage surrounded by its hedge of hazel bushes and sheltered beneath three large oaks. Indeed,

Grandmother's residence was impossible to miss. Aside from being the only dwelling for leagues around, the eaves of the cottage had been strung with lanterns that blazed both day and night, serving as beacons for those who passed. As the wolf knocked with false familiarity upon the front door, he wondered what kind of foolish old woman bothered with outdoor lighting in the middle of a sunny day, especially in such a low-crime area.

"Who goes there?" came a creaky voice from inside.

The wolf cleared his throat in readiness to reply, only to be interrupted before he could do so.

"Art thou a huntsman?" The voice sounded slightly stronger the second time, the note of hope in it unmistakable. It was followed by a clamorous clattering and clanging, as if the occupant of the cottage was in the midst of preparing for an unexpected visitor.

The wolf shook his furry head in amusement, for it appeared that the old woman possessed the same aspirations as her lively granddaughter. Of course he had no way of knowing that Grandmother had in her youth worked in a bawdy house on the south bank of the village docks — an establishment heavily frequented by huntsmen. It was in these very surroundings that the fertile seed of some nameless huntsman had caused her to beget Little Red Riding Hood's mother, a fact that probably accounted for the latter's concerned vigilance for her red-hooded daughter.

"'Tis I, Little Red Riding Hood," answered the wolf in the lilting soprano of the young lass he had met in the wood. "I have brought some nice teacakes and a pot of tasty strawberry jam."

The clamor inside the cottage abruptly ceased, only to be replaced by a deep sigh. "Alas, I am far too ill to greet thee properly. Pray, lift up on the latch and come hither," instructed Grandmother from her sickbed of pink satin, a ragged cough setting her ancient bones to rattling within their cage of withered flesh. Before she could haul herself up into a sitting position, a monstrous figure of fur loomed over her. Fortunately a pair of clouded eyes saved the ailing woman from the horror that would within moments befall her.

The wolf soon made himself comfortable upon the slippery, satin-covered mattress, adjusting the unfamiliar garments of his most recent repast on his oversized limbs. He placed Grandmother's floppy nightcap atop his large head, taking care to tuck his ears beneath it. Because of their pointy nature, they sprang right back out again, and any further attempts to camouflage them were subsequently abandoned. Thusly settled, the sly creature pulled closed the bed curtains, sealing off both himself and the bed in a cozy cocoon of chiffon.

Unable to locate any blossoms whose petals might send Grandmother into an expeditious slumber, Little Red Riding Hood made her way back to the footpath leading to the cottage, resigned to an afternoon of listening to the old woman croak out a detailed description of each malady. Upon arriving, she discovered the front door standing wide open and the interior of the tiny cottage silent save for the sound of heavy breathing. "Hello!" she called cheerfully, receiving no response. Perhaps Grandmother was sleeping and had not heard her young visitor arrive, in which case Red could leave behind her gifts and beat a hasty retreat.

Placing her burdens upon the bedside table alongside the cup used to hold the old woman's teeth, Little Red Riding Hood carefully drew back the wispy curtains enclosing the bed so as not to disturb her relative. Rather than snoring peacefully, Grandmother lay in a slothful sprawl against the pink-satin sheets with her garments all askew, a salacious expression distorting her bristled face. Never had the granddaughter seen the old woman in such a state, and she wondered if her elderly relation might have taken to ingesting some of the strange mushrooms one often stumbled upon in the wood. "Why, Grandmother, what big ears thou hast!" Red cried in astonishment, for they stuck up most uncharacteristically.

"All the better to hear thee with," came the cackling reply, the bloodshot eyes beneath the night-cap widening as the red-hooded visitor moved closer.

"Why, Grandmother, what big eyes thou hast!"

"All the better to see thee with," the wolf replied with a suggestive wink, his ungrandmotherly paws fluttering in a flurry of palsy at his sides.

"Why, Grandmother, what big hands thou hast!"

"All the better to hug thee with," croaked the disheveled figure in the bed, reaching out with false affection toward Little Red Riding Hood, the pink-satin duvet working its way downward toward this sly impostor's furry haunches. A furious thumping had begun against his partially sated belly, its point of origin growing larger and larger at the thought of what lay beneath the pretty granddaughter's skirts.

"Why, Grandmother, what a portly member thou hast!" squealed Red. For the great hairy thing writhing and wriggling before her bore scant resemblance to the sleek specimens belonging to the handsome young huntsmen from the village. She wondered whether this might be characteristic of those who lived in the wood — in which case she would henceforward confine her activities to the village!

The wolf thrust his lap lewdly upward. "All the better to fuck thee with," he growled, his tongue darting in and out of his salivating maw.

Such unseemly language and gestures were not at all what Red expected from a sickly old woman. In fact, up until this moment they had only been directed toward her by the sweaty bricklayers down at the docks. However, she soon realized that there was something else very much out of the ordinary about her aged relative. "Why, Grandmother, what a big mouth thou hast!"

Now *this* was what the cunning beast had been waiting for. He sprang forth from Grandmother's satin-covered sickbed, hurling Little Red Riding Hood to the floor and swallowing in all its flavorful and hooded entirety the savory morsel that had been the cause of so much pleasant rumination on this fine day. To his delight, it had grown even riper since morning, and his carmine tongue fed greedily upon the sweet juices flowing abundantly out from beneath where it sprouted. How wise he had been to save this delicacy for dessert!

Once the wolf's hunger had finally been appeased, he returned to Grandmother's bed for a much-needed rest, his satisfied snores shaking the cottage walls and dislodging several shingles from the roof. He would sleep so soundly that he failed to hear the approaching footsteps of a huntsman.

Attracted by the blaze of lanterns and alarmed by the discordant noises coming from within, this concerned citizen decided to check on the cottage's elderly occupant. He knew that the woman lived alone and was of a very advanced age. He also knew she had a granddaughter, for he had heard many stories in the village tavern about the young damsel's famous red hoods, one of which she did not wear upon her head. Intending to get into the old woman's good graces, the huntsman brushed the woodland detritus from his garments and straightened his feather-tipped cap before making his approach. Only whom should he discover snoring contentedly in Grandmother's bed and wearing

Grandmother's clothing but the crafty wolf he had tirelessly pursued for far too many days? "Ah-*ha!*" cried the huntsman in victory. "I have found thee, infernal rascal!"

As he cocked his gun in readiness to fire off a shot, it suddenly occurred to the huntsman that this plague of fleas and fur might have eaten the feeble old thing in whose pink-satin bed it had taken up residence. So, setting down the weapon, he reached into his sheath for his knife and before the snoring beast realized what was happening, the huntsman proceeded to carve a line down the wolf's meal-swollen belly. A bright flash of red appeared within the incision, and as he continued to draw the blade steadily downward, the huntsman saw what looked to be a hood of red velvet. Before he could reflect more fully upon an explanation for its presence, out leapt the nimble figure of a pretty lass.

"Oh, kind sir, I thank thee with all my heart!" cried Little Red Riding Hood. "For it was black as pitch in there and smelled unspeakably!"

"I am pleased to have been of assistance," bowed the huntsman, tipping his feathered cap in respect. The eyes of the little damsel who had occupied the wolf's fattened belly reminded him of stars in a winter night's sky, so brilliantly and with such clarity did they shine. With faltering fingers, he reached out to touch the pale softness of her cheek, surprised that so innocently intended a gesture should leave him quaking like when he was a young lad on his first visit to the bawdy house down by the village docks.

Red stepped out of the steaming viscera of her prison, using the hems of her skirts and pinafore to dry the grateful tears from her eyes. She spent several long moments doing so, peering stealthily through the weave of the cloth to gauge the huntsman's reaction. In the event his eyesight was not up to usual huntsmen standards, she raised up one foot and set it atop the fallen wolf, bringing further into the light what even a blind man could not have failed to miss.

All at once this helpful passerby spied what had been the focus of the wolf's desperate hunger. A cherry of mouth-watering proportions burst forth from a modest garden, sporting a hood even brighter and redder than the one atop the wearer's head. It had been draped quite jauntily, leaving much of the pulpy flesh beneath exposed to view and effecting considerable consternation in the mind and body of its beholder, who at this moment felt very much like a wolf himself. This must be the lass of whom he had heard his fellow huntsmen speak.

Before the huntsman could pluck the fruit out from the downy vale and sink his yearning teeth into its delicate barrier of skin, a garbled squawking from within the depths of the wolf's knife-rent belly stayed his hand. Unless he was mistaken, it sounded like the cries of an old woman. Although he would have preferred to ignore them, they stubbornly refused to be ignored. On the contrary, the cries gained in both intensity and pitch, becoming a monotonous series of *Help me*'s that grew ever more impatient and irate as he dawdled. *Dash the feeble old witch!* the huntsman grumbled inwardly, praying for the incessant wails to cease before the doubly hooded lass had taken heed of them and let her skirts back down. At the moment this Good Samaritan had far more pressing matters deserving of his attention than undertaking another rescue. The saliva of desire pooled in his mouth, making him giddy as a drunkard. How could he draw another breath without at least a little nibble upon the glossy riches flaunting themselves beneath a heart-stopping flash of skirts?

"Art thou a huntsman?" came a muffled voice, which was followed by the sight of arthritic fingers as Grandmother clawed at the bloodied sides of the wound the huntsman's knife had created. Indeed, she struggled with a spryness long unknown to her, for she recognized the feathered cap of a huntsman when she saw one. Apparently all that money from her old-age pension that had gone toward the cost and mainte-nance of the lanterns had finally paid itself back.

Ergo the huntsman found himself obliged to reach inside the wolf's fetid belly to save its remaining occupant. With the same blade that had freed its two unwitting victims, he promptly skinned the beast, cer-tain that its pelt would look quite elegant upon the floor before his hearth, to say nothing of providing comfort for whoever might wish to lie beside the fire. As he departed the cottage with a hearty wave, he thought that perhaps one day the old woman's granddaughter might choose to pay a call to offer her thanks, at which time the huntsman planned to seize the opportunity to sample what had ultimately cost the wolf his life.

Grandmother was at last allowed to enjoy the teacakes and strawberry jam Little Red Riding Hood had brought from home, pausing between bites to inquire with unprecedented vigor as to the whereabouts of the handsome young huntsman who had been their rescuer. As for Red, she had begun to regret that the old woman had not been left inside the wolf's stinking belly. Of course, had she known about the wolf's pelt being slated for use as a rug, she might not have been so keen to pursue a relationship with the huntsman. Although Red harbored no great fondness for wolves, she disapproved most heartily of animal fur's being employed as a form of decoration.

After many sunrises had passed, another wolf with a wicked gleam in his sanguinary eye accosted Little Red Riding Hood on her way to Grandmother's. Ignoring his friendly *good day,* she kept straight to the footpath, striding resolutely onward with her skirts dancing high about her thighs. Aside from being very much on her guard against lupine lechers, she knew that the hunting season was now in full swing. Reaching Grandmother's cottage unmolested, Red rapped soundly upon the door, knowing that the old woman's hearing was fast failing.

"Art thou a huntsman?" came a raspy, albeit hopeful voice from inside.

"'Tis I, Little Red Riding Hood," the red-hooded caller replied in exasperation.

Grandmother could not hide her crestfallen expression at seeing the nubile young figure of her granddaughter breezing through the door. For she was also well aware that the hunting season had begun and did not think it at all unreasonable that a weary huntsman might seek out her tiny abode for a brief repast or possibly even a bed for the night. In anticipation of such an occurrence, the old woman had appealed to her granddaughter several times to bring with her a bottle of French scent on the occasion of her next visit, only to be deluged with yet another delivery of stale teacakes and sour jam. It would seem that the lass believed her mind to be as feeble as her body!

As grandmother and granddaughter sat in the parlor drinking their tea and eating their teacakes, Red relayed what had just transpired with the wolf. Not wanting to take any chances, the two conspired to draw the bolt across the door, refusing to open it to this opportunistic creature who—like his less auspicious predecessor—proclaimed himself to be Little Red Riding Hood with some teacakes and jam for Grandmother.

Possessing a highly persistent nature that would ultimately be the cause of his downfall, the wolf refused to be put off by his cold reception. Had he been wiser, he might have declared himself to be a huntsman, thereby guaranteeing the door being thrown open in welcome. Instead, this furry trespasser prowled around the hazel bushes, eventually clambering up onto the shingled roof of the cottage to wait out the remains of the day. Darkness was close upon them, and the old woman's granddaughter would soon be making her way home, granting the sly beast his opportunity to strike. He had overheard many tantalizing tales about the succulent, rosy delicacy beneath the charming damsel's skirts, the huntsman who had recently murdered his lupine colleague being most loose-lipped when in the company of his fellow killers.

Grandmother guessed the wolf's clever scheme from the scuttering-about taking place above her and her granddaughter's heads. It sounded like the sneaky beast was plotting to slip down through the chimney, whereupon they would both be done for. Wishing to spare her granddaughter such a fate, the elder pushed the younger out the door. That was when Little Red Riding Hood saw the wolf placing one of his furry feet inside the chimney. Obviously she could not leave her poor old gran behind to face certain death, so she did the only thing she could think of. She sprang out into full view of the beast, calling

up to him a succession of nasty jeers and dancing fear-
lessly about with her skirts held high in taunting
merriment. While she was at it, perhaps she might
also catch the attention of a passing huntsman, in
which case her efforts would be doubly rewarded.

The wolf peered eagerly down over the lantern-
lighted eaves of the roof, leaning farther and farther
out in an attempt to glimpse the famous hood of which
the chatty huntsman had spoken with such lip-smack-
ing relish. The previous night's rain had left the mossy
shingles quite slippery, and suddenly he felt himself
lose his footing. The wolf went tumbling to the
ground, landing upon his head and dying instantly.

Grandmother cooked him up for that evening's
supper, convinced that the smell of fresh wolf stew
would bring a huntsman to her door. Being a strict
vegetarian, Red declined to stay — much to the relief of
her grandmother, who could do without the competition. After helping the old woman put a fresh set of
pink-satin sheets upon the bed, Little Red Riding
Hood went skipping merrily home through the woodland, hoping to meet a huntsman or two along the
way with a mind to pluck her hooded cherry. ❧

THE TRAVELING COMPANION

"The Traveling Companion" has been attributed to many tellers of tales and appears in many variants worldwide. Classified as a riddle tale, it features as its most popular character the riddle princess, who either poses a riddle or solves it. A number of these tales got their start in India, making their way into Persia, North Africa, and Europe. Yet it would be in Scandinavia that this tale was creatively reworked into what is likely the most widely known riddle tale of all time.

Considered more a writer than a collector of fairy tales, Hans Christian Andersen based his version of "The Traveling Companion" on the Danish folktale "The Dead Man's Help." Although the theme of upward social mobility has always been prevalent in folktales, for Andersen it seems to have held particular importance. A social outsider with a slavish admiration for royalty (for he was the humble son of a peasant cobbler), Andersen was attracted to stories that contained protagonists of lesser standing who sought the attentions of a beautiful princess.

By reaching for the unattainable, his characters likewise reflected his own life.

Because of the late conversion of the populace to Christianity, the countries of Scandinavia developed more independently than those in the rest of Europe. This resulted in a more authentic form of folklore, with the Scandinavian folktales evolving primarily from ancient mythologies and the influence of the landscape rather than from external influences. Of course, exceptions can always be found. Although Andersen patterned his story on a folktale from his native land, the adventures of his two traveling companions closely parallel a tale from Brittany. Perhaps the most significant element in this variant is the presence of the magic potion a soldier uses to help a young nobleman who wishes to put forth a riddle to a princess—a magic potion featured quite prominently in Andersen. Had it not been for its existence, Poor Johannes might never have been successful in winning the princess. This use of alchemy can also be seen in the animation of the puppets, indicating a possible connection to primitive cultures, whose folklore was filled with elements relating to the magical and metamorphic.

Like its Danish counterpart, Grimms' traveling duo in "Das Rätsel" (The riddle) set off on an adventure, which leads to the proverbial princess, who offers the challenge that she would accept as husband any man who proposes to her a riddle she cannot solve. In the manner of Andersen's princess, the German one relied on methods not entirely ethical in her desire to solve the riddle, taking the bold action of sitting alongside the traveler as he lay asleep in bed in hopes that he might divulge the answer—an act the puritanical Grimms and their editors somehow appeared to have missed as inappropriate.

However, not much else would be missed. Like those who worked on the *Kinder- und Hausmärchen*, many editors and translators of Andersen's tales came from the Victorian age, therefore any indicators of passion or eroticism failed to make it into print. Even a kiss on the mouth would be modified into a kiss on the cheek. Such pristine examples of physical emotion can be seen in a number of fairy tales that have made their way through the Victorian age (and past the Victorian editor). Be that as it may, neither Andersen nor his editors displayed any objection to physical violence, as for example Poor Johannes's traveling companion makes ample use of the switch against the riddle-posing princess, even going so far as to draw blood.

This punitive whipping with birches can be traced to the old peasant tradition of the "wedding bath." A purification ritual designed to cleanse the bride of harmful influences (such as the princess's contact with the troll), the process consists of the bride being whipped until all evils have been purged from her, whereupon she is bathed with milk. Indeed, it appears that this practice may have been widespread enough to have made its way into folk literature—and hence into "The Traveling Companion."

In keeping with the spirit of Andersen, I, too, have made generous use of certain punitive measures, for, like the Danish princess, the one in my version protests unconvincingly (if at all) against their frequency. ❧

The Traveling Companion

POOR JOHANNES WAS A GOOD SON. Therefore he saw to it that his father was placed respectfully beneath the rich green earth when Death arrived to claim him. With little remaining to keep him behind but memories and the freshly turned soil of his father's grave, the bereaved son decided to seek his fortune far from the safe environs of home and all that he had ever known in his young life. As the sun cast its golden rays upon the breeze-swept leaves in the churchyard, Johannes bid his father a final farewell, certain they would meet again in the afterlife.

The next morning, the orphan packed a small parcel containing everything he owned in the world. After hiding his modest patrimony within his belt, he embarked upon his adventure. Since Poor Johannes had never been away from the village of his father, he allowed himself to be guided by the experienced flutters of doves' wings. The faces of the flowers in the fields smiled their encouragement as he passed, straining their slender necks to receive the kiss of the sun against their petaled cheeks. As darkness fell, Johannes was obliged to make for himself a bed in a haystack. Yet not even this untoward accommodation could diminish his good cheer, for above him he had the moonlit sky and beside him the sweet fragrance of wild roses and below him the comforting rush-and-tumble of the river.

The insistent tolling of bells finally roused Poor Johannes from his peaceful slumber. It was Sunday morning, and the farmers and their families could be seen wearing their best garments as they walked toward a tiny chapel in the misty distance. The orphan joined the procession, intending to offer a prayer for his father. As he approached the gate, he suddenly noticed a beggar loitering outside the churchyard. Despite the fellow's destitute appearance and out-stretched palms, none of the parishioners paid him any mind. Without a moment's thought for his own difficulties, Johannes bestowed upon the bedraggled specimen all the silver coins he had in his belt — indeed, nearly half of his paternal legacy — and then quickly rejoined the others as they entered the chapel. Exhilarated by his selfless act of charity, Johannes remained oblivious to the snickers of the beggar, who flagged down a passing hackney coach and jumped inside, followed by a pair of heavily painted women who had been waiting hopefully on the corner.

Later that afternoon a frightful storm erupted, and the fatherless young traveler decided to seek shelter before its black wrath engulfed him completely. Arriving at another little chapel, he went inside to wait out the night in an available pew. However, he was awakened shortly after midnight by a heated argument, the subject of which concerned a dead man in a coffin. Unable to bear the sound of voices raised in anger, Poor Johannes intervened at once, only to learn that the coffin's occupant had cheated the quarrelers out of money owed to them by dying before the debt could be paid. As a result, the men wished to cast the deceased out into the rain and chop up his coffin for firewood. Having been a good son to his own father, Johannes could not permit such a sacrilege to be committed upon the father of another, so he made an offer of money to pay off the debt—the entire remainder of his inheritance—the agreement being that the debtees leave the debtor in peace. Chuckling at this outsider's soft-headedness, the men agreed, snatching the precious gold coins from Johannes's outstretched palm and leaving him in the company of the dead, who had already been left in the coffin far longer than advisable.

Once the storm had seen fit to blow off toward the distant foothills, Poor Johannes set off once again without waiting for the arrival of morning, relieved to be leaving behind the gamy remains of the chapel's lifeless parishioner. A silvery moon lighted his way, showing the orphan that he was not alone. Naked elves frolicked to all sides of him, undisturbed by his presence in their wooded glen. They danced around him in carefree circles, which caused the young wanderer's spirits to rise and his step to bounce. Indeed, he did not even take offense when they used their tiny elfin nozzles to spray him with their special elves' milk, for they said it brought prosperity — and prosperity was exactly what Poor Johannes needed. As the moon began to relinquish its post to the sun, the wee creatures scurried back inside the flower blossoms in which they lived, and Poor Johannes emerged from the shadowy glen into the full bright yellow of morning. Before he could adjust his eyes to the light, a voice greeted him heartily, inquiring of his destination.

"I am but a poor orphan out to seek my fortune in the world," answered Johannes, the stark contrast between his previous actions and his stated objective apparently lost on him.

"Aye, I am of a like enterprise. Shall we keep company together?"

Poor Johannes eagerly agreed, pleased to have found a companion upon his lonesome journey. The two immediately became fast friends, although it would soon become evident that this congenial stranger was very much the wiser of the pair. He had traveled the world many times over and knew intimately of its capricious nature. In fact, there seemed to be no subject unknown to him.

As the sun lifted itself high above their heads, the travelers settled their weary limbs beneath the shade of a tree to partake of a meal, which had been thoughtfully brought forth from the stranger's knapsack. At the same time, an old woman could be seen hobbling up the grassy slope toward them, the weighty burden of wood upon her back causing her to become more stooped than she already was. She came to a groaning halt before the two lunchers and leaned unsteadily upon her walking stick, the logs shifting threateningly along the hump of her spine.

"Good day," replied Poor Johannes, tipping his hat respectfully as his father had taught him.

The old woman nodded warily, suspicious that this fresh-faced young laddie and his older and more polished accomplice might be of a mind to steal her handbag, which dangled precariously from one of the logs. While she stood there perusing them with eyes that had long ago lost their focus, a fly stopped to rest upon the tip of her nose. Reaching up to shoo it away, she lost her hold on her walking stick and collapsed in a spindly heap at their feet. From the grievous manner in which she shrieked, the two travelers realized that the old woman had broken her leg.

Johannes proposed they carry her home, for she would perish if left to her own devices. However, his worldly-wise friend appeared to have something different in mind. He rummaged around inside the worn burlap of his knapsack until his hand emerged with a jar, which he declared to be a special salve capable of curing any malady—including that of a broken leg. Scooping up a portion of the ointment in his fingers, Johannes's traveling companion proceeded to rub it high up beneath the broken-limbed woman's skirts. Almost immediately she began to writhe and moan. The leg that had lain broken and useless stretched slowly out and away from its healthier twin, twitching and jiggling with renewed life. The jar's benevolent custodian continued with his ministrations, no doubt determined that the cure should be complete. By now the old woman's legs were kicking like those of an excited colt, her withered thighs flung wide as she endured her restorative treatment from this stranger. With a cry like that of crackling parchment, she sprang up from the ground and sprinted off down the hill, leaving a trail of logs in her wake.

With their bellies full and a good deed done, the two travelers continued on their way, moving toward a range of dark mountains whose tall peaks snagged the passing clouds. Although they looked fairly near, it would require the entirety of a day to reach the dense black forest that marked the entry point to the great metropolis located at the far side of the range. Ever mindful of the dwindling daylight and the resultant drop in temperature, Poor Johannes and his companion decided to avail themselves of a modest inn they found along the way. A puppetmaster was in the process of setting up a little theater inside the taproom, and everyone had gathered around to watch, including the inn's new arrivals. Unfortunately, the burly butcher from the village and his slobbering bulldog chose to settle themselves directly before the miniature stage, thus procuring for themselves the best seats in the house and blocking a good many views, including that of Poor Johannes, who contented himself with half a view rather than complain.

The play got under way, its central characters being those of a king and queen. Other dolls had been positioned at points to the right and left, playing the roles of courtiers and ladies-in-waiting. As the queen arose from her throne and glided crossways over the miniature stage, the bulldog suddenly let loose with an angry barking, only to bound forward and, hence, away from the reach of its master. Seizing the delicate figure of the queen within its powerful jaws, the animal gnashed its sharp teeth together, cracking the puppet at the neck. Satisfied with the carnage, the dog trotted proudly back to the butcher, whereupon the two made a hasty exit—although not before alerting the innkeeper that the boyish presence of Poor Johannes would provide payment for the chalk marks that had accrued upon the slate beside the butcher's name.

The show having reached its premature conclusion, the audience dispersed, leaving the inconsolable puppetmaster on his own with his broken queen. With great tenderness, he fitted her serenely smiling head back atop the jagged remains of neck, not daring to blink for fear it might roll off again. At that moment the stranger who accompanied Poor Johannes stepped forward, promising that all would be put to rights. As the puppet man looked doubtfully on, the worldly traveler removed from his knapsack the very same jar of ointment that had cured the old wood-collector's broken leg. Yet rather than concentrating the mysterious unguent's application upon the doll's headless neck, he rubbed it high up beneath its skirts in the same location he had the old woman.

Like magic, the puppet-queen came to life. Her dissevered head knitted itself back onto the splintered shards of her neck, leaving behind not a mark to indicate it had ever been separated. Fully restored to its rightful place, the doll's tiara-crowned head rolled recklessly about as she kicked her wooden legs and pumped her wooden arms—and all without the slightest pull upon her strings. The puppetmaster was absolutely delighted, for no longer did he need to orchestrate the movements of the queen doll at all; she could move about entirely on her own and, indeed, with a will of her own.

Later, after everyone at the inn had retired for the night, a lamentable sighing could be heard in the taproom. It carried on for so long that it roused the sleepers from their beds. Concerned that the bulldog might have returned, the puppet man sought out his little theater, since it was here whence the sighing seemed to originate. Yet what he discovered would have made him question the rightness of his mind had not the two travelers also borne witness. Scattered every which way across the stage were the puppets, their wooden limbs intertwined like a heap of kindling. The king and his courtiers along with the queen's ladies-in-waiting had been reduced to a jumble of confusion. It was *they* who sighed so piteously, their glass eyes staring entreatingly at those who had come to investigate. For like their queen, they, too, wished to be rubbed with the magical ointment.

At the sight of such terrible anguish upon the prettily painted faces of his wooden friends, the puppet man could only stand there weeping and promising to give the stranger with the knapsack his entire takings for the month if he would anoint his cherished dolls with the miracle-producing salve. But the prospect of money did not interest Poor Johannes's traveling companion, who instead proposed to the puppet troupe's tearful orchestrater that he relinquish his sword, which glittered sharply at his side. By now the plaintive wailings of the king and his subordinates had grown so grievous that the puppetmaster would have been willing to pay *any* price to put an end to it. Hence a bargain was struck and the jar of ointment brought forth.

No sooner did the traveler unbutton the dolls' breeches and lift their skirts to apply the embrocation than a celebration erupted. After much flapping of arms and kicking of legs, the male puppets hopped up onto their wooden feet to dance with the flesh-and-blood ladies who had gathered in the taproom, the female puppets taking a turn with the flesh-and-blood gentlemen. In all the excitement, Johannes's worldly friend had not been given an opportunity to refasten the courtiers' breeches, thus their pink appurtenances normally kept concealed bounced wildly and discourteously about, severely stiffened by their curative rubbing. The ladies-in-waiting danced with their human partners, demonstrating equal if not greater abandon, their skirts swirling higher and higher up their wooden thighs and revealing smaller and daintier versions of this appurtenance. As for the puppet king, his majestic representation rose out from his braided breeches, only to be attended by the rouged mouth of a comely barmaid, as would the queen's rosier counterpart. It proved to be a merry eve for all.

The next morning, Poor Johannes and his traveling companion resumed their journey. Together they ascended through fragrant stands of pine and juniper until they could ascend no more. To the far side of the summit, a new world lay before them, offering mile after mile of exciting adventures to the two trekkers. A city with many towers of crystal shimmered in the distance, and from its center arose the turrets of a magnificent castle. It was in this direction that the travelers would go, although not without stopping once again for rest and refreshment.

As with most inns, the proprietor was of a mind to bend the ears of strangers, which is how it came to pass that Johannes and his friend learned that the monarch whose castle they had espied from afar had a daughter—a young woman with a most blood-thirsty reputation. Through her calculated wickedness, many men had lost their lives, for, whether prince or pauper, Princess Hannibella—for so she was called—invited all and sundry to woo her. If the prospective suitor could provide the answers to three riddles the Princess put forth, she would condescend to marry him. If he guessed wrong, she promised to dispatch the failed candidate to the executioner's ax, if not perform the deed herself.

The monarch had long ago removed himself from his daughter's personal affairs, therefore he could do little to halt this slaughter of innocent men. Despite having been warned beforehand of their possible fate, none shied away from the challenge of the three riddles that might win the bloodstained hand of Princess Hannibella. However, all who made an attempt had failed, and over the years many heads had been collected by the murderous Princess, several of which still retained the scream of death upon their shrunken lips. As the innkeeper relayed with undisguised relish this gruesome tale to his audience, Johannes found himself bristling in affronted anger. Did the fellow take him for a fool? For such an outrageous yarn could not possibly be true.

The innkeeper was interrupted by an exaggerated roar of adulation coming from outside the walls of the inn. The two travelers followed the other patrons into the road, curious to learn the reason for the clamor. An open-topped carriage of hammered gold rolled slowly past the swelling crowd, the team of horses drawing it as black and sinister as the river Styx. Seated high upon a velvet banquette was the daughter of the monarch, who acknowledged her subjects with a menacing wave. The overhead sun turned the rubies in Princess Hannibella's crown into fiery sparks, their reflections making it look as if her hair had been formed from the flames of Hell. The mantle cloaking her fine figure had been sewn from the flesh of her victims and remained open in the front, exposing the steel breastplate she wore as protection when she went out in public. Hanging from one slender wrist was a small pouch made from the scrotum of her most recent suitor—the innkeeper's brother-in-law. It was rumored to contain her cache of riddles.

The commotion drew Poor Johannes to the dusty edge of the road, where he felt his heart softening to jelly inside his chest. Surely this breathtaking creature could not be the bloodthirsty Princess of whom the garrulous innkeeper had spoken. "I, too, shall endeavor to answer Princess Hannibella's riddles," he vowed. "For I am desperately in love!" Of course everyone tried to dissuade him, including his older and wiser companion, who genuinely feared for the innocent orphan's life. Alas, Johannes's smitten ears chose to deafen themselves to these well-intentioned warnings. Making himself as presentable as his humble parcel of possessions would allow, he set eagerly off for the city of crystal towers and the castle at its center, heedless of the town crier's pronouncement of "Princess Hannibella strikes again!"

Known for his equitable nature, the monarch received the young traveler most cordially. But when he realized that upon his doorstep had arrived a new aspirant for his daughter's murderous hand, he commenced to weep in a most unregal manner. Indeed, here was yet another head to be added to his offspring's grisly collection. To think how many lives might have been spared if only he had never agreed to adopt her!

The monarch begged Poor Johannes to reconsider, even going so far as to escort him into the private gardens of Hannibella in hopes that this might dampen the orphan's youthful spirits. For suspended from the branch of every tree was the head of a former admirer, many of whom had been handsome princes from neighboring kingdoms. Flowers and vines sprouted haphazardly from the graying skulls of those that had been dangling for some time in the garden, twisting and twining sinuously outward from the vacant sockets — sockets that once held eyes that had gazed in adoration upon Princess Hannibella. "Do you not see what will become of you?" bemoaned the monarch, who strongly suspected that his adopted daughter had not been entirely ethical in her dealings.

However, Poor Johannes had a plan.

Upon being informed that she had a gentleman caller, Hannibella came out into the courtyard, whereupon the fatherless son knelt to the ground in a respectful bow, his love for her now greater than ever — especially when she presented her foot to receive a kiss from his worshipful lips. The Princess entertained her guest in the drawing room, where he was plied with sweetmeats and petit fours before being presented with the challenge of his first riddle, the answer to which Hannibella claimed to have written down on a slip of paper beforehand. Although as hopelessly in love as one of only so vernal an age could be, Johannes knew his limitations when it came to matters of the intellect. Therefore he had taken the precaution of borrowing from his traveling companion's burlap knapsack the jar of magic ointment.

By the time Hannibella had put forth her first riddle, Poor Johannes had already scooped up a generous portion of the salve in his fingers and, when her attention momentarily lay elsewhere, slipped them high beneath her skirts, rubbing in the approximate vicinity he believed his worldly friend had done with the old woman and the troupe of wooden puppets. To his surprise, his fingertips alighted upon something warm and wiggly that stood straight up like the fin of a fish. It seemed to grow warmer and more voluminous with his ministrations, turning increasingly pliable as he worked. The fin-like object felt quite pleasing to the touch, and Johannes found himself rubbing it with substantially more vigor than he had witnessed being demonstrated by the keeper of the miracle-producing unguent.

As expected, Princess Hannibella kicked her legs recklessly about and flapped her arms like those of a crazed bird, prompting a sigh of relief from Poor Johannes. Why, in her state *any* answer he proposed would be the right one! It was then arranged for the resourceful orphan to return the following morning, at which time he would submit his final answer and learn whether he might be allowed to keep his head for another day—or at least until the time came to solve the Princess's second riddle. For neither prince nor pauper had as yet managed to draw a breath beyond the first.

Now it just so happened that Poor Johannes's traveling companion was very concerned about the fate of his young friend. Not wishing to place faith in the fickle hands of Providence, the worldly-wise traveler decided to take matters into his own capable hands. Wishing to do good where it could best be done, he departed shortly after supper for the castle, determined to intervene before Johannes was obliged to take permanent leave of his foolish head. To make certain he would not be followed, he had plied the lovesick orphan with enough drink to keep him in blissful slumber until the arrival of daybreak.

It was an unseasonably warm night, and the traveler had no difficulty in locating an open window, in fact, several open windows, one of which belonged to Hannibella herself, for he saw her restless figure hovering before it. He waited for the great clock in the city center to chime midnight, at which time he planned to enter her bedchamber and exert whatever influence he could on the Princess. But before the bell managed to alert him of the hour, the room's lethal occupant had already departed through the window.

Johannes's traveling companion blended himself into the shadows, waiting until Hannibella had gotten clear of him, only to set off after her in stealthy pursuit. He did not need to keep too closely on her heels, as the white cape she wore billowed around her like a ship's sail against a sea of indigo sky. For nearly an hour they walked toward the mountains, together yet separate, until at last they could go no farther— whereupon the Princess strode purposefully up to a boulder set into the mountainside and rapped against its adamantine surface as one might a door. All at once a terrible rumbling could be heard. When it sounded as if the earth itself would open up to swallow them both, the boulder swung inward, the hermetically sealed interior of the mountain releasing a puff of fetid breath into the air.

Just beyond this blackly gaping mouth lay a deep cavern. Its corrugated walls glistened wetly in the moonlight, the moisture forming tiny blue icicles. Having already come this far, the traveler decided to follow Princess Hannibella into the stygian bowels of the mountain. An unwholesome smell irritated his nostrils, worsening with each footfall. He stifled a sneeze, puzzled that the bothersome effluvium seemed to have no effect upon his quarry's highborn nostrils. Its origin would soon become known, for at the end of the cavern awaited a troll. A swarm of fat flies buzzed happily about his stunted person, drawn to what had so thoroughly repelled his clandestine observer. Hannibella placed her foot forward, allowing the unsightly creature's withered purple lips to kiss it. Poor Johannes's traveling companion pressed close to the jagged wall, resolved to learn the reason for the Princess's visit and praying he would not be discovered in the process.

"I am in need of a second riddle," declared Hannibella. "For I have a new suitor who appears quite resourceful and may have already guessed the first."

The troll nodded sagely, his stench growing stronger within the airless confines of the cavern until the traveler found himself choking on it. "This new suitor...does he come to thee generously equipped?"

"Oh, Poppa, what does it matter, since I only wish to kill him anyway?"

"In that case, thou must choose something so simple it would never occur to him," advised the troll in a voice as thick and rattling as rancid curd. "Then the Princess shall gain for herself another handsome head for her fine collection. And prithee, Daughter dearest, do not forget to bring me his manhood so that

I may fry it up in butter with some fava beans and wash it down with a nice Chianti."

The traveler's head ached from all he had seen and heard, the noxious interchange leaving him greatly confused as to why the daughter of the monarch should have addressed the troll as if *he* were her father. Returning unobserved with her to the castle, he again stationed himself outside Hannibella's open window until enough time had passed for her to get into bed for what little remained of the night. Hearing the silence for which he had been waiting, Johannes's traveling companion entered the Princess's bedchamber to find her exactly as expected—sound asleep in her bed. She appeared to possess not a care in the world as she lay upon the embroidered coverlet, her breathing steady and without the inflections indicative of a troubled sleep. The first thing he noticed were her feet, the elegantly arched soles of which glowed pinkly and innocently in the moonlight. The finely woven lawn of her nightdress had ridden up to her waist, exposing a pair of graceful thighs and the corresponding hills above. Trembling with indignation and perhaps something more, he drew back his arm in heartfelt readiness as he intended to seek redress for the obliquity intended Poor Johannes.

Indeed, the peacefully slumbering form positioned with such indecorous abandon upon the bed ignited a raging conflagration within its beholder's soul, hence the worldly-wise traveler wielded his hand with enthusiasm, spurred onward by the milky mounds before him and the fiery red splotches his actions imprinted upon them. The prone recipient cried out with every resounding smack of his palm, her legs kicking every which way, her arms flailing uselessly at her sides. It might even be believed that she welcomed them, for she raised herself up to meet each strike, falling back down again with a sated sigh.

Poor Johannes's traveling companion slept soundly that night, as did Princess Hannibella, who dreamed she had melted into a warm puddle. That morning as Johannes shook off his drink-enhanced slumber, his friend greeted him with unusual tenderness, for, thanks to him, the lovesick orphan would live to see the dawning of another day. After enjoying a tasty meal of sausage, eggs, and black bread served courtesy of the innkeeper's wife, it came time for the Princess's latest suitor to depart for the castle. The itinerant stranger saw his trusting ward off at the door, confident that his less-than-tender ministrations of the wee hours should have persuaded the Princess to exercise far more liberality when weighing the answer to her first riddle.

Johannes found himself being ushered into the grand salon, where a team of judges awaited him, along with the teary-eyed monarch himself, who, in anticipation of the unsuspecting orphan's fate, sniveled through many a kerchief. The moment Hannibella entered the room, this petitioner for her hand felt his heart soaring with love. The Princess's cheeks had taken on a fine rosy glow—a glow similar to that which heated the cheeks she now struggled to sit upon. She extended her foot for its reverential kiss, her manner all sweetness and benevolence. Yet for Poor Johannes this was to be no mere social call.

As the monarch wept into his kerchief and the judges mopped their sopping brows, Johannes took a fortifying breath. Ascertaining that he had gained the Princess's full attention, he placed a fingertip against his right earlobe and wiggled it about in suggestion of his earlier ministrations with the salve upon the little fin he had located beneath her skirts. Hannibella's eyes widened in acknowledgment, and she bit the pink plump of her lower lip in remembered ecstasy, the slip of paper containing the riddle's solution tucked inside her perspiring palm dropping to the carpet in a wet ball. Only then did Poor Johannes put forth his answer.

The Princess (who had gone quite red in the face) nodded helplessly at the judges, whereupon the monarch burst into cheers of joy. For the sparing of a life, however momentary, was a thing to celebrate. Johannes next received a command to join Hannibella in the drawing room so that he might be presented with her second riddle. Once again he had taken the precaution of bringing along his traveling companion's jar of magic ointment, and once again the words had barely left Princess Hannibella's lips before he had his fingers high up in her skirts rubbing the now-familiar fin they met there. It grew bigger than ever beneath his fingertips, and the fatherless orphan soon found himself working the whole of his arm up to the shoulder joint.

That evening the worldly stranger did not need to ply his young friend with spirits, for the day's exertions had sent Poor Johannes to bed very early, and his exhausted snores could be heard all the way to the inn's front door. The traveler sallied forth to the city with greater haste than ever, determined to reach the Princess before she sought out the venomous troll for a more foolproof conundrum to have ready as insurance in the event her latest attempt to stump her suitor also met with failure. Since it was to be her second riddle for which the fatherless orphan would be risking his silly head, Johannes's traveling companion thought it might be of benefit to put into practice *two* hands instead of just the one.

Hannibella had taken to her bed for a much-needed respite after her encounter with her suitor, only to discover that there would be no respite as her midnight caller brought his palms savagely down upon the symmetrical swells of her nether cheeks in a steady *one-two* motion, refusing to let up until the strength had ebbed from his arms. Fortunately, the clock in the city center quickly rejuvenated him, and the traveler matched each strike of the midnight hour with a strike of his own, the twin mounds of milky flesh launching themselves high into the air, flushing redder and redder with every persuasive blow. It would not be until the predawn hours that the resonant smack of palm against flesh had finally been silenced. Indeed, Princess Hannibella's feet would do much kicking about on this night.

The following morning, with a carefree bounce in his step that left heads shaking in disbelief, Poor Johannes set off on the road to the castle, where he was once more ushered into the grand salon to hear his fate. Having been briefed by his worldly friend beforehand, he offered up an answer of ridiculous obviousness—albeit not without first securing the Princess's attention by twiddling the lobe of his ear with a readily available fingertip. Hannibella's sharp intake of breath sliced through the stillness of the room like a scream. A crumpled slip of paper rolled from her hand onto the floor. Had those present bothered to unfold it, they would have discovered it to be blank. Twice thwarted in her acquisition of a new head for her garden, she nodded in flushed affirmation toward the anxious team of judges, thereby gaining for Johannes another reprieve.

The sight of the orphan's brazen finger manipulating the dangling lobe of flesh had caused the Princess to grow quite faint, and she bade Poor Johannes to lead her to a settee so that she might rest. It was from here that she posed her third and final riddle, her palm-tenderized nether regions too ill-humored to allow her to even sit up properly. How could it be that she was suddenly helpless to thwart the young man who sought her hand? Finding herself without the foul counsel of her blood-father the troll, Hannibella did the best she could, calling upon the resources of her own mind. "What is it I am thinking of at this moment?" she inquired languidly, not entirely certain of the answer herself, but comforted by its conveniently transitory nature.

However, Johannes's salve-anointed fingers were already journeying high beneath her skirts, rubbing and kneading the voluminous fin they had come to know so well—a fin so fiery hot that it singed his enterprising fingertips. Princess Hannibella's legs were flung every which way upon the settee, offering no resistance and, in fact, making her suitor's ministrations all the easier to perform. It was not long before her arms flapped like broken wings at her sides and her feet kicked the air. Despite his success, Johannes refused to desist from his labors for a moment. If his response to her third and final riddle was deemed correct, not only would he live to see another day, he would also receive the Princess's hand in marriage. With so much at stake, he massaged more and more of the magical ointment beneath her skirts, not stopping until he had emptied out the jar.

Just before midnight, Poor Johannes's traveling companion paid a final call to the Princess's bedchamber, knowing that the morning would determine whether his young friend should live or die. Although a storm appeared to be brewing in the east, he was not the sort to allow a few raindrops to deter him. He discovered Hannibella cloaked only in nature's garb as she lay face down upon her bed, so depleted of strength she could not even summon a maid to assist her into a nightdress. These circumstances would suit the traveler well. Rubbing his hands together to warm them for the task ahead, he raised them high into the air, hesitating briefly and with unexpected relish before bringing them down against the twin hills before him, the sharp crack of thunder creating an alliance with the sharp crack his palms made upon contact. A flash of blue-white lightning illuminated his target, revealing a veritable chaos of reddening splotches and inspiring their wrathful administrator to add several more in a stormy crescendo of blows.

Hannibella gasped for breath, pushing herself up from the embroidered coverlet so that she might meet these cruel kisses, their stinging burn reactivating the burn induced by her suitor's earlier application of ointment. The pink bottoms of her feet flew about in maddened circles, and her fists pummeled the pillows until she eventually lost consciousness, only to be revived by still more priming from her intruder's able palms. For Johannes's peripatetic companion had no intention of allowing the Princess's writhing body a reprieve until he was certain he had earned one for his friend.

That sunrise before Poor Johannes departed for the castle for the very last time, the owner of the jar of magic ointment presented the orphan with explicit instructions that he should clap his hands sharply together when the moment came to provide an answer to Princess Hannibella's third riddle. Indeed, the palms of his own were cracked and peeling, indicating they had been given good usage. Not understanding the significance of this piece of advice, yet not wishing to appear ungrateful, Johannes nodded his humble thanks, suddenly experiencing a terrible sense of guilt over having borrowed without permission the special salve — the empty jar of which was still contained in the pocket of his coat. Perhaps, if all went well with the Princess, he might make amends to his itinerant friend by having his future father-in-law offer him a knighthood, particularly since the traveler had already managed to procure his own fine sword.

As Poor Johannes approached the castle, he noticed a delivery coach double-parked outside with two men unloading a coffin. Before he could inquire as to who in the monarch's household had passed away, he was escorted into the grand salon, where the tearful monarch sat hunched forward in misery upon his throne, his unregal trembles visible to all. The covey of judges chewed their quills in dreaded expectation, their stern faces creased with more worry than usual. The deliverymen Johannes had seen earlier arrived and just as swiftly departed, having placed the empty coffin discreetly in a corner. After several strained minutes, Princess Hannibella made her entrance, her face the white of chalk, her eyes ringed by dark circles. With considerable effort, she lowered herself onto the settee, wincing when contact had been made. "Pray, persistent Sir, what have I been thinking of since you last came before me?" she inquired of Poor Johannes, her voice so enfeebled that all had to strain to hear it.

As the judges and the monarch looked in hopeful eagerness toward him, rather than answering with words, Johannes brought his palms sharply together as instructed by his worldly friend. For additional insurance, he also tweaked both earlobes between thumb and forefinger until they had turned bright red with blood. At the sight, Hannibella fainted dead away—although not without first flapping and flailing her arms and legs in the frenzied manner so familiar to the one whose actions had incited it. This time, the Princess's hand was conspicuously empty of any slips of paper.

The chorus of *hurrahs!* from the grand salon could be heard as far away as the inn, where, in an upstairs room, Johannes's traveling companion smiled with heartfelt pleasure, taking pride in the role he had played—a role that would allow the fatherless orphan to keep his head. With the wedding celebration at the castle already underway, he sallied forth toward new adventures, the burlap of his knapsack slightly lighter upon his shoulder with the absence of his jar of ointment.

It never occurred to the Princess's victorious suitor that without the oleaginous contents of the jar and the traveler's secret midnight spankings, the marital bliss he had hoped to enjoy with his new wife would be severely limited. Indeed, Hannibella found herself greatly disappointed with the quality of her husband's insipid fumblings beneath her skirts, to say nothing of his lack of imagination regarding the appropriate application of the palm. What Johannes did not seem to realize was that he had won the Princess under false pretenses.

Sadly, all that effort put forth by his well-meaning traveling companion would come to naught, since in the end Hannibella beheaded Poor Johannes anyway. ❧

THE TURNIP

Tales that contain as their main protagonists a pair of brothers have always featured prominently in folk literature and narrative. Although tales of brothers can be found in nearly every European country, their earliest written form has been discovered in the papyruses and steles of ancient Egypt. Since folktales are generally considered to have arisen from the wishful thinking of the poor and the unsuccessful, perhaps it should not be surprising that one of the most commonly occurring themes is that of the poor and virtuous brother happening on sudden riches, thus allowing him to gain parity with his wealthy, but less virtuous, brother.

A widely known example of the rich brother/poor brother tale is "The Turnip" by the Brothers Grimm. Unlike many of the stories they collected over their lifetimes, the Grimms' "Die Rübe" may genuinely stem from the true German folktale tradition—one characteristic of which is the concept of a man of little or no means achieving equal footing with his financial betters by rising in social class as a result of his industriousness. Given the prevailing social order of the day, one often sees this emphasis being placed on an individual's industriousness, an industriousness that in turn was tied to the agrarian pursuits of the peasantry. For the basic structure of most folktales appears to stem from the social situation of the agrarian lower classes.

Although "The Turnip" clearly corresponds to the German tradition, the Grimms rarely provided the names or dates of their sources, therefore the origins of many of their tales have been difficult to trace. No doubt the reason for this lack of disclosure relates to the fact that the majority (if not all) of their sources were family members and friends of literate middle-class backgrounds rather than the peasant narrators from whom the brothers claimed to have collected their tales. Furthermore, since the Grimms apparently saw fit to destroy the manuscripts that had been used for the first edition of their *Kinder- und Hausmärchen*, it has proven impossible to confirm that the original source material for the text of their stories received accurate treatment. It is believed, however, that substantial discrepancies do exist, and that these discrepancies flourished with each subsequent edition of the *Kinder- und Hausmärchen* as the Grimms continued to stylistically revise and edit their tales up until the seventh and final edition. Hence we may never know the true origins of tales like "The Turnip," let alone know whether such tales are, in fact, German.

As one of the few fairy tales containing no female characters, "The Turnip" demonstrates that the feminine presence is not always necessary to make a successful story. The feminine presence is surely not needed in *my* version...or at least, not needed by the bachelor king. ❧

The Turnip

I N DAYS OF YORE WHEN GREAT WARS WERE
fought in exotic lands over exotic bounties, there
was never a shortage of men willing to take up
the lance and shield. Those of a clever nature pros-
pered from their situations, leaving others of simpler
character to perish. During one of these conflicts, there
were two brothers who happened to serve honorably
as soldiers in the same bloody battle. Upon the final
laying down of armaments, one emerged a rich man,
the other poor. To free himself from the weighty
shackles of poverty, the less fortunate of this fraternal
pair decided to take up the plow, for the agrarian life
seemed a logical way to feed himself, not to mention
profit from the feeding of others. The fellow managed
to purchase a small piece of land, which he sowed
throughout with turnip seed. It so happened that
turnips had become very popular in the kingdom and
were served at the King's supper table every night.
Therefore, the decision in favor of the turnip would be
an easy one.

Farming was hard and, indeed, hungry work,
and the aspiring farmer liked to chew a few of the
seeds as he hoed and sowed, since many an hour

remained before he could sit down to partake of his own supper. Despite the many hardships he endured, the impoverished brother believed that all his long hours of sweat and toil would one day prove worthwhile. And his dedication to the soil served him well. As the seed took hold, turnip leaves began to display themselves in abundance along his modest parcel, their thick roots burrowing happily downward into the dark rich earth. Only the farmer would have far more success than he had originally bargained for. There was one turnip in particular that grew and grew until it looked as if it would never stop growing. Although this should have provoked great joy in the poorer of the two brothers, it instead provoked great dismay. For this most vigorous of vegetables did not sprout from the ground as had its leafy companions, but from the farmer himself.

Indeed, it surged aggressively forth from beneath the pale paunch of his belly, its stout base surrounded by a dense cluster of leaves that shaded the equally pale flesh of his thighs. The turnip would become so heavy that this devoted tiller of the soil eventually found it difficult to walk, let alone hoe his plantings or climb a ladder or perform any of the normal tasks of daily life. Each time he sat down for a meal, it bumped the underside of the table, upsetting the weathered rectangle of pine along with everything that had been placed upon it. It got so that the farmer had to slide his chair so far back that he could barely reach his plate. Soon the wearing of trousers became an impossibility. He would be forced to either cut away the buttoned flaps at the front or go about trouserless, the latter option proving most distressing whenever a chill wind blew.

Perhaps the poor brother should not have eaten so many turnip seeds. For what other reason could there have been for this curious phenomenon? The root that sprang out from his overburdened groin eventually grew to be so enormous and cumbersome that, to simply move about on his land, the farmer had to place it atop a cart, which would then be drawn by two strong oxen. Even a trip into the village necessitated a harnessing of the beasts, a fact that probably explained his ever-increasing reluctance to undertake the short journey. The aggrieved fellow did not enjoy being a public spectacle and enduring the titters of tot and parent alike. Yet as the days passed and the size of his leafy burden increased, he began to wonder whether such a seeming misfortune could possibly be turned into an advantage. Although the farmer could likely sell the vegetable at market for a tidy sum, the prospect of making a gift of it to the King held more appeal, for His Majesty's fondness for turnips was well known. Why, there could be no telling the rewards he might reap from so reverential a gesture!

So it was that early one morning the turnip farmer harnessed up the pair of exhausted oxen. After carefully situating his weighty impediment inside the wooden confines of the wobbly cart, they set creakily off for the palace. Doubtful as to whether he would even be granted an audience with the King—for indeed, he was only a humble man of the soil—he traveled with greater haste than might have been advisable under the circumstances, overturning the cart and its clumsy cargo several times along the way, to say nothing of causing considerable anxiety to the two oxen. To the farmer's surprise and delight, the King agreed to receive him immediately, having been informed by his courtiers of the unusual nature of the call. Because the cart and its grunting beasts could not be allowed inside the palace, two of the brawniest courtiers were dispatched to assist the caller with his encumbrance.

"Many wondrous things have these eyes of ours borne witness to, but never such a monster as this!" squealed the King when the farmer and his turnip were presented to him. "How did this miracle come to pass?"

The farmer bowed his head reverently, not daring to meet the monarch's astonished eyes—which gleamed with a brightness rather in excess of the occasion. "It is as much a miracle to His Majesty as it is to me," he said deferentially in response.

With a nod, the King indicated for his nervous subject to carry on and the farmer took a deep breath in readiness to put forth his offer. "Unlike my elder brother, I am a poor soldier who has naught but a tiny plot of land upon which to make my meager living. Therefore I would be most honored if His Majesty would accept this turnip as a token of my humble obeisance."

"Indeed," replied the King, his moist, beef-colored lips quirking up in one corner. "Might we be allowed to touch it?"

"By all means!" effused the farmer, both flattered and embarrassed at the same time. "It is His Majesty's to do with as he wishes."

The King reached forward a be-ringed hand and traced with his fingertips the purple-tinged waxiness of the turnip's surface, shuddering violently as he did so. Beads of moisture had broken out upon his brow, and he mopped them irritably away with the monogrammed kerchief he kept tucked beneath the cuff of his doublet. "This is truly a most lusty specimen," he croaked, clearly overcome by a powerful emotion. The farmer flushed with pride and glanced modestly away toward the royal courtiers, all of whom stood silently by wearing knowing smirks upon their normally impassive faces. Suddenly the King grabbed hold of the proffered turnip, his great hands dwarfed by its massive bulk. He began to squeeze it all along its length, as if testing for quality. "We shall be most pleased to accept this fine gift as a token of your loyalty."

"His Majesty honors me," wept the grateful pauper, his breath inexplicably quickening at the touch of the King's fingers. At that moment he would have bent to kiss the monarch's feet in appreciation had not the impediment surging out from beneath his belly prevented him from doing so.

Arising from his throne, the King tapped the kneeling man's head with his staff. "Thou shalt be impoverished no more." And with that, he ordered his courtiers to arrange for his turnip-bearing subject to be moved into the palace posthaste.

The lowly farmer was given the fine suite of rooms adjoining the King's private apartments, since His Majesty had as yet no queen to inhabit them. As if such luxuries were not reward enough, he also had bestowed upon him large sums of gold as well as the most fertile of green pastures to do with as he pleased. However, the farmer no longer had any need for the tilling of soil or the sowing of seeds. Instead he sat back and watched as his fortune grew and grew in startling conjunction with the growth of the turnip attached to his body, until he discovered that he could no longer leave the sumptuous confines of his quarters. Many a time did he respectfully propose to the King that the turnip be removed, for, upon his initial offering of it, this had been the farmer's intent. He even used a gold coin to bribe one of the servants to bring him a knife from the palace kitchens so that he might get an advance start on what was certain to be an arduous task. Surely His Majesty should have preferred to have the great root at his full disposal, particularly since his interest in it seemed to center more on the corporeal than the culinary.

Indeed, the King's unnatural fixation with the turnip had begun to prove most embarrassing to the simple farmer, who was not at all accustomed to being in the intimate company of such important personages, to say nothing of being party to such curious pastimes as those His Majesty had devised. For whether morning, noon, or evening, the portly monarch insisted upon saddling his doughy posterior atop the turnip, where he commenced to canter up and down, accelerating his movements to a wild gallop, his shouts of "Go, horsy, go!" reverberating all through the palace and broadening the smirks of the royal courtiers. The poor farmer's scrawny thighs would nearly be pummeled flat beneath the weight of the King, so forcefully and with such enthusiasm did the gleeful sovereign hurl himself down upon his turnip-bearing subject. It would not be until the King had trumpeted his last "Ye-hah!" that he finally leapt off, only to amble unsteadily away from the florid-faced former soldier without so much as even a cursory nod of thanks.

The farmer's sudden and undesired position as court stallion further served to convince him that the moment had long since passed for him to remove the cumbersome growth from his body, for what had originally been intended as a gift had now become a curse. Yet no matter how tactfully he put forth the helpful suggestion that the turnip be harvested, His Majesty refused to hear of it. In fact, he went quite red in the face at the mere mention of any type of excision being performed, until the farmer, who dared not risk further offense, was forced to drop the matter.

News of the poor farmer who had been taken in by the King traveled far and wide, and the prosperous soldier eventually came to hear of his brother's good fortune, which by this time greatly outrivaled his own. He wondered how the gift of a simple root could stimulate such royal generosity. Why, if his pauper of a brother had been able to gain so much with so little, imagine what a wiser and wealthier man like he himself could do! Therefore he, too, set off for the palace, bringing along with him the shiniest of gold pieces and the swiftest and blackest of steeds with which to impress His Majesty, for he had heard that the mighty monarch had become quite the equestrian.

Although the King accepted these gifts with typical good grace, he replied that he had no item of great value or rarity to offer his generous subject in return. "*Nothing?*" choked the brother, certain he was being made an ass of.

Now this set His Majesty to thinking. "Hmm...perhaps there might be *one* small thing." The courtiers were then instructed to show the caller into an adjacent room.

As he waited for his reward, the soldier realized that he occupied the King's bedchamber. Never had he expected to receive such an honor. Indeed, his riches were trifling compared to the stately opulence he saw all around him. Oriental carpets of varying shapes and shades crisscrossed one another upon the gleaming wood of the floor, each more intricately woven than the next. Tapestries of extraordinary richness and beauty hung from the silk-upholstered walls, relaying tales of bloody battles fought by previous realms. A damask-covered settee fashioned from maple and inlaid with mother-of-pearl had been advantageously situated before a hearth within whose marble borders a fire popped and crackled with merriment, suffusing the soldier with a comforting warmth. Yet most spectacular of all was the place where His Majesty rested his head each night. For directly beneath a soberly executed painting of the mighty King himself was a large four-poster bed, its elaborately carved teakwood encrusted throughout with opals that reflected iridescent rainbows against a coverlet of red velvet.

And there upon this plush red counterpane lay the soldier's brother, naked and bleary-eyed with exhaustion, the enormous growth below his belly weighing him to one side. The heavy damask draperies at the window had been drawn back to welcome in the fine spring morning, and streaks of incoming sunlight cast the turnip in stark relief, showing the enormity of its size and the greasy yellow slickness coating its waxen flesh. A porcelain bowl of lard had been conveniently placed upon the bedside table; it was nearly empty.

Upon seeing the familiar face of his brother, the farmer tried to raise his hand up from the bed in greeting, but even this small effort was too taxing. The opportunistic soldier fled the palace in horror, leaving behind his gold and his horse — and leaving behind, his brother who, upon the death of the King some years hence, would find himself possessing more wealth and commanding more courtiers than he could possibly have use for. Nevertheless, no amount of wealth could free him from the burden he was forced to carry day after day, until at last he was allowed to experience the blissful release of death. ❦

THE
SLEEPING
BEAUTY

❦

"The Sleeping Beauty" can be found in various incarnations worldwide, making it almost as popular as "Cinderella." Although the names most linked to the story of the sleeping princess are Charles Perrault and the Brothers Grimm, the tale can be traced to medieval days, with its most essential elements possibly reaching back in history to tribal societies.

Like "Rapunzel," "The Sleeping Beauty" is considered a puberty tale, with the young princess also finding herself confined at the age of puberty—a confinement that in primitive cultures would often be imposed on a young girl at the onset of menstruation. Yet instead of having an awareness of her surroundings like her golden-haired counterpart in the tower did, the princess in "The Sleeping Beauty" undergoes a long sleep cast on her by mystical means—an element that may offer further proof of the tale's primeval origins, for the practice of sleep magic filled the folktales of tribal societies.

Undoubtedly the most major and, indeed, erotic fore-bear to "The Sleeping Beauty" can be found in Basile's "Sun, Moon, and Talia." Rather than the proper prince of later versions, an adulterous king comes upon the sleeping and virginal Talia. Unable to resist her, "...he felt his blood course hotly through his veins in contemplation of so many charms; and he lifted her in his arms, and carried her to a bed, whereon he gathered the first fruits of love...." Having been in a state of sleep, Talia knows nothing of what has transpired. This unawareness of the sex act likely stems from the influence of Christianity, prompting Basile to bestow on the sleeping female an immaculate conception of sorts, for Talia's ravishment results in the birth of twins whom she calls *Sun* and *Moon*. She finally awakens when one of her infants mistakenly suckles her finger, drawing out the fiber from the spindle on which she had pricked her finger. Returning for another pleasurable dalliance, the king comes upon Talia with their children. When his wife (an ogre) discovers the reason for his absences, she plots to gain possession of the twins so that she can have them cooked and inadvertently fed to her philandering husband.

However, long before Basile put ink onto paper, "The Sleeping Beauty" existed in the story of "Brynhild" from the *Volsunga Saga*. According to this Old Norse myth, Brynhild falls into an enchanted sleep after being pricked by a thorn, thus preserving her youth and beauty for the man brave enough to make his way through the flames surrounding the castle in which she lies asleep. Despite these parallels to "The Sleeping Beauty" structure, one can locate an even more obvious precursor to Basile in "Histoire de Troylus et de Zellandine" from the fourteenth-century French prose novel *Perceforest*. Here a prince takes unbridled sexual advantage of the sleeping princess Zellandine, on whom a curse has been laid and levied out by means of a distaff of flax. Having satisfied his desires, the prince abandons her, whereupon Zellandine later awakens to find herself with child.

Indeed, these copious references to the spinning of flax may have far greater significance to "The Sleeping Beauty" and its historical counterparts than its popular use as a vehicle for the levying of curses. In primitive societies, spinning was considered a sacred female initiation act. It became common practice in some countries for women to expose themselves to the flax and ask it to grow as high as their genitals, for in so doing, the flax would supposedly grow better. Hence spinning came to represent the essence of female life, with all its fertility and sexual implications. It may be that the princess's inadequacy at spinning was meant to signify her lack of sexual development—a deficiency that would be long gone by the time of her awakening.

As the French literary tale came into vogue, Charles Perrault would put forth his own version of the princess's story in "La Belle au Bois Dormant" (The sleeping beauty in the wood). Only this time the protagonist appears somewhat more animated than her predecessors, for "the princess awakened and looked at him [the prince] with fonder eyes than is really proper at first meeting...." Like her folktale ancestors, she, too, gives birth to two children, albeit with far more cognizance of how this phenomenon came about. Of course Perrault would have been all too aware of the inappropriateness of telling a story at the court of Versailles about a married king who sexually ravishes a sleeping maiden, only to leave her pregnant and alone. Instead he continues his story in Basile-like form, in which, on learning of her son's marriage, the prince's mother (an ogre) seeks out her grandchildren to eat them and afterward make a meal of her daughter-in-law.

No doubt the best-known and best-loved version of "The Sleeping Beauty" tale has to be "Dornröschen" (Brier Rose) by the Brothers Grimm. It is here that the princess finds herself charmingly awakened by the famous kiss. Absent of the cannibalistic characters from earlier versions, the brothers departed from their predecessors in other ways as well, excising the sexual content in the story. Yet let it not be said that "Dornröschen" has been rendered barren of the erotic, for the beauty of the princess so stirs the prince that he is inspired to kiss her—a kiss that up until the Grimms had not made an appearance. Perhaps this kiss might be representative of a young woman's sexual awakening, just as I have chosen to make it in my version in a conspicuously more complex form. ❧

270

THE SLEEPING BEAUTY

I N A CASTLE FRINGED BY A MEANDERING river of blue, there resided a King and Queen who spent their days with only the members of their court for company. It would be an arrangement that was not a result of their own choosing, for the couple yearned more than anything to have a child to brighten their empty eyes and fill the interminable hours of the passing years. Yet with each change of the season, no such child was forthcoming, and a cloud of sadness settled permanently over the castle and its occupants.

Word of the royal couple's barren status quickly spread, and an endless succession of wily opportunists came forth to offer their aid. There were those who hailed the reproductive properties of snake oil and others who swore by onion suppositories. Indeed, the poor Queen was nearly at her wit's end — as was her husband, who did not much care for the odor of onions wafting from his wife's womanly parts.

On one unusually warm winter's morn, the Queen went down to bathe in the river that burbled past the castle. Afterward, while she sat drying herself in the sun, a frog of the brightest and most iridescent green hopped up onto the stony bank beside her. Her initial impulse was to shoo the slimy little creature away lest it be of a mind to wipe its muddy feet upon her queenly flesh. Moreover, its raucous croaking had begun to annoy her, as did the stink of spirits on its amphibious breath. But what transpired next would stay the Queen's hand as the nonsensical sounds emanating from the frog's ballooning throat abruptly took on the form of words. "Despair no longer, my good Queen," croaked the web-footed interloper. "Before the year is through, a daughter shall spring forth from thine imperial loins."

"Pray, tell me what I must do to make this so!" the Queen implored, ready to embark upon any means necessary to increase her fertility. Although repeatedly chastised by her husband for being gullible, she found that it made perfect sense that if the frog possessed the ability of speech, it was just as probable it possessed other preternatural abilities as well.

"A night with Her Highness is all I ask," the frog stated with a telltale burp, its watery eyes bulging in appreciation of the rosy flesh left exposed both above and below the fluffy towel with which the royal bather attempted to cover her modesty.

This was not the answer the Queen had been hoping to hear. So far, she had washed in the blood of pregnant women, eaten afterbirths for breakfast, stood upon her head after performing her marital duty, and endured onions stuffed within her person. Granted, she might have been desperate for a child, nevertheless, she *did* have her limits. The mere thought of this slimy green creature huffing and puffing on top of her set her flesh to crawling. Bad enough to have to endure it from her husband, the King. "I think not, frog."

The frog shrugged its shiny shoulders, apparently nonplussed by the Queen's reaction. Over the years it had grown accustomed to these rebuffs, therefore it always made certain to have a backup plan in place. "I ask then for a simple reward. A mere pittance." And perhaps it *was* a pittance, for the frog requested that the royal household supply it with a lifetime's supply of spirits. According to the amphibian grapevine, the castle cellars were stocked full of fine port and brandies and even several kegs of ale, which should surely see the frog into its golden years. Seeing no alternative, the Queen agreed to the creature's terms, whereupon the frog disappeared with a gaseous splash into the sparkling blue river as quickly and unexpectedly as it had first appeared.

Being of a practical nature, the King refused to give credence to such a prophecy. As a result, it took quite a bit of convincing for him to relinquish the precious contents of his cellar to a frog, who, rather than coming in person, had dispatched a team of amphibious cohorts to the rear door of the castle to collect this special honorarium. His Highness watched solemnly as the bottles and kegs from his cellar vanished downriver upon a caravan of lily pads. Expecting nothing in return, the King himself was astonished when the frog's prophecy actually came to pass. For nine months later his wife gave birth to a baby girl so beautiful he wept with joy each time he looked upon her perfect, pink form.

To wish the infant well in her new life, the proud father ordered a feast to outrival all feasts, inviting friends and relations from near and far, along with the local wise women, whose presences were considered an absolute *must* upon such occasions. As one might have imagined, the guest list grew and grew until no more guests could be accommodated. Because the household had remaining to it only twelve place settings for what should have been thirteen wise women, this meant that one would need to be left out. In the single-mindedness of his joy, the King failed to anticipate that something so ostensibly minor would be interpreted as a major snub.

The festivities were celebrated with great lavishness, with food and drink aplenty and laughter and good cheer all around. When it came time for the wise women to present the child with their gifts, the first gave virtue, the second beauty, the third wealth, the fourth grace—and on it went until the infant girl had been given everything her parents could have wished for her. As the twelfth wise woman stepped up to the royal crib to offer her gift, a disturbance arose as the uninvited thirteenth elbowed her way inside the grand hall. She felt most vengeful on this day, having taken considerable offense at the absence of her name from the King and Queen's guest list. As number thirteen, she had experienced a lifetime of being the odd one out. Even at home, when her twelve colleagues paired off each night to their respective bedchambers to bill and coo beneath the bedcovers, she would be left on her own to entertain herself...and without so much as the comfort of a bed to do it in. Ergo this latest exclusion was the last straw.

Forgoing the respectful bow demanded of all those who came before the royal couple, the thirteenth wise woman marched directly up to the happily gurgling infant and put forth her gift, saying, "In her fifteenth year of life, the King and Queen's daughter shall prick her finger on a spindle and die." Whereupon she spun about on her heel and departed, leaving the guests gasping and clutching their throats in horror. Indeed, she was quite pleased with herself, having no fondness for the royals, let alone their pampered progeny.

The wise woman who had been interrupted hastened forward in a panic. Although she could not cancel out the curse that had just been wished upon the child, she might be able to alleviate some of its sting. It was also a matter of pride, since she had no affection for the thirteenth member of her group and would not have liked for the woman to get the last word. The twelve had grown weary of number thirteen's endless rantings and ravings about abolishing the monarchy and creating a state in which the producers possessed both political power and the means of producing and distributing goods. Why, if such a system actually came into being, where would that leave wise women like herself?

Touching the infant's forehead, the twelfth wise woman offered what she hoped would be a remedy. "The King and Queen's daughter shall *not* die, but shall fall into a deep sleep to last one and ninety-nine years." Not given to take the pronouncement of any wise woman lightly, the child's father issued a proclamation commanding that all spindles in the kingdom be destroyed forthwith, convinced that by doing so, he had outsmarted the vicious gate-crasher.

As the little Princess grew older, each gift that had been given her by the wise women befell her. She would be beautiful and kind, clever and virtuous, musical of voice and light of step. Yet as each of the twelve gifts came to pass, it was inevitable that so, too, should the thirteenth.

During their daughter's fifteenth year of life, the King and Queen found themselves called away on urgent court business. This would be the Princess's first occasion to be alone without the watchful eye of a parent upon her, and, having an enterprising nature, she planned to take full advantage of the situation. The custodial eye of her father had become stifling over the years, and it frustrated her that she had been prevented from participating in activities her young peers so freely enjoyed. Why, other princesses her age were already keeping company with handsome suitors, whereas she was still keeping company with dolls! Although her first thought was to invite a prince or two to the castle, the servants had been ordered not to let anyone pass through the gates, especially young men with a special gleam in their eye.

With no other form of amusement available, the bored Princess embarked upon an investigation of the majestic structure that had been her home since the moment of her birth and from which she was never allowed to leave. She entered every chamber and parlor and opened every door, as well as every lid and drawer. Not even the den of a dormouse could be kept from her. The Princess's explorations eventually led her to a crumbling old garret in a part of the castle that had long ago fallen into disuse. She ascended the narrow stone steps winding around the tower, each dusty footfall bringing her closer and closer to an arched door located at the top. The rusted iron of a key had already been set into the lock, inviting her inquiring fingers to give it a turn. And this she did, dispensing an expert clockwise flick. The door creaked open upon antiquated hinges, revealing a room of diminutive proportions. Inside, the hooded figure of a man dressed from head to toe in black sat before a distaff.

"I bid thee greetings!" hailed the Princess. "May one inquire as to the nature of thy labors? For it appears most interesting."

"I am spinning flax," replied the man without looking up.

Stepping closer the better to examine the apparatus, the Princess noted that the spindle had been placed conveniently in the spinner's lap. It was long and sturdily constructed, the topmost portion containing a tiny hole through which the finished threads came out. The man operated the device by moving his hands up and down in a brisk, steady motion. Since her arrival, he appeared to be applying himself to the task with greater vigor than before. Fascinated — for she had never observed anyone spinning — the Princess grabbed hold of the rapidly bobbing spindle and attempted to spin a thread herself. Yet no sooner had she touched it than she experienced a strange fluttering in her belly that made her go quite woozy. Within moments she collapsed onto a straw pallet that had been set beneath the soot-covered window, falling into the deep sleep foretold by the twelfth wise woman, who had apparently been successful in counteracting her colleague's lethal spell.

For rather than pricking her finger on a spindle and dying, the young Princess had fallen asleep by touching a prick.

Upon the King and Queen's return and their discovery of the events that had transpired in their absence, the wise woman who had spared their only child's life by altering her predecessor's spell was immediately summoned. Powerless to rouse the sleeping Princess, wise woman number twelve did the next-best thing. Ergo the very same state befell the parents as well — as it would the whole rest of the court, along with horse and hound alike. Even the flies spiraling about the kitchen became affixed to the walls in a buzzless slumber. The fire in the hearth gave one last sickly sputter as the pheasant roasting upon the spit stopped turning. The red-faced cook fell asleep over a mound of chopped parsley, his ravishment of the scullery maid not yet having reached its blissful conclusion. Beyond the thick stone walls of the castle the wind stopped blowing and the river ceased to flow, freezing into a gelatinous ribbon of blue. Not a leaf stirred in a tree. The twelfth wise woman had placed everyone and everything into a deep sleep so that when the Princess awakened in one hundred years' time, she would not find herself in a house of death.

Yet even in slumber the King's fervent protectiveness of his daughter continued unabated, for he had earlier arranged with the wise woman further warranties against harm's coming to the young Princess. A protective hedge of thorns began to encircle the castle, growing higher and thicker until every stone and turret vanished behind it. Not even the royal banner waving from the castle roof could be glimpsed. Indeed, the King would sleep a peaceful sleep, secure in the knowledge that no man could possibly succeed in getting through the deadly hedge — and thus getting to his precious daughter.

Over the years, amazing tales came to be heard in the surrounding countryside about a beautiful Princess who could not be awakened, such accounts inspiring many a passing prince with an ear tuned to the local chatter to fight his way through the hedge of thorns. Alas, such herculean efforts were generally to no avail. The moment anyone put a foot through the hedge, the prickly brambles came together, intertwining and interlacing around the struggling figure and holding it fast. Generations of promising young potentates suffered a miserable end in this lethal enclosure, which only made the story of the sleeping Princess travel farther and encourage still more adventurous sons of kings to meet the challenge of this thorny barricade.

As for the occasional few who managed to defy death by reaching the little garret room where the famous Princess lay in slumber, their successes went unreported and their fates remained a mystery. At the intrusion, the Princess would come briefly awake — for she had always been a troubled sleeper — only to discover her visitor seated at the distaff spinning flax. Indeed, she would be amazed at the variety of spindles to be had. Some were long, some short, some fat, some thin — yet each needed to be worked with a vigorous and relentless pumping of hands. Wishing to master the art of spinning, the accursed Princess seized hold of the bobbing spindle so that she might spin a thread herself...whereupon she fell back into a deep sleep all over again.

A number of births and deaths occurred before a prince from a very poor kingdom happened by. While stopping off at a tavern for a tankard of ale, he overheard an old peasant talking of the hedge of thorns and the castle, behind whose walls of stone a princess — or so it was said — had lain in sleep for nigh on a hundred years. The peasant had been told many stories by his grandfather about the sons of kings who had forfeited their lives battling to get through the deadly copse in their desire to locate the Princess, as well as stories of those who had disappeared in the process, their fleshly remains likely having been picked over by the castle's hungry ravens. "Perhaps I shall succeed in reaching the Princess, for I am not afraid," announced the visiting Prince, downing the last of his ale with youthful bravado.

Naturally, the old peasant sought hard to dissuade this naïve newcomer, who knew naught of the terrible dangers awaiting him at the castle. But no amount of pleading from the peasant or the other patrons had any impact upon the Prince, who hoped to achieve fame and fortune by becoming what he believed would be the first man alive to cast his eyes upon the legendary Princess's sleeping form. The descriptions of the daughter of the King and Queen had greatly piqued his interest, therefore he was most keen to be the one to finally awaken her. Undoubtedly her parents would be so grateful they would make him their son-in-law — a situation that should please his father, who made no secret of the fact that he regarded his son as little better than a ne'er-do-well more interested in chasing butterflies than accruing wealth for the kingdom.

All the while, the one hundred years' sleep the twelfth wise woman had conferred by amending the evil thirteenth's sentence of death was reaching an end. As the Prince approached the castle, rather than the cruel hedge of thorns he had been led to expect, he was greeted by a colorful myriad of blossoms. Like the thighs of a waiting lover, they parted willingly at his approach, granting him permission to pass through to the other side unharmed. Finding himself inside the hushed courtyard, he made his way toward a side entrance to the castle without the slightest mishap. It was all so easy that he could not understand what all the fuss was about, and he wondered how it could be that so many before him had failed in their attempts to reach the Princess.

The entrance the Prince had selected led him to the kitchen, where he came upon the stout figure of the cook, who had fallen forward with his head resting against the chopping table, the pile of parsley before him having dried to a dusty green powder. Beside him a scullery maid remained bent over with her skirts hiked up to her waist, her fingers clutching the feathers from the crumbling bones of a guinea fowl she had been in the midst of plucking. Continuing on into the grand hall of the castle, the

Prince next encountered the members of the court, along with the majestic presences of the King and Queen themselves, who slumped sidewise in dreamless dormancy upon their thrones, their chins crushed against their chests from the weight of their crowns. At their feet lay the royal hounds, their sleek forms curled into tight balls. Indeed, it certainly appeared that he had come to the right household.

After undertaking an exhaustive and fruitless search of the castle proper, the Prince next moved in what he believed to be the direction of the turret he had observed from outside, a process of elimination indicating that it would be here that the sleeping Princess could be located. His heart pounded with a sickening force as he climbed the winding steps, his footfalls muffled by the thick coat of dust blanketing the worn stone. The silence in the castle was so profound that the sound of his breath rang out like the clanging of church bells. The door of the little garret stood part of the way open, as it had for the past one hundred years, and the first thing the Prince saw was the abandoned distaff. Behind it upon a straw pallet lay the figure of a young woman. Her pale limbs were sprawled every which way as an incoming ray of sunlight from a small window illuminated her motionless form. He knew instantly that she had to be the daughter of the King and Queen.

Tresses of burnished copper formed a frame for the perfect ivory oval of the Princess's face, spilling across the sun-faded brocade of the pillow supporting her head. The delicate blue-tinged lids of her eyes remained tightly closed against the intruding shaft of light, making it appear as if she had just lain down for a nap. The scattering of dainty freckles adorning the bridge of her nose overflowed onto her cheeks, although they would not reach as far as her lips, the pale pink of which reminded the Prince of a blush not yet come to fruition, prompting an invisible glaive to pierce his heart and the region directly below his belly. A gown of a diaphanous silk draped the young Princess's sleeping form in elegant folds, the lustrous threads clinging to her curves so precisely that one might have thought a team of silkworms had spun the garment expressly for her. Two gentle hillocks rose outward from her torso, the serene rise and fall of her respiration causing the tender pink nibs at their peaks to etch graceful swirls into the garment.

With great care, the Prince lowered his weight onto the straw-filled pallet. Although awakening the Princess had been his original intent, he now desired for her sweet slumber to continue without interruption. Pinching the finely sewn hem of her gown between trembling fingertips, he slid it slowly and deliberately upward, his knuckles grazing the soft warm flesh his bold actions uncovered. It would not be a particularly lengthy journey, the garment having only been cut to knee length. It had likely been intended for use as a nightdress and was, as such, not a suitable item of attire to be worn in the company of others, especially young sons of financially strapped kings who rarely had the funds to enjoy the pleasantries of female companionship.

A pair of gracefully rounded thighs came into view, their pale ivory as smooth and polished as an Oriental carving. Concerned that she might awaken and discover him in a position of compromise — for he suspected that his furtive movements might be deemed inappropriate and possibly deserving of an affronted slap to the cheek — the Prince kept an attentive eye on the steady up-and-down movements of the Princess's chest, which had quickened ever so perceptively since his arrival. The translucent hem continued its steady ascent, offering to the incoming sunlight and the Prince's eager eyes the entirety of the sleeping figure's thighs as well as the discreet V located at their crest. All at once he cried out in delight as the pearly silk of the gown uncovered a little pink butterfly.

A pair of gossamer wings began to slowly unfold, as if readying themselves for flight. However, no such enterprise would be forthcoming, for it appeared that the fragile creature was being held back by two fuzz-covered pods, which had closed fast around its struggling body. Perhaps it had alighted upon this predatory plant and, like the many ill-fated sons of kings who had endeavored to break through the prickly hedge of thorns outside the castle, found itself hopelessly and helplessly trapped. Not wanting to cause damage to the delicate wings, the Prince placed his thumbs against the sericeous surfaces of each pod and pried them gently away from each other. To his surprise, they yielded quite easily, revealing an interior as smooth and pink as their faltering victim and unmarred by even a hint of fuzz. Once the Prince had gotten them separated as far as they could go, he noticed yet another reason for the creature's plight. Indeed, no wonder it could not fly, since the means that should have propelled it had been weighed down with moisture.

Like a worshipper in prayer, the Prince bowed his head in readiness to flick away with his tongue the beads of dew that had collected upon the fluttering instruments his thumbs held exposed. Although it might have been more efficient, he dared not risk using the sleeve of his doublet for fear of causing damage. Applying the benevolent tip of his tongue with caution, he dabbed it along the surface of each dew-speckled wing, accelerating his efforts by allowing it to slither up and down and from side to side, even attending to the sinewy niche whence the two gleaming appendages branched away from one another. Confident that they had been sufficiently dried, the Prince lifted his face from the divided pods, their downy fuzz tickling the moistened tip of his nose. To his astonishment, still more droplets had managed to form. Despite his lack of success, he did not feel at all presumed upon at having to expend additional effort. Granted, the Prince might have spent more time on his labors than necessary—a fact that would be made apparent once the butterfly began to struggle in earnest beneath his fiercely licking tongue.

The sleeping female figure lying upon the pallet trembled and twitched, her eyes swimming frantically from right to left beneath their sealed lids, the muscles of her throat constricting in silent entreaty. Slender fingers reached blindly out to claw the mattress, tearing out clusters of ancient straw. With a rapturous cry, the daughter of the King and Queen awakened. Her belly hurled itself upward, her hands coming down to grasp the back of the Prince's head and pressing his dew-bespattered face against the source of the heavenly sensation taking place in her loins. The Prince shouted out a warning, which became hopelessly muffled by the pods. When the Princess finally loosed her grip, he permitted himself to open his eyes, fully expecting to be met with Death. Instead, the tenuous wings beneath him stretched themselves wide, showing their relieved observer all the vibrancy of their true nature. Only this time there were more drops of dew upon them than ever before!

The Princess smiled drowsily up at her visitor, and their lips came together in a tender kiss, his own tasting of a sweetness she could not identify, but very much desired to savor. "Have you come here to spin flax?" she asked dreamily, for she could see that the

Prince's spindle was already standing straight up from his lap and had been spewing out threads by the bushel-full.

In the grand hall of the castle, the King and Queen arose from their lengthy slumber, as did the rest of the court, who glanced at each other in hazy confusion, as did the hounds, who wagged their tails and leapt about like fools. In the kitchen the flies resumed their hungry buzzing, for the wood in the hearth had once again sparked into flame and the pheasant upon the spit began to turn. The cook gaped in bewilderment at the fine green dust he had been chopping. Regaining his wits, he set about the business of locating some fresh sprigs of parsley and happily resumed his ravishment of the scullery maid, who lethargically plucked the last of the feathers from the withered remains of a guinea fowl.

Naturally, a good deal had changed in one hundred years, since not all who had risked the deadly hedge of thorns in hopes of awakening the sleeping Princess were entirely unsuccessful in their endeavors. Over time the household had gained many new occupants—men of every age, shape, and temperament. Some walked more slowly than others and were even quite stooped as they hobbled along upon walking sticks, leaving behind them a potent trail of flatus that set the royal hounds to howling. The King and Queen discovered that they had amassed a sizable collection of prospective sons-in-law over the years, many of whom were considerably older than themselves.

With her father's reluctant blessing, the Princess came to be joined together in marriage to the Prince, who by virtue of youth had been deemed the most suitable of the candidates. Indeed, from the moment he had placed his spindle in his lap and commenced to spin flax, the Princess's interest would be irrevocably piqued, for his was the most impressive of all the spindles she had seen. With a fine spindle such as this, perhaps she might finally master the art of spinning. Therefore she insisted upon taking over the task from her new husband, only to fall right back into yet another deep sleep, the duration of which no one could predict.

For rather than pricking her finger on a spindle and dying as originally foretold, the Princess would continue to fall asleep by touching a prick. ❧

Ͳhe Ͳwelve ϺonͲhs

The theme of reward and punishment can be seen in the folktales of many lands. One particular offshoot of this theme that has been put into standard usage is that of the kind girl and the unkind girl. As patriarchal beliefs and attitudes found a stronghold in Europe, it was only a natural progression for such beliefs and attitudes to find a stronghold in European folk literature as well. As a result, the kind and respectful girl and her rude and ungracious counterpart soon became prevalent in tales like "The Twelve Months."

It appears that the story of the twelve months and the two female characters who encounter them most likely originated in Mediterranean Europe. It is here that the tale appears to be the most typical and, as such, shares the same essential elements. However, many of these elements may have entered the tale from the savage cultures of prehistoric times. The twelve month-men and their miraculous ability to control the weather bears an obvious correlation to the legendary magicians and holy men of the past who were believed to possess the ability to suspend the laws of nature—a tradition that goes back to the shamans and professional magicians of primitive tribes in

Europe and Asia. The element of the club employed by the twelve brothers in "The Twelve Months" may also be related to this function via its application as a charm to bring on a change in weather. Talismanic charms were often used by primitive cultures and would continue to be used by peasant and aboriginal communities up until modern times.

As one of the earliest recognizable versions of "The Twelve Months," Giambattista Basile's tale "The Months" tells a rich man/poor man story of two brothers, Gianni and Lisi. Lisi (the poor brother) finds himself aided by the twelve months, whom he encounters in a tavern. Hence the adversarial relationship between the two protagonists was one based on economics rather than temperament or, indeed, sexual rivalry. Nevertheless, sex roles and attitudes would undergo great change since Basile's collection *Il Pentamerone*, so it should not be at all surprising that the two male siblings in his tale evolved into two siblings of the female variety—and, in the process, developed the exaggerated characteristics that the patriarchal society of nineteenth-century Europe imposed on them.

Perhaps no better example of this can be seen than in the version of "The Twelve Months" collected by the Brothers Grimm. In "The Three Little Men in the Wood" (also known as "Saint Joseph in the Wood"), a girl sent by her stepmother and stepsister into the forest on a series of impossible errands receives assistance from three men, whom she repays by performing chores and sharing with them her meager meal of bread. Seeing that the girl has accomplished the tasks allocated her, the stepsister insists on paying a visit to the three men—although, unlike her kinder sibling, she treats them with callous disregard, refusing to perform any of the chores requested of her. The stepmother next sends the girl to rinse yarn in a frozen river, where a king happens by and marries her. Hearing of the girl's incredible good fortune, both stepmother and stepsister ingratiate themselves at the king's palace, disposing of the new queen so that the stepsister can take her place. But the deed is soon discovered, whereupon mother and daughter are disposed of, with the queen returning to her rightful place. No doubt the Grimms found the punishment of the unkind sister to have particular appeal—just as the reward granted to the kind (and therefore *obedient* sister) would likewise have appeal. For, by their actions, the sisters served as stellar examples of what *was* and was *not* considered appropriate behavior for females.

Known as "the Slovak Grimm," nineteenth-century writer Pavol Dobsinsky composed his own equally patriarchal version of "The Twelve Months," a version conspicuously lacking the royal marriage and its subsequent production of an heir that his German contemporaries, the Grimms, included in their tale. It is the story of his Maruska from which I received my inspiration. For it only goes to prove that kindness (be it from man or woman) most definitely has its rewards. ❦

The Twelve Months

I N A RUSTING OLD TRAILER SET ALONG THE edge of a snowy moorland, there lived a woman and her two daughters. As the eldest and (in accordance with tradition) the first in line for a husband, Holena was the fruit of her mother's womb and, indeed, was very much like her in appearance and temperament. As for the junior of the siblings, Maruska was merely a stepdaughter and thus of little consequence. In fact, the mother could hardly bear to cast her eyes upon the latter, whose prettiness so outrivaled her own flesh and blood that even the sound of the girl's voice brought her pain. Had it not been for the conditions of her late husband's will, the woman would have sent her to a workhouse a long time ago.

Because of the absence of mirrors in the household, Maruska did not realize she was pretty — and it did not behoove the members of her family to tell her so. In her mind, she and her sister were the same, which only made all the more baffling the cross expression that fixed itself upon her stepmother's face each time the woman looked at her, or the bitter venom spat from her stepmother's tongue with her every word. Therefore Maruska did everything she could to please her displeased parent. She did the cooking and cleaning and washing and ironing; she mended and sewed and raked and hoed; she even looked after the scrawny goat that provided milk and cream for the tiny household and, if it ever gained some fat around its middle, might have provided the meat for a few stews. (Suspecting this, the goat rarely ate a morsel.) Meanwhile, Holena whiled away the hours dressing up in garments she never had occasion to wear and gossiping with anyone who had been unfortunate enough to have come to the trailer's front door.

As Maruska grew more pleasing with the passing of years, her stepsister grew less so, thereby necessitating much fawning over by the occupants of the little trailer. Concerned for her blood-child's well-being and marital prospects, the mother decided that it might be wise to get her nubile stepdaughter out of the house and, hence, away from the line of sight of any young man who might come courting, fearing it would be the lovely and sweet-natured Maruska with whom they would fall in love, not her precious Holena. So mother and daughter began to plot out a course of strategy on how best to rid themselves of this female thorn in their sides. *Permanently.*

One day, in the bleakness of a harsh January winter, Holena suddenly experienced the unprecedented urge to smell violets. "Sister, dear," she trilled with false affection, "go and fetch me some violets."

"*Violets?*" cried Maruska in disbelief. "Wherever shall I find violets growing in the snow?"

"You worthless good-for-nothing! How dare you speak to me in that manner!" screeched Holena, her unprepossessing face purpling with rage. "If you do not bring me what I ask for, I shall beat you till you are black and blue—and then I shall beat you some more!" To reinforce her daughter's words, the mother thrust the girl out into the bitter winter's morning, slamming the trailer's rickety screen door against her.

Shivering with the cold, Maruska stumbled through the unwelcoming moorland, knowing she dare not return until she had performed the impossible task demanded of her. The entire world had turned to white. All she could see for miles around was snow, with the leaden gray sky above threatening to spill still more of the icy stuff onto her uncloaked head. She had barely managed to trudge a short distance before her footsteps got covered over with an all-new layer of snow, obscuring the trail she had left and making her fear she had lost her way.

Just when she thought she would have to turn back to face her stepsister's wrath, Maruska glimpsed a reddish-yellow light in the endless landscape of white. Its friendly flickerings drew her toward it, leading her to the crest of a craggy hill—where she discovered a blazing campfire. A dozen rocks of varying heights had been positioned around it, and upon each one sat the stoic figure of a man. Three of them, all in a row, looked very old, possessing long white beards that reached nearly to their toes. The next three beside them looked slightly younger, and the next younger still, until Maruska's gaze finally came to rest upon the remaining three, who were by far the youngest and most agreeable to the eye, their smooth, handsome faces untenanted by whisker or wrinkle.

Unbeknownst to Maruska, the occupants of this cozy circle were the twelve months. With the arrival of each new month in the year's cycle, the men changed places, each moving over one space to an adjacent rock—and so on and so on as the months followed the course of a year. This being winter, January held court upon the tallest of the rocks, his hair and beard as fluffy and white as the snow covering the ground, making it difficult to determine where the fleece on his face ended and the earth itself began. In one gnarled hand he held a club, which rested at his side.

The sight of the twelve months gave Maruska a start. She was not accustomed to the company of gentlemen, especially so many at one time. The family's trailer rarely received guests of either gender, and on those infrequent occasions when a man *did* come to call with some lard or a slab of bacon to sell, she found herself locked inside her room for the duration of the visit. Even a toothless peddler might be considered marriageable material, and her stepmother did not wish to forfeit any opportunity to make a match for Holena. As the winter wind bit cruelly through the inadequate protection of Maruska's nightdress—for she had not been given time to don her coat and wore only the thin gown in which she had slept—the fire offered so much heat that she forgot her apprehension. "Please, kind sirs," she stammered, "may I be allowed to warm myself by your fire?"

Taking note of her pitiful state, January indicated for this waif-like figure to move toward the flames. "And what might a little thing like yourself be doing wandering about the moor in this foul weather?" he inquired. Indeed, a considerable amount of time had passed since he had enjoyed the company of anyone other than his eleven brothers.

"I am searching for violets," answered Maruska, only to realize how completely ridiculous such a prospect must have sounded.

"*Violets?* Surely you must have noticed that we are waist deep in winter snow."

"Yes, but if I dare to return home without them, my stepsister says she will beat me till I am black and blue!"

"I see..." mused January, his knotty fingers combing thoughtfully through the long white tendrils of his beard.

"*Beat* you?" cried another brother from several rocks down, his youthfully unlined eyes suddenly bright and feverish.

"There may be something I can do to assist you," offered January, directing an impatient glare toward the month who had interrupted. "Yet before I do, perhaps you will be so good as to prune this for me?" With a telltale dip of his fluffy-haired chin, he indicated his lap out from which the gnarled branch of a tree grew lopsidedly upward. "For my old joints pain me too greatly to perform the task myself."

"I would be pleased to assist you. But as you can see," Maruska held out her palms in dismay, "I have no implements with which to do so." Now for certain she would be made to return to the trailer and receive the terrible beating Holena had promised.

"Perhaps you might consider using your teeth," came the elderly brother's helpful suggestion.

With the details settled, Maruska knelt between this most senior of the twelve brothers' knees and set to work, only to find that it demanded far more effort than she had anticipated. The dense nest of white in January's lap offered her the most difficulty, although the pruning of the branch itself would not be too arduous a process — especially after she had mastered the technique of absorbing it into her mouth. Unfortunately, old January had much to complain about with regard to the sharpness of her teeth.

Nevertheless, such complaints did not deter the others. For the instant Maruska stood up to brush away the debris January had left upon her nightdress, yet another brother felt compelled to call upon her. "Prune *me!*" demanded February, pointing frantically toward his lap whence a similar limb surged resolutely forth, speckled and distorted with age and the ice of too many winters.

"I am in need of a pruning as well!" piped March with even more boisterousness.

"A pruning would be most beneficial," concurred April with a mischievous grin.

And on it went around the circle, with each of the months clamoring for Maruska's horticultural services. Twelve specimens of varying shapes and textures came to be offered to the violet-seeking girl, whose teeth would be rattling in her gums by the time she finished. The older months in particular seemed in need of the most care and attention, whereas their younger siblings sloughed off their deciduous residue quickly and with little necessity for additional attention. A gasping and wheezing December had not even gotten halfway through his own turn when January arose from his rock. "Brother March, come and take my place," he instructed, passing over his club.

Settling himself upon the tall rock vacated by his elder brother, March waved the conferred club over the fire. The flames rose higher and higher, growing so hot that the surrounding snow melted almost completely away. The exposed earth had sprouted tiny buds, forming a patchwork of green. Winter had turned to early spring and violets pushed upward from the craggy ground. "Make haste!" cried March, his voice unnaturally high with the strain of his deed.

Maruska plucked flower after flower from the viridian patches beneath her feet until she had amassed a collection of violets worthy of the most finicky and disagreeable of stepsisters. After thanking each of her new friends with an affectionate kiss to the cheek, she hurried happily home, nearly colliding head-on with a gypsy tinker who had made the mistake of calling in at the trailer to offer his knife-sharpening services.

Already annoyed at having yet another potential husband slip through her fingers, Holena was even more put out upon seeing Maruska and her lavish offerings. A scowl of dismay took root upon the faces of both daughter and mother as a beaming Maruska came prancing through the front door, the sweet perfume of violets overwhelming the cramped rooms of the trailer within seconds of her arrival. "Wherever did you manage to find them?" choked Holena, rubbing the fragrant petals between thumb and forefinger as if suspecting they might be fake.

"On the top of the moor. There are hundreds of them!" cried Maruska, her joy at having been able to bring pleasure to her family streaming from her eyes.

Alas, such a joy would be all too fleeting. The very next morning Maruska was once again summoned by her stepsister, who, along with the mother, refused to be thwarted in their goal of ridding the household of this unwanted sibling. "Maruska, I do believe I fancy some strawberries. And I fancy them *now*."

"But, dearest sister, wherever shall I find strawberries growing in all this snow?"

"You worthless good-for-nothing! You dare to answer me back?" roared Holena, her homely features distorted with hatred. "If you refuse to do as I ask, I shall beat you to a pulp—and, indeed, take great pleasure from doing so." The stepmother grabbed hold of an astounded Maruska by the scruff of the neck and hurled her outside into the freezing cold, the trailer's screen door clanging cruelly shut behind her.

Without even a dressing gown to warm her, Maruska roamed the moors for hours, the thin nightdress cloaking her shivering form clinging to her like a sodden skin. She thought of the old wood stove at home and the figures of her mother and sister in a cozy huddle before it with their third hot toddy of the day. The sky chose that moment to open up its gates, spilling still more of its snowy burdens onto this lone wanderer. Surely she would perish out here in the cold and wet, for there were no strawberries to be had, and yet she dared not return to the trailer without some. Just when all hope seemed lost, she saw a reddish-yellow light at the top of a craggy hill—in fact, the very same light that had drawn her to it the day before.

Maruska followed the familiar pathway up the snowy slope on two frozen sticks of leg, praying she would locate the warmth she sought before Death stole her away. She found the twelve months seated in their usual circle before the campfire, with January continuing to occupy the tallest of the rocks. "Kind brothers, may I be allowed to share some of this heat with you?" she asked respectfully.

January beckoned for the quaking figure to move closer, only to recognize the charming seeker of violets who had stopped by the previous day. "And what brings you here again, pretty one? You should be at home and in bed, since the bed is what you are attired for!" he chuckled good-naturedly, winking meaningfully at his brothers. As if to confirm his words, a pair of tiny nibs the color of port thrust through the thin bodice of Maruska's snow-saturated garment, hitting home to the brothers just how long it had been since they had last been in the company of a female.

"I am looking for strawberries," explained Maruska, suddenly feeling very silly standing about in a wet nightdress expressing so absurd a venture.

"*Strawberries?*" January reiterated in disbelief. "But strawberries do not grow beneath the snow."

Maruska nodded in defeat. "Nevertheless, my stepsister wishes for me to pick some strawberries, and if I do not, I shall be punished most severely. I beg you, kind January, to direct me to the nearest patch lest my poor bottom be tanned by the leather of a strap." And indeed, Maruska was not overstating the fact, for Holena owned a whole assortment of leather straps, which she kept conditioned with a special oil to guard against the cold. She kept them inside her hope chest along with a gas mask and a black silk negligee that had yet to see wear.

The brothers took to mumbling among themselves, especially the younger of the twelve. For these springtime months possessed a more randy disposition than their elders who, by virtue of age, had gained more experience in the world and had thereby learned to better temper their masculine desires. A whisper began at one brother's ear, making its way around the campfire until it reached the last brother's ear. All nodded in silent agreement, their eyes riveted to the two points visible through the strawberry-seeker's sopping garment. The month Maruska presumed to be April because of his youth and uncompromised handsomeness seized her hand in his strong fingers, asking, "And what will you give us in return if we decide to aid you in this quest of yours?"

Maruska stared humbly down at her slippered feet, which had become wet through from her long trek in the snow. It shamed her that she had so little to offer when her new friends had already given her so much. Why, she could not even extend to the brothers an invitation for supper, since the family's trailer was far too small to accommodate so many guests at one time. "I do not know what I can possibly offer, for I am without wealth or possession. However, I place myself entirely at your disposal."

This would be all the jaunty month of spring needed to hear. Maruska next found herself straddling his lap, her legs draped awkwardly to both sides of the rock upon which he was seated. Something rigid burrowed into her tender place, making it wet and sticky and even a little sore. The hem of her nightdress had been turned into a collar for her neck as April's smooth hands squeezed the exposed knolls rising outward from her chest, his fingertips tweaking the port-colored prongs that crowned them until they tingled with heat. As he bounced enthusiastically up and down upon his rock, Maruska bounced right along with him, oblivious to the commotion her presence created and likewise oblivious to the indecorousness of her pose, for the other months commanded an unobstructed view of yet another port-colored prong that had earlier been hidden by her nightdress. Occasionally the brother whose lap she occupied would roll it about with a fingertip, evoking many a wriggle and giggle from its genial proprietor. Never had Maruska imagined that sitting upon a lap could be so enjoyable.

Maruska made her way from season to season, leaving each month to lean back against his rock for a much-needed rest. After a time, the branches that she had so scrupulously tended only the day before lay wilted and defeated in the laps of all twelve brothers, oozing with a sticky sap. Had it not been for the corresponding presence of sap at her tender place, Maruska would never have believed any of it possible!

"What did you say you were looking for?" queried a breathless January, who wondered how many more of such visits he could possibly survive.

Maruska tidied her rumpled nightdress. "Strawberries, kind sir."

"Ah, yes...*strawberries*. Brother June, I beseech you to take my rock."

June, who still had considerable energy remaining and many notions of how to make use of it with their pretty guest, grudgingly exchanged places with his elder. Accepting the club, he waved it over the fire until the snow surrounding them melted away, leaving not a trace of frost in its wake. The song of birds filled the air, along with the fragrance of strawberries. From north to south and east to west, it was summer.

Conscious of June's tenuous hold over the elements, Maruska moved quickly, gathering the little fruits in the hem of her nightdress until it could hold no more. Waving her thanks to the twelve months and sending a kiss through the air for June, she set off with her tasty treasures, her heart filled with happiness at the thought of how pleased her stepsister and stepmother would be. As she made her way across the once-again-wintry moorland, a warm liquid trickled down the insides of her thighs, only to freeze when it reached her knees, puckering the skin and making it awkward to walk. No sooner did the first sticky trail crystallize than another went cascading over it. Yet Maruska paid this bothersome phenomenon little heed, secure in the knowledge that she would soon be safely at home basking in the warmth of the stove and the praise of her family.

Seeing the crop of fresh strawberries tucked into the hem of her stepsister's garment, Holena's equine jaw dropped to the floor. Maruska had barely gotten a snow-caked toe in the door before their sweet aroma permeated the little trailer, overpowering the strong scent of leather coming from Holena's room. "Wherever did you find them?" screeched the older girl in horrified disbelief. Although she very much desired to savor their delicious flavor upon her tongue, the desire to be rid of this detested family member was significantly greater.

"On the top of the moor, dearest sister. They are so plentiful that my slippers are stained with their juices!" To prove the truth of her words, Maruska upended a foot to proudly display its pinkened sole.

Snatching up the strawberries, Holena and her mother consumed the fruits until their well-fed bellies could accept no more, not even deigning to offer a single one to the hungry waif who had brought them.

The next morning as Maruska prepared a pie from the last remaining strawberries, Holena unexpectedly appeared. The elder sister rarely darkened the kitchen with her presence. Like her mother, she preferred to leave any form of domestic labor to her younger sibling. "Sister, I do believe I have a craving for red apples."

"*Red apples?*" gulped Maruska, her mixing spoon clattering to the floor.

"Go and fetch me some this instant!"

"But wherever shall I find apples in the wintertime?"

"You dare to answer me back? Perhaps your lazy bottom might like to be introduced to a leather strap, aye, little sister?" snarled Holena, her eyes gleaming with sadistic malice. Indeed, she was most keen to try out her newest strap, which had arrived just that morning by special delivery. Unhappily, when she had shown it to the delivery boy in hopes of enticing him inside the trailer, he had taken off down the moor in a sprinter's run.

"No, Sister," answered Maruska in a frightened whisper.

"Then do not show your ungrateful face again until you have brought me some apples. And do not presume to bring green ones, as I shall accept only the shiniest and reddest of reds."

Once again Maruska found herself being hurled out the trailer door and into the bitter cold by her step-mother. Clad only in her nightdress stained with the pink of strawberries, she stumbled across the harsh moorland, her slippered feet sinking deeper and deeper into the snow. Yet rather than wandering aimlessly about as she had done in the past, Maruska made directly for the welcoming light on the hill, where a blazing campfire awaited her—as did the twelve kindly brothers.

Seeing the bedraggled figure staggering through the snow toward them, January's fluffy white eyebrows shot up in surprise. Had not the girl already gotten her fill of both his and his brothers' company? "Now what might you be doing out in weather like this?" he inquired.

"I am looking for red apples," croaked Maruska, whose voice had frozen inside her throat.

"Surely you realize that apples do not grow in the wintertime."

"Yes, but my stepsister sent me to collect some, and if I fail, my bottom shall receive a terrible beating with a leather strap!"

"A leather strap, you say?" repeated January, his words strangely garbled.

Maruska nodded miserably, feeling the phantom sting of leather against her tender flesh. If she returned to her family empty-handed, Holena would see to it that she could not sit down until the arrival of spring — or even summer.

"And where might this strap be applied?" asked October in a high-pitched squawk.

"On my bottom," mumbled Maruska, hanging her head in disgrace. "Oh, can you not help me, dear brothers?"

She was answered by twelve nervous clearings of throats, followed by a good deal of fidgeting about upon their rocks by the brothers. At last January broke the tense silence, for he appeared to be the only one who still had any command over his vocal cords. "Perhaps it might be helpful if you show us the precise location in which your stepsister plans to beat you so that we can gain a clearer understanding of the situation."

"Yes, show us!" piped the younger months, suddenly finding their voices.

Maruska pulled up the back of her nightdress, bringing into exposure a pair of gentle rises that together formed the shape of a heart. "I think I am beginning to get the picture," January replied thoughtfully. As the girl moved to let down her hem, he stopped her. "No! Leave it thusly so that we may contemplate your fate and decide how best to alter it."

By this time the throat clearing had turned to a low rumble as the brothers discussed the situation, apparently reaching a swift and unanimous decision. January bade the anxious apple-seeker to approach. Unlike the occasion with the strawberries, he preferred to exert the seniority of his position rather than placing matters in the hands (and in the lap) of a subordinate. "We are all of a mind to assist you. But for us to be successful, you must be willing to do your share as well."

Maruska exhaled with relief, grateful to have found such caring friends so willing to help her—*and* to help with little thought toward any personal gain to themselves. "I shall do whatever work is needed. I can cook and clean and darn and weave; pray, tell me what it is you require!"

The twelve months chuckled in unison, causing Maruska to blush pinker than the strawberries she had fetched for her sister. Could it be that the brothers considered her guilty of braggadocio? Yet she had put forth no claims to which she could not live up. Just as she was about to set them to rights on the subject, January interrupted. "I do not believe any of those tasks will be necessary," he proclaimed. "For all we require is your charming company."

"Yes, your company!" cheered July, who tumbled off his rock, so great was his enthusiasm.

"Come, sit upon my lap to warm yourself," invited the senior brother, flinging his long white beard out of the way. A gnarled branch with a fluffy copse of curls at the base sprang into full view — as did those of the other months as they, too, pushed their beards to one side. Those who did not wear a beard or whose beards had not yet attained such spectacular lengths merely needed to alter the drape of their garments to accommodate the growths in their laps. The months of spring possessed the straightest and, indeed, the most *upstanding* specimens; therefore these youngsters sat proudly upon their rocks, basking in the envious glances of their elders, who looked back with bittersweet fondness to days when similarly endowed.

As Maruska lowered herself onto January's lap, she groaned with the strain. Never had she experienced such terrible difficulty in the simple act of sitting.

Sensing her troubles, January fitted his hands to her waist, guiding her slowly and steadily downward. Little by little the crooked limb disappeared until all that remained was a thicket of snowy white, which tickled Maruska like dozens of tiny fingers, summoning from her an impish giggle. Perhaps, she mused, January had planted his misshapen old bough inside her bottom so that it might be given an opportunity to grow as long and straight as the smoother-barked versions of his younger brothers. For what other reason could there be for its presence in so peculiar a locale?

Maruska next discovered herself impaled upon February's lap as he, too, endeavored to entrench himself as deeply as had his brother. This sowing and reaping continued with each of the months, although it would be the youngest of the twelve who caused the most problem. Indeed, Maruska could not fathom why such mighty limbs should even be in need of cultivation. (It so happened that the following morning when she awakened in her bed, Maruska fully expected to find a tree growing out from her bottom. Instead, the sole evidence of the previous day's energetic tillings was a sticky puddle of sap on the sheet beneath her — a puddle she dutifully gathered up with a spoon. Just imagine what a treat it should be for her family to enjoy some on their griddlecakes at breakfast!)

As Maruska pried herself off December's dwindling lap with a distinctive *thwock*, January suddenly remembered why she had come to their hilltop encampment in the first place. "Brother October," he called, "come and take my place."

Accepting the club offered him by his senior brother, October waved it over the fire. The flames leapt higher and higher, their increasing heat melting the snow. A brisk wind blew in from the north, turning the moors a deep orange. Autumn had arrived, bringing with it an apple tree that dangled two shiny red apples. "Hurry!" urged October, his voice cracking with the exertion of holding off the encroaching winter.

With a kiss to all and both apples tucked safely inside the hem of her nightdress, Maruska hastened through the newly falling snow toward home, where her stepsister and stepmother waited—indeed, waited with the smug certainty that this time their undesired relative would *not* be returning. Holena had already drawn up blueprints to convert the cramped room Maruska slept in into a torture chamber. However, a familiar pounding on the trailer door set their hearts to sinking in their chests. "But how? Where?" croaked mother and daughter in astounded accord when they saw the shiny red bounties the ecstatic girl carried within her garment.

"They were on top of the moor. Is it not wonderful?" Maruska cried excitedly, waiting for the praise that was surely her due.

"Why did you bring back only two?" barked Holena, who scraped at the skin of the apples with a fingernail to determine if its vibrant color had been painted on.

"It is all the tree had to offer."

"You selfish good-for-nothing! You must have eaten the other apples. Perhaps I shall go myself and collect some more."

"Yes," urged the mother. "Do that, daughter dear. For it is clear that this ungrateful wretch has stolen them from our hungry mouths."

Donning her warmest fleece coat and cloaking her head with her warmest fleece hood, Holena went stomping off through the snow, annoyed at having to leave behind the cozy warmth of the little trailer. Despite her younger sibling's frequent forays into the moorland, it would not be an easy journey to make, and she grew tired very quickly. Just when she decided to turn back, she noticed a reddish-yellow glow at the crest of a craggy hill. With the tangy taste of the apple still fresh upon her tongue, Holena clomped irritably upward toward its source. This must be the place of which her miserable stepsister had spoken...although she could see nothing even remotely resembling an apple tree. There was, however, a fire, and Holena fully intended to make use of it.

Gathered in a circle around this fire were twelve men at various stages of life, some quite young, some quite elderly. Strange that her detested relative should have made no mention of their presences! — particularly when there were so few men of *any* age about, other than that dreadful gap-toothed peddler with whom her mother kept trying to fix her up. Without asking for permission, Holena stepped boldly up to the crackling flames, only to seat herself comfortably before it. She even went so far as to remove her fleece-lined boots so that her large, flat feet could be more efficiently warmed.

"And what brings you out today?" inquired January, for it was hardly a day to be taking a stroll on the moor. In fact, it had almost come time for him to pass his club to his brother February.

"Mind your own fucking business, Gramps!" snapped Holena, sticking her middle finger up in the air for emphasis. Pulling off her thick woolen socks, she set about massaging her benumbed toes, which resembled a sequence of paddles of varying sizes.

A scowl fixed itself above January's curly white beard. Because of his advanced age and the respect it commanded, he was not accustomed to being addressed in this fashion. Nor had he liked the look of that middle finger. From the manner in which this dis-agreeable Miss covered herself up, one might have thought she had something offensive to hide—as per-haps she did, if her toes were any indication. Suitably provoked, January waved his club high over his head until the somber sky above vanished behind clouds the color of smoke. The fire sputtered, dying out as a fierce wind blew through the small encampment, stealing away the last of the warming flames. Leaden balls of snow rained down from the darkened heavens, and within moments a thick blanket of the stuff covered the moor and everything upon it.

Including Holena.

Meanwhile, back at the trailer, the mother looked apprehensively out the window at the bleak landscape whose craggy contours were now completely hidden from view. Darkness would shortly be upon them, and still her blood-daughter had not returned from her visit to the apple tree. Finally she could wait no more. Dressing in her warmest fleece coat and donning her warmest fleece hood, she set off to follow the route Holena had taken, calling out the girl's name to the barren moor.

Day after day Maruska waited at home for the return of her stepsister and stepmother. Yet neither would be seen again until the spring thaw, when a passing bear desperate with the hunger of an overly long winter took an interest in the pair and made of them a most disappointing meal. With the loss of her family, the trailer now belonged to Maruska, as did everything both inside and outside of it, including the scrawny goat and the patch of scrubby land surrounding it. She lived there for a time by herself. Then one sunny morning a handsome young man came up to the screen door seeking directions. Rather than continuing on his way, he chose to remain behind with the trailer's pretty owner, who had taken an instant fancy to him. Indeed, he possessed a branch very much like the one handsome young April had had growing out from his lap—a branch of unswerving straightness whose supple bark oozed with a sap so sweet that Maruska could enjoy it on griddlecakes for breakfast, lunch, and supper.

Had she been more observant of the weather, Maruska might have realized that springtime had passed unusually swiftly this year—in fact, so swiftly that winter seemed to have gone directly into summer. For the young man she so willingly sheltered was none other than the month of April himself. ❧

About the Author

Mitzi Szereto is best known as M. S. Valentine, author of such erotica titles as *The Captivity of Celia, Elysian Days and Nights, The Governess,* and *The Possession of Celia.* Her work has appeared in *Joyful Desires* (Masquerade Books), *Wicked Words 4* (Black Lace), *The Erotic Review,* and the *Shiny* magazines. She is currently editing an anthology of erotica and writing a novel. She resides in the San Francisco Bay Area.

JUST FOLKS
Earthy Tales of the Prairie Heartland

VOLUME I

Jerry W. Engler

Illustrations
Sheri Schmidt

JUST FOLKS
Earthy Tales from the Prairie Heartland
©2005 Jerry W. Engler

Published by 6-mile roots
1429 260th
Marion, KS 66861

Printed in the U.S.A.
Print Source Direct
Hillsboro, Kansas

Library of Congress Control No.: 2005906372

ISBN: 0-9771255-0-5

Table of Contents

Foreword

I FIRST MET Jerry Engler in the newsroom of the Topeka Capital-Journal, back when it was the newsroom of the Topeka Daily Capital and the State Journal and we were trying to report on and explain the world to the paper's readers—which shows how long our friendship has lasted, and which gives at least Jerry the right to refer to me as an "old" friend."

And it gives me the right to tell you how good he is before you sit down to find out for yourself.

For the benefit of you who are crossword puzzle aficionados, Jerry is a oner, a word my spelling checker doesn't like and which my desk dictionary doesn't recognize. But it means about the same thing as one of a kind. He is deep, he is wide, which you soon will discover for yourself.

And in the process you will have wondered why this book wasn't published years before.

Many of us know you can't play the blues until you've paid the dues, and that it takes a heap of livin' to make a house a home.

Well, then, after your dues are paid and you've done that heap of livin', you just might be ready to write a book like this.

And part of the lesson in that will be that you will know that you don't write like this so you can become wealthy, or so your name becomes featured on marquees or bulletin boards. You write because you have been given the stories and are obligated to share them around.

Should you become wealthy and your name be featured on marquees or bulletin boards, you may think you've succeeded. But the true success will have been setting them down so others can know them, and so others can know you.

As is true with these stories from Jerry Engler.

Merle Bird, Kansas author and editor

Author's Introduction

THE QUESTION readers most often ask me about my stories is whether a particular one is true. Well, to answer you fully in advance of your asking the question too, at least the names are changed to protect the guilty.

I make up names. I make up stories. Some of them are nearly 100 percent true while others are concoctions. None of them actually portray a real person. They all qualify as fiction. I can only consider it one of the best of compliments when a reader can't discern whether what they read was the truth, especially if it left them smiling.

I write about a bygone age that was close to me. I write about characters I think I knew. I write about the characters who are still all around us because part of what is easiest to love about humanity is the uniqueness of each individual.

Of course, it could be that I am only a character too in some grand play. Some of the characters I supposedly have created could be my peers. Consider Harlan Medlam. I don't think I'll ever reveal to you whether there really was an 85-year-old farmer who could nearly become a gymnast, even at his age, if a dollar bill was involved.

My son, Mark, pointed out to me that my story about Salty the drunk, and coyote hunter, became much more meaningful to him when he found out that the incidents Salty goes through, even though fantastic, are close to 100 percent true. Salty is a character based on the lives of three real persons who actually lived experiences nearly identical to those in the story. Nobody can be crazier than the Kansas coyote hunters who chased their prey with packs of dogs, and of course, the humor surrounding the drunk character is an American cliche. For anyone tempted to emulate Salty, I have to tell you the life of a drunk coyote hunter isn't very good. All three of the persons he is based on were dead by the age of 45.

It could be that I am crazy. It could be these stories are true, and it could be they're just therapy. To find out, I turned to two of my favorite characters, Ricky and Roland, with the question, whispering it in Ricky's ear one night while he was sleeping.

Ricky took the question to Roland, who promptly turned it around a little. Roland said, "Well, Ricky, I hate to interfere with anybody's personal belief system. If you want to believe in Engler, it's your business. Personally, I doubt Engler's existence because I can't believe anybody would create this many characters unless he fell in love with his own life, and found the people and animals in it really that interesting.

"Of course, if you want to believe in Engler, and we're only characters here having words put in our mouths, it raises the question of whether Engler has a creator too. If he does, I have an insight that one facet of his nature could be creativity, and that we are the end of a line of creativity, unless of course, you or I write a story too that places us as one more link in the creativity line. Then there's the possibility that he's playing with us right now, and he's a liar."

Hmmm, good answer, Roland. You always are a little smarter than I am. My greatest reward is knowing that someone read my stories, and enjoyed them. They are play time for me and play time for the reader, I hope.

I do want to thank my wife, Belinda, and my daughter, Sheri, who are always my first readers of any story. I thank my father, Wayne, his wife, Marno, my brother, Greg, my sons, Ron and Mark and their families, a number of cousins, old classmates and friends who all have helped support my illusion that somehow I was destined as a fiction writer from early on. My mother, Pat Engler, always enjoyed my story telling clear back to the days when I filled the blackboards during recess in Mary Stewart's first grade room at Auburn. Mom, I hope you can read these in heaven.

I thank Jonathan Holden at Kansas State University for telling me the work I did in poetry could help Americans hold on to the memory of a way of life, and I thank my old co-worker and friend, Merle Bird, for saying at the right time, "Hey, man, these stories are good." Another co-worker, Tom Stoppel, said my stories are unique to him when he reads them because he can hear my voice. I wonder if he hears Ricky and Roland too?

Two men who own the Hillsboro Free Press and the Hillsboro Free Press Extra at Hillsboro, Kansas, Don Ratzlaff and Joel Klaassen, gave me the support and encouragement to first run these stories in their newspapers.

Now, lest I continue on ad nauseum, let's allow the stories to speak for themselves.

Sometimes a Mazzoura feist is about all you can expect

Author's note: We owned a Missouri or Mazzoura feist named Abe. As an affectionate pet and as a varmint dog he was unsurpassed among the animals we've owned.

NEARLY a thousand miles from the Montana mountain headwaters of the Missouri River and 10 miles below the new Sunrise Mobile Home Court on the county blacktop, Burford Crumble lived along a little creek that had hollowed out a high stone bluff drainage above the mighty river.

Back 500 miles to the west, where a man spitting into the wind could be charged with starting the headwaters of the Smokey Hill Basin, Hermes Wayford lived below a yucca-covered slope with enough buffalo grass to call it a pasture.

They didn't know each other. But Hermes, trying to explain later, said, "You see my sister, Agnes, on a trip traveling past where this Burford Crumble lived, then some hours later past where I lived, on the way to where she lived in the suburbs below a rock-pile of a West-Denver foothill some developer called beautiful, had stopped at a Missouri walnut bowl factory outlet store."

Hermes paused, patting his fat paunch while leaning forward to look over his dark-rimmed glasses, "Whooey, this tale takes a lot of wind to tell.

"All this is to get around to the fact that she used her cell phone as she went by to tell me that while buying the bowl she'd seen an advertisement for rat terrier puppies at the checkout. The number for the puppies she passed on belonged to this Burford Crumble because, after years without a telephone, he'd finally gotten a cellular too, even left it on all the time. Terrible waste I know, but when it comes to gettin' phone calls, well, Burford Crumble seemed inclined to always be hopeful."

Hermes paused a moment to pull his glasses down to rub the bridge of his long nose.

"Well, let's see. Oh, like I say, this Burford's always got his phone on, and everybody knew I wanted a terrier, so I call Burford Crumble except I didn't know that before I called that I was calling Burford Crumble. It's just that he had the puppies so I called him. Yeah, I guess you are followin' me this far.

"You know, Georgia always would like to take a trip, but she said to me, 'Whooey, you mean you are really going to drive 500 miles just to buy yourself some little tri-color rat terrier puppy?'

"Well, I told her I always wanted me a rat terrier because I had me rat terriers when I was a little boy, and, whooey, rat terriers are hell on

9

wheels **if any** *dog is—varmit catchers* they are. I might go to maybe **even** *raisin'* regular registered rat terriers myself. You know, Georgia, honey, I said, we might even leave halfway through the day Sunday, stay in some luxury motel that night, take Monday off, then have a leisurely trip the rest of the day because when I called this Burford Crumble, he only wants $50 for a registered rat terrier. Whooey, that's cheap for registered, you know.

"So, the next day in church right after the preacher said, 'God is good,' and us people holler back at him 'All the time,' because he is or I

wouldn't have found this rat terrier of my dreams, Georgia and I get out of there fast because the old Pontiac is all loaded for the trip. The weather man said the weather was going to be nice, had a cold front comin' down from Canada and some warm, moist air comin' up from the Gulf, but nothin' to worry about because when's the last time we didn't have to beg to squeeze water out of the sky?

"We had three kinds of soda pop in the cooler, got corn chips, pretzels, potato chips, crackers, spray cheese, sour cream—and we figured if we went 75 after we got to the interstate, we could still stop for a nice dinner, and get to a nice motel in the eastern part of the state. Whooey, that weather man never knows what he's talkin' about or maybe he doesn't care about those folks further east.

"Well, we did get to stop for a chicken-fried steak dinner with extra gravy on the meat, spuds and bread, and Georgia's pattin' that little poochy out place under her chin thinkin' out loud how she was beginnin' to like the idea of a puppy too, when I notice it's spittin' a few rain drops on the windshield, and the car's digital thermometer says 30 degrees. Whooey, I said to Georgia, honey, you know, Baby, I hope we don't get a little ice.

"But, we did get a little ice, had to slow down for about 60 miles. It slowed us down enough before we ran out of it that we didn't make it to any city luxury motel. Instead we stop at this little town with businesses only on one main street, and a cheap little motel with a neon palm tree in the window advertising discounts for apartments by the week.

"Georgia's crabbin' at me while she's gettin' her curlers and cold cream on, in case the Burford Crumbles are nice people, just because I'm drinkin' soda pop, and eatin' crackers in bed while I watch the football game—so I know she isn't happy with the motel. Whooey, I said, Georgia, sweetie, didn't you like the turkey legs, cole slaw and chocolate pie we had for supper? Wasn't that swell? This isn't a bad place at all, few missin' floor tiles around the toilet isn't that bad. We'll find us a breakfast buffet tomorrow, and I bet you we get a pretty good puppy, and see some different country, too.

"Whooey, I got that right. But Georgia wasn't too happy the next day either on account of the heat blowin' on her head all night gave her a headache. She was even more crabby, just gruntin' at me when I said whooey, wasn't somethin' nice. I was just tryin' to have fun.

"Well, the next day we are seein' different country, kind of rolling ground with a lot more trees and every once in a while the highway goes through rocky cutaways in the hills. We hadn't hit more ice, but the sky's a real low gray with a cold, moist smell in the wind. I kept watchin' the thermometer hover around 33 for a while, then go down to 32.

At the Sunrise Mobile Home Court, I called this Burfurd Crumble for more directions, and he said, 'Oh, didn't you want a male pup?' And, I said that was right.

"Then he said, 'All I got left is one female pup, so there ain't no use in you making the whole trip out here.' To which I said, well I've already come 490 miles so I might as well see if I might want a girl pup instead. To which he said, 'Ain't no problem if you want her instead.' Then he gives me more directions. Whooey, was he a hard one to follow.

"He told me, 'Be sure to watch out for the hollar in the driveway. It'll look like you want to get over to the side, but don't do it or you might drop a tire in the hollar.' I ask him what's a hollar, but all he does is talk louder like I don't know English, 'A Hollar. I said STAY IN THE MIDDLE WHEN YOU HIT THE HOLLAR.'

"Then Georgia starts saying, 'Maybe we better just head home. It looks like more ice to me.' To which I said, I came here for a rat terrier, and I'm leavin' with one unless the whelp is a total loser. To which she starts gripin' again about how she wants a puppy too, but she wants to get home.

"You wouldn't believe that county blacktop up one big hill, then down another with none of the hills cut out at all. Why, there were times when I think the bottom of a hill had to be 200 feet below the top. Finally, we go down this Burford Crumble's driveway, winding alongside this stone-bottomed creek with two feet of water runnin' fast in it all the way. I stayed right in the middle of the road, which wasn't that hard because the trees squeezed right up to the edge so hard you couldn't have gotten off anyway.

"I was scared I might hit whatever this hollar thing was, and the whole time Georgia is alternating between sayin' 'Oh, isn't this a pretty place,' and 'Look out, look out. Don't hit the trees. Watch out for that hollar.' At least she forgot to gripe about her headache.

"Well, the only thing I see is this little erosion dip cutting through the driveway to the creek, and I thought about cutting out around it a little to avoid the dump, but I stayed in the middle so I wouldn't hit this Burford Crumble's hollar. It must have been a half-mile back to Burford Crumble's mobile home with a frame room built onto it with a stove pipe puffin' wood smoke out the top. The thermometer said 31 degrees.

"Burford Crumble stepped out to meet us, got a green head scarf tied over a blue sock hat on his head, duckcloth coat and high buckle over-shoes with the jeans tucked into them like he was expectin' a flood. Soon as we were introduced, I asked him where this hollar was, and he said, 'Why you're in the hollar.'

"Well, what about this hollar in the driveway? I asks him, and he said, 'Yessir, did you have any trouble with it?' And, I asks, are you sayin' there's a hollar in the hollar? 'Well that's obvious ain't it?' he said. 'Reckon there's lots of hollars in the hollar.'

"I tell you, whooey, it was like tryin' to talk Greek to a Chinaman when English is your language. This Burford Crumble meant hollow when he said hollar, and a hollar to him is anything from a little ditch to this whole cut of a little valley this creek made through the rocks. I was gettin' exasperated with him, and he was plain startin' to get a little snippy with me.

"The air got still about that time. It started to sprinkle rain with ice crystals in it. So, trying to move beyond this hollar business, I asked him, so where's the rat terrier? And he said, 'Oh, some other folks got her while you were on your way. First come, first serve, I always say.'

"Whooey, I was gettin' all fixed to start hollerin' at him in the hollar when Georgia hollers first, 'Why, what about these puppies here?' because here's a half-dozen puppies comin' out of a doghouse right beside the mobile home.

"They were little black and white pups, and I said right away, well, here's a whole litter of terriers here that looks ready to go, pretty little rat terriers.

"Burford Crumble said to me in an uppity, irritated tone, 'Why those puppies ain't rat terriers. They're full-blood Mazzoura feists.' I said, Missouri feists? And he said, 'Mazzoura, the word's Mazzoura, ain't no Missouri, and yes they're genuine Mazzoura feists. Best squirrel dogs there is.'

"Well, I liked the way they had a little broader, intelligent looking heads, obviously some of the best rat terriers I've seen, but he hadn't cut the tails off. 'You don't bawb the tail on a feist,' he explained. 'His tail curls up, and he cocks his head when he sees a squirrel to tip you off to where the squirrel is. Kills the squirrel if it gets on the ground.'

"This Burford Crumble starts gettin' under my hide a little about this time. He asked me $50 for a rat terrier before I left home, and now he wanted $100 for a Missouri feist.

Georgia picks up the male feist we both like the best. I knew I had to have him because he grabbed my finger with those little needle teeth, and tried to shake it, the makin's of a top ratter.

"The ice is starting to fall, and Georgia said, 'Just give him the $100, and let's get out of here.' But, whooey, he had my dander up, I'm not going to do it. I'll give you $75, take it or leave it I said, and got in the car to go, with Georgia lookin' all sour at me over her cute little nose, and Burford Crumble lookin' all sour at me over his big pointy nose with the hair pokin' out the nostrils. When I turned over the engine, the thermometer said 29 degrees, and I had to crank the defroster up to get the ice off the windshield.

"Finally Burford Crumble said since I went to all the trouble to come all that way, he'd respect my offer, and he snatches that $75 cash out of my hand, and hands me a genuine Missouri feist.

"Georgia cuddles my new little rat terrier— don't have squirrels where I live, just prairie dogs—in her lap all the way up that cruddy driveway, tires slipping on the ice here and there. When I get to the blacktop, whooey, it's like pulling out on a sheet of glass, the car fishtailing while I get moving even when letting up on the accelerator. I gritted my jaw though, and I made it, spinnin' here and there, almost to the top

13

of the first hill before I can't go any more. I have to walk all the way down that driveway to see if Burford Crumble has a way to pull us out of there.

"Well, he's got this old Allis Chalmers tractor that he has to hand-crank to get it started, which it does after only three or four tries. He's got chains on the rear tires so that Allis will walk right along on the ice. Whooey, I tell you, that was cold riding the rear end of an Allis up out of that hollar. Numbed me clear through the belly. It didn't make me feel better halfway up to finally remember I could have called him on my cell phone, don't even have to crank it because it's got more battery than the Allis.

"Anyway, Burford Crumble ties a log chain around my car's bumper to tow me out with the Allis. At the top of the hill, I figure we can make enough speed going down to get over the next hill, so I said to Burford Crumble, well, do I owe you somethin' for that? He said to me, 'I guess it must be worth about $25 to tow a genuine Mazzoura feist up out of the hollar.' At least he could have smiled instead of just lookin' at me while I handed him the money. The terrier, cute little guy with soulful eyes, had wet on Georgia's lap, so she was anxious to go.

"It was tough going. Sometimes I'd about stall out at the top of a hill. Georgia gave the puppy a couple of corn chips for luck, and he threw them up on her at about the third hill. She wanted to change clothes,and she was gettin' sort of obstinate about makin' it somewhere claimin' our situation was due to my bullheadedness. But we made it all the way to the Sunrise Mobile Home Court.

"They said they had a vacant mobile home they could rent us for the night if we didn't mind sleepin' on the floor, but they had to check with their new owner for a price to charge. It was this Burford Crumble, and he told them $100 for the night just special for us. Georgia said I had to clean the puppy poop off their rug the next morning.

"Whooey, I tell you, I bought myself a good rat terrier but when it comes to Georgia, my honeybunch, I brought a feist home too, don't know if I'll ever get her to take a nice vacation again. And that Burford Crumble is a Mazzoura feist if I ever saw one."

The fury of
a woman conned

Author's note: Fredda's language was cleaned up, and toned down for this story.

COMING UP the interstate, Martin B. Dusitter of the state bureau of water works noticed the new subdivision in what recently had been pastureland on the south side, right where he thought it ought to be.

And there was the Terrytown watertower on the hill above on the north side of the interstate, right where it could feed to both the subdivision and the old village of Terrytown down on the lowland where creek bottom began its convergence with river bottom.

Martin B. Dusitter thought everything looked just as the map said it should be. In his 45 years of life and 20 years as a state worker, he had learned it was very important for everything to look as it should be.

Perhaps that was at least as important as all the papers to be signed in his briefcase for one Freddy Verdun to receive grant money as owner of the Terrytown water system served by Freddy's Water Line.

Of course, that was very irregular. Martin B. Dusitter never in all his days had seen a private entity own a town's water system, but after careful study his department had determined there was nothing against sole proprietorship of a water system as long as it fulfilled the public need. There was a public need in Terrytown, and the business entity known as Freddy's Water Line did fulfill the need.

In fact, Martin's heart was warmed by the whole idea. He dearly wanted public health and needs fulfilled. He could hardly wait to meet this Freddy, who must be a very benevolent local businessman.

As he drove down the Terrytown exit ramp, he noticed a big sign over a restaurant, Freddy's Cafe, and down the frontage road at the first curve was Freddy's Machinery.

When Martin B. Dusitter stopped as he entered the main street of Terrytown between Freddy's Antiques & Grocery, and Freddy's Tires & Service, he began to feel the first pangs of confusion. Where would he really find Freddy Verdun? Oh, the service station, sure. That's where Freddy had listed the waterline office.

He stopped at the station and stepped out of the shiny new dark blue state car. Right away a uniformed attendant came out.

"Can I help you, sir?"

"Yes, I'm Martin B. Dusitter of the state bureau of water works, and I have business with Freddy Verdun. Are you he?"

"No, I ain't he. I'm Lester. I work for Freddy. Freddy ain't going to be here now. Do you think you could come back later?"

"Well, could Freddy be at one of these other businesses that say Freddy on them? My goodness, I don't know why the place isn't called Freddytown instead of Terrytown."

"No, sir, Freddy ain't going to be in one of those businesses right now either. Freddy just ain't available right now."

"Maybe Freddy's gone home for lunch or a break. Could you tell me where Freddy lives, and I could drive out there to see."

"Well, sir, I ain't likely thinking that Freddy's going to be at home now either, and I'm afraid to tell you to take a chance going out there. You see I'm afraid to tell you to go out there the way things are now with Freddy ain't going to be anywhere."

"Well, just give me the directions, and if Freddy's not at home right now, there's no harm done."

"Guess I could do that, and hope there's no harm done. You just go on down the main street here until it turns into a gravel road, and goes over the creek on the steel trestle bridge. Then you go left two miles, then right one mile, and you come to some grassland, and in another quarter mile, there's a driveway to the right with a mobile home on top of a little knob. That's where Freddy and Fredda live."

"Freda—that would be his wife?"

"No, you're saying Freda, pronounced like F-r-e-e-d-a, but this is Fredda pronounced like Fred, and then da. That's the lady's name, and she doesn't like to be called Freda."

OK, Fredda, not Freda, Freddy and Fredda—had to be a marriage made in heaven because the odds of those two names getting together had to be millions to one, thought Martin B. Dusitter as he drove over the steel trestle bridge.

As he drove up to the knob where the mobile home set, a short, square-built woman was out front with long pruning shears snipping bushes. She turned to look at him, slightly frowning from a wrinkled flat face with small, turned-up nose as he opened the car door.

"Hello, ma'am. My name is Martin B. Dusitter. I'm from the state bureau of water works. Would you be Fredda Verdun?"

"Yes, I would be, Martin," she replied, coming up to him to stand an inch too close in his comfort zone and smelling of sweet rose perfume. "And what can I do for you?"

"Actually, ma'am, I'm looking for your husband, Freddy Verdun, in fact looking forward to meeting him he must have such a fine sense of public responsibility, and—"

The flat face krinkled into pale, vivid fury, and Fredda Verdun grabbed a very surprised Martin B. Dusitter by the necktie, and jerked his head down to her level.

"You got some nerve coming out here asking for that sorry jerk," she hollered in a voice that could have made a drill sergeant shy.

"Ma'am, if you could let go of my necktie.... I don't understand, I only—"

"You sorry, snotty fancy pants. I ought to yank your tongue out, and tie it to your necktie."

She let go of the tie.

"You march back to that car before I change my mind about dropping these pruning shears, too," she shrilled, looking him meaningfully in the eye while she dropped the shears to the ground.

"You just find that Freddy, tell him I'm coming to town, and I'm coming right away. He can try to run, he'd better not try, because he can't hide. I'll find him, and you can take a new definition of road kill back to the state with you, fancy-pants Martin. You hear me, Martin? Run for your life, and find that Freddy."

Martin jumped back into his car a plain-old-scared but also incensed Martin. He was finding everything about this place contravening, confusing and unexpected. He barely saw anything as he started back down the driveway, only wincing when a rock thrown in a hard curve hit the side of the car. That woman had an arm on her.

The application, he thought. It listed an attorney, Melvin Singleton, and a banker, Howard Hartglow. Maybe one of them would know where to find Freddy quickly. Martin was ready to get it all signed and get out of town.

It wasn't difficult going up the main street to see the bank, and down the street a few doors across the street was an office with a sign for Melvin Singleton, attorney. He would try the bank first.

"Mr. Hartglow's on the phone right now, but I'm sure he'll see you in just a moment, Mr. Dusitter," the receptionist said. "Wait, what's going on? That's him trotting down the street."

Martin looked out the window to see a man in blue suit and tie, his silver-gray hair blowing in the wind, trotting down the street. Martin didn't pause, he went out the door, and trotted down the street to catch the banker.

As the banker passed the attorney's office, another man came out in pin-striped suit and close-cropped dark hair to fall into a trot alongside the banker.

Martin ran hard, puffing with the exertion as the two men turned into Freddy's Tires & Service.

"Where's he at, Lester?" Melvin the attorney was appealing as Martin came into the drive.

"Come on, Lester, we have to know—she's coming!" shouted Howard the banker as Martin panted alongside him.

"And, who are you?" the banker asked, looking at Martin.

"I'm Martin B. Dusitter of the state bureau (puff, puff) need to find Freddy Verdun (puff, puff) and that woman, his wife (puff, puff)."

"We understand, we understand," Melvin said. "But run, run. Get in the back room. Here comes her car! Lester, tell her nobody's here!"

The attorney, the banker and the bureaucrat ran through the station, into a dark back room, and stopped before a metal door, which the banker kicked a couple of times before announcing, "It's no good. It's locked."

"Just stay quiet," Melvin said.

"What's this all about?" whispered Martin. "Why is this woman in such a rage? Why are we all hiding here? Where is Freddy?"

"I'm Freddy's banker. And this is Freddy's attorney, Melvin. It seems his wife, Fredda, inherited a couple sections of land. Freddy needed big money for his water line and purification plant. Found out he could make a good margin on the water. He mortgaged the land to us, and I loaned him the money on it. He gave me the legal descriptions, and it didn't have a mortgage on it before. He said it was his.

"Apparently she was just handed warranty deeds out of some kind of trust, and we didn't know what Freddy was up to until the deeds office started calling us all, including her.

"Trouble is, we all trusted Freddy. He's done business here a long time. He's a good bluffer at poker too. His name wasn't on the deeds. It's Fredda's land. We have to figure out how to straighten it all up so Freddy doesn't go to jail and Fredda doesn't get a hold of us beforehand.

"This town can't afford to lose Freddy or Fredda, either one! If they split, it could take us all down. Why, I could do jail time or Melvin could do jail time, or we could lose our credentials! You think you're confused. We're all confused, and we need time to think!

"If only we could get through that metal door. It's an old safe-room from when this was a freighting office. It's Freddy's poker room now where we all play. Nobody knows about it, but us boys."

"I'm afraid you ain't going to make it through that door any way you try, boys," said Lester as he appeared in the doorway with a blue glow all around him and a clanging sound. "I'm pulling the acetylene tank, and Fredda's got the cutting torch right behind me. Now, if everybody will take it real easy like...."

"This is Fredda talking now, banker-boy, lawyer-boy and bureaucrat-boy. You all just get across to the other wall, and stay real still. Nobody's getting hurt because I'm going to need you all doing your regular jobs in your regular offices.

"Now, you!" her voice changed to a higher pitch but still calm. "Freddy, I know you're in the safe room. Did you think I was so stupid I never knew this place had a safe room? Come out of there now before I have to use this torch to get in, and end up burning the whole place down around you! You aren't going to get hurt physically if you come out now."

The safe door slowly creaked open, and a short, pot-bellied man in coveralls with a ballcap tilted back on his head stepped out.

"I'm sorry, Fredda," he said. "I didn't mean anything. You know I only needed the money for both our good."

"I know you're sorry. You were sorry the first time I laid eyes on you. You'll be sorry the last time I lay eyes on you. Now, everybody march over to the bank. Not you Lester, you take care of the torch. These guys understand who's in charge now, don't you. Everybody bring your paperwork with you."

It was only two weeks later that Martin B. Dusitter came driving back up the interstate to Terrytown in the shiny blue state car with the barely perceptible place on the side where a dent had been repaired. His office had performed in record time to change all paper work on the Freddy Water Line to the company's new name, the Fredda Water Line.

As he drove by the Terrytown watertower, workmen were standing on a suspended platform painting out the name, Terrytown. At the exit ramp, the sign calling it the Terrytown exit was gone.

At Freddy's Cafe, the "y" had been painted out, and an "a" painted in its stead. The same was true at companies now called Fredda's Machinery, Fredda's Antiques & Grocery, and Fredda's Tires & Service.

Melvin Singleton was waiting at the bank door to walk in with Martin B. Dusitter.

"Good morning, Martin. Good to see you again on this happy day."

"Good morning, Melvin. Looks like there are some big changes going on around here in the business world."

"Yes, indeed, big changes."

"What's happening at the water tower and with the highway exit sign?"

"Well, at Someone's insistence the citizens of the town came up with a petition overwhelmingly in favor of a name change, and at Someone's insistence I put together the required papers in short order. You're no longer in Terrytown. You're in Freddatown."

"But not even Freddy could have the town's name changed, I thought."

"This Someone was able to insist more than Freddy could have insisted."

"By the way, where is Freddy? Is he OK?"

"Oh sure, he's fine. I think this is his day to wash dishes at Fredda's Cafe. You know hell hath no fury like a woman conned."

Be thankful for
friends in all forms

Author's note: A number of people tell me this story is their favorite. My son-in-law, Carl Schmidt, tells me this, and he came from urban New York, a radically different scenario in time and place. How can you fathom The Grateful Dead rock group and Aunt Edna being favorites of the same person? We are complex. I saved the story nearly as Aunt Edna told it—as close to 100 percent true as fiction ever gets.

SHE WAS in her 80s in the 1980s, a pretty, vivacious lady with silver hair and bright, warm, big brown eyes behind her glasses and above a short nose that people must have called "cute" when she was young.

Edna listened to the chattering conversation of the people around her this Thanksgiving Day. But when one of the youngsters finished talking enthusiastically about horse-riding lessons, Edna's face also glowed with a memory as she began to speak.

She said, "I remember a Thanksgiving time, too, when I had a horse, actually a pony, and another animal friend. They probably saved my life. It was so very long ago, and the world around here has changed so much. You children can hardly know how it was for us."

"Well, tell us Aunt Edna," the other adults and children said. "The pony really saved your life?"

"Yes, I think there's a chance he probably did. But as much as anything, my story is about faithfulness. It made me forget my own selfishness and self-concern, and remember for the first time on a Thanksgiving that somebody is watching over us. He gives you friends from throughout the creation, sometimes before you even know you have them.

"It was a lot different here then. We didn't have automobiles. People traveled by horse and buggy, rode a horse, or walked. There wasn't any paved roads, no gravel roads either, just dirt roads—or mud when the weather was wet.

"It had been wet nearly all that fall, and the dirt was churned into globs of mud by the traffic. At least on the road back to my house, it wasn't very well traveled, and a strip of grass was growing down the center you could walk on until you got to the main road. Usually, to get to school in the mornings, I would start that way, but then I would cut across the fields and pastures where I could. The school was over three miles away.

"Lots of the kids rode horses. In summer, the farmers would fill the school shed with hay for them, and the kids would tie them along a rail, and each would give his horse some hay from the shed before going in. The farmers would take turns during the school year bringing more hay to the shed so we didn't run out. At other times, they would bring loads of firewood.

"Most kids rode big horses, lots of good sorrels and bays. My folks gave me this dumpy-looking little pony gelding with a gray-brown mousey kind of color, and my daddy said he looked like kind of a smudge on the grass standing out there. So that was my pony's name because it stuck, Smudge.

"We had this big old funny-looking dog, too, white with black spots, a body like a greyhound, but with a big, old, rough, wide head. He was just all over the place all the time, had a hard time remembering not to jump up on ladies, he liked them so well. Daddy called him Mutt, and that stuck, too. Of course, then I was stuck, starting out to school every morning with Smudge and Mutt.

"I thought I was getting to be quite a young lady that year going into seventh grade. My mama and I had made me a couple of new calico dresses from flour sacks for school, and I was feeling kind of elegant. It made me feel really ashamed at the idea of riding such a dumpy little pony into school with a bouncing big ugly hound alongside.

"So, all that fall when I got to the point just before where other school friends traveling the road might see me at a high point in a prairie pasture, I would climb off Smudge, and slap him on the rump to send him home.

"He was stubborn, and not wanting to work either, so he was always just really happy to trot off for home.

"Mutt was another story. Usually, I would start hollering at him, trying to make him go home, where we went around a cornfield half-way up our road. He'd just smile at me and pant until I wanted to kill him. Sometimes he'd fall back a little, then he'd meet me up ahead—really irritating. If he put his nose against my lunch pail to try to smell it, I'd slap his face.

"When I joined the other kids, I'd ignore Mutt like he really wasn't with me. One time, I'm shamed to say, I even giggled like he was a stray when a couple of the boys threw dirt clods at him. Mutt would be there to meet me every afternoon when school let out, which made me feel even more humiliated. Everybody caught on that he was my dog.

"But at least Smudge went home, and Daddy would scold me every once in a while because he would have taken his bridle off to put him back in his pen. 'You ought to be happy to have a pony,' he'd say.

"There came the morning when we were all excited about going to school because the next day we would be off for Thanksgiving. I had slapped Smudge on the rump to send him home earlier, just like usual.The clouds that day were dense and gray, hugging the earth. It was cold, but almost eerily still. The weather that fall had been mild, with only two or three freezes, and lots of sunshine. Of course, there was no radio, no weather reports.

"Everybody must have felt the cold because when we got to the one-room school, the teacher and the older boys already had a hot fire going in the stove. The boys carried the fuel up from the cellar, where there was one bin for coal and another for wood.

"Finally, one girl looked up at the window, and called out, 'Look, it's snowing.' Almost right away, there was a big sigh, as though the whole world breathed out, and the frame of the schoolhouse creaked as a wind began to come up.

"The teacher let us all take a break to look out the windows. It was the first snow of the season, and it was heavy. You could scarcely see the privies across the school yard.

"The wind kept coming harder and harder, and the teacher let us all pull chairs up around the stove while she read stories to the little ones, and most of us older ones read books on our own. 'Don't worry,' she told us, 'it should let up. It's too early in the year for a big snow.'

"But she was wrong. There was a half-foot on the ground before two hours were up, it was coming down heavy, and blowing. There were big soft drifts forming up around the building. A farmer came by to get his children, and the teacher told us all that school was out early. 'You all need to go home now as quickly as possible, and be careful,' she told us.

"I delayed. I didn't really want to get out in that. I dreaded the walk home. I hugged the stove, and kept trying to read my book. I should have walked out with the first ones to go so we were all together. The teacher kept looking at me until she finally said, 'Edna, you have to go now. Don't just keep sitting there. Go home. I'm closing the school up.'

"I had a sort of sick feeling when I walked out that door. The wind nearly reeled me over, and the snow was stinging against my face like blowing sand crystals. I could hardly see three feet in front of me. I began to feel very afraid of the walk home.

"I remember shuffling down the porch steps, wondering if I could even see the road in front of the school when a big heavy thing hit me right in the chest. It was Mutt jumping up on me he was so glad to see me. He hadn't waited until the usual time. He was three hours early. I took hold of the scruffy hair on his neck with my mittened hand, it was such a relief to find him there.

"We lumbered along together through drifts, where I could see another big shadowy shape through the blowing snow. It was Smudge. How or why the two of them showed up back at school, I'll never know. My folks said they never came back home that day like usual, but Smudge didn't follow me either. It was pure serendipity, as though the two of them had a conversation with God somewhere along the way, and been told to come back for me.

"That's what I'll always believe, anyway. I've never been happier to see anyone in my life than I was to see the two of them that day.

"I got on Smudge, and Mutt leaped in the snow ahead of us, coming back to check every few yards. I couldn't see our route any part of the way. I never saw the other kids on their way home. The snow covered everything so you couldn't tell the difference between road or grass or cornfield. Smudge just trudged along, Mutt leading, and I hung on. They took me straight home.

"I'll tell you all since it's Thanksgiving. This is going to be preachy, but you'll all listen to your Aunt Edna won't you?" she paused while the rest of them waited to listen.

"My prayer for you is that each one of you will remember to give thanks for your friends—no matter who or what they are, no matter what they look like—because they're a gift to you, and you're a gift to them. Never be ashamed."

Driven by love
to sleep on a bench

Author's note: This first Harlan Medlam story started as a poem that I thought of as "The Harlan Medlam" even though that wasn't its title. Now it's a group of stories that recall some of the familiar scenes of youth. I like Harlan and Florence better all the time.

YES, HARLAN Medlam was driven by love to sleep on the bench in the elm-green dappled shadows at noontime.

But he was also given to sitting up from time to time, rubbing his stomach where his dinner digested, then rubbing again at his gray-black hair as he listened to his wife of 55 years, Florence, still washing pans in the kitchen.

His shiny dark eyes followed her silhouette moving beyond the window screen, and he nervously smacked his lips, grimacing and ungrimacing his farmer's nut-brown face a couple of times.

The woman worried him. At dinner she'd said, "You know that bungalow house the Pattersons want torn down is 30 by 30. Whoever does that gets all the lumber for the work. You know that's thousands of board feet of lumber— probably easily more than $500 worth. And if we don't get it, somebody else would."

She swept back her long gray hair and grinned at him under her pale blue eyes, glowing with avaricious need.

"If you have the wheat planted within the next two weeks, we could work on it every day after milking before we had to be back to milk again, and we could have all the lumber home before it was bitter cold, before Christmas anyway, or only a little into January.

"Of course, I'd be sorting it with you," she added. "The worst of it could be some stove kindling, too, and you could still get some time to cut wood down in the timber, and take care of hogs in the meantime."

"Dad-rat-it, Florence, you know the two boxcars out here are each half full of old native lumber we haven't had a need for yet."

"But we will some day," Florence said. "You can't ever have too much. This has been a good hay season, so you've rented the second barn to Paul down the road, but we still have the pole building. You can move all the lumber there together so it's more available, and you're more likely to use it or we can sell it. We'll get it organized. Then we can do something different with the box cars."

"That's a lot to expect from an old man," Harlan Medlam said with a sigh. "Besides, the old truck's in the pole building, and it has junk all over the floor already."

"You can do it—we can do it—just get at that disking. Get it done."

Harlan Medlam smacked his lips unhappily, remembering the conversation. Then reaching down the bench where he had settled in for his noon nap, he picked up his false teeth to pop back in his mouth and his cap to put on his head.

Before he could move, Florence was popping out the kitchen door to call, "Harlan, Harlan, you'd better be getting back to the field. You need to get it disked as soon as you can. Can't turn the next cash over if you don't move on."

"Move, move, move, dad-rat-it. Can't get any rest around here, dad-rat-it. Turn that dime, grab that nickel, all the time, dad-rat-it," Harlan griped.

But he moved just the same, slowly and stiffly. Soon the orange Allis

tractor was roaring down the driveway with the disk squealing behind it like usual because Harlan Medlam didn't use much grease.

Hearing those squeals down the road, Paul looked at the young guys who had been bucking 70-pound bales for him, hooks at their sides as they sat on the edge of the hayrack wagon behind the green tractor following their dinner.

"Sounds like Harlan's headed to the field, boys. Doesn't spare much grease for the machinery, that's for sure. Jimmy, Joe, Rick—you guys remember, greasing and maintenance pay."

Soon Paul's crew was in the alfalfa field, walking alongside the wagon to stick hooks in bales, and throw them on. In the distance Harlan turned the black earth in fine furrows, ready for a final harrowing before the wheat was sowed.

The hay boys stacked the latest load in the big tin barn that gleamed in the hot summer sun at Paul's, stuffing the last few bales up in the peak of the roof.

"Look here, boys," Rick said. "This meat thermometer I brought out says it's 135 degrees in here."

Wearily they finished.

"At least this afternoon we'll start on a new barn at floor level at Harlan Medlam's," said Joe.

Their shirts were sweated through. They sucked from the water jug eagerly, but careful not to be so fast they became sick either. They brushed the stems and leaves from hair and clothes while standing to let the breeze cool them as the rig moved to the next fields.

They pulled into the gate next to where Harlan Medlam had pulled in to go disk. There, to their surprise, set Harlan's orange Allis— parked, but running with a roar at full open throttle. Underneath the Allis lay Harlan, eyes closed and mouth open.

"Is he dead?" Jimmy asked, his eyes growing wider.

Paul, who had gotten off the tractor to come stand beside the boys said, "No, I don't think so. You can kind of see him breathing, his chest moves a little. And there's his teeth on the tractor seat. He's OK, just asleep. He wants Florence to hear the tractor so she thinks he's working."

Paul paused. "Dad-rat-it," he added smiling at the old man who began to snore.

But later that night, Harlan learned that Florence had wondered in the distance at the steadfastness of that hum which failed to strive with clods, no up-and-down roars where the earth was tougher.

"Harlan," she said, "guess you ought to have that field ready tomorrow. I'll come out toward evening to see you finish it up."

Harlan looked at her, smacking his lips, "Guess I ought to have it done. I'll get up early to make sure."

And at gray daylight, he was on the doorstep knocking at Paul's.

"Paul, thought you'd be about ready to go by now, be six in another hour. Been thinking about how you might not have enough storage for all the hay. Guess I could trade with you so you could use those two box-cars at my place too."

"Well, maybe, Harlan. What do you have in mind?"

"I have to finish that field I'm on fast, really fast. How about you spare a tractor and disk, and one of those boys to run it while I run mine, and we'll call it an even deal, your disk and a man for a day for the boxcars."

"Sounds fair enough, Harlan, although it's a tough time to spare one of the boys when we're hauling. But, we'll just do it."

So, Jimmy and Rick watched a little enviously as they drove by sweating and tired with loads of hay while Joe ran a John Deere and disk up and down one side of the field with Harlan Medlam's Allis on the other side.

By five that afternoon, the last round of disking was done. Harlan headed home to bring Florence back in the truck to look at the field. Joe took the John Deere home, and rejoined the hay crew.

By eight that night, the weary hay boys were finishing up the last load before going home.

"Tomorrow," Paul said, "we'll be ready to start putting the hay in those boxcars."

The next morning, Paul caught up with Harlan as he was beginning to leave with the harrow for the wheat field.

"Harlan, those boxcars are half full of lumber. We can't pull hay in there."

"Golly," said the old man, "I kind of forgot about that. Well, at least you have a good crew of boys and the hayrack here. You can stack the lumber on your wagon, and I'll show you where to put it. It's a little inconvenient for me to go to the extra trouble, I guess, but you'll have the boxcars then. See here in this pole building, just move that junk out of the way, and stack the lumber there. That'll be OK. Hadn't ought to take those boys long. I'd help, but you understand I got to get this field harrowed."

The hay boys were tired with loading the heavy native lumber, and unloading it before they ever got to any hay that day. To make up for lost time, they all worked a little later that night, and showed up in the morning twilight the next day to begin earlier.

They were near stumbling as they finished stacking the last load before dinner, one bale at a time through the narrow boxcar doors while the mud-dauber wasps they had disturbed buzzed around them.

"I'm so hungry, I could eat two horses," said Jimmy, big rolls of sweat carrying down dirt and hay grit toward his eyes while he mopped his forehead with a sleeve.

"Me too if I don't throw up or die first," said Joe.

They climbed on to the hay wagon while Paul started the tractor to drive through the barnyard. He stopped because Florence Medlam was standing by the orange tractor and harrow looking at him while Harlan was on his back on the bench under the elm tree.

"Everything OK, Florence?"

"Oh yes, everything's fine. I'm headed out to harrow for a while so Harlan can take a nap. The poor old dear's worn himself out, all this tractor work, and somehow he even got all that lumber moved out of the boxcars."

Paul raised his eyebrows, and the hay boys looked at each other.

Then they all looked at Harlan Medlam as he sleepily raised to one elbow to grin at them exposing his pink gums.

"You boys have a good day," he said. "Wish I was a strong young buck like you again, but now I need my rest. Work's good for you, but sometimes I overdo it."

Yes, Harlan Medlam was driven by love to sleep.

Or, as Paul noted to the boys later, "You know, he's such a nice, nasty old man."

When Mercy
and justice met

Author's note: You could do this too. First I recommend wrist strengthening exercises for you and a hydrophobia check for the animal. Skunks are notorious rabies carriers.

HEAVY-WRISTED Joe was sitting on his front porch, big old hairy legs spread over the steps and his huge arms folded over his large belly.

Ted, known as Twisted Neck, had admired Joe since the high school days when he was champion shot put, discus and javelin thrower, and ambled up to him in the hot summer heat looking for conversation in the shade of the over-hanging silver maple.

"Whatya know, Joe?" Ted asked, his long neck bobbing like a pigeon's.

"Nothin', nothin', at all," Joe answered, letting his chin nod to his chest as though a nap was exactly what he had in mind.

"Hey, Joe, what's that stickin' out from under the steps between your feet? Looks mighty like a skunk's tail to me, all black and bushy with that white stripe."

"I think it is a skunk's tail. Must be old Mercy takin' a nap under the porch."

"Why you say Mercy? Is he your pet?"

"Naah. When my old lady saw him come across the yard the first time to go under the porch, she said, 'Oh mercy, mercy, would you look at that,' and we been callin' that skunk Mercy ever since. Guess I ought to call the cops to come shoot him, but I just never got around to it...busy, busy, busy, everything takes time," Joe said with a yawn as sweat rolled over his gorilla brows.

"Looks to me like he could wet onya, Joe, you just sittin' there like that, could stink everything up."

"Naah, if I just sit here quiet like, he's probably tired too, probably used to us by now, been around for a couple of years."

"I hear, Joe, that a skunk has to have its back feet on the ground to wet anyway. Can't get organized, can't get its feet on the ground to spray you if its back feet ain't right."

"That right," Joe mused, putting his hands on his knees, and peering over his belly at the skunk's tail. "Must be a powerful sleeper too, us sitting hear talkin', and him not movin' a bit. Probably doesn't know his tail is out here. Surprise, surprise, surprise is the key to it, Ted."

And with that, Joe went into coordinated motion that did his old athletic ability credit, reaching down to grab the animal's tail, springing to his feet almost simultaneously, and swinging the skunk round and round above his head in a circle.

"It is the skunk, Joe. It's him, all right. Mercy, mercy what we gonna do now? His mouth is open, and he's surprised all right. Mercy, mercy!"

"Yeah, it's old Mercy all right," Joe said, making a wide arc with the twirling skunk. "And you're right," he panted. "He ain't wetting at all cuz I got him without his feet on the ground."

"But whereya goin' with him, Joe?"

Ted, his neck twisting back and forth, his head bobbing, was dancing several feet from Joe as he advanced across the yard, still twirling the skunk.

"Down here by the street, where I can give him a really good toss far from us. Otherwise there'll be no mercy from Mercy for us!"

"Good throw, good throw Joe. Looks like 50 or 60 feet, anyway."

It was that far as the poor skunk twisted through the air, and through the open window of Miss Marsha's white Chevy to land with a thunk on the passenger-side maroon seat covers, his tail and rear propped high against the seat-back, his back feet still off the surface.

Miss Marsha, the plump but good looking, driving along at 20 miles per hour, and wearing her best pin-striped dress, jumped a little as something came through the window, and flopped on the seat.

But she was no more surprised than the skunk called Mercy, who just sat in place, dizzily moving his head from side to side, stunned from his awakening.

Miss Marsha looked at the skunk, and said, "Mercy, mercy. What am I going to do now?"

Her answer was to accelerate to Main Street, running the stop sign at 40 miles an hour, and thereby drawing the attention of Harold the Hardhat, the expert-on-nearly-everything police officer, who was sitting in his patrol car awaiting just such a ticketing opportunity.

Thus it was that Miss Marsha pulled into Ralph's gas station with a patrol car flashing red lights behind her, and a skunk called Mercy propped tail-up in her front passenger seat blinking his eyes in the breezes.

Much to Officer Harold's dismay, Miss Marsha failed to stay in the front seat to wait his "What on earth are you doing?"

Instead, she threw open her door, trotted around the front of her car on her little white high heels, opened her other door, and trotted to where Ralph was washing the driveway with his new air-compressor-driven high-pressure water hose.

Ralph, the bald and scrawny, looked at Miss Marsha, and so did Harold the Hardhat, who was running up behind her trying to hold on to his hat with his ticket book blowing above his head in the breeze.

She screamed, "Skunk, skunk in my car!" just as the confused skunk, Mercy, hopped out to the wet pavement to stand blinking in the bright sunlight.

Harold, known as Hardhat for the stylish helmet he preferred, spied opportunity. He had two boxes of shells in his car, but only his lucky bullet in his pocket. With the skunk now between him and the cars, he pulled his revolver out to push the lucky bullet in its chamber.

"Quick! Quick, Ralph! Hit him with your water, and get him away from the cars and the buildings so I can get a clear shot at him without damaging anything. Quick, quick! Mercy, mercy don't let him get away! Together now, forward."

The hard-water-spray hit the skunk broadside, nearly pushing him down the wet pavement, his hair moving up and down in sloppy, wet waves as the water hit him. Then he trotted toward the gas station building.

"Oops, oops, he's turnin' his tail toward us, Ralph! Shoot him in the rear with the water. He can't go on us if he's gettin' hit.... No good, no good, hit his head, got to turn him away from the building. Can't shoot him if I might hit improvements according to ordinance—let's see, I think that's ordinance number 101205-H or was it 06," Harold said as he bounced in step alongside Ralph, holding his pistol forward in the classic shooting stance.

"Oops, oops, hit him in the tail again. Don't want him to stink us. Ah, I think we got him, almost to the corner there where maybe I can pull off a shot."

"KERBANG," went the loud pistol, and almost as instantly there were sounds of "PING, WHANG, KERBANG," and then a low "wheeze," as the lucky bullet ricocheted off the concrete drive to the interior concrete wall of the station bay to go into the motor of Ralph's air compressor—a clear, clean kill considering the bullet trajectory.

Harold looked at Ralph with the dwindling water coming out his hose, and Ralph looked at Harold, and said, "Oh, mercy," while the skunk staggered, his wet hide and plastered hair quivering, around the building by the car wash.

Heavy-wristed Joe's wife, Joan, the stringy blonde, was there finishing up the vacuuming of her newly washed car with all four doors standing open as she returned the vacuum hose to its stand.

The chilly, wet, stunned skunk took the first entrance to shelter he could find, and that was into the backseat floor of Joan's car. There he huddled down to take stock of the situation, as Joan closed the doors, and he probably would have said, "Mercy, mercy," if skunks talked.

As Joan drove her car past the front of the gas station, she saw the blinking red lights of the police car, and Harold Hardhat entering the building with pistol drawn in a squatting shooting stance as he walked, and Ralph the bald and scrawny rubbing his noggin as he shuffled at full-height behind him, and Miss Marsha the plump but pretty peeking out through the station plate glass window.

Joan decided she was glad she was going home, away from whatever trouble was going on there.

Joe, big arms folded over his paunch, and Ted, head bobbing and weaving, were still standing in the yard talking as Joan drove the car into the driveway, and got out.

"Oh, guys," she called, "would you have some mercy on a tired woman, and unload the packages and groceries on the backseat of the car? I washed it too, and I think I'll just go lay down inside for a while."

"Sure we will, Hon," said Joe as he walked to the car with all the grace of the athletically heavy. "Ted you get'em from that side, and I'll go for this door."

Joe opened the back door, and bent over for the first bag to where an anxiety-ridden, soaked skunk that had just ridden home in chilling air conditioning waited with a suddenly very full bladder.

Mercy the skunk had his feet on the floor and his tail in the air when the two doors opened, and he sprayed his opening salvo with bitter, eye-blinding pressure into Joe's face, and twisted with skunk-coordinated vigor to get the car interior and the underside of the bobbing chin as Ted's head hit the car roof for the second time.

A wave of acrid, nauseating odor drifted across the yard as the skunk marched past the stumbling men to his home under the front porch.

Mercy was returned with a seat of justice.

Ricky and Roland find their way as 'Santy Claus' and his helper

Author's note: This was the first Ricky and Roland story, written at Christmas. But it was followed immediately by the one written for Valentine Day that follows it which drew more commentary.

"HERE COMES Santy Claus, here comes Santy Claus," Ricky sang, and gyrated with his fingers in the air to the rhythmic "chuu chu, chuu chu," of the milker cups on the cows.

"Why don't you just settle down," Roland said, looking at him dejectedly as he slipped the cups off a cow's teats before turning her loose and giving her a fond swat on the top flank. "You'll scare the cows. They aren't used to idiots."

"I'm gettin' myself in the spirit, man," Ricky said, stroking what had been his red beard that he'd dyed white the night before. "You should, too. You'll look really cool with your hair dyed green and your skin a sort of olive—really, really elf-like."

"Elf, shmelf. I'd say your idea of how to color me up wasn't that great. I look more like a goblin. I don't know where you got the idea that Santa's helpers are green elves anyway. I thought they were supposed to be just ordinary little people—maybe like a dwarf or a midget or something. I don't know why the cows didn't run away when they saw me."

"Everybody's going to know you're a helper elf. Haven't you watched cartoons? Santa's helpers always have pointed ears like elves."

"But I have my own round ears."

"Don't worry. The children will catch on quick. They're just little preschool kids anyway. My sister, Rita, said I'd look just like Santa if I only had white hair," Ricky smiled, and batted the blue eyes in his big ruddy face. "And since you're a head shorter than me, being smaller will make you look more like an elf when you put on that costume that Rita left. We'll get into our suits when our milking shift is done. Little kids are sharp. They'll catch on."

"The milking's almost done, and I see out there the sun is coming up, so I guess at least we'll have time to get to the city. And, it was nice of Conklin to put other milkers on for the other shifts. Gosh, it's freezing outside."

"Time to get our suits on, too. Santy boots, suit and hat for me, and green elf tights, pointy green sock hat and green jumper shorts for you. Santy Claus is comin' to the Choo Choo Preschool for all the little boys and girls."

"We'll look stupid. People will think we're crazy. Are you sure that old boat of a car of yours can even make it up 50 miles of interstate to the city?"

"Come on, Roland. Everybody will love us. It's the holiday spirit. Either they'll love us or they won't pay much attention to us because there's decorations and stuff everywhere. And sure my car has problems, but good night, it's a Crown Victoria—a Crown Vic, the highway patrolman's choice."

"Yeah, but I bet a patrolman's car has good tires and doesn't backfire every time he turns the switch off."

"You're just negative, Roland. Try to have a good time," Ricky said as they walked across the crusty snow to crawl into the old pale, blue car with the dented sides. Holstein cows loafing along the steel rail lot fence watched them go.

Later, as Ricky the Santa, now in full garb, climbed back in the driver's seat, his elf was still griping.

"Good night, Ricky, where did they get this shirt for me? It's so tight I can hardly move."

"It's one of Rita's old blouses— the only thing they could find in glossy green. It's harder to find elf's suits to rent than it is Santa suits."

"I might be smaller than you, and I know I'm thin-framed, but even I'm bigger than Rita," Roland moaned, rolling his big almond-brown eyes as Ricky tromped the accelerator going up the interstate ramp. "When's this car going to warm up anyway? I'm freezing in these shorts and tights. They aren't anywhere near as warm as my coveralls."

"It loses a little antifreeze along for some reason. Maybe it's a little low on coolant to warm the heater. I'm comfortable, anyway. You'll warm up, too. Sing now.... Here comes Santy Claus, here comes Santy Claus."

"I don't want to sing. I can't anyway because my teeth are starting to chatter. Good night, have you really got this old bucket up to 70 miles an hour? Slow it down."

A young woman driving a small red car went around them.

"Ya haah, there goes our bear bait!" Ricky shouted as he stepped on the throttle to move past 75.

"Bear bait?"

"Yeah, she'll drive point for us, in case there's any smokies—any patrol—ahead."

"Are you nuts? A speeding Santa Claus with a green elf at his side— do you think they're really going to look at her first? You'd better drive a little under the speed limit."

"Yeah, I guess you're right. We are a little obvious. By the way, I think that green stocking hat I found for you really sets you off. Pull it down on your ears a little if you're really that cold. Here, watch this trucker coming around us to see if he notices us."

"He's not even looking at us. Just watch how you drive this piece of junk. I want to stay alive. Try turning the heat up and down. Maybe it will come on. It can't be above 20 degrees out there."

"Here comes a car around us. Got stickers on it, college kids headed home for the holidays. Aah, they're coeds, pretty cute girls. Thaar she blows. That one noticed us, ah hah, hah, hah," Ricky laughed as the girl in the glass next to him first clapped her hand over her mouth, and then started laughing too as she pointed them out to the others. The girls all started clapping their hands, and pointing.

"See there, Roland, I told you people would get a kick at the sight of us. Come on, wave back at them."

"Would you quit waving, and watch the road? I smell antifreeze."

"That one's waving with both hands. Hang on to the wheel for me, Roland, while I wave with both hands."

"No, I won't. You watch your driving."

"That's OK, I can steer with my knees. See!"

"There's steam coming out from under the hood. It's fogging the windshield."

"OK, OK. We'll pull off at this convenience store here. Keep wiping the steam off the glass with your hat so I can see. You got to admit they were cute girls. Let's both go in at the store while the car cools down. It'll be good for a few laughs."

"No, it won't. I just need to use the restroom, OK? And that's all I'm going to do."

"Ho, ho, ho," Ricky said winking at the clerk in the store. "Where's your antifreeze?"

"It's right over there, Sweetie," she said, grinning. "And, what's your little green friend here?"

"Why, he's a helper elf."

"I just need to use the restroom," Roland said, grimacing.

"It's in back," she giggled. "I didn't know elves went to the bathroom."

"Why, where else would lime juice come from?" Ricky roared, slapping his stomach."

Back outside, Ricky came back from having his head under the hood to look in the door at Roland.

"I'm sorry, Roland. The heater core leaks. I had to shut the coolant off to it, and top the radiator off with antifreeze. We aren't ever going to have heat."

Roland rode in his green blouse covered by a green Conklin dairy jacket with his arms wrapped around himself, and his green stocking cap pulled down over his ears. People who passed the Crown Vic either ignored the occupants, or paused alongside to smile or wave.

"I bet they think it's odd to see a Santa and a green elf in a car with a bumper sticker that says, 'Jesus is the Reason for the Season,'" Roland said.

"This is America, Roland. It's OK to be odd here."

"You have to admit, it's sort of fun, anyway," Ricky was saying when the car lurched to the right with a flop, flop, flop bouncing action. He rolled to a stop on the shoulder.

"Looks like you've had a tire separate. It's dead flat, and split with wire showing," Roland said while he jumped up and down for warmth outside on the passenger side.

"There's a spare tire in the trunk. I guess you need to change it, Roland. We can't mess up a rented Santa suit, and you're wearing clothes we put together ourselves."

"Why don't you just get back in the car, Ricky. I can't stand these cars honking at us because of the way we're dressed. You're too obvious standing out here in a red Santa suit, especially if you have to pat your belly and wave."

"As if you aren't obvious, my little green elf."

"Oh, when I tightened that nut, I think I felt the little green blouse start to split up along the back."

"You have a little grease on your face. Probably nobody's going to notice it much anyway when you're green."

They finally pulled into the Choo Choo Preschool parking lot. As Ricky turned the key off, the old Crown Vic sounded kerbang with a backfire and a thunk.

"That didn't sound too good, Ricky."

"Hurry, hurry, we're all ready for you," called a short, red-haired woman from the front door.

"Ho, ho, ho, we're here, Rita," said Ricky, swinging his arms as he assumed what he thought must be a Santa-type stride. "Santa and his favorite elf helper are here."

More than 30 children, ages 3, 4 and 5 sprang to their feet as they entered, mobbing Santa Ricky Claus as they grabbed him around the legs.

"Catch me, catch me, help hold me up, elf. Ho, ho, ho, you kids are about to knock me down."

The children began to back away, losing some of their enthusiasm as they stared in wide-eyed, half-frightened expressions at the green person.

"Roland," Rita said, "Why don't you help one of the other ladies bring refreshments in from the next room. See, children, Santa's helper-elf is going to help bring in treats from the next room, and we're all going to sit on the floor around Santa while he sits in a chair. We'll take turns sitting on Santa's lap, and telling him what we want.

"Now, just several of you at a time, get up, get your juice and cookie, then sit down. That's it, follow the elf."

Ricky was just taking an order for a GI John Super Destructo doll when he heard the first splash, then some more thunks, and a lady calling, "Children, children, stop it. That's enough. He isn't going to hurt anybody. It's just Santa's elf."

"What happened, Roland?" Ricky asked when he got to his feet, and saw his partner standing there with the juice dripping down his suit, and the shattered cookies at his feet."

"The little green blouse split the rest of the way when I bent over to pick up a tray, Ricky—I mean, Santa. That little blonde girl there yelled that I was 'hulking out' and needed to be cooled down quickly. Then they started throwing everything at me. I don't think Santa has elves for helpers, Ricky."

By the time preschool was dismissed, and Ricky's car was towed away with bent piston rods, and they ate a hamburger, and they found a flannel shirt for Roland, and Rita drove them home, it was getting close to midnight.

"What time is your milking shift, boys?" Rita asked.

"We have to get up at 3," Roland said, still hugging himself and yawning.

"Are you going to try to wash off?"

"Naah, guess we can just stay colored if it means getting a little shut-eye, huh, Roland?" said Ricky.

When his friend only stared at him, Ricky added, "You do have to admit though, it was kind of fun."

What a man does for Valentine's Day

RICKY contentedly stretched his legs out a little further in front of him in the reclining chair, took another drink of soda pop, and reached with a corn chip for another scoop of dip off the plate on the little table.

"Who would ever have thought our lives would end up looking like this?" he asked, looking across the table to his partner, Roland, in the other reclining chair.

"What do you mean? There isn't anything wrong with our lives," Roland replied.

"No, there isn't anything wrong with our lives—that's what I mean," said Ricky as he muted the television commercial. "Here we are, watching the Super Bowl in my own living room. And each of us, we got married, and there's our wives visiting in the kitchen," he said motioning through the doorway to the next room. "It's so domestic, so normal-like."

"Yeah, who'd have thought you would ever meet your future wife dressed as Santa Claus, and me there with you dressed as a green elf? Who would ever have thought that a preschool teacher would get interested in somebody so all-over-the-place like you?"

"Well, I have to admit, it probably helped that she already knew my sister, Rita."

"Not to burst the bubble of your contemplation, but have you considered, sitting here watching the football game, that Valentine's Day is coming up soon, and you need to get your wife something?"

"You bet. This year I'm ahead of the game. I'm finally catching on. The first year, I think I got her some candy, and it was OK. I think it was the second year I forgot all about Valentine's, and Carol was upset with me. So, I try to make amends, and explain that in my family when I was growing up, we just didn't get each other gifts, but that didn't help."

"No, I can see that it wouldn't. Just sort of oafish."

"I asked her, 'What can I get you, what can I get you that you'll like in the future?' And you know what Carol said? She said, 'Just get something practical so I know you remembered me.' So I got her a toilet plunger, and she cried."

"You really aren't too discerning, are you?"

"Well, I put a red bow on the handle."

"Naah, that wouldn't work."

"No, it didn't. And it didn't work either in later years when I got her the ice-cube trays or the electric mixer. I thought they were really practical. She even said the electric drill I got her to install her cabinets was obviously really for me.

"So, the next year I decide to go really big on romantic, but stay really practical too. I went down to a discount store, and got not one, but three 5-pound boxes of the cheapest candy on sale I could find. Ended up tasting like paraffin stuffed with sugar. Carol said quantity wasn't the issue at Valentine's, and not to get her candy any more because she was getting too fat."

"Gosh," said Roland looking back into the kitchen, "I don't think she looks fat. Well, maybe she's a little plumper than when we met her."

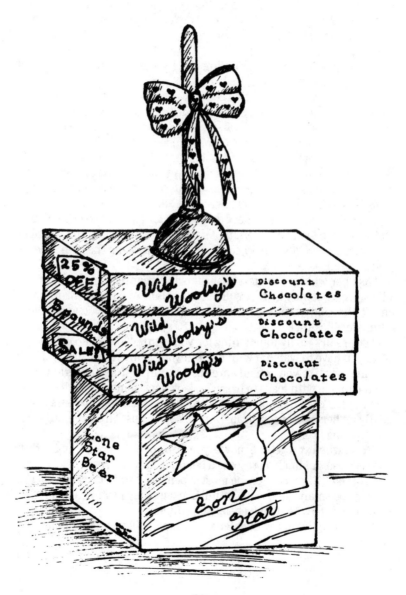

"Anyway, she said I needed to listen to her, meet her needs, take account of how she feels. So, I did. I got her a good gift this year."

"So, what did you get?"

"Well, I've been really paying attention. And, several days ago when they were interviewing people on the television news, getting ready for the Super Bowl you know, the people were drinking Lone Star beer because of it being from Texas, and Houston being involved in the football game, you see. Then Carol said how her brother drank some of that Lone Star when he was in Texas, too, because so many of the people there drank it. So, I took the hint. I went down to the liquor store, and special ordered her a case of Lone Star—good 6 percent too, not even 3.2."

"Ricky, Carol doesn't even drink beer! She isn't going to like that, and there's nothing romantic to it."

"But I figure it must be like getting wine from a special place—and besides, that's not all I got. Since she's feeling sensitive about candy and getting fat, I got her a pound of special beef jerky down at the locker plant to go with the beer. This time I've listened to her."

"No you haven't. You haven't listened to her at all. I tell you, Ricky, a woman wants you to listen to her with your heart. The ears don't do well when all that's between them is your big stretch of head. You have to feel—and if you can't, you have to get help.

"At Valentine's, when I need something for Nancy, I go down to the video store to look for a clerk that's the sweetest young thing—preferably in her early 20s—that I can find. Stay away from the men. They're just as dumb as you are.

"Ask her what is the most gushy-gushy romantic film they have, usually starring some guy that will make you almost want to throw up looking at him, and a really good looking girl. That's what you want, their ultimate chick flick.

"The really, really tough thing for you is this: There's no getting out of it, you have to watch it with her. Put your arm around her, and look at it intently like you actually are absorbed in it. If she looks at you during the movie with tears in her eyes, look back somberly with expression in your eyes like you might get sick or something, and kiss her gently on her hair or forehead. Don't kiss her lips. This is feelings, no love making.

"Now, when you get the movie, you also go to the florist, and get her one red rose. A bunch of roses is a bouquet, and one rose is elegance. You got that? Then get her the most expensive, exquisite candy they have in the smallest, most beautiful package they have. Practical is investing wisely, not being cheap and stupid."

"You do all that for Nancy, Roland? I can't believe it. You sound almost slick."

"I'm telling you, she likes it all, Ricky. Get the jerky and the beer out for us. I'm the man for that, Carol isn't."

Nearly two weeks later, Ricky walked into the video store, looking all around for an available clerk besides the bur-haired man behind the counter. Almost out of nowhere, a young woman, perhaps around 25, appeared in front of him.

"Can I help you, sir?"

"Well, yeah, I guess you can. You look like somebody I ought to talk to. I want to rent a real chick flick for Valentine's Day for my wife to look at—with me, I guess. Yeah, I'd be looking at it too. Something really gushy-gushy, you know."

The young woman smiled warmly. "That's so romantic, sir. And I have just the right movie for you. She'll love it, I know."

Ricky looked at the movie cover picture, and Roland was right. The man shown was one of those hair-swept-back types with oversized eyes and thin lips set in a thin face, stomach-churning looking, but the woman was a babe. He rented it anyway.

He thought about picking up a cactus at the discount store with the small, round red top grafted to a tall, green bottom—but he caught himself, and made a trip to the florist's for a nearly black-red rose, long-stemmed and elegant.

At the candy store, he almost couldn't make the purchase. "The most elegant and decorative piece of candy we have, sir, is this white chocolate bon bon with coconut cream exterior and a cherry-mash almond filling. As you can see, it's wrapped in laced, gold foil, with curled pink, cotton ribbon top."

"Good, good, I think. How much is one of those bon bons, or do you sell them by the box?"

"No, sir. We don't sell them by the box. They're $9.99 each."

"Good Lord, 10 bucks. OK, give me one."

Carol positively gleamed in her smile at him that night when he handed her the rose and the bon bon. The hug and the kiss she gave him were way beyond anything he had received for any previous Valentine's gift—even the toilet plunger when she had finally kissed him after laughing at him.

He put the movie in the videocassette player, put his arm around his wife, and endured the scenes of skin-crawling, passionate gazes, and ardent embraces with the irksome hero. When he felt himself dozing off in boredom, he bit his lip. And at that exact moment when Carol looked up at him with tears gleaming softly in the corners of her eyes, Ricky bent over, gently kissed her on the forehead, then gazed at her with the most luster that he could muster.

"It worked, Roland," Ricky told his buddy the next day. "I've never seen Carol so happy with me at Valentine's. I don't know how you knew what to do, or where you learned so much, but it worked."

"Good, Ricky. I knew it would work for you. I'm glad now that I told you."

"I only have one question."

"*You do, huh? Wouldn't it be better* to just accept how to please her at *Valentine's, and forget* questioning."

"No, I really want to know. How did you learn that? How did you know the way to a woman's heart?"

"Ohhh. I was afraid you'd ask me that. I can't lie to you again, even for your own good. We've known each other too long. Why don't you forget you asked."

"No, really, tell me."

"Well, Nancy and Carol drilled me on what to tell you. They made me memorize everything. I outdid myself with my performance. They said you weren't ever going to get it on your own. They even had Nancy's niece at the video store to give you an extra little push to get you started. I'm sorry."

"No, that's OK, Roland. I might have suspected you couldn't be that slick. But, it's OK. The results were worth it."

"No, I mean I'm really sorry. You responded so well that Nancy wants me to do the same thing for her next year."

Spook and the
nonexistent cougar

Author's note: Yes, there is a reality close to Oswald K. Underfoot. Don't smile if you're foolish enough to tell him you read the story.

LEON DIPPED a rag in the bucket to soak up another application of epsom salts solution, and then began to daub it in the wounds of the huge, white, whimpering dog beside him.

"I don't know what I'm going to do, Leslie," he said to his blonde-haired friend who sat beside him. "Look at what they did to my Pyrenes last night. Usually he'll kill any coyote that tries to get the sheep, but this time they tore him all up. Darned near tore his ear off. Must be a pair of problem coyotes working together to have a chance fighting him, or maybe it's dogs. But I'm losing a sheep about every fourth or fifth day."

Leon motioned at the 200 white, wooly animals that grazed winter wheat pasture on nearby slope. "I have a good sized flock, but I can't stand these losses for long. Usually between my dog and my llama, they keep any coyotes away."

"Look, Leon," said Leslie to his big, square-built friend, his face suddenly krinkling up in anxiety, "I know of somebody who can help. At least when we had a problem coyote, he trapped him right away."

"Great! What's his name? Do you have a phone number?"

"Well, I'm not really sure I should give it to you, but maybe it would be OK."

"Why not? What would be better than to take care of whatever problem coyotes or dogs it is, so I can get on with business? Doesn't the guy work for anyone?"

"I don't know whether he'll do it for you or not," Leslie hesitated, looking at his friend worriedly. "I guess I could give you his name, but the one thing is, you can't tell him who told you about him. I suppose he's harmless, but still, I don't know if I want him to know I told about him. Just say you saw his name on a bulletin board somewhere."

"For crying out loud, why?" asked Leon, gently cradling the dog's head on his lap.

"Well, they call him the spook. Only don't say anything about spook around him. You'll see when you meet him, he's like he has a sixth sense, kind of spooky. He calls the coyotes 'charlies' like he's back in the Vietnam War or something. As a matter of fact, anything that's against him or that he's after seems to be a charlie. You'll see. Just be careful, and remember I never said a thing. Let's see, here's his name and number in my wallet, Oswald K. Underfoot."

"Yeah, Oswald K. Underfoot, not Ozzie, not Mr. Underfoot and not Oswald Underfoot, but Oswald K. Underfoot, and never say anything about spook or spooky even if he does."

With that description, Leon hesitated, but when another ewe disappeared in four days, he made the call.

"Hello, this is Leon Gambel. May I speak to Oswald K. Underfoot?"

"Who gave you my name?"

"Mr. Underfoot?"

"Hssss, never call me that! Mr. Underfoot was my father."

"I'm sorry. Are you Oswald K. Underfoot?"

"Who gave you my name?"

"I saw it on a bulletin board, and I guessed you were really good, and I'm having lots of trouble with some dogs or coyotes killing my sheep. I need help, please."

"Liar! Nobody would put Oswald K. Underfoot's name on a bulletin board. It's the charlies made you desperate, huh? You called me cuz you need charlie dead, right? Why should I help you?"

"I'll pay you whatever your fee is for fair work done. Please, I need help. Usually my dog or llama puts a stop to any sheep killing, but—"

"Hssss, I'll do it. Be there tomorrow morning."

The next morning opened with gray overcast sky and a steady north wind. Leon was down in the long tin barn checking the lambing pens where individual ewes stayed with new lambs or awaited birthing. He heard a vehicle's engine, and looked out the door to see a two-tone yellow and white 1970's-type International truck parked in the driveway with nobody in it. Then he heard someone clear his throat, "Ummh.

"Oswald K. Underfoot here."

"Oh, you came up behind me. I didn't see you. How did you get in the barn behind me anyway?"

"Oswald K. been circling," the small, dark man under a huge black and red cap with earflaps replied. "Always circling to see where charlie's been and where charlie's going."

Oswald K. Underfoot raised his bushy dark eyebrows, looking Leon up and down as he tilted his head sideways making a snuffling noise through his long nose. Leon could swear he was sniffing him from three feet away.

"Was you ever in the Nam?"

"Excuse me?" replied Leon. "You mean Vietnam? No, I was too young. I was just a kid during that war."

"Hmmm, at least you didn't run away. I think I might like you OK. You just call me Oswald. But you don't ever lie again about bulletin boards. Tell your sneaky friend, Leslie, Oswald K. Underfoot can bite back nasty, sneaky charlies. Oswald has been in tunnels after charlies. Yes, I know he's been here. I sniffed him out. Show me where the sheep stay," Oswald said, drawing his lips back over strong, white teeth.

Leon walked the perimeter of the sheep pasture with Oswald K.

Underfoot who at times stooped, and bobbed his head up and down, then paused sniffing the wind. He would turn to study the ground on both sides of the fence, then look up to study the horizon both ways.

"Now, Leon, we'll drive out to that hedgerow way over there, and Oswald will pick the places for traps. Lock your dog up so he doesn't get hit by friendly fire."

The bed of the International was covered with an assortment of traps, stakes, ropes and other paraphernalia. "Just push those bottles on the floor out of your way, Leon."

Oswald K. Underfoot started tiptoeing at the first big spreading tree in the hedgerow, hands extended, palms downward, in front of him, turning his head from side to side to look warily around him.

"Now, old charlie, he's walking up this hedgerow, snuff, snuff, and he's hungry, really hungry, poor old belly shrunk up under his ribs, snuff, snuff. Can't just jump out there though, Somebody might see the poor old coyote. Snuff, snuff, ah-haah, halfway up the hedgerow, what's old charlie smell, snuff, snuff. Sheep, there's sheep for the eating out there. But what's charlie going to do about that dog cuz he's a whole division just waiting, snuff, snuff.

"Now charlie stays low, walking out here in the grass, and here's this big clump here where charlie's going to turn. Ah-haah, then he puts one foot down here to raise his head like this, and sniffs the sheep he's going to eat, and looks around for that dog, and—clank! We gets him because we put a trap here, don't you see, Leon? And charlies is as good as dead right here because we'll be out for him. But oops, oops what if charlie moves this way. We still put a trap here, and then one here so we get another chance at him.

"Aah, but what if charlie has a partner that's a good coyote partner, and it's going to be back here a ways, backing charlie up for the final rush, and he's ducking down here to watch, so we put another trap here. And, ahh, what's this?" Oswald K. Underfoot jumped excitedly up in the air.

"What's what?" asked Leon, still puzzled over the entire performance.

"It's a bigger charlie, much bigger. You're lucky Leon. Oswald K. Underfoot has wanted this charlie a long time, old and hungry, mean and lean. Oswald's got you now," the little man ran in place, waved his arms, and gave a jump.

"What? What is it, Oswald?"

"Old and desperate, belly caved in, gone to sheep cuz they're easy, not fast like deer. Oswald's got you in the throat. You're dead, big charlie."

"What do you mean?"

"Cougar, mountain lion—you got a big cat, Leon. It says so right here."

"Lord, that's spooky."

"That's what? Snuff, snuff, what did you say to old Oswald K.

Underfoot? What's that you said," Oswald said sticking his face up under Leon's throat.

"Nothing, Oswald. I didn't say anything. I mean, this is unusual. The government says there's no mountain lions in the state."

"Government's always said charlie isn't here anymore, just in Oswald's head. But let me tell you, Leon, Oswald K. Underfoot knows charlie is here. Got him now, I do. I'll take you home now, then Oswald will be back to lay the traps. Can't leave lots of scent around. Surprise, charlie, Oswald K. Underfoot is here."

"Wait a minute, Oswald. We have to call the government. It's illegal to kill a cougar."

"You said it, Leon. Isn't any cougars here. Oswald can't kill something that isn't here, can he? Just poor old Ozzie the spook killing charlies, smile, smile government, but not you, Leon, cuz poor old Oswald K. Underfoot might cut your heart out," the small dark man said, smiling at him wolfishly.

Four days went by, and Leon saw no more of Oswald K. Underfoot. He began to feel a sense of relief. Maybe it would be better to just get out of the sheep business if any more were killed.

Then on the morning of the fifth day, as Leon came out of his house, the yellow and white International was setting there with Oswald K. Underfoot leaning on the hood watching him.

"Oswald K. Underfoot is here for his fee. Your sheep are saved," he said, and held out a big cat's paw seven inches across for Leon to see. "The thing that wasn't here isn't here anymore, and isn't buried out by your hedgerow either. Only us spooks here now," he said with a grin.

"Gosh, I guess that's good, Oswald. But I hope we don't get in any trouble."

"No, Leon Gambel, only charlie is in trouble because he met Oswald K. Underfoot out in the dark, charlie and—only time will tell—maybe your sneaky friend, Leslie."

Frosty knew politicians and badgers

FROSTY LOVED Republican politics and bromegrass. He usually didn't care for Democrats or badgers.

Maybe he was called Frosty because of the way his white hair was brushed back below the crown of his Panama straw hat or the way his white eyebrows laid over his dark-rimmed glasses.

But it also might have been because of the pipe he carried with the bowl cut to look like a corn cob mounted on the stem, like Frosty the snow man.

Take any issue, and the pipe would drop to one side while his opposite hand rested on his hip to prop up his concerned, indignant slanted pose, his head tilted up and to the side, the eyes intently holding yours through the top of the glasses while he launched into the discussion.

As the intensity of thought grew, Frosty's pipe got tapped out in one palm as he talked, then puffed out big squat clouds of smoke as he informed you of the insider talk of Republican ideas. And everyone listened, whether in necktie or overalls, because Frosty was knowledgeable.

He'd always called Bob Dole about the afternoon before about the current concern. Mention Dr. Bill Roy, the leading Kansas Democrat at the time, and the arms would fold as though holding a pain, the elbow of one arm slowly propped into the palm of the opposite hand to raise the pipe to the lower lip for a pause before a big puff. Then eyes raised to the very top of the glasses, Frosty would explain in a softened hurt voice the evils of the welfare state and the machinations of the supposed malcontent, Dr. Roy.

Mention bromegrass, and the pipe frequently would go out while Frosty spread his arms, and smiled at how this wondrous perennial crop was capable of producing pasture, hay and seed to sell, sometimes in the same year if the rains came. He'd bought this 80 acres or that quarter-section, put it all in terraces and waterways just like he would for any dirt crop, but then planted it into a good stand of heavily fertilized income-producing brome where hardly a grain of soil washed or blew away.

Then someone had to mention the badger, and the guys in ties and overalls would barely suppress smiles, because they knew Frosty didn't know this badger— beside which Dr. Roy could glow in innocence— nearly as well as he knew politicians.

The eyes arose to new height looking over glasses' dark rims, both arms folded and gripped tightly for maximum hurt, the pipe gripped with teeth in one corner of the mouth while both the smoke and the explanation burst out.

"Well, you see that badger was digging holes in my terraces, tearing up the grass everywhere. I'm telling you, I would drive my station wagon out there, and it was rough, holes all over.

"I drove out there one afternoon, the brome about six inches tall and I'm telling you it looked beautiful, and there he was. He's just out there in my grass waddling along.

"Well, I had my cowboy boots on, and I figured I could stomp his head. So I gets out, I walks up to him, and what do you figure but he turns around, scrunches up, raises his head, his fur's all sticking out, and he goes 'huugh' at me.

"Well, I raise my boot to stomp his head with the heel, and what do you think he does? He grabs my heel in his mouth with those pointy teeth, and I can't put my foot down. He backs me up, 'huugh," and I have to hop.

"There we go across the field, him scrunching up, going 'huugh,' and me hopping, and durn-it, he won't turn loose of my heel. When we get 20 feet from the stationwagon, he turns me loose, and wowee, I have to run for it.

"I tell you he chased me, and I barely got in the car without him. I had to go back later for my good straw hat. I was about winded. In 60 years I've not seen anything like that.

"I'm telling you, next time I'm out there, I'll have my shovel with me. Then we'll see who goes huugh."

People flocked
to see rodeo dog

Author's note: *Here's a story that shows truth can be
as interesting as fiction. Yes, the dog did these things.*

THERE WERE cowboys swinging ropes in the arena, or riding horseback
in pairs, talking to each other. The rodeo clown was walking the fence
shaking the big powder puff he would use on bulls at youngsters. A lady
barrel racer was going up and down showing her horse the fences. It was a
fine, busy pre-show to watch.

Then a bull-rider Cherokee cowboy named Mickey and his dog
named Dawg walked to the side of the arena.

Mickey, at 18, had thick black hair, fine features, and that jockey-type
slender build just right for horseracing or rodeo topping out at 140 lb.

Dawg, at 5, had that black-and-white marled medium-length hair typical of his breed, with the brown around the muzzle and the chest depth
and strong hind quarters just right for cow herding at 50 lb..

Mickey probably was seven-eighths European heritage and one-
eighth Cherokee. Dawg was exactly half Blue Heeler and half
Australian Shepherd.

Mickey said in an earnest moderate tone, "Now Dawg, I'm gonna be
busy for a while.

I want you to jump up here on that arena post, and watch the rodeo
until I come back for you when it's time for the bulls."

He hadn't made any motions, just talked to old Dawg, so the people
that could hear were interested to see Dawg obligingly jump up on the
big square-topped post, and sit.

Mickey walked away.

And Dawg just watched from atop that post for an hour while even
the most active events, like calf roping and steer wrestling, went by.
Men and women wondered when he would jump down, and small children wanted to climb up there with him.

Finally Mickey came back to call, "Dawg, it's time."

Dawg jumped right down, and went straight to the side of the bull
chutes. He barked once or twice when Mickey climbed up on a huge
brindle Brahman cross, then quietly watched the wrenching ride until
Mickey was done.

When the rodeo was over, half the crowd saw Mickey drive his
pickup truck down main street with Dawg panting and grinning out the
side window until they reached the pink-painted Ern's Beefhouse Diner.

Mickey and Dawg went into the diner, and Mickey pulled out the
chair across from his at the red vinyl-topped 1950's table for Dawg to sit

up. The crowd hushed, and many of them wondered who would say something about a man bringing a dog into a restaurant.

Judy the pert, small blonde waitress knew what to say but she paused, giving Mickey time to speak first.

"Ma'am," he said smiling shyly because Judy was pretty, and had big dangly round silver earrings that dazzled his eyes, "I'll have the roast beef dinner, but Dawg here will just have a hamburger with only pickles, no onions."

Judy said, "Sir, we can't have a dog in here. It's against health rules."

Mickey blushed. He looked down at the table. Dawg just smiled up at her, and sat quietly.

"Mam," Mickey said, "if Dawg isn't good enough for your place, then I sure ain't either."

Judy looked around the room at all the folks dressed up in their rodeo kerchiefs and jeans, and everybody was just still. A little curley-top girl in the back said, "Mama, that rodeo dog still isn't moving."

Judy blinked first.

"OK, sir, you both can stay—as long as he keeps in his chair, doesn't cause any problems, and nobody complains."

Everybody agreed that Dawg was quite fastidious and polite, only nibbling small hunks of hamburger at a time, while Mickey had never learned not to hold two pieces of silverware at once.

Back in the kitchen, Trudy, the hamburger flipping cook with red hair, freckles and turquoise beads in her ears, said to Judy, "Isn't he cute. He may be about the sweetest one we ever had in here."

Big Ern, the restaurant

owner, said, as he played with his neck hairs,"He looks like a plain old cowboy to me—maybe a little thicker black hair than usual, but no better manners. Look at the way he chews with open mouth, and big wadded chunks of food still in his cheeks—yuck!"

"Not the cowboy, silly," said Judy,"we're talking about the dog aren't we, Trudy?"

"We sure are," said Trudy. "To tell you the truth, I never even noticed the cowboy, but I suppose he's OK, if he's your type. His ears stick out kind of funny, don't they? But, notice the dog—doesn't he look smart when he holds his ears up to look at people going out?"

"You're right," said Ern. "That dog shows real refinement, real manners and intelligence—he's kind of refreshing just to see, isn't he?"

Apparently the people going to the rodeo agreed. The word spread.

On the second day of the rodeo, the crowd across the entire grandstand paused to watch Dawg jump up on the post.

On the second day at Ern's Beefhouse, Judy said, "Well, hi Dawg," when Mickey and Dawg came in. "You know, you have quite the shine in those eyes," she added taking his face between her hands to look at him after he jumped up in the chair.

"Thump, thump, thump," went Dawg's tail against the back of his chair, and he hung out his tongue in a big grin."

"That dog shows real character," Ern said. "I can't say I ever admired an animal more."

"I just love him," said Trudy. "He's the only reason I went to the rodeo today."

"I find I'm looking forward to seeing him just all the time," said Judy as she checked her eyes, and touched up her lipstick in a mirror before going out to the tables again.

"Well, are you going to have your same old hamburger today?" Judy said leaning over to Dawg when she went out again.

"I think I'm ready to order too," said Mickey.

On the third day of the rodeo, Judy, Trudy and Ern stood by Dawg's post with a dozen kids as he waited before Mickey came to get him. When Dawg went to the bull chutes, the crowd applauded him.

Dawg was proud to stand by Mickey when the cowboys lined up in the arena afterwards to receive their awards and prize money. Mickey was bruised, bone-sore, and beaten by the bulls, especially by a big, black animal named Satan that threw him to put him down in the point spreads. But he did get third prize and a $100 check.

They made up a special grand prize purple ribbon just for Dawg, and he got a breeding dog page in the cow dog registry with a photo of him sitting on the arena post. A dozen patrons asked to bring their female dogs to him to get pups at a fee of $200 per live litter.

Dawg also got a year's supply of hamburgers free anytime he came in at Ern's Beefhouse Diner.

Later, Mickey asked Judy if she would take a truck ride with him and Dawg after work. "You'll have to sit in the middle though," he said. "Dawg always rides by the window, so he can look out."

When it was time for the truck ride, Dawg jumped into the middle of the seat, and wouldn't move even when Mickey pushed on him. Judy rode by the window, and Dawg smiled the whole way. Mickey finally smiled too.

People asked Mickey about his dog training methods. "I don't know," he always said, "I just talk to Dawg."

It wasn't long before Mickey realized Judy was talking to Dawg more than he was.

Mickey and Judy have Dawg's big purple ribbon and pictures of his progeny hung over Mickey's bull riding ribbons in their home now.

Sometimes Mickey wonders why a girl like Judy was ever attracted to him, a plain old bow-legged stub of a cowboy. He was just lucky or blessed, he guesses.

As for Dawg, he doesn't have to guess. He knows why.

Taking the horn
by the bulls

Author's note: This is another animal story where, yes, the bull really did these things, and he was a frighteningly powerful animal.

THERE WAS one ceremony in writing articles about farm and ranch operations in those days we all dreaded.

It was the laying-the-hands-on-the-bull ceremony.

I call it a ceremony because it seemed to have assumed an almost psuedo-religious repetitiveness that halfway through any interview with anybody who raised any kind of Brahmin-crossbred cattle, that person was going to invite you to pet the bull.

Usually the guy insisted. Brahmin breeders wanted you to know their bulls weren't the bucking, snorting animals trained for rodeo, and were safe for any farm.

The fellow would lead you into the lot for some photos, and to show you his long-eared cattle. First thing you knew you'd be next to some gray, black, red or brindle one-ton monster, and the Breeder would say: "See, he's gentle. Go ahead, and pet him on the side there. He ain't gonna hurt you."

Bird and I always knew that if the bull just flung his nose to the side to shoo away a fly, one massive horn could whack a body in two. Besides, one eye on the bovine horror always seemed to roll at you as if to say, "I know the guy who feeds me, but who are you?"

Bird and I had petted Beefmasters, Brangus, Santa Gertrudis and pure Brahmins in Arkansas, Oklahoma, Missouri and Kansas.

The dread of Brahmins seemed to have reached a perfect peak in us when Mickey, our Cherokee cowboy friend, invited us to ride in his truck with him—for enjoyment mind you—while he did a short job.

I call him a Cherokee cowboy because he came from Oklahoma, he had some Cherokee Nation genetics in him, he was in rodeos until the bulls bouncing him on his head gave him occasional blackouts, and he still did local cowboy work.

People would call him to get cattle out of pastures when they couldn't, or to rope a problem animal for veterinary treatment. Sometimes he and his big gray gelding, Pilgrim, were there with other horsemen to bring cattle home from pasture just because the pasture ground was rough.

So, Mickey came by at the close of work one day with Pilgrim tied in the front of a 20-foot gooseneck trailer, all saddled and bridled with a lariat hanging on the horn, and his old gray-muzzled dog, Dawg, riding on the flatbed three-quarter-ton truck pulling it.

Mickey was in a fine smiling mood. Bird was tired and I was tired, but we took the Pepsis Mickey offered, and tried to smile too.

"Well, what are we going to do, Mickey?" Bird asked, squinting through his glasses at him, and then at me while he loosed the top button of his shirt.

"We're going to get my bull out of a pasture, Bird. He's a cleanup bull I rent out."

"What kind of a bull do you have, Mickey?"

"Oh, he's crossed for vigor, Brown Swiss, Limousin and Brahmin—a real go-getter. He puts a little ear, longer and floppier like a Brahmin's, on his calves so they know which ones they are."

Bird's pink face was quite a bit pinker, and he was looking at me over the top of his glasses, his lips pressing to drive the blood from them, and then coming back near red again.

"Swiss and Brahmin in the same animal, huh? Sounds like he's double-wired."

"We aren't hands, you know," Bird said. "We can't do much for you."

"You don't really have to do anything much," Mickey said. "Don't worry, he's gentle."

Bird's glasses had about slid off his nose, and he was biting a lip.

But before we could bring ourselves to talk more, Mickey had already pulled up to a pasture gate, and then drove through to a big open place in the grassland. He dropped us off, drove the rig another 200 feet away from us, then stopped to open the rear door of the trailer.

"Now I guess we'll see some real horsemanship," I said.

"Yeah, if we live that long," Bird said. "There isn't much place to go to for cover here— just prairie, prairie and prairie. Maybe if we cover our eyes, he won't mess our faces up much for the funeral."

The horse was still tied in the front of the trailer, Dawg was taking a nap on the flatbed, being ho-hum about the situation, and Mickey was calling: "Here, Larry. Here, Larry."

Over the top of a slope came an enormous black and brindle bull in his prime, with the typical Brahmin dewlap and upswept foot-long horns.

Bird and I, like the trained troops we were, had swallowed our nerve to hold our stomachs in place.

"There you are, Lawrence," Mickey crooned by the trailer door. "That's a good boy, Larry, com'on, com'on."

The bull came on at a full trot into the back of the trailer, which bounced with the great weight while Mickey closed the door. We waited to see horse blood spewed all over.

But when Mickey drove the truck and trailer back to get us, we could see Pilgrim and Larry standing side by side. Mickey gave a small, wry smile, and winked at Bird.

"They were raised together," he said. "That horse and bull love each other like brothers. Besides, Lawrence always knows he's going to a new bunch of cows."

Hard Times Hattie
wins in the end

Author's note: She was one of the ladies who pre-dated the humane societies. I saw it happen.

HARD SELL HARRY contentedly inhaled a deep draft of tobacco smoke down his lungs from the cigarette he held as his white station wagon kicked up a dense cloud of gravel dust on the road.

A third of the brushes he had to sell in the backend of the car was already gone.

Harry, the man. Hard Sell, Hard Shell, Hard Hearted Harry, his peers called him all these things.

He glanced in the rearview mirror at the harsh, triangular face with butch haircut, clenching the cigarette, and smiled. Yes, he really was his own beautiful Hard Sell Harry.

He'd kept his last customer, a harried poor housewife with squalling children, an entire two hours until she squandered an appalling portion of her monthly budget on his brushes. It had been beautiful.

Now he followed his usual practice of beating the party telephone warning calls that there was a salesman in the neighborhood to skip two or three farmsteads while he grabbed a smoke. He'd get back to them.

His next selection was down a long lane with a red barn to one side and a white-fenced yard with a green-roofed, green-shuttered house to the other.

A curly gray-haired woman, wearing a white apron over a flowered yellow dress followed by a big collie dog, was stooping to pick up a wicker bushel basket in the yard.

She was frowning, looking over the rims of bifocal glasses at him as he walked to the gate. The dog had barked, but she'd told him to be quiet. Kittens of all sizes and colors were darting around at play or running around the yard.

Harry rejoiced inside. He knew this type. He might just sell half the remaining brushes.

He paused as he introduced himself and his wares because the basket she had been tugging at was covered with a lid, and he could detect movement inside.

"I'm Hattie, Harry," she said. "And, I just don't have time to talk to you until we get these kittens all caught. This is sorting day. I can't feed all of them. I have to buy cat food. Don't keep a cow anymore, so they don't get milk. You can help me catch them, and then I'll listen to you while I sort."

So, for the next half-hour, Harry helped Hattie catch kittens, black ones, white ones, gray ones, calicos and other two-tones. Some were easy to catch while others ran under white board lawn chairs or the porch, went up trees, or into rose and lilac bushes. Harry thought he had never seen so many kittens in one place. He and Hattie kept gathering them until they had stuffed kittens into three bushel baskets.

"Well, Harry that was warm work," Hattie said. "I'll get us some cold drinks and cookies, and we'll sit out here in the lawn chairs while I begin to sort kittens. I make my cookies with lard, but you won't mind that, will you, Harry? You ever had hard times, Harry? Once we had hard times, and we sure were glad when we got some lard to eat. Lard's good for you when you've had hard times."

Harry occasionally had to stuff a kitten crawling past the lid back into a basket as he waited. His salesman instincts were rising. He would go for blood. A half-hour of kitten catching was nothing. He's done worse to make a sale.

Hattie settled into a lawn chair, took a big sip of tea, and motioned the collie to sit upright at her side.

"Okay, Mr. Harry, you can begin," she said, actually smiling at him, "I can sort while I eat cookies."

Harry was already pointing out the number of bristles at each juncture on each brush as she pulled the first kitten from a basket.

"Oh, my goodness, a calico," said Hattie. "Look at this, Shep," she said to the dog. "I never let go of a calico this pretty. Now, you get going little girl," she said as she lowered the kitten to release it on the ground.

"Mam, I was just saying about this laundry brush," Harry said.

"Yes, yes, Mr. Harry. You go right on ahead. Oh my, a gray kitten, a solid gray kitten."

Hattie put down a cookie to raise the gray kitten above her face looking thoughtfully at him over her bifocals. "Gray cats are good mousers, but I have enough old gray ones."

"Shep, do it," she said, handing the kitten to the dog who took it in his jaws, gave a great crunch, and dropped it lifeless to the ground.

"My God, he killed it! He killed that kitten," Harry cried.

"Why, yes, he killed it, Harry. That's what he knew I wanted him to do," Hattie said. "He's a good dog, didn't take any pleasure in it, just did what he was told. It's hard times, Harry. I got too many kittens, and everybody's got enough cats, they don't want anymore. With this many kittens around they'd just get the St. Vidas dance or some other disease, and I'd lose them anyway."

"He killed that kitten. You killed that kitten," Harry said.

"Why, yes I did," said Hattie as she munched a cookie. "That's the way life is, Harry."

Hard Sell Harry drove his car down the gravel road at a subdued speed that didn't kick up much dust at all holding a cigarette in his mouth that he scarcely puffed on. A kitten crawled over the foot he held on the accelerator while more kittens played on the seat beside him, and even more were crawling out of the baskets in the car.

Hard Sell, Hard Shell, Hard Hearted Harry had been outsold by Hard Times Hattie.

Twister 'some kind of predicament'

Author's note: It was not only a predicament, but the biggest thing I thought I'd ever seen.

POP WILSON raised the broken arm tucked inside his overalls for emphasis, and patted the bandaged pad on his bald head with his good hand before beginning his story.

His pale blue eyes twinkled, and his broad grin showed his delight as he gazed at the half-dozen people around him. It was rare to have such audiences continually gather around him.

Pop said: "Well, you'll all remember it was just a typical June day, kind of hot and sticky, but yeah, that is typical.

"I was about ready to go to the house to see how Mom was coming with supper sometime after six o'clock when I noticed what breeze there'd been had plumb gone dead. I'd finished milkin' the cow, you see.

"I was steppin' up on the porch when I looks out to the west, and I could see some little clouds comin' from the south and some little clouds comin' from the north. And I says to myself, 'Well, that looks peculiar.'

"Old Shep wants to go through the door with me, and I thinks to myself, that old dog doesn't usually want in.

"I goes into the house with Shep, and I says to Mom, 'Maybe we ought to switch on the TV, and see if they're givin' any weather.'

"Well, they was givin' tornado warnin', said there was reports of a twister damagin' a farm out west.

"So Mom and I go look out the window, and there she was, the biggest thing I ever saw in my life. I tell you that twister filled the whole middle third of the horizon like a big old column. It wasn't no little elephant's trunk. I says to Mom, 'Well, isn't that somethin',' and Mom agreed.

"Well, this big old tornado was all pale gray, almost white at first, so it almost didn't show up like you were seein' what you were seein'. Then, as it kept getting closer, you begin to see it must be sucking up stuff because it was getting blacker and blacker.

"Well, you know, we never did have a basement, not even a cave or a crawl space. I remember once I said to Mom, 'Well maybe we ought to have a basement. They seem real nice.' Mom said goin' up and down stairs don't seem real nice at our age, and I guessed she was right seein' as how we'd always got along without one.

"Anyway, this great big twister's a-gettin' closer and closer, and blacker and blacker, and I could tell by Mom's face she's startin' to get concerned.

"So I says, 'Mom, don't worry. You see that little knoll over there below the big hill? That's right, the one that looks like a hay meadow—

someone probably will cut prairie hay there this summer. Well, them tornados always give a little jump when they hit that knoll, and they'll go right back up in the clouds. She'll go over us.'

"Well, Mom and I was watchin' as the twister came up to that knoll, and boy, were we ever surprised. She just come over that knoll like it wasn't even there, and the doggone thing was almost to us.

"I says to Mom, 'Well, wasn't that unusual?' and she nods at me. But it's startin' to get hard to hear because it's a roarin' at us.

"So, I says to Mom, 'Maybe we ought to go crawl under the bed,' and she agrees. So, we do, and I tries to put my arm over Mom, but you know it's kind of tight under a bed even though neither one of us carries much weight. So, I ends up just layin' my face down on my arms, and waitin', and I s'pose Mom was doin' the same. I guess I prayed a time or two because I was startin' to get nervous.

"Mom had made the bed up real nice that mornin' like we was havin' company, but don't s'pect she'd figured on a twister. Don't know where Shep was.

"Well, I s'pose it was closer and closer because I couldn't hear anything anymore. Then I just sort of come off the floor, and I knew I was

goin' up in the air. I tries to look for Mom, but it didn't feel like I could open my eyes. I move my arms and my legs, and they'll move. I says to myself, 'Well, this is interesting, but it's some kind of a predicament.'

"Then somethin' hit me in the head. I tell you it's like to be the hardest I ever was hit in the head. Oh, I've hit my head on stuff like everybody has, and once a cow kicked me, but this was harder than any of that. I just sort of blacked out.

"Well, I finally comes around a little, but I still can't see, and my arms and legs don't want to move. I thinks, well, if Mom and me's stuck through hedge trees like a twister puts straw in the wood, at least we won't need toothpicks for supper no more.

"Then I realized there wasn't anymore roarin', and there's somethin' wrapped all around me so I can't move very well. I starts to hollerin' for someone to come help me, and to strugglin' with it. I finally gets an arm out, and gets to unravelin' myself, and, what do you know? I was wrapped up in our own bed sheets, and my other arm's hurtin' because I broke it, you see.

"Well, I starts lookin' around for Mom when I see this other lump of sheets just five feet from me. I unwraps it, and it's Mom. She just looks at me while I get her up, and wonders where we're at.

"Well, when we climbs out of there we could see, that twister had dumped us in our neighbor's basement, but their house wasn't there on top. Now wasn't that a funny way to finally get a basement?

"Our house wasn't there anymore either. In fact, that big twister had landscaped the place so different it was hard to see exactly where we was at or where anything had been. All the trees was either busted, or pulled out by the roots, or just plain gone. The sun was shinin' on that little knoll.

"The rescue people came, and took us to the hospital by and by. They checked us, and taped us all up. We never did see the cow or the chickens again. Old Shep came back after a week.

"You know, that big tornado killed some people, and sure killed a lot of animals, hogs, horses, cows— all of them. Me and Mom, well, I guess it just wasn't our time to go.

"But I told Mom there's at least one good thing to come out of it. You can talk about your John Glenn and all of them other astronauts. But I'm the first man to spacewalk in this county."

With that, Pop Wilson grinned again at his audience, and did his best to shake hands with as many of them as he could.

Barry liked Audie
more than baseball

Author's note: This guy could also hit a baseball straight down the center of a gravel road for a quarter-mile if you told him that's what you wanted him to do. He could do it the very first time, and you could spend a boring afternoon waiting for him to miss once.

BARRY WAS just a plain big brown-haired kid. We'd never thought of him as anything but one of us, doing all the same playing, carrying on and teasing everybody did.

Except, come to think of it, he never did tease—just some artful name calling, which is maybe part of why we all liked him.

He was a head taller than any of us, and his shoulders were a third broader across than the next biggest boy's.

Lying there in the cool, knee-deep brome grass by the old school house, waiting for the first lightning bugs to come out, Barry was usually first to see a star appear in the evening sky. Later, we might have learned the star was the planet Venus. Barry just said it was so pretty he hoped no "Japs" lived there.

Old war movies were special fare on television, and Barry was obsessed with shooting Japs and Nazis long after the rest of us ceased to talk about them. That might have clued us.

Another clue might have been that in third and fourth grade, when Miss Langdon said everybody had to stay in from recess until they memorized the times tables, Barry was still there two weeks after everybody else had learned them. He still didn't know them past the threes.

We just felt sorry for him because he'd missed so much recess, which was the most important reason for being at school.

Sometime after that they sent him to his own special school, but we still played together in the neighborhood.

Somebody told Barry you could tell Germans apart from regular Americans because they had blue blood, especially those with Nazi tendencies.

Terry said he was part German.

Barry asked him: "Will you cut your finger so we can see? You can use my pocket knife. It doesn't hurt much. I did it once."

"I ain't a Nazi, though, and I'm probably mixed up with Englishman," Terry said.

He was right. The blood was red.

Barry said Japs seemed sneakier than Germans, but they weren't because you could tell which ones they were even without uniforms.

He added that if we wanted to see the real thing, the movie "Audie

Murphy" (known in Hollywood as "To Hell and Back") was going to be on television that afternoon starring the real Audie Murphy, a real war hero.

Once, we were standing there in the farmyard, legs spread far apart facing each other, playing stick'um with pocket knives, when Barry noticed a pig rooting a Nazi helmet around with his nose. Our father and uncles had dumped the helmets in the hog lots when they came home from the war—in retrospect now, probably as a final insult to the fallen enemy.

"Wow, lookee," Barry said, his teeth shining widely in his big round face. "A real Nazi helmet, swastika, eagle and everything!"

"Yeah, Barry," we replied, "and there's one there, and another one over there, and there's one in the shed."

Then we shamefully added, "and their bodies are down there in all that mud."

"Bet you I can get'em again," Barry said, and he picked up a stick, hit a piece of gravel with it, and the rock sailed out there to strike a helmet—"ping" it rang.

"Bet you can't do that again," everybody said, and Barry obligingly hit rocks three or four more times with the stick to ping those helmets.

We were amazed, but we forgot that incident—along with our interest in war movies, all except Barry that is—as the years went by.

Barry started throwing hay bales for local farmers before the rest of us could lift them. Then, as we got into our teenage years with enough size to buck bales, we began hauling hay too, sometimes with Barry down on the hayrack to throw bales to us through a hayloft door because he was the strongest.

The only complaint we ever heard about him was that nobody could get him to stop drinking too much water between loads, so he got sick.

One day he'd really slowed down on the wagon because he was heaving. He'd talked incessantly about whether we could quit early because the Audie Murphy movie was going to be on the afternoon movie. Jim got disgusted with Barry, and pushed a bale back out the loft door onto him.

Barry jumped off the wagon, picked up a stick, and hit a rock through the loft door to strike a beam over Jim's head.

"If you'd a been a Jap, I wouldn't've missed," Barry yelled.

Remembering that earlier incident, we called to Barry, "Bet you can't do that again."

He did, and the rock hit the beam in the same place.

Everybody seemed to have the same idea at once. We got Barry down to the Kawtown community building below the high school. We gave him a bat, and one of the guys got on the mound to pitch to him.

"Where do you want me to hit it?" Barry asked.

We kiddingly told him to hit the side of the fair building down south, knowing full well that even the best of the older guys on the fast-pitch town team didn't hit the ball that far.

On the first pitch, Barry hit the ball, and it hit the side of the fair building. On the second pitch, the ball hit the fair building. On the third pitch, Barry hit a high foul.

"It's easier than hitting rocks though," Barry said.

We got old Jake from the town team leadership to come watch for a while.

Jake wrinkled his forehead between his glasses and forehead, so we knew he was impressed.

"Boys that kid could be a pro. We got Henry, the softball fast-pitch king against us Saturday. We'll sneak that kid into the lineup some-where in the middle of the game, and give old Henry the surprise of his life."

We were all excited for Barry. He was going to get at least the break a small town could give him.

Saturday we got Barry into the bleachers behind the town team. The older guys on the team would look up at us smiling from time to time as they came in from the warmup with gloves hanging at their sides.

Barry had his red ball cap pushed back on his head, and sometimes he would smile back at them. We would change him to the team's blue-and-gold cap later.

Henry was amazing in his warmup. Never had we seen a ball sizzle over the plate to crack in the catcher's mitt that way. Of course, the guys all said, the harder it's thrown, the harder it can be hit.

We fed Barry popcorn and a Coke, and asked him: "Man, aren't you excited? This is a big chance for you."

"Yes, I am excited," Barry said, his brown eyes rolling from side to side to not miss anything. "And Audie Murphy is going to be on televi-sion today."

"Yeah, but you've seen Audie Murphy before. How many times have you seen that movie anyway?"

Barry thought for a moment.

"Oh I've seen it maybe three times three is nine—a really lot of times. But I want to see it some more."

The game proceeded at a slow pace through the first three innings. It was 3-0 with the town team down because nobody was hitting off Henry. Barry was getting fidgety so Terry took him to the stand for another Coke.

Finally Jake gave us a wink, and a come-on with his hand, and we hurried down to get Barry and Terry back from the stand.

We found Terry standing by the ball field. He'd left Barry standing in line for the Coke. But when we got to the stand, there was no Barry there.

"Have you seen a big guy in a red cap?" we asked the girl running the stand.

"Yeah," she said. "He was a friendly big galoot. He got a Coke, and told me all about how Audie Murphy was the greatest war hero, and he was going home to watch his movie now."

Sometimes you have to wonder if what might have been one of the great professional baseball hitters of all time never got the chance because he liked war movies better than playing ball.

They don't have many of the old war movies on television anymore, but Barry has videotapes.

A battle of Will...
and Carmen

WILL STARED through the window at the big bay gelding in the steel-pipe corral, and snorted to himself.

Well, I've fouled myself up this time, he thought, tapping the toe of his cowboy boot on the hardwood floor. I've got no choice but to call Carmen.

"Charmin' Carmen the crafty...," Will stopped just short of adding crook, but he thought of it anyway. He didn't believe in labeling someone a crook unless they were caught outright. But the closest thing to a crook, he knew, is a horse trader.

Will was hoping Carmen the horse trader would give him a good price for the gelding without too much haggling because he didn't want to take the time for advertising the horse or waiting for a good horse auction.

The transmission on Will's old car was going out, and he was buying a brand new Chrysler New Yorker. "Brand spanking new, nothing else will do," he muttered.

And he would pay cash. Will always paid cash because he'd learned the hard way what being in debt was like. His slush fund was about enough for the car, but the money for the gelding would put him over the top with a little boot before the next bunch of calves sold. He and his wife, Edna, would pick up the new car tomorrow morning.

Some of his other money in savings had given Will the reputation among neighbors for having "deep pockets." But that money was untouchable for something like a car or a horse that wasn't absolutely needed. He had other horses—all of them registered Quarterhorses—both for himself and his hired help.

Will smoothed down a shock of the graying red hair tumbling over his sunburned forehead before picking up the phone. Cash was the deal for a cow-calf man. Didn't owe for the cows or the calves, and not much for land. Land was different. If a fellow ever had a chance to pick up a little more land at a price he could live with, borrowing was OK.

"Carmen...Will here," he told the horse trader's answering machine. "Got a prime good-colored gelding here with cow sense to sell. I'll be home if you got time to look."

Will slipped on his Stetson-type straw hat to do morning feeding, and spent the next two hours kicking bales of hay to calves and horses before finally ending up at the gelding's pen.

Yes, that horse was a picture of symmetry. He set right on his hocks, moved around the pen with ease, and even the four black stockings on his legs cut off nearly even below the leg joints.

Will sighed, and almost came to relent in his decision to sell the horse, but he'd only owned him a couple of weeks, so there wasn't too much attachment yet. But he'd ridden him several times, through cattle and on open ground, and he knew the lustrous intelligence reflected in the horse's big eyes proved out in performance, too.

Then Carmen drove in, right up beside him, and rolled down a window. Where Will's features were fine and thin, Carmen's were heavy, high-boned and broad like some extra-thick ancient Sioux chief. Will steeled himself. Get set for charm.

"How you doin', old buddy?" Carmen was smiling at him from under spectacles on a big nose. "Got a good horse to sell, Will?"

"Sure do, Carmen."

"Well, where is he?"

"Why this is him right here."

"Broke to lead is he? By the way, how's Edna? Frances has been meanin' to come see her."

"Lead, heck. He handles like a dream. This is a cow-cuttin' horse. Now look here, I said he was good. If you want to try to put some yack on me, let's just stop here."

"Now, now, Willy, boy, I wuz just checkin' your pulse. If you say he's good, he's good," Carmen said, gimping his big frame out the car door while holding on to another straw hat that was just like Will's.

As they stood side by side eyeing the gelding, Will was painfully aware of Carmen's big paunch and bow legs over cowboy boots, and his own developing smaller belly. Lord, he hoped he stayed in some kind of shape.

Carmen had pulled a camera out of the car with him.

"You care to let me take a few pictures of you on him puttin' him through his paces, if don't you mind saddlin' up, Will?"

"That'd be OK, unless you care to ride him yourself." Will allowed a smile inside himself. Riding the horse would almost be too much work for Carmen the Charmin'. They'd known each other since childhood, and he knew Carmen would always rather gab for a living than actually do something.

"No, no, I'll just take a few shots here."

So Will rode, while Carmen shot. Then Will posed while Carmen shot.

"Are we done yet, Carmen?"

"I guess. What kind of price you figurin' on?"

"I hate to take so little for him, but if you're going to take him outright here, I'd take $3,500 for him."

"Oh, my gosh, Will. I am sorry, but I got to be able to make a profit with him. I'm makin' my whole livelihood buyin' and sellin' now. Couldn't possibly give you more than $2,000 for him."

"Now, Carmen, I figure that somehow you're going to end up with about $5,000 for this horse, and I want my money."

"I don't know if I could possibly do $2,500 or not."

"I said $3,500, and I mean it."

"I tell you what, Will. Let's sit on it overnight, OK? You're my old buddy, let's see what we can do."

Then Carmen proceeded to ask about cattle and neighbors for another half-hour before adding, "Write you a check for $2,000 here and now, Will?"

"Naah, we'll do better than that."

"So, $2,500 just cuz we're old buddies make you happier," Carmen said, grinning.

Will smiled back. "Happier wouldn't be hilarious enough."

By the time a cloud of dust closed behind Carmen's car, Will was tired.

The next morning dawned with anticipation at picking up the new car. Will felt a rush because he knew Carmen wouldn't let a horse like that get away from him.

Edna smiled at his sudden enthusiasm over breakfast, and asked, "So you really think Carmen's coming back for him?"

"Sure he is. He's into the trade now." Will actually went out to feed whistling a tune that died quickly on his lips as he came to the gelding's pen.

Will looked over the gate at four feet sticking up in the air. The horse was dead. He walked disbelieving around the carcass of what had been a healthy animal wondering how on earth this had happened.

He went to the house to call the veterinarian for a post-mortem when suddenly a better alternative came guiltily to him. The horse was dead anyway. Why not get that Carmen for just once?

He called, and got Carmen's answering machine. "Hey Carmen, Will here. Think I was too hasty. I know you got to make money too, buddy. I'll take your $2,000 for the gelding. I'm going to pick up a car now, but I don't have to be here. You just come on over, and pick him up."

"Will," Edna said as they drove to town, "do you think that was really the right thing to do to poor Carmen? He's not going to know what to do either when he sees that horse dead. How's he going to feel?"

"I don't know. I was feelin' real bad about that horse. But right now, I just sort of want to enjoy it." Will actually chuckled a little.

When they returned home, the horse was gone, and Will didn't hear from Carmen that night or the next night.

Two weeks went by, and Will became afraid to call Carmen. What if Carmen flew into a rage, or told all the neighbors that Will was a crook? A crook calling a crook would be awfully believable.

By the time a month had gone by, Will had lost most of his enthusiasm for the new car, and he was feeling petrified of seeing Carmen.

He nearly jumped off the ground one day when Carmen drove in while he was feeding.

Will walked to meet him as Carmen got out of the car, and he was surprised to see Carmen was smiling.

"Hey, Will, old buddy. I'm sorry I took so long to get back here. Took me a little while to get a deal put together on your horse. Here's a check for you for $2,500. Felt like I said I would go that extra $500."

"But, Carmen, that horse was dead. I'm so sorry. How can I take your money for him?"

"Don't you worry, Will. I'd already sold him before you called. Did real well too. I hate to admit it, but you were right. Actually got a little more than $5,000 for him."

"But he was dead. You couldn't sell him like that!"

"Well, you see I got me a bunch of jars, cut slots in the lids, put pictures of you ridin' him on them, put me a sign on them sayin' put your address and a dollar in here for a chance of gettin' this horse, and put them in stores up and down 200 miles of highway. People filled those jars clear up because you were right, Will. He sure was a flashy, good lookin' horse. I'd give a dollar myself just to see you ride him again," Carmen said with a grin.

"But Carmen, that horse was dead. You had to have a winner or you were running a crooked game. Not even you could do that. What was that winner going to say?"

Carmen looked grieved for a moment, but then his grin was restored—a big satisfied grin that cut his broad face in two.

"Now, Will, you know I've always been fair to everybody I dealt with. Yeah, the winner was unhappy alright. But I gave him his dollar back. Fair is fair."

Christmas Eve thaw

A SOFT BUT heavy wet snow had fallen all Christmas Eve day of 1956 covering completely the brick sidewalk in the half-block between the two houses.

But still Mary delayed.

She had her two grandsons and their parents for Christmas and the night before, and she knew her husband's sister, Cora, dearly wanted to see the little boys.

It was Rinaldo, her husband's brother, that she didn't want to see or particularly have around the boys. Rinaldo was in a wheel chair with a requisite list of illnesses from the doctors for being there, but Mary believed the truth behind his sickness was his debauched life.

It was true that the doctors said his downhill slide in health had begun with exposure to mustard gas in World War I. But that didn't excuse the man for all the other things he'd done in life. He had even driven her own husband to work harder on the farm, hurting his own health, and taken money from him.

Rinaldo couldn't abide a filter cigarette, but still rolled his own, even chewing and swallowing the stubs. He drank incessantly—beer, wine, anything else he could get his hands on, and had wasted his youth and middle years in corrupt wandering. He'd divorced two wives, neither of whom Mary had much approved of to start with.

Rinaldo had become bitter hard as winter with his hard black eyes shining almost savagely from inside the deep wrinkled eye folds of experience. His swarthy skin was freckled with brown age spots, and here he still tried to throw back his head arrogantly to look at her as though he had youthful vigor. He even made poor Cora still dye his hair, and comb it back in black strands.

Besides all that, Mary thought angrily, batting her light brown eye-lashes, when she asked to bake cherry pies in their oven for the guests coming, even bringing an extra pie for Cora and Rinaldo, the nasty old man had insisted she bring down her own bucket of coal so their supply didn't dwindle.

Cora on the other hand was a good and godly poor widow who had taken this reprobate in, caring for him, feeding him, and keeping him clean.

By 3 p.m., Mary could delay no longer. Randy, the blonde 7-year-old could just about pull his own galoshes on for the short journey, but Steven, the dark-haired 4-year-old still needed help with overshoes and coat.

Finally they were started down the walk, the boys stomping, and turning to see the deep imprints they made in the snow. She could see Cora looking outside the kitchen window, and then rushing to the back door off the porch-room to the kitchen as they arrived.

"My goodness, look who's here," Cora cried, holding her hands to the gray sidewalls of her own black hair. "It's Grandma, and this must be Randy and Steven."

"Yeth, it ith," said Randy looking up at Cora with a grin that revealed a row of missing front teeth.

Old Rinaldo sat in his wheelchair at the back of the kitchen trying to eat a spoonfull of oatmeal from his shaking palsied hand, pausing to look at the boys with tight-lipped smile set in determination.

He looked for a moment at Mary with bright, knowing black eyes, slightly nodding his head, then losing control one moment with his head rolling to the right, the smile becoming a scowl.

The boys unfearfully walked right up to him. "He's sick," Steven said solemnly.

"Yeth, heth either thick or heth got a ditheath," Randy said.

"He's sick or he's got a what?" Cora questioned.

"A disease," Rinaldo laughed. "Didn't they teach you how to spell ditheath in school?"

Rinaldo grinned sardonically at the two women, then broadened his smile with a little genuine warmth at the boys. "You fellows want to play with a toy truck. Get them that toy truck out of the closet, will you Cora?"

"Rinaldo, that thing hasn't been there in years. Actually I think I gave it to their father when he was little.. You've spilled oatmeal down your face. Now hold still, let me wipe it off." Cora wiped Rinaldo's face and hands with a wet rag while his body swayed, and the hands shook.

Both boys watched him.

"We won't stay long, Cora," Mary said. "I know you have a lot to do," she said looking again at Rinaldo. "I just wanted to make sure you saw the boys."

"Smoke, smoke, Cora, I need a smoke,"Rinaldo called, his head going side to side, both hands shaking, and his knees raising just perceptibly under his coverlet. Both boys backed up a step.

Cora handed Rinaldo a tin of tobacco and a square of thin ciggarette paper. He took them with hands suddenly gone steady, and his head was still. Rinaldo carefully poured a row of tobacco up the paper, glancing once at Mary. He didn't come to her house because he wasn't allowed to smoke there.

Surprised at the steady control in his hands for the long-practiced habit, both boys stepped back up by the wheelchair.

Rinaldo held out the tin of tobacco for Cora to take with one hand while with the other he steadily held the paper to lick the edge and roll it, still all one handed.

He smiled broadly at the boys, black eyes gleaming.

Cora handed him a book of matches, and he struck one, holding it carelessly to the new cigarette while he watched the boys.

He inhaled, and puffed great clouds of smoke. Then he inhaled even deeper, and blew out a great smoke ring.

The boys looked in surprise at the ring. While the women visited, the boys put their hands through rings, or batted them in the air, following them around the warm kitchen. Rinaldo tipped his head to the side or up toward the ceiling to send the rings in different directions for them.

"Randy, are you in a Christmas play or anything?" Cora paused to ask. " You're in school aren't you?"

"Yeth, I am a king who lookth for Jethuth under the thtar."

"Hah," guffawed Rinaldo looking at the boy in fond delight. "Quite a whelp, ain't he now?"

"That isn't all you say either, is it Randy?" Mary asked, for once smiling back at Rinaldo.

"No, a verse too," Randy said raising his eyebrows and grimacing.

"Mary put him in thwaddling clothe in a manger cuth there wathn't room in the inn or thomething like that, Matthew theven."

"And why is that important?"

"Cuth he ith the newborn thavior who ith Chritht the Lord."

Mary was surprised to find a pleasant feeling inside herself even after being with Rinaldo as she and the boys kicked through the twilight snow that was turning hard and crystalline, and beginning to blow.

The next afternoon she was surprised to see Cora behind Rinaldo and the wheelchair tracking through the snow to her house.

While Mary and Cora, and Mary's husband and children visited, they looked through the window to see Rinaldo, with his earflaps pulled down tightly, blowing smoke rings in the still icey moist air left from the storm for two dancing boys. Rinaldo smiled back at them, even at Mary.

The next day, Rinaldo asked Mary if she could come down to his house before her grandsons left. Leaving the boys in her husband's care, Mary tramped once more through the now packed snow to the other house.

The old man blew a great smoke ring toward her as she entered the kitchen, and then folded his hands, still holding the cigarette in his lap. He stared at her a moment with noncommital eyes that seemed open to the soul.

Cora handed Mary two sacks and a heavy envelope.

Rinaldo spoke slowly, "Mary, that's a silver dollar for each of the boys in the envelope and a bag of candy for each of them too. I had Cora pick them up for me.

"See those silver earrings she's wearing? They came from France when I was there years ago. There's another set of them on the table for you. Don't tell me thanks," he added batting his eyes. "I ain't in the mood for thanks now.

"You know they signed the armistice for that war what, 36—maybe 37 years ago. I think I'm going to call it over with also before I go and die here. Even the snow out there's got to thaw sometime, huh?"

"Rinaldo, I..." Mary tried to begin.

But he held up the hand with the cigarette at both her and Cora, steady as a rock. Then he inhaled deeply on it, threw back his head, and blew his biggest and finest smoke ring into the room between them.

"Go on, get out of here. Spend some time with the grandsons.

"Hey, that was a good cherry pie. Maybe after the kids leave I can buy the coal for the next one."

Banker with a heart of gold

Author's note: The cinamon rolls really were that good. I like them with raisins, and I favor a big, doughy roll from the center of the pan.

HOWIE OWNED the majority share of a state bank in one of those little Kaw towns where the main street is paved, but the side streets are gravel-covered dirt.

He'd had the bank built himself. He loved to see the waxed glow of its hardwood oak floors every morning when he opened the front door from the main street sidewalk at 6:45 a.m.

That gave him time to switch the radio on in his office to hear the 7 a.m. commercial from the national bank in the county seat 10 miles away advertise itself as "the bank with the heart of gold."

"Yeah," Howie always muttered, "cold, hard and shiny."

Howie was an early riser, and he kept the bank opening to the public at 8 a.m. when most banks opened at 9 a.m. He came in with thick brown hair brushed to perfection and necktie carefully windsor-double-knotted in a town where the rule was bald heads and open-necked work shirts for the older end of middle-aged men. By 7:30 a.m., Alice, his right-hand clerk, would nearly have the bank crew ready to open the front door.

The bank building included a couple of features just for Howie's office: a big window where, with the blinds half shut, he could watch across the side street to the grocery store to see who was coming and going and, more important, a side door where he could slip out of the building without going through the front lobby.

The cafe a block north of the bank was his destination at 9 a.m., and no customer sitting in the lobby would ever keep him from slipping out the side door to walk the distance from the back of the bank to enter the back door of the cafe for a home,baked cinnamon roll and coffee for an hour with his friends.

At 7 a.m. he usually started getting any of the state and federal forms out of the way he hated so much—"I guess they think they know my business better than I do!"—and by five minutes before 8 he was ready for his daily prayer. "Lord, give me mostly investors today, and only enough borrowers to get by."

Howie was tired of fighting the world and of hearing the words of the hopeful who only had a minimal business chance, although he always listened to them with a smile.

But by five minutes before 8 one cold January morning, when refrozen ice clung to the gutters of main street and little flurries of sleet came around from time to time, Howie was already beginning a less-than-routine day.

Alice buzzed him to tell him Fred from National was on the line.

"Hello, Howie. Fred at National here."

"Hey, Fred. Glad to hear you're up for the day. How's the weather there?"

"About to freeze my gold-plated posterior, Howie. Listen, got a little thing for you to cover today. It's Jake again.

"OK, how much this time."

"Yeah, it's the same thing again. He got one of our counter checks at the sale barn, memo says for black cow-calf pairs. We got him covered, so I assumed you're going to cover us for him again."

"Sure, how much?"

"It's $10,855.33. You ought to just open him an account here with some of that half-million he's got in your bank, Howie."

"Sure, when hell freezes over. But yeah, sure, it's covered."

A quick check with Alice showed that Jake only had $15 in his checking account. Howie couldn't transfer money for Jake from other accounts, so Howie went back on the phone.

"Hello, Hazel, this is Howie. Is Jake in?"

"No, he's taken the pickup somewhere."

"I assume that means he's out looking for a retirement spot, maybe moving you to sunny Southern Texas. You know, a guy that's past 80 has to stop buying cows sometime."

"Stop your dreaming, Howie."

"Well, tell him I need him to stop by the bank as soon as he can, OK?"

It was already past 8:30. Howie carefully peeked around the hall door frame to see the lobby. Good, there wasn't anybody out there.

But then he looked through the window again to see a young couple with two small children getting out of a car.

"Good Lord, not them again," Howie thought. "How could any real-estate agent in her right mind be showing them a quarter-section without checking to see that they only had $500? That wasn't enough for the earnest money, and if they put it up, it would be gone—young hopefuls with not enough dollars and experience to hope with, nice kids with little sense."

"Go to the grocery store, go to the grocery store," Howie muttered, watching the couple with the kids who would sit in their parents' laps for a moment, and then go poking around his office. But they went east to the corner of the bank building where they could round the front to come in the door.

Howie peeked around the corner to see them entering the lobby. He heard Alice say, "Can I help you?" Then there was a moment's pause before she added just a little more loudly, "Well, you'll have to wait a moment while I see if he's in."

Good old Alice—just that moment's delay, and Howie was out the side door headed around the back for cinnamon roll and freedom.

At the cafe, he sat for a blessed hour in the far dark corner at a table chuckling with his friends, and filling with the warmth of coffee and roll. Then it was time to go to the bank again.

No use being cautious this time—he was fortified. Howie went right out the front door of the cafe, down the main street sidewalk, and into the bank's lobby with no interruptions.

"They're gone," Alice said, smiling knowingly at him.

At least that was a relief, but as Howie sat down, he looked out the window. Their car was still there. He had no more noticed it when he heard Alice proclaim, "Well, you'll have to wait a moment while I see if he's in."

When Alice looked through his door, Howie just shrugged. He couldn't run down the sidewalk all day if the youngsters were that persistent.

Howie welcomed the family into his office with his dark brown eyes sparkling and the kind of smile that gave people hope even when he felt none. Howie hated saying no. He handed Tootsie Rolls to the children who politely said thank you, and stood there unrolling them while their father handed him the paperwork that listed assets and liabilities, and all the other cash flow information that Howie had asked from them.

They actually owned a half-dozen calves, their old car out-right, and the man worked a good job.

"Well, Jeff and Teresa," Howie said, "I can see you're still struggling with the world. As for me, I gave up struggling long ago. It's easier just to go with the flow of things, and to accept the way things are."

Just then, Howie's side door came open, and an old bent gray-haired man stepped through wearing six-buckle unsnapped overshoes, and removing a hat with earflaps.

"Thought, I'd catch you coming in this way, Howie," he said, peering myopically through horn-rimmed glasses at the young people. "Oh, sorry about that. Didn't know you'd have company.

"Name's Jake. Oh yeah, I've seen you kids at the sale barn buying calves. How you doin' with them?"

Then looking at Howie, he added, "What's this old bugger doing, giving you the fighting-the-world speech?

"Guess I forgot to make a deposit again, huh, Howie?" Jake took a bunch of wadded and crinkled checks from his wallet, and began bending over Howie's desk to endorse them, then handed them over one at a time.

"Jake, this check's six months old. You have to get them in here."

"Yeah, yeah I know. I just forget," Jake said, reaching for a tissue from Howie's desk and blowing his nose. "And then I see those cows were going low. Might make a little on them if I can take care of them. Pull me up a chair there, Jeff, will you? I knew your folks you know."

"Jake, I need to finish with Jeff and Teresa here."

"Yeah, I know, sorry I interrupted." Then turning to Jeff and Teresa, he added: "Got $500,000 on paper with Howie here, so he cuts me some slack. Tell me what kind of deal you got here."

So Howie listened to Jake interview the couple for the next hour while the children wandered to the lobby to carry magazines back in or smudged handprints on his window.

He heard all about how Jeff and Teresa would have a cow herd someday while he twiddled his pen between his fingers, and finally ate a Tootsie Roll himself.

He was returning to a consciousness about how he might get everyone out of his office when he heard Jake winding things up.

"Now I tell you what. Let's go look at this ground you want, and I'll show you the new cows. What do you think of this? We can shake hands right now. Howie and me will buy this land for you, and you make the payments right here at the bank. I'll lease you cows for a share of the calves. Can't owe for land and cattle both. Howie will stay here, and draw it all up."

Howie was numbed to the core by this announcement.

"Now wait a minute, Jake, their asset ratio doesn't near match up...."

"Ratio, smatio, Howie. Got to do something for the future don't we? They'll learn, they'll learn. You and me will guide them. Get your stuff together, kids. Get some of your rusty old money out, Howie, not the bank's money, your money, or I'll be doing it myself anyway. Here I am, can't remember nothin' anymore, and you're sneakin' out the door in a town where even the main street's turnin' to dirt soon.

"Got to resolve to do something for a future, don't we? Ain't any shame in startin' with nothin'. You'll work hard, won't you kids. All of us goin' out of the world with nothin' anyway."

"But, Jake, I can't do a deal like this."

"Sure you can, Howie. Let's put some of that heart-of-gold garbage to work."

"But that's another bank."

"I know, cold, hard and shiny. But Howie, you got a mind set like a steel trap—tight and rusty."

Memory of a mason

Author's note: *This story is nearly the direct quote from a man who really existed with a few elaborations for descriptive purposes.*

CLAUDE WAS 95 that June of 1970. He was sitting there, waiting while watching traffic, in a white-board lawn chair under his favorite cherry tree in the old family front yard along main street.

The place wasn't difficult to spot because of the unusual stone fence around it, made of great slabs of precisely cut white limestone squares that were topped with red, round granite glacier boulders. Here and there the top was interrupted with limestone squares between the boulders with various patterns carved into their faces—sometimes a floral pattern, or a cross or a dove.

Claude stood to shake hands, although he had to lean on a cane to do so. "I've been waiting for you about long enough to eat a dozen cherries or so," he said, pointing at the ripening fruit. "Pick a few for yourself."

His hands were still rough and calloused from his trade because Claude was always picking up rocks he saw that interested him. Sometimes he took a hammer and chisel to them, or some of the many other tools that lined his work benches.

In contrast, the weathered skin of his face had thinned with age and blue lines of veins showed through it. The years of close work hadn't seemed to dim his eyes, still green-brown flecked, although behind spectacles.

Claude was a rarity, one of the last of the old-time stone masons, those people who had carved many of the old limestone buildings that lined the streets of Kaw towns. He had worked other jobs, mostly for the railroad, but rock cutting was his life's work.

He loved to walk the hills and creek valleys, picking up rocks to see what might be in them, or shoveling dirt from a bank to see what was underneath.

North of his town was what had been the leading edge of a glacier, and to Claude it happened like yesterday as he explained how this rock might have begun its journey being pulled south by a glacier from the Dakotas.

South of town, the Flint Hills ascended above the creek and woods with their limestone outcrops adding to Claude's diversity of life.

Nothing interested Claude more than to look at the rocks he recognized as having been worked by those who came before, the native Americans, the Indians.

"This might look like just another rock to you," he said, "but it was a grinding stone. See how it's been shaped? This was a cutting edge, but it's been broken—too bad. Here's what everybody looks for, an arrowhead. Pretty good shape, too."

Claude rubbed the gray stone up and down his hand while gazing at Main Street.

"Let's talk about them a little bit," he said. "You know, I saw the last bunch of them to come through here right down this road in front of us. I was born in 1875 right here. My daddy built this house, and my mother had me right here, in the back room of this house.

"I don't know how old I was, just a kid. I know I already ran all over town, and I was already interested in rocks, throwing them, and getting paid to pick them up in some farmer's field—not much because they didn't pay much, and I was too little to be worth much.

"It was cold—a kind of wet sleet was coming out of the north, and them coming with their backs to it. It had been wet all fall, and their horse's hooves made sucking sounds in the mud because there wasn't any pavement then. They had three or four wagons, and the hooves and the wagon wheels made about the only sounds because they were quiet. Some of the men rode horseback.

"They didn't look a lot different than a lot of us because they wore a lot of white men's clothes and hats, except they were dark and most of the men had long straight hair without mustaches. There must have been 30 or 40 of them.

"The blankets made them look different. They had lots of blankets, and they seemed to like red blankets. Even the men on horses had blankets around them.

"They went on through, and of course I followed them just like a few other people did. They came to the end of town, where the ground flattens out for the creek, to a place where a man named Johnson had three or four acres of saw-wood stacked and a barn with a blacksmith shop in the middle.

"This wood was all kinds of firewood for Johnson to sell people in town and to the railroad and such. Then there were kind of medium lengths and great big logs of oak and walnut because Johnson had a kind of sawmill, too. The wood was in great big piles, some of it seven and eight feet deep, because he had a lot of it.

"Well, these Indians come into the wood lot, stop and look around, then there's a bunch of them that kind of let out a low moan almost all at once so it's like there's ghosts with them in that damp. The men get down off their horses, but they're just quiet again looking around at the wood, the steam coming off their horses.

"Some men and kids that walked down to see the Indians are standing around watching them, and customers of Johnson's start coming out of the barn to join them.

"Finally, Johnson himself walks out toward the Indians, people making way to let him through, and calls out to ask what's going on.

"Some of the Indians go to a wagon, and help this old woman get out.

She's all slouched over wrapped in a red blanket until she gets up to Johnson, then she gets up to him talking loud, and pointing back at some of the wood piles.

"It's Indian talking, so nobody understands her, but she's impressive with long gray hair, standing about a third taller, and talking out real loud and clear like she's giving Johnson and everyone orders.

"The Indian men are standing around, and the rest of their people are watching from the wagons like they expect us all to do something. But Johnson and the rest of us don't have any idea what she's talking about.

"Then some of the Indian men started talking, too, and they began to sound kind of angry, and some of our men are edging closer to each other or kind of tensing up.

"Finally, Johnson shrugs big with his hands up in the air, and everybody stops talking for a little while. One of the men said he knows an old man a couple of miles out of town that used to be able to talk some Indian, and figures he can get him back there soon.

"Johnson and some of the others make talking signs with their hands, and downward motions like to sit down and wait. The Indians watch the man ride away, go quiet, but none of them move away, even the old woman who just pulls her blanket back up around herself, and stands there.

"I decided to go find Daddy because I thought he ought to know about all of this. When I get up by the church, I see him going in, and there in the church I find him and about 20 other men all standing around with their hunting guns in case there's trouble down at the wood yard. They're just quiet, and waiting, too.

"They asked me all about what happened, and Daddy leaves his gun with them to go back down with me to see what happens if the man comes back in to talk to them.

"I don't know what kind of Indians they were, but when the man that rode away comes back with the old man, he walks right up to them, looks them over, and seems to say just the right things to them. That old woman began talking real fast to him.

"It turned out they had people buried there under the wood piles. Men came from all over town to help move the wood to where Johnson and the Indian talking man told them. They brought some mule teams down to pull logs. The Indians helped too. A big bunch of the women brought down lunch for everybody, and the Indians ate like they were starving even though they didn't look like it.

"When the wood was all moved, everybody stood back while the Indians, men, women and children stood around a space and sang a kind of little sing song up and down.

"One of the men made a sign of the cross like a priest, but I don't think they were Pottawatomies—some French among them, you know. I figure they must have been from one of the nations that had to move south. They all got back to their horses and wagons, and rode that way. We never saw them again.

"Johnson never put wood on that space again, but he's long gone now. The county widened the road there, and hard-surfaced over the area we cleared a long time ago. Doesn't matter because they're all gone, and I suppose the ones in the ground are long past caring now.

"I wish I could have talked about rocks with them."

Claude died four years later in 1974.

The triumph
of Polyvinyl Bert

BERT WAS already more delighted than most folks would ever be to walk off the black asphalt parking lot steaming with new spring rain to what to him was nearly a magic kingdom—a new, multi-departmental hardware store.

There were aisles and aisles of power tools, new gadgetry, hand tools, nails, nuts and bolts, the things he already knew about and loved. But it was a more fateful day than most because Bert made a great discovery, the art form of his life—PVC pipe.

Polyvinyl Bert had a pencil-pushing, keyboard-plunking type of job that paid very well, but it was no match for the passions unleashed by the pipe discovery in the city hardware store along the river bottom road that took him to his small-town home.

His home, where he lived with his wife, Jane, and their four small children, had been one of his other dreams—two huge square stories, a full third-story attic, a full basement and wrap-around porch set in Victorian splendor among tremendous trees.

But now the home was to become even better, the perfect art object for the perfect art form— PVC pipe.

Granted, you could argue that Bert was a little stressed on this fateful day because he was being faced with what he thought was going to be a great expense—getting a plumber to repair the iron pipes of the first plumbing era leaking here and there in his big home.

But out of great problems come great ideas, and this was to be no exception to that rule.

Bert didn't exactly break into a big Hollywood dance scene there in the hardware department, but he did push his glasses back up his nose to ask the clerk, "What is this stuff—plastic pipe?"

"Yes, sir.... Well, no sir, it's PVC."

"Comes in different dimensions, huh? Three-quarter inch, inch, and here's joints, and joint compound—this stuff glues together? This pipe's white, and that one's gray. How come?"

"Different uses, sir. Heat resistance...."

"You could bend this stuff all over if you didn't kink it, couldn't you?"

"Well, here's some manuals on its use, sir."

Bert came home with an armload of pamphlets, books and pipe samples to show long-suffering, stoic, patient Jane the new dimension that was added to their lives.

What Jane looked forward to was a series of get-togethers with friends that culminated each year with a single grand party for friends and neighbors at their home.

That very first year of the grand party, Bert had a pipe running across the kitchen floor to the sink from the bathroom, which was built in an old pantry off the kitchen—as is typical for many old homes built before plumbing. He was running new water pipes to the kitchen sink.

Many a joke was told about getting somebody to stand in front of the partially open bathroom door when a guest needed to use it, because it wouldn't close with a pipe on the floor going through one corner.

The women looked at Jane to see how she was taking it, but she laughed with the rest of them.

The next year, guests going to the bathroom were surprised to find the room was back to its ancient use as a pantry again. Bert had moved the toilet into the coat closet at the front of the living room.

The sink was on the front porch, but only for the duration of warm weather, he told everybody. The tub was on the second floor in a child's bedroom.

The floor boards of the porch at the front entryway were gone for a few feet either way, and a person was required to step on cement blocks to go up or down to porch level.

Bert had needed more access to punch through the foundation wall to attach a big sewer pipe under the former closet. He had then run the pipe across the basement ceiling through a foundation hole on the other side, and then the length of the backyard, where he had dug a hole to the sewer.

No problem, smiled Jane as she stepped out of the closet toilet, out the front door onto a cement block, and then onto another cement block to step up to use the sink.

The next year, the bathroom was in the master bedroom at the foot of the bed—although for some strange reason the front cement blocks and sewer pipe were still in place under the missing porch boards.

Jane told guests they could lay their coats on the bed, but to knock first in case the toilet was in use.

Guests who cared to go with Bert for a tour of the ancient unfinished basement were shown a skeletal work of "plastic" pipe beginning to crisscross the ceiling and walls.

The years went by. Sometimes friends and neighbors would entertain themselves with wondering where Bert's and Jane's bathroom might be.

Once, the sink joined the tub while the toilet moved to a second floor closet. Then they were all in a child's room.

Another time, Bert had to augment the city water pressure with a half-horsepower electric pump because all bathroom fixtures were in the attic but showers were added on all other floors including the basement.

Besides that, Bert had added an irrigation system to the backyard so Jane could garden. It was made of plastic pipe.

Finally, years into the future, the fateful year arrived. Bert was bald and graying. Jane was brushing away the gray. The four boys were nearly grown, and had joined Bert in many of his weekend plumbing pursuits. His two daughters also helped by handing tools down through holes in the floor when somebody called.

It was time for the annual grand party. And Jane invited Mayor Shnubottem, the clean-up-the-city- all-tidy-and-neat Mayor Shnubottem, who tied her silver blonde hair in a bun, and puttied on eye shadow under ultra-thick glasses lens that hugged her face like over-sized goggles.

Bert and the boys were in the year of final touches. A plank laid

across a kitchen-floor opening, where guests walking across it could look down through criss crosses of white pipe to the basement floor and a full bathroom below.

As a matter of fact, every floor, including the attic had a full bath.

For one last time a sewer pipe ran across the living room floor.

Bert had decided the entire front-porch flooring had to be replaced, and it was about three-fourths done.

The front-room-closet flooring also needed replacing because it was gone. It didn't matter as long as a person only hung a coat on the rod, and didn't step into the closet to fall to the basement.

Mayor Shnubottem wasn't impressed with PVC pipe, the house, Bert's work, Jane's patience, or the work ethic the children had learned.

After the party, she called the city building inspector. The building inspector, after examining the house, gave Bert 90 days to clean it all up, or the house would be condemned.

Everybody looked to Jane, the one who lived with the mess, the one whose patience must finally be wearing thin. Here and there a few people wondered if she and the children might move out.

Bert went to the hardware stores and came home with loads of pipe, lumber and large tarps. He and the boys hung tarps from the shade trees, and ran ropes from tree to tree to hang more tarps. The house and the front yard were hidden from the street.

Mayor Shnubottem and the building inspector didn't like not being able to watch what was happening from the street. The police chief advised biding their time because he couldn't see any indication of illegal activities.

Bert carried in electric pumps and heavy-duty cords. He and the boys buried all the pipe in the back yard, and put in ordinary water taps.

Bert asked for, and received, approval for a nighttime meeting with the building inspector to look at the house again.

Jane sent out invitations—the biggest, most extended, most major guest list in the family's history. All of the friends, all of the neighbors, Mayor Shnubottem and the entire town were invited.

Somewhere along the line, the building inspector and Mayor Shnubottem noticed the time and evening for the party coincided with the building inspector's appointment. They called the police chief to make sure he honored his invitation.

As the big day approached, most of the tarps were taken down. The house looked good, its front porch completed. Only one massive section of tarps remained suspended by a triangle of ropes from two shade trees and the third-story roof.

Bert and the boys went in and out of this tent until the last day, when they brought out ladders, full black trash bags and tools.

A reception preceded the final inspection as darkness approached. Bert's boys safeguarded the front-yard tarps as guests crowded the big house for cookies, tea, punch and coffee.

Everybody was amazed—even the building inspector as he happily munched an extra Oreo. The house was finished, the porch was finished, there were no holes, all bathrooms and plumbing worked, and new paint reflected the light in a steady sheen.

As the final hour of inspection approached, Bert's boys set a small platform by the porch. Bert and Jane stepped on the platform, and an automatic hush came over the crowd.

The building inspector began, "Well, Bert, you seem to have met most of our requirements, but these big tarps hanging in the yard, I don't know...."

"Just a minute, sir," Bert said. Then looking at the crowd, he said, "I want everyone here to know this is my final creation. I respectively donate it for the aesthetics and appreciation of the entire community."

At that, Bert's boys and daughters pulled ropes so the tarps fell, and one of them threw a valve and a switch.

A PVC-pipe tower climbed into the air looking like an oil derrick, or giant monkey bars with turning wheels of pipes bent in geometric patterns on it. Fountain sprays of water shot from yard sprinklers attached to the wheels and the top of the construction, and other wheels with colored lights that turned shined through the sprays in golds, blues, greens and reds.

The crowd stepped back in collective gasp, then gazed in hypnotic fascination at the splendid machine.

Jane's face shone with raptured joy.

"Now you can all see clearly what I have been able to see for years," she said. "Bert's creativity knows no limits. He is our true genius, our Michelangelo."

Mayor Shnubottem left early. She approved the building inspector's decision to give Bert another 90 days to tear the contraption down.

Bert makes PVC patio furniture and playground equipment now.

When Bogart met Bogart

Author's note: I know that bears are supposed to be more ferocious than this, and I don't recommend that anybody try this with one. But the bear this is based on seemed to be content to let the humans in his life get by unscathed. It goes to show what a good home life with pets to settle your nerves can do for you.

BANDER BUILT a concrete block house with wrap-around porch on a bluff shaded by big sycamores and bur oaks above a bend where the creek entered the river.

He lived there with his wife, Bertha, four rat terriers, a bunch of cats and one pony.

Other than those animals, Bander and Bertha, big square ruddy-faced people, lived alone until one summer when they took a rare vacation to the Black Hills of South Dakota and bought a baby black bear. They saw him climbing a stump in a pen with a bunch of other baby black bears at Bear World, where for only $5, you could drive your car in among bears and wolves, and see the baby bears on sale for only $400 each at the end.

The Bear World man told them Blackie and Borus were the most common bear names, but Bander and Bertha favored Bogart after the biggest businessman in the town three miles northeast of them across the river, and because they liked Humphrey Bogart the actor.

They'd already been through an Indian phase, naming two terriers Cochise and Geronimo, and a Civil War phase, naming the other two Sherman and Jeb. The biblical name went to the pony, old Moses.

So Bogart the black bear rode nearly a thousand miles, got neutered, and grew to more than 400 pounds eating dog food, like a fat house cat, with four snappy, yappy terriers he thought of as the grownups.

Bogart spent happy evenings on the porch, where sometimes Bander would let him put one big clawed foot on his knee, and get sour with him if he licked. On much rarer occasions, Bogart would climb into the back seat of the car for an afternoon ride.

Bogart loved pie, cookies, sandwiches and cokes—and going to sleep with dogs and cats on top of him who had learned he was a warm perch.

Sometimes on hot afternoons, Bogart liked to go the creek or the river for a swim. But he often went alone because the heat-lazy terriers, who by this time had learned to go with Bogart most times because he was good at digging up rodents, preferred to stay under the shade trees.

So, it was that one afternoon after a swim and rub-off-roll in the grass, Bogart wandered a mile upstream where Tom and Jack had parked their car while fishing. Not knowing a Bogart bear with his own habits was around, they'd left a back door open while going back and forth down to the bank getting loaded to leave.

So, the bear got into the car.

Bogart pulled a cooler lid open, crushed a can of Coke in his teeth, then ate the remaining sandwiches while he was at it. He felt so warm and at home, he stretched out in the back seat for a nap.

Jack had never arrived back at a car to find a black bear in the back seat, so he was feeling distressed by the time Tom got there, too.

Tom looked at Bogart, and said: "Oh, don't worry. That's Bander's black bear. Been hand raised. You open the door on the other side, and I'll push on him. I think he'll go right out."

Only Bogart didn't want to get out. He hunkered down without moving, even when both men pushed on him—managing only to shove the bear's back end up a little while the front end hung on. He moaned a little and gave a grunt, so Jack jumped.

"Are you sure he's not gonna turn on us? Cripes, he's big. Time you feel him through the hair, he's so big and fat all over."

"Take it easy. Don't act scared. He'll be fine just as long as he thinks you're calm like his folks."

Jack said, "I got to get back to town before it gets much later. What are we going to do with this bear?"

"We'll just have to take him with us, and I'll call Bander tonight to come get him. Don't worry, he's tame as can be. We'll just roll down the back windows so he stays cool, and we don't have to smell anything."

After Tom pulled into his alley parking space, he decided to leave his back doors open so Bogart wouldn't tear up his seat covers if he wanted to leave. And Bander and Bertha weren't home when he called because it was diet club square dancing night.

So Bogart the bear decided to look around in Bogart the businessman's town.

Bogart wandered up and down on mowed grass, cement walks, asphalted streets and dirt alleys while dogs barked. The air was permeated with strange smells. He'd come out late enough that nearly all humans were in bed.

He found an ice cream dairi-ette, but finally left it when it became confusing to scratch on the plate-glass windows. Bogart climbed into a nicely treed backyard to take a nap, but a growling rottweiler tried to bite him until Bogart smacked him upside the head with one big paw. His terriers were snappy and bossy, but none of them had attacked him like this guy. Bogart was upset. He wanted to be somewhere comfortable with food, and then a nap.

He ambled back to the downtown area, managing to cross the main street unseen after a couple of cars had gone by. Wandering up an alley, he saw one of those familiar things that were a comfort—an automobile with the back door left invitingly open.

Bogart stuck his big head in to sniff, and discovered a box of doughnuts, just like home. After eating the two dozen of them, it was nap time on a back seat again with some stacks of annoying files pushed onto the floor or shoved around more comfortably for added padding.

Bogart the businessman was inside the building gathering up some final files and going through some figures in his head while rubbing his thin face thoughtfully. He was upset, too—with his wife. She had called him a work-aholic before he left home, and greedy.

"God wouldn't give you a wife and two daughters if he didn't expect you to spend time with them," she'd said.

"Well, just maybe God wants me to provide for them very well, and that's his expectation," he'd replied. "Maybe he can just send me an angel if he intends differently, or a demon if you think that's more fitting."

She had just glowered at him like he was a demon.

Bogart the businessman knew very well that some people in town did consider him a greedy demon, but it didn't ruffle him until it came from his wife. He watched what other people were successful at, then imitated or improved on what they did. He'd just opened a discount hardware store at this location when he observed a new discount hardware store that had opened across the street doing very well. The owner there hated him, but Bogart smiled thinly: that's competition.

Bogart had begun business in small-engine repair, then sales, and then opened a used-car lot. Now he owned half of everything up and down main street. Why should he care if his auto-parts store had nearly ruined the old one? Business is business. He was careful with his money, and always had more to provide start-ups than most people. He was moving into other towns, thinking of consolidating under a corporate banner.

Bogart the businessman decided to call it a night, placate his wife, or maybe she was asleep. He slammed the back door shut as he walked by, and threw the few remaining files he had carried out on the front seat. Then he buckled up and turned the key.

Little did he know that the consolidation of Bogart and Bogart was imminent.

Bogart the businessman had just pulled his auto onto the main street when Bogart the bear gave a silent yawn, feeling all warm and loving. As he raised in the back seat, he laid a friendly but heavy paw on Bogart the businessman's shoulder.

All the adrenaline Bogart the businessman owned rose to his noggin, and his mouth went wide in a silent scream. Bogart the bear felt this surge of fear and discomfort, and reassuringly slurped a big-tongue lick across the side of the businessman's head.

Bogart the businessman had learned that if you ask you might receive, and Bogart the bear had learned that not everybody is just like Bander.

The businessman leaped out of the car and didn't look back as he ran down main street. The car rolled across the street, and the engine died as it hit the curb. Bogart the bear had to squeeze over the front seat, crunching it and slashing seat covers as he made his way.

A south breeze was stirring, and Bogart raised his nose to smell the river. He knew the way home. The bear swam the river, pausing on a sandbar to look primordial in the moonlight before continuing on his way.

Both Bogarts had had quite a night, but when Tom called Bander the next day to tell him his bear had gotten away, Bander said: "No he hasn't. I can see him right here out the window sleeping with the terriers. I think he's been here all night."

Bogart the businessman told his wife he would be spending more time with her--better that than live with his personal demons.

Watching out for Hoagie

Author's note: I played the trombone.

A S SUMMER waned into the last great heat of September, with the smells of new-turned wheat ground and ripened corn permeating the air, it was time again for Mr. Timmer's great stress.

Stress because it was the beginning of school, stress because the century-old community fair was a month away, and Mr. Timmer was the perfection-ridden genius music teacher who must put together a combined band of grade school and high school kids to march up Main Street in the fair parade.

He truly was a genius, and that was part of Mr. Timmer's problem. He could play every instrument in the band beautifully, from trombones and coronets to clarinets, flutes and saxophones.

Sometimes he was restless, and yearned to do more. Yet he held himself together, and endured, because he had to make a living, and he loved children even though every squawking tone and mistake coming from their play made his nostrils flare and his eyes half close below his butch haircut.

As early as July, evenings came when he would sit at his desk, laying his face in his hands at the thought of the fair to come in October. This year, he thought, maybe the children would march in straight lines, in step, executing the great left turn onto Main Street perfectly, and play with outstanding gusto, "Military Escort," the one march they could play nearly flawlessly.

And every September, Mr. Timmer would grow rigid with helplessness as he marched forward, backward and around the band himself, realizing he could only make it as good as it could get.

Every morning in the beginning weeks of school, the high school kids would come by bus to the grade school, and Mr. Timmer would line them up on the school driveway.

The largest high school kids went to the right outside, and the smallest grade school kids to the left inside, so that when the two left turns were made, the short-legged people could nearly march in place while the long-legged people would pace the long sweep on the outside.

Of course that had to be balanced by sections—the clarinets together, the trombones together and so on—with trumpets and coronets to the front to blare out the great opening crescendo of "Military Escort."

Mr. Timmer would give instructions on how to line up, then stand back to eyeball the band before putting his hands on the shoulders of individuals to move them here and there, pronouncing, "You will be great here."

They believed him too, "the great stone face," down to the smallest kid squirming here and there while looking up at him with big eyes.

The drums began the march roll, Mr. Timmer shouted, "Forward march," and the band marched down the driveway to the first left turn entering the side street, a practice before the big left turn on Main.

Came the order "Left turn march," and Mr. Timmer was looking up and down the lines. "Straighten out there. Watch out the corner of your eyes for the people next to you. Come on, you're doing it."

He would console himself with thoughts of, "Well, that wasn't too bad was it?" And, "They really are trying."

But on the outside, Mr. Timmer's face became set in a great frown.

By the time they made the second left turn, the big one onto Main Street, the rows of sunbrowned farm and small-town kids did really seem to improve. They marched down Main, the snare drums and bass pounding the rhythm, to the old store, where they would stop to begin playing the march.

But before they even got there, they might face a huge distraction bursting out the door of the two-story white frame house beside the grocery: Hoagie shouting and hollering at the top of his lungs.

Hoagie held his head slightly sideways, and angled down, one arm out from his body in an almost twisted broken-arm appearance, and the other hand waving in the air.

He danced, skipped, jumped and ran excitedly around his fenced yard, saliva dripping down his face, a thick shock of brown, gray-flecked hair hanging out from under his sideways red ballcap.

"Ignore him, ignore him, ignore him," Mr. Timmer croaked out of the corner of his mouth as he marched up-down the length of the band. Year after year, it seemed, the kids were able to ignore him too with an air of tolerant adult reserve designed to show understanding.

A few of the smallest kids would twist their heads to stare in wonder at the howling Hoagie, but the word would pass down the ranks from the big kids: "Korean War, shell shocked, he's just happy that we're here, let him have fun, nobody look."

Then the trumpets began the opening salvo of "Military Escort": "Taa ta ta taa, ta ta taa taa taa," and Hoagie would pull on the fence, raising his voice to howl even more loudly.

When trombones slurred in their "taa-ump" that brought in the rest of the band, Hoagie was yowling, jumping up and down, hanging on the wood gate that a grape arbor grew over, and rolling his eyes back.

Sometimes his mother would quietly open the front door, wiping a dish with a towel, and smile at the band while at least one or two little kids over at the side were wondering if he could get loose.

Other times, Hoagie's married sister would sit on the porch to watch, or, often as not, he would come out alone.

When the last strain of "Military Escort" died away, the band would march down the street with the howls of Hoagie sounding in the background over the roll of the drums.

They stopped to play "Military Escort" again at the street by the church with the sounds of Hoagie slowly rescinding behind them.

That's the way more than 20 practices went, day after day after day—forward march, one left turn, continue marching, the big left turn, "Military Escort" with Hoagie howling, forward march, "Military Escort" again, then on for dismissal at the high school, where, on fair day, each kid would be given a candy bar and bottle of soda pop.

Every day, 99 percent of the eyes in the band shifted sideways to see Hoagie come out his door.

Since the school couldn't afford uniforms, on the day of the parade all the kids dressed alike: white dress shirts, blue jeans, white socks and white tennis shoes. Mr. Timmer consoled himself that the clothes looked somewhat like real uniforms.

They played "Military Escort" in the grade school gymnasium one more time before filing out to line up for the real thing—the practice called a "warm-up" although its real purpose was for Mr. Timmer to feel assured they could still at least halfway play the tune.

The band lined up behind costumed children and floats, but ahead of farm machinery and horses because they were the climax of the show—and nobody expected a band to walk behind horses in street shoes.

On the first left turn, it seemed the band was the sharpest it had ever been. Almost everybody was in step and the lines were straight. Mr. Timmer's confidence began to grow.

On the second great left turn to Main, they were even better as the huge crowd lining both sides the length began looking for their marching kids.

Hoagie burst out in a new print shirt, and hit the fence hard for the opening "taa ta ta taa." As he did, a hundred sets of kid eyes glanced at him as they concentrated on pushing air through their instruments.

When the trombones hit the "taa-ump," an unprecedented thing happened. Hoagie hit the gate, and it swung open. For a moment he was stunned. Then he screamed, and kept on screaming as he danced in a high skip round and round the band.

Not a kid broke ranks.

When the drums began the roll at the end of the march, Hoagie raised his head as high as he could, laughing and yowling in delight. There was no sign of anyone coming out of his house.

Mr. Timmer marched in his assigned position at the side of the band, correctly looking straight ahead as they came down Main Street. Hoagie was at his side, facing him in a strange sideways skip that let him keep pace as he hollered into Mr. Timmer's ear.

Then Hoagie noticed the carnival a short distance away, darted off to the crowd, and disappeared into it.

When the band started "Military Escort" again, back came Hoagie, screaming, yowling and dancing.

Every kid in the band was wondering what would happen to Hoagie when they stopped playing. What if he wandered off, and his mother couldn't find him? Did he know not to run in front of a car? Did anybody know how to take Hoagie home without putting a rope around him?

Mr. Timmer was wondering the same things, and he came to a revolutionary decision.

"Band, right-turn march, and 'Military Escort' again and then again as we continue to march."

This was truly a revolutionary decision because these were orders the band had never before heard in any practice. There was such a short time to get ready for the fair at the beginning of the school year that they didn't practice right-hand turns, and they didn't try to play the tune, and march at the same time.

The big kids—now suddenly on the inside for a turn—held it together for the opening "taa ta ta taa" as the little kids on the outside for the first time scrambled in jumping steps to keep up. The "taa-ump" and what followed was a little ragged as the band tried to walk in step while reading music.

Hoagie howled, "Yaaaoool," and danced by Mr. Timmer who, for the first time in a parade, smiled.

The band played and marched, and made two more right turns as well as they could as they took Hoagie home. Then the kids played in place until Hoagie's mother and sister, who had never been able to catch up with them through the crowd, arrived to take Hoagie in.

They brought the candy bars and the pop to the band that year, and Mr. Timmer smiled at them as they enjoyed the treats together.

He was satisfied.

One step ahead
of his neighbors

HARLAN MEDLAM didn't keep a bull, but he usually had about 30 cows on hillside pastures that bordered the creek.

Much to the annoyance of his neighbors, Harlan Medlam seldom kept up his end of the fences. The neighbors continually had to enter his pastures to look for their strayed animals, and make the minor repairs he should have made.

Their bulls got over the fences for dallies with Harlan's cows. They fought each other fearsomely, with one large bovine engaged in pawing, head-butting and injury against his neighbor. The barbed-wire cuts from going through fences were many. The neighbors often had to separate their animals before bringing them home.

And, all of Harlan Medlam's new calves every year resembled the neighbors' bulls, the quality animals they had invested in to improve their herds.

His neighbor Paul was represented in the Medlam herd offspring by his black Angus bull, his neighbor Sam by the offspring of his red whiteface Hereford, and his neighbor C.J. by the offspring of his Shorthorn.

In the fall, Harlan would watch with a smile on his weathered wrinkled face as his neighbors gathered their cattle to take to winter quarters.

Then he would brush back the hair on his old head before catching a nap, and say to his wife, Florence, "We sure have a fine bunch of calves this year."

Later, he might ask one or two of those neighbors for help in bringing his own cattle home.

So, it was at coffee one day that Sam said to Paul and C.J., "That old Harlan Medlam."

They all shook their heads.

"You know, we shouldn't let him do this to us year after year. It's about time the old stinker bought his own bull."

"Well, I guess I could run calves in that pasture this year, and that way he wouldn't have the benefit of my bull."

"That's a good idea," the other two men said.

That spring, they all began to bring calves to the pastures.

Harlan Medlam awoke to that fact on a warm spring day after taking a nap under a hedge tree where he had parked the tractor and trailer. Florence had sent him out there to pick up firewood they had cut before rain made it muddy.

Florence had worn him out through the winter pulling on a two-man saw.

The honey bees were already buzzing by for the tree bloom, and Harlan yawned deeply. He looked across the fence and saw a herd of calves—no cows, no bull.

After a hurried tractor ride home, he and Florence drove around the area in his old black pickup.

"You're right, Harlan," said Florence. "They all have calves on the pastures. Guess we have to change our management plan to keep up with the neighbors."

Harlan's mouth gaped in a big smile at her suggestions.

That night Paul got a call. "Oh, hello Harlan. What's up?"

He covered the mouthpiece and whispered to his wife. "It's Harlan. I bet he's asking about the cattle."

"Paul," Harlan said, "I was wondering if you could bring your truck over to help me get a critter tomorrow. I've bought a bull from an old friend, Evin Pritcher. I'm past 80 you know. Don't know if I can handle it."

"OK, sure, Harlan, I guess I could do that." Upon hanging up, Paul said to his wife, "Well, this is an event. Harlan Medlam has bought his own bull."

The next morning, with sunshine burning off a morning fog, Harlan stiffly raised himself next to Paul on the truck seat and gave him directions to reach the Pritcher farm 30 miles away.

"What kind of a breeder is this Pritcher—got a good purebred line?" Paul asked.

"Naah," replied Harlan. "Old Evin has all kinds of cattle. Milks some Jerseys—nothing prettier, you know. Got a beef herd. Even got an old Brahmin crossed-up bull from somewhere. Looks like an old race horse to me with them legs."

Harlan smiled, enjoying the conversation.

"He never castrates anything because he says the difference in price for a bull calf instead of a steer calf isn't enough for him to take the trouble. He lets 'em run together all the time, so he's always got calves that have grown enough to sell. Gives him a monthly income."

"Good lord, Harlan, that's terrible management. I don't see how he stays in business—the calves must be so lousy. Say, what kind of a bull could he sell you anyway?"

"Oh, he said he'd be a good one. And it won't cost me near as much as a purebred. Don't need anything like a purebred to get calves."

Once there, Harlan and Evin visited a while, thumbs hooked in their overalls, while Paul looked in horror at the worst bovine in the corral that he'd ever seen.

The bull couldn't have been much more than a yearling, but it was hard to tell on its lanky legs with ridge-topped spine.

The bull snorted and pawed at him through the fence, then shook his horns on the strange square Jersey with a Brahmin long-nose head shape.

"Hey, he's bucking now," Harlan said, as he handed $300 cash to Evin. "Looks like a good one, Evin. Ought to have a lot of vigor. Lucky I got good neighbors to help me with him."

On the truck ride home, Paul sat in tight-lipped silence, staring through the windshield while Harlan mused from time to time on what kind of weather it would be this year, and how the seedling crops looked.

When they stopped in Harlan's driveway, Paul stepped up on the sideboard to look at the bull again.

"You know, Harlan," Paul said, "I think I might know a situation at a sale barn where I could make a profit on that bull. Wouldn't want to hurt you or cut you out, though. You gave $300 for this bull. I could give you $350 if you'd let me have him."

"Guess I could let you have it," Harlan said. "If the deal's that good, give me $400, and we'll call it even."

"OK, Harlan, deal. I won't even unload him, just take him there now, and drop you off because I won't have time tomorrow. I need to get those calves off my pasture, and move the cows in—and the bull, too, of course. Guess you'll be fixing some fence soon too, huh?"

"I don't know, Paul. You know it's terrible hard to get things done at this age. The joints creak, you move slower. Got to get lots of rest."

Harlan Medlam yawned, and then grinned, and patted his pocket where Paul's check for $400 set.

He said to himself, "Well, it's been a tough morning, all that riding. But it's dinner time anyway, and I'm sure Florence will see that I need a nap."

Painful truth about
one day fishing

Author's note: Sorry about that, June.

MEL HAD his line in the water on the upper reaches of the river, but he was thinking that it might be better if the fish just didn't bite.

It was just too nice of a day to do anything, but sit in the folding woven mat chair he'd brought along, watch the sun sparkles on the current ripples and the reflections of the willows in the still dark green deep pools.

Mel was relaxed, barely hanging on to the fishing rod. This was what retirement was all about. Sometimes his chin would sink into his chest, his eyes would close, and the warm world would just carry him along in short, sweet slumber, nodding, nodding, not a care in the world.

If sometimes his glasses slid down his thin nose or a breeze-blown gnat came close to his ear, he just didn't care.

But something big and dark was cutting a swirl in the water, and when it hit his hook, the rod nearly was jerked from his hands. That caused Mel to jerk back, and he set the hook in the creature's mouth really well.

The rod bent, and Mel gave the line some slack—"got to play him, got to play him"—pulled back again, and reeled in a little.

It was going to be big, probably the biggest fish he'd caught in some time.

Mel kept playing the line, reeling in, until he could see the top of a fin in the water, and the tail that occasionally broke the surface to thrash out foam.

Finally he was able to get his net under the big catfish, and pull him to shore.

"Look at you, you're a dandy," Mel muttered at the big black-green white-bellied fish. "Must be about 14 or 15 pounds."

Mel tried to grasp the fish behind the head just as it gave a quick jerk sideways, and he was stuck with a fin bone in the finger for his carelessness.

"Ouch, doggone you bugger," Mel said as he waved his finger in the air.

"Got to get that hook out."

Mel held the fish with his foot while he grasped him again, and put his fingers in to grab the head of the hook. He was surprised when the big catfish bit down, and bit down hard.

"Ow, ow, ow," Mel yelped as he danced around a little. Blood was running down a slice in his hand.

"Doggone you," Mel repeated as he kicked the fish a good one. He could almost feel the nasty squish as his toe bent sideways, and pain ran up his leg from the toe.

This time he got his pliers to get the hook out, and he kept the fish in the net as he lowered him into the cooler.

Mel limped in pain as he tried to load everything up the bank to his car. He finally sat down on the bank to take his shoe and sock off over the swelling foot. He could hardly believe the black-blue toe with more blue lines running up into his ankle.

"I guess God didn't mean for fools to kick big fish," he said as he got his things into the car in a kind of shuffling hobble.

Mel bent down to pick up the fish in the cooler, and, as he pulled up, leaning at an unusual angle because of the toe, his bad back went out.

"Aah, sciatica," he moaned trying to stretch back after lifting.

He rode back to town, a wounded senior, breathing short gasps, no longer relaxed, muscles cramping up.

At home, he had problems uncurling to get out of the car, and finally honked the horn until his wife, Gertrude, came out to help unload him and everything else.

"Just leave the rod and tackle here on the lawn until I can come back for them. But open that cooler, Gert, and just look at the fish I caught. Ain't he a dandy? Except I think he's trying to kill me back."

The catfish thrashed once in the cooler before they could slam the lid back on, and it threw water on the front of their clothes.

"Better call Charlie to come over, and filet him for me, Gert," Mel sighed. "It's embarrassing, but I don't think I can handle it right now," he added as he gimped along with his wife under his arm to get into the house. "At least ask them to come over for fish dinner afterwards,"

The toe didn't stop swelling. By the time Mel and Gert got home from getting the bone break set at the doctor's, Charlie and his wife, Lavina, had fish frying.

"He weighed 14 pounds, Mel," Charlie said. "He really was a dandy, but look at you, poor guy, foot all wrapped, Band-Aids on your hands. Ha, I guess you were right, he really was trying to kill you back. But he dressed out nice, fileted easy, got all the bones out of him. It's time for you to just sit back, and enjoy your catch while the rest of us serve the meal."

Maybe it had been worth it, Mel thought. The fine delicious flaking fish meat almost seemed to melt in his mouth, and it had been a beautiful day most of the time. The pills were helping his back really relax, the muscles were unclinching.

Charlie was looking out the picture window.

"Mel, didn't you leave your rod, reel and tackle box on the yard? There goes the garbage truck, and I think they just picked them up."

He turned around as he began to hear Mel coughing violently, and Gert was slapping him on the back.

"I think he's got a fish bone in his throat," she said.

Bringing down
Pop's old silo

Author's note: The arsenal may not be the same, but, yes, they shot it down.

THE BIG square-built man in a shining silver-and-blue pin-striped extended-cab four-wheel-drive truck drove up to a large suburban ranch home where a man who looked just like him stood among an assortment of rifle cases and small boxes on the close-clipped grass.

"Morning, Dennis," said the driver as he stepped out of the truck while tapping the bill of his red ball cap.

"Morning, Lennis," replied the other man, also tugging slightly at the bill of his identical red ball cap.

They grinned broadly at each other as though each looked into a mirror with a fleshy, ruddy face laughing back, occasional silver-filled teeth glinting in the morning sun.

"Guess if you got old Silver warmed up, I'll leave the Thunder wagon at home," Dennis said pointing at his own custom-ordered blue-and-silver pin-striped truck still setting in the driveway.

Then Lennis pointed at one of the rifle cases on the ground, and they both laughed "heh, heh, heh," at the same time, and hollered, "Thirty-aught-six!"

"This is going to be some kind of fun, Lenny."

"No use hiring a bulldozer to ruin a fun day, Denny."

"Got your Chinese along?"

"SKS, you bet—wouldn't miss firing a few rounds automatic. You too, huh?"

"Yeah, and even a forty-five. Got plenty of ammo?"

"You bet, this is going to be some kind of morning. Pop never would have expected anything like this."

"Well, let's load you up, go get Stanley, and pick up some coffee and doughnuts on the way out there. About time Stanley quit having such a poker face about it, and had some fun, too."

Stanley was met standing in the yard at his own home with a single rifle bag under his arm. He stood tall and thin like a pine-stick rod, his solemn thin-lipped look a quiet contrast to the jocular attitudes of his twin younger brothers.

"I tell you," he said as his brothers stepped from the truck, "Pop wouldn't like this. First, the old house is gone, then we tear down the barns, and now you're really going to shoot down the old silo? Pop wouldn't like this."

"Get a grip on it, Stanley," Lennis said. "Have some fun out of it. The thing needs to come down anyway. Heck, it's starting to crumble at the top. Got a tree growing out the middle of it. Nothing lasts for ever. Is that all you got? I suppose it's your old single-shot twenty-two."

"Yes, it's the single-shot. I remember when Pop put that silo up. Said it was a symbol of progress. Showed the farm operation was moving ahead."

"Simple thinking, Stanley," Dennis said. "Nobody uses upright silos anymore, and even feeding cattle silage is going to be a thing of the past. You're being too sentimental for your own good. Make it a fun day together, just us brothers."

They munched on doughnuts as they arrived at the silo, 40 feet tall. Deep-green leaves of an elm tree barely stuck out the top of it, and the side doors were visible because the crumpled tin side chute that once covered them had dropped to the ground. Tall clumps of weeds and grasses grew around it where the earth hard-packed from years of traffic allowed plant penetration. The sight was a ragged testimony to years gone by.

"Remember Pop crawling around the edge of that thing to hook up the block-and-tackle to pull the blower pipe into place?" Stanley asked. "Remember that? Gosh, heights never bothered him at all. Just always ready to do the work at hand."

"Huh," Lennis grunted. "Remember sweating and itching in that crud all day, pulling off silage with a fork, and wondering if the day would ever end so you could go to town? Life's a sight better now."

"Well," said Dennis, "at least if we did the work Pop would give us the keys to go to town—and a little cash besides. He let us have fun."

"Well, he wouldn't do that if he could see you now," Stanley said. "He'd probably take the keys away from your big old silver truck, and ground you for a week. I just don't think Pop would like this. He was proud of his work, and he wanted us to respect it, too. That silo was a symbol. It could still stand here for years."

"But it isn't going to," Dennis said. "We'll start shooting wherever we want down around the base. It's concrete cinder block of some kind— it'll crumble, and the whole thing will come down. Just don't shoot high. Hard telling where the rounds could get to.

"Just for you, Stanley, we'll start with the twenty-twos."

The twins pulled rifles from cases and loaded up while Stanley stood there looking at the silo.

"I used to love climbing up there in the winter, that sweet ripe smell of the silage when you scooped it down the chute, the smell of the cows when you fed it, and the steam coming from their nostrils and off the silage in the wagon," he said. "That stuff put off a lot of heat."

"Yes, and I remember how the cold puckered the goose bumps on my behind climbing up that chute, and how cold my hands would get, and how Pop said his knees hurt from all the years climbing it," Lennis said. "It's going to be a pleasure seeing it crumble in the dirt."

"I still don't think Pop would like it," Stanley said.

The twins stood, and fired twenty-twos in unison with powder and flakes of concrete blowing away from the sides of the silo almost instantly. Stanley sat in the grass.

"Aren't you even going to shoot?"

"No," said Stanley. "I'd just like to sit and relax. You guys go on ahead. It's OK."

The twins fired away, changing weapons together, their rounds sometimes just puffing up a cloud of dust, and at other times blowing whole concrete blocks apart. The top of the silo sagged here and there, or collapsed in heaps along the edges.

Stanley just watched, and only grimaced for the brief time the twins fired bursts of automatic rounds.

When the twins paused for a drink, laughing and whooping together, Stanley said, "I wonder if we'll see Pop's cornerstone when the thing falls down. Remember that?"

"Oh, just kind of vaguely," Dennis said. "Why would you need a cornerstone for building a silo? It's round."

"It was just a piece of limestone, and he plastered on concrete with his name and the date," Stanley said. "It was a mark of starting to build the thing, a cornerstone of the progress of the farm Pop told us. Boy, I don't think Pop would like us taking that silo down this way."

"I'll tell you what," Lennis said. "When the silo comes down, we'll blow the bottom of that tree away, then we'll find that cornerstone, and blow it away too."

Stanley just looked unhappy.

After a while the concrete blocks began to blow away easily, and the concrete dropped in great thudding hunks. The base of the silo was gone, pulverized to powder and chips with a pile of debris around it. Everything had fallen in a circular outward pattern easily exposing the tree trunk that began to sag to the side in the unaccustomed open exposure to breezes.

"Whoo, look at that boys," cried Dennis.

"We sure made short work of that," yelled Lennis.

And the twins stomped together smiling at Stanley, who only looked sadly at the remains. "Well, I guess that's kind of the end of the old farm," he said.

"Not quite," said Lennis as he pulled up a rifle, and began to fire at the tree trunk.

Dennis joined him, and in short order the tree trunk was blown away as if shattered with a giant axe.

"Now let's find that cornerstone," said Dennis, and all three brothers walked up to the silo's edge.

The cornerstone was fully exposed inside the silo's front edge where the leverage of concrete falling from above had pulled face blocks and years of soil and silage away to expose it. As if just done yesterday, the concrete etching on the stone face preserved by years under silage glowed white under the sunshine with its message, "Lester Denny, June 2, 1945."

"Amazing how good that looks," said Stanley.

"Well, it won't in a minute after we shoot it," Lennis said.

"Don't you think we ought to dig it out, and take it home like kind of a memorial?" Stanley asked. "I think Pop would have liked that."

"Naah, it would be too much work," Dennis said. "We'll just have a high loader put it on a truck to haul away with everything else. Let's shoot it. What do you think, Lenny—thirty-ought-sixes together?"

Dennis and Lennis grinned at each other while Stanley searched for a word of protest that might slow them down.

The twins laid down side by side, aiming their rifles from the prone position. Stanley flopped on his belly beside them.

"Now, Lenny, we'll hit her square, head on, blow her to kingdom come—ready, fire!"

The rifles exploded at the same time, and in the briefest instant something also exploded behind them, with shattered glass flying and a resounding whack of metal on metal as the silver truck's windshield came apart, and a bullet penetrated through the hood to the block from two ricochets.

The three brothers raised on elbows to look grimly back at the truck.

"I told you Pop wouldn't like it," Stanley said.

Carmen takes it
to the house

Author's note: There was something elegant about see-
ing the innovations in a turn of the last century house.
It didn't seem right to bypass the old water tanks for a
modern water line.

CARMEN THE horsetrader wanted to be thought of as an "old
buddy" by the people he dealt with, and not as the great rascal, as he
felt down deep in his bones that they sometimes did.

Truth was, he sometimes barely got by. He had learned all the make-
do secrets of farm and ranch life: tying things together with baling
wire, whether it was a muffler to a car, a steel post that propped up an
older wooden one, or sturdying up the blower on an old machine when
the original bracket rusted through.

Could he help it he was such a good trader that it was tough to
remember that those not so endowed with his talents might suffer
before the force of his accomplishments? Sometimes he did make thousands of dollars.

Horses are horses, and money is money, and making a great trade is
sweeter than honey, he told himself.

Would a rascal take such great pleasure in sitting visitors down on
the broad front porch for cold or hot drinks—depending on the preference and the weather—and describing the old three-story white house
he lived in? Could a rascal love an old house like he did, and take care of
it so well?

No, no, no, Carmen told himself as he stroked his thin-haired noggin
under the cowboy hat above his high cheek-boned face. To love this soaring house with the Victorian-era brown woodwork was a testimony to
his higher character.

He would fold his hands over his large paunch, lay his undersized
bow legs on his favorite little porch stool, and stare meaningfully into
the eyes of a visitor.

"Let me tell you about this house. It might have been finished in 1910,
but it was way ahead of its time. This was the first house out here to
have runnin' water. Know how? No, don't s'pect you do.

"Why, they put big bridge timbers across the floor up in the third
floor attic, tied them in to them big supports in the frame—not your
modern little skinny lumber, but big hand-cut walnut from right here—
and put four 300-gallon stock tanks in. That's 1,200 gallons of water.

"That big windmill yonder in the back yard pumps the water up to
the tanks when you flip the lever. The pipes from the tanks run down

through the house to the toilets, the kitchen, and everything. And it all still works.

"Frances and her brothers wanted me to replace it with an electric pump and pressure tank. I wouldn't.

"Then Frances wanted us to tie into the new rural water line, and I told her, 'Now Frances, honey, if the Lord had intended us to have rural water, he wouldn't have blessed us with a plentiful producing well, that big windmill, and the genius of the person who put them tanks in the attic.'

"So, come on up here. Stairs ain't much of a climb."

Then for an hour Carmen would show the visitor the big tanks full of clear water, the pipes running down through the walls, and maybe flush the stools for them in a display of the plenty. No, a rascal couldn't receive the blessing of a house like this with a water system like this.

But there **came** a day when the blessed water system needed a repair. Frances was the first to notice a spreading water stain across the ceiling wallpaper of their second-story bedroom.

"Not to worry, not to worry," Carmen told her. "I'll find the problem, and probably I can fix it myself. I'm good at fixing things."

See there. Could a rascal be so reassuring to his wife, and be able to fix things his own self? No, no, no, he couldn't, Carmen told himself.

So, he went to the attic, crawled round and round on his knees over the water-stained flooring until he found the problem. There it was, just a little trickle of water coming out along the bottom seam of one of the tanks. It was hard to see. But he could lay his finger across it, feel the chill of the water and, by pressing on it, see the flow of the water over the edge of his finger.

Now how am I going to fix this? Carmen was no hand at welding or soldering, and it would be unhandy to have someone with a torch up here anyway. All the tanks were very old, probably only been replaced once or twice in more than 90 years. Tanks would be a great expense, probably cost more than a dollar for each gallon they held these days. Might be $1,500.

He knew the answer almost before he asked himself. Carmen had done it before in the animal feedlots. Why, you just pour a half-foot of concrete over some reinforcing wire in the bottom of each tank. Seals them up tight. Carmen could do that himself.

It was tough to lose a day's work, but Carmen spent the entire next day on the project. He went to the lumber yard and bought heavy sacks of concrete. He even carried them all the way to the attic himself, stopping to puff, and breathe, and sit rubbing his knees at each floor.

He got 5-gallon buckets and filled them with water for mixing concrete once the big tanks were drained. He rolled up a section of old range fence to use for concrete reinforcing, and hauled it up to the attic. He took the steel wheel barrow up. He carried up buckets of sand and gravel for the mixing.

It was tough to lose a second day's work, but after hauling everything up, Carmen was too tuckered out the first day. Besides, it was easier to watch the water level drop in the tanks a little at a time instead of draining them all at once. But he had to finish draining them anyway, opening all the water taps on the first floor to do so.

It was tough to lose a third day's work—and listen to Frances gripe. Why was she doing that? He'd filled buckets of water on every floor for them to use, hadn't he?

Carmen got the job done, sweating nearly without ceasing, hand mixing and pouring the concrete across the wire in the bottom of the tanks 6 inches deep. He was so dead tired that night, he hardly heard Frances asking when she would have tap water again.

"The concrete's got to cure out," he told her.

Finally, after a couple of more days, Carmen flipped the windmill levers and the water came out in great bursts at the attic to fill the tanks. A pint of water is a pound of weight, eight pounds to a gallon times 1,200 gallons is 9,600 pounds on top of heavy, newly cured concrete. More than five tons of weight settled on the old beams.

Carmen was pleased, but still ready to die from weariness. Would a rascal work so hard and do so well? Every tank held water, and the floor around was dry.

Carmen fell heavily asleep that night, only slowly rising to a sleep state with satisfying dreams of his own merits and work ethic. He slowly became aware that the wind outside must have come up because the old house was groaning, and creaking as it sometimes did in wind storms.

"Do you hear that?" Frances asked, grabbing his knee and bringing him fully awake.

Eeeeagghcreek, sighed the great house throughout the ceiling above them.

"Must be a heck of a storm," Carmen said, rubbing his great belly where the muscles still ached.

"It isn't storming."

Creek, crack, crunch. A board that connected to the rafters at one end of the room popped loose right through the plaster, sending a great shower of the material down at one end of the room.

Carmen received a moment of insightful enlightenment.

"The weight," he said. "The concrete was too much more weight!"

But then the ceiling split, and a great splintered bridge beam stopped only a foot from his nose in a resounding boom that overpowered the sound of hundreds of gallons of cascading water pouring over Carmen, Frances, the bed and the floor so that they were scarcely aware in the washout of the overhanging danger.

Half-drowned, and sucking to breathe through the water that had so recently filled their mouths and noses, they clung to each other as they descended the stairs in nightgowns wetly plastered to their hides.

The great rascal was baptized for his transgressions, and shielded from the total potential damage of their results. As for Frances, she was washed clean as a result of her love and loyalty.

And Frances got her reward, even though it took a lot of horse trading to rebuild part of the house, and hook into the rural water line. It was unbelievably difficult for the workmen to bust up the concrete-filled water tanks that hung on the beams, and get them out of the attic.

"I tried, though. I really tried. I did all the work, and I didn't swap out of any part of it," Carmen would sometimes murmur to himself. "My house, my poor old house. One little mistake, and all that history's gone. Lord have mercy, am I really such a bad old rascal?"

Starla shows her plucky side

Author's note: Strange things always did happen when cousins came to spend the night.

THE HIGH-CEILING rooms with their broad, cool linoleum floors were where the boys liked to hang out as the early days of spring began to give way to the close, humid heat that foretold the coming of summer. They lay lackadaisically, hanging over the ends of the couch, reaching to feel the chill of the floor surface with their toes, not quite resting and not quite stirring, just waiting.

Rickey and Roger were waiting on their cousin, Starla. Starla was a 10-year-old tomboy with power in the shoulders, forearms and torso to rival any boy her age. She was so quick with the comebacks that she could get cousins into conflagrations with other boys by the force of her tongue, and choose to join the fight or walk away.

Her weakness was her Aunt Margaret, Rickey and Roger's mother. Somewhere in Starla's deeper recesses was a respect for Aunt Margaret as a lady, and she loved staying with her, loved her cooking, especially fried chicken and fried steak, would cheerfully do chores for her in the kitchen or around the farm, in fact she adored Aunt Margaret. She came to play with Rickey and Roger, but she actually came to see Aunt Margaret.

Starla arrived, getting out of the car with a mischievous grin for the boys and a bright, never-been-bent-up cardboard shoebox under her arm. Wiping her nose with her forearm while shoving back her blonde curls in the same motion, Starla crinkled into a smile that included both eyes and mouth. Looking up at her well-combed Aunt Margaret in a rose-pattern apron, she asked, "Want to see my new tennis shoes?"

"Why, I sure do," said Aunt Margaret. "Did you just get them?"

"No, I've had them a couple of days. But they're pure white so they pick up the dirt easy, and Mom says I should keep them clean to go places until my old shoes wear out on the bottoms too instead of just the sides."

Starla sat down, took off her old stained tennis shoes, and put on the bright white ones. "You probably won't see me in them much unless we decide to go do something nice."

With that, Starla again changed shoes, went to the bedroom where she would sleep on her overnight stay, and pushed the new shoes under the foot of the bed. Then she followed the two brown-haired boys on a running tear through the yard with two dogs leaping alongside that scattered white and red chickens out of the path, pausing for a moment to aim a kick at one big rooster that tried to block the path, and fight, breast out, wings tipping down, and beak forward.

The cousins crawled through a barbed-wire fence to pretend to wade out to a dead elm tree on its side with all the bark slicked off to provide a white easily climbed skeleton work, a battle ship off to war.

All afternoon they hollered in mock battles, and climbed the dead branches to sight enemies. Before long, each youngster had a length of dead limb to serve as a sword, and at times they were squared off striking sticks together in sword fights.

By suppertime, they were ready to eat, and Starla delighted in one of Aunt Margaret's fried-chicken-with-mashed-potatoes-and-gravy meals, "eat the vegetable if you have to, and look at that cake and Jell-O for desert."

Starla was stuffed, but she still managed to show her white tennis shoes to Uncle Clarence too before tucking them away carefully under the bed again.

"Now tomorrow afternoon," Aunt Margaret said, "I have club to go to. You kids just play here, and I want you to feed and water the chickens and gather the eggs—you got that?"

Rickey and Roger wrinkled their noses, but Starla said, "We sure will, Aunt Margaret. Is that all you want us to do?"

"Yes, you just have fun the rest of the time. And stay out of trouble, and don't get hurt."

Aunt Margaret left the next day just as the pasture battleship was caught in a frightful crossfire between the British and a pirate, but the cousins had their chicken-tending instructions for when they crossed back through the fence.

They brought their white weathered swords with them, using them for canes as they gathered the buckets to pour water, carry corn and gather the eggs.

Rickey and Starla took the water in, but Roger stood outside with the corn buckets, shooing back the chickens that were beginning to gather around him in a hungry multitude.

"Why don't you bring the grain in?" Starla asked.

"We're going to throw it in handfuls on the ground out here, so they all have to come out to eat," Roger said. "That way they all come off the nests, and we don't get our hands pecked gathering the eggs."

"Gad, you big baby," Starla said. "Can't take getting your hands pecked?"

Roger grimaced at her sourly, and began throwing handfuls of corn around him while the chickens pushed for it on the ground in a melee of pecking and scuffling for position. Soon the three children were throwing corn all over in a 50-foot radius, sometimes still playing that the ship's cannon was now firing shrapnel that hit the chickens in blasts of corn. The birds only jumped momentarily, and kept on eating.

Then they went in to go down the rows of nests, picking up eggs to put in the buckets until Roger came to the last nest on the last row, and just stood there.

When he put his hand toward the nest there came the telltale sound, a rhythmic "puck, puck, puck," followed by the "caaw" warning from a broody hen with feathers all ruffled up to make her size look doubled.

"Just reach under her and get the eggs, Roger," said Starla.

"Nah, she'll peck me, or worse."

"Well I'll do it then," Starla said and slipped her hand right under the hen.

"Yeow, she pecked me—you old biddy!" Starla hollered, and swung her stick-sword, hitting the chicken in the head, and the chicken fell out of the nest to the floor where she lay still.

"I think you killed her," Ricky said.

"What's Aunt Margaret going to say?" Starla asked.

"I'm glad it was you instead of me cuz Dad would probably give me a spanking," said Roger.

"I want to cook it," Starla said. "Aunt Margaret's been cooking for me, so I'm going to pluck this chicken, and cook her a fried chicken dinner. They won't know which chicken it was, will they?"

"You know how to do all that?"

"Sure, you just pull all the feathers off, and then clean it."

"Isn't plucking all the feathers off the cleaning?"

"Naah, cleaning is when you take its intestines out."

"That's yucky—you aren't going to do that. You aren't going to want to cut its head off either."

"We don't have to cut its head off, it's already dead."

"We'll need some scalding water to get the feathers off."

"Naah, we can do it anyway. Just fill this bucket with cold water. No sense getting burnt."

Starla dunked the chicken in the cold water, and tentatively pulled some tail feathers out. "They're tough pulling out."

She grabbed bunches of feathers, and tried pulling them out here and there.

They heard an engine coming, and Roger said, "Uh oh, here comes Mom home. What are we going to do?"

"I know," said Starla as she went running into the house carrying the chicken by the legs. "Quick, help me get my shoebox from under the bed."

Starla pulled her shoes out, and hurriedly shoved the chicken into the box, pulling the lid down tight, and shoving the box back under the bed. "We'll figure out what to do with her later."

"Why Starla, you're wearing your new white tennis shoes for supper. What's the occasion?" asked Aunt Margaret.

"Oh, nothin'. I just thought I ought to break'em in better. Besides, my old ones are about clear worn out."

The children tried to eat quietly, avoiding looking at each other until finally even Uncle Clarence noticed.

"You kids are awful quiet tonight. You didn't have a fight or anything did you? Hey, what's that noise?"

They all heard a thunk of cardboard hitting the floor followed by a scratch-and-scrape noise coming through the rooms, a struggling sound as something came closer and closer.

"And what's this?" gasped Aunt Margaret as a chicken staggered into the room trying to catch it's balance on the slick linoleum, flopping first to one side and then the other with bare spots showing through its feathers which seemed to point off at odd angles instead of laying smoothly.

The chicken stopped, shook itself, and ruffled its feathers the best it could into an airy ball of indignation.

Then it went, "Puck, puck, puck."

No more horsing around

Author's note: Yes, old Bill did this. It's sometimes interesting to get the animal's perspective.

DOLLY MADISON stuck one big foot inside the barn door just before dawn, and right away, she knew things weren't quite right.

She got her front quarters in, and stood there with her bottom lip drooping, her ears laid back, looking into the dark recesses where the muscular man stood as the other horses paced behind her.

It wasn't right. Her grain was at the wrong end of the stanchion trough. It was just as if someone was to sit in your pew at church, or at your desk at office or school, or worse yet, in your chairs at the dinner table. It just wasn't right.

She had been the big, dominant mare on all team combinations on this farm for many years, and her place was at the right end of the stanchion, just like in the harness she took the right side.

The man was to pour her feed first. Then Queen Mary entered, and he poured her, and then, and only then was William Tell the gelding allowed to take his place in the middle by virtue of knowledge gained from bites and kicks from the big Belgian-cross mares when he was young.

That was the way it was always done by Chester, the master of the farm.

The truth was that this new Larry, the hired man, was doing this to throw the animals off balance because he enjoyed it.

Dolly looked to the man, and then, with her ears laid back all the way, she went to her feed. She was too hungry, and there would be too much work to do once the sun came up to wait longer.

Queen stepped in, and laid her ears back, too, as the man dumped her feed at the other end of the stanchion—the wrong end for her. Then, ears forward, she contemplated Dolly. She decided Dolly wasn't happy, but she was going to allow her the wrong place to eat. There wouldn't be any disciplinarian threats.

William Tell—Old Bill. the farm workers called him—wasn't quite so sure. Dolly was his mother and Queen was his aunt, and as the youngest, lowest member of the horse trio, he knew the adage, "If Mama ain't happy, ain't nobody happy," better than many humans ever would.

Larry grinned when, after pouring Old Bill's feed, the big horse hesitated—and then hesitated some more after glancing back and forth at the eating mares. Only when he decided that neither would throw an anger fit did he step to his place in the middle.

Larry joined the other hands and Chester, who were coming up from milking to eat breakfast.

Then it was time to hitch all three horses for heavy pulling to a hayrack for a day of hay hauling. Larry and another hand harnessed the horses, and hooked them in the hitch.

Chester noticed that every time Larry put a hand on an animal, it would lay back its ears even though each horse was too gentle and accustomed to work and handling to do anything more.

"I don't believe those horses like you," Chester said.

"I guess it's cuz I'm new."

"You've been treatin'em OK?"

"Sure have, sure have," said Larry, because in his eyes petty cruelty wasn't the same as major cruelty. He hadn't cut them or beat them—just rearranged their mentality.

The hot, long day plodded along slowly for both men and horses. The men forked hay from windrows onto the wagon, weighing it down to where the horses strained into the harness long before it went to the barn for unloading.

William Tell (Old Bill) had learned to pull his share long ago as a colt. If he hadn't done so back then, the mares would nip him, and aim side kicks at him to move him along. Chester knew, just as most farmers did, that the best way to train a young horse was to put him in harness with a hard-pulling old mare.

But Larry had decided Old Bill was the easy animal to keep picking on, taking time as he slowed down on his own work to pitch small pebbles and dirt clods ever harder into Old Bill's rump.

"Heh, come on you," Larry would mutter. "Pull into it. Carry your share of the weight. Psssssst, c'mon, move it, move it."

And Old Bill kept a steady pace between the two mares, pulling as he'd been taught, turning his ears only when the man spoke. The other hands began to cast disapproving glances at Larry, and looked to see if Chester was watching. But the old farmer only seemed to keep working at his own steady pace.

The noon meal passed without incident with another hand taking care of the horses' food while the crew washed up.

In the afternoon, Larry kept it up.

"Big dumb plug, get goin' there, heh, c'mon."

He curved a couple of clods into Old Bill's sides when Chester wasn't looking, and the hands were beginning to get angry.

"Seems like it's somebody else that ought to be carrying his weight," one of them said, looking into Larry's hard, thin face."

At high afternoon sun, just before the fiery globe would begin its descent down the sky, Chester called, "Hey now, let's all take a break. Larry, you unhitch the horses, leave the harness on, and take them to the shade trees there for some feed and water."

Larry, like all the others, was tired, and took the opportunity at the order to say "shoot," and whack Old Bill with one more rock.

As Larry took the reins to drive the team to the trees, one of the hands said, "Look at Old Bill's ears laid back. He sure doesn't like that guy" —and, looking meaningfully at the farmer, added— "and, Chester, I don't blame him."

The last words were no sooner said than Old Bill's back feet were arcing outward in a powerful kick that caught Larry in the chest, and threw him 15 feet where he lay still.

All the men ran to Larry, who was drawing in a great gasp as they came up. Chester ran his hands probingly over Larry's chest to feel his ribs.

The hands all looked up at Chester as he stood to pause while looking at Larry.

"Boy," he said. "You ain't dead, and you ain't broken. So, when you can breathe and get up, go get those feed bags for the horses. By the time you're done with them, we'll be done with the break, and you can go back to work with us. Guess, you're just lucky Old Bill commenced to train you as a member of the team before he had to get hard on you."

Stories amid the storm

IT WAS ABOUT time for the late afternoon lunch anyway when the first hot-day lightning cracked across the black clouds that were beginning to fill the west.

The hay was just unloaded into the barn. The hay boys, with their grimy, dirt-caked foreheads, and shirts soaked through with sweat, were happy to flop down with their hooks and gloves on bales or buckets—whatever was handy—glad they weren't caught in the field as the first rain-chilled wind began rushing in the barn doors.

From time to time one of them would look out a door as if at the storm, but really to catch the first sight of the car that would bring ham sandwiches, potato salad and ice tea. It was four hours since the meat and mashed potatoes of dinner-time, and four hours until the meat and mashed potatoes of supper-time.

Hungry hay boys knew if you worked for Uncle Art, he liked to work hard, eat a lot, and tell tales.

"Well," said Uncle Art, "well this storm reminds me about the financial start I got in life, so I could own all this ground, and you boys could haul all this hay."

A few of the boys begin to stick tongues in their cheeks, and raise eyebrows at each other, but they had no place else to go.

"You know the wind blows twice as hard out west as it does in these parts, and the storms are twice as mean, and they're always fixing to form up tornados whether they're big giants or nasty little dust devils. It's out where the farms are so far apart that everybody has to own his own tomcat unless they're lucky enough for a dust devil to carry one their way. And it's so flat they have to close the curtains at night so as not to embarrass a neighbor six miles away.

"Before I had anything, I was out there in an old long-bed truck my pop loaned me just so I could see it. A storm popped up, just like this one popped up, and the biggest, meanest twister you ever did see came out of it—nearly two miles across.

"It went to sucking and roaring across the countryside picking up everything off the farms it came to, a fearsome, fearsome thing."

Uncle Art paused as the squall line winds of the storm began clanging and vibrating the tin barn roof. Looking up meaningfully, he continued.

"Naturally, I joined everybody else with my truck going from place to place to clean up afterward, and what do you think? There was my big opportunity. That twister had sucked well holes and post holes out of the ground on every farm we came to. Nobody cared if I picked them up.

"Of course, I had to cut one other guy in on my idea because not all the holes had cleaned clear out. Some of the well holes still had a little water in them, and some of the post holes still had a little dirt in them, and it took two of us to pick them up, and shake them out, or the load would have got too heavy for my truck.

"Some of the well holes had run so deep we had to cut them in two, and still they over-hung the truck bed. We tied them down real well, and red-flagged the end of the load so some hot rod didn't tailgate me, and end up with his car falling in a well hole.

"We got back here with that load of holes, and I sold them all for a premium price. Not too high mind you. I don't believe in gouging folks. But people sure were glad to buy well holes they could stick right in the ground to get water, and fence holes they could poke down to slide the post into with no hard digging work. We had to go back for more loads, and it assured my fortune."

One of the hay boys guffawed, rolling his eyes, "Uncle Art, I don't think tornados are the only thing windy around here."

"Now, boys, boys. I'll tell you one more story, and it's the gospel truth if you can interpret it that way. Besides, lunch isn't here yet.

"There was another time out there I was hunting. It was so flat, and with no trees, and you could just see forever. I looked over on the horizon, and saw a black dot moving. Well, I just kept on hunting, walking along, and that dot starts getting bigger and bigger.

"Soon I could see it was the biggest, meanest looking old black bull you could ever imagine, and he was running right toward me. That rascal had spotted me from miles away, it was so flat.

"So I start to running too, and there's nowhere to go, no trees, no place, just more flat land. And that bull, he starts to gaining fast. I can hear him snorting, and when I look back he's got those big red bloodshot eyes and big horns. He keeps gaining and gaining. I know I'm in trouble.

"He's right on my back. I can feel his hot breath, and I know he's got me, boys. Then just in the nick of time I grabbed a low branch, and pulled myself up in the tree."

"Aww, Uncle Art! You said there wasn't any trees around. Boo!"

"Now boys, there had to be a tree or I wouldn't be here, would I?

"Good, here's the lunch car. Now, a couple of you boys run out there to get it, so she doesn't have to carry it through the rain."

Tireless talker never shut off the tap

Author's note: I think I've had coffee in the same place with this guy at least 136 times.

BIRD PULLED his car into a space in front of the town's only cafe next to a near-new Chrysler New Yorker shining brightly but covered with deep dents and scrapes.

Good, he thought, peering through the front-door glass, the cafe was nearly empty, and it had an interesting 1950s decor of black, red and white tile floor and vinyl-topped tables. Not too bad of a place for a tired fellow to spend a couple of hours before the next meeting drinking coffee, maybe reading a newspaper, and sometimes these small places would have rhubarb pie.

Man, rhubarb pie, that would be OK, maybe not even sweet, red rhubarb, but the old-time green, sour, pithy stuff of his youth out of somebody's old-time garden. Bird already was relaxing and salivating for pie as he stepped through the door.

"Hey, whaddaya know there, fella, whaddaya say? Howya doin'? Whereya from anyway?"

Tap, tap, tap, tap, tap.

Bird looked at the source of all the questions, who was sitting in the corner with a shock of gray hair sticking out the sides of a white broad-brimmed cotton golf cap, extra-thick glasses with great black horn rims over a pink striped shirt. His hand was doubled with a great horny-calloused short-nailed thumb tapping the table top in high energy, tap, tap, tap.

"I say there, hey whaddaya know, fella, whaddaya say? Howya doin? Whereya from anyway?"

Tap, tap, tap.

"Not much, nothing, hundred miles east of here."

"Good, good, good, well sit right down here. How's the weather been there, whaddaya do, whereya been, c'mon now, whadaya know, don't be shy. Sit down, sit down, make yourself at home, right here, right here, sit down, whaddaya know, huh?"

Tap, tap, tap.

"I just really wanted to sit down and rest a bit. You see, I have—"

"C'mon, c'mon, c'mon, sit down, sit down, don't be shy. Yer a good enough lookin' young fella, no need to be so shy, sit down."

Tap, tap, tap.

"I sawya look at the waitress when you came in. Gotta eye for the girls, eh? Yer a good enough lookin' young fella, no need to stay so shy. I said sit down, sit down."

Tap, tap, tap.

"Look, all I wanted is some quiet, some coffee and a piece of rhubarb pie."

"Rhubarb, huh, that's a good one, fella. I s'pect she does have rhubarb, but I don't think ya need to be lookin' at it. Yer a crusty one, ain't ya, fella, c'mon now, whaddaya know?"

Tap, tap, tap.

"Look," said Bird starting to flush red, "I don't know what you're try-ing to imply, but I—"

"Can I help you, sir?" asked the tall, thin black-hair dyed waitress, smiling tiredly.

"Reckon ya can, reckon ya can, Gladys. This fella's a crusty one, gotta lotta spice—ho, watch the fella now, watch the fella now, hide yer rhubarb."

Tap, tap, tap.

"Just coffee, thanks, black," said Bird, squirming around in the chair where he had somehow come to sit almost against his will.

"Testy, testy, young fella, hey relax, relax. Ya won't see me fightin' the world. No. Do I care when I pull in at the gas pumps when they make the drive too narrow so I hit the posts with my Chrysler? No, no, not me. An' I don't get mad when those semis drive like they own the world. I just cut'em off, and hang my head out the window, and laugh at them. Relax, relax, it's a great world, now whaddaya know, really?"

Tap, tap, tap.

"Why, you're nuts. You could get killed cutting off trucks."

"Nuts? Nuts? Ya tryin' ta start a fight or somethin'? Yer nuts, yer nuts, settle down, now tell me whaddaya know now. Yer a feisty one, and crusty, too. What are ya, a Democrat or a Republican?"

"Why, I'm not going to tell you that. I keep my politics to myself."

"An independent, huh? Meet me in the middle, round and round she goes, where she stops nobody knows, ring around the rosey, that's what ya are, dance clear around the circle. Ya piece of foggy fluff. Ya ain't a leftist, and ya ain't clear out on the right either, nothin' to ya, dance the dance of life, wussy, wussy, wussy."

Tap, tap, tap.

"Now, what are you talking about? True, I don't think of myself as a true conservative, but I'm no leftist either."

"Ah, yer one of those fuzzy heads that thinks politics is a straight line. Looky here, fella, the rule of this dimension is the circle. The earth is round, the universe is round, yer head is round, an egg is round, and so is Gladys. Ya wouldn't like any of 'em as squares or parallelagrams. Yer not a tetrahedron-lover are ya, fella?

"A circle is 360 degrees and what's next to the 360 on its right is the 1, round and round ya go, where she stops nobody knows. Somewhere right of Ronald Reagan and left of Ted Kennedy is the 360 and the 1.

"Why, Hitler was so close to 360, he was more nuts than nearly any-one. At the other end of it was Stalin. He was so close to 1 he was more nuts than nearly anyone, and they looked sort of alike, only they was in a different circle than our politicians, which is why it's unfair to com-pare. Their circle is the violent-nuts' circle. Even the moderate violent nuts like Francisco Franco are entitled to a place on their own circle separate from us.

"Our circle's the one of democratic republican capitalist socialist builders, the Jeffersonians and Hamiltonians still fightin' it out so we don't know what we are, keeps us safe. Now, tell me whaddaya know, don't tell me ya don't know nothin', fella."

Tap, tap, tap.

"I'm afraid that began to make a little sense even to me."

"Sense, sense? There ya go tryin' to start a fight again. Of course, of course, at the 180 the middle is empowered, and everybody's fightin' to complete the circle, take it away from the haves for the have-nots, chicken for everybody, give it back to them what stoled it. Ring around the rosey, round and round she goes, c'mon boy, when ya gonna tell me. Whaddaya know? Whaddaya know? What was the weather whereya came from?"

Tap, tap, tap, and he pushed the big horny thumb into Bird's chest.

Bird jumped, bumping his coffee, so it went all over his lap.

"Now look whatya done, all over yer pants, boy!"

Tap, tap, tap.

"I have to go now, and find a change. Sorry, we couldn't finish our, er, conversation."

"Nonsense, nonsense, fella. We was just gettin' started. We can mop ya up."

Tap, tap, tap.

"I'm sure you could, but I really need to go," Bird said, turning and walking away.

He paid the waitress listening to the sullen tap, tap, tap, tap in the background. As Bird came to the door, another man was entering.

"Take my advice," Bird whispered into the man's face, "just throw your coffee in your lap, and leave as soon as you can."

"Hey, whaddaya know, whaddya say, fella?" boomed the voice in the background to the new man coming in. "Howya doin'? Whereya from anyway?"

Tap, tap, tap went the thumb all the way to Bird's car.

Hard-sell Harry drives again

"**K**ITTENS!"

Harry nearly spat the word through a great plume of smoke directed at the fat, black, neutered tom cat curled near the air conditioning vent on the car seat next to him.

"That's OK, Hattie, we'll show them," Harry snarled, biting down on his cigarette, his blue eyes narrowing below his black cotton hat. "I named you Hattie so I'd never forget the cold, cold woman who gave me all those kittens, but it's just you and me now, Hattie, and nobody's getting away from us without buying brushes."

Hard-sell, hard-hearted Harry, they had called him until he brought boxes of kittens to give away into a sales meeting one day.

"How did you get the kittens, Harry?" they had asked him, and when he told them, they walked away with cold, lizard salesman smiles.

She had eliminated one kitten, allowing a collie dog to chomp it, and Harry's hard heart, the one that had kept him selling brushes to poor housewives until they cried, melted to make him take the kittens.

For a long time in sales meetings, he would shift his eyes and try to be subtle about turning his head to see who was going "meow" or "kitty, kitty" behind him. But they were learning that Hard-Sell Harry wasn't done. Push, push, push, persistent selling over long hours, and the reputation was returning as Hattie the cat aged.

The great dust cloud settled on the gravel road behind his station wagon as Harry pulled into a driveway in front of a white, green-shuttered house where an elderly woman was hanging clothes on the line.

Harry cracked the windows for Hattie in the shade of a giant elm tree that swayed in the hot, southwest wind.

"Ma'am, I'm Harry Blackhart representing the Southern Brush Co., blah, blah, blah, vegetable brushes, floor brushes, bath brushes, blah, blah, blah. We have brushes so soft they baby your skin, and brushes that can peel the paint off a board."

"Well, Harry, I'm Opal," she said from a face so deeply wrinkled she reminded him of a basset hound, and I don't know what I can buy here." She added, grinning, "I've asked the Lord to keep me poor to keep me humble, and he's always obliged.

"But come on in here to the house where it's cool, and let's look at your brushes. Don't mind the bed sheets all over the furniture. I'm alone since my dear husband passed away, and it helps keep everything clean. When I say I'm alone, Harry, I also mean I enjoy company, so show me all your brushes. You never know what I can use."

Ah, you're very, very lonely. Harry's brain was going off like a slot machine. This was going to be a big sale.

Great lumps of ghostly white furniture stood out in the half-light of the high-ceilinged, polished room.

"Actually most of the time I know he's right here with me, Harry. He said he'd never truly leave me," she said with a smile, stepping to the shadow of a stuffed chair. "Of course, I have neighbors and my pets.

"Come sit here on the couch, Harry. You can open your case there. Oops, oh, don't sit on that end. Roger's there."

Harry paused, looking at the empty seat beside him. "I don't see—"

"Oh, the ornery thing, if I have you move, he'll probably move too. Roger! You let Harry sit down. There, he's moving, he's moving, sit down, Harry."

As Harry sat down, he was startled to see a bulge, an indentation and a moving ripple in the sheet at the other end of the couch.

"That Roger, isn't he a card, Harry? He must like the looks of you since he's staying close."

"Let's hope so," purred Harry. Now jump in there, and sell this nut case, he told himself.

"Opal, if you ever really thought about cleaning this furniture, here's a little brush for you with microscopic turns in the bristles at the ends that blah, blah, blah...."

Harry felt the cushion next to him move. He felt the couch rippling behind his back. He refused to be deterred.

"I do want that brush, Harry, and that one, too. But let's move in here to the kitchen table for ice tea while you show me more, and just let Roger have the couch."

Harry talked for an hour. He drank one glass of iced tea, then he drank most of another. Once he heard a distinct thump from the living room. He thought he heard a knocking on the floor. But when he turned around while putting his glasses on to make a brush invoice list, there was nothing there.

He and Opal looked over the rims of their glasses at each other while he ran the calculator, and then she wrote a check, and he took his last sip of tea.

"Well, Opal, I think you'll find you've made a wise purchase with these brushes, a lifetime of service at your fingertips," Harry said, closing his brush case. "If you need anything more, give me a call. I really must get on down the road now to make another stop."

"Harry, hold very still. Roger is coming up behind your chair. No, no, don't turn around or make any moves, you'll scare him."

Harry heard a thump on the back of his chair, and the hair on the back of his neck involuntarily went up. Then something gripped his shoulder.

"Still, still, hold very still Harry. I think Roger wants to give you a kiss goodbye."

Harry felt a shock of hair touching the side of his head, then a moist touch on his cheek.

"Uugh," Harry sucked wind softly and stood as the grip tightened.

"Slower, take it easy now," Opal said as he grabbed her check, his glasses and his case, and began moving.

The grip changed, there was a chattered garbling in his ear, and something clawed the side of Harry's face. scratching it as it released him rushing out the door.

"Bye, bye, Opal," Harry hollered as he jumped in his car.

As he drove down the road, Harry trembled as he pulled his next cigarette out and patted the scratch on his cheek with a tissue. Harry sneered at black Hattie on the seat, and said, "Nobody can say you aren't a hard sell when you keep going with ghosts in the room. I get all the nut cases."

In the meantime, Opal offered a nut to the trembling red squirrel that sat in the middle of her kitchen table.

She softly petted and soothed him saying, "There, there, Roger. Harry didn't mean to scare you."

Oh for a piece
of that rhubarb pie

AWAY FROM home, away from his wife and children, and here Bird was sitting at a desk in a branch office typing at his laptop, and thinking of rhubarb pie.

Rhubarb pie, not pink and sweet, but the old-fashioned green really tart stuff like Mom used to make—that's what he wanted.

He'd cashed a $100 bonus for the good work he'd done since leaving home, and "Doggone it," he muttered, he'd about give it all for really good rhubarb. It seemed like everywhere he'd been, he couldn't get rhubarb pie.

He'd had coffee and a doughnut for breakfast, coffee and a hamburger at noon, and now, when work ended, he was ready for something that was good for him, plus coffee and rhubarb pie, succulent bite-you-in-the-back-of-the-mouth rhubarb, as sour as sour as can be.

At 4 p.m., he called down the aisle, "Hey, Herb, you got a restaurant in this town that serves really good pie?"

"Why sure, the motel place out on the highway."

At 5:30 p.m., he asked the secretary as they were leaving the front door, "So, you think that motel restaurant might serve something like rhubarb pie?"

She swore that she saw his eyes get larger. "You know, really good rhubarb pie," he said.

"If any place has it, that one does," she replied. "They have the best pie. Everybody goes there for pie."

Bird was sure it must be the place to go because there was a picture of a trucker on the window with a big piece of pie and a steaming cup of coffee that said, "Try Our Pie!"

"I'll try, I'll try," Bird hissed, fairly savoring the flavor.

It looked good inside, really good—lots of people, really clean, neatly dressed waitresses in clean green-striped uniforms scurrying around. There were people eating pie—tall ones, skinny ones, fat ones, all kinds. Pie, pie, pie.

"Hello, I'm Ruby, and I'll be your waitress."

Bird looked up into the sparkling green eyes of a twenty-something redhead.

"Well, Ruby, tell me, do you sell pie here?"

"Yes, we do, we have the best pie you won't believe—"

"Yes, yes, but do you have rhubarb?"

"We sure do, we have—"

"Never mind, never mind. Just knowing you have rhubarb is the ticket. Really good rhubarb. I can hardly wait."

"But, well, there's—"

"That's all right, Ruby, just take my order for the main course here, and we'll get to the pie in the tangy bye and bye. I better eat something really good, but not too fattening because I plan to really do some damage with that pie. How about this item, strips of white chicken with salad."

"Why certainly, sir, and wouldn't you like to order your pie now?"

"Nah, let's save the pleasure of that for later. Just some coffee, black, with the rest of it now. Maybe I'll be able to eat two pieces of that rhubarb pie."

"I think that wouldn't hurt you too much, sir," Ruby said wrinkling her nose at him in sweet conspiracy. "Maybe I ought to tell you that pie list now because—"

"Nope, nope, nope. Just march on Ruby Ruby, Ruby, Ruby, Ruby," Bird sang out a tune, he was feeling so happy.

"Heh, that was nice, sir. I suppose you sing often."

"Why that was a Dion song. You can still hear it on golden oldie stations."

"Sorry, sir, I'm a little young to go for golden oldies."

A little young for listening to golden oldies was she, Bird snorted to himself as he munched a hunk of chicken, lettuce and carrots all together. These kids didn't know the half of the good music they were missing. Bet she didn't even stop to eat the rhubarb they had here, good old rhubarb with a tang that curled your tongue.

He cleaned his plate off, drank the last swallow of coffee in the cup, and actually paused holding the cup in the air. The time was here, time for rhubarb.

"Are you ready for more coffee and that slice of pie, sir?" Ruby leaned forward smiling at him as if he was the sweetest old father figure she'd seen in a while.

"I sure am, Ruby Doobie Doobie, ready for the rhubarb. Bring it on, and see if I can stop at one piece."

"Well, all right, sir. Let's see, we have raisin rhubarb and strawberry rhubarb. Which one would you like, sir?"

Bird was stunned. He raised tall in his chair. "Raisin rhubarb and strawberry rhubarb? No, no, no, no, no! I want rhubarb, plain, green, tangy, sour, with just-a-touch-of-sugar rhubarb."

"I really did try to tell you the list earlier, sir. There's raisin rhubarb and strawberry rhubarb. That's it, makes it really nice and sweet, so—"

"No, no, no, no! I wanted plain rhubarb. Why would any right thinking American put big sweet dried up grapes in rhubarb? Gag! You can't be serious. You really wouldn't do that to rhubarb. And as for the other, you've ruined two good fruits."

"You should really just try it, sir. It's really good. People stop here special just for raisin rhubarb."

Bird took off his glasses, and sat with his face in the palms of his hands. It seemed he might cry or explode.

"Let me pour you some more coffee, sir, and you just sit here a minute, and think about it. Maybe I can bring you back the whole pie list."

Bird sipped coffee, staring ahead.

"I'm back, sir," Ruby said with an encouraging smile. "Would you like some pie now? Sir, want me to top that coffee for you, warm it up? ...A little out of sorts, are we?"

Bird rubbed his knees, and looked around.

"Sir, I go off shift in about 15 minutes. I sure would like to bring you that pie. I tell you what, why don't you try a piece of that rhubarb raisin on the house. I just promise you, you'll be back for more," and she wrinkled her nose at him."

"No, no, no, no," Bird said so softly that Ruby leaned forward to hear him. "How many pieces of rhubarb raisin do you have back there?"

"Why, I think there must be about 10 pieces, sir."

"I'll take all of them, just bring all the raisin rhubarb out, Ruby Doobie."

"Are you sure, sir? That's a lot of pie. They're big pieces, and they're $2.50 each. That would be $25 extra plus tax, sir."

"Yes, yes, I know, I know, and I'll give you another $25 to stay past shift, and help me at my table here."

"Sir, are you making a pass at me? Fifty dollars is more than most people spend in this place. I have to work here, you know...."

"No, no, no, no," Bird said, putting his hands up flat against the air in protest. "It's a question of pie, you'll see. Bring two plates with the slices, and two extra spoons, and more coffee, for you too if you want it."

"That's it, that's it, just set them all down here, Ruby. I count 11 pieces."

"You said you wanted it all, sir."

"That's OK, that's OK. Now let's get started. We'll each take a slice of pie at a time. Use your spoon, and pick the raisins out, and put them on that plate over there, eat them if you want to, or take them home, or throw them in the trash. On this plate here, we put all the rhubarb, and the crust too, it looks pretty good."

"You're crazy, sir, we can't do this. People are beginning to look at us."

"That's OK. It's good for publicity. And besides, the customer is always right. Do you have a lemon or some lemon juice in back? Nothing sweetened. I may want to pour it on this rhubarb. It looks a little sweet, Ruby Doobie."

Ruby smiled, and wrinkled her nose at him as she chewed. "Sure, I can do that for you. These raisins really are good, you know."

Ruby reached to pat his hand as she got up, and hit the edge of his coffee cup so the black liquid spilled in his lap as Bird sampled his first small taste of rhubarb.

"Oh, I'm sorry, I'll get a rag, sir. I'm so sorry."

Bird sat there in his soggy britches. "That's OK. You know this really isn't too bad, a little sweet maybe. Hey, Ruby—Ruby, Ruby, Doobie, don't forget that lemon back there!"

Sticky business at Copperhead Farm

Author's note: I think the guys were truly happy the snakes were cleaned up before they got stuck.

"WHY, THIS is the most beautiful little creek valley I think I've ever seen," said Jack as he looked out of the car window to white water tumbling over rocks below burr oak-dominated rocky banks on one side, and across a vista of flat bottom lands covered with late summer crops on the other.

"Huh, guess it is if you have stomach for it," said the old county agent, George, as he steered the station wagon around the next curve in the road that wound up and down following the creek.

"Beautiful big old trees, clear creek with rock bottom...why that rock would be great to climb up with the kids," Jack said. "I think I'll bring them out here, and my wife would love it too."

"That probably isn't a good idea right now," George replied. "You'll see, you'll see. You know, I've worked out here 30 years with these farmers. Maybe you will, too. Just listen to them. See how they do things. Don't jump in too quick. It's a tough area."

"Well, I am interested in seeing this farm. Strange to hear anybody advertising dirt-raised hogs anymore, raised down and dirty for disease resistance. At the college and most everywhere else I go, the talk is all about raising pigs in confinement. That's where the research is. Say, can we stop, and look at the creek a minute?"

"No, no, no, we won't do that— you'll understand when you see the name of the farm, Jack. Alfie and Essie will be serving us a good dinner too. Wouldn't want to be late. You're going to like their son, Albert. Young guy like you, be taking over the hog business, and be with you a long time if you hang on in this county. They're survivors with a sense of humor."

"OK," Jack said, looking at an especially beautiful big, deep slow-moving pool with a tumble of big rocks and logs around it. Corn on the other side grew nearly to the road surface."

Then a turn brought them out on a broad plateau above the creek, nearly a half mile across to the next trees shimmering in the distance amid the humid heat. Nearly the entire length was taken up by a huge expanse of stripped-bare, rooted-up area of hog lots surrounded and subdivided by a series of electric and panel fences. A white two-story house and out-buildings stood in the middle, surrounded by hog pens.

Pigs trotted alongside a fence next to the car, seemingly too occupied to join their fellows cooling in mud holes further down the slope, until the two animals in the lead pounced down, then came up with separate ends of a writhing dusky-red snake in their jaws.

One pig pulled against the other to keep the snake until they pulled it in two, and ran again, each trying to eat its end of the snake before other hogs could pull it away.

"Now you get it," said George, pointing glumly at the big sign overhanging the driveway.

The sign in big, black letters with a twisting metallic red serpent logo under it read, "Copperhead Hog Farm."

They pulled 30 feet into the lane before there was a gate to open, hogs wandering here and there across the drive. A second sign on the gate proclaimed, "Watch where you tread!"

Jack sat still—looking back at the hogs that had finished their snake meal, looking up at the signs, looking at George.

"Copperhead snakes, Jack. The whole creek area is full of them living in those rock ledges, crawling out here in the fields. Hogs can handle their poison, and they eat them. The only way these people could farm this place, live here, and raise live kids was to surround their home with hogs. You notice they even prefer Duroc pigs because they're red like the snakes."

George raised the flat of his hand toward Jack, pointing at his thumb underneath the nail where the flesh was sucked against the bone.

"A copperhead did that to me, Jack. He was hanging in this gate when I opened it, and he bit me in the thumb. Lucky old Alfie got me to the hospital right away, or I might have died. Sure felt like dying. As you can see, even then, the meat just sloughed off my thumb, marked me good. Now, if you don't mind, I'll let you open the gate. Don't much feel like it on my last visit out here."

Jack cautiously surveyed the ground all around him as he got out, and looked at the gate from several angles before grabbing the bolt to pull it open fast. He shut the gate, and did a sort of hopping walk to the car when it pulled to the other side.

The valley wasn't looking quite the same to him anymore, beauty hiding an evil side.

As they traveled down the driveway, Jack saw more hogs indolently chewing at a mound of brown substance while seemingly satiated fellows cooled in nearby mud.

"What on earth is that stuff?" Jack asked.

George smiled. "Looks like chocolate candy to me. These people sure got their own ways, Jack. They go to the new candy factory about 40 miles north to get surplus and stale candy for the hogs. Snake meat and chocolate, that's probably a different pig ration than you've studied, eh? You'll notice, there are grain feeders, too."

Alfie, Essie and Albert didn't look unusual at least—all three dressed in clean, cotton shirts and wearing blue jeans. And the smell of fresh-cooked ham was savory.

"So, you're the new guy are you? Pleased to meet you, very pleased," said Alfie, smiling under his close-cropped graying hair.

Albert reached out a hand to shake very seriously, then said loudly, "Oops, watch out pointing at the floor," so that Jack jumped back three feet from a rubber snake.

"Do that to all the first-time visitors," Albert said, finally smiling. "Sort of breaks the ice, and puts some humor on the place."

"Well, I guess it does that," Jack said, finally smiling, too.

"Let's eat, it's ready," said Essie. "We call this candy ham because the hog it came from probably ate chocolate, and it's a whole lot better than calling it snake ham."

The rest of the dinner turned routine, with inquiries about Jack's background as well as George's retirement plans and the hog business.

Everybody was full and happy until Alfie got up for another pitcher of tea, and looked out the window.

"What's the matter with that sow?" he asked. "She's trying to get up, and can't do it. Neither can the one next to her. There's another one struggling, and another one. What's wrong with them?"

"That's the sows that have weaned their pigs," Albert said, looking over Alfie's shoulder. "I got a big load of taffy from the candy factory yesterday. They look stuck in taffy."

"We're going to need some help," said Alfie, looking at George and Jack. "Those are 400-plus-pound hogs."

The five people ran out to where a half-dozen red sows were stuck in pink, yellow, white and chocolate taffy—sun-heated and melted from large mounds to cover the ground in a 20-foot-wide pile of ooze.

"Come on, Jack—we're the young guys. Help me!" hollered Albert, shoving on the side of the sow nearest the edge.

Jack joined in, lifting and struggling to push with Albert as their shoes stuck in the goop and their hands to the animal. The sow kicked, and struggled, too, finally getting to her feet and pulling herself out of the taffy.

Jack stepped out of his shoes, and began to try to walk to the next sow—wobbling, sinking and trying to pull his feet out—when he fell backward, splat on his back, looking into the blinding sun.

He tried to pull out, but couldn't. When he pushed up with his legs, he felt the back of his head sink deeper. He flailed out with one arm flopping and sticky onto Albert, who lay next to him.

"Help!" they hollered in unison.

"We're thinking, we're thinking," said Alfie from somewhere outside the circle of taffy glue. "You know, George, we've got to think about something quick, or those sows are going to die in this heat."

"What about us?" cried Jack.

"Settle down, settle down, we're thinking," said George.

"You know," said Essie, "I think you two men need to take the truck to get some hay out of the barn to walk on while I watch the two boys so none of the hogs take a bite out of them. Stop wiggling, boys. It makes you look like big snakes. You guys better get shovels and boards to pry with, too. How about a winch?"

"Jack," said Albert.

"Yeah?"

"I think I'm sinking deeper when I try to move. We better hold still."

"Yeah, I think so, too, but there's a fly on my nose—phgh, phgh, phgh, can't blow him away."

"They're landing on me, too. And this stuff's got on my mouth. This stuff don't taste like taffy, Jack!"

"Know what you mean, Albert. I'm sort of gulping now on the ham dinner we ate, myself."

"You boys just hang on—I can't reach either one of you," said Essie. "Besides, this taffy smells so sweet melting out here, I can't hardly stand it either. But I got you beat. I can wave my hand in front of my nose."

Finally the truck came back.

"What do you think, Alfie? You don't want those sows getting too weak. Shall we get them first?"

"Nah, better get the guys first. We might need their muscle to get the sows up."

One by one the men tore pieces of square bales of hay to make foot paths through the taffy to the two young men. Then they pulled them up one at a time to step out on the hay, trying to slop sticky taffy off their hands and heads while waving away flies at the same time.

They wearily made hay paths to each of the sows, and, prying and pulling together, they got them out. Albert didn't even wait to clean off before bringing a tractor with dirt shovel to heap soil over the taffy pile.

The entire crew sprayed themselves with a water hose, and scraped off taffy with everything from big kitchen spoons to ice scrapers. They took showers, and threw their clothes in tubs to soak before washing.

Everybody was so tired that nobody wanted to talk anymore.

George even opened the gate to go home while Jack sat wrapped in a bathrobe in the front seat.

Jack's wife shaved his head to get rid of the candy.

When Albert came into his Jack's new courthouse office next week with a shaved head, they laughed at each other's appearance.

Then Albert handed Jack a new t-shirt with print on it that read, "I Survived the Ultimate Taffy Pull on the Copperhead Hog Farm," a sweet memory that would live forever in their hearts.

Cotton men and the arithmetic hen

Author's note: *The carnies who used to come with the fairs seemed like hardened half-wild people with cynical knowing attitudes to us when we were kids. But they welcomed the rubes and their money. Nobody was more interesting than the one who took the time to describe to us how chickens have sharp eyesight for the things we are hardly aware we are seeing, and how they will work for feed. By the way, my friend, old Bill, tells me the number of kinds of meat in a turtle changes according to what you've been drinking.*

DOWN AT the Deerhead Tavern, the men were coming in one by one for their coffee out of the morning twilight of what portended to be another hot, dusty day.

As they gathered at the long table under the high, creaking ceiling fan in the middle of the room, they were talking the usual talk—what was in the paper, what the weather was and would be, who died, and wasn't he related to so and so.

Then Cody Clayton thought to ask the question of the day: "Hey, isn't this the day old Tall Cotton's brother comes to see him?"

"Yessir," replied Buster. "Old Tall was in here yesterday saying he was going to find something special to feed his brother cuz he was the only thing he loved in the world. Looked like he might shed a tear. Do you suppose he'll feed him turtle? I asked him, didn't a snapping turtle have 22 kinds of meat, and he said no, that I must have forgot the little dark part behind the gizzard."

"Toitle in the mawnin', toitle in the evenin', toitle at suppa time—good fo a body," Paul said in such perfect imitation of Tall that everyone smiled or chuckled.

"Do you suppose he's an old carnie like Tall?" asked Lester.

"Old Tall said he grew up, and spent most of his life on the carnival circuit, so I suppose his brother must have, too," said Buster.

"Look out now, see out the window," said Kelly. "Here they come now."

Half the men at the table got up to see two tall, shave-headed men with brown skin burnt and gnarled like beef jerky, dressed in shorts and muscle shirts that exposed blue and red tatoos accumulated over a lifetime between the wrinkles. They looked a lot alike, but they recognized Tall, the one looking adoringly at the stranger who carefully carried a cardboard box in the crook of one arm.

As they stepped into the room, the stranger surveyed the group with hard, shiny, knowing blue eyes.

"Gentlemen," said Tall. "I want y'all ta meet my brotha, Candy Cotton."

He paused and smiled, raising his hand. "Candy Cotton, the greatest chicken man evah with a cawnival, Cook Cawnival, Anderson Shows, or, or Royal American."

"I'm very pleased to meet all of you," Candy said. "You're Tall's friends he's told me about, and this fine community, and the good turtles you can catch out of your river. By the way, Tall, didn't you say a turtle has 25 kinds of meat?"

"Naah, it's 26. Ya musta fohgot the little piece of white meat wheah the toitle's shell hooks up."

"You don't have an accent like Tall does," said Buster.

"Naah," said Tall, "He don't evah talk like me. Ah talk a little bit of Floida, a little bit of Bama, an' even some Joisy thrown in from the East—everyplace we growed up. Candy, he taught himself how ta talk like the six o'clock news—kinda normal American."

"Gentlemen," Candy said, "we're both the children of Miss Kitty Cotton, the dancing queen of the midway and part-time tatooist, God rest her soul. She taught us well before she passed on when I was 12 and Tall was 10, and we had to finish getting raised by ourselves and the other carnies.

"She called him Tall because she was in tall cotton when he was born, and me Candy because life was sweet at the time—although she said sugar can turn bitter with age. She was a farm girl from Mississippi who forgot her real name, and said most of what comes out of Mississippi is cotton anyway.

"We been all over in most the carnivals of North America. I could whicker rubes like you when I was a baby, and in my sleep by the time I was 9.

"I'm really Candy because I'm sweet as life can get, and mean and tough enough to laugh at it—sugar and vinegar all stirred together. You learn that taking joy in where you're at is one of the best lessons the Good Lord gives you."

"Gosh, that sounds pretty tough," Cody said.

"Tough? Tough? My first spiritual experience was a good swift kick in the behind which I have held close to my heart and inner character ever since. The world's such a funny place, I don't know why I don't die of the hilarity.

"You've heard it said that anything's funny if it happens to somebody else? Heck, if I didn't laugh at what happens to me, I might cry, and if I didn't cry I might laugh.

"You've heard it said that when the world gives you lemons, make lemonade. I tell you, don't just drink the stuff, roll in it. Take yourself a bath in it. Pour pitchers of it over your head. Put the lemons in your pants, and sit on them to squeeze them if you have to. Get ridiculous.

"I was slicker than a weasel, and I bit like one too, but the Good Lord taught me to smile like a beaver.

"By the way, Tall, did you say a turtle has 29 kinds of meat?"

"Naah, Cotton," Tall was smiling widely at his brother, and fairly glowed. "A toitle's got 30 kindsa meat. Ya musta fohgot that juicy, dark piece behind the liver."

"Why did they call you the chicken man?" asked Cody.

"I'll show you that without further adieu," said Candy, carefully taking off the lid of his box to reveal a little black hen that blinked in the light.

"That's a common banty chicken," said Buster, crowding around with everybody else to look at the small chicken.

"Common? You say common? Up, up with you," said Candy, and the little hen jumped and flew to his shoulder.

"You're fortunate, most fortunate, gentlemen, that you are all friends of Tall instead of ordinary rubes, and I'm not in a betting mood, or I could leave town with all your posterity. This is the great Hennie Pennie, Hennie Pennie the magnificent, far beyond the scope of your common barnyard chickens.

"And she's so peaceful, one of creation's great peaceful animals. I love to hear her cackle in the mornings. Even when she's pecking a grasshopper apart, it's not malice, just another meal. But what's more amazing, gentlemen, Hennie Pennie is a chicken arithmetic genius.

"Hennie Pennie, fly down here to the table to give the gentlemen a demonstration, elementary at first. Hennie, what's four minus three?"

The little hen cocked her head a moment to look up at Candy, and then pecked the table once.

"Huh," said Cody, "so you taught her to peck the table."

"Hennie, these men want tougher problems. What's four plus nine?"

The black hen pecked the table 13 times, barely cocking her head to look at Candy again. The men watched him to see if he was moving a finger or anything, but he was merely watching the chicken with his mouth part-open as if in anticipation.

"And 10 minus three, Hennie?"

The chicken pecked the table seven times.

"Well, you got her doing addition and subtraction anyway," said Kelly.

"Ah, so you want the difficult do you? I told you she's magnificent, a genius. Pennie, what's the square root of two?"

The little chicken tapped a number, paused, and did the same thing in sequence after fluffing her wings once. Candy carefully watched her, mouth open, barely daring to breath.

"Gentleman, that first number was a one. Pennie fluffed her wings to indicate a decimal. And her final answer is rounded off to 1.414. And now, if there are final skeptics, Pennie, give me the constant number necessary for figuring the square of a circle."

The black hen repeated the performance with pecks and wing fluttering.

"That's exactly right, Pennie, and you are magnificent. The answer is the value of Pi, 3.14.

"And now, gentlemen, if you'll excuse us, I need to get ready to go turtle fishing with my brother, Tall. Hennie Pennie's birthplace was a nursey in the middle of Missouri, and I'll bring their catalogue with me tomorrow for everybody who wants to purchase their own peaceful little chicken.

"And, Tall, before you join me, I want you to take this classified ad down to your newspaper in town. Just say, 'Wife wanted. Will pay $10,000 down payment for woman of my choice this week at the Deerhead, selections made during morning coffee.'

"Gentlemen, if you think that's an attempt to draw a multitude of the ladies of this town, it isn't. I advertise everywhere to see if my first wife shows up. She'll go anywhere for money. She ran off with the bearded lady, and he was a fraud with a lot of money."

The coffee drinkers stood or sat quietly as Candy walked out, stunned at his performance, as Tall grinned expectantly, and looked from person to person.

"So, Tall, how does he do it? How does he get that little chicken to count the right answers? I watched him, and he just stood there. I didn't see him move ."

"Heh, you rubes ah jus' lucky ol' Candy jus' wanted to have fun, an' yeer my friends. It's his tongue. A lot of hours and a lot of feed for rewards while that lil chicken was growing up. She just watches ol' Candy count it out for her with his tongue. Any bird can pick a kernel of wheat out ofa bucketa beebees, got sharper eyes than y'all.

"An ol' Candy fohgot the toitle's tail. That'd be 31 kindsa meat."

When 'compassion' makes its move

NAN DID HER nails at noon each day. Then she ate her yogurt and apple. When the attorneys she worked for were safely gone to lunch, she did her stretches and tension exercises. Then she went to the restroom to touch up her makeup before going back to her desk to read a self-improvement book for 20 minutes.

These things were on her schedule. She made herself a weekly schedule each Saturday. The first item on her schedule was to also make a schedule for her husband, Bob, an accountant she had selected for his orderly numbered life. With her schedule he would know what would be expected of him during the week too.

Nan was dark-haired, pretty, petite and proper. She was by-the-numbers, no-nonsense Nan.

On the other hand, Caroline strolled the sidewalk in ponderous grace, her undulating hams moving in great waves of fat on her 300-pound-plus short body.

One day she wore a green John Deere hat with a pom pom that bounced along with her own brown curls, a purple jacket and a pink skirt. The socks above her white tennis shoes must have been snatched up carelessly because one was white and one black. Her white blouse would go with anything.

Caroline seemed to look intently at everything through black-rimmed glasses, but replied with a short, disinterested "Good morning," to most people who spoke to her.

Only one tall, thin man with short-cropped gray hair seemed to capture her interest, pausing to say, "Hello Caroline," as he stooped, and smiled. They visited intently for a time, at least it appeared they did to the casual observer.

Unbeknownst to the thin man, they did have an observer, and she approached him afterward. Nan had been watching. She'd lately been reading a self-improvement book about the compassionate heart. She was certain she could build a more ennobling spirit in herself by showing compassion and understanding for a less fortunate person.

Nan had added becoming more compassionate to her list. Caroline could be her less-fortunate person, somebody she could work into her schedule for weeks to come. Even before this book, she'd been thinking for some time that she really should appoint time for some kind of spiritual uplifting. Once she was uplifted, she could get Bob uplifted.

"Excuse me, sir," said Nan, "but could you tell me who that woman is you were talking to? I was rather intrigued by her appearance."

"Why, yes I could. I suppose anybody could be intrigued by Caroline

Pinkerton's appearance. I'm her pastor at First Presbyterian, Charles Parker. And you are?"

"I'm Nan, Nan Brown. I don't have a church right now, and I've been thinking about finding one."

"Well, you and your family would be most welcome at our church, Nan, and here's my card with time of services. I can about guarantee you that Caroline will be there. She doesn't like to sit back with everyone else, and she doesn't want to miss a word, so she's always by herself in the front pew."

Oh, the poor thing, Nan thought to herself. Her plan of compassion was going to be directed very well.

Why would that sad, sad woman expect to sit with other people in a public place when she dressed the way she did? And her weight! What lack of discipline, what lack of planning, what failing of sense and intelligence had made it so Caroline was burdened by that much flesh?

Obviously she was in need of a well-meaning friend to help plan her life.

Nan fussed with her hair a little on the way back to the office, and gazed from time to time in admiration at her nails. Her plan of spiritual success was well on its way.

Bob was just as happy to find going to church on his schedule as he was to find most of the things he found on his schedule. His only surprise was in being pulled to the front pew, and put in a place where Nan could sit next to him, looking down the seat from time to time at a heavy woman in white dress and white shoes.

At least the poor thing dresses herself better for church, Nan thought. Of course, Caroline's clothes didn't have the eloquence of her own ankle-length white dress with intricate floral pattern.

Pastor Charles Parker spoke on the compassion of Christ, beginning with the account of Jesus meeting the Samaritan woman by the well. Nan did her best to assume the face of compassion, and Bob wondered a little at her moon-eyed looks that bordered on pity cast sideways at the heavy woman.

At the end of church, Nan did her best to turn on the charm while glowing with the level of compassion she felt she was achieving.

"Hello, Caroline Pinkerton, I'm Nan Brown. I've been wanting to meet you. Perhaps we could get to know each other a little."

Nan was slightly taken aback by the hard, brittle gaze that met her suggestion. It might be tough to get such a dense person to be touched with her compassion. But Caroline allowed her to pat her gently on the shoulder, and follow her to the kitchen commons, where the congregation socialized.

There, Nan chit chatted brightly to Caroline while sipping coffee, attempting to draw her out with whimsical conversation that might help improve her.

For instance, she discussed hairstyles and dieting plans available, and how pre-planning and no-nonsense behavior worked to improve her life and Bob's.

A happy buzz of parishioners talking, and children playing was going on about her.

Pastor Parker came over. No doubt he must be impressed with her talented effort to penetrate the cloudy mind of Caroline Pinkerton.

"Nan and Bob," Parker said, "I hope you noticed in the schedule that we have a lecture here this week, 'The relationship of God and creation to the science of quantum physics,' given by our own Caroline Pinkerton, our most brilliant member, and, I might add, our most eccentric member," he said smiling at Caroline, who was beginning to look at the ceiling.

"She kindly condescends to speak to us despite her personally busy schedule, and her need to prepare to go back to teach at the university this fall."

Caroline looked directly at Bob.

"As an accountant Mr. Brown, you may be interested in some of the mathematics involved in the calculating of time passage as outlined in Einstein's equation—energy equals mass times the speed of light squared—given which you may have accepted the reality of the atomic bomb while failing to realize that an equal implication with measurable quantification is the effect of gravity and velocity on the passage of time. Given energy is relative-means time is relative, and is a fully measurable dimension in and of itself.

"As for you Nan, I promise I'll try to explain quantum physics in such a way that everybody can understand. You seem to be a very needy person, and all of us need understanding at our own levels. I've been reading a popular culture book about the heart of compassion, and I have to admit I've been entirely too focused on my studies, and just relaxing, and slouching around for the summer. But I'm sure I could help you."

Help her? The woman wasn't intelligence-challenged? No-nonsense Nan couldn't stand the nonsense of the moment. She lost hold of the handle of her coffee cup, so the warm, black liquid slopped down the front of the flowered, floor-length dress.

"Oh, I didn't expect this!" Nan said. "I must get to the restroom, wash off."

"It will be OK, Sweetie," said Bob.

"The restroom's this way, Nannie," said Caroline.

Oh, Nannie, what a horrible nickname to be called.

Nan slammed the door to the restroom behind her, and went to work swabbing the front of her dress with cold water while beginning to sniff in indignation. Her, needy? The idea was preposterous. I have to get home.

Nan pulled at the restroom door. She twisted the knob this way and that pulling on the door. She was locked in.

"Help me!" she wailed.

There was grinding and twisting in the door-lock from the other side, and reassuring noises coming from Bob, Caroline and parson with other murmurs in the background.

Then the door was yanked open revealing the knob in the stocky forearms of Caroline, who, after a moment, clicked her tongue in sympathy.

"Bob, get me home," Nan said, doing her best to keep volume out of her voice as she muttered in his face. "Can't you see this is embarrassing!"

Bob tried to put his arm around her as she turned, but put his foot down awkwardly on the back of the soggy dress that no longer flowed around her ankles. There was a resounding "r-i-i-i-p" up the back of the dress as Nan fell awkwardly on her bottom.

Caroline pulled Nan to her feet while wrapping a table cloth around her.

"There, there, honey. Let's get her to the car," Caroline said. "You're awfully thin, Nannie. Tell you what, let's go to the barbecue buffet at the restaurant before my lecture. You and Bob can ride in my car with me. Come to think of it, Nannie, where do you work? Let's have lunch together this week too. You'll love the thick bacon barbecue special Monday. We'll get some weight on you.

Nan began to whimper as she was led out the door. Her list was being re-done by a higher power.

Redemption for Jake the Joy

THERE WAS Jake the "Joy" and Jake the "Jerk," both living in the same little old dirt street Kaw town.

Fortunately, we're talking about Jake the Joy first because he was a sort of loveable old boy while Jake the Jerk was one of those tough-to-love people who try to get attention by pointing out the miseries and shortcomings of others.

But then sometimes you need to get a jerk to figure out there's a joy right in front of you.

Jake the Joy had an old house where he lived with his wife and an outpouring of children and all sorts of dogs and cats. The structure was nailed together just enough for the entire family to stay healthy and happy.

He loved his neighbors and everyone else he met—nice as him or not—and did what he could to help them overcome life's difficulties.

The smile and krinkles around his face were permanently set in lines and wattling skin that hung on him like he was a basset hound with a crew cut. Those lovely, warm, shining brown eyes that looked out through thick glasses only added to the effect.

Because people tend to respond to smiles and kindness, one year during the election, when the blank for township assessor was empty, enough people thought of Jake the Joy to write him in for the job. Thereafter when election time came, there was many a heartfelt glow as citizens marked their votes by Jake's name.

Come the right time of year, and Jake was out on the roads in his beat-up old red Ford pickup stopping at every farm and residence in the unincorporated town to fill out the assessment lists by interviewing the property owners. Every chicken, cow and pig, anything that was useful, had its place on the assessment.

Jake was usually fair and accurate on everything, until it came to the dogs.

In those days, the state taxed dogs, one dollar for a male dog and two dollars for a female dog. It was a tax that seemed ludicrous and nasty to Jake, although he didn't say much. He wished his neighbors well in the small pleasures they had, even if it was only a mutt for a kid to play with, a good livestock dog, or a good varmint and watch dog.

Jake thought life was harsh enough already without begrudging people joy in the little things.

So after leaning on the truck hood, filling out the assessment forms with some sunburnt young farmer for a while, Jake would go through the usual routine when he came to the line on dogs.

"I have to ask you here, Duane, how many dogs do you have?"

"We have two dogs. That other one over there's up visiting from the folks' place."

"OK, that's one male dog if I'm hearing you right."

"There's two dogs, and I didn't say whether they were both boys, but—"

"That's one male dog, Duane. That takes care of livestock. Now let's see what you have for machinery."

Jake always filled in the dogs like that, and year after year the state took his reports with the corresponding assessments for taxation of property.

But as sure as the earth keeps turning, there's always a time for a turning point. It had been a significant year anyway, the year Jake the Joy's oldest son was drafted into the Army while his youngest daughter was starting first grade.

Jake had the assessing done early that fall. The weather was still warm enough one Sunday to have an evening church outdoor basket supper with steel chairs arranged like pews and a center aisle leading up to the lectern where Pastor Peter Poudre would deliver a sermon after the meal.

Unfortunately, it was the same Sunday the Kansas City Star came out with a second section story on Jake's township, the only township in the state on the tax rolls reported as having 150 male dogs and no females.

Almost fortunately, Jake the Joy and his family hadn't read the Star before coming to the supper. Nearly everybody else in town had read the Star though, and, unfortunately, that included Jake the Jerk.

Jake the Joy was finishing his final bite of potato salad when Jake the Jerk, his smooth, narrow, ruddy face glowing with pleasure under his railroad striped hat, came sauntering up to the table with a Kansas City Star tucked under his arm.

"Hey, old man," the Jerk said. "Did you see here you made the paper?"

He pulled the page out of the paper with the short story highlighted with red crayon.

"Think the state will have everyone calling you Jailbird Jake before long, and me Straight Jake? Hey, Pastor Poudre, where's your dog. Isn't it a female?"

"She's locked up right now."

The pleasant happiness always evident in Jake the Joy's face faded as he read the article, and passed it on down to his wife and family.

Embarrassed, he barely acknowledged the greetings and nods of friends as his family took seats for Pastor Poudre's announced sermon of "Know the truth, and it will set you free."

The Jerk sat in front of the Joy, and occasionally tilted his face half back with his eyes raised while mumbling, "...or the truth could put you away for a long time."

As he finished the sermon, Pastor Poudre called for Jake the Joy to come to the front.

"Jake, I've called you up here because you're an example," the pastor said smiling at his congregation. "Everybody here can show examples where you have stayed true to yourself and true to your friends like an example of our Lord, and that truth has set you free, free to have joy in your life no matter what happens."

He was interrupted by a clap of hands and loud guffaw from Jake the Jerk as an unexpected group of participants began making their way up the center aisle. It was Pastor Peter Poudre's poodle-beagle mix, Pixie, who had been locked up because of her season, and was now making her way, after escaping, to her master's voice with 20-some potential admirers following in her path, panting in indelicate canine delight.

Pastor Poudre's spouse, Petula, stepped into the aisle to pick up the errant Pixie in her arms to carry back to the pen while two boys ran interference for her pushing the determined doggy suitors away.

Jake the Jerk made low dog sounds, "Arf, arf, yowl," while other people tried not to look at him.

Pastor Poudre closed the service with the congregation singing "Joyful, Joyful, We Have Found Thee" with his arm around the shoulders of Jake the Joy while Pixie went to the pen.

Jake the Joy never went to the pen. Pastor Poudre spent most of the morning Monday on the telephone waiting for busy signals to clear to get through to the state office of taxation just before noon.

He said, "I saw that article in the Kansas City Star, and I'm calling in to tell you I never told your assessor, Jake, that I had a female dog."

The voice on the other end said, "Thank you for calling in, Pastor Poudre. You'll be happy to know we have already received reports from 130 other people who said they never told Jake they had a female dog.

"About a dozen of them have told us about another man named Jake who keeps coon dogs, and sells pups. Do you know him?"

The state decided to solve a potential public relations versus legality problem by sending a letter of commendation for his years of service to Jake the Joy.

There isn't a dog tax any more.

As for Jake the Jerk, during the time his tax evasion case was being studied, it was also discovered he had outstanding warrants for unpaid parking tickets, speeding, public intoxication and petty theft.

The state's attorney offered him a choice between prosecution or going to the Army where he might get his life straightened out.

He went to the Army, canine corps, the dogface.

Big Jim chews it over

T HE LOCUSTS that did their long, lazy sing-song out in the woods and grasses were already beginning to ping the screens around the porch lights, and fall to the concrete as twilight faded around the gathered people.

The people sat in twos or threes or small groups out on the broad expanse of mowed yard, or around card tables up on the cement porch. They held plates on their laps, and along with the noises of eating, spoons clacking on plastic or glass, there was pleasant conversation with chuckles or bursts of laughter.

It was the annual picnic of the Valley Ladies Club at the Ford home this year.

Big Jim went inside the big screened porch where the deserts were carefully arranged along a long table. Herbert was there in Panama straw hat and khaki pants, standing contentedly, and eating dark-raisin pie.

"Hey, Herbert, hitting that pie pretty heavy aren't you," said Big Jim, grinning widely below twinkling blue eyes, the look that endeared him to people.

"Yeah, and this is my second piece," said Herbert. "I can't pass up good raisin pie. My mother used to make it, and I always look forward to finding some. It's rare that anybody brings it."

"That good, huh?" said Big Jim, running a large freckled hand over his short, red hair. "Guess I'll have to have a piece of it, too. Then we can stand here to talk, and maybe you can just hit a home run on your third swing, then Herbert, with another piece of pie."

They munched contentedly talking about this year's crops interrupted only by Iris Binion coming through the door with her plate to the dessert table.

"Jim, Herbert, you boys certainly seem to be enjoying yourselves— good, good," said Iris. "I see you've taken a liking to Florence's raisin pie."

Herbert stopped chewing at once, and the crinkles around the eyes in his square-jawed face narrowed. "Florence? Florence made this pie? Again, who did you say made it?"

"Why, Florence Medlam made it, dear. And it's just pretty good isn't it?"

Big Jim chewed and swallowed. "Well, I sure think so. Darned good."

They looked at Herbert, who had turned a shade of gray-green, and was spitting the contents of his mouth out on his plate, and looked like he might start gagging at any moment. He threw the rest of his pie in the trash.

Iris made a face, and walked out. But Big Jim put his arm on Herbert's shoulder while he continued eating his pie.

"What's the matter, Herbert?"

"It's that pie. I can't bear the thought of eating anything made by

Florence Medlam. I'm sick. I'm going to have to go home."

"Why, I can't see anything wrong with Florence's cooking. Heck, she has old Harlan come around every year with Christmas cookies and cake she makes, and we eat'm right down. Matter of fact, Paul and I are headed over there tomorrow with my tractor and scoop and both our manure spreaders to help Harlan clear off his livestock lots before winter. Florence will be making dinner for us."

"Have you ever eaten there before, Jim?" asked Herbert, his agony appearing to grow as he rubbed his rumbling stomach.

"Well, we've done work there before," said Big Jim, scratching his noggin. "But I guess actually I never have. We always ate before at my house or Paul's house."

"Maybe you'll understand. Yes, you'll understand. Good luck to you. I'm going home."

The next morning by 7, Big Jim was alternating filling three manure spreaders with scoops off the lot with his tractor while Paul and Harlan used their tractors to pull the loaded spreaders to the fields to empty them.

Big Jim worked a fast clip, and the other two men each usually found a loaded spreader waiting on them, or only lacking one more scoop. They hit a rhythm,, pausing only momentarily in those instances when variations in the workload made them overlap each other.

At noon, Big Jim shut his tractor off to wave at Paul, who had just come in from the last load.

"Dinnertime, Paul. I'm hungry enough, too. Hope Florence has a big meal waiting for us."

"Well, I hope so, too, Jim. But then I did four years in the Army, so I can almost eat anything under any circumstances. Seem to have an iron stomach."

"Hah! You must have seen Herbert last night after that raisin pie."

"Yes I did, but I've eaten here before, too. It never hurt me any, but I can understand Herbert, too."

Harlan drove in then, and the three men walked up to the yard to wash their arms off at the hand-pumped well before going in the house to wash hands a second time.

Inside the porch door, Florence had a big metal bowl of creamy brown water warmed for them to wash their hands in.

She stuck her head out the kitchen door several times, gray hair all tied up in a bun, to smile, and say, "Hope you boys are really ready to eat because I've been cooking a chicken dinner most all morning. Barely had time to pick fruit, feed chickens and hogs.

"I'd been out there helping you," she added, pausing momentarily to frown, "but I was sick last night. Stomach was just queasy. Thought I might throw up. You know I usually work hard in the fields. But just felt so bad last night, I took time off and cooked. Made some more of that raisin pie you loved so much last night, Jim," she ended with a smile.

Big Jim smiled, too, as she went back in. He paused looking at the bowl of creamy water. "Think we better dump this water out before we wash, boys. Looks kind of greasy, like it's been used before."

"No, no don't do that," Harlan said, his saggy jowl quivering beneath his leather-brown skin. "Florence is thrifty, really thrifty. She just boils the water over to use again. You know how it is in these parts. People are hauling water, with the wells all going dry again. Florence is trying real hard to save water. You don't want to haul more than you have to."

Big Jim shrugged, grabbed the soap, and began to wash. Paul was smiling a little half smile at him, his eyes dancing a little in delight.

Inside the door, the welcomed savory smells of fried chicken, mashed potatoes and gravy, and green beans filled the air, and Big Jim inhaled deeply while looking gratefully at Florence.

"This smells wonderful, Florence, and I'm really hungry."

She was beaming back at him. Everybody liked old red-haired Big Jim.

Big Jim stepped over to the kitchen stove where another two metal bowls, a big metal spoon sticking out of each, bubbled and simmered on the top heat.

"Ah, Florence! This gravy smells delicious," he said looking at the bowls of cream-colored liquid. They looked alike. Must be two bowls of gravy, Big Jim thought.

"Harlan," said Florence. "Bring the gravy to the table, so we can all sit down to eat. Mind the dish water."

Harlan picked up one bowl, leaving the other.

Big Jim looked at him. "That one's dish water?" he asked, looking at the one left on the stove.

"Yeah, dish water," Harlan said.

Jim whispered an aside to Paul. "How does he know?"

They sat down, and filled their plates. Big Jim filled a big spoon full of gravy, and poured it over his potatoes in a loose watery slush—no cream to it—that filled the plate.

He started to hand the gravy to Paul, who said, "No thanks, I just eat butter on my spuds."

"Harlan, you don't have your teeth in," said Florence, glaring at the old man.

"That's OK, got'm right here," Harlan said, pulling the pink gums with a set of white teeth out of the jean jacket pocket on the back of his chair.

Big Jim munched a piece of fried chicken as he watched Harlan slide the dentures into his mouth. Paul took a drink of water.

"I s'pose you got yours in?" asked Harlan, looking at Florence.

"Of course I do," she said, pushing the lower plate out with her tongue.

Usually, meals were noisy chatty affairs with Big Jim, but he sat quietly part of the time, eating more chicken and pieces of bread while he stared at the thin gruel of gravy on his plate.

"You know, this chicken turned out just OK," said Florence, trying to adjust her dentures with her tongue while she ate at the same time. "He was a sick one. We always sell the best ones, and cull out them that are a little smaller or weaker to feed on ourselves. He was yawning his beak at one time like we might lose him. But he seemed like he grew on out of it, and looky here, here we are eatin' him," she said with a grin as she bit a piece of meat from a drumstick.

"I was going to get Harlan up at break of day to kill him for me, but the poor old dear works so hard, he needed his sleep. I was up anyway, sick all night like I told you. You can see the chicken's head out there at the stump with the axe in it if you want to. The comb and tongue had a good color by now."

"Yeah," said Harlan. "I do need my sleep. Got to take care to rest at my age. Wonder if your boy might come up to drive one round for me after a big meal like this, Paul. Sometimes at my age, you can't get by without a nap."

"He might, Harlan. Got him disking, but he might be able to take a little time if we call him after lunch," said Paul.

Big Jim had gotten very quiet. He was manfully taking one spoonful of mashed potatoes and gravy at a time, and swallowing them quickly without much chewing before pausing to take another.

As soon as he had taken the last bite, Florence said, "OK boys, time for pie. Make space on your plates."

Harlan tapped his fingers on the table with one hand while he took his teeth back out of his mouth with the other to lay them gleaming by his plate. "Sure do love Florence's pie. But it's so nice and soft. Better chewing without my teeth in."

"You know, Florence," Big Jim said, "I ate so much pie last night, and with this good big meal you went to so much trouble to fix, I'm just too full now."

Big Jim sat silently, occasionally puffing his cheeks to let out a stream of air, and patting his stomach softly while the others ate pie.

Outside, Paul's boy joined them as they strolled toward the tractors. He was wondering at the gray-green pallor on Big Jim's usually ruddy complexion.

"Is it always that way there, Paul?"

"Yes it is, Jim. I'm afraid it's about always that way."

Inside, Harlan Medlam was stretching and yawning, looking fondly at Florence. "Guess, I'll go outside to take a nap on the bench. Nice weather out. I'll wake up to join them when a tractor goes out. That Big Jim's a hard worker. Doesn't eat that much either. Thought somebody as big as him would be hard to feed. He's an easy keeper, be good to get him back again."

"You're right. He's easy to have around. Good spirit. I'll be glad to cook for him again."

Paul's bull-and-pony show

Author's note: I kind of wonder if my brother's pony mourned that bull the rest of his life.

THE PONY and the bull became a sight to marvel at.

The pony came first. One early spring day when the grass was first beginning to green, Paul took a cow that had failed to calve to the sale barn. It was no small deal even for one animal because the truck was used for many functions, and it was a bit of a strain for one man to lift the heavy wooden stock racks into place, and bolt them all together. Then the cow had to be loaded.

By the time Paul got to the sale barn, and unloaded the cow, the auctioneer was in the final half-hour of haranguing the crowd with his chant over the grunts and dust of the hogs. So, Paul had time for a hot roast beef dinner in the barn cafe before the cattle sale.

When he took his seat above the sale arena, it was time for whatever miscellaneous animal might be brought in to be sold. That would be followed by the baby calves, a few old bulls ready to go for meat, and then the cows and cow-calf pairs.

He must have been really relaxed after laying back from the morning's work followed by a hot meal because his first unusual thought when they ran a dusty, brown Shetland Pony yearling into the ring was, "My kid could use a pony." He'd already said "no" to every request for a pony for several years.

The auctioneer in the white Stetson started the bidding at $10, a big grin pasted on his face because he knew the market price was low for the overpopulated world of small ponies. Breeders had overstocked on Shetlands, and it would take years for prices to recover.

"Looky here, looky here," he said. "Somebody's brought us a midget horse to sell."

In a twisted sort of way, it made it amusing for an auctioneer to try to sell a pony for the over-optimistic person who had brought it in. He had to drop the price to $9 to get a bid, but that got things started.

The bids seemed finalized with the auctioneer calling, "Hey, I got $12 here. Will anybody give me $13, gimme, gimme $13? Hey, how about $12.50, $12.50, $12.50? That's $12 twice."

Then Paul raised his hand to say, "$12.25," at the same time kicking himself for being so unbusiness-like to think of taking on even a small pony to feed.

The pony was nibbling on the rails of the arena panels in such a fetching way that some heart softened to call out, "$12.50."

A worker shooed his hat in the pony's face to make him move, and the pony bucked once,and kicked out with his hind feet, so someone else called, "$12.75."

149

The pony obviously was going to be ornery and stubborn, but Paul still gave the auctioneer the nod for a $13 bid. On the way home with the pony settling down in the back of the truck after a couple of practice rears, Paul thought more than once, "I need my head examined for this."

Of course, the rest of the family was thrilled. The pony named "Dusty" was already becoming legendary for his nips and bucks when the kids tried to train him, and for his wild, charging gallops, tan mane and tail flying in the wind, up and down the pasture, when Paul brought the next new animal home.

It was a yearling Angus bull, Oscar II, destined to become the next herd bull after Oscar I was shipped to the sale barn. The new Oscar was already heavily muscled with curly hair growing on his broad face.

Oscar II was worth considerably more money—both in purchase price and future reward to the farm—than a $13 pony.

Paul was growling to himself as he unloaded the bull into the pasture.

"That pony better not bite him, and pester him until he runs him through a fence, or by golly that pony is history," he said.

Sure enough, Dusty ran up to Oscar II first thing to bite him on the rump. But to Paul's surprise, the bull pivoted around, and punched his head squarely into the pony's chest. The pony whirled, and kicked his hind feet into the bull's head.

Oscar II gave a buck, and went right after Dusty, who dodged him and artfully bit him in the back. They never stopped. Dusty and Oscar II continued their play fighting day after day pausing only for long periods of grazing side by side or not far from each other.

When Oscar II left for his first season with the beef cows, Dusty walked the pasture, or looked over fences as if searching for his friend.

When Paul brought Oscar II back to the pasture again after some months, he had grown to a huge one-ton specimen. The whole family watched as the small pony whose head only came to the top of the bull's heavily muscled hump charged across the pasture.

Dusty whirled, and kicked the bull's lowered skull with both hind feet. Then he turned, and reared to come down with both front feet on the bull's head.

Oscar II rolled his large bloodshot eyes, then surged forward with his head under Dusty's head and belly to flip him over on the ground.

Paul and his family breathed in sharply at the sight.

But the pony jumped up to return to biting the bull on his shoulders and rump. Round and round they went, head to shoulder, teeth to rump, bucking, kicking, and stomping up the dust. When both were winded, they began to graze again side by side.

Paul's family became familiar with the sight of the bull and the pony playing their romping games. But it wasn't long before a somber, brown-haired woman drove her car into the driveway, came to the door, and said, "I think you should know there's a bull killing your pony."

"No, no he isn't," said Paul smiling with a lowered face. "Just sit here on the porch and watch. They're playmates."

It wasn't long before the concerned woman was smiling instead.

The callers came frequently to report the bull and the pony. As people learned the truth, there sometimes would be one or two cars pulled up along the road as their occupants watched Dusty and Oscar II at play.

Paul and his wife had visitors who stood in the picture window with them as the first winter snow began to fall to watch the pony and the bull.

The seasons turned to years. Every time Oscar II came home from a breeding season, the two animals resumed their friendship. Sometimes Paul complained a little when he had to go catch the pony for the kid to ride because he didn't want him in with the bull, but he was enjoying the spectacle and everybody else who stopped to watch did, too.

The final year came. It was time for Paul to take Oscar II to market and then buy a successor.

"I hate to see that bull leave the pony," his wife said.

His kid said, "Dad, are you really going to sell old Oscar?"

But business was business, cash flow was cash flow, bulls would come, and bulls would go. Oscar II loaded easily for the final trip. He always did load well. After one muzzle-upturned final bellow, Oscar II trotted up the chute ahead of Paul, and into the truck.

Dusty raised his head to nicker softly as the truck pulled down the driveway—as if he knew a life moment was passing.

The successor was introduced. A new big black yearling bull raised his head to glare at the pony.

The pony stood and looked at him awhile. He tilted his head at a three-fourths upward angle to look again. Then Dusty ambled off disinterested to the far end of the pasture to graze.

Paul watched, then lowered his head at the wistfullness that welled up in his chest. There isn't always room for sentiment on a farm.

"Times come, and times go," Paul whispered softly to himself. "Nothing's ever exactly the same."

Time to put the cards on the table

A THICK, HEAVY early-morning fog rolled down the dark streets of the town, obscuring outlines except where building fronts showed in the white and yellow glow of street lights.

Gary would always think of the place that way, a town half hidden by obscurities with a glow here or there.

Halfway down the main street, one door stood open on an old wood-front building, glowing light onto the brick sidewalk, and adding its own peculiar fog to the mix. When Gary arrived there, he nearly gasped at the smell of acrid fumes of melted lead mixed with a cloud of tobacco smoke.

Ella was at the linotype machine, one hand at the keyboard while another pulled at the workings, and a foot stayed on a floor pedal. Her blonde-gray hair was tucked under a ballcap against the Monday morning chill, and she looked over bifocals past the end of her puffing cigarette at the machine.

"I thought this was an offset newspaper," Gary said, as she seemed to be the only one in the place. "This looks like all letterpress."

"And you must be the boy from the college interning with Tim this vacation, I take it," Ella said, pushing the cigarette to the side of her mouth, and tugging at a type piece.

"This paper's hybrid as corn, letterpress and offset, and we need to get it stuck together by Wednesday—as you'll see if you get to sleep a little bit to be awake by then.

"I'm Ella. Tim ought to be at the train station by now, which is why you're here this early to pick him up. Key's in the truck out back. Drive out past the grain elevator to the station to pick him up. I got to keep going now. We'll talk Thursday."

"They still have passenger-train service here?"

"Just for the one guy, you'll see," she replied, eyes, ballcap and cigarette inclined toward him at the same angle as she continued type-setting. "Truck's choke doesn't work. Keep your foot down part-way on the foot-feed 'til she's warmed up, and t'other foot riding the clutch so you don't go too fast—four-speed, you got to shift."

Gary drove the truck, alternately roaring and bucking under his guidance, down to the south side of town to the depot, where the outline of a slumbering man showed up in his headlights through the mist. He was all laid back under the roof overhang of the depot with the collar of a duck-cloth coat drawn up tightly and a red hat with ear flaps pulled tightly down on his head.

"Don't shut the truck off. Don't shut it off!" called the man jumping to his feet. "It might not start again. Just scoot over, but keep your foot on the acc_elerator until I get my foot in there. I'll drive, Gary. I guess you're Gary since you're the only kid with my truck here to get me. I know I don't want to walk after not getting any sleep all the way to Chicago from Kansas on a freighter—played cards the whole way with the railroad boys. Saw a play about a guy who died with his head stuck in a bucket while the boys laid over. You like pinochle, Gary?"

"Yes, I'm Gary. I don't play pinochle. I guess you're Tim then?"

"What do you play then—hearts, pitch, spades, poker maybe? That would be good if I could play five-card to a fresh face. Those railroad boys are good. Sometimes, Gary, I like to sit down in the aisle between the paste-up tables around 2 a.m., and just play a little cards for relief, you know what I mean? Can you bluff, boy? Of course you can. What kind of newspaper guy wouldn't know how to bluff?"

"I don't know how to play cards, Tim."

In the light of the streetlights driving through the town, Gary could see the incredulity in Tim's bright, brown eyes, his bristly, newly whiskered face beneath strands of light brown hair poking out under the hat.

"Don't know how to play cards, huh? I'll be jiggered. Gary, you'll be covering county commission and city council followed by school board tonight. Them old boys and girls might not walk around with full decks, but they all know how to bluff, I guarantee it.

"You can start writing sometime Monday night if you want to, just so you have them all written by noon Tuesday. Maybe give you time for a feature story that afternoon before we paste up that night. Wednesday morning she goes to press, then you help with mailing and stuffing inserts.

"Then maybe I can start you out slow with some crazy eights to learn the cards. I hope you can keep a straighter face than you are right now. Thursday we sleep really late, but I like another game of cards while we drink coffee at lunch time discussing the next issue.

"Once a month you or Ella or someone picks me up like this when I been to Chicago doing a feature story on the railroad if me and the boys get caught. Right now, I clean up, and we eat breakfast," he said, leaning over and smiling into Gary's face to wink.

"Oh, I do pay you something while you intern with the stipulation that you learn poker, too. Wouldn't want you to go home with all your hard-earned money. You're kind of a big round-faced old kid, aren't you. Try not to smile much, and maybe you'll look more real."

After Tim shaved, washed and changed clothes in the back room at the newspaper, yelling questions from there while Ella "hmmphed" in reply, ignoring him, they emerged with the sunrise to get in the truck.

With the now warmed-up machine purring, they drove through a downtown climaxed by two giant warehouse-like buildings across the street from each other, "Gambo's" and "Lugini's" their signs said.

"What are those?" Gary asked.

"Furniture and variety stores," Tim said with a smile. "And Mr. Gambo and Mr. Lugini can't stand each other—good for competition and advertising."

On a U-turn at the end of town, two cafes were across from each other in such a way that customers of the one could see the customers of the other through the glass. Gary sipped his coffee, and slowly ate an egg while Tim wolfed down an omelette and platefull of pancakes, drank refills of coffee non-stop, and filled him in on the workings of the meetings he would cover.

Then, as they were finishing, he noticed a short, round-figured man with large nose and black hair get up from among a group of men by the big window.

The man walked to the window glass, slowly and deliberately folded his arms, and tilted his face upward wearing a great and arrogant frown.

Across the street, another man stood in that cafe's window, similar black hair and large nose only on a tall thin frame, glaring with his fists on his hips. Talk quieted in the cafe as people turned to watch the two men who stood posing as if the first one to walk away might lose something.

"What's that all about?" Gary asked, looking at Tim, who had quit talking to sit smiling with his hands folded under his chin.

"Looks like a furniture sale war to me," he said. "We'll be running a bigger paper this week. That's Mr. Lugini and across the street is Mr. Gambo. You run to your meetings fast now. You'll be needing to do a story on the sales war tomorrow."

That's what happened. Gary went to his meetings, wrote his stories, wearily typing the last lines, while down the street Mr. Gambo and Mr. Lugini lined up furniture on the sidewalks along their stores.

Tuesday afternoon, Tim was calling to him, "Quick, quick, get down there with a camera, Gary. They're nearly into it in the middle of the street. I have to help Ella. We have a full-page ad from each of them."

He took a picture of Gambo and Lugini leaning over the hood of a police squad car shaking their fists at each other while an officer leaned against the front door.

"Hey, you, reporter," Gambo called. "You come with me, and I'll tell you about the kind of sale I'm going to have, 30 percent off on most items."

"Come with me first," Lugini said. "I'll have 40 percent off."

Police Chief Garland chose for him to go with Lugini first.

"The crook is trying to run me out of business," Lugini said. "I tell you I won't be undersold."

"If he can't stand the heat, he should get out of town," Gambo said. "I tell you, nobody will miss him. I'll cut prices as much as it takes to see him go."

The second week, the second story, and the second set of full-page advertisements, everything was 50 percent off. People were driving to the two stores from 50 miles away to grab the bargains. Main street was filled with cars. Gambo was crying poverty. Lugini said he might be reduced to going to live with his widowed mother.

The third week, semi-trucks tried to pull up across from each other to deliver more furniture to each store, and Lugini was in the street hollering, "Get your truck out of the way, you animal. I need more furniture."

Gambo hurled a chair at him.

"No, no, officers," Lugini said. "I won't press charges, but I will press him under with the weight of competition—50 percent off, buy two items and get a third of equal value free. Free, absolutely free. I may go broke, but I'll take him with me."

"I've invited an observer from the attorney general's office to see that my sales are legitimate. I invite him to do the same," Gambo said.

Thursday noon every week, eating bolgna sandwiches at the card table by the coffee pot in the back room of the newspaper, Tim gave Gary more angles on feature stories to do about Gambo's and Lugini's while Ella took extra drags on her cigarette. Gary learned crazy eights when Tim skipped his monthly Chicago trip to do more Friday features.

The furniture stores each jumped their advertisements to two-page spreads.

Tim fell asleep playing cards between the layout tables at night. Ella snored at the linotype one morning while a puddle of lead formed on the floor. Gary fell asleep during a commission meeting.

Gary woke up one Thursday morning too tired to sleep late on the only morning after Wednesday that he was allowed to do so.

"Might as well go to the paper early and make some coffee," he mumbled to himself.

To his surprise, the front door was open although the interior was dark. Wearily he made his way to the back room door, and pushed it open. The lights in there were bright.

Around the crowded card table sat Tim, Mr. Lugini, Chief Garland, Ella and Mr. Gambo, each with a hand full of cards.

Tim smiled at him sheepishly, then widened the grin to wolfish dimensions.

"Hey, kid. meet the Lugambo brothers, alias Mr. Gambo and Mr. Lugini. They have quite an angle in volume furniture sales. Want to learn poker now? I need someone losing here besides me—as if any of us are going to lose, huh?"

With time,
Petunia blossomed

Author's note: *We had pet pigs before the pot bellies were introduced in the U.S.*

FRIDAY NIGHT was bath night, with the northwest wind pressing the big cedars over in the front yard, bearing their heavy loads of ice and frost, and the house was creaking and groaning with the blow.

Inside, predominantly red, green and yellow lights glowed from the tree in the otherwise dark living room. In the brightly lighted kitchen, big steel dishpans steamed with water that had been newly carried in with buckets from the hand-pumped well. The vapor curled around the ceiling or puffed in and out around the ice-glazed windows where the house breathed in and out around the frame cracks.

As the pans heated, the water was dumped in turn into the big tin tubs on the cracked linoleum, already full of naked children, taking up most of the kitchen floor. Jesse, as the older brother, shoved with his foot to keep Benjamin in his end of the long tub. Abigail and Amber each enjoyed the solitude of a round tub.

Mom was about to pull the fly swatter from the top of the refrigerator to enforce order when there was a fumbling at the front door to the living room as somebody struggled through the entrance with an awkward load.

"It sounds as though your dad is home," Mom said as she went to the living room. "Get your baths finished. Everybody use soap. He'll want his turn in the tub."

Then she returned with Dad, still red and ruddy in his coveralls from the wind and cold of hours of chores, to announce, "OK, everybody, let's dry off. Dad has brought a surprise, and it's under the Christmas tree."

"But Christmas is over, it's almost New Year's," Abigail said. "We already opened presents."

"But this is a special present," Mom said as they heard a slight stirring against cardboard in the next room. "Everybody wrap up in a towel, and we'll go into the next room to see."

And there in the next room was one of the things they least anticipated under the Christmas tree: a baby pig in a box, thin and awkward with an over-sized head, floppy ears laid flat against it, a kind of red-gold color with a dried umbilical still attached at the belly.

"What is it, a boy or a girl?" asked Amber.

"It's a little gilt," said Dad.

"That means it's a girl," said Benjamin, looking up with his brown eyes full of important knowledge.

Jesse, who had been reading too many Porky Pig comic books, said, "We'll name her Petunia."

Mom took a pitcher of cold cow's milk out of the refrigerator, yellow fat floating around the top, and poured it into a shallow pan to heat on the stove next to the water pans. When she felt it warm to the touch, she put the pan on the floor.

"Now Jesse, pick up Petunia and dip her nose in the milk until she begins to drink."

Soon the little pig was sucking noisily at the milk."

"What about Patches?" Abigail asked, pressing her nose to a window pane to try to see the shepherd-collie pup curled up on the back porch. "Will he like Petunia?"

"Petunia will have to stay in here and keep warm until she grows more," Dad said. "Then she'll have her own pen out at the shed. We'll all just have to watch Patches so he doesn't hurt her. Petunia's mother had too many pigs. She was the runt, so we'll keep her special."

In a few days, the little pig was crawling over the side of the cardboard box to run to the kitchen, slipping and sliding on the linoleum from time to time, to root her nose against cabinet doors looking for her milk, saying, "Uh, uh, uh, uh."

As the late days of January passed, Petunia joined the children running in the backyard. She sniffed noses with Patches. He nipped her nose. She jumped back giving a little grunt. The people scolded Patches. Soon Petunia was circling him, pushing up on his belly with her nose. Then she bounced on all four feet, turning around in a circle excitedly.

"She looks like a spinning wheel," said Benjamin.

Patches ran around and around the yard, playing like a dog does. But in a moment he had a pig running around and around the yard after him, playing like a pig does "oof, oof, oof," except a pig gets hungrier quicker.

Soon Petunia would be knocking her snout against the back door—and squealing—to ask for food again.

Eat a lot, play a lot, chase the children and the dog round and round under the big elm in back—it was a good pig's life. Petunia grew and grew on the regimen of milk, then grain and pig supplement as she was ready for it. She started looking not like a runt anymore.

By the first of February, Petunia had gotten too big for the house. She moved to the shed and the pen where Jesse, Abigail, Benjamin and Amber could hear her squealing whenever she needed more food.

"Whose turn was it to feed Petunia today?" Mom would ask.

Everybody wanted to feed her at first. Then Jesse got so he would say, "I think it was Amber's turn to feed her today."

"No, it wasn't—it was Benjamin's turn," said Amber.

"No, it was Abigail's turn."

By the first of March, Petunia partly solved getting her food on time herself. She learned that climbing over a board fence wasn't really so much more difficult for a half-grown pig than climbing over the side of a cardboard box had been for a baby pig.

At first squeal she would rear on her back legs to hang her front legs on a middle board, raising her red Duroc head in the air to go, "Arreah, eeee, eeee, oink, oink, oink, arreah!"

It took a terrible commotion on her part before she was putting her hind feet on the slatted boards, and climbing with her front feet to throw her red-haired body with the pink belly over the top of the fence.

By the first of April, the big cedars in the front yard were rustling in the gentle moisture-laden south breeze. The house's back door was opened to let the air fragrant with new growth come through the screen. Even though the first spring rains had been plentiful, the atmosphere was full of the promise of more to come.

Petunia was celebrating all of this new water down at the pig pen with a long dip in a slimey lime-green puddle that left a finely plastered coat of mud over her red coat when she stood to go check the food pan. It was empty, "Arreah, eeee, eeee...." But there were no children around to hear.

It was no problem for a pig with climbing ability. Over the fence Petunia went, and she headed up the spaced rock path to the house. It was no problem again, "oink, oink, uh, uh, ug," as she expertly bounced the screen door a couple of times with her nose until it widened enough to let her stick her head through.

Then it was no trick to trot her whole body through to the old familiar slick linoleum floor lined with rows of kitchen cabinets clear down to floor level where a sensitive nose could feel to pull and push where the cabinet doors fit against the tight-sealed cracks before finally bouncing them open.

Clang, crash, bang, went the pots, pans and roasters as the pig snoot rolled them across the floor. Splat, splash, ping, went the pieces of green mud as Petunia shook them off with her head and whole body against the cabinets and Mom's clean kitchen floor. Ahh, crackers, sharp pig teeth and grinding molars could eat them wrappers, box and all, lots better than the dried beans.

Then Mom came to the door with four children following carrying buckets with eggs just gathered.

"Oh, no!" hollered Mom as she swatted Petunia on the behind with her fly swatter.

"Uh, uh, uh," said Petunia, unafraid of Mom as she gave the screen door a shove that pushed the screen aside at the corner.

"Arreah, eeee, eeee!" called Petunia as she jumped on Benjamin, who was carrying a bucket of eggs. The football impact of the growing hog sent the boy to the porch floor a-flying, with eggs breaking around him. Eggs would do, thought Petunia as she smacked them down, rooting vigorously against Patches' shoulder when he tried to lick them up, too.

"It's time," said Mom to Dad. "That hog has to move on down the road to join the other hogs in the lots. She's too big. She'll knock the children down, and hurt one of them. She'll root up the back yard when she gets out of the pen."

Later, the children leaned over the high corral fence, discerning Petunia among 100 other fat hogs that wandered among the big steers that were being fed—discerning her because she was bigger than any of the others, a runt that had outgrown them all with her milk-added diet.

Other than that, all the hogs were red, muddy and rooting, occasionally shoving on each other to get at a tastier tidbit, squealing if they were the one that lost or got bit.

"Do you think Petunia knows us anymore?" asked Jesse.

"I'm sure she does," said Dad. "But she's a hog first of all. She's doing what comes naturally to hogs just like we do what comes naturally to us. She's happy to eat and sleep in contentment with the others. She had her place with us for a while when she needed us.

"But everything changes, and moves on. It's always been that way. You never know what change might bring—as natural as the seasons, winter changing into spring. So, you be natural that way too, and just enjoy the day."

If only banana trees grew in Kentucky

BIRD PAUSED his walk through the thick leaf pack dominated by fallen oak leaves to chew contentedly on his banana.

What a wonderful cold, crisp day with the winter sun shining brightly, but barely warming, to be on vacation in the cathedral-like still air and over-hanging limbs of a Kentucky state park forest.

It was invigorating to be with relatives who were friends—his wife, his wife's sister, Chatty they called her, and her husband, Dandy.

Bird listened to the occasional scurry of animal movement around the different kinds of oaks, sweet gums and other trees. He contemplated the geology necessary to uplift or erode away the rock chasms and rubble that showed through the forest, and almost smiled in his contentment.

Then he threw down his banana peel.

Chatty narrowed her eyes, and lifted her mouth to one side of her petite face, staring grimly at him.

"What?" Bird asked. "Do I have something on my face?"

"You are going to pick that up aren't you?"

"Pick what up? You mean the banana peel?"

"Yes, I mean the banana peel. We have trash bags along for each of us to carry. You don't leave your trash in the park."

"It will decompose."

"Pick it up."

"Let me see. I see leaves all over the place, a foot deep in lots of spots. They'll decompose. I know they will. There's too many of them for my trash bag anyway, and I really hate to carry extra stuff anyhow. There's acorns all over the place. That would be tree fruit. There's tree fruit all over the place. Bananas are tree fruit. But I don't see any banana trees. What you're really saying to me is that banana trees don't grow in Kentucky. It's out of place. That is what you're saying to me, isn't it? Banana trees don't grow in Kentucky."

Dandy didn't like confrontation. He walked on ahead.

Bird's wife rolled her eyes. "Bird, don't be a butt."

"I said pick it up, it's trash," Chatty said. "It looks trashy."

She grabbed Bird's bag, stuffed the banana peel into it, and shoved it into his pocket while he stood there grinning.

"I could have stuffed it into your mouth," she said.

"I suppose you're one of those people who think being conscious of taking care of the environment is all about appearance," Bird said. "You would really take up more ground by putting a banana peel in a landfill when it could rot here naturally in a forest, or be eaten by a deer or something. You know that paper is mostly cellulose, like these leaves around us. If we really wanted to be environmentally sound instead of just giving the appearance, we would do our best to throw all our paper out car windows to distribute it over the earth, like what's natural. Now that would be more environmentally sound than ruining more land to dig a hole to put masses of it in."

"Let it go, Bird," said his wife. "We're here to enjoy ourselves. Just put your trash in your bag, and be quiet. Forget it."

"Yeah, just shut up," said Chatty, who was smiling at him now.

"Oranges? Oh, do you have some oranges along to eat too," Bird said, moving his eyes around hurriedly to look at the trees around him. "Let me see, I don't see any orange trees for certain, so I guess orange peels will go in the bag, eh? Oh, and dried figs in plastic bags. Let's see, do figs grow in plastic bags instead of peels? Oh, I guess the bags go in the trash sack anyway because I don't see any fig trees."

The women shook their heads at each other. Bird walked the half-mile back to the car mostly silently behind them. But once in the car, Dandy at the wheel, he had to speak up again.

"I suppose you know if you were really environmentally sound you wouldn't use drive-up windows any more, all those cars setting there, idling, putting out fumes, waiting for a turn."

"But they're convenient when you're in a hurry," said Chatty. "I like them just fine because they save me time."

"Ah-hah! So you're only environmental if it's convenient for you. I suppose you like the interstate system, too."

"Of course I do. It's great to be able to go quickly anywhere you want to across the country. The interstates are great."

"One average mile of four-lane interstate uses 40 acres. Did you know that? Think of that—all across the country, hundreds of thousands of acres covered with concrete and asphalt. Why, when the Civil War ended, a lot of people wanted to give the freed slaves each 32 acres and a mule. Think of all the former slaves who could have used what the interstate system takes up—and we wouldn't give it to them."

"I like the speed and safety of four-lane highways, Bird," said Chatty, openly beginning to chuckle at him. "Think of all the human lives they've saved. They're much safer."

"You're being a bore, Bird," said his wife.

"I agree, if you mean an oink-oink boar," said Chatty wrinkling her nose. "We could all use showers after that walk."

Bird turned red. "And while we're on the subject of land use, think of the way we let shopping malls and housing leapfrog into the country-side, using up the farmland, killing the inner cities. We'll pay for our poor planning some day. We can't keep using up land like there's no end to it."

"Think of it," said Chatty. "We're short on land because banana trees don't grow in Kentucky."

"It's greed, plain and simple," Bird grumbled. "We let greed take

162

over. If somebody can make more money, get an advantage over some-body else, the heck with our land. And who said a shopping mall is a higher use of land than using it for farming or trees anyway?

"I tell you what we should do. We should have zoning requiring every shopping center to plant a big shade tree every sixth or seventh parking space. That would help. So what if the trees make a little mess when they drop leaves or limbs. We could put more people to work cleaning up after them."

"Sure, nobody would mind paying more for merchandise or taxes to put the people and the trees to work, would they?" Chatty said. "By the way, I thought I'd broil steaks for us, Bird."

"Sounds good to me."

"Well, how about all those cows you have out there in Kansas? Think about all the methane they're putting out."

"That's ridiculous. Why don't we let out contracts to bulldoze in the everglades in Florida. Swamps put out methane, too."

"Or for that matter, Bird, why don't we just put a cork in you," said his wife. "You're as impenetrable, tenacious and obscure as passing gas—a real stinker."

"Actually, the cow is under-rated on efficiency," Bird said. "They used to tell us cattle would fall into obsolescence because we couldn't afford the inefficiency of feeding them food that could be used to feed people. We would lose food energy with the step needed to produce meat. But that was before the energy crisis. The energy the old cow uses to har-vest grass by grazing looks pretty good stacked alongside the energy machines have to use to plant and harvest."

"We're having rhubarb pie tonight too, Bird. I guess you'll eat pie made from a plant that did better when we stacked cow manure around it, won't you."

"Sounds good to me. You know, rhubarb's efficient. By the way, banana trees don't grow in Kansas either, but rhubarb does even if it's not a tree. And, you just sort of let the rhubarb leaves lay there on the ground and rot."

"Next time just let him throw the banana peel on the ground, OK?" Dandy said. "It cuts down on noise pollution."

A public display
of good fortune

*Author's note: Remember when you do this that the pie
should be wrapped in a napkin first. Then the stickiness
doesn't bother you so much until you get home, and
have to pick little pieces of napkin out of the filling.*

HARLAN MEDLAM had a necktie. He only wore it to weddings, funerals, and that great special event that he and his wife, Florence, looked
forward to each year, the rural electric cooperative association annual dinner and meeting.

Their strategy would be the same as always in the big auditorium
with the white-paper-covered tables set end to end. And they loved the
prizes given away at the end of the meetings, including three electric
mixers alone that they had won over the years—one now in the kitchen
and two in the storage room.

The time in between when they talked about business, such stuff as
kilowatt-hours and election of officers, got dull. Harlan and Florence
mostly cared about their personal business, but they were patient and
persistent, and they were lucky. They had long ago learned that luck is
patience and persistence.

"Anybody can be lucky if he works for it long enough," said Harlan
Medlam in that rare moment when he wanted to look wise before others, sticking his tongue against the inside of his old brown, weathered
cheek, and tilting his head momentarily before speaking to give it
emphasis.

The necktie had been a celebration of that insight. It was his lucky
tie, purchased in the 1940s with the end of depression and the boom of
war. A luminescent maroon with yellow polka dots that had set off his
dark hair, he had bought it in one mad moment when the first time
came that he had saved $500 to buy a certificate of deposit.

He and Florence had been lucky to survive, clawing their way
through every situation for every advantage. They had let nothing that
could move them ahead pass them by.

As the decades passed, and each six-month notice of interest gained
on that CD came, Harlan would pause at the most protected spot in his
closet, holding the bank letter to run the lucky tie through his fingers.
The cord connected him to the harsh realities that had evolved into his
current wealth.

He had a suit, too, a different looking old dark, double-breasted thing
his parents had bought for him as a wedding gift. Harlan had stayed uniformly thin. Waste not, want not—now that was a saying a person could
tie his life to.

"We're lucky tonight, Florence," Harlan Medlam said, smiling as he knotted the lucky tie while Florence laid the fingertips of both hands on the front of her rose-flowered dress in a final shift before the mirror. "There's just a light shower of fine ice crystals falling outside, nothing to cancel a meeting for, but enough to keep a few more folks at home. Don't forget the sack."

They got out of the old, black pickup truck in the blackest of nights with a chill north wind pushing the flaky crystals to enter an audito-

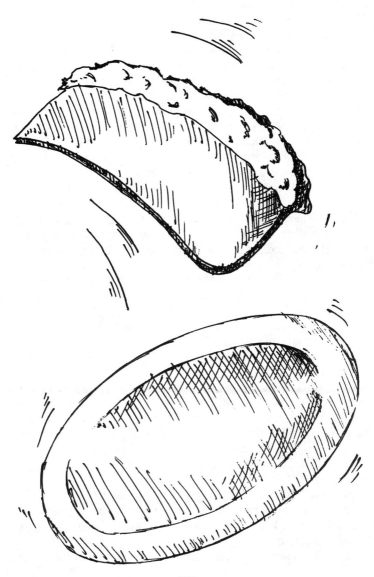

rium brightly lighted, and filled with the steady rumble of talk, coughs and laughs from the crowd filing to the tables.

On every table were the glasses of water, the coffee cups waiting to be filled, the bowls of carrots, celery and pickles, and a slice of pie at each place.

"Wait for it, wait for it," Florence whispered out of the side of her thin lips, patting the bun of white hair that hung on her neck, and nodding to people.

"Harlan, Florence, you two sure look nice all dolled up," said Paul, eyes twinkling as he ushered his family passed them.

"You're looking good too, Paul," said Harlan. "We're just waiting here a minute to see if they have plenty of room."

"Sure you are, real nice of you, too."

Finally Harlan nodded to Florence. "There we go, over at that last table," he said. "There's only a few people sitting at the front of it, most of it's empty, and nearly everybody's sat down."

Harlan Medlam, his gray-splattered dark hair shining in the auditorium lights, smiled in nearly open-mouthed mirth at the big slice of cherry pie in front of him. He rubbed the tip of his lucky tie between his forefinger and thumb. There was a slice of lemon pie at the empty space to his left, and at the empty chair across from him was blueberry pie. At the empty seat across from Florence there was a slice of peach pie.

The rural electric was mighty nice about spreading the different kinds of pie all around in case you and a neighbor wanted to trade, or, thought Harlan Medlam, eat different kinds if not enough people showed up.

"Here, what's this?" hissed Harlan to his wife. An old man with thick, white hair combed back so it stuck up in a most unkempt way, wearing a jean jacket with big pockets was walking up the opposite aisle. He bobbed his big angular face at Harlan trying to smile in a most congenial way. "The old fool looks like he might try to cut in."

The old man sat down across from Harlan, and began eating the piece of blueberry pie.

"Here, you're not supposed to eat that until everybody's eaten everything else," Florence scolded.

"Can't you see they're just starting to serve the main course at the end of the table?" Harlan asked. "It isn't seemly to eat dessert first, even though you're tempting me to. That pie does look good."

Harlan licked his lower lip glancing once at Florence for possible pie permission.

"Name's Harkin, and I'm hungry," said the old man.

Harlin Medlam opened one eye during the invocation prayer to look at his neighbor, only to see that Hungry Harkin had one eye open, too, looking back at him.

The caterers were setting the plates of roast beef, mashed potatoes and peas in front of them now. Ladies followed behind them offering to fill cups with coffee.

"Could you fill the coffee cup next to me, too?" asked Harkin. "That way you don't have to come back so soon, and I'm fierce cold after being outside."

He noisily slurped a cup of steaming coffee down in merely three gulps, and hurriedly chomped the rest of the meal without closing his mouth, occasionally emitting a noisy burp.

Florence raised herself in her seat, and batted her eyes while frowning disapprovingly at Hungry Harkin. Harlan glanced at her trying to look disgusted too.

Harkin put carrots, celery and pickles on his plate, then opened a side jeans jacket pocket to dump the rest of the contents of the condiment plate into the pocket.

Florence opened her mouth in amazement and worry, widening her eyes as she looked at Harlan, who looked back at her with concerned lips drooping in a frown. "Get the sack out he said."

"But folks are just starting to eat their pie, and they haven't even had the meeting yet," she said.

"Yeah, but we need to be ready."

Old Hungry Harkin scratched dog-like at one of his hairy, big ears sticking out from under the bush of hair as he reached over to scoot the peach pie across from Florence next to his plate. He started eating it.

Harlan looked protectively and meaningfully at the lemon pie at the empty space next to him, then stared at Harkin, who was sucking on his fingers.

"Did you folks get enough carrots, celery and pickles down there?" asked someone up the table beyond Florence.

"No, we could use some more," Harlan said, looking around her to smile. When the plate came down, he dumped its contents into the paper bag between himself and Florence.

Hungry Harkin put both hands on the table, and stared at them like he might come up out of his seat.

An uneasy truce ensued as the officers of the electric association cooperative introduced themselves, and began to talk about the progress of the last year. Harlan stared at his own hand pulling guard duty in front of the slice of lemon pie, and Hungry Harkin sat with his arms folded looking at him.

Harlan Medlam couldn't stay awake in meetings for long after a meal any more than he could working on his own farm. His head began to sag forward, his top denture drooped off the gum as he gasped, and drew in his first sonorous snore.

"The poor old dear works so hard," Florence explained to the person at her elbow.

Hungry Harkin grinned and slowly began to slide his hand across the table.

"And now," the speaker was saying, "I know these folks want to get onto the prize drawing. So if there is no further business, I will declare the official meeting adjourned."

With that, Harkin seized the lemon pie.

"Aagh," said Florence as Harlan Medlam came awake at her side reaching with a swift speed that belied his more than 80 years for the pie plate moving across the table. He grabbed the edge of the pie plate just as Hungry Harkin was raising it from the table.

There are those historic moments when the whole world seems to stand still as the telling event unfolds. People old enough remember where they were when John Kennedy was shot, when man landed on the moon, perhaps when they received their first romantic kiss, and certainly when lemon pie first took flight.

It was a little bit that way for the Medlams and a few other people here and there during that pause awaiting the first-prize drawing when a piece of lemon pie raised two feet above the far end of the far table, curling end over end before landing on the knot of Harlan Medlam's lucky tie, and sliding down its length onto his plate.

Prior to the announcement, those who would remember the lemon pie were either staring in disbelief or trying to look away.

"Harlan Medlam, come on up," called the electric association spokesman up front. "Harlan Medlam, you must be one of the luckiest people I know. You seem to win a prize every year, and here you already have the third runner-up prize, an electric mixer for you plus another one for the friend of your choice."

Harlan came forward still dabbing at the last of the lemon pie on his tie with his white handkerchief, and back leaving the extra gift mixer in Paul's hands.

In the meantime, while Florence was politely clapping for Harlan with the rest of the crowd, Hungry Harkin had taken Harlan's plate to scrape the remains of the lemon pie into his jacket pocket. Then he reached down the table for another piece of pie at a vacant spot.

The prizes over, the meeting over, the crowd was up to leave, visiting in a loud rumble as they made for the exits.

Harlan and Florence Medlam were hurrying down one side of the table putting slices of pie, carrots, celery and pickles in their sack while Hungry Harkin filled his pockets on the other side.

"You know," said Harlan ruefully rubbing his stained lucky tie as they stood at the exit glaring at Hungry Harkin at another exit a door down. "Some people have no manners, no finesse at all when it comes to making a public display of their good fortune."

Penelope and her Pekinese named Pau Pau were in a pinch

EACH MORNING at 10 after television jazzercise, Penelope showered herself and, dressed in appropriate pre-lunch dress with nylons, checked her blue-black bouffant hair in the mirror. She also dressed her Pekinese, Pau Pau, in his best purple sweater with matching leash.

Then, putting on her ankle-length charcoal coat with fringed gray fur, she put the pooper scooper and sack under one arm and, taking Pau Pau's leash with the other, proceeded down the pavement in pompadour refinement, parading atop clicking pointy high heels to central park.

At fire hydrants and trees, which Pau Pau baptized with contained eagerness, Penelope stood with all propriety looking around aloofly lest any person should mistake her interests in Pau Pau for an unseemly concern with dog nature.

If Pau Pau did more, the pooper scooper went quickly and skillfully into action, with the results going into the sack which Penelope would carry as casually as if it were a loaf of bread instead of noxious waste destined for a proper landfill.

At the park, with its broad expanse of clipped grass and carefully spaced big trees, Pau Pau would push eagerly ahead looking for one of the squirrels that had always been there back to his earliest memory, or for that matter to Penelope's earliest memory.

Or, Pau Pau would look for his first glimpse of the big pond where he might be allowed to shove his flat snout into the grasses growing taller along the moist shore.

If few other humans were within sight, Penelope sometimes would even allow him off-leash to bound in a short-legged way around the pond. Better that then her risking leaving a sidewalk to sink the pointy heels into soft earth.

Unfortunately, newcomers had taken up residence at the park over the last decade. There they were, trimming the grass in their fat gray-slate bodies, arrogant black beaks honking here and there all over the place, the Canada Geese.

Occasionally a goose would have the audacity to stretch, and flap its wings while Penelope was forced to watch its beady black eyes and continually squirting posterior. Pau Pau strained at the leash, wondering if he could possibly take a bite out of a goose, or if he was safer under restraint.

When the geese first came, there had only been a pair sticking mostly to the pond dam, where Penelope enjoyed seeing them. It had been a treat to see them swim the pond with newly hatched goslings cheeping between the mama and the papa. Penelope had almost broken down her reserve to think she might become a nature lover, but not quite.

A dozen geese returned the second year, then multiples of 10, until now there might be 500 in the park, hissing and snaking their long necks out as if they owned the place if she and Pau Pau got too near.

Worse than that, nobody followed the geese with pooper scoopers,

and they greased the sidewalks and grass with their green grime until a person could build up a crust to clean off even on a pointy heel or dog paw.

Penelope tried not to look at the geese so carefully anymore, but she growled in her throat when she saw them and their excrement almost as much as Pau Pau.

But on this day, with bright, warming winter sunshine that had melted even the thin skim of ice on the pond, it was too nice to worry about geese.

Penelope breathed the still-crisp air, and walked a little faster than usual, feeling nearly a state of enjoyment rather than propriety. Pau Pau felt the surge, and began to forget a little of his reserve and caution. At the pond, he pulled eagerly on his leash until Penelope released him.

He went rushing off nearly to the pond's edge, diverting his course from a newly planted tree with a zig-zagged tooth pattern of rust-red metal barrier a foot tall around it to protect it from intruders. Only there were intruders.

A mama goose sat on a nest of sticks, grass and feathers inside the barrier, laying her first egg of the season. The papa goose who guarded her came running, thump, thump, on webbed feet, wings extended at his sides in magnificent gander display, long black neck extended, honking at Pau Pau.

He chased Pau Pau for 30 feet before the chastened dog made it back to Penelope, who for once smiled at Pau Pau's adventure.

From then on, as the winter advanced into early spring, Penelope also thawed as she began to watch on every walk what she was beginning to consider her particular geese. Pau Pau off-leash always carefully detoured a long distance around the gander and his hen whether they were at the nest or grazing on the lawn near it.

The hen increasingly stayed on the nest more and more, and the gander increasingly honked his warning earlier and made his advance sooner toward Penelope and Pau Pau as the time approached when goslings would hatch.

Finally, one fine spring morning with the odor of growing grass caught in the vapors evaporating under the more intense sun, a group of small yellow-fluffed goslings with dark gray tops and shiny dark beaks circled around the inside of the metal tree barrier with papa goose on the outside honking, and mama goose circling broodingly with her wings to the ground offering shelter to her troubled brood.

"Ah, the poor little things can't get out," said Penelope, forgetting herself to talk to nobody around quite out loud. But the gander heard her, and he rushed right up to her to cause her to back up several steps with poor Pau Pau extending in the background to help pull her backward.

Say what you will about Penelope's aplomb, but she was no coward. As the gander ran back to his cheeping brood, Penelope released Pau

Pau, who stood in uncertainty while she pulled off her gray sweater and high heels to step onto the grass.

"Somebody must help the poor little things out," she said.

Penelope walked boldly in unaccustomed barefoot fending off the gander's first charge with a pooper scooper to the breast, Pau Pau dancing 30 feet out of range. She almost gave up when the gander made a leap toward her chest with beating wings that confused her. But a lucky pooper scooper thrust to the side of the head threw him off balance.

Pau Pau decided he could bite one of these things in Penelope's defense, but was sent away yelping with a gander riding his back and its pinching beak attached to his plump side, beating him with its wings.

With that diversion, Penelope decided she could make it all the way to the goslings. She ran to the tree barrier, fell to her knees, and begin reaching for the first baby. But the broody hen goose suddenly came alive and rushed forward to seize Penelope by the hair in a twisting beak fashion.

The gander, not to be outdone after releasing Pau Pau, noticed poor Penelope's pushed-up posterior writhing from side to side toward him with Penelope saying "Ah, ah, ah."

He attacked, biting down hard on first one side of the plentiful target in his great black beak while twisting his sinuous neck, then seizing the other side.

When Penelope "Yeowed!" and staggered to her feet to turn, leaving a wisp of hair behind, he leaped up her front to grab hold of the soft fold of skin under her blouse that protruded over her skirt. "Aai, aai, aai!"

Another goose, that had ambled over with several of its fellows from the park grass to watch, stood on her sweater adding insult to injury.

As Penelope and Pau Pau fled across the grass, the gander fell back honking the victory trumpet, and ruffling his feathers to join his family.

But the geese gathered to watch realized that the defeat was done, and hissed, flapped and nipped as Penelope, now grimly silent, swung retrieved sweater, leash, heels and pooper scooper around her.

"Dr. Cowper, can you work another patient in between appointments?" the nurse asked. "We seem to have a wounded woman and dog in the waiting room." She gestured in to where a bedraggled spectre with fallen bouffant stood with panting Pekinese in hand.

Later, Dr. Cowper was saying, "I certainly appreciate your patience in letting my colleague come in also to look at these wounds, Penelope. You certainly are flushed. I hope you're not hurting too badly for this.

"Now look here, Dr. Kurpaska, on each buttock, a half-inch diameter of skin gone with a ring of blood blisters around it. Have you ever seen such a pinch? And, now if you'll roll over, Penelope.... See here, an identical wound in the stomach, and look at the little dog too. He's got nearly the same wound, all of them due to a goose in the park."

Several days later, at 10 in the morning after television jazzercise, still sweating, Penelope pulled on her blue jeans, double-tied the bow knots on her new boots, strapped on her bicycle helmet, tucked her pooper scooper, sack and new baseball bat under her arm, and, with Pau Pau securely leashed, went to take a walk in central park to see the goslings that had somehow struggled up over the tree barrier swimming with their parents.

Just don't know
what to believe

"I DON'T know, I don't know," Buck Barnsworth muttered as he peered out at the early morning darkness after finishing his standard two fried eggs, toast, bacon, oatmeal, juice and second cup of coffee.

"You don't know, you don't know—for 60 years I've listened to you say that. I guess I'm used to the expression, but I wish you'd get a new saying," said Rosie on her way to the television set for the early-morning news. "Just don't trip down the porch on your way out this morning. Looks like it could be icy."

"What's that you said? Talk a little louder. I don't know what you said, I just don't know."

"I said, TURN YOUR HEARING AID UP."

"Yes, you're right, I didn't have it turned up. I don't know, just needs adjustin' or somethin'. I don't know."

"Have fun at coffee. Don't back into anything."

Buck shook his head ruefully, and scratched his thick white hair, "They should have known better than to park right in back of me. I don't know. I just don't know."

At the first cafe Buck went to, he sat alone at his table, drinking his coffee and waiting for the possibility that one of the older friends he started going there with many years ago might come in. People said hello to him, asked him how he was, and he said, "Oh, fine, fine, but I don't know, I just really don't know.

He caught snatches of conversation from the two big ruddy-faced men in seed hats who had been laughing hard while eating pancakes at the next table. One of them said, "I tell you, you should have seen old Ed Pasaquet when he read the letter from Penelope. He laughed so hard he nearly died. It was terrible, just terrible."

The man gave out a last "guffaw," then pulled out his handkerchief to wipe his eyes, and blow his nose. His partner coughed a couple of times from the effort of mirth.

"I don't know, I don't know," muttered Buck, shaking his head solemnly.

"What don't you know, Buck?" asked the waitress.

"I don't know, you know. I just don't know."

At the next cafe, Buck sat at a table with two old friends, Arthur and Daniel.

"Did you hear?" Buck asked, solemnly folding his hands around the steaming cup of coffee, "Poor Ed Pasaquet died in an accident while he was away at the city to see his sister, Penelope. Terrible thing, just terrible. I don't know, I just don't know. Just so terrible, I don't know."

"I bet it was on that new bypass," said Arthur. "It's just terrible. The traffic goes so fast, and there's all those construction zones."

"I tell you," said Daniel. "They need to slow those semi-trucks down, the way they drive in those great big rigs. They aren't safe, I tell you. It's a pain to be around them. Poor Ed, what an agonizing way to go. His family must just be torn up over this."

"I don't know, I just don't know," said Buck, rolling his eyes tragically under his spectacles. "I don't know how I'm going to tell Rosie about this. You know they lived just across the street from us. You see, you don't know, you never know, you just don't know."

"I'm glad you let us know, Buck," said Arthur.

"Yes, it's terrible isn't it. I just don't know. I don't know."

At the Deerhead Tavern, the cleanup man had just mopped up from yesterday's night crowd as the coffee drinkers left their quarters on the bar to go sit at the long table.

"Watch your step there, Buck, the floor's still wet," he said as the older man walked haltingly over his cane, gently wiping under his spectacles with his handkerchief. "Hey, you're OK, aren't you? Sit down, I'll get your coffee for you."

"I don't know, I don't know, I just don't know," Buck said more loudly than usual as he solemnly took his chair. The men lined up on either side of the table and looked expectantly at him.

"I don't know, I don't know," Buck said again, slowly shaking his head.

"You don't know what, Buck. Tell us. What's up?"

"I don't know," Buck said in a hush. "Haven't you all heard? Poor Ed Pasaquet and his family all died in a terrible, terrible accident, in terrible agony, in the city on the new bypass. A semi-truck speeding in the construction zone ran over their car. I don't know. It was terrible, I guess. Tore them all up. I just don't know."

"Golly," said Edgar down the table. "Ed lost his mother just a year ago. His father will have a terrible time handling this on top of everything else. A person shouldn't have to face so many things on top of growing old, but we all do."

"I don't know, I just don't know," said Buck, quietly shaking his head.

The bank was just opening as Buck walked in to see if his Social Security check might have arrived before he received notice of it.

"Have you heard about the Pasaquet family yet, Buck?" asked Shiela the teller. "We hear there was a bad accident, and I know you live across the street from them."

"I really don't know everything," said Buck. "I don't know, I just don't know. But what I heard drinking coffee this morning is that they were riding with Ed's father around the bypass down in the city. They say his father shouldn't have been driving, but his mother is such a dear, she asked them to let him. I guess he was too old, but I don't know, I just don't know. Anyway a semi-truck speeding through a construction zone ran over them when Ed's father changed lanes, and it was terrible, just terrible. Of course they say the semi-driver is in agony over it."

"We never know do we, Buck?" said the teller. "We just never know."

"No, I don't know. I just don't know. I don't think I ever know."

Buck drove by the parsonage to see if his pastor might come home with him to help tell Rosie the terrible news.

But the pastor's wife said, "I don't know what's happening yet, Buck. But Pastor's gone to the funeral home to see if the out-of-town family might have sent anything in about arrangements yet for the poor Pasaquet family. People have been calling us to ask if there's anything they can do. But we don't know yet, Buck. We just don't know."

"I don't know either, I just don't know."

Buck drove his car into his driveway very slowly and very carefully. How was he going to tell Rosie? It was a terrible thing to have to tell her because she liked the entire Pasaquet family down to the smallest child.

"I don't know, I just don't know," muttered Buck to himself as he stopped the car. He looked up and saw Rosie framed in the middle of the picture window, gazing out with a smile on her face. "Oh my, maybe she's heard, standing there kind of nutty like that. I don't know, I just don't know. What can I say to her? I don't know."

"Hi, Buck. Did you have a good visit at coffee?" Rosie asked. "You're just in time to watch television for a while with me. They're having a marathon of old television quiz shows on the cable today. They're playing the old 'To Tell The Truth' show. Remember that one? We'll enjoy seeing that one."

"Rosie, I don't know, I just don't know how to say this, but I need to tell you something."

"Just a minute, Buck. I'm watching the Pasaquet kids across the street. They've been skate-boarding, and now they're with their mom giving their dad, Ed, a hug before he leaves for work. They're so sweet, and so active being out there in this cold. I just love to watch them, don't you?"

"I don't know, I don't know. So they're all out there are they? Didn't I try to tell them? Didn't I try to tell them all that I just didn't know about all those rumors being passed around. I'd tell them I don't know, I just don't know about all of that? What a mess. What a mess for poor Ed Pasaquet to get straightened out. You can't depend on anything! I don't know, I just don't know."

"What is it you were going to tell me about, Buck?"

"Oh," said Buck, striking his cane angrily on the floor. "I'm just disgusted. I'm so darned disgusted I don't know. I just don't know."

"Why, you're disgusted with what, Buck? Don't hit the floor like that. You'll scratch it. I want to know what you're so disgusted with."

"It's those coffee shops and the coffee drinkers. I don't know. I just don't know whether a fellow ought to be going there, them and all their gossip. That's all they got to do with their time. A fellow maybe ought to stay home, and count on what he knows more. I don't know. I just don't know. Maybe watch the morning news with you. I don't know."

"Well, I guess I don't know either, Buck. That would be up to you. To tell the truth, I just want you to be happy."

Harlan Medlam milks a deal with Paul

THE AIR was still—so deep and penetratingly silent in the deepest soul-slicing cold of winter that you could hear a twig crack in the tree row 200 feet away or a cow licking at the frozen snow hanging from her hair. But it was bright beyond normal, as the early sunlight reflected against the white.

Some optimistic cattleman long ago had euphemistically called this early-spring calving season, no doubt looking forward to a better season ahead. Easy to see that he might not have called it so if he'd been one of the new baby animals dumped so unceremoniously from the warmth inside the cow to the frozen ground. However, the cattlemen also knew that once the calf dried off, this was healthier weather than the rainy months to come.

Paul loved these mornings coming down to the cow herd's winter quarters to drag hay bales from the hay shed into the bunk lines, breathing the clean, crisp air, the cows also exhaling clouds of steamy breath with ice crystals hanging on the hair around their muzzles. There were at least a half-dozen new black baldy, or white-faced, baby calves curled in hay litter with a couple of the cows contrasting in red, white-faced color by them for guard duty as the others came up to eat. The calves were the result of cross-breeding an Angus bull with Hereford cows.

Looking into the big lean-to area built for animal shelter against the shed, he saw no more animals. They'd all gone outside for the sunshine.

Paul would be back later, driving with supplement pellets. But this was the walking time, the time to watch for new-born calves, eyeball the herd for problems, and chop ice on the pond to reopen the drinking hole for the cows.

Down on the pond, where white lines ran through the gray-blue ice in the frigid weather, Paul could see, squinting against the brilliant light, that something was going on. A cow was standing on the ice, uttering the low moaning moo used in cow sound for encouraging a calf, and she was licking at a small bundle on the ice.

Having carried the axe stored at the shed to the pond, Paul began chopping the ice while watching the cow with the bundle that now transformed upon closer view into the shape of a curled-up newborn calf. He watched while the cow alternated licking and nuzzling the black calf, and looking toward him in nervous glare. She was a silly thing, he thought, choosing the pond to have a calf on. But then cows could choose strange places for the momentary isolation of birth.

Paul took the axe back, then walked back down carefully, stepping without slipping on the ice directly to the calf. The brockle-faced cow lowered her head, moaning, and shook it at him as he gently rubbed the calf's fur-like newborn hair coat a little with his leather-gloved hands.

The brockle-face was bluffed by her lifelong familiarity with Paul as the central caretaker and authority, and also by his apparent calm lack of concern that she might do something.

The calf was alive, but a little weak from lying unfed on a cold surface slippery to stand on. Paul knelt down, raising the calf to put one arm under its front quarters and the other under its back quarters, then carried it up the slope, the cow following uncertainly behind. Under the shelter of the shed lean-to, he set it on its feet at its mother's nose. In response to her nuzzling, it took two wobbly steps.

Then the calf moved to the cow's udder seeking to nurse. Paul smiled. It looked like everything would be OK as the calf found what it was looking for. He left to do the rest of the chores, coming back once to feed pellets, and again checking to see that the brockle-faced cow and her calf looked fine.

The next morning, the still air was replaced with a steady, harshly cold breeze, and the welcome sunny glow was replaced by a gray overcast. Paul wasn't smiling either as he looked toward the pond to see the brockle-faced cow standing on the ice again. This time the calf wasn't as strong.

"You crazy old heifer," Paul said into the breeze toward the cow.

Paul carried wooden panels inside the lean-to, and wired them together in a containment pen. Leaving one side temporarily open, he went to get the calf to put it in the pen with the cow following. He got the gate closed, got the calf on its feet, and steadied it as it tried to nurse again. Although more feeble, it finally began to nurse once more, even resuming weak head-butting against the cow's bag as it got its first tastes of milk. But Paul was worried for it. The new baby still lacked sufficient vigor.

He put down hay in the small pen, left some water there for the cow, and went on to do the chores. That afternoon during the pellet feeding, he checked to find that the calf was curled up comfortably in a corner, breathing well, and looked bright-eyed.

Paul had every expectation the next morning, as he stuck gloved hands in his pockets walking into the hay shed in a much more blustery cold wind, that the calf would be sufficiently healthy to turn it, and its mother, loose with the herd. Instead he found one of the wooden panels crushed from the top where the cow apparently had tried to go over it, broken boards hanging, and the panel knocked askew.

The cow and calf were gone.

Paul felt a grim reluctance to see what he expected, but there it was—the brockle-faced cow back on the ice again, the calf stretched out dead at her feet. When he picked up the dead baby, she once more followed along, softly moaning as though she expected the calf to awaken. Paul, breathing hard in the icy air, passed up the hay shed this time to go straight to a loading pen along the road in the wintering yard. The cow followed him and the carcass in.

"Whatya got there, a dead'un?" a voice startled him into realizing he wasn't alone. Paul looked up to see the old, lined, brown face of Harlan Medlam, who was wearing a red hat with earflaps and looking back at him under the top, heavy paddock board of the loading pen. The sharp, shiny brown eyes were looking at the cow. "What are you going to do with her, Paul?"

"Oh, truck her down the road to feed out with the fat calves, haul her to sale when they go this spring," replied Paul, the shepherd within him already supplanted by the businessman.

Harlan stuck his top denture out, clicking on it with his tongue thoughtfully before pulling it back in. "Born dead was it?"

"No, it was a good calf. But she had it down on the ice, and kept going back—you know how they can be when they get something in their heads. That's not good mothering ability so she's out of here," Paul said with a shrug, heaving the calf carcass over the top of the pen by the road so he could haul it away later.

He tried to show as he shrugged that he was indifferent to Harlan Medlam's interest, wishing the old man would go away at this moment of misfortune. Harlan was beginning to remind him of a scavenging coyote.

"So, she's a cull cow then," Harlan said, shaking his head. "Looks to be in pretty good condition though."

"Yes, they've all been fed well. She ought to finish off fine."

"Still go for slaughter cow price though, what a shame. I sure might like to buy her for a milk cow. We need one, if yer a'willin' to sell her at killer price. It'd save you feedin' her to get a discount on her anyway."

"She's beef breed, Harlan. You wouldn't get that much milk. If you want a dairy cow, why don't you buy a Holstein? Or if that's too big for your needs, get a Jersey for the high cream. Doesn't Florence still churn butter?"

"She does, she does, but no sense paying a premium for dairy stock when you got this nice cow here that would suit our needs fine. Be doing us a favor to sell her to us. I'd give you $300 for her. Know she was a $500-cow to start with, and maybe you'd still get $350 at sale time for her, but this would save you all that feed and time."

Paul was tired of Harlan and suddenly weary of the cold and the discouraging results with the calf. "You got yourself a deal, Harlan—$300 and she's yours."

Harlan Medlam took one hand out of a glove, reached inside one overall pocket for a checkbook and pen, and slowly wrote Paul a check while licking his lips thoughtfully in the chill air.

"Here's my check, that seals the deal," Harlan said looking again at the cow that was circling the loading pen, looking for a way out through the high sides. He added as he began to turn for the short walk home, "Oh, and, Paul, when you get your truck to bring her down this afternoon, we'll just stall her in the barn until she gets used to things."

Paul shook his head. How did he get himself into these deals with Harlan Medlam?

He was to wonder about that even more a couple of weeks later when his wife was reading through the classifieds in the city newspaper.

"Paul, listen to this advertisement in the want ads. It says 'Farm-fresh frozen lean hamburger for healthy eating. No implants or antibiotics. Only $1.49 a pound. Call Harlan Medlam at 555-2929.' Do you think he can get that for hamburger when it's 99 cents in the grocery store.

"Oh, he can, he can," growled Paul suspiciously.

He felt his suspicions being confirmed only two days later when he saw Harlan Medlam at the co-op, and the old man took his hat off to run his fingers through his black hair. He looked up at Paul, smiling broadly.

"Well, Paul," Harlan said. "I'm sorry to say things didn't work out with that cow. She was just too wild to be a milker. But don't you worry, we put every last scrap of her into hamburger, must have made 600 pounds with all the liver and such in it, too. We're going to get a lot of good eatin' from her, so we're going to make out on her even if I did make a good deal for you."

Sometimes the river can't be handled

Author's note: Definitely don't try this. These girls did grow up, but it's a wonder they made it that far.

BEYOND THE tall grain elevator leg and the outbuildings where calves loafed was the gray-blue river—sparkling in the sun or growing gray-brown muddy and sullen under a thunderstorm that could swell it quickly to a yellow torrent.

Mama would walk Ceilia and Ann through the grassy groves of walnut and ash to the river bank to where their father had already unsaddled his horse from a morning ride through the feedlots, and was stripping off his clothes for a swim.

Sometimes one or the other of the two little blonde-haired girls would protest, "I don't want to go swimming today."

But Mama would gently keep a hand on their shoulders to explain, "You have to learn to handle yourself in a river if we're going to live next to it. The river will always be there, and it will wait for your careless moment if you don't come to understand it and how it moves.

"You go to the river first because someday it's going to come walking up out of its banks to where you're at anyway. How do you think this old black ground got here? The river carried it from the uplands, and flooded out on this flat ground to put it here, that's how."

They would take hold of Daddy's long, slender fingers as he led them down the bank, out from the shore, on the sticky, smooth-mud river bottom with its occasional deposits of sand, gravel, rocks and tree branches. Mama sometimes sat on the shore or other times waded in to join them.

Then, looking down on them with his long, lean brown-burned face, Daddy would call out, "Now splash! Hands out to the side, splash hard. Who can splash it over my head first?

"OK, let's see who can remember how to float on your bellies, heads down, arms out, hold your breaths, now float."

He rolled each girl over on her back with his hand under her until he had one girl on each hand, floating beside each other, before gently removing his hands.

"Today, girls, we're going to learn to feel the river. This old river seems to have a soul, a spirit. The water that provided for all the plants and animals comes through it. I'm going to tow you out here on your backs in the current. You feel the river like it's alive under you, close your eyes, the warm sun on your faces like you're tucked in for a nap and the cool river moving under you. Put your ears back in the water, and listen to the river talking to you. Then quietly, quietly, let your bodies stay all loose like you really are asleep, let the river take you on a trip, you're a part of the river. I'll be by your side for a couple hundred yards until we're down by the big cottonwood tree on the bank cut-out, and I tow you to shore."

Ceilia and Ann learned to paddle and kick on their bellies, then to do the same on their backs, rolling from one position to the other without touching feet to the bottom.

"Feel the river, feel the river, it's alive and you're alive, alive together, roll, you're a part of the river," Daddy would say. "Now go straight up, and under, feel the river around you. See what else is part of the river. Try to touch a fish."

The biggest day for the girls was when they'd swum the current turning and rolling enough times to the cottonwood cut-out, Mama and Daddy joined them to double the distance downstream, all the way to the steel railroad bridge. They were becoming like young otters.

Mama and Daddy used similar methods when it came to teaching Ceilia and Ann about horses. They'd had them sitting behind saddle horns when they were babies, "feeling the horses under them," and handed them the reins as soon as they could hold on.

By the the time the girls were 11 and 12 years old, beginning to get long-legged, they regarded themselves as experts at swimming the river and at horseback riding. Their parents decided they were sufficiently skilled to do those things by themselves. Often as not, Ann would put a bridle on her gelding, Buck, and Ceilia would bridle Toby to ride bareback to the river. There, they would plunge with the animals into the water and splash them and each other in the summer heat.

Then they would turn the horses loose to return to graze along the banks while they went swimming before flipping over on their backs to ride the current down to the cottonwood cutout, watching dragonflies hover around them for a perch in the steamy haze.

"Ceilia," said Ann one day as the two stood in the shade of the cottonwood running their fingers through their long hair to squish out the water, "did I tell you that at school last spring that Miss Herndon said one day you and I are like young barbarians?"

"Why would she say anything so mean?"

"Oh, I don't think she was trying to be mean because she was smiling at me when she said it. As a matter of fact, she said she wished she knew how to swim, too."

"She had better learn to because she lives out here on the flat land too in that little cracker box of a house halfway to town. I don't care if it is up on a mound. Daddy says he's seen the river in that house before. At least we live in a big two-story house so we can be sleeping nice and dry upstairs if the water comes."

"Hey, Ceilia, know what we ought to do?"

"What?"

"Next time the river gets up high, let's go off riding the horses, but we'll really come down here, and get in the river when it's really rough. Daddy calls that 'wrestling the river,' when even the best swimmer can lose."

"Mama and Daddy wouldn't like it at all if we tried something stupid like that. There's undertows then that can take you under, and you can't swim out of them."

"But, Ceilia, we maybe could learn how to handle ourselves in it so if Miss Herndon gets in trouble we can help her, or even if Mama and Daddy get in trouble. Daddy says there's no other kids better than us in the water. I really like Miss Herndon, don't you? I wish my hair was red like hers, and she really smiles nice."

"Yes, I like Miss Herndon, but I don't know if we ought to go in the river when it gets mad."

"Scared?"

"No, I'm never scared of the river. I guess I feel like it's part of us. But Mama and Daddy say we hadn't ought to swim when it's like that. Look at it, it's happy now, just gurgling and rolling along. But you know it doesn't look like that when it's bank-full."

Not many nights later, Ceilia and Ann awoke in the night to a sound of thunder splitting the atmosphere like a heavy sledge. Through the curtains they saw continual lightning slicing across the sky. Rain pounded on the windows and roof. It was a four-inch frog strangler that had followed miles of drainage area up the river.

The next day the sun peered weakly through a misty atmosphere, and they could hear the river long before they came to it. There was no walk down the bank to get to the water because the river was 10 to 20 feet over its banks, depending on elevations.

Tree logs ripped by the water from crumbling banks, looking like long black battleships, were towed downstream in the grip of the river before they spun around in the roaring cascade, and got sucked under in whirling current.

"Maybe we hadn't ought to wrestle the river today," hollered Ann above the noise. "It looks awfully strong."

"You're scared," said Ceilia.

"Yes, I guess I am."

"So am I, but I'm going anyway. On the count of three we'll go together. See that big log coming. We'll swim hard to it together. Hang on, and swim back out at the cottonwood cutout. One, two, three!"

Ceilia plunged into water that immediately seemed to take the breath out of her, pulling her rapidly along in a current that surged over her no matter how hard she stroked with her arms and kicked. She glimpsed Ann once at her side, then couldn't see her again. She reached out to grab the log, felt its rough bark twisting around burning her hands with its friction and jamming a finger, then she went under.

Ceilia's lungs and throat burned with the effort to hold in breath that had been inadequate to start with as the water pulled her down, down until she kicked hard on the bottom mud to rise again. She sucked what air she could as she struggled to break the surface only to be drawn under again.

As she kicked off the bottom again, she could feel the tell-tale ache through her system that told her her body was weakening.

If I don't swim out of it this time, she told herself, I may be gone. And Annie, my sister Annie, where is she?

Ceilia broke the surface kicking and stroking with head down in the strongest style she had mastered, heading for the shore. Even though the last kickoff had moved her close to the shore, she was still swept downstream another 200 feet before she hit shoreline mud. Breathing hard, with a strong shot of adrenaline she pulled herself along the ground away from the river to lay gasping on her side. That didn't last long because, with alarm, she thought to look up for Ann.

Looking upstream, she quickly realized she had made land in a spot not used before because there was the old cottonwood tree with only half its length above the water surface at a sick 33 percent angle that suggested it might be soon to fall.

Downstream, she looked just in time to see a blonde head break the surface out in the middle of the river only to continue in the rush downstream.

Ceilia ran along the river trying to keep up, crashing through stands of weeds and shrubs, meandering pell mell around trees.

If only, I can catch up a little, I can get an angle on it to get Ann out, she told herself, still breathing hard. She couldn't believe it when she saw she was nearly to the railroad bridge already, but there it was with the water above its abutments, and the bottoms of the first of its structural steel beams barely into the wash.

And there was a girl with scarcely recognizable mud-gray hair plastered on her head, clinging weakly to the angle of a bridge beam as the current tried to pull her away.

"Ann, Annie!" Ceilia cried out. "Come this way!"

Seeing that Ann was too weak to move, Ceilia jumped in, swimming above the abutment to let the current push her into the base of the beam. She put her arm around Ann's waist to help hold her to the beam, and was relieved to see Ann look at her with open eyes even though watered-down blood flowed from a swelling on her forehead.

The two girls pulled themselves across the beam together, felt the concrete of the abutment under their toes, and tip-toed to help push to where they could grab onto grass and weeds to heave themselves to muddy ground.

How long did they lay breathing on the mud—five minutes, fifteen minutes, twenty minutes? When at last they stood up, still clinging together to stare at the river for a moment, they turned to look at each other. Ann leaned forward to murmur against Ceilia's ear, "I can't believe we're both still alive."

"I suppose we should go back upstream for our clothes," said Ceilia."

"No," said Ann with tears beginning to form in the corners of her eyes rasped red by the river. "We're too weak now. We'll have to tell Mama and Daddy the truth anyway. They'll forgive us. They probably expected us to try something like this someday anyway."

They walked toward home holding hands, pausing to turn around only once when a giant log crashed in the river's rampage against the railroad bridge abutment, and was lofted momentarily to stand verti-cally 30 feet in the air before falling to submerge in undertow beyond the bridge.

Irony of 'riffle water' is in the cards

Author's note: The secret to making this work is to leave the engine running all the time.

BAILEY AND Dodson came out of a late-night school board meeting to a world blasted raw by a 30 mph north wind that carried a steady stinging stream of ice crystal snow pellets.

They knew they needed the only hot caffeine available in town before the 50-mile midnight trip home.

"Caffeine," they said, because the only choice for a cup in town at this hour was the Deerhead Tavern, where coffee at night was a euphemism for genuine black coffee mixed with bourbon whiskey—which was tucked deep behind the bar safe from the eyes of state inspectors.

Ask for coffee, and the man behind the counter would ask how much cream you wanted—light, medium or heavy to make the mix that varied from amber to black.

Real coffee—what out-of-town people without cast-iron stomachs drank, with real cream—was straight black caffeine with milk.

The Deerhead was a warm, welcome break from the wind with a few German-looking, light-haired, Flint Hills cowboys with weather-burned faces sitting around the tables.

But on high stools at the end of the bar perched the Bison with the Gardener, like a walrus on the rocks with his pet parrot, their red caps with ear flaps laid out before them.

The Gardener, who would be the parrot referred to, looked neither to the right nor the left, but kept his black-wool head and thin frame stooped over his coffee sipping intently, coffee so yellow it looked like hot lemonade.

However, the Bison shifted his weight to rise another foot above his paunch, watching Bailey and Dodson intently with little eyes that looked a size too small in such a big face. His shocks of black hair stuck ridiculously out to the sides around his bald pate.

He resumed drinking his own coffee while Bailey and Dodson ordered their caffeine, and then went to a table to drink most of it, intent on private conversation about the night's happenings.

Dodson looked up in time to see the Bison, with a wily smile, whisper something in the Gardener's ear.

The Gardener exploded from his stool, shouting a string of obscenities. The cowboys around the room began quietly smiling.

The Bison had sat up straight again, but merely watched unsmiling, moving his eyes to every person while his friend performed.

"Don't want no mo' riffle water," the Gardener hollered.

The Gardener picked out the biggest cowboy in the place, a man who could stand two heads above him, and shoved his pugged nose into the man's face.

"Hey, you try'n to give me riffle water? I'll punch you bloody in the snow."

"No, Gardener," the man responded with all seriousness. "I wouldn't try to give you riffle water."

The Gardener then danced in front of all the younger cowboys in the room calling them milky little cowards and mama's boys, and saying how he could whip them all for trying to give him riffle water.

The Bison was smiling.

Finally, Gardener realized that Bailey was someone new, and he came waving his fists across the room to get in Bailey's face while once more shouting his question, "Hey, you try'n to give me riffle water?"

"And what would this riffle water be that you are referring to?"

"Hey, you try'n to get smart with me. You want to fight? Hey, c'mon I'm ready for you. Just c'mon. Get up out of that chair."

The cowboys were turning to watch as Bailey stayed in his chair, and Bison in his place at the bar grinned, and said, "Uh-huh," as he took a drink of Gardener's coffee and cream.

"No, I'm really curious about it, and I want to know what an obviously gifted person can tell me about riffle water. Please tell me, I really want to know," he said earnestly and calmly. He looked down his long nose motioning with his chin toward his companion, "And I'm sure Mr. Dobson here would like to know, too. He's uncommonly curious."

"Well, didn't you see my truck out there with the hood up? Didn't you see it? Radiator cap all pushed up with a big icicle under it. That fool over there," and he motioned at the Bison. "I tell him I didn't have the money to pick up antifreeze for my truck. He says don't go home and get any money for antifreeze, just go down to the creek. Just get you some of that riffle water that foams over the rocks. Put it in your radiator. 'You ain't never seen riffle water freeze have you?' he says. Darned fool. It froze up my whole block, and busted it. Been sittin' there ever since. Everybody's laughin' at me. You laughin' at me? I'll fight you right now, c'mon, get up."

Bailey shook his head slowly, thinking, trying to stay expressionless while Dobson carefully looked toward the opposite wall.

"No, no, no, in all sincerity I don't want to fight with you," Bailey said, reaching for his wallet to pull out a $100 bill, which he held and stroked meaningfully between his two hands. "I think you and your friend have just mis-timed your effort.

"I remember reading a historical account by the great scientific observer, P.T. Barnum, that in a given moment there are only so many persons born of your perceptive ability."

Gardener was absorbed watching the $100 bill. The Bison, seeing that much cash, had moved over by the table.

"You see," said Bailey, leaning forward meaningfully after a moment had passed with no reaction to his comment, "he helped form an investigative company with a member of my family that did great acts for the public good."

Then Bailey added, lowering his voice: "Drew a lot of interest from the government if, you know what I mean."

"I get you," whispered the Bison.

"I think I do, too," Gardener said.

"It's a big corporation now, called Barnum and Bailey," said Bailey. "And I can tell you a secret. There is riffle water that never freezes, and the government is very interested in it. My associate, Mr. Dobson here, can verify it if he will."

He motioned toward Dobson, who sat with his mouth in his hands. "You have to collect it for maximum ionization over the limestone at the precise time of night for correct moonlight. If they would pay $100 just for the first bottle, can you imagine all the wealth for just knowing when to collect it with the volume of water that stream carries?"

Dobson was shaking his head.

"No, it ain't so," said the Bison as Gardener looked at him while scratching his hair.

"But it is so. All you have to do is collect it in glass bottles like the ones your 'cream' comes in, and let nature check it for you. The bottles that aren't good will freeze and break. You only have to write down the time of night you collect the riffle water. Here's our card on it. Keep it with you. We'll be watching for your first results. Barkeep, one more caffeine for each of us, and a drink each for Bison and Gardener, whatever they're having, and put it on my tab."

Dobson was looking at his friend with his eyebrows raised.

"That's nice of you," Gardener said.

"No, that's not nice of me," replied Bailey. "It's an investment. I am only too anxious to see what two men of your obvious intellectual capacities might bring me in the way of perfectly ionized riffle water. Remember, you have to collect it at night, and no hour is too odd to be out there."

As Bailey and Dobson sat in the warming car watching the Bison stroll out with the Gardener teetering around carrying a box of empty bottles behind him, Dobson said, "I can't believe you said all of that without getting your lights punched out. I don't know who put on the biggest show, you or them. That Bison is a local businessman. He might be cold and stiff in the morning, but he might also remember this. It was just a weird night. I don't like drunks. What are you going to do if they ever show up?"

"I'm not worried," said Bailey. "I gave them your card.

Generosity has a downside sometimes

TOO MUCH generosity can be deadly. For whom, you might ask? Well, you decide. You see, Harlan Medlam had a nephew whose childhood photo was on his dresser.

Harlan only had a nephew because he'd had a sister, Susanna, who'd had a son named Steven. Generosity may not have had anything to do with Harlan Medlam having a nephew.

Steven lived up a headwaters branch of the creek, several miles north of Harlan Medlam—which, even though he did care for the old man, was sometimes just not far enough away for Steven.

Steven shared a trait with his deceased parents. He mostly liked to see Harlan Medlam at reunions and celebrations because if Harlan's old black truck pulled into the driveway, it either meant he needed his nephew to do something for him or he had figured out how to make some money from him.

Harlan Medlam decided that Steven probably was in trouble. But old habits die hard.

Harlan knew Steven had done the best he could do. It was all he could do on his clay-dust, pebble-strewn, upland fields bordering the creek headwaters. He didn't have the years of tightwad scrounging behind him that Harlan Medlam had to deepen his pockets.

When Steven looked at himself in the mirror each morning, he saw a face once a ruddy tan now growing gray with anxiety and sleeplessness. There were black circles under the eyes, a face somehow both puffy and filled with stress lines.

As he paused in the quiet air of one early morning to tap snow off the firewood he was taking into the house, he realized his efforts could be like his nearly totally dwindled pile of wood: not quite enough.

Low grain prices, low livestock prices and a long-term drought were catching up with him. The high land prices that had produced the financial equity to carry him for bank loans through the first few years of the hard times were coming down with only fellow farmers to bid for it.

Last fall, the same banker who had loaned him money to expand told him the next July payment from his wheat crop better be there. He hinted that it might be wise, considering Steven's cash flow, to consider other employment or possibly sell out.

And do what, Steven wondered. Who would hire a man in his late 50s who had never done anything else but what he did right now. He figured he was too old to start over, but too young to retire. There would be no more loans without radical change.

So, he had risked it all for one final effort. Wheat was the predominant thing he grew anyway, and he put all of his acres in it. He sold what few cattle he owned and the equipment to handle them. He kept a tractor, tillage tools and a planting drill for one more chance that things might get better. He could hire somebody else to combine the golden grain at harvest rather than own the expensive machine himself.

Steven kept enough money from the sales to plant one more wheat crop and barely cover personal expenses until next summer. He paid what he could on his debt.

The children were grown and gone. His wife, Jeannie, took a job in town at the library to do what she could do.

When the August sun scalded the earth in the waning days of summer, Steven got his equipment ready. He scrimped on using any more of the diesel fuel left in the farm tank than he had to. He warehoused the seed wheat in hopes that somehow there would be fall rains to germinate and grow the winter wheat as the seasons changed.

The heat of August continued through the fist half of September.

He delayed planting until the second half of September, watching the days growing shorter, and the season for planting the wheat turning late. He hoped for a fall shower to mellow the ground.

Finally, with the first chill of October, a quarter-inch rain fell. It was the best chance yet for enough moisture to germinate the wheat, Steven thought. Why not take it?

He drilled the seed wheat in powdery soil the small rain had barely penetrated, with clouds of dust billowing behind him.

Long days of riding the tractor, aching, tired and dirty at the end of each one, began to fill him with hope instead of despair. Doing something about the situation, taking action, was always better than the waiting.

In the evenings he would take his hat off to rub the front of his bare scalp, thinking about how much he had done that day. In the mornings before she left, he and Jeannie would pray for the wheat.

November came in dry, cold and blowing with no wheat sprouts showing. The soil blew in wave-type eddies along the surface of the fields on the gentler wind days. On the harder wind days it began to make dust drifts around the edges. Blowout, Steven began to tell himself. The wind would be his finish. An ice storm late in the month stopped the dust.

Steven got the chainsaw out to start cutting firewood from the deadfalls along his fence lines and the creek, hauling it back to the house on his pickup truck.

The ice scarcely began to melt when the first December snow fell. Christmas went by with Steven barely hanging on, smiling at the visits of his children but inside submerging himself to think, Hang on, just hang on.

Again, that snow barely began to melt when the first bitter great cold front of January brought blowing 3-inch snow over an earth so parched beneath that only the frozen crust of the earlier storms held it together.

Steven and Jeannie agreed to turn the thermostat down to 55 degrees so there would be fewer loads of household fuel to buy. They wore sock hats in the house. They dragged in an old wood stove from a shed, and hooked it into an existing chimney. They kept the stove fired up, especially in the evenings, for a time of warmth.

The end of January brought a brief two-day return of southern moist air. At first, it seemed the month might end in a thaw. Instead it met the cold air for a 12-inch heavy wet snow with big flakes that settled evenly over the ground with very little wind. Steven and Jeannie just watched it fall. She couldn't get to town to the library that week.

Ten days into February, it seemed like the weather might moderate. The top crust of the snow began to melt only to freeze a day later into a tough crust. The north wind began blowing hard bringing another 10 inches of much finer drifting snow with it.

The household fuel ran out as the outdoor temperatures fell to zero with continuous wind. Steven didn't want the fuel to be gone in such weather, so he checked everything twice, the thermostat, the furnace and the fuel tank.

They opened the damper further on the wood stove for more heat, and it ate the remaining firewood with quickened appetite. Steven and Jeannie shivered with thoughts of a future that seemed to grow more foreboding.

Steven realized that Jeannie's familiar rounded face under the brown hair was beginning to grow puffy and lined like his.

The south wind returned only to become stagnant with the chill returning as February prepared to turn to March. Jeannie returned to work on the day when there was only enough firewood left for two more days.

When she left, Steven was tempted simply to sit in a darkened room with his hands in his lap. But no, he decided, he had to take action again.

He put on his coveralls, coat, hat and boots, picked up his chainsaw, and waded through the deep snow along the timber by the creek. Down where his creek joined the main stream, he found what he was looking for. It was a deadfall of a tree variety at the westward limit of its native area—sycamore, distinctive with its mottled-white bark.

Steven had never burned sycamore before, but he looked forward to trying a new wood, seeing how much heat it threw and how long it lasted.

He cut sycamore most of the day, making a huge pile. It might last until warm weather returned if he cut only a little more to go with it, he told himself. Tomorrow he would get back to hand-carry it to the pickup at the road.

That night, he and Jeannie burned the remaining firewood at the house as though the supply was plentiful. He felt better.

Before bed, they stood on the porch for a while with their arms around each other, smelling a resurgent south wind that moaned through the yard trees with its strength. It carried a scent of green growth, a sure sign of coming spring.

At midnight, the end of winter was heralded with a boom of thunder, and Steven and Jeannie looked out the window in surprise at the gnarled devil's hand forks of lighting spreading across the sky. Then it began to rain, chilled and heavy.

Snow melt and rain combined. In the morning, the creek was a swollen lead-gray mass out hundreds of feet along its banks that could be seen a half-mile away.

Steven could feel comfortable sitting on the porch in the quickly warming air, a now gentle breeze caressing his face.

As the water lowered, he traveled downstream to see the next blow nature had dealt him. His sycamore firewood was gone, carried away by the water.

That night Steven and Jeannie sat in the chilled house, sometimes grasping each other's hands as a television program mercifully blotted out for the moment what the elements and the world seemed to be doing to them.

Jeannie only had a half-day of work the next day, Saturday. She arrived home, and was unloading groceries when an old 1950s-style black truck pulled into the driveway.

She came in, eyebrows raised shaking her head, to announce, "Steven, your Uncle Harlan is out there."

Oh my sweet lord, Steven thought, coming out of his despondent lethargy. With all of nature arrayed against me why on this day of all days do you remind me that I have an uncle like Harlan Medlam, as tight and opportunistic an old man as you have in all of creation?

The old man was just sitting in his truck, his flat hat pulled low on his brow. He was looking intently around at the buildings, missing nothing, with an occasional bowing glance out the passenger-side window to see if Steven was coming.

"Hello, Uncle Harlan," Steven said as the old man rolled down the window to motion him closer.

"Steven, think you might come down to help me a mite this afternoon? Got some firewood to load, and I can't find any of the neighbors at home to help me."

"Uncle Harlan, would you put your teeth in your mouth?"

"I got'em here in my pocket. Put'em in if it really bothers you, but it's more comfortable with'em out. I can eat OK without'em if I want to. OK, that better?" Harlan asked in a mouth-spread-wide grimace under his dark sharp eyes.

"Yes, that's better."

"I see you bet heavy on wheat this year. See you sold your cows too. If you're of a mind to sell land, you know I might be interested in a little more ground. Of course, it's not worth much now, maybe 50 cents on the dollar what you gave for it.

"Of course, if you're doing just fine," Harlan said, holding up a glass platter, "I brought this cut-glass cake platter along that your mother gave Florence. Jeannie could use it."

He looked at Jeannie who now stood behind Steven.

"Thought we'd take it to the antique dealer, but offer it to you first since it's family. We only want $200 for it."

"Harlan," Jeannie said, "why don't you just leave Steven alone? We don't have any money."

"She's right, Uncle Harlan," Steven said with a sigh. "And, why would you be interested in any more land anyway? You're in your 80s, and here I am only in my 50s wishing I could retire. I'll probably be working the rest of my life."

"Well, I ain't dead yet," Harlan said. "What's wrong with working the rest of your life if you get plenty to eat and take naps whenever you want? I need my rest, you know. But a body's got to seize every opportunity of the moment it can, don't it?"

"Uncle Harlan, I got to admit, I'm ready to give up," Steven said, putting his face in his hand as Jeannie wrapped her arm protectively around him.

"Well, have you gone west to look at your wheat field this morning? Both of you, get in this truck with me now. Don't just look at me," Harlan snapped. "Do what I say for once for the sake of your mother. Now get in here. Throw the rag on the floor, and stick my cigar in the glove compartment. It's only half-smoked."

At the top of the west hill, Harlan parked his truck to the side while they looked out across the broad wheat field, the snow washed away by the rain and warm air, a bright rainbow showing in the distance through the parting mists.

The warming sun illuminated the bright green mass of wheat growth. It had germinated under the snow.

Harlan Medlam grinned at them, his brown face crinkling in a mass of wrinkles around the white teeth.

"See there. Pull your backbone back together, boy. You got years to work yet, maybe do a little more for your poor old uncle along the way. Now unless you really got something in the oven, we'll drive down the creek to my place to pick up that firewood.

"I guess I could let you have half of it for helping. It was the darndest thing I ever saw anyway, all sycamore already sawed. Suppose you'd call it an answer to prayer. It was all carried down by the creek to stick in a pile at the stone bridge, just as pretty as you could see for me to pick up.

"Haarmph, let's see, let's see. I suppose Susanna would like you to have the plate. You're going to have quite a wheat crop. We really ought to keep it in the family, so you can pay me for it after harvest.

"You ought to have a few cows again. The neighbors had pretty good bulls last year, so I have some great heifer calves. Tut, tut, don't say anything now. I'm proud to help you out. They're really top quality, but for you, why they won't cost much over premium market price even as good breeding stock.

"I'm gettin' 3 percent on my money down at the bank. A fella's got to get more for financing somebody though, but I'll only charge you 5 percent. I'll be proud to show you how to load them when you come down with your truck to get them, and your payments won't even start until the wheat's sold.

"Now, now, I know you're breathin' a sigh of relief," Harlan smiled at them again as he licked his lips."But you don't have to just sit there looking at me like that. I know I'm a hard cookie sometimes, but even a hard cookie can crumble a little around the edges.

"And, hey, what's the point of having an old uncle if I can't be here from time to time to help you out in your time of need? After all, family's family. There comes a time for us to be generous to each other."

He was just a
tough, old bird

UNCLE HENRY sat on the edge of his lawn chair, hands folded over the top of his cane, as the children danced around him in the glows of sunlight and family love.

Their mothers held the birthday cake before him, candles all lit, and the children ceased their jumping to begin the call, "Make a wish Uncle Henry. C'mon, make a wish so we can eat the cake and ice cream."

Henry tilted his head to squint at them from his round face, reaching up with one hand to pull the white cap snugger over his bald spot. "OK," he said. "I've made my wish, but we need to get that cake cut in a hurry because I'll tell you the wish with a story of who I am, OK?"

They put his plate with the angel food cake, vanilla ice cream and strawberries on a tray in his lap, and spread the dessert feast on blankets on the ground for the half-dozen children in their tennis shoes and blue jeans to sit around him.

Abner, his brother, called from the folding table alongside where the adults sat, "Henry, remember, you're the birthday boy. You promised the kids a birthday wish story. We're all ready to listen."

"Ah, well, I did promise the story, didn't I," Henry nodded, his head tilted again as he looked into the face of his small brown-haired niece, Annie, with mouth stuffed to overflowing.

"Well, I would wish to be a small boy again when the warmth of April brings the grass new green shooting from the ground, and the roses begin to sprout on the grandest day of the year. For me it was a day at least nearly as grand as Christmas, what a wish that could be to have a day as great again.

"That grand day was the day to go get new baby chickens at the hatchery. First we would go to the lumberyard where you walked through the back part where they had piles of lumber on two stories of catwalks. You'd smell that pitchey smell of new-cut pine, all sweet and burny to the nose at the same time. I could smell things a lot sharper then, I believe. They'd have burlap bags packed full of sawdust from the same piney lumber back by their big circle saw waiting for folks like us.

"You could lay your hands on the bags while your Dad and the lumberyard man stuffed the car trunk full of sacks of sawdust, that rough burlap cloth with little stickery bits of sawdust coming through it, giving just a little when you shoved on it. The piney smell, like somebody had been able to sweeten turpentine, seeped through the whole car from the trunk going on to the hatchery.

"At the hatchery, the man and woman would put little yellow fuzz-ball baby chickens into the cardboard boxes with the round holes poked through the sides. They were going 'peep, peep, peep' all over that hatchery, so many tiny voices they filled the place with noise. They would let me pick one up now and then very carefully to put it in the box too. They were really soft, and you had to hold them soft so you wouldn't squash one. Sometimes the little chick would nibble at the edge of your hand when you held him, and tickled just nice.

"The chicks were all straight-run White Rocks for us to raise for fry-

ers, all little yellow chicks that would grow into white chickens with meaty frames. Straight-run meant they were like you guys, both girls and boys, pullets and roosters. They didn't sort them out. Even though they were meat chickens, my Mom and Dad would keep part of the pullets for egg laying. They laid nice big brown-shelled eggs.

"But you know what? I spotted something different. Right next to all those little yellow chickens was an open box full of little black chicks. They really caught my eye. They were cute, and they were beautiful, I thought. I started begging my Mama right away if I could please just have a couple of those little black chickens. She said 'No,' because the little yellow chickens were what we came after. I caught my Dad looking at me, and I decided to say I really liked those little black chickens just in case the folks decided to give me some slack.

"Finally the hatchery woman gave me a grin, and reached in to get two of those little black chickens. She said, 'Oh, here we'll give him a couple. They're Black Australorpe cockerels, and I doubt we'll be selling them anyway. They only wanted the pullets.'

"Well, I was just really tickled. On the car-ride home, Abner and I'd poke our fingers in the holes to get chick-nibbled, and lots of times the little chickens would poke their beaks through. I'd get down on the seat to try to look through the holes in the boxes to see my little black chicks, and Abner would try to say they were his too.

"At home, Mom and Dad backed the car up to the brooder house, a tin roofed quonset-looking building, and they carried the bags of sawdust and the boxes of baby chickens in. They spread that sweet smelling sawdust on the floor for bedding, all fluffy to walk through. They put the tin electric brooder with little red flaps hanging down out in the middle for the baby chickens to get under to stay warm. They put little metal chicken troughs with chick grower in it around the brooder, and turned glass jars full of water upside down on little chick water saucers so the water could come out whenever the chicks drank the level down.

"Then we opened the boxes to take the baby chickens out all together putting them under the brooder so they could get warmed up a little coming into their new home. We didn't want any of them to get chilled. And, there was my two little black chickens. I held them for just a minute before putting them in, and they gave me a few little nibble pinches around the rims of my hands, like getting little kisses.

"It didn't take many days before those hundreds of little chickens were scurrying all over running out from under the brooder to peck feed out of the troughs, get drinks or cuddle up with each other. I liked to play with them without getting too rough for their soft little bodies, holding them, putting a finger under their breast until they flapped their tiny wings. My black chicks got a lot of attention from Abner and me.

"The chicks grew fast. They'd have little fights with their necks stretched out looking at each other, then rearing with their feet at their opponents. I pulled for my black chicks to do well in these matches, and they sure seemed to.

" They grew little wing feathers and neck feathers first over the fuzz, and as they got bigger and bigger, the feathers began to cover their whole bodies. The brooder house had wired-in runways coming out a little chicken door in the front, so when the chickens got bigger, they could come out to sun themselves. We'd pull weeds and grass to push through the wire to them, and they sure did like the greens.

"When they finally got big enough, Mom and Dad would come down to catch a few in the mornings for Dad to cut their heads off. I'd check later to make sure the black chickens hadn't been taken. Mom would gut the chickens killed, and dip them in scalding pails of water before picking the feathers off. I tried to help pluck them, but I was slow, and probably not of much account. Neither was Abner. She would have tin cans full of alcohol on fire at the house so the alcohol burned off the surface to singe the chickens over to take any pin feathers off that were left. It smelled like really strong candle wax, not perfumed, just the plain kind.

"I was sure relieved when it came time to turn the pullets that were being kept loose to graze, and catch bugs with the other chickens, and there were my two black chickens with them, almost all grown up.

"They got great big as the summer past by, nearly as tall as I was. There came a day when I came out the front door to play, and there was one of my roosters, great big and beautiful black, with shiney green in the black where the sun hit him. He had a fine big red comb on top his head, and a red wattle tongue under his beak. I thought he had to be one of the most beautiful chickens I had ever seen.

"But when I came down the porch stairs to get a closer look at that rooster, he stuck his neck out at me, and then ran right at me. He jumped clear up my belly thrashing me with his great big wings, and scraping me on the chest with his feet. I hollered really loud, and tried to get away.

"Then here came my other black chicken from the other way, and he jumped on me too. Between the two of them, those chickens had me on the ground while I rolled around, them beating me from the head down to the toes. Let me tell you, I was really scared. Then my Mom came out with a stick, and whacked them away from me. She held me while I cried. That was that. They weren't cute any more, and I sure didn't like those black roosters ever again.

"Hey, can I have just a little more cake and ice cream?"

The children watched Uncle Henry, and waited as he began to eat. "Well, what happened, Uncle Henry?" called out his smallest niece, Annie.

"Yeah," all the children cried out together. "What happened to the black chickens?"

"Didn't you get to play in your yard anymore, Uncle Henry?" Annie asked pushing back a wisp of her dark hair.

"Boy," said Uncle Henry smacking his lips together, "that sure was a good birthday dinner, especially the dessert. Yessir, I sure liked going to get baby chickens.

"Oh, the black roosters. Yes, we ate them. I forgave'em, but I didn't forget'em. I asked Dad to cut their heads off, and he did the next morning. Mom let me help pluck them, and she said those feathers came off harder than they did on a white chicken.

"I sure do like roasted chicken with new corn on the cob and tomatoes."

Annie stood up, and stomped her foot on the blanket, a tear beginning to trickle down her face. "Uncle Henry, you're just like Aunt Mary says you are. You're just a tough old bird."

The rise and fall
of chicken pickin'

GREAT HERDS of chickens once roamed the prairies of America. Their eggs were taken, and they were slaughtered by the hundreds of thousands for profit, and for Sunday dinners.

Most herds were white chickens, but here and there were exceptions of red, black, golden and barred chickens. People usually call them flocks instead of herds unless they have heard the thundering thump of chicken toes in the great stampedes of hens chasing the last grasshoppers of summer.

You have to learn to peck your grasshopper, and swallow it fast if you expect to do well as a chicken among chickens.

Ralphie Roshband, who came to raise range chickens behind his little white house on a rocky knob, said that made chickens a whole lot like the office workers he used to be with. Then he would grin, and rough down the manes of red-brown hair left on either side of his bald head.

To explain how Ralphie came to be there, you have to realize that these great herds of chickens came about because every farm home once had chickens roaming around its yards, and going to sleep at night in its accompanying coops from coast to coast in America, no matter what the other special crops and livestock of each farm. The farm families who kept them were both their best predators and their best shepherds.

In the last century, it became less profitable to keep chickens, and more profitable for the ranks of farmers thinned out to lower numbers because of economics and government policy to specialize in what they produced.

The chickens that once roamed free, breathing the sweet country air, and helping contain bugs and farmyard vegetation in their grazing, were confined to long chicken buildings for mass production. The mass production became more and more massive.

The number of people involved with chicken predation became fewer and fewer while chicken consumption and the financial capital to be tied up grew until only a few corporate structures seemed to control chicken destiny. The executive urge for chicken control profits resulted in chicken parts wrapped up in nuggets, strips and patties. There were few chicken writers left to chronicle that people once ate recognizable necks, last of course.

But with the beginning of the 21st century, there were still old-timers left who remembered the pleasures of chicken shepherding, and eating

truly farm-raised chickens that once grubbed for part of their food themselves.

Ralphie, in a moment of passion because of being downsized out of a company when he was in his 50s, remembered the romanticism of chicken-raising youth, and, scratching his long hump-backed beak of a nose, told his willowy, blonde wife, Roxie, "I shall raise range-fed chickens.

"They will be healthy and robust. They will have the firm, meaty flavor I remember from my youth. They will never be washed out, falling apart and brown-boned like some grocery store mass produced-chickens we have had. And, it will be fun. I will love my chickens, and treat them like the noble beasts they were meant to be, running out in the sunshine with their social peers, not huddling and debeaked in some cage."

So Ralphie and Roxie worked hard tending to the needs of their chickens, giving them names, watching them grow, and talking to each other about the social development of individual chickens. It was nothing to hear Roxie say, "You know that Reginald rooster is smaller than most of his flock, but boy is he aggressive. He got four black beetles when I turned over a rock. I guess you could say he's a Cornish Rock hound."

They got the new baby chickens in, brooded them under a heater until they began to develop feathers, then put them outside under open-bottomed cages on the grass. Each day the cage was dragged to fresh grass, and grain added for chicken consumption, no drugs, no antibiotics. As they grew, they returned them to a building only to turn them loose each day to roam the yards, and lock them back up at night when they returned.

Everything was taken personally. Ralphie once said, "You know that pullet, Pennie the 10th, is picking on Priscilla the 13th precisely because the predominant cockerals pick on her. That's it, Roxie, we never buy straight-run chicks again, only roosters. Also, don't ever name a chicken Ralphie again, OK?"

They were romantically obsessed with the life of rearing chickens.

Bird was obsessed too, with the idea of eating chicken like he remembered it as a youngster, good heavy, meaty, crispy but juicy fried chicken, maybe with a little hunk of yellow fat here and there, firm enough to catch in the teeth once in a while. Aaah, chicken and mashed potatoes and chicken gravy like Mom made, he thought, that would be heavenly. Maybe he'd have it with good rhubarb pie, and of course garden lettuce or perhaps celery would be OK. Or maybe he'd have chicken with green rhubarb cobbler, or if the season was right, sticks of rhubarb fresh out of the garden to dip in salt. Aaah, rhubarb and chicken, chicken and rhubarb, now there were some dreams worth having.

Bird had heard of range chickens too, and he read Roxie's and

Ralphie's advertisement in the Dirt Duster Weekly for chicken "The way it used to be."

So, one pristine golden bright sunny day Bird drove the gravel road out to the rock knob for his own range chicken, fairly salivating in anticipation as he went.

He caught Roxie and Ralphie out by the mailbox getting the mail.

"Hello," he said, rolling down the window. "Are you the folks selling chickens?"

"We certainly are," replied Ralphie. "I am Ralphie and this is my wife, Roxie. And your name would be?"

"Bird, just call me Bird, nothing else."

"Pleased to meet you, Mr. Bird. How many chickens will you be needing?"

"Oh, just one. But I'll probably be back for more if it's everything a range chicken is supposed to be."

"Don't worry. It will be. Our chickens are our perfection, all organically grown. So, you're a Bird here for a bird."

Bird looked at him, tight-lipped and grim. "I don't like puns on my name."

"Oh, sorry Mr. Bird. I didn't mean anything by it. We just try to be friendly on our tours here. So, you want to come out back, and we'll start where the baby chickens come in?"

"I don't want a tour. I just want a chicken, and if you raise any rhubarb, I'd be interested in that too, especially green, bitey-sour rhubarb."

"Yes, we have some rhubarb like that," Roxie spoke for the first time. "I could cut a sack of it for you. Ralphie could give you a tour of the chicken facilities while I do it. Everybody enjoys that, and usually people like to pick out their own chickens, and we sort of introduce them."

"The rhubarb sounds great, just great. But, if you don't mind, I'll just wait here by the car while you get the chicken and the rhubarb. I just want to relax, and enjoy this fresh air."

Ralphie stared in surprise for a moment looking at the round man with the noggin even more completely bald than his own. "Well, I guess we could do that if that's the way you really want it."

It wasn't quite 15 minutes later he returned with a white rooster tucked submissively under his arm.

"Mr. Bird," he said, holding the chicken outward nearly at arm-length close to Bird's face. "I want you to meet Chuckie the 16th, only the 16th because we run a lot of groups of chickens through here.

"Now Chuckie was precocious as a chick. He ate and drank right away when he came in, and he was the first of his group to grab an earth worm when they came out of the ground after a big rain. Chuckie has been as fast a growing chicken as ever a Cornish Rock could be. In fact he's the biggest chicken in his group, which is why I brought him out."

Bird looked away from the rooster that was tilting its head to look at him with shiny beady-black eyes while cackling lowly and nervously.

"You might notice that Chuckie has a large breast, and very round, large drumsticks."

"Look, I'm sure this chicken is an example of prime poultry, but I don't need to know it personally. Get it out of my face, will you?"

Ralphie looked with surprised open mouth at Roxie who was just returning with a sack of rhubarb. "Bird doesn't like Chuckie."

"No, no, I don't like or dislike this chicken any more or less than any other chicken you might have. Please, just take it back, and get me another chicken that you haven't tried to parade out here for me."

"You don't want Chuckie?"

"I couldn't give a whoop about Chuckie. I just want a chicken to eat."

"You want to butcher him yourself, or do you want us to process him for you?"

"Do it for me, won't you? I really don't feel like doing a chicken myself. You two just run along, get me a chicken already dressed for me to take home, and I'll try to enjoy what's left of this experience just waiting here at the car with the rhubarb. OK? The rhubarb does look good."

"That's alright, Roxie. You wait here with Mr. Bird, and I'll get him a chicken," said Ralphie, still with a wrinkle of puzzlement across his brow.

He returned later with a processed chicken in a plastic bag to find Roxie and Bird both munching on pieces of raw rhubarb. "Mr. Bird convinced me to try a stem of rhubarb this way," Roxie explained. "It's very good, but puckery."

Ralphie gave Bird the chicken, and Bird handed over the cash to complete the transaction. "I don't want you to feel badly that I didn't look around, and comply with your chicken routine," Bird said. "So, there's a dollar tip for you too, and don't worry, I'm sure this will be such good eating that I'll be back."

"Well, what do you think of that?" Ralphie asked as he and Roxie watched Bird's car speed away. "I introduced Chuckie to him and everything, and he just wasn't really interested, was he?"

"That's OK, Ralphie. Every customer's going to be a little different. You can't take it personally. So, which chicken did you finally get for him?"

"Why, I gave him Chuckie. We couldn't let a stranger eat him."

Knock-doc takes a whack at a sore mule

Author's note: A chiropracter tells me I actually got this one right. I'll be darned.

THE BIG man smelled.

That was the first thing Olive Primwaite noticed in the gust of wind he made hurrying through the door of the Manipulative Mechanical Medicine and Nutrition Center to her reception counter.

At least most people cleaned up before coming in, she thought looking at his disheveled green shirt, the chest hair poking from it up to his collar as curly brown as the 6-inch mop of hair on his head.

"Does the knock-doc work on animals?" he almost whined plaintively in a deep, gravelly voice.

Olive sniffed, and raised her penciled-black eyebrows at the crinkled face framed by oversized hairy ears above her.

"Dr. Dunhop is our doctor of chiropracty, and we are quite busy today. I know he has worked on dogs before, but I'll have to see if he'll depart from schedule to work on an animal today. You'll probably have to arrange a time later even if he's willing to work on your beast, Mr... uhh...."

"Oh, Muhlesburg's my name, Buzz Muhlesburg," he said with a smile hewn with oversized square white teeth. "And that's my wife, Gertrude, just now comin' in your door."

He gestured toward a short, thin-framed mousey woman wearing a blue denim hat with a pink artificial flower in it.

"Well, it's about time for Dr. Dunhop to take time to eat and have a break. This is new patient day. We may have 20 people coming in at one o'clock," Olive said. "Let's see if he might have time to talk to you now."

Olive stared at the petite Gertrude standing primly with purse held in front of her at chest height, not even as tall as Buzz Muhlesburg's shoulder.

"How about you, dear? Would you care to have a seat while your husband talks to Dr. Dunhop?"

"Oh, no thank you," Gertrude replied in a thin little squeak of a voice. "I helped load the big mule, and I want to see the treatment."

"She sure did," Buzz rasped, clapping a big meaty hand gently across the thin little woman's back. "She slipped the winch cable down over his neck and chest to drag him on the trailer with while I held him up."

"You call your husband Mule? Or are you saying you brought a mule with you?" asked Olive putting her fingers on the penciled eyebrows that were rising too high by far.

"Why, we brought the knock-doc a mule to treat, lady," Buzz intoned

while grinning with what sounded like a load of gravel rising in his throat. "Our mule, Ebenezer, he's down in the back, can't get up. He's been such a good old mule, looks at you with those big old eyes almost teary-eyed. Why, just couldn't haul him off without trying to do something for him.

"The veterinarian was going to put him down, or have me haul him off to make meat scrap for dog food or Frenchmen. They send a lot of horse meat across the water, why not mule, huh? But old Ebenezer's nearly family, so I figured a knock-doc's worth a try."

"You brought me a mule to work on?" asked a little man from the doorway behind Olive, a sandy-haired man, nearly as small as Gertrude, wearing thick glasses. "I'm Dr. Dunhop. I'll take a look at the mule. I'm intrigued by cross-species treatment integration."

"Come on, Doc. We got him out in the alley on a two-wheel flatbed behind my truck."

Ebenezer was a big John mule, one of those thousand pounders, all stretched out gray-brown, rear legs to one side, front legs underneath him, on a 12-foot-long flatbed trailer little more than two feet off the ground.

Dr. Dunhop showed no hesitation, hopping up on the trailer to probe with his fingers up and down Ebenezer's smelly, long, broad bony spine, pausing to work and dig his knuckles deep into some vertebrae a third of the way up from the bushy tail.

Haaaw, Ebenezer moaned softly, laying his long ears back to try to turn his head to look at tiny Dr. Dunhop, who seemed dwarfed by the big mule's dimensions.

Dr. Dunhop worked his way to Ebenezer's hairy face, nearly as long as his own body, while the animal drooped his lower lip, and looked at him with big, brown sad eyes.

"Aah, poor old fellow, in pain aren't you?" said Dr. Dunhop, fairly cooing while he looked back through thick glasses. "Yes, it hurts doesn't it?"

He put his fingers on the mule's face to press down hard. Then he began to rub.

"The knock-doc's got a way with animals, huh, Gertrude?" Buzz noted.

"Sure does, sure does," squeaked the small woman poking her tongue in the corner of her mouth. "Just jumped right in there with that big mule. Not scared of him at all, poked his fingers right in his face."

"I'm not just poking him," said Dr. Dunhop. "This is myofacia release. It helps relieve the pain. We're relaxing Ebenezer before we adjust him."

"How are you going to adjust him, Doc? He's kind of big to just pop into place isn't he?" asked Buzz.

"Tell you what, Buzz. You go over behind the building there, and get me one of those 2x4s, about an 8-foot sturdy stud will do just fine. Better bring two of them. And, you wouldn't happen to have some kind of hammer like a big mallet in that old truck of yours would you?"

"Sure do, Doc. I got a short-handled sledge hammer I've been using to drive electric fence posts."

"Yes, that will do. That will do just fine. Now, Buzz, I'm going to have you grab a big wad of Ebenezer's tail to pull up on. Gertrude, you and I are going to slip those 2x4s under him to pry up. We'll just all lift together so I can slip his rear legs under him. I want him all stretched out with that spine in a straight line, all together now, lift, lift (puff, puff), aah."

Haaaw, replied Ebenezer softly.

"Not quite right, but close. Now, Buzz, you tie your rope around Ebenezer's tail, pull tight, and tie it around that utility pole over there. Then get in your truck, and give one or two more clicks on that winch around his front end. I want to straighten him, and get a little more pull on him.

"That's right, that's right. Now hand me that 2x4 and the mallet. Um hmm, um hm, got to wedge the end of the 2x4 against this vertebrae just right."

Dr. Dunhop pushed the 2x4 snugly into position on Ebenezer's back, then stood a moment, changing the angle of the board up and down, side to side, squinting down it to get it correct.

"Lordy, this is going to hurt," said Gertrude, an octave higher than usual. She was holding her hands to the sides of her head.

"No, Gertrude," chuckled Dr. Dunhop. "It won't hurt us a bit."

Then, holding the 2x4 steadily in one hand, he swung the mallet overhand in a mighty blow to the end of the board, and there was a resounding ker-pop noise.

Eeee-haaaaw, bellowed Ebenezer as he suddenly began trying to bounce on the trailer with the previously numb hind legs.

"Praise the lord, praise the lord," hollered Gertrude, jumping up and down. "The big mule's cured."

"Quick, Buzz, get that rope loose, then let's get that winch loosened," Dr. Dunhop called while pushing his glasses back in place.

His bonds loosened, Ebenezer the mule got shakily to his feet. Then, with a couple of tentative kicks, scattered the 2x4s 20 feet apart. Ebenezer's big white teeth shown for one moment in the sun as he turned to bite Dr. Dunhop—to give him myofacia release, of course. But Dunhop deftly hopped out of the way.

"Yeow, he almost got you, Doc," squealed Gertrude still hopping up and down hanging onto her flowered hat."

"Ooh, Doc," said Buzz holding onto his back. "This all kind of got to me too. Think you could work me in for a quick treatment inside before we go?"

"Sure, Buzz," said Dr. Dunhop, smiling and still swinging the mallet in his hand with the joy of the healing as he and the others walked away with Ebenezer stomping on the trailer behind them in newfound vigor. "It's good to see him respond so quickly. Maybe I could come to the farm for his next treatment instead of you going to all this trouble. We'll need to put both of you on a treatment schedule."

The waiting room was already full, and Gertrude plopped herself down beside a large, plump woman. After Buzz and Dr. Dunhop went into the back, Olive could see Gertrude motioning toward the other people still jabbering with excitement.

"I tell you, we just saw a treatment you wouldn't believe," she said. "It was a near miracle the way he got up. But of course, the knock-doc wants him back for more.

"The big mule. I had a heck of a time getting him in here."

"He was awesome all right," whispered a girl across the room to her mother. "I just saw the big hunk come through."

"Had to winch him in," said Gertrude. "Ooh, you got to be a little rough when they're so big, the great bristled beast, got those big old hairy ears you know too."

The little woman squeaked in an ever-higher pitch as she continued, putting her hands to the sides of her head to wiggle them back and forth like mule ears.

The tall, thin man in the corner was bending forward to hear what she was saying. So was the young man in jogging shorts. The old man and woman on the far side of the room turned to look at each other every time she spoke. The plump woman had her hand on her mouth. Gertrude liked a good audience.

The old man put his hand to the side of his mouth to murmur to his wife, "What's that little woman talking about?"

His wife replied, "She says her husband's just a big rough old mule. Couldn't you smell him when he went through?"

"I knew he could be mean," Gertrude added. "He tried to bite the knock-doc with those big white teeth later on, you know."

Gertrude pursed her little pink lips and shook her head. "Don't I live around him all the time? I know he can be mean. But there was the Doc up there unafraid, giving him that myofacia release for his pain.

"Then the doc gets the 2x4, and sticks it in his back, and pounds it with the mallet. I tell you, that made the big smelly mule kick."

The old woman was whispering to her husband with a shocked expression. "She says the chiropractor used a mallet and 2x4 on him."

The phone rang. After Olive answered it, she hurried into the back treatment room away from where the visitors waited to say,

"Oh Mr. Muhlesburg, quickly, quickly you must go. That was the people across the alley. Your mule is off the trailer, pulling on your winch, and bucking. They say he's about to drag the whole rig off."

Buzz jumped to his feet, and ran to the door. "Got to stop Ebenezer," he brayed in his long drawn-out rasp as he dashed past Gertrude.

"Wait, wait," said Olive. "You're forgetting your mallet."

"I'll catch up to him with it," said Dr. Dunhop, grabbing the mallet to trot with it through the waiting room. "Buzz, Buzz, wait," he hollered. "Buzz Muhlesburg, wait on me."

"Lordy, lordy, the big mule's gotten away," yelled Gertrude, jumping up and down before running out the door behind Dr. Dunhop.

The old man looked at his wife, and said, "Looks like he made a break for it. Help me up. Let's get out of here before the doctor catches him with that hammer."

The plump woman looked for a moment with open mouth at Olive behind the reception counter. The thin man stood, hesitated, then trotted for the door, where he and the young man in the jogging shorts struggled to get through at the same time until the plump woman pushed them through to completion. She was followed by the remainder of the 20 new patients.

None of them ever came back except for Gertrude and Buzz Muhlesburg, who were put on a regular mechanical manipulation schedule.

Harlan Medlam gets an adjustment

OLIVE PRIMWAITE had been pressure massaging beneath her closed eyes to stop an oncoming headache when she sensed somebody watching her closely. Too closely.

She nearly jumped a foot backward from her reception counter at the Manipulative Mechanical Medicine and Nutrition Center when she opened her eyes to find the nose of an elderly woman a scant four inches from her own.

Obviously she was a country woman, Olive thought—no make-up, long white hair tied sternly back in a neat bun, roughed calloused hand, like a man's, on her counter.

Olive raised her own penciled black eyebrows above carefully blushed cheeks and lipsticked mouth to say, "Oh, you startled me. Can I help you, ma'am?"

"Why, I sure hope you can. I'm Florence Medlam, and I was wondering if the knock-doc might be able to work someone in real soon today."

"Knock-doc? Knock-doc, indeed," Olive said, frowning. "I don't know what it is with people around here that they would bestow such a title. Dr. Dunhop is a chiropractor, a doctor of chiropracty, an educated man. He doesn't just knock people carelessly around."

"Well, excuse me, sweetie. But I still need to know if he can work someone in."

"It isn't an animal, is it?"

"Oh, you mean like with the mule?"

"You heard about that already?"

"Sure did, honey. I heard the doc did real well, too. That's why I'm here. I figured any chiropractor who could work on a mule might be able to work on my husband."

"My name is Miss Primwaite, not sweetie or honey. And, what is your husband's name?"

"My husband's Harlan Medlam, and he's hurtin' real bad. I got him laying down on some hay in the back of the truck. He's going to have a hard time walking in."

"Was he injured in an accident?"

"Well, he got hurt, but I wouldn't call it an accident since he did it to himself on purpose. You see, we had a fierce big wind storm, and it knocked a big limb out of our elm tree.

"My husband," continued Florence, "the poor old dear, just works terrible hard all the time, and after dinner he always goes out to take a nap on the bench under the tree. Well, sometimes he takes a nap before dinner, too, if the crops are in, and I haven't told him what else to do—

although most of the time he can count on me telling him what to do. Time waits for no man, you know.

"Anyway, that broken limb let a big beam of sunshine right through on the bench. Harlan was too tired to move the bench since he was waiting on the neighbors to come help pick up the limb, and he figured they might as well move the bench while they were at it. So, he laid down on the gravel, and he woke up with a big chunk of rock in the middle of his back that must have pushed his backbone out."

"Well, if he is in pain, I suppose Dr. Dunhop will see him right now," said Olive.

"Oh, he's in terrible traumatic pain." Florence paused, and lowered her voice to a conspiratorial whisper. "See here, Miss Primwaite, the knock-doc isn't a Jap, is he? Because I know lots of them are short, and I hear he is?"

"No, I think Dr. Dunhop's ancestors were of the Swiss persuasion. Why, did your husband see action in the war?"

"No, but a couple of neighbor boys did, and since Harlan bought their farms out at bargain rates when they had to go away, he always figured it was becoming of him to hold it against the Japanese. He could have held it against the Germans, but the neighbor boys were of German ancestry just like we are, so that becomes harder to hold onto. Anyway, Harlan won't abide going to Asians except for the times we sold eggs to them."

"I see. Well, perhaps Dr. Dunhop would be willing to take your husband during his lunch break which begins in about 45 minutes. Would that give you time to get Mr. Medlam?"

"Oh, that won't take any time at all. He's just out front laying in the back of the truck on some hay, right where me and a couple of neighbors put him. I think he fell asleep on the way to town, and he's peaceful except when I try to talk to him. Then he starts groaning.

"Now, the knock-doc isn't going to stick any needles in him, is he, because Harlan doesn't like needles in him? They had to give him a couple snorts of morphine to hold him still to get his teeth out. Matter of fact, he's a little leery of coming to Dr. Dunhop, but I convinced him it was worth the money so he could work sooner."

"No, no, the practice is strictly manipulative, no needles or bodily intrusions of any kind at all, Mrs. Medlam. The doctor will take some x-rays, look at them, and give a treatment to help Mr. Medlam recover from his sleeping accident."

"No, Harlan won't need the x-rays or anything else—except just the basic treatment to pop him back in place. We can't afford much," Florence said, assuming a plaintive look, half-lowering her eyes. "Just how much is the basic treatment, Miss Primwaite, honey? Oh, excuse me, I forgot, no more honey."

"It's $20 for an adjustment."

"Ye gawds, $20. Harlan Medlam will be fit to be tied. He's never spent as much as $20 at once unless there's a way for us to make money from it. But he's got to be helped, there's no way around it. He's in his 80s, so we hadn't ought to expect him to get back to work without help."

"I think you'll find that $20 is a very modest charge, Mrs. Medlam."

"You can just call me Florence, Miss Olive Primwaite. You are a sweet-looking girl, you know. You should have been married a long time ago, but I know times are tough."

"Yes, well, perhaps you could just have a seat in the waiting room until Dr. Dunhop's ready. You can call me Olive, too, if you'll remember not to call me honey."

"Naah, I'll just go out, sit on the tailgate, and talk to Harlan about my plans for harvest, and for getting another cow for him to milk, and for getting some used lumber to build another pig hutch, you know, wife talk. When Dr. Dunhop's ready, just have him hop out there to help unload Harlan."

Soon, Dr. Dunhop was ready.

"Aaaagh," wailed Harlan Medlam as Florence grabbed him by the ankles to drag him toward the tailgate.

"Wait, wait a minute, ma'am, I think we can ease him off more gently than that," said Dr. Dunhop, holding his hands above his short frame, and grimacing. "Let me reach up in there, Mr. Medlam, sir. I think you may have caught a piece of baling wire around your overalls strap as you were dragged."

"Florence, get my teeth off the dash of the truck so I can talk plain to the doctor here. I guess you're the doctor aren't you?" asked Harlan, neck cords standing out on his dark, scrawny throat as he tried to raise his head to see. "You're kind of young to go messing around with people aren't you?"

"Well, Mr. Medlam, I'll never see 30 again, and I'm fully credentialed with some years of practice behind me."

"Stop pulling at my feet, Florence, and hand me them teeth. You aren't thinking to use a hammer and a 2x4 on me like you did Buzz Muhlesburg's mule, are you? He told me all about it, cuz he says he likes to stop to see me since he doesn't live next to me."

"No, Mr. Medlam, I just use my hands on human beings."

"You can call me Harlan if you're thinking of getting close enough to put your hands on me. And you aren't going to try to stick needles in me or anything, are you?"

"No, Harlan. Just calm down, and try to relax. I don't do anything like that, and you need to be calm to be treated best."

"Oh, I'm calm all right. But are you really going to take hold of me, and just pop me by the backbone, horrible, horrible to have to be seized up like that?"

"It doesn't hurt, Harlan. I just gently probe, and feel where the problem is, and manipulate you back into place. There are some quick shoves on your back, but most people feel relief right away."

"I knew it, you're going to pop me. Here, Florence, get up here in this truck, and get me dragged to the front. Let's just go home. I can't bear the thought of my backbone gettin' snapped. Reminds me of once when a tomcat got under the back tire—terrible, terrible."

"Please, Harlan," said Dr. Dunhop. "You need help. I can guarantee you'll feel better, and this won't hurt a bit."

"Well, you must really need new patients."

"Harlan, I'm here to help heal people."

"Come on, Harlan," said Florence. "You need the help or we aren't going to get anything more done. You won't even be able to be comfortable taking naps."

Harlan paused. "Well, that's true, Florence. I need my rest peaceful. How much do you charge, Dunhop?"

"The basic treatment, just like my receptionist told your wife, is $20."

"Gaawd, that's awful. A person could work and connive all week, and still have a hard time making $20. Merciful heavens, that's terrible, it's manipulatin' all right. We can't throw money around like that. Drag me to the front of the truck, Florence, let's get out of here. How could you act like we're going to do a thing like this for $20? Twenty dollars—that's just unbelievable."

"Look, Harlan," said Dr. Dunhop brushing his fingertips against the beads of sweat collecting along the front of his sandy-haired crewcut. "You need treatment. If $20 is unaffordable for you, we'll adjust the price. Just let us get you in there."

"How much will you adjust the price?"

"We'll talk about it in the treatment room, OK? Let's just get you in there."

"Oh, ho, ho, ho, ho, aaagh," moaned Harlan,simmering out the side of his mouth, as Dr. Dunhop supported him under one arm and Florence under the other arm in a gimping hip-hop limp to the clinic door.

"OK, Harlan, let's unbutton your overalls straps, and pull the front down over your shirt before we lay you on the bench," said Dr. Dunhop, Olive running ahead to open doors.

"Naked? You're going to get me naked for this? You didn't say anything about getting me naked, especially not with this new young woman around. Florence, get me back to the truck. Let's just go home. I'll heal."

"The ladies can both leave the room, Harlan. I only need to have the top of your overalls down, so I can feel through your shirt easily. You won't be naked. You'll just lay face-down on my adjusting bench there while I check, and manipulate your back."

"But I could smother. You going to make me put my face between those cushions there on the tissue paper? A body could smother like that. And say, what about my neck? You aren't going to try that deal where you take hold of my head, and pop my neck are you? Florence, get me to the truck, and—"

"Harlan," said Dr. Dunhop. "If it will make you feel more comfortable. We'll just forget the $20 entirely. This will be just an introductory session. I promise you, none of this will hurt. You'll breath easily. You won't smother."

"Well," huffed Harlan. "I guess that can make me a little more comfortable."

"Now, ladies, after you help me get him down here, you just go out into the waiting room, and close the door behind you."

"I hope he'll feel better so we can get back to business," Florence said to Olive in the outer room.

"Oh, he will—they all do," she replied as they heard Harlan moaning a soft "oooh" in the next room.

Twenty minutes later, Harlan shuffled out hunching his shoulders as if loosening up. Dr. Dunhop stopped in the door to watch him walk.

Harlan grinned at Florence. "Feel 10 times better already. I'm a little stiff but I'll loosen up. The neighbors will have moved my bench back under the shade by now, so after supper, a little nap should help."

Harlan popped his hands together after crawling in the front seat of the truck, and opened them to show Florence a five-dollar bill.

"Where did you get that, Harlan Medlam?"

"Dunhop the knock-doc done gave it to me to get me to let him do my neck. It was worth it too. My neck feels a whole lot better. Not bad for a half-hour's work—$20 credit, $5 cash, $25 ahead.

"Guess we ought to stop at the co-op on the way home for me to get a cigar to celebrate."

Buck Barnsworth's driving days end with a final thump

Author's note: My apology to everyone out there who has reached an age where you feel you just can't do as much as you used to. Are we humorous, tragic or admirable? Certainly these traits aren't far apart.

"WATCH WHERE you're going, Buck," said Rosie to the small white-haired man humped over the steering wheel next to her, looking over his silver-rimmed glasses at the interstate. "You were driving over the center line."

"I don' know, I just don' know. Did you say something?"

"I said, TURN UP YOUR HEARING AID, and quit saying 'I don't know' to me. I'm sick to death of it. You were driving over the center line. Aaaagh," hollered Rosie.

"Aaaagh," hollered Buck, looking first at her and then out his side window. "Stupid 18-wheeler's comin' awfully close to us. They let them kids out on the road without enough practice these days."

"Watch your driving, and look where you're going. He probably had to get close to us to get around us. Look at the gap between the right side of the car and the right side of the highway. You can move over."

"Don't know why the idiot had to get around us so fast anyway. Look here, I'm drivin' 45 miles an hour. That's over the minimum speed on the signs. I don' know, I just don' know."

"What don't you know? Why do you keep saying that? I repeat, what is it you don't know?"

"Why, where we are? I don't know where we are. I never took the interstate before, but the boys at coffee said it's the quickest way to go. Where were we going, anyway? I don' know, I just don't know, I think I forgot."

"Why, we're going to our son's home, Dan Barnsworth. You've been there hundreds of times. He and his wife, Sheila, invited us over. Our other son, Bub, and his wife, Angie, will be coming over, too. Are you really that mixed up, Buck?"

"I don' know, I don' know how we got to goin' the way we're goin', going this way."

"How do you expect me to tell you? For once, I don't know either. I wasn't watching, and I've never come this way. Are you sure you went the right way? Get off at this exit, and let's ask directions."

"I don' know about that, I just don' know. What if they don't know Dan?"

"You don't ask them if they know Dan. You just tell them where he lives. That's right, just pull into this little shopping center here. Pull up into that space at the side of the building, Buck. Buck, Buck, slow it down a little, Buck."

THUMP.

"My goodness, you jumped the curb, and thumped the side of the building."

"I don' know, I just don' know that it really hurt anything. Let me back up here. Naah, see there, nothin' really hurt, just peeled a little paint off."

"Buck, put your foot on the brake while you're looking. Stop the car."

CRUNCH.

"Oh, great, super. You've hit the door on the car behind us."

"I don' know why you're so worried. I just don' know. I can see that car in the side mirror. We didn't hurt it any. Come on, we're just gonna get back on the interstate, and find the way ourselves, maybe, I think so anyway, I just don' know."

"Buck, do you really think we should have left back there without saying anything to anybody? Hey, you'd better get back up over 40 again getting on here, watch it, now watch it, Buck. Can't you see there are cars coming?"

"Jeez louise, why are they all honking at us? I don' know, I just don' know why they can't tell I already know they're going to go around me."

"Breath easy now. Let's both just draw deep breaths, and try to think. We'll surely see something familiar, or think where we're going here soon."

"I don' know, I just don' know that anything's lookin' familiar. I'm signaling left now. We're going to drive down through the grass strip in the middle of this road, and go back the other way."

"Do you really think we ought to be doing this, Buck? I mean, somebody told me once that only policemen could do this legally on an interstate."

"Why can't they all quit honking at us every time we move? Jeez louise, I just don' know why they do that? We made it through the grass, didn't we? And, I'm going the right way, just like the other cars going around us. Aaagh."

"Aaagh."

"Jeez louise those big trucks can come close to you, can't they? I just don' know, I just can't figger what it is with those guys."

"Buck, there's a highway patrolman behind us."

"Yeah, I see him. I don' know what he's doin', thinks he's going to a fire or something, I just don' know."

"I think his red lights are on because he's trying to tell you we have to stop."

"I don' know, I just don' know about that. Looks kind of dangerous to stop here to me with all the trucks set to buzz a person. We'll get off here at this exit, and pull into that motel restaurant lot. Watch to see if he follows like maybe he wants to visit with us or something. I don' know but what it looks like he's following, I just don' know."

"Let's just park right here in the middle between the white lines, Buck, so we can't hit anything with the patrolman watching. That's right, dear, just put it in park. I think the patrolman's tapping on your window. My, he was fast getting up here, wasn't he?"

"Hello, officer. I don' know, I just can't quite recall this countryside. I just don' know where we're at. It's real fortunate you came along here, cuz I think I could use some directions, but I don' know, I really can't say for sure if we might have got it worked out anyway."

"Sir, I stopped you because you were weaving around on the interstate, going slower than the minimum speed part of the time. We've also had reports of a vehicle matching this description going over the center line much of the time, going through the interstate medium in an illegal U-turn, and being involved in possible damage in some parking lot collisions. Sir, did you leave the scene of an accident?"

"Well, I don' know, I just don' know whether we can determine what was legal or not."

"Sir, may I see your driver's license?"

"Sure, sure, don' know why you didn't ask in the first place. Got it right here in my wallet. I thought I did anyway, here someplace, I don' know, I just can't see it. Rosie, have you done something with my license?"

"No, I didn't do anything with it, Buck. But you had it out the other night when you were telling me you just didn't know about all this identity theft going on."

"Oh, I did, I did, but I just don' know—yes, I do too know. Officer, here, take my keys, and open the trunk. Look under the spare tire. I put it there so nobody could find my identity. I didn't know it would work so well."

"OK, sir, I found your license. Where were you going?"

"To my son's house—to Dan Barnsworth's house, that is. But I don' know right now, I just can't recollect where it is unless you know him."

"I tell you what, sir. I'm just going to keep your license, so we don't have to press any charges. You won't be driving anymore. Perhaps your wife can give me your son's telephone number. We'll call him to come get you. I'll give your keys to a waitress I know in here named Ruby. She'll hold on to them until your son gets here for her to hand them to him. I'll be telling her not to give them to you. Do you understand, sir?"

"I don' know, I just don' know what's not to understand. You think I can't hear either? Hand me my cane there, Rosie. Let go of my arm, I can walk into a restaurant myself."

Buck Barnsworth watched the patrolman talk to the red-haired waitress, and tip his hat to them as he walked out. The waitress came over to them, a young 20-something, regarding them warmly with her green eyes, and smiling.

"Well," she said, "the officer called your son, and he'll be here soon to get you. Would you like something to drink or eat while you wait?"

"Tell her we don' know, we just don' know, Rosie," said Buck. "We didn't come in here to eat. I don' know, I just don' know but what we just been dumped here."

"Aah, come on, sir, it's not going to be that bad," said Ruby the waitress. "I'd guess that your son loves you, and he's coming to help you out. After a nice visit, you'll go back to your own house in your own hometown, and there will be people to help you out. Come on, at least have a cup of coffee, or a piece of pie. I'll treat if you're short on cash."

"I got my wallet, and I got money. I don' know much, but I know that," Buck grimaced.

"Got any rhubarb pie?" Rosie asked.

"Sure do, ma'am. We have strawberry-rhubarb, raisin-rhubarb and even some straight green rhubarb we keep back in the freezer for a customer who shows up from time to time. I can microwave you a piece of that."

"No, we'll have fresh strawberry-rhubarb."

The pie and coffee were consumed, and Ruby had served second cups of coffee when Dan and Bub walked in, followed by their wives.

"You guys, are you OK?" asked Sheila, curling her fists on her sides to give them a big hip shake.

"Mom, Dad, are you alright?" the boys blurted in unison.

"I don' know, I just don' know, yes, I suppose so," said Buck.

"Sure, we're fine, full, fat and happy," said Rosie.

"And now, young lady," said Buck, giving Ruby his own hip shake, "I'll be handing you a tip, and you'll be handing me my keys, I think, I know."

Dan was nodding his head at Ruby from behind his father as Ruby handed him the keys.

"Now, I don' know, I don' know for sure, but I suppose you all rode over here together."

"Yes, we did, Dad."

"Here, Dan, you drive my car, and Mom and I will ride home with you and Bub while the girls take your car. I don' know, I just don' know how tired I am. Why don't you just take us back home."

The drive home started in silence, but soon the conversation began.

"Dad," said Dan. "The patrolman told us he's not giving you your license back."

"He recommended we don't give you your keys either," said Bub. "Mom already gave up her license years ago, so do you even want to keep the car?"

"I don' know, I just don' know what I'm supposed to know anyway. Just take the darned thing if you want it."

"Dad, we don't want your car. We could sell it for you, and we'll take turns coming over every day, and maybe the neighbors could look in on you, too. If you want, we could even get somebody to come in to stay with you. You can live here in your own neighborhood for quite a while even without your car."

"I don' know, I just don' know, I don't know what we ought to do. There's our house. I don' know, but I think it's nearly 2:30 already, isn't it?"

"Yes, it is, Dad. Let's just all go in together, and talk about this, OK? Mom?"

"I suppose you're right, Bub. Everybody just come in. Here are the girls, too. Tell them to just come in."

"I don' know, I just don' know what to think about all of that. It's 2:45 isn't it? Everybody just sit down here now, I don' know what you want to do."

"Well, let's talk, OK?" asked Dan.

"I don' know, I just don' know if I know what I know, but it's got to be pushing 3:00 isn't it? You all just pass the time here, and I'll be back soon. I don' know, won't be long."

The five people sat in silence with their thoughts for a few moments to be interrupted by Angie as she looked out the window. "Guys? Isn't that your dad riding down the street on a bicycle? At his age? Can he do that?"

"I don't know," said Dan. "I mean I didn't know he did that anymore. Mom, does Dad still ride a bicycle?"

"Why, he hasn't ridden a bicycle since you boys left home."

The boys caught up with him only two blocks from home, waving their arms out the window of the car to stop him as he pedaled stiffly.

"Oh, fine," said Buck, pulling next to the curb. "Now you guys are the cops. I don' know, I just don' know where you're headed."

"Dad, are you in good enough shape to ride a bicycle?"

"I don' know, but I did, didn't I?"

"Where are you going?"

"Why, it's coffee time at the Deerhead Tavern. I go every day. I'll be back soon. Your Mom always waits."

"But, Dad, we had important things we wanted to discuss with you— how you're going to live, what to do with the car."

"I don' know, I just don' know yet about all that stuff, but I do know you boys must be confused. It's coffee time. Why, you can't tell the frills from the fundamentals."

Alfie gives Harry the old brush off

HARRY BURNBLACK pushed the hairy black tail curled under his chin back from his face, and inhaled his cigarette smoke with great satisfaction. He looked at his own thinly lined, long-nosed, blonde, butch haircut face in the car's rearview mirror, and fairly purred to himself, just as the big black cat curled over the top of the car seat behind his neck purred, "Ah, Harry, you can be a devil."

He loved it when a pressured housewife became teary-eyed with the frustration of too little money and desire for brushes, and he could harangue her into buying more than she should.

"Ah, ma'am, what am I to say?" he mumbled at himself again looking at the mirror. "The opportunity to buy brushes of this quality is a once in a lifetime opportunity, and they may last your lifetime, indeed. You won't find brushes like these in a store anywhere."

She had been so young, so vulnerable, so innocent, so distraught with two young children hanging on her legs when he wouldn't leave, and kept shoving brushes in her face. He'd crushed her.

"Ya, hah, hah, yes, Harry Burnblack, you are a devil of a salesman, Hard-Hearted, Hard-sell Harry, pitchman deluxe, the peddler's ideal, the very best at selling housewives, and many times househusbands, more than they need."

He glanced again in the mirror to check the knot on the recently purchased blue tie carefully chosen to match his bright, blue eyes.

"Get off my neck, Hattie, you cuddling curse of a tomcat, you'd think you were a girl. I wish I could have you neutered twice. Get under the other air conditioning vent. You bother me. You better hadn't have gotten hair on my new black suit. At least you're black."

Call after call had gone like that this week. He'd had to go back to the city to load the station wagon with more brushes. And, now here he was, 30 miles west of his usual territory, the first salesman from his company here in 20 years.

He was driving up this beautiful tree-lined little creek valley where he could almost savor the purity of the very air itself for the idyllic life the locals must lead. He only hoped that he could wipe out a portion of their savings they had never meant to spend.

His only guide to this territory was the black book left from back then by Lester Pingham, co-owner of the original firm of Pingham, Dingham and Leevam before the upstart Wingingham had come in to change the name.

Those were the good old days when, as a new salesman, Lester wouldn't give him his first day's commissions at 5:00.

"You call this sales?" Lester had asked him. "Boy, you don't come back until you've scored at least $300 in a day. I'll be here for you at midnight."

The rest was history. Harry had found a woman too loose with funds in the suburbs whom he had sold into a hysterical frenzy of buying. His star had risen. And, he was the first salesman back to an area only Lester had sold. Lester Pingham and his wife, Leena, had been good, hard people.

Now the creek valley road followed the creek itself meandering down through oak, hickory and walnut covered rocky ledges while on the other side of the road the vista opened into a broad fertile valley with new bright, green spring crops growing before the eyes in the intense heat and moisture.

Around the curve, there was a driveway going down through the valley with huge lot areas on either side of it surrounded by electric wire. Hundreds of hogs of all spots and colors ranged through the lots, most of them hunkered down in mud holes with the heat.

A big wooden sign overhung the entry gate at the driveway. It read, "Copperhead Hog Farm" in big black letters with a metallic red twisting serpent logo displayed. Underneath it, a second sign read, "Watch Where You Tread."

"Hallelujah," said Harry because he smelled not pigs, but opportunity. Anybody who would display a sign like that probably showed pigs from time to time too.

And, what did they need to clean the pigs off for show, make them shiny and bright? Why, they needed brushes, of course, and Harry was just the man to sell them to them.

"Eureka, I've struck it rich—brushes for the pigs, brushes for the house, brushes when we jigs, and when we gets a louse, har, har, har. I'm a poet now, Hattie."

Before he got out of the car to open the gate, Harry opened Lester's black book to see if there had been an entry for Copperhead Hog Farm 20 years before.

"Here, out of the car you go, Hattie, while I check the book. Don't go far to piddle, or I'll leave you here, you gutless wonder."

Here it was. Why, the repeated sales at the hog farm went into the thousands of dollars. But what was this? A balance never paid was left of $13.27. Lester had left someone owing a balance. That man never would have left anyone who owed 27 cents, let alone another $13. And, Harry was his disciple.

He was incensed at the idea of uncollected debt. He got out of the car to pace while he smoked, half-heartedly kicking at his cat when Hattie tried to purr against his leg.

"This is unheard of, Hattie. Just think of the interest that could have accrued against $13.27 by now, or the gratitude Lester could have capitalized on to sell more brushes if he had genuinely forgiven the debt. But uncollected counts for nothing. I won't have it stay this way," Harry proclaimed as he made a rapid stride for the gate with Hattie trotting in front of him.

Only a cat was quick enough for what happened next. A fat, lustrous red-brown snake struck out faster than an eyeblink at Hattie who jumped high in the air away from the fangs even faster.

"Stupid snake," growled Harry stomping with his shoe heel on the snake's head while it was extended. He bent limberly over the back of his foot holding the snake to blow smoke in the reptile's face.

"I'll show you what we used to do to snakes. You're lucky you didn't hurt my Hattie or I'd have killed you a lot slower," he added raising his heel, and grabbing the snake's tail in a fluid motion to snap the animal quickly like popping a bullwhip so hard it split its side.

The pigs that had been lounging across the fence in a mudhole under a boxelder tree came running as they saw what he had done, and Harry tossed them the snake.

Harry watched as the swine grabbed hunks of the snake from each other to chew them down.

"That will teach you, snake. Golly, that felt great. I'm up for big things now, Hattie. Let's collect that debt, and sell these pig people their next thousands of dollars worth of brushes."

Down at the house, Harry walked rapidly for the door, deeply breathing the acrid odor of pig, turning to smile momentarily at a white cat that had jumped on his car hood. It raised its back to hiss at Hattie, who had crawled up to the inside dash to hiss back.

"That's a boy, Hattie," he mumbled lowly. "We're going to ping these folks for good old Lester."

The older man who opened the door took one look at Harry, and before Harry could speak, asked, "Whatya sellin', boy?"

"Brushes, sir, the best brushes this side of heaven for scrubbing everything from dishes to hogs."

"Say, you ain't one of old Lester's brush salesmen are you?"

Harry smiled. "You're talking to one of his old timers. Lucky thing because the youngsters might not have known who you're talking about."

"I'm Alfie, and Lester's a favorite of mine. I always bought a lot of brushes from him, showed lots of hogs at fairs and trials back then. It took a lot of brushes for scrubbing every 100 head of hogs. What happened to him anyway? He just never showed up again after coming out here for years," Alfie said scratching at the bald spot between two sheaves of gray-streaked hair."

"Lester passed away. He's dead, caput."

"Is he now. Sorry to hear that. Well, Lester, if you're listenin' in, I hope you're getting along fine down there wherever salesmen go."

"Down there?"

"Well, I don't suppose he went up there unless you can take advantage of the fact that God invented the sense of humor. Lester was Lester.

I s'pose he's in a fix though, if some folks are right, and humor's just the tension between good and evil. Anyway, Harry, I'm glad to see you. Sell me some brushes."

"You are? Good, I'm glad. There is a matter of $13.27 that, according to Lester's black book, you still owed before we can get started."

"Hmm, just s'pose we waz square. OK, I'm game. You just start out with that for your stake."

"My stake?"

"Sure, after you sell to me. Lester and I always played poker all afternoon after he sold to me. I'm alone today. Everybody else went to town, so it's a perfect day. Don't worry, I'll probably buy double your daily quota, and there's a $2 limit on every game, $25 limit for winnings on the day. Of course, there's been a lot of inflation since then, so let's play $5 and $50. I don't fully understand the $13.27 because Lester usually took his winnings in frozen pork, and I took mine in brushes. Want a piece of candy?"

"Yes, I guess so," Harry said, furrowing his brow at the turn of sales to social occasion. This didn't seem normal.

"What kind of candy is this anyway, almost crisp but chewy, pink and yellow wrapped around a little soft chocolate? Never ate any like this before," Harry chewed even more thoughtfully as he sank into a big stuffed chair."

"It's surplus candy from the factory up north of here. I suppose this bunch is a couple of kinds of taffy they dug out of the auger ends twisted together, and wrapped around some melted surplus chocolate bars. We get it for the hogs. They want it so bad when my son, Albert, hauls it in, I thought it looked good. I started busting me up a couple of shovel fulls in a bucket to bring in the house. Good, ain't it?"

"Yes, surprisingly so."

"Now, Harry, I don't care much to hear about all the kitchen brushes, toilet brushes, clothes brushes, and all that sort of thing you got. Just spare me your diatribe. Just put me down for two of each of the whole variety. However, we do still show a few of our dirt-raised go-getter pure-bred swine, and I want to know if you have anything new in 20 years time to scrub a hog clean with."

"We do, we do have a super brand new brush you won't believe, the No. 9 composite nylon and ceramic scrubber brush that lasts and lasts."

"But will it get a hog clean in minimal time, Harry?"

"I guarantee it, Alfie. Do you suppose I could try another piece of that candy? Mind if I smoke a cigarette, too?"

"Sure, Harry, and can you give me a cigarette, too? Just don't smoke around my hogs. Second-hand smoke's hazardous, you know. In the meantime, let's get you out of that suit. I have a pair of coveralls you can slip into."

"Why would I do that? You do something else besides poker?"

"You have to brush a hog, wash it off, son. I want a demonstration."

"I can just slip the coveralls on over my suit."

"That's what Lester said for the last new brush, too. OK, boy, just pull them over the suit if you want to. It's your clothes. Take your shiny shoes off, and slip those rubber boots on."

Outside, the two cats were laying down squared off on their respective sides of the windshield.

"Your kitty cat going to be OK, Harry?" Alfie asked. "It can get awfully hot in a car?"

"The windows are cracked. He can get down under the front of the seat if he wants to."

"Well, I know howya must love your kitty cat letting him ride around like that with you."

"Love? I don't love a cat."

"See that big sow over there?"

"Good night, she must weigh 800 pounds."

"That's Lady Bertrand, purebred Chester White. You'll scrub her so we can take her to town for the grade school kids to see tomorrow. They can't believe a hog could get so big. I tell'm there's a hundred pounds of just bacon there. Climb right in there, and we'll herd her up on this concrete along the dirt here, and squeeze her in a little with the hog panel. That's right, Harry, get your hands on her rear, just push a little to get her moving. Careful about waving the flies off your face. You're slinging a little mud."

Huh, huh, huh, grunted Lady Bertrand as her enormous hams swung in a stately walk."

"This mud is horrible," said Harry. "It's nothing but green slime, and boy does it stink. Look there, where it's watery in the middle of her swim-hole. It's even bubbling."

"That's because it has manure in it, Harry. A pig's gonna go where a pig's gonna go."

"You'll see, the No. 9 brush will take it off anyway."

"OK, Harry. She's all squeezed up. I'm turning the water hose on. Take that bottle of liquid soap, and just squeeze a little out along her back, and work down on her. Remember to get the gunked up stuff from between her hooves."

"Now, you notice the bristles on the No. 9 brush have a special slight curvature for maximum contact."

"Save your spiel, Harry. I'm not interested. Just wash the hog."

But Harry didn't know how not to sell. "You'll notice the fine way the soap beads up without being removed until you apply the water, blah, blah, blah, blah," on and on for a half-hour.

"Harry, don't give me the spiel. I don't know that I see much improvement in this brush over the old one."

"You must have some reason for feeling that way. Perhaps let me show you the unique hand-grab capabilities of the handle of the No. 9, blah, blah, blah."

"Harry, I said can the spiel. I don't want a sales talk. Just finish Lady Bertrand up there. I hope that water's not getting through the coveralls to your suit too bad. I still will take some No. 9s. Harry, be quiet."

"I'm certainly glad you are appreciating the qualities of the No. 9, blah, blah, blah."

"That's it, Harry. I can't take anymore. You salesmen just can't be quiet. Areeeah, reeeeeeah, reeeeeeeah," squealed Alfie in imitation of a caught or hurt baby pig.

Harry paused as a great rumbling growl from Lady Bertrand's body turned into a "huh, huh, huh, snuff, snort," as she turned her nose toward him. Harry was shoved stumbling backwards as the panel popped behind him.

"Areeeeah, reeeeeah," squealed Alfie one more time as he scratched his head.

Harry tried to break into a shuffling run as the great sow nose lifted him under his rump before he tumbled face-down in the green slime.

"Heah, pi', pi', pig, whoooee, pi', pi', pig," shouted Alfie in the candy call that made Lady Bertrand forget her ferocity to turn back toward him.

Harry pulled himself up, and took a step after one boot pulled off in the mud to stumble once more into the center of the bubbling liquid.

"Gee, I'm sorry, Harry. I just wanted to quiet you down. You salesmen just can't stop. Lady Bertrand's really pretty gentle. I didn't think she'd eat you even if a salesman is close to as poison as a copperhead snake at times."

"Poison? You have poisonous snakes down here? I thought the snake I killed up at your gate was just like the bullsnakes we used to have back home."

"Why did you think we surrounded ourselves with hogs, Harry? Let me help you out of there, and let's play some cards. I'll take all the No. 9s you got with you."

When Essie came home, she was introduced to Harry, who was wearing her son's blue-striped bathrobe while he played cards. Finally she asked, "Where's your clothes? What's that you have going in the washing machine, Alfie?"

"Oh, that's Harry's suit and tie, Essie. The hog stuff got inside his coveralls. Harry and I don't usually do our own laundry, but I figured I could get it washed while we played so Harry could get on his way."

"Alfie, you don't wash a suit."

That evening Harry drove home still dressed in a borrowed bathrobe, his entire stock of brushes sold, his frozen pork winnings in a sack in the back seat, while Hattie curled sleepily on the shrunken suit in the seat next to him.

When he got there, he called Leena Pingham to tell her how he had followed in the tracks of her husband, even down to collecting the $13.27.

"Oh, Harry," she said. "I don't think Alfie owed Lester that money. That was Lester's dry-cleaning bill for his suit. They charged him double the usual. He wrote it down because he said he was going to win it back from Alfie for getting him rolled by a hog in the mud."

One beautiful way
to escape a debt

ONE OF Rathburn Lettergoh's notorieties was his lack of talent as a bookkeeper.

Oh, Rathburn was a hard worker, all right. You never saw anybody who could hold his tongue in the corner of his mouth, and strain so hard on the end of two bars to take a semi-truck tire off the rim like Rathburn.

He tried to keep tickets of the things he charged or paid by throwing them on the floor of his old Ford truck for collection later, or giving them a toss onto the heap on top of the ancient desk in the corner of his gasoline station office.

The tickets in the truck stayed there until they got kicked out, blew out a window, or got sucked through the hole in the floor where his plyboard patch job had rotted out behind the gas pedal.

Rathburn seldom looked at the tickets on the desk again until the two or three times a year his wife, Bertha, insisted they go through them. He had a little table by the window where his spiral pad checkbook set, and access to the checks was all he really needed.

At least most of the time Bertha stayed happy despite Rathburn's peculiar carelessness, laughing and jolly with the customers, all three of her fat-folded chins shaking at the really good jokes.

Sometimes looking at her good-humored large brown eyes under the curly brown hair, the customers decided that Bertha had to be just plain good-natured to be born in the 1960s with an old-fashioned German name plus getting stuck with Rathburn to boot. In her own mind, she had chosen to be steadfastly kind to everyone.

Bertha wasn't at the station yet the early morning, with the sun still red in the east, when Rathburn had already paid several thousand dollars in checks. He sent off a utility bill, paid the soda pop delivery man, and took the cash on delivery load of gasoline he customarily got in weekly.

Ledborn Gotterbach came in on his usual morning stop for coffee to ask, "Whatya doin', Rathburn?"

Rathburn used eight fingers to brush back his still uncombed bristly brown hair to answer, "Bettin' on the futures market."

"I didn't know you played the futures. Are you into stocks too?"

"No, I don't have either one. I'm writin' checks bettin' by the end of the day they'll all be covered."

"Aren't you afraid you'll bounce a check? How far down's your balance?"

"Naah, I don't worry. I won't balance it until the end of the day, or tomorrow maybe, or Bertha will do it on the weekend. Just a sec', the candy man's waiting up front for his check. Don't step out on the gas island while I'm busy. Here comes Everett with fresh dings on his Chrysler."

Ledborn watched as the old man in the drooping-down cotton hat pulled his New Yorker alongside the two gasoline pumps coming within an inch of hitting the guard posts set in concrete. The sides of the otherwise shiny, newer car were pocked with dents and scratches.

Rathburn left the station to lift the nozzle to Everett's gas cap. "Fill'er up, Everett?"

"Nah, just $10 worth. That's enough to get to the city. Gas is cheaper there, ya know. I come here cuz you'll pump it for me, ya know."

Rathburn looked across the street at the six-pump convenience store where commuters were in line for gasoline at two cents a gallon cheaper than he was selling it. And all Rathburn had currently was this one old man.

"Yeah, I know, Everett. I understand."

The phone was ringing as he finished, but luckily Bertha was down, smiling at Ledborn with his hatchet-thin face, just in time to answer it. Her face had turned glum, and she was downcast as she answered, "Yes, sir," and "No, sir," into the receiver.

"Who was it?" Rathburn asked.

"It was Howie down at the bank," Bertha replied. "It's 9 a.m., Rathburn."

"So?"

"Your gas supplier, old Polk, was there to cash your check as soon as the bank door opened. You're short $1,500 to cover it. Howie told him to come back at 2. Howie says to tell you to have it covered by then or you could face a criminal charge. Howie says he's doing you a favor to hold it even that long. He could have just handed it back, and told him the odds of it being good are close to nil. Polk wasn't happy, but Howie says he put his faith in you on the line to hold him off, told him you'd be in. But you better come awful close to the $1,500 because he can't cover you again."

"Gee, Rathborn," said Ledborn. "This sounds harsh. How many times have you had overdrafts anyway?"

"Oh, not more than four or five a month. They usually cover me."

"What are we going to do, Rathburn?" Bertha said softly. "I think maybe you've gone too far this time."

There was a long pause as Bertha and Rathburn looked at the floor, then at each other, working their tongues back and forth, then looked back at the floor.

Ledborn glanced back and forth at the two of them waiting on a resolution before he paused to stare at the floor a moment himself, pulling softly on the bill of his gray ball cap.

"I got your solution, Rathburn, Bertha. Just give me a half-hour to get back," said Ledborn.

It took 40 minutes for Ledborn to get back, 40 minutes in which Bertha and Rathburn sat silently in their chairs on either side of the station door with only one customer in for a candy bar. It was looking like Howie's attempt at faith was terribly misplaced.

But Ledborn did come back with his pretty, blonde, 18-year-old niece, Lottie Gotterbach, in tow, her well-endowed figure covered in a beige overcoat.

"Rathburn," he said. "You'd give me $100 for having all of your problems solved for the day wouldn't you?"

"I guess it would be darn sure worth that much, Ledborn," replied Rathburn.

"Good, because that's what Lottie still owes me for me helping buy her a car. I told her your situation, and she agreed to help in return for me forgiving the money. Behold, Rathburn, Bertha, your solution, my niece, Lottie, pumping gasoline for you. You know Lottie, right?"

"Yes, we know Lottie," Rathburn said, smiling and blinking his eyes in rapt flirtation. "I've pumped gas for her, and she's come in for coffee with you once or twice."

With that Lottie opened her overcoat.

"Good lord!" said Bertha. "You're naked."

Rathburn didn't speak, but he nearly bit off his tongue, which could cue you in to a second reason for his notoriety.

"She ain't naked," said Ledborn. "She's covered top and bottom. This here yellow thing is a Brazilian thong swimsuit. You mark my word. Customers will come here to see our Lottie in a thong. You know this will work. You've seen Hollywood tell you it works over and over. Show them your smile, honey."

She did, and Rathburn was smitten backward two steps.

"The deal is," said Lottie, "the customers can look, but nobody can touch."

Ledborn was right.

Lottie stepped to the gas pumps, and old Everett, who was driving down Main to head for the city, did a U-turn to pull into the station so fast he put a crease down his left fender on the guard posts. Lottie stepped back fast, and Everett forgot everything when she washed his windshield.

The customers across the street watched Everett's turn-around, then left the convenience store pumps to come to Rathburn's.

The cars backed up to get gasoline lined up first down the block, and then around the block. The Mulvane brothers came through the line 10 times getting $3 worth of gasoline each time.

Everett came back with his riding lawnmower, hitting it on the front post after driving up the island curb on one wheel, came back with his wife's Pontiac denting it on the left rear against the curbside electric pole, then with his son's pickup with the tailgate down conveniently pinging it against the rear post.

"You're a godsend," Bertha told Lottie as she brought her Coke and ice when the sun's heat built up at noon.

Lottie, who was already tired, red and flushed, said, "You're the god-send, bringing me a Coke right now. And you seem like a godsend to your husband, too. You seem like a really sweet person."

"Without you, my Rathburn would go to jail."

"I'm doing it this once because Uncle Ledborn's forgiving me $100. Maybe by now it's for you too, Bertha. You've been good to us as kids, too. More than once you spotted me a dime for a candy bar when I didn't bring enough money with me. The way your Rathburn looks at me, maybe he ought to go to jail. He didn't even notice me when I was younger. You can tell him I'm fine in my tennis shoes. I don't need your white heels."

"Look how her freckles stand out when she flushes," said Everett, who had run out of things to put gasoline in, and now sat eating a candy bar.

"I've never seen anything like this," said Everett's wife, Elaine, one of the women who were beginning to come to watch, too. "Thanks for telling me about it."

"The freckles sure do stand out," said Rathburn. "I think I'll take her the next Coke while Bertha runs the register."

"Better yet," said the guy in the fourth chair down who was drinking a Coke and eating a candy bar, "as soon as I'm done with this, I'll buy me and her both the same thing again. Your potato and corn chips and your peanuts are all gone, Rathburn."

By 1 p.m. Rathburn deposited more than enough money in the bank to cover his problem, and he was back calling Polk to bring him another load of gasoline before the day ended. He was also calling the soda pop and candy suppliers to bring more supplies out.

By 3 p.m., Polk hadn't come, and Rathburn was out of gasoline, so Lottie sat in a lawn chair on the island selling quarts of oil to admirers.

"Well, that's it," said Ledborn at 5 p.m. as Bertha handed him $100.

"I'm exhausted," said Lottie as Bertha handed her one more cup of Coke. "I'm hungry for something good, too. You know I've hardly had anything except for the candy bars all those guys bought me."

"Gee, we should have thought of that," said Rathburn looking up at her from his chair. "I tell you what. Come back tomorrow, and we'll do the same thing. Except this time we'll send out for a chicken dinner for you, and you can have the $100, too, instead of your Uncle Ledborn.

Lottie smiled at Rathburn as she slowly poured her Coke onto his lap.

"Tomorrow, Rathburn," she said, "you hire yourself a bookkeeper."

Pranks of an old snake in the grass

Author's note: These guys couldn't just throw away a find as unique as a boa carcass.

JIMMY OATS and Jimmy Allen ran two county mowers in the early summer months when the yellow sweet clover, grasses and weeds reached a rampant peak in growth on roadside ditches.

Jimmy Oats, everybody agreed, always looked like he was "sowing his wild oats," with his cocked grin in a youthful tanned face turned up at one corner of the mouth and wide blue eyes sparkling and mirthful. He drove the smaller gray tractor, bouncing as fast as it would go, mowing road shoulders with a single bush hog.

Jimmy Allen, everybody agreed, looked more like you'd caught him just after swallowing a belly-full of green persimmons, with his broad mouth burned into a face of old leather. Jimmy Allen drove the big red tractor with three bush hogs coordinated by hydraulics, slowly and carefully.

Jimmy Oats loved the new world of computer screens, cellular phones, and people keeping exotic animals as pets almost as much as he loved just being out in the open air.

Jimmy Allen knew how many days and hours were left until retirement because he counted them on the hour. He kept his cell phone off so nobody would call him. His constant admonition to Jimmy Oats was, "Slow down, you're gettin' too far ahead," although he was actually happier not to eat Jimmy Oats' dust.

It was Jimmy Oats who kept the fun at the county shop rollicking with practical jokes, such as crawling up on his belly behind Jimmy Allen's metal folding chair when he drank his coffee with his toes resting on the frayed plastic table cloth of the break-room table. He tied one of his shoe laces to a chair leg, so he would be pulling the legs together when he took his feet down.

It was also Jimmy Oats who brought a BB gun one day so everybody could try to take a turn pinging shots at the rats they could hear crawling through the walls of the building that occasionally stuck a nose out a broken stucco hole.

Jimmy Oats was way ahead on his tractor one afternoon when he saw his front wheels fast approaching what looked like a most peculiar pole half hidden in the grass, all brown and cream mottled colored. He stopped the tractor, stopped the mower blades, and sat there blinking for a moment before he began to guess at what he was looking at.

It was a snake—perhaps the biggest snake Jimmy Oats had ever seen *outside a zoo.* He got off *the tractor,* and approached the snake carefully. There was still no movement. He walked close until he could see there was 15 to 20 feet of thick snake body stretched out.

Jimmy Oats clapped his hands, and sang "Wally Wally Wampum" once to see if the snake responded. But it stayed still. Finally, he stretched out one foot to give the resilient snake body a push with his leather boot toe with still no response.

"Whoop!" hollered Jimmy Oats, taking a step closer to give the snake a good solid kick. It looked like he had himself a dead boa constrictor that had gotten loose from who knew where. The body still moved loosely under the impact as though the snake hadn't been dead long.

Jimmy Oats pulled his ball cap off while he mopped perspiration from his forehead under the thick sandy hair in the 90-degree heat, and slowly began to grin his biggest crooked smile. A dead boa constrictor could be a great tool for a prankster.

The thing was very heavy, funny to the touch, slick but roughened skin all at the same time. It was warm from laying out in the humid mid-day sun. Jimmy Oats got the tail to trail over his shoulder to the ground in front so he had a heavy section resting on his shoulder, and he began to drag the snake. He curled the body, one length at a time around the top of his bush hog deck.

When he came to the snake's head, he took the big club of a thing up to his own face for a moment to look at the eyes. They were still there all dark, but filmed over. This was a great thing.

Jimmy Oats fired up the tractor, and started the mower, looking back from time to time to make sure his boa constrictor was riding along fine. The weight held it most of the time with an occasional stop for him to go back to recurl it in a heap if the vibrations began to work it across the deck.

He quit a little early for the day, waving at Jimmy Allen as he met him, and just grinning when the older man raised his wrist to point at his watch to tell him it wasn't time to go in yet.

At the shop, Jimmy Oats dragged the snake across the floor that was empty now but soon would be full of workers coming in to quit for the day. He curled it under the break-room table, carefully putting the edges of the checkered plastic cloth back to the floor to hide the boa. Then he got a soda pop out of the vending machine to wait for the others to come in.

A dozen men were in the room before Jimmy Allen arrived, shaking his head sourly at Jimmy Oats. "Why'd you quit early? You know that ain't right. You need to keep out there after it 'til quittin' time, ya know?"

"Wait, wait, listen," Jimmy Oats said in a hushed voice as he rose to his feet. "I hear one of them wall rats under the table, boys. One of you get your hands under the other end of the table to help me pick it up when I say go. Jimmy Allen, grab that hammer over there to hit him with it when he runs. Ready, Fred? One, two, three, go."

"SNAKE!" hollered Jimmy Allen on a diving run backward as he flung the hammer sideways at the boa carcass.

"Gawd, almighty!" hollered one of the others as the room cleared of everyone but a hee-hawing Jimmy Oats, bent over and slapping his legs.

"Jimmy Oats," said one of the first half-dozen men to come back in the door. "Where did you get that big old stinkin' thing? By golly, those eyes freak me out."

"Hey, it don't stink, but it's dead," said Jimmy Oats. "He's deader than a doorknob. But he's sure got a lot of fun left in him. Here, a couple of you boys help me put him in the back of my pickup. Then follow me down to the Deerhead Tavern."

"Wait a minute, Jimmy Oats," said Jimmy Allen in a dry voice. "I liked that. It gave us all a real thrill. That's probably the best prank you ever played. The supervisor will be here in a minute. Let's haul your snake in there for when he puts his legs under his desk to log the day in."

"What are all you guys still hanging around here for? Isn't it time to go home?" asked supervisor Dick as he came in the door.

"Oh, just yacking to each other, boss," said Jimmy Allen in the dead-pan only a normally humorless man could manage. "Just havin' a last drag on our soda pops. It's been a hot day out there."

"What are you all peeking through my door for?" asked Dick. He kicked off his shoes like he usually did, and wheeled his chair to slide under the desk, like it could shield him from their eyes. "Hey, are you up to something...what's this?"

Dick kicked his socked foot against the snake's big solid side, and bent to look under the desk into a boa face propped up on a coffee can. "Hey-yaaah!" he hollered, causing Jimmy to grin at Jimmy in a most satisfied manner.

Down at the Deerhead, the whole gang went in for drinks while Jimmy Oats went in to ask the girl running the register. "OK if I bring my pet in? He's well behaved."

"Sure, Jimmy Oats. Just don't let him jump up on people."

Jimmy Oats came back in dragging a great long snake across the var-nished oak floor by a leash with a dog's chain choke collar.

Jimmy Allen was delighted when the register clerk was at first oblivious to the presence of the snake, and he had to yell "SNAKE!" to send her climbing onto the bar.

Some of the men followed Jimmy Oats around on his tour for a while, but they had to go home before the fun ended. Dick the supervisor was shaking his finger at him when he left, but smiling too.

Jimmy Allen helped him stack the snake coils on the passenger side floor, and sat on his knees hanging the first three feet of snake out the window like he was trying to hold him in for the benefit of everyone they met.

At the drive-in, when Jimmy Oats saw the boy coming with his hamburger, he pulled the snake's head over the sideboard of his truck hollering, "Help me, somebody help me!"

Then he and Jimmy Allen had to run giggling to catch the boy before he dialed 911.

"Lord, that kid about came uncorked, didn't he?" commented Jimmy Allen before he had to go home for the evening. "You're goin' to bring him back to the shop tomorrow, ain't you? Don't throw him away yet."

At his parents' house, Jimmy got his father, who was known by the nickname, "Quaker," to leave his shop to see him give a satisfying jump when he looked into the truck bed at the snake all curled up with its head propped menacingly against the sidewall.

"Now, I'll get Mom," Jimmy Oats snorted.

"Wait," said Quaker. "Let me go in to take the grandbaby from her first. We don't want her to drop him when she sees that thing."

Jimmy Oats whirled, clapped his hands over his head, and whooped when his mother screamed a drawn-out "Aiiiiih!" She grimaced, and slugged him on the shoulder.

"Thanks for coming out to look, Mom," he said.

"You're 21, Jimmy," she said. "It's time you quit this kind of stuff. Get rid of that thing before you scare somebody to death."

Jimmy Oats' uncle wouldn't come out to look when he asked him to see what he had in the back-end of his pickup.

"I know you, Jimmy Oats," he said, "and I'm afraid you got a snake or something in that truck. I'm scared of snakes."

It was quite a job for Jimmy Oats to drag the boa constrictor up a flight of stairs to his apartment. It was remarkably flexible for something that had been dead all day. Surely he could get one more day of good from it before he had to throw it away.

He laid it on the living room carpet, and contentedly dozed off and on beside it while watching a TV show about best home videos.

"Too bad I didn't video all this today," he whispered, grinning crookedly. "You know old snake, if I was to play a joke on myself I'd rig it up for you to have me half-swallowed when I wake up again."

That's what he began to dream about when his eyes closed heavily. His legs were stuffed through the snake's mouth nearly up to his navel in its gullet. The dream became so vivid, he could feel the snake's muscles undulating to swallow him more squeezing against his arms, pulling him in around the throat.

In the dream, Jimmy Allen, Dick the supervisor, and all the other workers were standing around laughing while it happened.

"Ain't that Jimmy Oats somethin' else carryin' the joke into gettin' swallered himself," guffawed Jimmy Allen.

Good old Jimmy Allen, thought Jimmy Oats as he slowly began to blink himself awake. He had a sense of humor after all. Why this getting swallowed was downright comradely.

There was something kind of strange about this dream because the more he came awake, the more he realized the laughter was real. It was the late night show on the television with the audience laughing at the host's monologue.

But what else was real was that sensation of something undulating against the sides of his body. Something was gently caressing his arm. There was a brushing across his neck and cheek. A lump was squeezing up and down on the inside of his shirt like there was a blood pressure pulse outside his own body.

"Oooooh," Jimmy Oats shuddered as he forced his eyes open to find himself looking into the veiled eyes of the snake carcass where he had rolled. His legs seemed numbed at first by the suggestion of his mind, but he jumped to his feet with baby snakes falling from his body.

Jimmy Oats ran in a dancing shuffle for the bathroom shuddering all over, looking back to see if the big snake carcass was moving to come after him. It had nearly scared him to death because his heart was throbbing.

No, it wasn't moving. The snake was still dead. Nobody had told Jimmy Oats that a genuine boa constrictor is one snake that bears its young alive, and if someone is kind enough to keep it flexing around, the babies still might come out when the parent is dead.

The boa constrictor had punished the perpetrator, playing its final joke on Jimmy Oats himself. He kept one of the 26 baby snakes he found for his own pet.

It took a couple of months for the men at the county garage to stop watching the hole in the break-room wall after Jimmy Oats stuck a half-dozen of the snakes into it.

They don't have rats anymore.

Harlan Medlam's way to get ahead

OH, TO BE ahead of the game, to have money, health, the wealth of everything.

That's what Harlan Medlam wanted, and that's what Harlan Medlam believed he had. He always had $5 in the front of his wallet, and another $100 hidden in the pocket behind the front, plus another $100 usually hidden here and there on his person. You never know when a deal requiring a little cash might arise.

The farm and lands he and Florence owned were paid for, as well as every head of livestock and every machine they supported. The old couple agreed: debt was the scourge of Satan, and God was "pretty lenient" for those who helped themselves.

Everybody has to have a philosophy, Harlan mused to himself, and it might as well keep you persistent as well as comfortable.

Health? Harlan was in his 80s, and he considered that he still had very good health for his age. Not that he had any doctors telling him so. Doctors cost money, and there was no need messing with them until they were absolutely needed.

Oh sure, he'd had false teeth for 20 years now, he thought as he patted his coat pocket where his dentures lay, and ran his tongue thoughtfully over his gums.

He could see well too, but he'd finally condescended to buying a pair of dime-store glasses for the fine print.

And, Harlan could move his thin, wiry frame—not too much in front of anyone else, mind you. If he was sure Florence and the neighbors weren't looking, he could raise one leg from the ground, and lay his heel flat on the bed of his truck. Now, that's limber for an old man, ain't it, he thought.

Last summer he had watched the boys hauling hay step to radio rock-and-roll music while they were on lunch break, and had spit his chew from a leftover stub of cigar as though he couldn't understand their enthusiasm.

But in the twilight of summer late evening, when he turned the cows out to pasture from milking, Harlan Medlam had crawled up on the flatbed of his truck to try it himself with no radio, just a memory of the music to go from.

He grinned for a moment, flitting his shiny, dark-brown eyes back and forth, thinking of his big secret that nobody would ever know. Harlan Medlam could do the Harlan Shuffle, and he was nearly supple when he did it if he used his cane—especially on the shuffle to the left.

Best of all, Harlan Medlam was mentally sharp. He multiplied, divided, added and subtracted through visualization and number break-downs in his head without benefit of pencil and paper. He could hide the fact that he knew mathematical answers before those around him had figured them to maximize his financial benefit.

He was a survivor.

Harlan's memory was phenomenal, too. For instance, he knew that in the south shed was a set of Model T wrenches on the dirt floor just inside the front wheel of an old car which had the remains of a hay mower and a dump rake shoved up against it with a pile of lumber piled over the top of them. Some sheets of tin and a canvas tarp covered most of the roof of the car, but if you looked at it in the right light, along about sunset, you could still make out a corner of the car roof.

Harlan had left the wrenches there himself, he remembered, in 1925—May of the year, he thought. His father had been helping him then.

But the wrenches weren't the complete set, and that was part of the problem. One wrench lay on the rim of the gray concrete silo 40 feet in the air where he had left it himself while hooking up the silage blower for the last time in 1969. He'd used a Model T bolt so he needed a Model T wrench for a makeshift job of hooking up the blower.

Now he needed all of those wrenches, and somehow he was going to have to use most of his abilities to get them himself because a small fortune was involved. There wasn't any harm involved in occasionally getting a small fortune without Florence Medlam involved was there? It was $100, and $100 was a lot of cigar money, maybe even pipe tobacco, and gasoline for a few extra runs in the old truck when nobody suspected.

Harlan smacked his lips as he read the newspaper classified one more time to steady his nerve. "Will give $100," it said, "for a complete set of Model T wrenches, call 555-3415."

Harlan had called, with one eye cocked toward the door to watch for Florence, who'd gone out to feed chickens. The froggy-voiced man said he'd be out this very afternoon, which was handy because Florence would be at club.

But the situation eliminated many of his usual resources. He had no time to finesse his favorite neighbor, Paul, or any of the others into somehow doing the work for him. He could hire young guys to get to the wrenches, but it would be unseemly and foolish of him to pay much of a percentage of his $100—he nearly considered it in pocket. Granted, most of them could have the lumber carried away from the machines in an hour. Then they could hook a log chain from a tractor to the frames of the machines to pull them aside to get at the wrenches.

Bruce Bondin down the road the other way from Paul's might get it done in less time. He was young, and a good hand. God knew it would have been easier for young Bondin to climb that silo than it was going to be for Harlan Medlam.

Patience, patience—wait for the situation to be right, Harlan Medlam told himself as he stretched out on his bench under the elm tree for a nap after dinner. Let Florence Medlam get her flowered dress on, and stand out here waiting for Paul's wife to give her a ride to club. She'd pull her bonnet here and there a half-dozen times before she left. Then she'd go, and he'd almost jump into action, quick as he could go before the froggy-voiced man arrived with his $100.

"Your nap time about ought to be over, Harlan," said Florence, pacing up and down in the flowered dress while pulling thoughtfully at the white bonnet to get the right tilt on her head. "Hadn't you ought to be getting the tractor ready to go the field?"

She'd bought the white bonnets at a hardware store sale in 1939, in September he thought, and there were still several in the cedar chest waiting to be worn. Even he had noticed that white bonnets were nearly extinct in the stores by the 1970s, so she'd been wise to stock up.

Ahh, here came Paul's wife. He sat up on the bench.

Florence pointed meaningfully at the tractor as the car pulled away. But she was hardly out of sight before Harlan was headed toward the silo as fast as he could go on two legs and a cane. He'd even thought of a safety precaution—a 30-foot rope, about the only one he could find in a short time.

He knotted a loop of the rope securely around his chest, under his armpits. He could see from the ground that the lip of the silo showed crumbled spots, and here and there some steel-reinforcement sucker rod was exposed.

Harlan checked the ground first to see if the wrench might have fallen with some of the lumps of concrete on the ground. But, no, it must still be up there. So, he climbed up the steel ladder, rungs inside the metal side chute, one rung at a time, dragging the rope behind him—puff, puff—with a breathing pause at the 10th rung.

Harlan already was wishing he was back on the ground. He'd never had bad muscle cramps before, but the right leg, the same one that rebelled on the shuffle to the right, was feeling uncomfortably tight.

One side of the 11th rung had pulled away from the silo on the right side, but the left side still felt securely bolted, so up he went. At the top rung, Harlan Medlam stuck his head out of the chute into the open air to a welcome new breeze with a touch of chill to it.

No sense hurrying to the point of foolishness, take time to gasp in a little of that air. My, but he was in his 80s wasn't he, despite being in good shape for the age. The climb was nearly too much. And now, there was the climb out on that rim to face, only 8 inches wide with a 40-foot drop to either side. It looked like about a 20-foot crawl to the blower where the wrench ought to be.

Good thing he had thought of the rope. Harlan pulled it up, letting the excess tumble over the edge of the chute against the side of the silo, until he had the end to square-knot securely to the top rung.

It was hell getting that right leg over the top of the chute. Hell, hell, thought Harlan Medlam—sorry about that, God, when you've made life so convenient. He had to lay his belly over the rim, looking down into the long drop, while he lifted and pulled on the leg at the same time. The tip of his cane where he had stuffed it down the back of his overalls poked his buttocks when he strained forward.

He squished the leg down on the metal and the side of the silo both, making it take up less space to yank the foot out with one hand. The metal took a hunk of skin away just beneath the sock from the feel of it.

Then Harlan Medlam did a slow twist to the right on his belly, pulling the left leg out of the chute easily so that his legs dangled, one on each side of the rim.

As he pushed to sit up, Harlan decided he needed to steady his nerves a little, so he pulled a cigar stub out of his overalls pocket while he studied the situation.

He chewed, letting some of the brown juice dribble down his lined brown chin while he breathed deeply. There was no choice but to push up with his hands to scoot on his rear a foot at a time along the rim. He dug his heels in on the sides to help lift, and steady himself. The curved handle of his cane stuck out above his head like a flag, the length of the cane propping against his back like he was reinforced.

Half-way there he hit broken pieces of concrete. He took a short breather, then continued to scoot along with the pieces growing jagged under his rear. A pigeon landed on the rim, and paused to look at him curiously before flying away—dad-ratted smart aleck darn bird.

From five feet away, the concrete had broken away in bigger chunks, and there was exposed steel, not much to sit on. But there the wrench was, too. He could see it laying on an intact piece of the rim. Two more feet to go, two feet more precarious than any feet crawled before this, with chunks of concrete beginning to break away to the sides and a point of sucker rod that stuck him good.

Harlan Medlam laid on his belly, trying to hold on as tightly as he could with his feet to the side and left hand wrapped around a piece of the steel. Then he reached up with his right hand to pull his cane from the overalls. He gritted his gums against nothing because he'd swallowed the last of the cigar, and pushed himself half-way up. Then, holding steady as he could, he reached out with the cane to tap the wrench to the side.

Harlan Medlam watched in great satisfaction as the wrench fell heavily to the ground 40 feet below, kicking dirt in the air. He was successful. No, he was almost successful. Now Harlan had to get himself down.

He couldn't go forward because of the broken-out rim, and turning around was going to be tough. So, he decided to try to go backward, push up with the hands while gripping with the feet to shove his seat back. It was slower, and he was much more weary. He definitely had the beginning of a cramp in the right leg now, and the left leg wasn't far from doing the same. His arms felt rubbery from the unaccustomed work.

He dropped his cane, and watched it flop over so the curved handle hit the ground first. It took a big bounce before landing. Guess that's how it would be for me, he thought—the heavy end would hit the ground first.

Back he went—back, back, until there was only 10 more feet of backward crawl to go. Then a chunk of concrete fell. It startled Harlan, but it could have done more because it fell away from the steel right where he had sat to reach out for the wrench with his cane. A new crack ran on a slant down the side from where the chunk fell, and that section of the silo wall began to lean inward. Inward, huh, thought Harlan. The old silo could implode someday.

He felt like he was beginning to lean to the inward of the silo himself, and then as he tried to straighten up, he realized he was. Harlan Medlam sighed as he began to loop the rope in tightly. He took his ball cap off to loop the tightened rope around it into the grip of his hands. No use burning his hands more than he had to. He'd been a fool not to get help. Florence might as well had part of the money, too.

He got his left leg over to begin a slithering fall against the silo that jerked his arms and shoulders hard when he hit dead weight at the end of 10 feet. The fall continued as he swung into the side of the metal chute. But Harlan Medlam held on, and there he hung on the outside of the silo. At least there wasn't any concrete dropping on him.

It must have been adrenaline helping because Harlan was able to let the rope slide through his hands as he kicked off the side of the silo. He ran out of rope, and was left dangling with the loop under his arms 12 feet off the ground. At least the knots held, and he was alive, dadburned the situation. It wasn't God's fault. It was his own for making a predicament out of an easy thing.

He'd never been as happy to see Paul drive in as he was at this time. He tried to holler, "Paul," as his neighbor got out of the truck. But it sort of came out "Paaaugh," like a strangled sheep crying.

Paul pulled his truck up, climbed up on the roof of it, and pulled Harlan Medlam in to take the rope off him. Then he lifted the old man down to the truck bed where they sat for a moment, breathing.

"How did you do that to yourself?" Paul asked. "I stopped by at club for a minute to have a piece of pie with the women, and Florence asked me to stop by to see if you were OK because she couldn't hear your tractor in the field. I'll call them to get down here while you breath a minute more. You think we need to get you to the hospital?"

"No, no, dad-rat it I'll be fine. Call Bruce Bondin for me too, will you? I need you fellas to help me for about an hour. I'll even pay you both."

At that Paul raised his eyebrows, but he did what Harlan wanted.

Harlan Medlam explained the situation to a furious Florence

Medlam, who stood hands on hips glaring at him embarrassed in front of her neighbors.

"You were totally unbecomin', Harlan Medlam," she said.

Paul and Bruce were clearing the pile away to collect the wrenches just as the froggy-voiced man drove up in his white Chrysler. The wrenches were just where Harlan said they were, behind the wheel of the old car, and they made a complete set with the wrench from the silo.

Harlan wearily watched them work from a lawn chair they pulled up while his wife stood at his side with her arms folded.

"You still have to go to the field today, Harlan Medlam," Florence said.

Harlan Medlam had rope burns under his arms, his arms were sore, his ribs felt stretched, and he had muscle cramps running up both legs. There would be no Harlem Shuffle for some time. He knew Florence would take his money, and possibly he would not have supper except what he scratched up himself. "Oooh."

"Why, that's a Model T under there," said the small froggy-voice man with hair combed down both sides of his head. "When was the last time it was driven?"

Somewhere in the deep recesses of Harlan Medlam's mind, habitual predator instincts were making their way to the surface. Old machinery isn't worth much either because it's worn out or something new has taken its place. But the man was paying $100 for wrenches, so what would the old car be worth?"

"Yeah, it is a Model T, a 1925," Harlan said, his eyes losing some of their weariness to gleam again. "It was only driven once. We had a good wheat year that year, bought it new. Matter of fact, bought two of them. Pop and I put it together. Then he bought a Chevrolet because he liked the new three-speed shift instead of the foot-operated transmission. We drove the Chevy, and let the Ford set. You see, my pop was a bit of a spender," Harlan added, looking apologetically at Florence.

"It just set here?" asked Froggy in his scratchy voice, patting the hair on one side of his head, and narrowing his eyes. "My god, look at it," he added, as the men pulled the last of the lumber away. "It's nearly perfect except for the dirt. It doesn't even look like rodents have chewed the wiring. It might run."

"Sure it might. Probably will with just a little work," said Harlan Medlam, rising to his feet. The pain was all going away. He tapped the ground with his cane looking into Froggy's eyes while he touched a finger to his chin."

"I'll give you $2,000 for it," Froggy growled amphibiously.

The full killer instinct slid into place. The elements of the universe, including Harlan Medlam, had flowed to their rightful places.

"Take $4,000 for it," said Harlan.

Florence Medlam was smiling at him. He hoped his teeth hadn't dropped out at the silo because he was going to eat steak tonight.

"$3,500," said Froggy. "It's too much money, but this is beautiful."

"Yeah, it's been a beautiful car for sure—$3,750."

"Thank you, thank you so much Mr. Medlam. But you said there's a second car?"

"Yeah, under that other wood pile over there. But Pop and I never got it put together. It's still in the crate from Ford, so guess it would cost you a little in labor to put together. I know it took us a long time. But, look here, it's still worth quite a bit."

"My god, still in the crate, maybe all the original paper work in there, right from Henry Ford's own company?"

Harlan Medlam went for the throat. "Reckon I'd take $10,000 for it."

Paul turned to Harlan, a look of unbelieving shock on his face. Bruce dropped the board he was carrying.

But Froggy's face was shining. "It's a terrible price for antique cars, but it's worth it, it's worth it. Of course, Mr. Medlam, an opportunity like this only comes by once in a lifetime."

He didn't bother to correct Froggy as he wrote out the check for $13,750, but the man was wrong, thought Harlan. The opportunities of a lifetime came by, not once, but day by day. God truly was lenient. All you had to do was keep reaching out, and he'd lay them right in your lap.

Harlan was patting the check in his pocket. Florence Medlam was patting him on the shoulder. "You poor old dear," she said. "You've had a big day. Why don't you come in, and lay on the couch while I start supper. You could have strained yourself, you know. But you'll mend, you always do.

"The men can finish up here. As a matter of fact, Paul, Bruce, why don't you tell your families to come for supper.

"That field can wait until tomorrow, Harlan, if you're up to it."

As a matter of fact, he was starting to shuffle to the left, but then softly groaned "aah," as though it was a spasm, when he noticed the others were looking at him.

Revenge of the Doobey brothers

Author's note: Take note that this is the first story in a sequel of four stories. I recommend you read them in order for full effect. The real Doobey brothers and their mate, Kukumba, raised some nice goslings on our farm.

CHARMIN' CARMEN the horse trader wouldn't have hired Hard Luck Pete if it hadn't been for the tri-color paint bronco he spotted. The animal was partitioned off by itself in the top front of Lucille Lillie's double-deck semi-load of killer horses headed to Texas for the eventual edification of French cuisine.

Lucille wouldn't have stopped either, but she'd had a flat tire burn up on the rear of the trailer. She bounced out of her tractor seat, boiling-over angry over the tire, and cussing under her bleached-blonde hair. The display was most unladylike—if Lucille had ever claimed to be a lady, which actually she never had thought of. Lucille concentrated in dollars of product shipped over the road, not in ladiness or unexpected stops.

Carmen walked up to her, fascinated as always by the green eyes set in a leathery tan face with pink blotch spots, and asked, "Why you got that old horse penned up separate from the others up front?"

"He's a troublemaker, Carmen. He's a ferocious son-of-a-gun, always whirling to kick out with his hind feet at the other horses. Plus that, he's a biter. Maybe that's OK out on a pasture, where the other horses can get away from him. But I don't want my product torn up or crippled before I get to the Gulf."

"Mind if I climb up there to take a look at him?" Carmen asked, puffing as he pumped his bow legs one over the other up the slatted side of the trailer while going "ssh, ssh" at the horses inside as though he could calm them down. "Lordsey may, lordsey may, why they got to make these trucks so high?"

Carmen pulled his white cowboy hat off to hang to the side one-handed and two-footed, pushing his long Siouxian-type nose through the slats to get a closer look. The horse had looked red and white paint when he first spotted him, but now he could see the black streaks and spots too—a real tri-color, maybe even more color than that with the brown-red turning to streaks of beige.

The brown eye that turned toward him rolled nervously, but then the horse turned his head to reveal a blue, white and brown rolling eye on the other side.

"Whooey, Lucille, he got the evil eye. Look at that thing rollin' around in his head. Got good legs too—good, heavy-boned thick legs like somebody bred him to be cushioned to be a jumper or a great rodeo bucker. Or, maybe he's got some cuttin' horse background? I don't know about that, Lucille. Them boys sure love their sorrels and bays, and maybe the occasional Appaloosa. But this bronc ain't no Appaloosa by any stretch of the mind.

"You let me have him at killer price, would you? Maybe me and Frances could get him worked into a gentler state for some fancy cow-

boy horse with those colors, or for one of them lady barrel riders that wants the sturdy legs."

"I know your wife works horses in the round pen to tame them down, Carmen. But do you really want your Frances in the pen with that bronc? Come on."

"She'll be OK. Frances knows her horses. And I'll be helpin' her. I work the rascal, too. Got to work'em a little yourself if you're gonna trade them."

"Killer price plus $50 for unloading that crazy animal, Carmen. Have to unload all the others off the top in your lot to get him off, you know. That's a lot of trouble."

"How about I says $25 plus killer price, and I get a couple of my boys to do the unloadin' while you and I sit in the shade and sip a couple of cold ones each, Lucille. Hey, what you think of that deal? Don't mind cuttin' you a little tip money, eh?"

They were sitting in the shade, sipping their third cans of Lone Star beer. The boys had rigged all kinds of trip ropes on the tri-color bronc before finally adding a loop over the rear end, then dragged him with the tractor to a high steel-rail round pen.

Ernest had joined Carmen and Lucille—beginning the business of sipping suds himself, his long, lean shadow stretching across the lawn.

"What you think of him, Honey Bunch?" Carmen called to Frances, who was turning around in the center of the arena with a lariat while the tri-color bucked and galloped around her.

"He'll calm down, Carmen," Frances said, shading a hand over her black-rimmed glasses. "I'll have him coming up to me in a week. But I'm not too sure about being the first one to climb up on him. He's pretty spirited."

A small flock of gray Toulouse geese with a rear-guard of two large ganders waddled across the yard in front of the beer drinkers, the ganders pausing to go "hsss, hsss," toward them.

"Stupid Doobey brothers," Carmen said waving his hat. "Go on get out of here. Leave us be."

"Doobey brothers?" Lucille asked.

"Yeah, that's Frances' geese. I call them two ganders the Doobey brothers," Carmen said. "I kind of like to watch them workin' those long necks to clip the grass, but I can't abide them stupid Doobey brothers hissin' at me. Old Carmen here figures one of them ought to get slow-roasted for Christmas. But who wants to eat a Doobey brother when you can have good beef?"

"You know, Carmen," Ernest said. "You'd better get Hard Luck Pete when it comes time to sit on that horse. Pete can do it without getting busted up. He's a prime broncbuster if that critter goes to throwing a wild one."

"Hard Luck Pete? Ain't he the one they tell about riding a wild horse two miles only to get thrown off in a patch of prickly pear cactus?"

"Yeah, he's the one. But they only tell it because it's uncommon for Pete to get throwed. Usually his bad luck happens after a ride. He couldn't get hurt on the prickly pear anyway because of that rear end of his."

"What about his rear end?"

"Well, you heard the television commercials about exercises giving people buns of steel? Ain't anybody got an iron posterior like Pete's after decades of bronc bustin' and rodeoin'. Plus, I went skinny dippin' in a pond once with him and some other guys, and that Pete's got ridges of calluses across his behind. Nobody had to pull any cactus needles out of him. They just took a razor, and sliced off a quarter-inch of calluses. Yessir, I'd sure get old Pete," said Ernest.

"I don't know if I'd do that if I was you, Carmen," said Lucille. "I hear about Hard Luck Pete, too, and I hear he's plumb dangerous now because he's commenced to praying before he rides. It's real serious. If he doesn't have the hard luck, it's got to go somewhere else on them that wasn't praying when Pete was. I hear lots of folks are having uncommon bad luck when Pete's been around. You'd better get another hardhead to sit that tri-color for the first time."

"Phsst and phooey, I don't believe that kind of stuff," Carmen said. "I'm a horse trader, ain't I? That means I know my stuff, do my homework, and I play the odds. There ain't no such thing as luck. It's all in the odds, and I know my odds. This is simple odds.

"That tri-color is a good lookin' horse. If he don't work out, he'll get shipped down to Texas on another truck load, and I'll be out my $25 unless a 50-50 chance hits of the slaughter market going up—them Frenchies are still eating, ain't they? Hard Luck Pete it is.

"Hey, Lucille, come look at my brand new red three-quarter ton pickup truck before you leave. Got it all polished up, and it's a dandy."

So it was a month and a half later, when Frances with a little bit of help from Charmin' Carmen had the tri-color following her around the round pen like a big dog, that Hard Luck Pete himself drove into the yard for the first ride.

The bronc looked calm out there. He'd been gentled enough that he even held still when he was shoed in anticipation of riding him. Carmen had confidence in him.

Carmen had taken the luck warnings just seriously enough to allow Ernest to drive his new red truck around back to park it under a lean-to shed against the barn for some protection. No sense taking unneeded chances.

And now what do you know? Here was this Hard Luck Pete climbing out of a new red three-quarter-ton pickup truck identical to Charmin' Carmen's. He was almost a sorrowful spectacle of a little man with sagging, brown cheeks, long chin and long nose on short legs even more bow legged than Carmen's, the feet tucked into boots that looked oversized for the body. Only the jeans fit tightly against his thin legs and oversized rump.

The Doobey brothers came flapping their wings across the yard, hissing and honking as though overjoyed that here was a victim worthy of full attention. Pete paid little attention to them, but pulled his hat off to lay it in the truck bed, and turned with both hands on the truck to lower his head in prayer.

After a couple of tugs at Pete's behind, the Doobey brothers gave up to stand turning their stupid heads in unison at their own reflections in the shining truck finish.

Carmen came up to stand while the small brown-haired man finished his business meaningfully clearing his throat at last before Hard Luck Pete turned around to face him. The man's brown eyes were amazingly bright and shiny in the sagging bulldog face.

"Had to pray on my truck special hard," Pete explained. "It's the best thing I ever owned other than a spotted dog that got run over by a train one time after I rode, and a new saddle I'd just shined before the hogs got out, and ate it. Is that your bronc with that woman leading him into the arena."

"Yeah, that's my wife, Frances," Carmen said gesturing to the tall, slender brown-haired woman leading the tri-color into the arena. "She's got him all saddled, and ready for you. You need anything special? Anything we can do for you before you get on him? Got your $50 cash for riding him right here, but I don't want you getting hurt either. Just want him good, and geared down before somebody without your expertise gets on him."

"No, no, I'm fine. Ain't no bronc going to hurt me. Looks fine like he is."

Pete followed the tri-color into the arena where the earth had been freshly disked up to slow the horse, and provide a softer landing cushion for a rider. He walked up to the horse while Frances and Ernest held him.

Pete bent forward to sniff noses with the tri-color, sucking in some of the bronc's hot breath while blowing his own wind back into the broad nostrils. He ran a hand down the horse's long neck and withers where the tough skin still rippled over hard muscle from the landing of a horsefly.

Pete gazed with his brown eyes into the soft brown eye of the horse. Then he walked around to the horse's other side to see that tri-colored eyeball rolling at him. Pete did a short step backward to make the sign of the crucifix over his chest at the sight of the eye.

Then he swung forward with uncommon grace for such a small body to land effortlessly in the saddle seizing the reins as Frances and Ernest backed away.

The bronc stood stock still for a moment, then turned in a half-circle. Pete pulled his head up to rein him the other way before all hell exploded under him.

Carmen saw he was correct that those heavy boned legs held the ability of a rodeo bucking bronc because the tri-color went straight in the air effortlessly before churning around in a bucking, kicking twist. Around and around he went trying to dislodge Hard Luck Pete. Then he crow-hopped with arched back across the arena. Pete stuck tighter than a cockle burr.

It seemed like it was going to last forever, but when the horse reached the level of running around and around the pen in circles, everybody knew Pete had made his ride. Hard Luck Pete tightened the reins and extra rope to turn the tri-color's head the other way. Back and forth they went changing directions until the bronc was worn out. He stood there huffing while Pete got down.

Pete went up, breathed in the tri-color's nose again, then jumped back into the saddle to squeeze his legs into the horse to make him go again. Three times he did that before the small man came out of the arena to stand in front of Carmen quietly, his shining eyes darting reluctant glances all around. The only sound was an occasional "thump, thump, thump" out behind the barn.

"Reckon my part's done here, Carmen," Pete said. "Doubt the next person to ride him will have quite as much problem if they ride him right away. He kind of likes Frances anyway."

"Thump, thump, thump. Thump, thump, thump."

"You shore did ride him good, Pete," Carmen said. "Reckon I never did see better horsemanship."

"You hear that sound," Frances asked, "that kind of thump, thump, thump? There it is again, thump, thump, thump."

Hard Luck Pete rolled his eyes. "Reckon I better go if you'll kindly give me my 50 bucks."

"Sure, sure, Pete," Carmen was saying just as Ernest ran up.

"Carmen, Carmen," Ernest hollered. "It's the Doobey brothers, they got to pecking at their reflections on your shiny new red truck, and they've pecked most the paint off the sides."

"Oh," said Pete. "Oh no. You got a new red truck too?"

"Pray, Carmen, pray quick," shouted Ernest grabbing his hat off to flap it in the air. "Hard Luck Pete done prayed, and now his bad luck's gone to your truck."

"Those stupid Doobey brothers," moaned Carmen pushing back his wisps of thin hair under the cowboy hat. "They've about ruined the finish on my new red truck."

"Carmen, the tri-color bronc's got out," Frances yelled. "One of us must not have put the gate pin in good."

"There's four of us. Herd him, herd him, let's just get around him now," said Carmen. "Darn it, he's goin' around back. Headed for the barn lean-to. Easy now just squeeze him up under the lean-to. Oh, look at my poor truck. Those stupid Doobey brothers."

The tri-color was just fine getting squeezed in backwards, Frances softly murmuring "there, there," to him, when a stirrup on the side caught over a nail-head sticking out of a supporting post, and tugged the saddle sideways.

The bronc didn't like the unaccustomed pull of the saddle, and kicked out hard with his steel-shoed back feet, "whump, whump, whump" into the shattering grill-work of Carmen's new red truck.

It took the talent of Hard Luck Pete to walk up to the tri-color, softly blowing in his nose before unhooking the stirrup, then climbing on his back to ride him back to his pen.

"Now, now, Mr. Carmen," said Hard Luck Pete. "Quit your moaning and crying, OK? You can just keep your 50 bucks. Honest, I didn't know you had a brand, new red truck just like mine before I started, or we'd have prayed over it too.

"It was just too identical a thing for my kind of luck."

How the cat business became profitable

Author's note: This is the second story in a sequel of four stories.

THE COUNTER man was pushing the last sawdust out the door with a big sweep, completing the cleanup of a particularly messy night before at the Deerhead Tavern as Doc Frenchie stepped in.

Actually, he only had to take about 15 steps to get inside the door from his own office because Doc Frenchie's veterinarian office was next door to the Deerhead.

With a name like Frenchie, you might think of the classic French look, perhaps slender and dark, but old Doc Frenchie appeared exactly the opposite, with a big, broad, ruddy face and body. He plastered down his sandy brown hair on his large cranial dome, so it fit neatly under a white Stetson-style hat.

His fat nose and crevassed face were pitted with white blemishes as though he must have once held his head inside a sand blaster. Doc walked with that particular pinched slow stroll peculiar to many who wore cowboy boots. He looked like his customers, the cattlemen of the grasslands.

Doc Frenchie was a large animal veterinarian by profession and by choice. Oh, he'd occasionally work on a dog, especially if it was the farm or ranch dog of the cattle-herding breeds—English Shepherds, Border Collies, Australian Shepherds, Blue Heelers and so on.

By profession, and by choice, he avoided other small animals, especially of the feline variety. His specialties were cattle and horses, and a hog or a sheep if he really had to.

By habit he was so quiet that people actually listened when he spoke. Doc Frenchie could sit at the coffee table in the Deerhead under the creaking ceiling fan for an hour without saying a word beyond two-syllable replies while the conversation droned around him.

His wide, thin mouth—used mainly for sipping coffee—promised an event if it happened to begin turning into a smile. Most often the mouth could be described as glum. Doc's mouth-loosening times usually occurred in the company of Jim Beam coffee and a deck of cards, after a good fish catch, or when settling up with hot, dirty ranchers after working cattle.

When Doc sat down, Johnny Beauregard was agonizing this day over what to do with all his money. Johnny barely paused his monologue to acknowledge, "Good mornin', Doc." Doc replied with his usual, "Hmmp."

Johnny continued, "I don't like to take certificates for more than 90 days, but that means you always have to watch for the best rates. I don't know, I might move some of it this time from down at the savings and loan to the national bank over there. I almost put money in First State one time, but they promised me a real good deal on anything over a hundred thousand, and then they backed down."

Doc Frenchie was beginning to smile, so 20 men up and down the table automatically stopped talking or listening to anybody else to turn toward him.

"Johnny," Doc said. "You got $100,000. You know, I could learn to call you Daddy..... Daddy."

"Well, Doc, if I was to have a baby boy," Johnny said, "I could hardly imagine him looking more original than you."

"Well, I'd love you, Daddy. For sure, I would love you at least $100,000 worth. What are we going to do today, Daddy?"

"For sure I know what one of you is doing today," said Donnie Dector, down the table. "You got a customer, Doc. Look what's getting out in front of your office."

With the first glances out the window, the chuckles and knowing laughter grew beyond what it had been with Doc's little jab at Johnny. That was because Doc's apparent customer was a suburban looking woman in sandals and shorts with short dark hair. She was unloading a cage holding two big, overweight, neutered house cats out the back of a green mini-van.

"Kitties, Doc," said Johnny, savoring the chance diversion in conversation. "Looks like you get to work on some nice kitties, Doc."

"Oh, good night," said Doc.

"You don't seem to be getting up, Doc," said Johnny. "You'd better go open up shop for the lady."

"Umm, phht, darn," said Doc. Then he just sat there.

"Looks like she's looking in your door, Doc," said Buster Noggins from further down the table. "She's tried the knob. It's locked. Now she's reading your hours. Better get over there, Doc. Those cats might get hot setting out on the sidewalk like that. Oh, good, good, she's moving them to the shade from the car."

"C'mon, Doc. Go help her out," said Johnny.

"Baah," said Doc, sipping another swallow of coffee. "She'll go away. Hey, is the sports page still with that paper down there? I wasn't stayin' in town this morning anyway. Got to go out to Charmin' Carmen's to give injections to some yearling quarterhorse colts he got in."

"She ain't lookin' like she's leavin' anytime soon, Doc," said Buster. "Hey, I kind of like that one cat, big old orange tiger-stripe fellow. Look at him, Doc. He's pretty. So's the fluffy gray one. She looks like a nice lady too, Doc."

"Hmmph. Who you gonna pick this fall? Oakland? Might have to slip into my place through the alley door if she doesn't leave soon. Got to get my stuff loaded."

"Kinda looks like that problem's solved for you too," said Johnny. "Here's Charmin' Carmen himself pulling up in his truck. Hey, what's that old scoundrel got in that cage in the back of his truck? Looks like two big old gray geese.

"Now he's got the lady looking at them. Look out, lady, you must have a money smell to you for Charmin' Carmen to show you anything. Look at the old horse trader admire her cats. Oh boy, she's looking at the geese again, and givin' Carmen something. Uh oh, Carmen knows your habits, Doc. He's opening the door up front for her."

"Got to go to the bathroom. If they ask, tell them I'm not in here," said Doc Frenchie.

"Hi, boys," said Charmin' Carmen. "I'd like you to meet Mrs. Marcelle Eulinger, owner of them fine-bred pussy cats out there on the sidewalk. She's lookin' for...."

"He ain't here. Ain't seen him at all," said Johnny.

"That's right," added Buster. "And he ain't never been here, either."

"You mean Doc Frenchie? That's who she's lookin' for, aren't you, Mrs. Eulinger."

"That's right, Carmen, and I really appreciate your help. Carmen tells me the doctor is very particular when it comes to treating cats."

"He shor is, ma'am," said Johnny, grinning. "He might show up here after a while. Why don't you and Carmen just pull up here at the end of the table where the half-drunk cup of coffee is. Just shove it aside. One of the guys had to leave quick. Doc will probably come in here soon. He always comes in."

"I was so fortunate to run into Carmen with his geese. I've been wanting some waterfowl for the yard, and I had no idea they could be purchased so reasonably, only $15 each for.... What was it you called them, the Doobey brothers?"

Buster slapped his knee, grinning, "I knew it was a Charmin' Carmen deal, the same geese that picked the paint off the sides of his new truck."

"Curious," said Carmen, "uncommonly curious—that's what they were, a mark of real intelligence in geese. All you have to do is let them have plenty of yard space to run in, and things to look at, and they won't get in trouble."

"I thought you were raffling the Doobey brothers for Thanksgiving dinners," said Johnny, pointing at a money jar on the bar.

"Well, I was taking them down to the locker plant, but I was stoppin' by to have Doc give them a checkup."

"Yeah," said Buster. "The two of you were probably going to have a drink celebrating them being processed. I've heard you say you couldn't stand them Doobey brothers, and Doc say they're nearly bad as cats."

"Now, now, you boys quit funnin' with old Carmen here. That's all they're doing, Mrs. Eulinger, is teasing. I got to go to the restroom. Ma'am, if you'll go open the back of your minivan, I'll be back out to help you load them prime Doobey brothers and your cats. Me and Doc will come by your place this afternoon so he can treat your cats, and we'll be bringin' you a prime load of kittens too."

"Kittens? What do you mean, kittens?" Johnny asked.

"Now, now boys, ssh, ssh, fun's fun, but let's stop now. Shucks, Mrs. Eulinger, everybody knows old Carmen raises the best gooses and cats around, and Doc Frenchie is just the best vet to get to take care of them."

The men were smiling at each other, and beginning to guffaw as Marcelle Eulinger walked out the front door. But as for Charmin' Carmen, he was already running for the restroom.

"Doc Frenchie, Doc Frenchie, Doc, you come out of there now. Old Carmen's got us a gold mine on the hoof. That woman's a genuine California millionaire that's moved here. She's into companion animals, companion cats, companion gooses, and we can get her graduated into companion horses."

Carmen came out pulling Doc by the arm.

"Doc, I told her I had cats just like hers at home, and she tells me she gave $50 each for those buggers. Doc, Doc, she's a-goin' to give us $5 each for kittens cuz I was honest, and told her things are cheaper here. She says it's a bargain.

"You got to help me. We're headin' out to my place to catch all the barn kittens we can find, and if we can find any on your farm, we'll get them too. That fine lady deserves selection. She already gave me $30 for them stupid Doobey brothers."

"I got some kittens at my place," hollered Johnny.

"Me, too," said Buster.

"I know where there's some giveaway kittens," said Donnie.

"Have them all here at the Deerhead by 2 p.m.," said Carmen. "If she takes yours, too, I give you 50 percent of the money for them. Now, it's my deal. Mine and Doc's.

"Doc, I know you told me how much you hate a darned cat, but I tell you it appears there's money to be made in the cat business if you get the right person. I hate them stupid Doobey brothers too, but looky here, I done right by them. Now this lady needs a good cat veterinarian if she's gettin' all these kitties."

"I know I could learn to call you Daddy, Doc, for the sake of the cats of course...Daddy," said Johnny.

Carmen had Doc Frenchie by the arm and was pulling him toward the door. A couple of other sets of hands were gently pushing his back and shoulders to move him along.

"Hmmph," said Doc Frenchie, but he was walking.

Educating Mrs. Marcelle Eulinger

Author's note: This is the third story in a sequel of four stories.

MRS. MARCELLE Eulinger stood amid the maize of a dozen pet carriers and cages at 2 p.m. in the Deerhead Tavern, mopping back her short black hair while smiling gratefully with white-toothed grin set in perfect complexion at the men around her.

The carriers and cages were full of all colors of kittens—black, white, gray and orange, Siamese pattern, striped and calico.

"You are such dear men, so honest and, well, true, to bring me kittens, all of them at only $5 each when I've confessed your local price is way below what I'm used to. I paid $50 each for cats where I lived in California, and I feel I have to let you know, that was very low there because it was from an individual instead of a pet store."

Charmin' Carmen rubbed a finger under one high cheekbone, and pulled off his cowboy hat to rasp, "And we're only too glad to help you, Mrs. Eulinger. You choose your kittens, then ol' Doc here will help us carry them next door to his place for distemper shots."

Beside Carmen, Doc Frenchie stood stoically with his fingers hooked in his pockets, his broad pit-marked face looking straight ahead, his hat still on his head.

"You know, I'm just glad I've moved to this town," said Mrs. Eulinger. "Everything is so reasonable here. I feel like I'm taking advantage of people. The bungalow I bought over on West Street—you may know it, the Smith place. Where I came from it would have been worth $300,000. They had it advertised for $80,000, and I just snapped it up before anyone else could get it."

Cough, hack—"You paid $80,000 for that old...," said Charmin' Carmen. "Lordy, lordy, I had a couple of other places I could have showed you. No matter. Yes, ma'am, we're just full of bargains here, ain't that right, Doc?"

Doc Frenchie looked almost sadly at Marcelle Eulinger as she sat down in front of them, crossing her tanned legs below her crisp white shorts as the first kitten was lifted into her lap.

"Ma'am," he said, frowning his wide thin lips into a stretch. "You know it always pays to shop around."

Johnny Beauregard spoke up. "Mrs. Eulinger, that calico baby is one of the kittens I brought. Don't you think she's a good'un? Well worth $5, ain't she?"

"What do you think, Doc?" she asked, turning her brown eyes

upward to smile again. "You're the veterinarian. You want to take this kitten, and look at her, too. Isn't she sweet?"

"Truth is, ma'am, I'm not much for cats," Doc said looking toward the ceiling and removing his Stetson to brush back his thin hair. "It's not that I hate them like some would tell you. I like animals or I wouldn't have become an animal doctor. I just like to see a cat out in the barn, not sleeping with people. Truth is, just handling them today, my sinuses are swelling a little. I think it's just pretty, though—I mean nice or whatever—that you like cats. I guess I'm just saying I'm not much of a cat man, more of a horse and cow man, ma'am."

"Come on, Doc," said Johnny. "We all know how you hate a darned cat. He don't even want to work on 'em, ma'am. Old Carmen got him to help get these cats. You ought to get another vet to work on 'em."

"Shut up, Johnny. You're always yappin' when you ought to shut up. I said I would work on Mrs. Eulinger's kittens, so I will. Give them all their shots for you, ma'am."

"Doctor, that's so sweet. It's fine that you're such an honest, upstanding man."

"He's honest all right, Mrs. Eulinger," said Carmen. "Does all my work, and never overcharged me. And believe me, there's folks who would like to get to a poor, honest, hard-workin' horse trader."

"I know I would," said Donnie Dector. "Mrs. Eulinger, just take a look at those black kittens I brought you."

"Now, now, boys," said Carmen. "I know they's all fine kittens, but everybody knows there ain't no finer bred-up cat than a Siamese, and looky there, ma'am, I brought you at least three-quarter bred Siamese kittens."

"It's so hard to pick," said Marcelle Eulinger. "There must be more than 50 kittens here. I know I want these here—and oh, look at those white blue-eyed ones. Doc, are you sure you can't help me out? Are there any health tips to watch for? I'd really just like to take all of them."

"Mrs. Eulinger," said Doc, his sunburned face turning a much heavier shade of red that spread down his neck in a blush, "I think I can help you. Just leave the kittens for a minute, and come over to that corner table with me to talk. Boys, you all just stay over here away from us while we talk."

"What about our cat deal?" asked Carmen. "Don't you think we need to get this all taken care of?"

"Yeah," said Johnny. "These kittens are pretty young, Doc. We need them to get loaded up soon so they can go to Mrs. Eulinger's to rest."

"We'll get her kittens taken care of so she can load them up in just a little bit, boys," said Doc. "I just need to give her some cat advice."

"You know, she's a good lookin' woman," said Carmen, nodding to the corner where Doc seemed to be speaking intensively to Mrs. Eulinger, gesturing with his hands for emphasis.

"Yeah, and she's a rich one too," said Johnny. "I hope that old cat hater ain't talking her out of our deal. By now I'd like to sell cats once in my life."

They looked back at the corner where Marcelle Eulinger was leaning forward, gesturing with her hands, talking back to Doc, who was sitting up rigidly looking at her. Suddenly, the big red face of old somber Doc Frenchie split open in a big wide grin, and he was talking back to her without bothering to return to a frown.

"Look at that," said Johnny. "I don't know how, but I'm afraid that sour old sodbuster's spoiling it for us. I don't like seeing him grinning. She's chuckling too, I believe. Why did he have to take her over there?"

"I don't know, I don't know," said Charmin' Carmen. "I ain't feelin' anything, and I tell you I usually got the sixth-sense instinct for these deals. Only time I ever lost my sense recently was when Hard Luck Pete came to visit, but even then I ended up gettin' rid of those darned Doobey brothers. Sssh. Here they come, here they come."

Marcelle Eulinger stood smiling, her head barely coming up to the top of Doc Frenchie's chest, while he held up his hands.

"OK, boys," said Doc Frenchie. "Mrs. Eulinger is taking all these kittens—just get a count on them. Looks like 50-some head at the agreed-on trade price of $5 a head. After they're counted, just get them all over to my office where you can all help hold them while I give them shots.

"Marcelle will watch the count while I slip into the restroom to wash off a little," he added smiling at the woman again.

"Marcelle," Carmen whispered into Johnny's ear. "Did I hear Ol' Doc call that little lady Marcelle— her first name, not ma'am or Mrs. Eulinger?"

"You sure did, Carmen. I heard it too. Marcelle is darn sure what he called her, Marcelle no mistakin' it. Hey, hold on there, Donnie. That's my cage of kittens. I want to be in on countin'em."

"Hmm, you check the count on my kittens, OK, Johnny. Ol' Carmen here needs to slip into the restroom a minute myself, got to check up on that Ol' Doc."

Doc Frenchie had obviously just scrubbed his face, and his hat was laid to the side while he slicked down his thin sandy strands of hair with moisture. "Hmmp," he said, seeing Carmen come in the door. But then he smiled again despite himself.

"What'd you just do out there, you old coyote?" Carmen asked.

"I spilled the beans on you boys. Told Marcelle she was being taken advantage of because she could watch the papers for all the free kittens she would ever need in this area. Told her she needed to watch her step in moving to a new area because she way overpaid for that cruddy old bungalow house. Told her you're an old scoundrel, and the only honest things she got from you was the price of the Doobey brothers because that's what geese really bring here, and you didn't know she was rich and naive yet."

"Naah, you didn't tell her that did you? Jeez, that's terrible."

"Yeah, but she said she liked you all anyway. Said she'd been havin' fun watchin' true aboriginal fellows. Said she'd knowed that she probably was being taken advantage of somehow, but it was fun anyway. She knows what you are, Carmen, and she still enjoys you. Quite a lady, that. Said she appreciated my honesty, and she thought I was a well-educated attractive fellow."

"Naah, she didn't tell you that, did she?"

"Sure did, then she asked me over to supper."

"Doc, no, you can't go. You're the naive one. She's probably figured you're a single fellow. Doc, I hate to tell you now, but that lady's a widow."

"I know," Doc said, smiling again. "She's a good talker, too, and she's got a shed out back where all the kittens can stay."

"But you can't be interested in her. Pretty woman like that ought to be able to see you're gettin' kind of old. You must have blindsided her with all that honesty."

Old Doc Frenchie smiled so broadly that Carmen guessed it must have been the first time he ever saw his teeth exposed like that—pretty good teeth, too, except for the gold-capped one.

"I told her, Carmen. Told her I wasn't a spring chicken anymore. Told her I was 55 years old."

"And it didn't make any difference? Gawd, Doc, I hate to say it, but you ain't very pretty. That good lookin' woman didn't think it made any difference you're such an old goat?"

"Naah, she was honest with me too, Carmen. Women like her got their own market specialties a clod like you don't know nothin' about. She'll be 60 next month."

Charmin' Carmen turns generous

Author's note: This is the fourth story in a sequel of four stories.

YOU COULD cut the humidity with a knife.
Way down, where the creek joined the South Fork, a streak of lightning slashed across black rumbling clouds that were disappearing over the horizon. But the crowd didn't care.

There was just enough breeze to blow a hat off if you weren't careful, enough to take the moisture away from the bodies in the bright shirts, white western hats and blue jeans. It was enough breeze to charm the nose with the combination of horse sweat, horse manure, and sawdust and sand used to dry the wet earth of the arena.

Possibly the man who cared the least about the trickle of sweat around the band of his hat was Charmin' Carmen the horse trader because he considered this his special day of the year. He and his wife, Frances, had built this arena on their own place for a bronco-riding and steer-roping event, a great move to sell more horses to the people who bought horses for recreation and work.

They even made sure the announcer had a good sound system and a viewing stand at the end of the arena—just like at a big-time rodeo or fair. A truckload of Longhorn calves with 6-inch horns had been brought in for the roping.

Doc Frenchie and his new wife, Marcelle, a pair Carmen took credit for introducing each other to, were posted with their newly painted white veterinarian truck that read "Cats, Dogs, Horses and Cattle, Our Specialties" down by the gates in case an animal needed help.

There was even a nurse from the hospital with a bottle of peroxide and first-aid kit if a cowboy got wounded to the point where somebody griped about it.

Best of all, Carmen's and Frances' truck-driving friend, Lucille, had brought in a load of horses Carmen had been buying up, down and around the city suburbs a few months before.

City people were notorious for putting a good horse on too few acres to feed him, and then forgetting him when the newness wore off. Carmen bought the starving horses, fed the weight back on them, and Frances worked to bring their training up.

For the horses that weren't going to work out to ride, Lucille was available again. She hauled them in her semi, blonde curls bouncing down the interstate to the Gulf, to go to the killer plant for frozen boxing of export edible cuts for the eventual edification of French cuisine, of course.

Carmen got her to bring back a whole trailer load of Lone Star Beer with the understanding that she only got six six-packs to drink on the trip from her personal cooler.

He also made deals with the local soda pop bottling plant and coffee vendor to stock his little refreshments booth by the arena. That way he could watch the sales of all the drinks from his position in the top of the bleachers going to the eventual edification of his and Frances' bank account.

Frances also had cut a deal with the local bakery for cinnamon rolls to sell in exchange for training a horse. For all the money-making tricks Carmen hadn't thought of, slender, brown-haired innocent Frances could think of them hands down.

Carmen and Frances had 300 horses they could sell from among those they bought or raised, a near-record for the ranch. They were becoming big-time—arena, cash flow and all.

Now Carmen sat in the top of the stands, smiling like a pot-bellied

catfish in a Stetson, watching all this prosperity float by. He was a study in benign salesmanship ready to pounce on the prey in a laid-back charming way up by the horse pens after the show events were over.

"How-da-dooh, how-da-dooh, good to see ya here," he nodded to everyone who came near. "Good to see that rain steered around us, ain't it? Looks like a fine, fine day for our little party here, don't it? Be glad ta give you a little tour around the little ranch here if ya want to after the events."

The preacher was coming into the arena to offer the prayer for the events, and all the cowboys and cowgirls who would participate were marching in on foot to form a semi-circle around him facing the stands. Always good to bring God in on your side, thought Carmen.

Carmen was just dwelling on the God picture—thinking of all the likely sales he would have with it this evening, imagining himself a little pot-bellied figure with halo before the pearly gates, dollar bills showering down on him—when he saw the cowboy with the bulldog hangy cheeks. The cowboy was pulling his hat off with the others, slouching with his big rump protruding over bull legs and high-heeled bronc busting boots.

The announcer had just asked for quiet before the invocation when a bellow rang from the stands.

"Stop! Stop! Don't let that feller pray with everybody else. Stop that Hard Luck Pete. Where'd he come from? He wasn't invited, was he? We can't have him prayin' on our place."

The whole crowd paused in place, then turned to watch Carmen bull his way down the bleacher seats with people standing to make way for him, still shouting, "You stop that, Pete! Don't you go to prayin' again.

"You got your red pickup here? Ernest, where's my red truck? Remember them stupid Doobey brothers geese peckin' the paint off my truck last time you wuz here cuz it looked like yours, and everybody knows your bad luck got to go somewhere, and if you pray it ain't goin' to be on you, but stuck on all the poor innocents around you which could be me.

"Don't you go prayin' here on me again, Hard Luck Pete. Somebody get that rascal out of here."

But nobody else moved. They didn't know what to think of their raving host. So Carmen huffed and puffed his way right to the arena gate. He swung it open, and marched right up to Pete, who had his bright, brown eyes fixed on him like everybody else.

"What you doin' here anyway?" Carmen demanded.

"Why I come to ride a buckin' horse, and rope a few calves for the fun and the prize money just like all the other boys," said Pete.

Charmin' Carmen paused a moment looking at the crowd of people leaning forward to see what this was, and realized he was disrupting his own event and his own potential sales.

He stepped up to look Pete in the face, his own big Siouxian nose next to Pete's long skinny one.

"You gonna leave or what, Hard Luck Pete?"

"Why, Carmen? Why I gotta go? I'm just here to have fun with everybody else."

"Sssh, sssh, everybody's listenin' in here. It's cuz, Hard Luck Pete, you took to prayin', and every time you do that, your hard luck goes to someone else. Only way I ain't gonna drag you screamin' and kickin' from this ring instead of gettin' your fanny floated by a bronc is for you to pray for me too when you pray. Pray I get what I got comin' to me."

"Uhh, Carmen, I couldn't do that to anyone, pray that they get what's comin' to them. You wouldn't want that either. How about I pray that you get what you need?"

"That sounds fine, too. You promise to pray for what I need, and you can stay."

"Done deal, Carmen. Yer in my prayer."

Charmin' Carmen walked from the arena in his gimpy, bow-legged gait waving his hands in the air that it was all over. "Everybody pray now, ya hear. Give us a good one parson." And he muttered under his breath, "You give us a good one, too, you Hard Luck Pete."

While everybody else was praying, Carmen was doing his own under his breath. "You hear that, God? I know you're up there listenin' to that old Hard Luck Pete even if you ain't listenin' to the rest of us cuz ya know that scallywag really needs you, and is sincere. Ya hear him talkin' about me? I'm ready, Lord. Let them old blessings fall all over me cuz I could use a great cash flow year."

The broncos bucked, turned and twisted just like they were supposed to. Carmen watched with satisfaction as Hard Luck Pete hit the ground from his second horse just like everybody else did some of the time. Apparently the boy wasn't perfect.

The calves dodged, and turned making the horse and rider that got ropes over their necks stand out as experts. Pete roped them some, and missed some too. Good, the boy wasn't perfect. But I guess God doesn't ask for perfection, just faith, Carmen thought to himself. When you had luck like Pete's just surviving to ask protection was faith.

Carmen's cell phone rang. "Hello, dag nab it. I'm in the middle of some events here. Can't you call back another time?"

"Carmen, don't hang up. This is your brother, Larson. Look, I'm desperate. A deal just fell through for me, and I already wrote a check to cover it for $5,000. You know I don't normally ask you for favors. But that's larceny if it ain't covered, isn't it? And I can't have people calling me Larcenous Larson. Loan it to me this once please?"

"You want $5,000? That's a lot of money, Larson. How soon you going to get it back to me if I wuz to help you."

"Couple of weeks, Carmen. Just a couple of weeks, and I'll have it back to you. Just don't tell my wife or anyone, OK? Send it in the next hour, OK?"

"Well, I guess you are the other kid our mother had. I'll bail ya out. Call in to my bank to wire it to you now. Just let me get down here behind the stands."

Carmen had no sooner made the wire when the preacher came up.

"Carmen, I'm wondering if you might be able to help us out? Looks to me like the good Lord has blessed you a lot here, all these friends, all these horses, this ranch. We're trying to finish the building project down at the church, and we're behind on our budget dispositions at the same time.

"A big donor is giving us money contingent on us coming up with matching money within an allotted time. Nobody's stepped forward with the money needed to finish the match, and I'm hoping you might have the ability to. Normally, they don't have the parson ask for money, but I'm here, so I thought...."

"Never you mind, never you mind at all," said Carmen. "What ya need, big money ya say, fifty bucks do you?"

"No, Carmen. We need $7,675.52. I know it's a lot, but I'm guessing with all the trading you've been doing that I see here, you could do it at least so you'd be well covered before the day is done. The Lord will truly bless you for that kind of giving, Carmen."

"Gee whillikers, you think I'm made of money? Think all these horses and this stuff happen without lots of hard work and connivin'? Lordy, lordy, preacher, you think I should be the one to come up with that kind of money? What could you be thinkin' of?"

"All I know, Carmen, is that right after the prayer, God put it in my heart that you were the one to ask for the money. I know he plans to bless you from it."

"Bless me, bless me I bet. Here, preacher. Before I change my mind, I'll just write you out a check for $7,675.52. And bet me, I better get a blessin' from it, cuz old Carmen plays the odds. If this God of yours ain't cut out for tradin' you can bet you better not come back here askin' for money or even to pray over this shindig cuz a horse trader never forgets the times he gets beat."

"Thank you, Carmen. And, God bless you, too."

Charmin' Carmen was just about to turn the corner when he saw Frances running up to him.

"Carmen, Carmen, now don't be mad, OK?" she said.

"Mad about what, Frances? Now don't tell me you went and gave away a bunch of money."

"It was our boy Wilbur, hon. He and Fannie got the chance to buy the house of their dreams, but they got to make the down payment today to hold it from getting taken by another buyer that's ready to pay now. I had to wire them the $10,000 now, so I called our bank. I knew you'd understand that it was for the kids."

"Lordy, lordy what's that dirty old Hard Luck Pete done to me? I don't get it yet, but somehow he's done turned God himself loose on me. Look here, God, stop it. Stop it right now, ya hear? I know you knowed I wuz flush with a little money left after all those deals I cut to make a killin' today. But all my cash is almost gone. Ya hear me here, God? Cut it out. Don't do no more listenin' to that Pete."

"Hey, mister, mister," said a little red-headed girl pulling at Carmen's jeans. "Can you give me 50 cents to go with my 50 cents to get a drink? I can't find my folks, and I'm awful thirsty. They say the old boy that does this fun show doesn't sell any drinks for less than a dollar. I know arithmetic because I'm in the fourth grade. Help me, please? I'll tell my Daddy to pay you back."

"Ain't gonna leave old Carmen alone, huh, God. Here little girl. Here's a whole dollar for a drink, and here's 50 cents so you can buy your old daddy one, too. There ya go, God. How was that? We gonna get rid of all my money are we?"

"Excuse me, Carmen, but I thought I just heard you mumbling something over there with that little girl about giving away money," said Alice Tenswerth. "You know I'm a 4-H leader, and it sure would be nice if you'd give us a big discount on one of those horses for a worthy member."

"Sure, sure, and I s'pose ya think I should just give away the whole darned horse?"

"Why thanks, Carmen. Did you have a particular horse in mind to give us, or should I just pick him out? This is really generous of you."

Carmen stopped himself. He'd really just given away a horse, too? This was getting ridiculous. Not only that, he was stumbling around talking to God just like the situation and Hard Luck Pete's hard luck were just as they seemed, just like somehow that prayer was coming true. Time to sober up, but a deal's a deal. "Nevah you mind, Alice. I'll help you pick a gentle one."

Somebody else tugged at his shirt from behind. What now? Why, it was old Hard Luck Pete himself smiling at him.

"I heard ya, Carmen, I heard ya. You was bein' generous. That's just what I told God too, that I wanted him to give ya what ya needed. He whispered back to me it was generosity. Generosity, Carmen, that's what ya needed more than anything. If someone gets a lot, it's a responsibility. Of course, Generous Carmen don't have quite the same ring to it that Charmin' Carmen does, does it?

They sold all 300 horses that day at record prices. Even Doc Frenchie bought six for his new bride, and the preacher bought one because he said it was time he learned to ride, too. Hard Luck Pete was so pleased with himself he bought a fine palamino, also.

The preacher and Alice Tenswerth went around the crowd the rest of the day talking about what a generous soul Charmin' Carmen was.

His brother, Larsen, showed up to sniffle about how his brother had always been there for him.

Wilbur and Fannie arrived to show anybody who would look pictures of the house their folks were helping them buy.

A little red-headed girl's daddy brought Carmen a Lone Star from the stand.

Everybody agreed you could trust to buy a horse from a man who was so generous.

"Isn't old Carmen just charmin'?" they asked each other.

Aunt Edna remembers the best kitchen sweat ever

THANKSGIVING was over, and it was one of those Saturdays when the women got together to go Christmas shopping. The men either opted to find chores to do, went with the women, or the more dedicated couch potatoes clung to the sports on television.

Everybody ate supper together, almost as though it was a third holiday. To Aunt Edna it seemed that way, as she helped clean dishes after the meal. She was in her 80s in the 1980s, and to her, any get-together relieved some of the aloneness of widowhood.

It was getting warm in the kitchen, and she patted down one of her silver curls as she smiled with warm, sparkling big brown eyes from behind her glasses at a trio of her chattering nieces carrying in piles of plates.

Behind them, Gracie, the hostess this time, said, "My, this kitchen is getting hot. It's really beginning to make me sweat. Aunt Edna, you look a little hot, too. Maybe it's time for you to sit down."

"Reminds me of a kitchen sweat from long, long ago," said Aunt Edna. "My, but I loved a good kitchen sweat. Everybody did. It was such a relief from the winter, and it was really special near Christmas time. There was one of those, a very, very special one for me," said Edna with her face glowing to the point where a sort of youthfulness began to replace the lines of aging.

"Well, tell us. Tell us about your kitchen sweat," said Gracie. "Everybody come in here. Aunt Edna is going to tell us about a kitchen sweat. What on earth is a kitchen sweat? How do you make a kitchen sweat? Throw water on the floor?"

"No, no, dear," said Edna. "A kitchen sweat was a dance at someone's house. You have to understand that in those days homes weren't evenly heated, and sometimes they weren't heated at all in rooms like the bedrooms. Everybody had to dress more warmly.

"But the kitchen was the exception. The cooking stove was heated with the smallest wood, almost like the kindling to start a fire. And, most kitchens had a heating stove, too. The kitchen was the warmest room in the house.

"It usually was one of the larger rooms in a house, too, sometimes the very largest. So, when you moved the table and chairs out of it, and maybe a few other things, there was a dance floor. When I was a young woman in a new-made dress of flour-sack calico, we could all sweat our clothes clear through when Clarence Biddle played his fiddle at a kitchen sweat.

"The one I am going to tell you about actually had its beginnings at Thanksgiving because of the boys. I came home from normal school—

that's where you learned to be a schoolteacher—at Thanksgiving. As you all know, I had four younger brothers: Peter, Roger, Frank and Russell. They were only two and three years apart in age, and all becoming good workers.

"But, my, they were praying for vacation to end so they could go back to school, and they were dreading it when Christmas vacation would begin. They just wanted it to be over with because of the wood even though they liked the food, get-togethers and gifts in between.

"I think Frank liked to talk about how Jesus came into the world even back then, even though he was the hardest for Mama to make get ready for church. He's the one who became a preacher, you know. Best dancer of the bunch too, you probably didn't know.

"Anyway, the boys got terribly tired of wood cutting. Daddy had rules for wood cutting, and one was that the work began when the weather got cold. It was cold enough at Thanksgiving and Christmas, and those were the holidays for the boys to be home for long periods of time for wood cutting.

"Daddy's next rule was that 15 rods of hedgerow—that's close to 250 feet—had to be cut, and separated for use every winter for the following year's use. We were always burning at least year-old wood.

"I see you shaking your head back there, Ruthie. You don't know what a hedgerow is? Well, that's hedge trees planted close together. About every 20 years they were ready to be cut again if you wanted a few posts—sooner than that if you just needed firewood. They call them Osage orange trees too, or beau d' arc because the Indians prized them for making bows.

"They have really hard, yellow wood that doesn't rot away easily, and it burns hotter than any other wood. A good hedgerow is a really, really valuable thing to have. You all might want to get yourself one for when the oil is gone. I know Russell said that a hedge tree's just a big pasture weed, but Russell always did have trouble showing appreciation.

"Daddy and either Peter or Roger, since they were the two biggest boys, would start with the two-man cross-cut saw on the bigger trunks of a hedge, stopping to chop off the little thorny branches in the way with an axe. They would use smaller saws and axes to cut the littler pieces. The two smaller boys would help cut, or go together with the horse team and wagon to take a load of wood back to the woodyard out west of the house.

"Daddy separated the wood as they went. The biggest, straightest trunks and branches would be kept in 10-foot lengths for fence posts. A hedge post can last 100 years you know. There's still some down at the end of your subdivision that Daddy put in the ground.

"The next smallest wood would be cut in foot-and-a-half lengths for heating stove wood. The stuff a little smaller would be separated out for the hot fires in the cook stove. The very smallest stuff was saved for kindling to get fires going. Daddy didn't waste much, or leave much of a hedgerow behind, only the stumps in the ground to start growing all over again. Not many trees can start over again. I tell you, a hedge tree is a valuable thing.

"It didn't take long for the boys to get red-faced with the heat of that work, even with sparkles of snow-shine blowing around them. The two oldest ones would be blowing out long clouds of steam trying to keep up with Daddy.

"I believe the team of horses they used that year was a couple of sorrel Belgians—really pretty with their blonde manes and tails, Bill and Dolly. They always looked so nice standing there with their red hair coats against the snow. The dogs we had then—two rat terriers named Dot and Dimple and a shepherd-collie, old Teddy—liked wood cutting too. The rabbit hunting usually is good around a hedgerow.

"Anyway, Russell would get to whining when he and Frank drove Bill and Dolly out of sight of Daddy on the way to unload at the woodyard about how they ought to get more time for fun. Frank would tell him to shut up, that they'd go play on the pond ice some evening, and to just hope it was time to go back to school soon. It was hard for Russell to appreciate how good they had it. Daddy had to cut wood when he didn't have help, too.

"At the woodyard, the posts were propped up in tepees, and the other wood was stacked. By the time they unloaded the first wagon, and returned, there was another load ready for them all to take it in for dinner. Of course, they would get another two loads in the afternoon before milking cows and supper. It seemed that except for the dinner on Thanksgiving and the dinner on Christmas, the boys were always going after the next wagonload of firewood.

"It must have been that way at the Winsley house, too, because Joe and Virginia came over with their buggy and bay trotter mare at the end of Thanksgiving to tell us that they had decided to break up the woodcutting with a kitchen sweat the day before Christmas Eve. It would start after cows were milked, and last until the last visitor flopped on the floor or out the kitchen door. Clarence Biddle had said he'd bring his fiddle, and Fiener Haugesloh would play the banjo.

"It worked. The boys stopped thinking about woodcutting, and started thinking about the kitchen sweat. Even Russell wondered if they'd still be able to hear the music if they went down to slide on the pond ice at Winsley's.

"The Winsley place was neat to visit anyway. They had apple orchard three-fourths of the way around the house. There was a big, wraparound porch with two porch swings. They had the biggest kitchen of anybody for miles around. The food would be great with everyone bringing some.

"We thought about, and looked forward to, the Winsley kitchen sweat for weeks. For once, the boys started counting the days until Christmas vacation would begin. Russell even marked it off on the calendar, and started acting more like a kid again, lifting Dot and Dimple into the wagon with him on the way to the hedgerow.

"Daddy said we would take the wagon to the Winsley's instead of the buggy to help stay warmer, and carry more of a load. The boys took the high sides off it so we could see out sitting flat on the bottom. Mama and I had ham, potato salad and pickles to take, so if you stuck your head under the blankets on the wagon ride, you could smell the food in anticipation.

"Poor dogs. Daddy hollered at them to stay home, and they sat on the driveway watching us go. But Bill and Dolly had their heads up and ears forward, moving willingly at a fast rate as though a kitchen sweat was something special for horses, too.

"We got off the road to cut across the big field below Winsley's to save time getting there, and you could look up at the stars, and faintly hear the fiddle and banjo in the distance. Biddle and Haugesloh didn't miss the opportunity to play together by idling around while others made their way to a kitchen sweat.

"The house was brightly lit with several kerosene lanterns running at once along the kitchen cabinets, and in the adjoining rooms, an extravagance for the Winsleys. The table and chairs, and whatever else was moveable, had already been pulled from the room. People were laughing and dancing with sweat already running down their faces.

"Outside, all of the horses the people brought were whinnying and snorting at each other. Horses liked a good social, too.

"The Winsleys had brought jugs of the apple cider they made up out of the stone-arched cave, where it cooled without freezing, to heat at the stove or drink cold. Most of it burned the throat anyway. The cider had begun to make jack. But ham or some cookies off all the trays people had brought softened it some.

"I don't mind telling you—I'm not embarrassed easily anymore—that I had been wishing there would be a young man there, somebody of my own age group, somebody I would be pleased to dance with. And there he was. I spotted him right away, I think maybe before he ever saw me.

"He was Tom—sandy haired, a head taller than me, always was even tempered his whole life. Oh, he had his ups and his downs, but he was kind. He was living with the Winsleys then as a hired man, came over from the next county. He asked me to dance right when Biddle seemed to hit his high note for the night, and Haugesloh had his bald head turned down almost into the strings picking fast with the sweat rolling.

"When they propped open the kitchen doors to let some of the heat out, we waltzed right out onto the porch and around it with the snow sparkling under the stars and moon in the apple orchard. My face only seemed to burn more in the cold.

"It seems right, now, that almost all I can remember of the night is Tom's face and the sound of his voice. Oh, other things happened.

Russell got sick on too much jack, and bruised his back end badly on the ice. In my mind, I can still see Frank holding up on his legs while the other two boys pulled Russell into the wagon.

"But Tom, oh Tom," said Aunt Edna as she paused looking down at the table, a tear trickling down her face.

"Aunt Edna," said Gracie, "was that Uncle Tom? Was that the night you met him?"

Edna nodded, and took off her glasses. The room was quiet for a moment.

Then Fred, Gracie's husband, laid a large hand on Edna's shoulder. "Aunt Edna, would you care to dance with me? It won't be Biddle and Haugesloh, but we do have some CDs over there. How about we start out with a little Elvis Presley.

"Hey, you guys in the next room. Turn off that football game, and get in here. Carry the table out of the room here. We're going to have a kitchen sweat for Christmas."

Fred took Aunt Edna's hand, and put an arm around her waist. "Do you think we can start off slow, Aunt Edna? Elvis is singing 'Blue Christmas.'"

Harlan Medlam's missing teeth

HARLAN MEDLAM lost his teeth.
It wasn't that he set out to lose them. It was that he just took
uiem out for one of his usual activities, such as chewing a cigar stub or
taking a nap, and they just plain disappeared.

By the way, if you happen to find a set of teeth during this story,
Harlan's teeth were false. That is, they weren't the ones that sprouted on
his jaws naturally. Through the course of nature, perhaps through some
quirk of youthful nutrition or lack of dental care, Harlan had already
lost those first teeth that supposedly come permanently attached.

That is, 20 years ago a dentist took them out at great cost, and
replaced them with false teeth at great cost, and nothing injured the
sensitive memory of Harlan Medlam so much as that of great cost.

Losing a set of false teeth could bring a replacement cost the price of
a good cow. On the other hand, not having a set of teeth could cost the
ability to chew a piece of good steak, except for the part where you pulverized the last piece of fat to liquid with your gums.

The whole predicament agitated Harlan Medlam.

He could even remember the guy who made the teeth singing to him,
"You've traded your sins for a crown," and his joy wasn't about
Christianity.

If his wife, Florence Medlam, found out that they might have to pay
for another set of teeth for him through his own carelessness, she might
be furious.

Florence Medlam was cautious. She had gone through the same
tooth replacement of natural with false, and she would never risk losing
her teeth to have to pay again.

The first places to check for his teeth naturally were in his jean
jacket pocket and his overalls pockets. He'd already done that, and now
he scratched the black and gray hair of his old head in puzzlement that
the teeth weren't there. His pockets were always the first places he put
his teeth.

Harlan ran into the bedroom to check the nightstand where he took
the teeth out at night. The only teeth there were Florence Medlam's
spare teeth lying safely in a glass of water on the stand by her side of
the bed.

She had gone to the great expense of having two sets of teeth made at
the same time so she would have a spare, an extravagance that Harlan
still couldn't believe of her. Why, it was as bad as if he'd done something
foolhardy like having two sets of eyeglasses made. He could only see

through one set of glasses at a time, and he could only chew with one set of teeth at a time. Still, she was stable most of the time.

Harlan looked for his teeth on the tractor. They weren't on the tractor seat, and they weren't wrapped with the wrench in a grease rag on the tractor foot platform. They weren't in its toolbox either. Harlan remembered putting the teeth in the tool box once when he took a nap under the tractor out in the field.

Ah, that must be it. He also had set the teeth once in the branch of a hedge tree along the field while he took a nap. He had done that several times in the same tree. It had a handy heavy branch where he could drive the tractor next to it, and lay his teeth on the branch from the tractor seat. He quickly drove the tractor out to the hedge tree, but the teeth weren't there either.

He searched under the bench under the elm tree where he took his naps after dinner. Then he pushed with his toe and his cane all through the grass around the bench.

"Harlan...Harlan Medlam, what are you doing stumbling around like that out there?" Florence called from the kitchen window.

"Nothing, nothing at all, Florence. I thought I saw a strange-colored toad you might like to see, too, and I was looking for him again. That's all."

"Good night, I've heard you take off with the tractor once, and fumble around all over the place. Haven't you gotten anything done? The day will get away from us. It's almost dinner time. I'm starting to fry chicken."

Fried chicken. Harlan's mouth salivated at the thought. He was going to need his teeth for a bite of fried chicken. Florence might suspect if he tried to eat chicken without his teeth in.

The hayloft in the barn—he hid extra smokes in the loft, cigars accumulated from dozens of trips to town. Florence Medlam didn't need to know about an extravagance like extra cigars. A fellow just had to be careful in front of her to show that you weren't wasting the cigar you were smoking currently, taking it clear down to the shortest stub possible to let it cool before chewing.

Harlan hung his cane on the back strap of his overalls as he breathed huffing on the climb on the wooden ladder into the hay loft, the sweet dry dusty odors of alfalfa and prairie hay mingling in the air. There wasn't anything tucked behind the board on the wall by the loft door but cigars. Although he climbed a side ladder twice to check where the beam joined the wall, there wasn't anything there either but another box of cigars.

The silo—Harlan had climbed to the rim of the silo to look for a wrench from a Model T to sell. It had been agonizing to climb around on that rim, so maybe, just maybe, he had taken the teeth out in that agony. It seemed he'd had them in his mouth since then, but maybe it wouldn't hurt to look.

So Harlan huffed, and he sighed, and he stopped for rests twice as he climbed the silo ladder to the top. He stuck his head out the top of the silo chute to look round the rim.

There were no teeth there.

Maybe he had taken them out when he took a nap in the stall next to where the sow had her pigs.

No, they weren't there.

Maybe the teeth were in one of the fruit trees around the garden where rows of potatoes were growing shooting green from the earth. He had taken a nap there just yesterday while hoeing the potatoes.

"Harlan, time for dinner," came the call from the house. "Harlan, come on in and eat," yelled Florence Medlam.

It was time to behave normally. Harlan Medlam always came right away to eat. He never took a chance on missing a meal or a nap.

He sat in his chair, and tied a dish towel around his neck to protect his clothes. Florence Medlam believed in keeping clothes as clean as possible.

"Look here, Harlan," she said. "The first frying chickens are ready to eat, so I butchered one this morning when you took the tractor out to the field. I was so glad to see you ambitious like that in the spring of the year, I figured we'd eat extra good today. Look here, potatoes and gravy, and I brought a canning jar of green beans up out of the cellar. I made bread, too. Smell it in the oven. Just sit down there. I know you're tired and hungry. You've just been flying all over out there this morning getting ready for spring planting. I don't remember a year like this in recent times when you've so much get up and go that I haven't had to remind you to get to work."

Harlan tried not to look directly at her. Sagging lips could be a dead giveaway that there were no teeth behind them. He ate potatoes and gravy first, and then some green beans and bread.

"What's the matter with you, Harlan Medlam? You haven't touched your chicken yet. You always eat meat first."

"I'm just saving the best 'til last, dear. Aren't you going to sit down too?"

"I am, I am. I'm just going to pull out another loaf of bread here. I thought we better have extra on hand in case you want a slice before your afternoon nap."

Harlan Medlam contemplated the brown, crusty drumstick in front of him. He wanted to eat it. Florence was watching him. He tried to keep his face down.

He quietly reached for his knife and fork, and began cutting chicken away from the bone.

"Harlan," said Florence as she sat down reaching into her apron pocket for her false teeth, "Harlan, what are you doing? Why are you cutting that chicken up instead of picking it up for a bite?"

"Nothing, dear," said Harlan, cutting the chicken into smaller pieces.

"Just thought I'd cut it up to keep it small and tender today."

"It's plenty tender without cutting it up, Harlan. Harlan Medlam, look at me."

Harlan looked up at her.

"Where are your teeth?"

"I guess I lost them, Florence."

"Lost your teeth!? Harlan Medlam, don't you remember what a set of teeth costs? Why, we could spend a cow for a set of teeth. How could you be so careless? Me, I'm always cautious. I always know where my teeth are. See, they were right here in my apron. I got my spare teeth in the water glass in the bedroom.

"You shouldn't have more cigars 'til we've made the price of more teeth. I'm going to have to look for more work for you to pay for more teeth. How could you, Harlan? How could you lose your teeth? Have you looked everywhere you could think of," she asked as she put her own teeth in her mouth to savor the first bite of chicken.

"I've looked everywhere, Florence. I just can't find them. The only thing I can think of that I might have done different with them is I washed 'em here at the kitchen sink last night because I dropped them in the dirt out at the potatoes. Oh, I forgot that before. I did wash them last night. I remember that now. I washed them right over there. What's the matter, Florence? Why are you scrooching up your lips like that?"

"My teeth don't fit right, Harlan," said Florence. "They seem like they're a little too big, and the top ones almost stick out over the lower ones."

Harlan Medlam smiled. He reached over, and took the teeth from Florence Medlam's hand when she took them out of her mouth. Then he popped them in his own mouth to take a first bite of chicken. He tried not to look too happy.

Florence Medlam lost her teeth.

It wasn't that she set out to lose her teeth because teeth are expensive. At least she had gone to the great extravagance of having a second set to wear.

The first place she looked for her teeth was under the towels in the lower drawer of her kitchen cabinet where she kept her grape, butterscotch and peppermint hard candies hidden so Harlan Medlam wouldn't find them. Harlan Medlam usually never looked through kitchen cabinets because they represented a whole new line of work.

As she moved on to look in another cabinet, she looked out the window to where Harlan lay taking his nap on the bench under the elm tree. He better not be smiling, she thought.

Help sometimes comes the lard way

THE BOY already was chilled in the steady north wind that bent the ends of the huge thick limbs of an elm tree above him so they creaked and groaned.

For the first time in his life he raised his blue eyes in understanding at the great age of the tree, many times his own age, with icons of the past marking the deep, brown bark.

There was a branch that was shattered to a stub in a great storm 20 years before with four branches already large growing from it, an imbedded piece of No. 9 wire covered in rust sticking out of the trunk 6 feet up, and then further up, perhaps 10 more feet, another piece of iron, this time thick and round—a foot across, but no more than a couple inches thick.

There was rusted cable dangling from the round iron, and it was suspended from the branch on a heavy rusted iron chain that had been there so long that the wood of the branch had covered where it was tied in great lumps of growth.

The tree was an American elm, of a type that cut into good hard, red wood, a last survivor among what once had been many of its kind on this farm. Dutch elm disease had nearly exterminated these elms, but along the fencelines here and there seedling trees still struggled to make a comeback. This tree was a last of its kind, a healthy living colossal memorial to its farm.

As he went up the porch steps to go into the house, the boy realized he looked back at something special. The tree covered 100 feet of shade area in any direction. It dominated the driveway, the black silhouette of its tall figure covering a large portion of the gray clouded sky.

"Grandpa," he said to the old man in the rocking chair as he pointed out the picture window. "Look at that tree."

"Yes, I have many times."

"It's huge, and it has pieces of iron coming out of it."

"Yes, I suppose it has," Grandpa replied, his blue eyes sparkling with silent amusement at the boy's solemnity.

"There's a round piece of iron high up hanging from an old chain."

"Well, son, that's because that's the hog hanging tree."

"The hog hanging tree?"

"Yes, back when I was your age, and a little bit older too, I've seen as many as a half-dozen hogs hanging from that tree at a time, although usually there were only two or three."

"Why, Grandpa? Why would you hang a hog in a tree?"

"Well, to butcher them. They were already dead when we hung them

in the tree. We cut them up for meat—you know, bacon, ham, pork chops. You like all that stuff, don't you?

"And then there was the lard. The lard was important back then. We cooked everything with lard instead of vegetable oil. My mother was in charge of rendering the lard, and I'd eat cracklins afterward—eat so many I'd get sick eating so rich while I smelled that lard cooking.

"You know, this takes me back to when some of that lard was really special to a family. It was during the Great Depression, a hard time for everybody, but worse for some than others. We didn't have much money, but we always had enough to eat because we were a farm family. Some people had a terrible hard time having something to eat.

"We had to butcher in cold weather for the meat to keep, and of course there's no flies in winter. I was your size then, but that tree was there already big and old. The round piece of iron you see up there is a pulley, what's left of a block and tackle.

"There was more here on butchering days. There were always stands to hold 50-gallon steel barrels of boiling water on them with hedgewood or fuel-oil burning underneath. There were hooks on stout ropes tied in the tree so you could slip a rope into the hook to quick-fasten a hog around the elbow of his hind leg. Of course there was a table with knives in hot water ready for use.

"They'd herd the hogs down there with gates from the feedlot, one or two at a time. They were big old red hogs usually—Durocs. The men would ease them along, pushing them with the gate so they'd just grunt a little as they came, trying to root at the dirt at the same time with their noses. It would be kept gentle so the hogs weren't excited.

"Down here by the tree either my father or one of my uncles would shoot the hogs in the head with a rifle. Then they'd hook-rope each hog higher into the tree pulling him up with that block and tackle. They'd stick him in the throat with a knife to bleed him out."

"Gross, Grandpa, that's gross."

"No, it wasn't. The men made sure the hogs didn't suffer any. It was all kept clean. I'm sure it was better meat than what we get to eat today.

"Anyway, they'd make a slice down the hog's abdomen then, his belly, to take out his intestines and organs. Things like the liver would be saved."

"I don't like liver."

"Sometimes we'd fry that liver first as the best meat of all. Anyway, they'd lower the hog again into the hot water to loosen the hair to take it off, maybe have a second barrel there to dip him in after he was cleaned. I can remember those cleaned hogs hanging there waiting to be cut up into what we would eat, all chilled down and nice. I'd think about what that meat would taste like, and my mouth would water.

"As they cut the meat up, they'd trim all the fat out, and us kids would help the women carry it to the house in clean milk buckets for lard rendering. Like I said, I didn't care much about eating the meat later after getting stuffed on cracklins.

"But like I also said, there were those people around who weren't getting stuffed on much of anything. That was the year I found out about the Jolkinsens. They were a family that lived up north of here—below where the watershed lake is now—in a house that might have been a shed first. It was built of logs covered with wooden planks and red asphalt sheeting.

"My father needed to go to town, and my mother said why didn't he take the Jolkinsen family by a can of our new lard since we had more than enough to carry us clear through to next winter. So Pop hitched up the horse, and loaded a five-gallon can of lard in the buggy.

"They had about four kids, if I remember right—all of them pasty-white, thin-faced, but tall with really dark hair but oddly pale blue eyes. The boy that met us was about my age. But even if he was built like a stick, he was still a little taller than me. Their mother was hard-grim looking with wrinkles before her time, but she smiled when she saw my father. I remember because she had a couple of her front teeth gone, poor thing. I didn't think much back then about what being hungry could do to you.

"He pulled that can out and told her he had a can of lard for her because we had plenty. She tried to fumble around trying to turn him down a minute, but she looked like she might cry she was so happy. The girls in the family were even taller than the boy—except for a little one—and they all seemed to stretch a head taller looking at the can of lard he was carrying in.

"My father set it on a wooden table in the middle of the room, and pulled the lid off to show Mrs. Jolkinsen. She told him the only food they'd had left to eat for a couple of weeks was potatoes out of the cellar. Her husband was off trying to find work, she said. That lard was so pure and white, and the saliva was about running out the mouths of those kids.

"That boy couldn't stand it any longer. He reached with his hand, and scooped a couple of table-spoon's worth of that lard into his mouth. Here I was so full of cracklins still that I could hardly contain them watching him eat that lard.

"Mrs. Jolkinsen started to make a noise like she was going to tell him to quit it, but she couldn't get it out in time. When the girls saw she couldn't say no, they all scooped a mouthful, too. Then all the kids were scooping lard, and eating it down as fast as they could go.

"The tears were running down Mrs. Jolkinsen's face, and she looked at my father and asked him to excuse her. Then she took a mouthful of the lard to eat too. She didn't take another mouthful, just sort of rolled her tongue around, and told the kids to quit before they got sick until we made ready to leave. Then she told that boy to fire up the wood stove while she cut up some potatoes to fry in lard.

"Later on, my folks decided my father better go back with some meat for them too. He told Mr. Jolkinsen they would trade them some meat along in trade for help if he wanted to. As I remember, my father said he was quite a good help when he was needed there for a couple of years.

"The boy was Harry Jolkinsen. We caught bullheads fishing together the next summer. He moved to the city later.

"Things got better. It doesn't seem that it was long after that when my mother drove the horse and buggy home from town so my father could follow in our first automobile.

"Funny how we try not to eat too much fat now, isn't it son? But people have to eat some fat, and those Jolkinsens were starved for it. I've eaten lard on bread before myself, but it doesn't sound too good now.

"We only figure we're better without something when we don't have to have it anymore. How about a bowl of ice cream to tide us over?"

Salty's bumpy ride to justice

Author's note: If you're in the habit of skipping intro-ductions to books, go back now. You'll find my comment on Salty there. You may not find him likeable, but he was real.

IN THE EARLY fall, when the cottonwood leaves begin to leave the stems like soft yellow lemon drops and the prairie grasses assume rusty brown hues—that's when the supercharged guys appear like seasonal climactic events.

Salty Fraedenhaup was one of those supercharged guys who became known through his self-medicating as a periodic binge-drinking town drunk. He had to be heir to the old-time cowboys who rode behind the cattle from Texas, working long, hard hours, only to cut loose in one hard Kansas binge.

Salty had to work hard, play hard, and then cut loose, especially if everything had gone right. He just couldn't contain it all. He was even colored like the season—soft lemon-yellow hair curled over rusty brown lean skin burned in from the summer heat.

This was one of those years because Salty was ready to explode. He'd sold all his calves at record prices instead of carrying any into winter. The crops were all harvested with decent prices. The machinery was greased and shedded for spring.

And best of all, he'd really begun his tear on the day before, when he was first on the scene after the airplane spotted a coyote loping through a big pasture. He'd cranked the old Ford into high gear with his pack of yelping brown and gray wolfhound-greyhound crossed dogs bouncing with excitement on the truck bed behind.

Salty hit 70 miles an hour before he was done, knocking off rocks, and jumping a gully to break both rear shocks on the recoil bounce. He'd brought the dogs to within sight of the panicking coyote that now looked back on the run. Then he pealed into a half curve, busting one tire off the rim on a piece of jutting limestone, before jumping to the rear to lower the dog-box gate.

Luckily for Salty—not for the coyote—the tall, lean dogs caught the coyote within their range of sight since the truck was immobilized. He already was pulling the bottle out from under the seat when the throat dog, old Dan, grabbed the coyote, and the pack fell on him to tear.

When Salty's coyote hunting buddies caught up with him, he'd finished one bottle. He called to them, "Hey, when Salty Fraedenhaup spots a coyote, you babies get out of the way before you get hurt. Whoooey, you should have seen how Sweet Sally put on the speed to shoulder-roll him, and then how old Dan, my throat dog, went for him. Hey, come to think of it, watch out city, old Salty's coming to town. What you loafers smiling at? Let's get my coyote and my dogs, get this tire fixed so we can get going. Jack, there's a couple more bottles under the seat. Drag'em out."

Actually, it took three bottles to get the truck repaired to the point of getting out of the pasture. Then Salty drank just as much when he got to the Deerhead Tavern that night—the same night he showed them how to do the Charleston from the top of the bar and was gently moved to a back room after falling asleep on the floor.

Five months of relative spring and summer sobriety with occasional drinks had been tough for Salty to take.

By early evening the next day, Salty had wrapped his long brown fingers around at least a couple more bottles, and chased them down with a six-pack. He was stoking the furnace, and his friends wished he'd go home. But down in the city, they got this club called the Jumbalai that had a bouncing dance floor mounted on heavy truck springs.

"Don't bother me boys, I'm headed for the Jumbalai," Salty said as he tore open, and emptied a 50-pound bag of dogfood into the dog box, and heaved up a 5-gallon bucket of water to the dogs. "Me and the pups are loaded for bear. I'm a'gonna dance on that bouncy floor 'til it caves in or the rapture comes."

The big, lanky dogs were quiet as Salty's truck bounced into the broad asphalt parking lot of the Jumbalai. Vapor lights shone strangely in the night air, and the moon was nearly blotted out behind the changing neon signs. This wasn't a coyote dog's kind of place—contentment lay in napping in the truck bed.

More then one head turned as Salty, lean and tall with grinning white wolf teeth himself, jumped on the dancing floor. The stringy-haired band with the cowboy hats pulled low on their heads was so loud, Salty thought he might go numb from the tips of his ears to the tips of his lips. Or, maybe that was the whiskey.

There were women in the place, but Salty didn't need any female partner to be able to dance. When they rock-and-rolled, he did a sort of Charleston-tap dance routine on his boot heels between draws on the bottle. When they did the Oh Johnny Oh, he swung himself off the floor instead of swinging a sweet corner maid.

"No drinking on the dance floor, buddy," a burley bouncer with curly brown beard and ear rings said, tapping Salty on the shoulder.

"Well, don't just stand there then, buddy," said Salty. "Get me to a table, and let's have a bottle there."

It was 1:00 in the morning when the bouncer and one of his buddies helped Salty out the door by the armpits while he held the last two bottles he'd bought. He hung on the truck for a minute while the dogs licked his face.

"Now where we gonna go, buddies?" said Salty. "It's time to celebrate."

Luckily, at least for Salty's needs, the route from the Jumbalai to the interstate went by the 100-acre grounds of the veteran's hospital. There, across the grassy yard, Salty saw a familiar form trotting—a coyote, right here in the city. What blessed luck, he said to himself.

Then he stomped the accelerator to jump the curb and dodge the carefully spaced trees. The coyote actually stopped to look, he was so surprised to see native fauna like Salty in the city. Possibly he was a specimen who had never met his natural enemies, drunks with dogs.

Whatever the case, Salty only had to hit 40 to get across the lawn, and go into the classic curve before jumping out to dump the dogs right in front of a central heating plant with steam pouring out the stacks. Funny how city grass smelled all sweet when it was torn up, even in the fall when it ought to be half-died back.

The coyote got the message that something new had arrived in town, and he took off with a dozen dogs stretched to full run behind him. Fortunately, the sidewalk was broad enough that Salty could drive the truck right up it, only dodging off once between two trees to avoid the railing of a handicapped ramp.

This was a smart coyote. He got across the street without the dogs getting him. But then old hunt-wise Sweet Sally caught on to his dodges here where the city offered trees and lamp posts to wrap around. She figured where he would hit the straight-away to cut the coyote up the front steps of a house where the bunch of younger dogs crashed into him like a train wreck. Unfortunately for the coyote, dogs don't drink like drunks.

By the time Salty jumped the curb back into the street, then turned down the side street to catch up with them, it was all over. The lights in the house came on as the pack pulled the carcass down the steps. Salty was contentedly taking a swig from his bottle, and loading his last dog when the police drove up.

Now, why did they have to do all of that? Salty hadn't caused any trouble, had he? Doggone, didn't they want coyotes killed even in the city? Sure he was drinking, but he hadn't hurt anyone or done any damage other than a bark peel on one old tree that got in the way.

They took away Salty's driver's license, and called a couple of his buddies to get him and his truck home if they didn't want to see him spend the night in the drunk tank. At least that was fortunate. He couldn't have kept on celebrating if he'd been forced to sober up in jail.

Why, he even gave those folks $20 to get their front steps cleaned. After all that, he was still officially arrested, and would have to see a judge. Salty was wondering about the justice of life.

He had brunch at the Deerhead of cold ham and potato salad with another bottle. It was kind of good to be home. But nobody wanted to see him dance in the daytime, so he had to put a coin in the juke box to dance with himself in a corner. Darn, this place was dead. At least the Jumbalai in the city was a place where a guy could come alive.

His buddies had taken his truck keys. His dogs were home safe in their pens. It took two bottles to walk home for the tractor.

As the neon lights blazed red and green through the falling leaves that nobody saw of an ancient cottonwood overhanging the asphalt lot of the Jumbalai, a big dual-wheeled diesel farm tractor belching black smoke jumped the curb. Salty was back in the city.

There was a crowd at the Jumbalai. The parking lot was full except for one parking space between two cars, and the tractor was just too broad to fit. So, Salty left it parked like it was, so it blocked three cars from backing out.

Then he walked into the Jumbalai to see that dancing floor jumping and rocking to a hundred people stomping on it. There were all kinds of hairstyles and clothes bouncing to the rhythms. Every once in a while, Salty could even focus in on lips and eyes, but it was getting tough.

He was just getting through the first part of his next bottle, just beginning to tap his toe to jump on the floor. Heck, he'd even noticed a brown-haired woman in a silver dress who looked back at him. He might have even danced with a partner. But the evening was ready to end.

A young cop came in to ask the curly bearded bouncer, "You know who drove that tractor in? He's blocking some people in, and I have reason to believe it might have been reported with somebody driving it up the median of the interstate."

After Salty's eyes rolled back in his head, the cop and the bouncer carried him out together. At least they have coffee in jail.

Salty did some tall thinking while he sipped his coffee. He even called his attorney at home, old O.B. Goodfellow himself, to fill him in on his ideas. He did a lot of thinking about life, and what he might do with the extra money. It looked to him like he had this city dead to rights, treating a fellow like this. At least the cops assured him his tractor was OK in the city impound.

O.B. Goodfellow wanted too much up front to get in on the deal. He didn't even want Salty's case for the percentage of the take he offered him. It was just as well. Salty could represent himself, and get all the money. Maybe he could get another truck, or even a trailer with a second dog box for a few extra dogs.

So, when the young cop took off his hat to ask him if he wanted to make bail, Salty replied, "Heck, no. I got you fellows right where I want you. I want to see the judge right away before this goes any further. You tell him I'm suing the city for $100,000. Just send me down the paperwork, and I'll get it filled out."

"Well, sir," said the young policeman, staring at him from unemotional dark eyes, "you might just want to tell his honor about that yourself. Court's in session. I'm sure he'll want to hear about your lawsuit, and possibly advise you about bail himself."

"So, if I understand you correctly," said gray-haired Judge Edward T. Gooken, tilting his head to look at Salty over his glasses, "you don't want to make bail. And you say you want to sue the city? What could you possibly be suing the city for?"

"Why that's easy, judge, I got this city over a barrel. They're just lucky I ain't going for a million dollars. Can't you see what they've gone and done is unfair, unconstitutional and unheard of justice-wise?"

"No, I don't see that. Please tell me what you think the city has done?"

"Why, they've gone, and arrested me twice on the same drunk. Now that ain't fair at all. I caught 'em at it good."

Salty got 30 days in jail, and he had to take the driver's test over in a year to get his license back.

They wouldn't let him have anything but beer at the Deerhead, and then it was a two-can limit after 8 p.m. with a buddy there to drive him home. Any other time there, he was served coffee, tea, water, juice or soda pop. Remember, they reserve the right not to serve anyone, even when they stomp their boot heels on the wooden floor really hard, and turn red.

They barred him from the Jumbalai, but of course it wasn't home.

The dogs were glad to see Salty. The tractor worked fine for spring planting.

Hermes' home life is for the birds

Author's note: *I'll end this volume for you as you started it, with Hermes and his feist out on the Great Plains.*

HERMES WAYFORD sat in his sagging reclining chair and looked glumly over his dark-rimmed glasses at the blue bird sitting on his elevated gray-socked foot.

The black and white terrier on the carpet at Hermes' side yawned as he looked at the bird, glancing only once at Hermes as though this was a common occurrence.

His visitor, the Rev. Wolford Wongamuff, had regained his composure after being startled by the whirring wings that had brought the bird to a landing in this spot.

Before, the parson had just been wondering idly why Hermes had built his house so the picture window faced the yucca-covered pasture slope behind the house instead of the driveway and road in front of it.

"It's my cows," Hermes said. "In the summertime I like to sit and watch them if they come here to graze. I reckon it's like watching the dollar bills accumulate as they turn the grass into pounds of beef."

But now Hermes was wiggling his toes, then bobbing his foot in the air, saying, "Go on! Get out of here, Joseph, ya troublesome bird. Go to Mama.... Georgia, honey, you in the kitchen? Your little bird is in here, just in case you don't want him leaving his black and white calling cards all over the house.

"Whooey, I tell you, Reverend, ya just never want a bird in your house. They're dirty. They're messy. You have to change the newspapers in the bottom of their cage—and it gets really nasty if your sweetheart wants you to do that. And while you're at it, you discover a comic strip you never got to read, and they've gone and messed it up. Had to hold one next to the window glass just the other day to read it, and then I had to clean the window, too—whooey, nasty, nasty, but it was good. Peanuts, I think. I like that dog, he's smart like my rat terrier feist dog here, Burford.

"Whooey, where was I? Got to catch my breath here now. Anyway, I guess it was a flash of iridescent blue and the sun shining off one of those pink breasts that started this whole thing about two years ago—bluebirds are beautiful things...to some folks anyway...especially to them that put their hair up every night, and cage it with bobby pins to make daily bouffants. Yes, I see you noddin' your head cuz you know that the latter would be none other than my Georgia honey, my sweet lamb. She ain't hearin' me tell you this ya don't think?

"Yes, we was stayin' one night in one of those Illinois towns in the

286

black-earth belt west of the Kankeekee, where the corn grows right up to the back door of your motel. Whooey, it's a strange part of the world compared to here. They even get rain in August, a fella there told me.

"Anyway, we got taken with travelin' the surroundin' states now and then after we bought my dog, Burford here, from a fellow named Burford Crumble over in Missouri—or Mazzoura if ya listen to him. The fella's got a speech impudiment. Don't raise your hand. I know folks usually say impediment, but this guy was impudent.

"Anyway, we decided we were liking seeing different kinds of countryside. So like I say, outside this motel we catch the flash of this bird going by, and there he was, a genuine bluebird. And Georgia says to me, 'HERmes, isn't that beautiful?'

"Well, I knowed I was gonna be in trouble somehow because Georgia never accents the first part of my name like HERmes instead of a normal Hermes without some predicament steppin' in.

"This bluebird heads down along the corn field to where there's a whole line of birdhouses facing southeast, each about 20 feet from the next, and all mounted on five-foot tall posts. Whooey, I knowed that somehow we was needin' to get out of there, so I whistled Burford into the front seat, which he does right away cuz he's smart enough to realize a priority for departure.

"But, Georgia, she just ain't jumpin' when I calls to her to load up in the back seat. That's the way we ride a lot of the time, Reverend—me and Burford in the front cuz we like the same radio stations, and Georgia in the back so she can stretch out without mashing her hair. Ya know, sometimes I think I even catch that Burford wagging his doughnut tail in time when I play the tape I put together myself—starts off with Buddy Holly and Merle Haggard with a Guy Lombardo tune throwed in there to break it up.

"Whooey, let's see, where was I? Oh, yeah, she's a lookin' at those bluebirds and birdhouses, and I realize I can't leave yet cuz the cooler with the pop, chips and frosty doughnuts in it is still in the motel room. So, we ends up goin' to the motel desk so Georgia can ask the clerk, who's takin' curlers out of her hair, where we can find us some of those cute little bluebird houses. She asks her if them beautiful birds come to wherever there are houses.

"Well, the old gal sends us down the road to this hardware store where the gal behind the counter, a younger one this time with earrings punched in the tops and bottoms of her ears as well as sideways, tells my sweet Georgia, that 'Oh yeah,' them bluebirds is easy to attract if you put bluebird houses out. Trouble is those houses are $19.95 each and their little poles are $4.99 plus Illinois tax which for sure ain't no better than home.

"Whooey, I says to Georgia, well honey that settles that. She says 'You bet it does,' and tells the gal we'll take 10 of 'em. I tell you, Reverend, I liked to have talked out of church most unchurch-like. But Georgia, my

sweetie, tells me that if I can go to Missouri to buy a Mazzoura Feist what wetted on her lap as a puppy from old Burford Crumble with the hair growin' out his nose, then she, Georgia Wayford, certainly wuz entitled to a few lousy birdhouses which she could fill with birds free just by placing them correctly.

" I said OK, but I don't think my Burford liked the part about the wetting cuz since he hit his current maturation level he's really careful. Oh, he's been known to heist his leg on a salesman's briefcase, but wouldn't we all like to.

"Anyway, there we are goin' over the border into Missouri across the Mighty Mississippi, my Burford pup on his hind legs lookin' over the backseat at Georgia playin' with her birdhouses, when I make the mistake of sayin' even that Burford Crumble could have sold us birdhouses cheaper cuz I think he owned a woodworkin' shop, too.

"My Georgia looks up, touchin' the little hangin' down part of her throat too much like she does when she's thinkin' or excited, and says, 'Ya really think so?" Oh no, oh no, I really said that, whooey, I says to myself—big, big mistake. Burford lays down on his back in the seat with his feet in the air he's so embarrassed at my gaffe.

"Nothin' would do, but she has to call that Burford Crumble on my cellular phone right away to see what he can do. He says bargain time—$10 houses, and no Missouri tax, actually no Mazzoura tax—if we come out to the farm cuz what the government don't know won't cost'em.

"So it actually goes pretty well for dealin' with Burford. She gets 10 more houses for $10 each with 10 more hickory poles he remembers he has custom-built special for her at $15 each—sounds mighty like Illinois in the balance don't it? I got to pay him $10 to fix a flat tire I got down in his hollar, but at the same time I'm likin' it cuz my Burford is hidin' down below the seat from him.

"Old Burford Crumble finally spots my Burford, and allows how he's sure a fine lookin' feist if I care to part with him—says he shouldn't have sold him to me. But, I like the little fella too much to sell him even though that other Burford thought I was tryin' to be coy bargaining with him. I got the last laugh as we drove away holding my dog's paw up, and hollerin', say goodbye to Daddy, Burford. Don't reckon I better go there much anymore.

"Whooey, you sure are good at listenin' long, Reverend. Hope I can hang with you cuz I'm gettin' parched. Georgia honey, if you can hear me would you bring us some tea, and get this Joseph off me so I can uncurl my toes so he don't bite me through the hole in my sock. I'm gettin' to that, Reverend, I'm gettin' to how this here Joseph is an ungrateful, bitin' wretch. You see this little scar on my earlobe?

"Anyway, we get home, and I'm out there bolting all these little houses on to poles I had to auger holes for—all facin' southeast, all around our house—when I hear Georgia give a whoop from the door.

"She's been on the Internet researchin' bluebirds, and she tells me we're facin' a terrible calamity. Doggone the Internet anyway. It's a terrible pestful thing. I just hauled one satellite dish to the dump that had more television stations than I could watch anyway, and Georgia had to go gettin' another one full of a Worldwide Web—whooey, sounds like spiders waitin' to crawl all over you, don't it?

"Anyway, Georgia says, 'It says right here on the net that house sparrows are gonna move into my birdhouses, and keep the bluebirds out. You, know, English sparrows, European sparrows. Come on, don't be so ignorant, Hermes. It says they can even corner bluebirds nesting in the houses, and kill them. It's terrible, Hermes.'

"And I says, whooey, you mean them little spatsies that eat the milo off the ground at the grain elevator? Them little birds are killers? And I gotta keep them out of the birdhouses? Look here, it's tough enough just puttin' the houses up. I'm exhausted, and Burford is worn out marking the posts. I know he's a feist that was bred to hunt squirrels, but he's used to prairie dogs, and there ain't been many trees here for him to worry about. Whooey.

"Well, I can't believe it, but that spring Georgia was right. Them killer spatsies that look so innocent like little chirpin' birds started movin' into the birdhouses, and we never see any bluebirds. Whooey, it's like magic. Me and poor old Burford wuz kept busy just goin' up and down the line yankin' grass and feather nests out of those birdhouses, and just as fast the spatsies wuz rebuildin' them behind us.

"Georgia shows me a plan off the Web for putting fish line in a pattern over the birdhouses that will confuse the spatsies so they stay out, but which a bluebird is cunning enough to get through somehow. I tell her I'm headin' to town to the hardware to get fish line, but she says monofilament is $1.39 a roll there, and it's only 99 cents a roll at the discount store in the city. Whooey, I says to her, but that's 110 miles away.

"Well, I think I told you before, Reverend, about how my sweet magnolia, Georgia, can be a feist, too. She called down there, and the fish line at the discount store was a bargain. She said I wuz a piker not to go spend the gas money to save her some money. Whooey, go figure.

"Anyway, I go get it. Whooey, I about die out there pullin' the nests out of birdhouses, and stringin' that fish line. Burford got so tired he didn't even want to go back to the waterdish to refurbish himself, and he quit keepin' both ears up at the same time for a while.

"That fishline works maybe four or five days, but those spatsies are clever like bluebirds. They learned how to get back into the birdhouses, and I'm back to pullin' nests again. Finally, Georgia says it's time for mass murder. I got to learn how to make traps for the spatsies, and dispose of them when she isn't around, she says.

"Whooey, I don't really want to do that cuz I'm startin' to admire those tough little spatsies. Besides that, they're the only birds livin' in our yard.

"Anyway, I drive in to the county agent, and tell him he's got to give me some kind of plan for a spatsie trap. And, he says, 'Spatsie trap?' like I'm speakin' French or somethin'.

"Whooey, you know—house sparrows or English sparrows or European sparrows whichever ya wanta call'em. I got to get rid of them cuz they're takin' over Georgia's bluebird houses.

"Well, that agent looks right at me, and says, 'Hermes, we don't have bluebirds here. This is the wrong part of the country. Now to the east of us they got eastern bluebirds and to the west of us they got western bluebirds and mountain bluebirds, but right here in yucca country, we ain't got bluebirds unless you're a'goin' to be uncommonly lucky.'

"Well, whooey, doggone it anyway. I had to tell Georgia the news, and Burford, the little coward, wouldn't even come in the house with me when I done it. She starts to wailin', all disappointed. I tell her not to worry, that I'll take all the birdhouses down so the spatsies can't have them. Would you believe it? She says, 'Whooey,' and slugs me on the arm a cut, and says I am so selfish—that the least I can do is leave her bird-houses and her sparrows alone so she can enjoy what she does have.

"Whooey, you go figure that one, Reverend.

"I got to do something, so me and Burford loads back in the car for that 110-mile trip to the discount store again to find somethin' that will make her happy, and I spy this Joseph here, a little blue parakeet. The clerk—I should have knowed what wuz comin' cuz she had rings in the tops and bottoms of her ears too—holds this Joseph on her finger, and he nibbles on her lips to give her a kiss. I bought him, bargain price, $8.95 plus Kansas tax and whatever their local politicians got tacked on. His cage was only $17.95, but at least I didn't need 20 of 'em.

"I get home, and I pull out this box, and I tell her, Georgia, honey, look here what I got you, your very own bluebird that you can keep. Well, I reached in to stick that little bird on my finger, and when I grabbed him, he sank his crooked little beak right in the end of my finger. Whooey, I was scared I might have twisted his cute little head right off pullin' that piece of meat out of me.

"Then I says, don't worry, Georgia, honey, watch what else he can do. I tell you, Reverend, if you thought the finger was painful you should have seen that parakeet punch into my lip for one of the most powerful kisses I ever experienced, whooey. And Georgia's dancin' around me while I'm jumpin' up and down, and she's hollerin' to let him go, 'Let him go. You just don't know anything about birds.'

"Well, Reverend, whooey, I tell you, I knew somethin' about her old Joseph here, and that wuz I didn't want him givin' me lip kisses any-more. I thought I about throwed him half-way across the room with my lip meat.

"Anyway, he sits on Georgia's finger now, and on her shoulder, and on her hair where he practices nibblin' for her lips on the bobby pins.

"Now, I do like the spatsies—whooey, I'll admit that much. And

291

Burford likes how the birdhouse posts fill in for trees. But I can't hardly abide this rascal, Joseph, and neither can Burford.

"See how he's got his wicked little head cocked at my toe?

"Reverend, I'd dearly appreciate it if you'd look into the kitchen to see if my Georgia can come in here. And, if she can't, would you please just bring me the flyswatter off the refrigerator?"